ARIADNE'S CHILDREN

ARIADNE'S CHILDREN

Roderick Beaton

St. Martin's Press New York

Library of Congress Cataloging-in-Publication Data

Beaton, Roderick.
Ariadne's children / by Roderick Beaton.
p.   cm.
ISBN 0-312-30457-9   (hardcover)
1. Crete (Greece)—Antiquities—Collection and
preservation—Fiction.   2. British—Travel—
Greece—Crete—Fiction.   3. Archaeologists—
Greece—Crete—Fiction.   4. Family—Greece—
Crete—Fiction.   I. Title.
PR6052.E1768A75   1996
823'914—dc20   95-26163   CIP

First published in Great Britain by
The Orion Publishing Group Ltd

First U.S. Edition: April 1996
10 9 8 7 6 5 4 3 2 1

This fiction has long been promised to

FRAN

I have dreamed of man's state, of his courteous and enlightened social state; behind which, in the temple the horrible blood-sacrifice was consummated.

. . . from love . . . alone can form come: form and civilization, friendly, enlightened, beautiful human intercourse — always in silent recognition of the blood-sacrifice.

Thomas Mann, *The Magic Mountain*
trans. H. T. Lowe-Porter

CONTENTS

AUTHOR'S NOTE

This is a work of fiction and the intimate lives of the characters who appear in it have no basis other than in my own imagination. On the other hand, I have tried to be as true as possible to the real history which shaped the lives of these fictional people, as it has also shaped the lives of many more who really lived. The characters in this book often abut against that history, and it should not be surprising to the reader to find that aspects of their *public* lives may here and there run parallel to the public careers of real people no longer living. Nothing whatever of the fictional, inner lives and private actions of my characters has any foundation in the lives of real individuals, living or dead.

Similarly with places: the hilltop on which the remains of Ariadne's Summer Palace are supposed to stand is a real location in north-central Crete, though innocent, so far as I know, of real Minoan remains. Other places, such as Sarajevo, appear with their real names, although the places themselves may be just as much the product of imagination. The Cretan town called Kastro here shares its history and much of its topography with the better-known Heraklion but acquires, I like to think, a life of its own in these pages to which the older, unofficial name of Kastro seemed to me more appropriate.

1 THE ROAD FROM SARAJEVO

IT started with a bang.

The report was so loud, and so close to Lionel Robertson's head, that his first thought was that he himself had been shot. At his back was the plate glass of a Viennese cake shop, at which he had been peering only a moment before. Reflected between the golden curlicues that announced the shop's name and its wares, he had watched carefully as the cars drove one after another, at unexpectedly high speed, towards him up the Quay. The first had slowed with a screech of tyres to negotiate the crowded junction where Lionel was standing. Rumours had been flickering through the crowd like stray electric currents all morning. Would the motorcade turn right according to plan, or had the Heir Apparent had enough, would they turn the other way, across the bridge in a short cut to the Konak? The second car followed the first, turning right into the narrow winding street named after the reigning emperor. It was then that Lionel turned, to see the third, an open sports car with the flag of Austria Hungary fixed to the running board, and perched precariously just behind the flag a colonel of the Austrian army in full dress uniform, come to a hesitant stop not ten yards from where he was standing. People seemed to be shouting at the driver; fingers were pointing. In that moment Lionel had his first and only glimpse of the Heir Apparent, sitting bolt upright on the leather upholstery. He looked like nothing so much as a bad-tempered turkey on Christmas Eve, thought Lionel, as he eyed the large frame barely contained within the tight folds of its uniform, the heavy face and brows dwarfed by the plume of feathers that all but hid the imperial helmet.

Lionel could not have told how many shots were fired. For a split second all motion seemed suspended. The two plump, ripe royals in the car still sat upright, staring before them: the Archduke and the Duchess Sophie. Nothing had happened. Except to Lionel's head, which now throbbed terribly on one side. Then, as the Duchess's hat slid slowly, fondly, to nestle on her husband's shoulder, Lionel saw. The blood on the Archduke's lips. He seemed to be speaking and bubbles of blood welled up below his moustache. The tall colonel on the running board was leaning forward solicitously to wipe them away. Everywhere now was shouting and movement. The car engine roared; in a cloud of dust and exhaust it was out of sight over the bridge that led across the river to the Konak. But well before that Lionel had ducked down below the heads of the crowd. Almost before he had registered the blood on the Archduke's lips, Lionel's mind had gone into action. Whatever was done here was done. There would be photographs; there would be arrests; lynchings, maybe. He, Lionel Robertson, had no business being in Sarajevo at eleven o'clock on the morning of 28th June 1914. For a time Lionel Robertson would have to become invisible.

And it is a remarkable fact that none of the photographs and none of the many witnesses' testimonies that have ever come to light have revealed any trace of an Englishman, six foot three inches tall, in a white tropical suit and straw hat, who a moment before the assassination had been standing intently eyeing the cakes in the Viennese pastry shop at the corner of Franz Josef Strasse and the riverside Quay.

The only person to take much notice of the Englishman on that fateful morning was the attendant of a Turkish bathhouse at the top of a narrow, cobbled street in the Muslim quarter of the town, that smelt of mule dung and warm mare's milk. The old woman, who had no teeth and had probably never before seen anyone so tall and so white, both in skin and dress from head to foot, muttered something as she took the proffered money and handed over a set of starched towels. Removing his straw hat, the apparition in white strode purposefully into the steam and was lost to view.

Fatme never told anyone what she had seen. She knew it was an apparition because, although she remained at her post that day, like every other day, until the quavering voice of the muezzin had sounded from the neighbouring minaret for the last time amid the lengthening shadows and it was time to gather up the towels and lock the doors for the night, the tall white infidel never appeared. Impatiently, she counted the clammy, warm towels that would have to be washed and pressed and starched again before dawn tomorrow. All that remained of the improbable stranger was the imprint of his long naked body on the towel where he had lain. Familiar with the smells of the bathhouse, Fatme detected a peculiar whiff that didn't belong there. In the new bazaars, where the stalls had forbidding glass fronts and the electric trams came clanging along the street and frightened you out of your wits, her nostrils had picked up this unfamiliar scent before. Knowing neither of carbolic soap nor *eau de Cologne*, Fatme had found her own word for it, although she couldn't have said what it meant. That word was *Europe*.

By the time that Lionel Robertson emerged from the bathhouse the bells of

2

the churches from across the river had begun one after another to toll. The streets in the upper part of the Muslim quarter were almost deserted. Although the minarets were silent, rumour had already travelled swiftly, and the meaning of that dismal peal could not be in doubt.

Lionel now wore the sleeveless woollen zouave jacket, crumpled breeches and one-piece *opanka* shoes of stout leather of the Bosnian shepherd. On his head he sported a red fez, set at a jaunty angle. The only thing that might have given him away – and which could easily be jettisoned in an emergency – was the haversack slung lightly over his shoulder, whose contents would certainly surprise any inquisitive Austrian official.

And so, no stranger to the roads and mountain tracks of the Balkans, Lionel Robertson set out to walk the sixty or so miles to Mostar, across the mountains in Herzegovina. From here, he judged, it would be safe to resume his own identity and make his way more speedily, by train, to the coast.

That evening, high above the main road that shadows the single-track railway, he had his last glimpse of Sarajevo, its graceful minarets and the brash square of the Austrian barracks above the town flaring pink in the last rays of the sun while the town itself, huddled steeply between the surrounding hills, already lay in shadow. It was a moment of extraordinary peace. The small detachments of cavalry, their pennants flying, that he had watched earlier in the day, scurrying about the valley and raising clouds of white dust, had retired. Only on the far hillside, where the occasional scatter of whitewashed houses, at this distance no bigger than boulders, betrayed a village, did a pall of dark smoke rise ominously to hang in the still air. Immediately below him, as the shadows deepened in the valley floor, the river seemed silently to burst its banks before his eyes. It was the evening mist, that had gathered quickly above the river in the warm air and now began, as Lionel watched, to spill over its winter floodbanks in a ghostly tide.

That first night, Lionel walked until the moon set. In the distance, as he walked, dogs barked. Mindful of previous experiences with wild sheepdogs, he had broken himself off a heavy branch of poplar, and as he went he whittled it into a stick, in passable imitation of the knobbed staff that Balkan shepherds carry. Few of his friends in England would have recognized Lionel Robertson that night, as he lit a fire in a deserted sheepfold, drew his knees up to his chin, laid his head against his haversack and fell at once into a deep sleep. Those who knew him affectionately as 'the old rogue' would probably have guessed, however, that he was happy. It would be for others now to unpick the tangled skein that had begun at Sarajevo that morning. Lionel was once more in his element. In his dreams a small boy in knee-length short trousers untied the painter of a fishing boat as the tide came up the beach, and crouched out of sight in the for'ard locker. Without oars, his heart in his mouth, he waited, ready for whatever adventure the tides and currents of the darkening Stour estuary would bring, as he had waited, ready, now throughout the dreams of more than thirty years.

In previous treks across this wild, mountainous country Lionel had been the hunter. Then he had fearlessly penetrated into spots where few Europeans could have been before him, to set up his tripod in a dusty village and catch on bromide the astonished, embarrassed faces of a group of Muslim children to send back to the *Illustrated London News*, or with the help of some cheaply hired and cheerfully willing local labour explore a cave that had been inhabited in prehistoric times, the ruins of a Roman temple in a remote outpost of empire that turned out to be full of the most exquisite statues. The miscellaneous booty from these expeditions – flint axe heads, bones and antlers of extinct wild beasts, the head of a bear that he had himself shot in Montenegro, brightly coloured *kilim* rugs, even the gods and goddesses of Olympus in bronze and marble – had periodically been boxed up for transport to the nearest railhead, to arrive many weeks later at the port of Harwich. While lively accounts of these doings were published in the learned and popular journals of the day, the trophies and the treasures had found their way to Upland Grange overlooking the Stour, which in its owner's absence was rapidly turning into a museum.

But now Lionel was the quarry. Even the British passport, that he carried like a talisman in an inner pocket of his Bosnian breeches, could not be relied on to work its magic in these troubled times. Lionel had fallen under the suspicion of the Austrian police in the past, and knew the four-square, literal-minded persistence of bureaucratic questioning. His passport was innocent of the telltale stamps that would have betrayed his movements during the last few months. But if questioned he could not, this time, fall back on the bland, bluff honesty that had got him out of such scrapes before. As he trudged, head held high, but dirty, thirsty and gnawingly hungry, past little fields of wheat and maize and groups of white-kerchiefed women winnowing and stacking hay, Lionel held firmly to his resolve to keep out of the hands of the Austrian authorities.

It was the fourth day of his trek, and the hottest part of the afternoon. Lionel was descending briskly now towards the flowering valley of the Narenta. The only food he had tasted was wild cherries and the occasional ladleful of sheep's milk or a knob of soft cheese laconically shared by a passing shepherd at a crossroads. Round a bend in the road, behind a clump of cypresses, he came upon a humped-back bridge. By the parapet lounged a sentry in dusty uniform and forage cap. In his hands he held, idly, a rifle with fixed bayonet. It was too late to turn back.

The sentry slouched to attention. '*Alt!*' The meaning of the outstretched, upheld palm was clear enough. Lionel continued to approach. Outwardly he allowed his very real fatigue to show. His head drooped, he passed a hand

4

wearily across his eyes, squinting in the hot sunlight, a vacant expression, at once interrogative and submissive, on his face. But his mind was racing. He came right up to the soldier, who had scarcely moved from the stone parapet. He had to come this close, to be sure of what lay beyond. Suddenly Lionel leapt. Vaulting over the parapet, he launched himself into space. The river bank was steep, but not too steep. Bruised, his pulse racing, Lionel slithered with a crackling of breaking branches and an avalanche of pebbles until he reached the river. A deep channel ran between whitened outcrops of rock. The bank was thickly overgrown. As he darted, soundlessly now, through the shadow of the undergrowth, he heard a shot and the vicious richochet as the edge of a boulder splintered near him. He was a good fifty feet below the parapet of the bridge, and he knew the sentry must be firing blind. But it was with a deep sense of relief that he scrambled down a further drop, the sounds he made more than drowned by the waterfall beside him, and the bridge was finally out of sight.

The riverbed was less than half full at this time of year, but it was slow going, clambering downstream over boulders and gullies worn smooth by winter floods. At last the steep banks began to open out, and he saw open country ahead. The river spread out too, to fill its course more amply, and he found himself more than once obliged to wade up to his waist. Ahead of him through the trees he caught sight of the corner of a building. He hitched himself up on the bank, and approached cautiously. Water dripped from his torn breeches; his arms and legs were cut and grazed. He sank down in a patch of shade and breathed long and deeply. So far so good.

He was ready to fall asleep there, on the soft grass in the shade of the chestnut trees that grew tall along the river, but hunger drove him on. After a few minutes he scrambled to his feet, and warily began to approach the building he had seen from the river. It was an old stone mill. A blank, moss-grown wall rose above the millrace; the wheel was motionless. On the side away from the river a flight of wooden steps led down from the mill into a little courtyard where Lionel could see chickens running about. Beyond was open farmland. The crop in the nearest fields had already been harvested, and in the distance he could see clouds rising from what looked like a threshing floor. Where there was a mill there would be flour; and where there was flour there was a good chance of finding bread. On his way out he would strangle a chicken to deal with later. The saliva began to surge in his dry mouth, his hands were shaking. Like a man in a dream, as though magnetized by the unanswerable craving for food, Lionel began to move towards the mill.

His conscious mind was still working, even if it was no longer in control. From the shelter of the trees he scouted carefully along the two sides of the building and the courtyard that he could see. But soon even this much caution became too much for him to bear. The mill was empty. There was washing strung out between two trees. He felt it with his hands. It was quite dry and stiff. A low door at ground level stood open.

In a flash he had crossed the open space that separated him from the building. He stood for a long moment, his back flush with the wall, the open door to his right, listening. There were the sounds a wooden-floored building makes on a hot afternoon, a rustling, perhaps of mice at the grain. There was no one here. More boldly now, Lionel went in. As he had expected, there was nothing for him on the ground floor, which in effect was the basement of the mill. Equipment for washing lay about the earth floor; in the darkness beyond he could make out the wooden machinery that drove the millstones upstairs. He felt his way in the semi-darkness to a flight of steps that creaked alarmingly under his tread. At the top was a trapdoor. He eased it open, and peered through the crack. Bags of flour were stacked along the walls. On a table was a torn-off hunk of dark, gritty bread. An aroma of baking – one, two, maybe three days old – still lingered, and faint though it was, it made his head swim. Lionel pushed up the trapdoor and entered the room.

The bread on the table was hard to the touch. Ordinarily, it would have to be soaked before it could be eaten, but he seized on it ravenously, just as it was. Dry crumbs showered to the floor, it made a cracking noise as it broke between his fists, but Lionel didn't care. He crammed as many of the pieces as he could into his mouth, and waited for them to soften enough that he could swallow them.

It was now that he felt the eyes upon him. He could see nothing beyond the sacks ranged round the edges of the room. But there was no mistaking that sensation; the hairs rose all down his spine and on the backs of his hands. He was being watched. And then he saw them: two jet-black eyes set in a smooth dark forehead that might have been carved from wood, and framed by a white kerchief. They were staring at him over the top of one of the sacks. From his position half crouching over the table, where he had been cramming his mouth full of bread, he slowly straightened and turned to face the eyes. His first thought was for his appearance. Dripping wet from the waist down, scratched and dishevelled, his cheeks bulging and his mouth stopped up with stale bread, he was conscious of being at a severe disadvantage. The eyes and kerchief slowly rose from behind the sacks. The face that came into view was veiled. So the miller's family were Muslims. The only other thing he could tell about her, as she stepped forward hesitantly into the room, was that she was tall. Everything else was concealed by the wide, shapeless blouse and full-length skirt of the Balkan peasant woman.

He addressed her in halting, but authoritative Serbian. 'I need your help,' he said.

Her eyes, still without blinking, continued to bore into him. 'Who are you?'

'Not Austrian. A friend.'

'A foreigner.'

Lionel bowed his head. The voice that came through the veil was neither young nor old. As the bread forced its way painfully down his oesophagus, he felt an unexpected stirring of something more than hunger.

'The *giaour sultan* is dead in Sarajevo,' her voice went on. 'The Austrians have taken my husband. It is not safe for a man. Come.'

She led him, unresisting, into another room where a pile of sacking had been spread over a low wooden divan. She was standing very close to him; he tried to outstare the jet black eyes but failed and had to turn away. Amid the smells of stale baking and flour and not-very-clean sacking his nostrils caught hold of something else, a blend of summer flowers and slight sweat on a female body that sent his senses swimming.

She pointed urgently at his soaking breeches and shoes. 'Give those to me. You must rest now.'

Suddenly the unaccustomed food and the simple warmth of her presence overwhelmed him. The sacking would be full of lice, he knew, but it was a bed, after three nights in the open. With a last lingering flicker of anxiety, he quizzed those impenetrable eyes. Could she be trusted? But already she had turned to leave him. Throwing off his clothes, he sank at once into the deepest, most delicious sleep of his entire life.

It was the barking of dogs that roused him first. She was bending over him, shaking him urgently. From below came a furious clucking of hens, the sound of running feet and male voices. Her eyes, so close to his, were enormous. 'The Austrians. With my husband. Quick.'

As he leapt up, she thrust his clothes into his arms. A miracle: they were dry and warm. Without a thought of shame he dressed in front of her, scarcely taking his eyes from the burnished marble of her brow and those eyes of pitch that still would yield no clue to her age.

The sounds from outside were getting closer. She bustled him to the trapdoor. By now he had his shoes and his precious haversack. 'In the near field,' she hissed at him, 'the haymakers have finished. Hide there till dark.'

It was no moment to linger. But Lionel could not rid himself of the fascination of those eyes, of that young-old face, of the alluring gentleness beneath her rough peasant clothes, that was such a provocation.

He reached a hesitant hand toward the veil where it hid the line of her cheek.

'Won't you,' he was struggling to find the Serbian words, 'won't you show me your face?'

He heard her sharply indrawn breath. A second later he was down the ladder and the trapdoor had slammed shut over his head.

Only just in time. From above his head came the sound of heavy boots and harsh, questioning voices. Clutching his clothes and haversack, Lionel hugged the outer wall of the mill, keeping out of sight of the courtyard, and

7

entered the field that had been only partly visible to him as he approached from upstream. Here, as the woman had said, the reapers and winnowers had done their work and moved on. The straw had been gathered into loose bales, some of them as high as a man. Thankfully, keeping the bulk of the packed straw between him and the mill, he burrowed into one. It was an acutely uncomfortable refuge: the straw scratched his flesh and invaded his ears and nostrils. His nerves were at full stretch, his thoughts in turmoil.

The shouts and the tread of heavy boots were coming nearer. Cautiously he tunnelled through the straw that covered him, to peer out. Could the woman have betrayed him after all? About a dozen peasants with wooden pitchforks were being harried by an NCO and two or three privates of the Austrian army, in full kit, their forage caps drawn down low over their eyes. In their midst stood a little man, bareheaded and bald, who kept pointing helplessly this way and that, shrugging his shoulders and raising his face to the sky as though calling Allah to be his witness. Lionel had him cast in his mind as the miller. But now he had to burrow as deeply as he could into his haystack and lie very still. He heard the swish of pitchforks probing the straw. Instinctively he curled himself up like a hedgehog, his arms over his head to protect his face. He felt a searing pain in his left buttock and bit deeply into his arm to prevent himself from crying out. His hiding place heaved once more under the assault of the pitchforks, then the sounds of the search began to recede. His nether regions were on fire; something hot was trickling down his leg and soaking into the straw. He disengaged his teeth from his flesh and let out a groan. He had drawn blood, he noticed, and spat out a piece of skin.

He was especially troubled at not being able to see his wound. The pain covered the whole of his buttock, and a tentatively probing finger revealed only that he was losing blood. His greatest fear was that the blood would seep through the outer layers of straw and give away his hiding place. Gritting his teeth against the pain, and the waves of nausea that now accompanied it, he rolled his drawers up tight into a ball and wedged them against his bottom to staunch the bleeding. From time to time, as darkness fell, he heard sounds of movement and shouts from the mill. But for most of the time he drifted, almost peacefully, in and out of the blank darkness of unconsciousness, punctuated only by a powerful throbbing at the top of his thigh.

The waning moon was low in the sky and the lights of the mill had long gone out when a sudden tremor shook one of the straw bales in the neighbouring field and into the stillness silently irrupted a limping figure, six foot three in his socks and more in the stout *opanka* shoes he wore. Hobbling painfully, Lionel Robertson headed for the undergrowth that lined the river, determined to put distance between himself and the mill. History and rueful recollection would ever afterwards dub his injury 'the old rogue's war wound'.

★

Two days later a tall Englishman in a slightly crumpled tropical suit and straw hat walked boldly, but with a pronounced limp, into the railway station at Mostar and demanded a ticket to Ragusa. The day was hot and dusty, but Lionel had allowed himself, today, the stored-up treat of a bath and a shave. Gone were the soiled breeches and, with a pang of regret, the dusty *opanka* shoes that had brought him over the mountains. A travel-weary but determined tourist was returning to Ragusa from where, so the itinerary in his wallet declared, he had set out exactly a week ago. Mindful of the worsening international situation, Lionel Robertson was cutting short his tour of Herzegovina and Dalmatia and would tomorrow, God willing, be embarking on the next steamer to leave Ragusa – bound, with any luck, for Venice.

True to his role, he had gone early that morning to stand on the old Turkish bridge that spans the rocky channel of the Narenta in the centre of the town. Lionel had been here before in happier times. His photographs of the river swollen in spate had been well received in England, and had accompanied an account of the legend of the bridge's building that had briefly aroused the interest of comparative folklorists. The master builder and his apprentices had toiled by day to span the current of the Narenta, but each night their work had been miraculously undone. At last the *vila* of the river (*a type of the guardian spirit familiar from the dryads and hamadryads of antiquity,* Lionel had glossed for the benefit of his less erudite readers) had appeared to the master builder and laid down her conditions. If the bridge was to stand firm it must be founded on a sacrifice of human blood, and the bloodthirsty *vila* had demanded that the victims should be a pair of young lovers, whose strong hearts and the strong bond of love between them would bind the fabric of the bridge indissolubly for ever. In writing up the story Lionel had rather relished its sensational aspects and invited his readers to imagine the tragic plight of the pair, chosen, perhaps by lot, the story didn't say, to fulfil a terrible destiny and lie together in the foundations of the bridge for an eternity that must surely only rarely be vouchsafed to the brittle bonds of human love. But he had rounded off his flight of fancy with a more judicious conclusion; the words came back to him now, in the July sunshine of 1914. *We may confidently assert,* Lionel had written, *that legends of this type, of which many variant forms are to be found throughout the lore of the Balkan peoples, preserve memories of a time far more distant than the days of Suleiman the Magnificent when the bridge in question was constructed. Whether indeed such inhuman sacrifices as my informant recounted to me in Mostar have ever been practised in historical times must remain a matter for rational scepticism.*

Having secured his ticket and a seat in a first-class compartment, Lionel scanned the newspapers at the station's rudimentary bookstall. Yesterday's Dalmatian papers had arrived on last night's train, together with a selection of Austrian and German ones, several days old, that had presumably come by steamer via Trieste. Nothing from Belgrade, he noted, was on sale here. He bought several, and as he settled himself in comfort in his carriage and the train started off on its six-hour journey to the coast, Lionel began carefully to read. The assassination in Sarajevo eclipsed all other news, and several papers carried photographs of the assassins, who had already been captured and paraded before the magnesium flares of the press. He scrutinized the angular, stubbly, above all young faces of the conspirators, and carefully pieced together the full list of those who had been arrested, clicking his tongue reproachfully as he did so. He recognized none of the faces, but several of the names were not unfamiliar to him. He had not been so badly informed, he thought sadly.

The pale features of Gavrilo Princip, only twenty years old, stared at him through the grainy texture of the photograph. This was the man, the paper informed him, who had fired the fatal shots. The high cheek bones, the smudge of a moustache, dark eyebrows and shock of short black hair could have belonged to any of a million sons of the peasants and former serfs of this oppressed outpost of Europe. Princip was a student, apparently; and in the thin, sloping shoulders and large hands, in the bewildered hope he fancied he saw in the eyes of the photograph, Lionel divined from experience the strong roots that must bind this young man to his peasant forebears, and his doomed struggle to free himself by picking a crazed aspiration out of the air. It was the face of neither a fanatic nor a madman, but of a tragic little clown. In later years, Lionel could never watch the films of Charlie Chaplin without being reminded of that face and reckoning, as he began to reckon for the first time now on the train between Mostar and Ragusa, the cost of that missed vocation.

It was late in the afternoon when the train began its slow, steep descent into the province of Dalmatia. The air was sticky and thunderclouds were gathering over the sea. Below, the orange-red roofs of the old town of Ragusa came into view, clustered round the harbour. Ragusa had been built by the Venetians – founders, like the British, of a maritime empire – and been built to face the sea. From above, the town seemed to Lionel hemmed in but also attractively safe within the massive fortifications of white stone that closed it off from the hinterland.

As the train descended to the railhead by the modern port, the roofs and bastions of Old Ragusa disappeared from view. It had grown suddenly dark, and as Lionel stepped out of the station the heavens opened. He hired a landau to take him the short distance across the headland to the old town. The smell of cypresses and suddenly drenched earth, and the looming walls of the town as he passed through under the old Venetian gate into its narrow, medieval streets, brought back a rush of memories. It had been here, just over fifteen years ago, that he had brought Hermione for their honeymoon. Here that they had rented a spacious flat up three flights of stairs. Their balustrade had looked out over the harbour and Lionel had become accustomed to waking in the morning to the changing moods of the sea reflected on the bedroom ceiling. Here, too, the débutante sparkle had faded from Hermione's eyes when she asked him for the third or fourth time if he'd bought the tickets for the return journey and when they were going, and he had stopped evading her and explained gently and firmly that they weren't going. He was going to write a book about the ancient Illyrians, he planned to travel all over the country. 'And me?' Hermione had demanded, her pale lips trembling. He had commended her to the wife of the British vice-consul, reminded her of the several ladies whose acquaintance they had made at garden parties during that summer. Hermione liked to paint, didn't she? She could take her easel round the old town and up on the headland among the cypresses where you could see the whole bay spread out below you. It would be a success, she'd see, and he had pecked her drily on the cheek. *She* would be a success. *You'll see.*

But it had not been a success. The book on the ancient Illyrians was never written and the flat overlooking the harbour was soon up for rent again. Mrs Robertson was due to be confined in the early months of 1900, and as the century drew to a drab and windy close the Robertsons had embarked from the modern port of Ragusa on a packet steamer bound, eventually, for Harwich. Hermione was continually sick on the voyage, but no more so than she had already been on land: it was a difficult pregnancy. But Lionel had suffered almost as much, and vowed never again to trust himself to a long sea voyage if it could possibly be avoided.

It was the more remarkable then, that in July 1914 he should have been so impatient to embark for Italy.

His first stop was at the British Consulate.

Here he was surprised to find, despite the pelting rain, a nondescript mob thronging the outer courtyard of the former Venetian *palazzo* from whose balcony the union flag proudly flew. He had no umbrella, and was distinctly wet as well as travel-stained by the time he had cut a path through the crowd to the barred gate of the consulate. It required some sharp words with the two policemen on duty there, and the production of his British passport, to gain entry. Inside the building it was almost dark. Lionel had a sense of muffled, dignified alarm in the comings and goings that, after a short interval, brought him into the presence of the consul.

'Ashby.' He was greeted by a tall, puffy-cheeked and very pink young man who shook him energetically by the hand. Career, Lionel judged at once; young enough still to be piqued at not getting into the diplomatic corps and not too old to try again. 'And what brings you to Ragusa? You're something of a celebrity in these parts, aren't you? I've read your articles. Jolly good, if I may say so.' Ashby blushed easily, and his already pink face turned a shade pinker as he said this.

Lionel, who was not indifferent to praise, although he knew that the young man exaggerated, said simply, 'Thank you.'

'Sherry?' Ashby continued in a rush. 'It's too late for tiffin.'

Sherry was brought – Empire sherry in tiny, old-fashioned glasses – and Ashby's nervous smalltalk poured out unabated. Lionel was reminded forcefully of the reasons why he had chosen to live for so many of the last few years away from England.

When, finally, the consul repeated his initial question, Lionel took his cue. 'The truth is,' he said, 'I'm in a hurry to get over to Italy. It's rather an emergency. I thought you might be able to help.'

The other laughed drily. 'I don't know where you've been during the past week. Most of the time I've been evacuating British subjects as though tomorrow was the end of the world. Worse, I've got half of Ragusa camping on the doorstep claiming British protection and you can imagine how sympathetic the local police are to that. You can try the port offices and the steamship companies if you like, but I'm up to here. No can do, old boy.'

Lionel looked grave. They were standing by a long french window looking out over the harbour. Sheet lightning slashed through the rain and darkness. Seeing his expression, Ashby clapped him in comradely fashion on the shoulder. 'I should sit tight and wait for it all to blow over. The same thing happened back in 'nine. You must have been here then, weren't you? I wasn't. They're a touchy lot, these Austrians. But all they have to do is strengthen their grip on their Balkan provinces, which they only wanted an excuse to do anyway, tighten the noose on Serbia, maybe break a few heads, that's all. Austria's got more to lose than gain by going to war.'

Lionel said nothing. He was beginning to comprehend, beneath the breezy cheerfulness of the consul, the atmosphere of a place under siege that he had sensed as soon as he came in.

Ashby turned to him, a frown beyond his years puckering his high, smooth forehead. 'You don't think there will be war, sir, do you? You're something of an expert on these parts. I'm just a raw recruit. I've only been here a year.'

'I don't envy you your job at a time like this.' Lionel was not unsympathetic, but he was conscious that he was in much greater danger than Ashby and, although he was not gifted with foreknowledge, he still had precious little comfort to offer. He continued patiently, 'So, you can't get me out. Then there's something else you can do for me. I want you to send a cable to London. No,' he held up a hand as the other was about to interrupt, 'it's a special cable and it has to go through you. Tonight.'

Ashby looked surprised. 'We don't – as a rule—'

'On this occasion you do. I doubt if you'll get a reply before morning. I'll

12

come back. And there's something else. My luggage has been mislaid and I've very little money. I should like you to lend me some.'

Relief appeared on the other's face. This was a situation he was used to. 'Just see Carruthers on the way out. He'll see you right. Oh, and – you'll have to sign for it, of course.'

'Of course,' said Lionel, without a smile.

'Oh, and—' Conscious that his lapse into officialdom had been a lapse of courtesy, after what had gone before, Ashby added with a further social lurch, 'what about a spot of dinner?'

'I have been travelling for a week, and as you see I am not properly dressed. If you would pardon me, perhaps another night?'

Lionel then took out his pocket book and extracted a small folded square of cigarette paper, which he handed to Ashby. 'I'm sure I can rely on your discretion,' he said, as he left the room.

The storm had passed, but it was now fully dark by the time Lionel left the *palazzo*. Thunder still rumbled around the hills, but the cobbles were beginning to dry and the summer night was pleasantly cool. He had transacted his business with the inevitable Carruthers and had money in his pocket with which, among other things, he would buy a suit of clothes tomorrow. But for now, and until the answer to his telegram should arrive, he was once again outside the precarious assurance afforded by the consular walls; once again, as he had been on his hike across the mountains, at the mercy of the wolves.

Next morning Lionel returned to the consulate. The crowd in the courtyard seemed to have grown during the night, and to be more unruly than yesterday. From the street outside, two or three mounted police looked on. Lionel's new clothes were somewhat dishevelled by the time he reached the gates and once again he had to raise his voice against several others before he was ushered, rather abruptly, inside. While he was waiting for Ashby to summon him, an official brought him a telegram on a tray. Anxiously he opened it. It contained only numbers, nine neatly-typed sets of digits.

Having nothing better to do, as Ashby continued to keep him waiting, Lionel withdrew the pocket-sized New Testament he always carried these days from his waistcoat pocket and began decoding. His first reaction as the message resolved itself before his eyes was of pure joy, tinged with exasperation. *Wait Milan*, was the laconic response from London to his cable of the night before. Milan was fine, Italy was where Lionel wanted to be. But how was he going to get there? He supposed sorrowfully that those shadowy people in London on whose orders he depended for the time being would not concern themselves with details such as that. Then he understood. Angrily he crumpled the piece of paper and flung it at the opposite wall. Milan was Milan Petkovic, the Serbian jeweller from whose obscure little shop he had received instructions once before. They had thrown him to the wolves.

It was then that he was summoned into the presence of the consul. Lionel was in no mood for pleasantries, but he was unprepared for the complete change that had come over Ashby since the night before. Standing rigidly behind his desk, his plump cheeks and indiarubber frame exaggeratedly puffed out and his naturally pink features some three shades darker, the consul delivered himself of a tirade that was meant to be haughtily indignant but to Lionel's ears sounded merely peevish.

'Mr Robertson,' he began, 'I consider your visit here most inopportune. Most inopportune indeed. Last night I understood you to be a British subject in need of consular assistance and, in view of your past connection with these parts, could not but be honoured to make your acquaintance. Your request to me as you left was highly irregular, how irregular only became apparent to me when I passed your message to our telegraphist for transmission. Mr Robertson, the consular service does not transmit cables in code. Our activities are entirely open and honourable, and have to be understood in that light by our hosts. Were any suspicion of – underhand – activities to come to the ears of the authorities, that would make my position here extremely difficult. Extremely difficult indeed. And in times like these, I need hardly tell you, it could be that the fate of hundreds of British subjects could hang in the balance, jeopardized, Mr Robertson, by a thoughtless action such as yours.'

Averting his eyes, Ashby continued, 'Please do not attempt to exculpate yourself. I want to know nothing whatever of your – activities, or your purpose in coming to me last night. I wish you good day, sir.' At the last moment his voice modulated into something nearer the confiding tone of the night before. Lionel thought he caught a momentary look of wistfulness in Ashby's eyes as he added with a gulp, 'And good luck,' and suddenly stretched out his hand.

The shop where Milan Petkovic did business was at the top of one of the steep, narrow flights of steps that lead upward from the cathedral square towards the landward walls. Weeds grew among the worn Venetian steps and the faces of the buildings rose sheer and blank for several storeys. Here and there a flying buttress spanned the alley, probably quite literally to prevent the tops of the buildings from touching. Looking back the way he had come, Lionel had the sensation of peering down a narrow shaft. Only in the distance did the view open out over the red-tiled roofs around the harbour. Beyond, the sea glittered without colour in the morning heat-haze: his road to freedom that might as well have been on another planet.

The jeweller's shop was in a tiny side-alley where the sun could never penetrate. Moss grew unchecked on the lower walls; the windows were thick with dust. Lionel pushed open the door to the accompaniment of chiming sheep bells. He was angry, he was frustrated; for the first time since agreeing to undertake his mission he felt the hopelessness of it all. It wasn't the relative failure of the mission that oppressed him. He had taken that on as almost a wager with himself; whatever the outcome had been, he would not have taken it personally and could have shrugged off either praise or blame. No, it was his own situation that now for the first time seemed irredeemably bleak. Throughout the last three months every stage, every contact, every moment of danger, had led on towards a climax or a resolution that was always ahead. Now only the danger remained, and it was all around him. He had nothing to do but stay alive, and he foresaw a long, hard course ahead.

'Milan. It's me. The *inglits*.' The semi-darkness was alive with the ticking of a hundred clocks. The diminutive Serb emerged from the back of the shop, a pencil shaft of light emanating from the tiny electric torch he wore on a band on his forehead.

Milan Petkovic was of a piece with his shop, unaired and dusty. He fussed nervously over his visitor, went to the door to look up and down the alley, before whisking Lionel through a bead curtain that led to an inner sanctum even darker, it seemed, and more crowded with miniature mechanical objects than the shop itself. Milan, it seemed, abhorred silence as much as nature abhors a vacuum.

There was a wary excitement in his eyes as he held out a crumpled newspaper for Lionel's inspection. 'You read Serbian, don't you?' Lionel squinted at the Cyrillic script in the dim light. With Milan he spoke Italian, which was still the *lingua franca* of Ragusa and in which he was fluent. What he could make out from the paper shocked him. The facts, and the Charlie Chaplin face and figure of the Archduke's assassin, were as he had read them the day before in Mostar. What should not have surprised him, but did nonetheless, was the crude exultation with which they were reported. In Belgrade, Gavrilo Princip was a popular hero, even though the Serbian government had disowned his act. No wonder that the Belgrade newspapers had disappeared from the bookstalls here.

He looked up at the little jeweller. 'How did you get this?'

Petkovic shrugged his shoulders almost up to his ears. 'Oh, this has passed through many hands. They cannot stop up our ears and mouths entirely, you know.'

The jeweller was a fierce Serbian patriot and of the Orthodox religion. For the first time it occurred to Lionel to wonder how far his ideals were compatible with those of the Catholic Dalmatians among whom he lived.

'Milan,' said Lionel with easy familiarity, 'I need to stay somewhere safe, out of sight. I'm waiting for a message. Unless, of course, you have one for me already?'

The same exaggerated hunching of the shoulders. 'I, Excellency? Does the English government communicate with me, a simple jeweller of Dubrovnik?'

'I don't know,' snapped Lionel irritably. 'Somebody must communicate with you or I would not have been sent to you before.'

'Very true, but that was in peacetime. Now, soon, any day now, it will be war. Already it is not easy to be a Serb and an Austrian subject. Do you know that they have taken Serbian patriots from their villages and hanged them on the hillsides? You can see how it will be. The Austrians will make war on little Serbia. But: can England stand by and watch a little democratic country in its swaddling clothes destroyed?'

Lionel had a good idea how little the fate of Serbia weighed with most of his countrymen, and he modestly considered that if just a few extra hundred of them now knew where Serbia was and could call to mind half a dozen anecdotes of that country's past, then the credit was largely due to him, Lionel, and a decade of articles in the popular and learned press. On the other hand, the last time he had been in England, which was less than a year ago, he had been appalled by the belligerent mood of almost everyone he met. No, he supposed, England would not stand by. Lionel was a rationalist of his time, trained to look beneath the outward pretexts that masquerade as rational decision-making. Europe was ripe for a bloodletting. She was overcrowded and too many of her people lived in ease and comfort. Therefore the deep instincts of the tribe were on the warpath. Statesmen might think they went to war for this or that cause; delicate missions such as his own might be devised with the more or less realistic hope of altering the course of events. But all this, Lionel knew, was fine-tuning, not untinged with pomp and vanity. If Milan Petkovic thought the nations of the world were going to fling themselves at each other's throats to decide the fate of Serbia, so be it.

'If there's a war,' he said levelly, 'I think that England will fight.'

The Serbian's steely, short-sighted eyes were on his face. 'They are saying – I have heard it said, that your secret service had a hand in the assassination. Is that true?'

Lionel laughed his large, generous laugh. 'I've absolutely no idea. If they had, I'd be the last person to know of it. And if by any chance I did, do you think I could tell you?'

The Serbian's expression didn't change. 'But you were in Belgrade. And Sarajevo. That is a fact, surely?'

'Milan my friend, you are being indiscreet.' Lionel rose and clapped the jeweller on the shoulder with a heartiness he did not feel. 'Now, let's be practical. I have to stay here for a while. You – don't worry, I understand perfectly well – don't want me here. I – let's be quite honest with one another – don't want to stay. But neither of us has a choice.'

The jeweller was stammering now. 'How – how long? How long will you stay?'

'That depends. How likely is that you'll get a message for me?'

'There will be no message now,' the jeweller muttered with finality.

16

'Well,' said Lionel unhelpfully, 'I have to wait for one. Unless, of course—'

'Unless what?'

'Unless you can arrange my passage out of here.'

The little Serb brightened at once. 'Have you money?'

'Fortunately, yes.'

'How much?'

'That's enough now, it's agreed. I will wait here for the message you say won't come. In the meantime, you will arrange a safe means for my departure from here. If, by the time all is arranged, no message has come, I shall leave anyway. If a message does come, I may be able to leave sooner. So you see, it will not benefit you to suppress any message you might receive for me.'

The Serbian looked pained. 'Do you distrust me so much?'

'No more than you do me. You don't know whether in helping me you are helping a friend of the Serbian cause or an enemy. But you do know that you cannot betray me to the Austrians without betraying yourself and the cause you believe in. So, is it agreed?'

He offered his hand and shook the Serbian's desiccated claw vigorously.

There was an attic at the top of the building, reached by a perilously dark staircase, which the jeweller owned and which served him, he explained, as a storeroom. It was here, as the days passed and summer turned to autumn and far away the armies of Europe marched triumphantly to war, that Lionel made the discovery that would determine the whole course of his life from then on.

The roof of the attic sloped steeply, and the irregularly shaped space was lit by a skylight. The view beyond was limited to the blue of the sky and at night the stars, until the rains came and the light turned grey and wet. Here, too, there were clocks, but these the jeweller did not keep wound and so Lionel was saved from the perpetual ticking and chiming that, downstairs, would soon have driven him mad. During the first days he felt all the anger and frustration and bewilderment of the wild beast caught in a cage. Lionel was nothing if not a man of action. If he was to be thrown to the wolves he would rather (he now began to think) pit his strength and ingenuity against theirs in the wild places of the mountains he had just crossed, than hidden away in this dingy gazebo at the mercy of the jeweller's likely duplicity and with the certainty that if he was betrayed he would be caught like a rat in a trap.

On one of his first days there Lionel stood on a chair beneath the skylight and silently, with infinite care, prised it open. The sticky summer breeze from the sea, mingled with cooking smells from the street below, flooded into the attic space. For a long time he hung there gasping, gratefully drawing the living air into his lungs. Then, after taking the precaution of locking the door that led down to the jeweller's quarters, he hoisted himself through the aperture and carefully surveyed the neighbouring roofs. It might, when the moment came, be possible to make his escape that way. It made a difference to know that. But the moment was not yet. It irked Lionel intensely to be under orders, something he was not at all used to. But there it was. His orders were to wait. And in an agony of impatience Lionel paced up and down the wooden floor of the attic, as the last days and hours of peace ebbed away, until he awoke one August morning and knew, even before Milan silently laid the newspaper in front of him, that it was too late. Now he really was on his own. The jeweller had been right. No message would come from London now, and no help either.

A great numbness, a terrible sense of exhaustion, crept over him. Time had run its course. The bright world that had illuminated his thirty-nine years, the world beyond the limits of this tiny attic, was gone beyond recall. Lionel harboured no illusions that this war would be over by Christmas. God knew (and God, Lionel knew, was but the reflection of that bright world, accumulated over centuries in the minds of men) how long it would last and what would be left when it ended. Almost without his realizing it, Lionel's restless being began to accommodate itself to the enclosed space of the jeweller's attic. He would explore the intricate, tiny riches of this miniature world that was now the only world there was. There was no urgency any more, in a place where all the clocks had been stopped for so long.

So Lionel, with all the time in the world, as it seemed to him then, began to penetrate the half-light under the eaves, to prise open one by one the dozens of boxes and crates of every size and shape that were piled up there. In the loneliness of his surroundings it was not unlike exploring a cave in the Montenegrin mountains, or entering a royal tomb of the ancient Moesian kings that might yet prove to be unplundered. It was a strange assortment of objects that Lionel found keeping him company in the attic. Before long he had separated out the precious stones – agate and amethyst and garnet – whose remarkable quality was due very largely to nature alone. Beautiful though some of them were, the hand of man was evident in them only in the relatively straightforward task of cutting and polishing. By these Lionel was little moved. It was, as in previous expeditions against the grander backdrop of the plains and mountains of the Balkans, the traces of his fellow men that drew him on. And there were many objects in the attic, most of them tiny, in which human agency had indeed been more fundamentally at work. There were gold signet rings of many epochs, many of which he recognized and was immediately able to classify; carved beads of jade and amber, torques of gold and silver, cloisonné enamels and filigree work minutely executed. The jeweller must be a collector after his own heart.

One night Lionel was sitting up late by the light of the paraffin lamp. He had been examining the same oval, polished agate for some time. His right eye was watering from the effort of focussing at such short range through his monocle, the brightly coloured striations in the stone seemed to dance before

18

him. When he held the gem to the light at certain angles he thought he detected a hint of another pattern behind the swirl of reds and greys and blues, the glint of another surface etched into the smooth plane. He had been teased before by gems like these. Had they or had they not been shaped by man? Jumping to his feet in his impatience – and only just remembering in time to duck his head to avoid the low beam of the ceiling – Lionel swept up the stone in his right hand and furiously clenched both fists. The tension of those still, silent days had built up in him to an unbearable pitch. Outwardly he had forced himself to fit within the confines of the cage that held him. But below the surface he was at breaking point. Tears stood out in Lionel's eyes as his hands tightened, until it seemed the sinews must snap. He arched his head back, stretching his spine, and let out a long deep breath that was almost a sob. What was he looking for, among all this debris of a world that had vanished overnight? Lionel clenched his hands more tightly still: was it not that vanished, beautiful, civilized world itself he was clutching, with the spasm of sexual gratification, with the desperation of the climber who clings to the frayed end of a rope above the abyss?

Abruptly, Lionel pulled himself together. *Nerves*, he told himself sternly. *This will never do.* As he eased his fingers, quite painfully now, apart from his palms, he heard something drop and roll away over the wooden floor. He had forgotten the tiny agate he had been holding all this while. Idly he glanced at the skin of his right palm, that was white like parchment in the moment before suspended circulation came surging back. Clearly etched there, before the impression faded, Lionel for the first time saw the stylized lines of the charging bull, its head lowered, the upward curve of its horns marking the rim of the tiny oval space, and poised in perfect balance, arched in a flying handstand over its back, a lithe human figure, an acrobat with what perfect confidence, with what supreme control of body and mind, vaulting to safety where another figure stood waiting with outstretched hands to steady him behind the beast's tail. But already, while he stared in amazement, the impressed lines on his palm faded and were gone. In a moment he was on hands and knees, scrabbling about the dusty attic floor. Where had the gem rolled when it fell from his hand? He was in an agony of impatience, it would be too bad to have made such a discovery and then to lose it by such carelessness. At last Lionel's fingers closed over the smooth surface of the agate, still warm from his fist, and he bore it triumphantly back to the light.

The lines of the engraving that had shown up so clearly on his flesh had retreated again behind the hectic natural colouring of the stone. Only the glint of a cut surface that had teased him before was visible through his monocle. Impatiently, Lionel lit a candle from the paraffin lamp and poured some of the wax on to the table. Carefully he pressed the surface of the agate into the cooling wax, and held it there for several seconds before prising it loose. No, he had not imagined it. Once again, this time more permanently in the solid wax, the lines of the extraordinary image were there. And Lionel, in his lonely attic, perched high above a world at war, a world in which he himself was now an enemy alien, lost his heart to the exquisite beauty and proportions of these ancient lines impressed on wax, and even more to the extraordinary skill of the artist who had carved so much life and detail into the surface of a stone to be all but invisible to the naked eye.

There were more, many more. Now that he had cracked the secret, Lionel ransacked the jeweller's boxes once again, and began feverishly pressing the smooth faces of gemstones into candle wax until the table was buried beneath the white impressions. The gems were oval in shape, some almost round, other elongated or with pointed ends; the largest were scarcely an inch across, and many were less than half that size. Now, when he heard the jeweller's tread on the wooden stairway that would herald the arrival of coffee and a newspaper in the morning, or the nameless pungent stew with huge hunks of bread floating in it that sustained him later in the day, Lionel, after satisfying that sixth sense that even now had not been completely doused, that the shuffling step on the stairs was indeed the jeweller's, would barely glance up from the table where he sat engrossed. More often than not when Milan came back an hour later the coffee would be cold and untouched, the soup congealed in the bowl, the newspaper still folded where it had lain. To the consternation of his unwilling gaoler, the *inglits* seemed to have lost all interest in the outside world, and, more to the point, all interest in his escape. Instead, when he took notice of the other's presence at all, Lionel would question the jeweller intently about the objects with which he shared the attic. 'How did these things get here, Milan? Some of them are as old as civilization itself. I have studied these things. I know.'

The Serb shrugged at what may have been a compliment. 'They have been in these boxes a long time. I have not seen these boxes opened since I was a child, so high. Most of what is here was collected by my father. He was a jeweller too, of course. He had the shop before me. It is ten years since he died.' The jeweller crossed himself reflectively and fell silent.

'Did he travel? Do you know how he came to possess these things?'

'I think my father was not a good businessman. He was, you might say,' another shrug, 'a collector.' The nearest that Lionel had seen to a smile appeared momentarily to soften the jeweller's gaunt beak. 'But my father didn't travel, oh no. He was a poor man. Like me. His life was those objects you see – and of course the great dream of the Serbian people. He used to buy his things in the flea market. Especially when the foreign ships came in. Ships from Trieste, ships from Venice, ships from the south, from Albania and Greece. The sailors would sell trinkets and sometimes little stones like those, for the price of a few drinks or a visit to the brothel.'

It was not a very satisfactory explanation for Lionel, but he had to be content with it. Where the jeweller was of more help was in identifying the

20

different stones and their properties. As they pored over these together, even Milan seemed to be entranced by the scintillating lights and colours, and to cease the anxious wringing of his hands that so irritated Lionel whenever he first came into the room. There was rock crystal, colourless and translucent, that seemed to emanate a suffused, misty glow. There was blood-red haematite and pale green jasper. As the hours passed like this, Milan seemed even to forget the dry, hollow cough that no doubt also betrayed his fear.

Once, before leaving, he cleared his throat. 'Excellency—' he began.

Recognizing the abrupt change of tone, Lionel slewed round impatiently. 'Yes?'

The jeweller lowered his eyes, then spoke suddenly in a rush. 'Excellency, if the Austrians find you here in my house, you realize it will be the finish for me? They have never trusted us Serbs. Now we are at war. They will kill me, they will take away my livelihood. Do you see? Excellency, you must leave before it is too late. Surely you understand that?'

But Lionel was serene. He had found more than a refuge, he had found a whole other world, a world he could believe in, a world both infinitely remote and utterly his own, a world that possessed him and, for as long as he inhabited the space of the jeweller's attic, he in his turn possessed. Peering hour after hour through his monocle until his eyes swam and he no longer remembered where he was, Lionel had the sensation of growing smaller and smaller until the tiny dimensions of the sealstones came to seem fully lifesized. He entered into the strange perspective in which the artists of the remote past had drawn their subjects to fit the space available to them. A lion was foreshortened with enormous, high hindquarters, its four paws drawn in towards the same spot, and its mane turned majestically to face him. A priestess stood on a high rock, the piled pleats of her skirt seeming to continue the tapering contours of her vantage point, her waist unbelievably slender and her breasts bare. Around her, worshippers stretched out their arms in supplication and bent their bodies backwards at an acute angle. To Lionel this was an extraordinary world composed of colour, line and texture. The craftsmen who had carved these gems had had a love of beauty and perfection, a sense of power and grace, of flowing speed and hieratic majesty, combined with a technical skill and attention to detail, that Lionel had never seen surpassed in the art of the civilized world. He entered into the awe of the solemnly posed figures, guessed at the rapt devotion that held them transfixed before some now unimaginable rite. His blood thrilled to the movements of the chase where lions or bulls were the quarry or where, in the absence of man, the wild beast hunted and caught a deer or a goat.

Who were the people who had carved their delicate imprints on these gems, to be imprinted in their turn on softer, more perishable material, unchanged through the ages? From the clearer but cruder impressions on candle wax Lionel had been led back to the glowing, translucent lines of the originals, to trace shapes and forms made by man but almost invisible to the naked eye. Somewhere in the remote past, the originators of these originals had lived and worked and died: the craftsmen in their workshops, the hunters and priestesses, the wild and solemn animals. When? Where? What was the origin of that scintillating world whose images had been stamped, it seemed for ever, and given a life of their own, upon the tiny inanimate objects he held in his grasp?

Irritably, Lionel dismissed Petkovic and his fears. The jeweller was supposed to be making arrangements for his escape, wasn't he? Heaven help him if he should betray him!

He would always declare in later years that he owed his life to his immersion in these minute gems. The shouts and the heavy tread of boots on the stairs seemed to come to him from a great distance. As the police with drawn revolvers swept through the attic space that had been his home these past, uncounted weeks, Lionel knew with complete conviction that he was invisible to them. He had entered that other world of life and light and beauty. However it was, he was able to climb out through the skylight undetected. He came to, to find himself clinging to the steeply sloping roof in the wind and rain. Still with no clear sense of who and where he was, he inched his way along the ridge of the roof, and slithered down a precipice of crumbling tiles to land on the lower, flatter roof of an adjoining building. Here, out of sight of the skylight from which he had emerged, he sat huddled for some time, as the rain whipped his cheeks and the wind flapped the loose tail of his shirt. Cold began to seep through him, and with it hardheaded consciousness returned. He was an alien in hostile territory. And with no clothes and no money, only the loose shirt and trousers he stood up in, on a tiled roof fifty feet above the Venetian alleyway below and with no obvious way down, Lionel Robertson came face to face, at last, with fear.

Feeling in his pockets, his hands closed over a number of tiny round objects that were hard but also warm to the touch. It was extraordinary what warmth of courage spread through his whole body as he did so.

He had thought he had evaded his pursuers but now there came a shout. The chase was on. The alley that separated the buildings at ground level might have been ten feet wide. The roofs overhung slightly but it was still a yawning gap. Gathering himself for a leap he flung his body across the void and landed spreadeagled on the tiles on the other side. He heard shots, not far behind him, and scrambled on, over the ridge. Here another chasm awaited him, this time spanned by a buttress, a gleaming slippery bridge of hair in the pelting rain. He was across, he was out of sight of his pursuers and there was nothing to tell them which way he had gone in the maze of steeply interconnecting roofs. His 'war wound' was fully healed now, but he collected others in his headlong flight. His knuckles were bleeding, his trousers torn at the knee and he was bruised all over. At last, with his heart in his mouth, he entrusted himself to an overflowing drainpipe and amid the deluge of rainwater splashing over his arms and head, lowered himself hand over hand into an overgrown backyard. From here it was a simple matter to scale a crumbling outer wall, launch himself into the branches of a sickly fig tree growing at an angle out of the ruin, and so to reach ground level.

There were few people in the streets in wartime Ragusa in the rain, but those that there were, most of them struggling to hold on to unwieldy umbrellas, seemed intent on their own business. It was unnaturally normal. Lionel paused for breath and did his best to adjust his appearance. He shook the rainwater from his hair and pressed his knuckles to his eyes. Then he continued his flight at a more dignified pace. He knew these streets and steep alleyways of the old town, and knew how to reach the walls and lose himself in the busy crowd passing through the old Venetian gate without drawing attention to himself. Once outside the town he took to the woods, and half walked, half ran over the headland and down into the modern port.

He got into the heavily guarded docks riding in a coal truck, burying himself up to the neck in coke to avoid being spotted from the cranes that towered above him. When he emerged, covered in coal dust from head to foot, he was well camouflaged in the autumn dusk and the blowing smoke from the funnels of ships and dockside engines. He reconnoitred quickly. The Greek flag on the stern of a grubby tramp steamer attracted his attention. He would have only one chance. He would have to gauge it right.

'Laska!' The gangplank had been withdrawn, the steamer was small enough not to need a tug. Nothing but the crew and the skipper stood between Lionel and the open sea. He judged his moment carefully, as the bow began to swing outward into the murk. A gap opened between the sternrail and the quay. He waited for the thudding of the engine to deepen into a throb. Once he had way up, the skipper wouldn't want to turn back. Lionel began to run. He almost tripped on a rail, but gathered himself without stopping. At the edge of the quay he launched himself, not for the first time that day, into space. His hands closed over the metal rail, his feet swung wildly. The screw was beginning to churn the water into foam, if he fell he wouldn't even have time to drown. With a sob, Lionel put all of his waning strength into his arms and shoulders, and slowly, painfully, raised himself until he could rest a knee on the edge of the deck. He was aboard.

His exploit did not seem to have been noticed from the quay, or if it was it provoked no response. But it caused a stir on board the steamer. As he hauled himself over the rail and stood upright, Lionel found himself at the centre of a semi-circle of unshaven, brutal faces.

'I'm working my passage,' Lionel said between gasps, in his passable Greek. 'To Greece.'

The faces opened into incredulous grins. They were all excitedly questioning him at once. He told them he had been first mate of a Greek coaling ship that had been impounded by the port authorities. The company hadn't paid their dues, he didn't know, anyway, here he was with no ship and no job and Austria was at war and he had to get back to Greece which thank the Lord was still a neutral country.

Lionel knew that his Greek would not pass muster with an educated speaker of that language. But he seemed to have passed this first test. Now for the skipper.

This time he traded assurance for deference. He told the same story, but he told it differently. He was asking for a favour; he was willing to work his passage, he didn't mind how long it took, he had worked on ships, he didn't mind what he did, until they reached their first Greek port.

But the skipper was no fool. He dismissed the men and took Lionel on to the bridge, where he nodded curtly to the helmsman and rang the engine room: full speed ahead. 'I've a full crew and a clean record. I don't take passengers and I don't do favours for people I don't know. Is there anything you want to say before I order my men to throw you overboard?'

'Just this,' said Lionel softly, and reaching into his pocket drew out half a dozen tiny gems. 'I think these are worth a passage to Corfu. Or shall we haggle?'

The skipper glanced at them where they lay in Lionel's hand. Then he took one and held it up in the dim light of the bridge. 'I've seen those before,' he said thoughtfully. 'Got funny shapes carved on them, haven't they? There's some crazy foreigners will pay a lot for those. Digging up whole fields they are, in my part of the world. They've found a lot more like that. But they still pay good money if you find one. Shake on it. A passage to Corfu.'

They shook hands.

'Tell me, you haven't got any more of those, have you?'

Lionel was ready for the question. 'Tell me,' he said, 'what *is* your part of the world, where the foreigners are digging up these things?'

'Crete,' said the skipper curtly.

Lionel delved into his pocket once more. 'All right,' he said, 'a passage to Crete.'

2 FOUCAULT'S PENDULUM

OR so it seems to Dan Robertson, through the perspective of seventy years and the adventure stories of his childhood, that it must have been. Nineteen eighty-four was supposed to be the year of Big Brother and the triumph of the thought police. In the event it is the year of a bitter miners' strike; the homeless have crept out to join the rest of the litter on the streets of London. Three million are out of work. Many more, including Dan, go to work each morning with that knotted feeling in the stomach. Will today be the day that brings the letter of dismissal to his desk? Strictly speaking, Dan ought not to be worrying. He has a 'job for life'. But privilege, even the meanest, is not a thing to count on in the 1980s, and Dan doesn't. He often has that knotted feeling in his stomach.

Dan is a worrier.

Dan is fortysomething.

All his life Dan has diffidently, conscientiously, lived the life allotted to him on a crowded planet. Not for him the flamboyant successes of his grandfather Lionel, still affectionately remembered in what survives of the Robertson family as 'the old rogue'. Dan is impotently indignant about the human flotsam across which he has to step to reach the door of the Institute each morning. There is one in particular, to whom the secretaries sometimes take out cups of tea in plastic mugs, an unshaven man probably younger than Dan himself, who sleeps with a plastic lower leg and surgical fitting propped against his sleeping bag. Distaste discourages Dan from trying to find out: is this a prankster on three legs (we hear a lot these days about scroungers and bogus claimants on our pity) or a hopeless case on one? Dan has never seen him out of his sleeping bag. The Institute has recently invested in an iron grille that closes off the main entrance at nights. It gives a bad impression to foreign visitors, the Director says. It gives a pretty bad impression to Dan and his colleagues too, but he has work to do and if he's honest with himself (which he often is, he has to concede, honest to a fault) he doesn't know why these people are there. Dan votes Labour at elections, goes to church on Christmas Eve, gives sparingly to charities (there are so many, you can't give to them all).

There is also, just at the moment, a new emptiness in his life. The divorce that he and Margaret had many years ago conceded would be in the best interests of them both and the logical conclusion to a marriage already ended, without rancour, in mature friendship, has come through in the summer. It ought to mean freedom. With Lucy set to go to university next year and no ties other than his work (which he might, come to think of it, carry on at any of a dozen institutes around the world, it's only habit that ties him to London), Dan is a free man as he has never been except perhaps in his student days. And even then, he'd been in such haste to find himself a place in the immense rush of new impressions that was the world of his late teens, he'd hardly given himself a chance. Dan had done well at school, he'd worked hard, and been rewarded by termly reports that his mother used to read out to him with proud pleasure: *Daniel has potential. Daniel shows great potential in this. Daniel has shown that he has the potential to . . .* But what it was that he had the potential to do Dan has never been quite sure. And how he used to hate being called Daniel. It had been his father's name, and his father had not been like other boys' fathers.

Because Dan's father was dead.

The name of Dan's father, from the time of his earliest memories, has been as much the object of taboo and reverence as the name of the deity.

But Dan still remembers this potential sometimes and wonders what has become of it. Is it perhaps something like the electric current that, as a child, he used to be convinced would seep out of the socket if the switch was left on overnight? His greatest achievements had always somehow been measured in terms of access to further, shadowy achievements ahead. And all his life Dan has worked stolidly through the set of hurdles put up in his path. Unlike most of his contemporaries at university in the days when 'you'd never had it so good', he lived at home. Unlike many students in those years when the sixties were gathering momentum to swing, he lived a lonely, serious-minded existence between the labs and lecture halls of Bloomsbury and the straitened circumstances of home in South London. The daily scrimmage on Southern Region, jolted standing upright on filthy trains with (in those days) the smell of other people's cigarettes ingrained in your hair and clothes for the rest of the day, began early in life for Dan. Although there were some years in between, the transition from swotting for finals in Chemistry to holding down a job in the somewhat whimsical environment of the Institute of Chronometry, has long since come to seem, in some moods, seamless. In others, Dan will remember with a terrible vividness how his life has been bisected by two summers at the end of his univerity career – in fact, the first two summers he ever spent away from home. What happened during those

26

summers has its place in this story and will be told. But the hard light and the bright white dust of those months spent in Crete would leave an indelible imprint not just on Dan's memory, but on the whole future course of his life, which is still unravelling.

He owed that, of course, to the old rogue, though Lionel himself had been dead ten years when Dan first set foot in Crete.

Dan can remember his grandfather. Everyone had called him the old rogue. Dan didn't know what a rogue was and it didn't seem the kind of thing you could ask. He supposed it meant someone with that peculiar unwashed smell of wrinkled, mottled skin, perhaps also who collected medicine bottles like Grandpa did with liquid in them of every bright colour. That was before they moved to London. His memories of Upland Grange are less vivid than of Grandpa and his smells and the old threadbare screen on casters that hid the bed with the mound of untidy cushions. The room ended in a huge semi-circular picture window (it seems huge to Dan now, he has never been back). Dan can recall vividly the stooped frame of his grandfather, that must once have been tall, leaning forward in his rocking chair by this window. Outside it is getting dark, the trees are bare, a thrush is singing. (He knows it is a thrush, his mother has already begun teaching him the names of things.) Below the window the meadow descends to the dark waters of the Stour. The tide is high, just beginning to turn: you can tell from the quickening eddies as they flicker in the last of the sunset. Grandpa is a wizard teller of stories. His stories always begin here, at the house, but as he sets out, by boat, on foot, by royal barge – even, once, by seaplane – he leads Dan gently into a world of words that never was, a land of make-believe where anything can happen, where witches gobble up castles and giants come down beanstalks, and Dan, open-mouthed, sits for hours, sometimes on the old man's knee, sometimes nestling on a cushion at his feet. With the old man's voice in his ears his five-year-old bare knees beat a path through the long wet grass of the meadow, down to the shore where a boat with its phantom crew is always waiting. Cheerily he greets them and clambers aboard and as darkness falls the lights of an imaginary land come up, brighter than day, and he's off, off on one of Grandpa's adventures that never end.

'Far away in the dark sea,' – Dan would always remember this one – 'is an island with a hundred buried cities, and great mountains, and rich plains. Around its rim a metal giant walks and keeps watch. No ship can enter or leave port without the order of the king. This order was made long ago, no one now remembers how long. Centuries have passed since anyone last saw the king, and the cities that were once gay have fallen down and been covered by the earth. But the giant still keeps watch, and picks up the ships of strangers by the prow and hurls them and their crew far out to sea, where the men drown. Only one ship is ever allowed through. Each year at midsummer a terrible human cargo comes to the island. This had also, once upon a time, been an order of the king. At midsummer seven young men and seven young girls from across the sea have to be taken to the king in his palace. And now comes the terrible part. This king lived so long ago that his palace has become a ruin, a maze of broken-down passages, half buried in the earth. And the king sits without a throne, in the middle of this maze, under the earth, turned into a horrible monster. The young men and women know how to find him in the maze because they can hear him bellowing like a bull. And when they find him, at the very heart of the maze, do you know what he does? He eats them, one by one.

'Until one day . . .' And in this way, lightly transformed by Grandpa's always fertile imagination, Dan first learns the story of Theseus and the Minotaur. The beautiful Ariadne uses her wits to help the hero thread the maze, and the monster is killed. But Theseus is thoughtless in success. First he abandons the girl who helped him. But the end of the story is sadder still. When he set out on his dangerous voyage, determined to kill the Minotaur, the hero had promised his father, old Aegeus back in Athens, that if he was successful he would change the black sails of his ships for white ones, so that the old man should know his son had come to no harm. But Theseus, in his excitement at coming home in triumph, forgot his promise. His father sat watching the sea every day from a clifftop near Athens. When he saw the black sails approaching, his heart broke and he threw himself to his death at the foot of the cliff.

Grandpa had left Upland Grange for the last time, and Dan had moved to a school in South London, before he learned that the island in the story really existed. Its name, Crete, and its long straggly shape in the middle of the sea, as he traced it on a map in the geography lesson, brought a frisson to the eleven-year-old Dan. In history he had tried in vain to correct the teacher's mundane retelling of the legend of the Minotaur. It wasn't like that, Miss, you see . . . And Dan had been gently brought into line amid the mockery of his peers.

Now, in the emptiness of November 1984, at the Institute of Chronometry where he inconspicuously works, the first hint of what Dan will later term 'the scandal' is about to break.

The Institute is not easy to find. It inhabits the no-man's-land of narrow streets between what was once the notorious Seven Dials district of Covent Garden, at this time undergoing the dubious transformation known as yuppification, and the tawdry glitz of Soho. Squeezed incongruously between, on one side, a tall derelict warehouse that has not yet, in 1984, been converted into a macrobiotic flourmill and dried fruit store and, on the other, a deep-pan pizza outlet with wide glass frontage and pink-tiled interior, its squared white stone rises for four storeys in the pharaonic gothic style that, on a larger scale, dominates Bloomsbury in the form of the London University Senate House. Everything in the building is four-square. The interior décor uses polished granite, and all the fittings are of massive, stained oak. The upper storeys are supported around the central hall on lotus-headed columns, and here and there the canine features of Anubis or the wise old owl Horus peep from dark corners. The focal point of the building, and the first thing the visitor sees on stepping into the high galleried hall that is also the Institute's reception area, is the Foucault pendulum suspended from the apex of the stained glass dome high above his head. This feature of the building's architecture and furnishing had been an essential condition laid down by the founder, and seemingly the subject of long wrangles with the learned gentlemen of the University Senate, who even in the less straitened days of the thirties had had some inkling of the disadvantages inherent in high building costs and an open-ended commitment to maintenance. But Leonid Spengler had had his way. A wealthy German-Russian Jewish watchmaker who had failed, in tragic circumstances, to save his family from the Nazis but had managed to arrive in England in 1936 with the clothes he stood up in and a suitcase containing minute gems to a value that has never been fully disclosed, Spengler had at once set about earning himself an honoured place in his adopted country by offering a gift in perpetuity to the University, to set up a specialist institute that would both commemorate the profession on which his wealth had been founded and further the progress of human knowledge. This was to become the Institute of Chronometry, at whose heart the Foucault pendulum inexorably, silently, imposingly, beats in daily proof and measurement of the rotation of the earth, on which all our experience of time is based.

The nature of the work carried on in ground-floor laboratories and more genteelly furnished offices on higher floors is a mystery to most people. Posts in an establishment committed to interdisciplinary research in obscure and sometimes intersecting branches of the arts and sciences, free from the interference of teaching timetables and even from any tangible pressure to produce results, had been highly sought after in the expansive sixties and seventies, when the Institute achieved its worldwide reputation and, in the process, more than doubled its size. A sourness has lately crept in, however. Leonid Spengler has been dead these last fifteen years, and it has become clear that there are no more goodies at the bottom of that legendary suitcase to fund the consequences of expansion. Even academics, outside the Institute, have been known to cast envious glances at what is, in the chill 1980s, beginning to be termed a sinecure, and Dan is uncomfortably aware that neighbours and friends take a still more cynical view of the work he does for a living. His 'job for life' must sooner or later be on the line, and he knows it.

Work at the Institute is organized into nothing so conventional as departments, but there is a general sense of progression upwards from the ground floor, where Dan and a heterogeneous group of colleagues share a preoccupation with data collected from the ancient world, to the airier upper storeys where research is carried on into such topics, unique to our own century, as Proust's *Recherche* and the interior constitution of black holes in space. Scholarly communication and human relationships tend, as a result, to take place on the horizontal rather than the vertical plane. And it is with these lateral, that is to say archaeological, colleagues that Dan is lunching in the Institute's canteen on this November day in 1984.

The canteen is a cheerless place, lit by artificial light in a semi-basement. Here the multifarious researchers of the Institute foregather in desultory groups throughout the middle part of the day. They cannot afford the pizzeria next door except on special occasions. Much of the talk is of pay and conditions, of such abstruse and soon to be outmoded notions as tenure and academic freedom. But Rex Prebble, who does Mediterranean bones, and Jennifer Southern, who is Scottish with piercingly earnest eyes and voice, have been discussing something else when Dan sets down his tray at their table.

'Are you two plotting, or can I join you?' The cliché is worn threadbare, but the Institute is founded upon a tissue of shifting and interlocking patterns of power and mistrust. A seemingly casual chat over coffee in the neutral space of the canteen may be the visible manifestation of untold cracks and fissures with which the human fabric of the institution is shot through.

Rex is just back from a long summer that has stretched from one end of the Mediterranean to the other. He is regaling Jennifer with the tale of his passage through customs at Dover after driving non-stop from Tangier with the selected bones of thirty species of sheep and the whole, and only recently dead, hind quarters of a donkey in the back of his Land Rover. This last trophy, Dan is in time to hear, has now been transferred to the deep freeze in the basement of the Institute.

'All of which,' Rex cheerfully concludes, 'adds up to the bones of a paper for the Royal Archaeological Society. Ha-ha,' he adds in a stagey aside, apparently hoping to make Jennifer laugh, which is impossible. 'No, seriously,' he is an easy-going chap this Rex, his bad jokes conceal real enthusiasm. Dan likes him. 'I've got a whole lot of new stuff about meat eating and meat preparation in the Neolithic. I've even got some indications about the average weight of meat different animals must have produced. In a lot of places it seems to have been almost entirely sheep and goats, but they sure did eat a lot of them. There's a late Neolithic site in Turkey where we've got a stratified deposit – it looks like the knacker's yard for the whole site for a period of two or three years. We can work out average per capita consumption on that basis. Then there's this new thing in Crete . . .'

Jennifer removes a piece of gristle from the side of her mouth and skewers Rex with her eyes. 'You mean the Minoan cannibals?'

'I did look at that evidence. It's hard to know what to make of it. Anyway, that's the sort of thing that gives archaeology a bad name.'

Dan rather agrees. He is, he has always insisted, a scientist who happens to apply his expertise to the study of the ancient world. Graphs and figures have a magic for him because in their depths always lurks the possibility of discovering the pattern that will explain. Dan has always tried to confine his serious thoughts to the realm of the explicable. Which does not, in his view, include human behaviour.

'But they did,' Jennifer presses forward in her soft voice, 'find the bones of children with the marks of butchers' cleavers on them. I mean, the flesh had been systematically stripped from the bone.'

Rex, who has finished eating, tips his chair back reflectively. 'I've found very little evidence throughout the whole Mediterranean to suggest that cannibalism was ever widely practised. Odd stories like that one grab the headlines. I daresay that's what people out there want to hear. Maybe the taxpayer would stump up more readily for *News of the Screws*-type stories about our savage ancestors. That new Lindow Man sounds quite a hit, doesn't he? Garrotted some time before the Romans came, bled, and pickled in a peat bog. But I wonder what the archaeologists of the future would make of *us* if all they had to go on was a time capsule filled with the *News of the Screws*? You'd hardly get the groundswell of material progress, would you? One thing is quite plain,' Rex is suddenly vehement, 'Neolithic, Bronze Age, even later: eating people may not be *wrong*, but it never becomes a factor in economic development.'

'Then how do you explain these isolated cases?'

Rex shrugs. 'Let's just say "ritual", shall we? Archaeology-speak for I'm damned if I know.'

Dan pushes the remains of a far from tender pork chop to one side of his plate. 'No,' says Rex, turning to him, 'what I was going to say was about your particular neck of the woods. I thought it might interest you.'

'You mean Ano Meri?'

'Uh huh. The family seat.'

'You know that site's got nothing to do with me or my family any more.'

'OK, sorry. But you do still take an interest in your grandfather's excavation?'

It is Dan's turn to shrug. He would like to say: No, Ano Meri is no more to me than a minor source of data. My grandfather was an old rogue in his day and those who remember him at all, like you for instance Rex, are pretty superior and a little bit pitying when you talk about him: the gentleman archaeologist. Nothing the gentleman amateur can't do, that sort of thing. All terribly old hat. My grandfather had money, you see. Lots of it. And he spent it on an excavation that by today's standards was too amateurish for words. Spent the lot of it and a bit more. Didn't think to leave any for Mother and me. Petty, Rex, isn't it, but that's what I feel about Grandpa and Ano Meri. Professionally, it only interests me as a source of data. But I wish he hadn't poured all his money down the tube.

In still more private moments Dan will concede another anxiety: that he owes his present position to the fame – or perhaps even the notoriety – of his grandfather. He has always tried, doggedly, to make his own way. It has become an automatic reflex to feel a sense of threat whenever his grandfather is mentioned. *Robertson – not related to* the *Robertsons, by any chance? Oh how super* . . . But of course he doesn't say anything of this to Rex and Jennifer. Because the other thing is also true. The archaeological site at Ano Meri is part of his life. It was there that he spent the two summers that indelibly stamped the end of his adolescence. It was there, dammit all, so he has been told and he has no reason to disbelieve it, that he was born.

So Dan merely shrugs at Rex's question. 'What were you going to say about Ano Meri?'

'They've been clearing out this pit the last few seasons. It goes right down from Late Minoan IIA to the Neolithic. It's still going on, and they're starting to wonder if it doesn't extend all the way to the subsoil. That's about seven metres at Ano Meri. It's unglamorous work, but the finds are pure gold to a bone fancier like me. It looks like all the palace bones throughout the last period of occupation. It's the butcher's back yard all right.'

Jennifer is peering intently at his face. 'And were they cannibals at Ano Meri?'

Rex is clearly irritated by the interruption. 'Not to a statistically significant extent, no. But there are some human bones mixed up in that deposit. Nothing like a whole skeleton. Just bits and pieces.'

'What you might call *membra disiecta*,' says Jennifer with unmistakable relish.

'Of course, we don't know how they got there. Some societies do throw away human bones after a certain length of time. I wondered what you thought of it, Dan?'

'Not my field,' says Dan. 'Which I'd better be getting back to.' And he gets up from the table.

Dan's field is pots, or, more precisely, the clay that pots are made of. Spectrographic analysis is his speciality, and in conjunction with the latest techniques in computer mapping he has turned it into a formidable art. Dan can match up the tiniest sample scraped from a potsherd with the clay composition at any of a thousand prehistoric kilns around the Mediterranean and tell you with a margin for error of less than two per cent exactly where your pot was made. Dan is happy doing this work. It helps to stave off the emptiness that he knows is lying in wait for the end of his working day. Perhaps he'll stay late tonight. People do, often showing a marked reluctance to quit the spaces of the mind watched over by Foucault's silent pendulum.

But Dan is not one of those denizens of the Institute for whom the outside world has been wholly ousted by the intricacies of chronometry. As he works, a part of his mind strays first of all to his mother. Although the event is no longer recent, Dan always knows exactly how long ago it was that she died. Almost imperceptibly exchanging one sort of serenity for another. After what he imagines must have been a glittering early life, and the hero's death of her husband, accepting widowhood with surely more than stoic resignation, almost like a higher calling, with poise, with knowing tenderness. Severity, too. She hadn't been an easy mother. It had been too late, after the war, to go back to the singing career that had shown such promise twenty years before. But Dan remembers his mother singing – by herself, softly, at the piano after he had been sent off to bed; at some occasion with people standing round in suits and bow ties amid sparkling chandeliers and great mirrors, with an ear-piercing strength that shocked him then, but everybody was clapping and shouting for more and he held himself still and wondered: quietly, shyly proud of his mother standing all alone at the heart of the music. And as Dan grew older the operatic arias, the snatches of oratorio half heard between waking and sleeping, burrowed deep into his dreams. He may not be able to tell his Bellini from his Bizet, as he will self-deprecatingly declare nowadays, but the coiling seductiveness of the Habanera or the crystal purity of the priestess in *Norma*, carelessly introduced on *Desert Island Discs*, is enough to turn his insides to jelly and summon up a jumble of sensations too deeply buried to be named. Dan has no gift for music, but when Paola comes to London he makes her go to the opera with him.

Paola, who can afford to pay for tickets for the two of them at Covent Garden, indulges his passion with brisk good humour. 'All that fuss about a poor old hunchback,' she chides him after a performance of *Rigoletto*. 'It's so *primitive*. Don't you think so?'

He has long been prepared to think almost anything that Paola thinks. She is on this occasion wearing large pearl earrings beneath her short-cropped, jet-black hair, and a dark red dress through which the contours of her firm nipples and unsupported breasts can be traced by the discerning eye. A minimal time later, in a hotel room expanded to infinite size by mirrors entirely covering the walls and ceiling (she always has the same suite, when she comes to London), Dan will unzip this dress from the nape of her neck down to just above her buttocks, ease the fabric off her shoulders and feel his member rise against her panties as the dress slips to the floor and his hands reach round to cradle those tinglingly soft breasts with their nut-brown aureoles and nipples hardening already as they blaze at him from the mirror opposite. He has asked her, in mild exasperation, and not for the first time, what she means by *primitive*. Paola, he well knows, likes her pleasures to be complex. Magritte and Pirandello, Fellini and Stockhausen. *When the music becomes big, you become big. When the music becomes small, you become small.* She has made him try this, with his eyes shut, as the four huge speakers in the corners of the room bombarded him with, it seemed, the whole range of sound perceptible by the human ear. At the end he begged her to stop. It was a horrible, jangling invasion of himself, he felt annihilated, cut and mangled by the intersecting planes of sound. But Paola finds this sort of music exhilarating. Assuredly it is not primitive, although he has on occasion teased her with the irony that the most sophisticated aural experiments of the twentieth century should so much resemble the primeval din of the jungle.

In the arts of love Paola's tastes are not simple either, and it is some time before he comes gasping to rest, lying on his back staring up at the two naked bodies that look down at them, equally exhausted, from the ceiling. Now is the time for confidences, as they lie like stranded fish, just touching. The bedclothes have long since slid to the floor. Neither makes any move to gather them up. They look at one another only in their long reflections on the ceiling. The human form is curiously anonymous like this, Dan often thinks. Long and white, with a shock of hair at the top and another half way down. In the gyrations of lovemaking too, which are silent but for an eloquent and several times repeated crescendo of gasps and moans before Paola comes to orgasm with a whimper or sometimes a series of *Sì, sì sì sì Sì* and a sharp cry, he is happy to lose himself in the anonymity of the species. Their coupling bodies endlessly reduplicated in the walls and ceiling of this marvellous room might be Adam and Eve, satyr and nymph, any and all of the great or tawdry lovers that people human history. He is not he, she is not Paola; they are the poles in an eternal and all-consuming exchange of energy. It is something both more and less than love. So it is always a relief to lie like this now, still, beside her while the surge recedes from their perspiring bodies. As they begin to talk, desultorily, disconnectedly at first, then with the easy exchange of two people who have known each other, off and on, for twenty years, Dan is glad to retreat within the boundaries of his sole self. Often, at this point, one or other of them will reach up and pull the cord to turn out the lights. It is only now, when the mirrors fall dumb in the darkness, that he feels he truly, intimately, has her to himself.

It was on one of these occasions that he first told Paola about his separation from Margaret.

Her voice out of the darkness seemed not to be responding to his: 'Soon I will be forty.'

'I'm already forty,' he replied, with a trace of impatience. 'There's nothing wrong with being forty.'

'For a man, maybe no. I think when I am forty I shall become a nun.'

'Don't you dare.' Was she evading the subject? Should he try again?

'Old age is ugly, you know, I won't be able to help it. Do you think you will want me when I am fifty?'

They have studiously, throughout most of those twenty years, avoided the vocabulary of love. This is not because of a lack of love, so far as Dan is concerned at least. But love, in his experience, is a term much compromised by duties and obligations. Love is what has bound him to his mother, after all, and still binds him now that she is dead; it has had to make do for his devotion to his daughter Lucy, at this time well embarked on adolescence. Love is what he has always said he felt towards Margaret, and she, trying hard no doubt to save what could be saved of a bankrupt marriage, for many years reciprocated, until the currency has become debased. With Paola once: there was a time when she passed a half-chewed grape from her mouth to his and he had eaten it slowly and spat out the seeds. They had talked quite a lot about love, then.

'I think you're terrific as you are. Just think how much more we know, now, than when we were twenty. About ourselves, I mean. About each other.' And now he risks it. 'I'd like to be with you always, Paola.'

In the silence that follows he realizes that she is crying quietly. He sits up and turns on the light, takes her gently shaking body in his arms. It is true, she has lost nothing of her lean, clean figure. Only a thickening of the thighs, an inevitable relaxation of the waistline that hardly ever shows when she is dressed, a change in the texture of the skin that suggests the weathering of experience rather than incipient wrinkles, and which he finds actually exciting. He cradles her head and strokes her back. For years now he has been closer to Paola than to anyone he has ever known. But he knows she has her own life – perhaps, from things she has laughingly let drop, more than one. She once told him, apparently in all seriousness, 'I trust you absolutely, silly. When I'm not there, I know you don't exist. So what could you possibly get up to that would upset me?' Perhaps he has drifted into the same habit of thought. He is intrigued, occasionally titillated, by the titbits of her life she chooses to tell him. But he has no means of knowing whether what she is telling him is truth or fantasy, or a mixture of the two. For him it might as well all be happening in a book or on a cinema screen.

He tries to mend the fence as best he can. 'The divorce won't be for at least a year. Lucy's still at school and we're both being very sensible . . .'

Paola's sobs now become audible and she turns her face away from him. Try as he might, he gets no more out of her that night.

These, then, are the contours of the emptiness that will face Dan at the end of this working day in November 1984. But first comes a tap at his door. Following the genial practice of the Institute, his door is always left half open. Rex enters with a bundle of papers under his arm and sits down uninvited.

Dan is grateful for the interruption. He prefers archaeological problems, and guesses that Rex has come to consult him with some technical question about material remains. He is quite unprepared, however, for the particular problem that Rex now lays before him.

'Listen, I didn't want to say any more back there with Jennifer probing for ghoulish morsels. Anyway, it's nothing to do with what we were talking about. But something rather odd has come up at Ano Meri. I wondered if you knew?'

Dan shakes his head.

'This is difficult to say, Dan. It's bound to affect your family – posthumously, if you see what I mean. Have you been following the new excavations?'

'Not specially, I must admit. This is the new European Community team, isn't it? There's a sort of poetic justice in the EC staking a claim to the Villa Europa. The dig's too new to have produced much that's come my way yet.'

'OK, well listen. The first season, last year, was spent in clearing the perimeter of the site, mapping the extent of the unexcavated portion. They provisionally identified a new complex of rooms immediately south of the Great Court. This summer they went in there, on quite a big scale. Horst – that's the guy in charge, he's a grizzled Prussian but he has a soft side, I rather like him – anyway, where was I? Horst was a bit puzzled at first to find that some of the deposits had been disturbed. It looks as though someone had made a hasty exploration of a few of the rooms and then filled them in again. Being a methodical man, Horst checked. There's nothing in the published reports from your grandfather's day. Nothing in your father's excavation notebooks in the Fitzwilliam. He asked the Greeks. No record of anything in that area since the war. Then he came to Room H. Horst's labelling, not your grandfather's. He got to it at the very end of the season, last thing in September, they were all on the point of packing up. Nobody had noticed, I suppose because it's been overgrown all these years. Horst had time to dig a trial trench. Room H had already been systematically excavated, down to a sunken floor level, and the whole thing filled in from the spoil heap and levelled off.'

Rex, despite his urbane manner, is by now quite excited. 'Don't you see, Dan? Your grandfather, or your father, excavated a part of the site, kept no record of what was found, and *then covered over the traces.*'

'Isn't that rather jumping to conclusions?'

'Horst isn't a man to jump to conclusions. He's slowly consulting his team, who're at this moment scattered in ten universities in different parts of Europe. He won't do anything in a hurry. Probably not before next summer's season. But I'm tipping you off now. You're bound to be asked to help in the search. For the missing records.'

'This is serious. I mean, you're not joking?'

Rex shakes his head. 'I'm not joking. Yes, it's serious. At the best, if the records have simply been lost, it's the kind of carelessness that no archaeologist can afford – not even, sorry, Dan, a dead one. At worst – well, there's no knowing. The Greeks are bound to be upset about the finds. What happened to them? Any suspicion that something valuable, or especially important, was found and spirited out of the country would do terrible harm to all of us.' Rex runs a hand through his hair in bewilderment. 'It's quite out of character isn't it? Your grandfather's supposed to have been meticulous, and your father after him. So why, Dan, *why*? Have you any idea?'

And so, on this November day in 1984, the 'scandal' as Dan will always privately term it, stakes its first insidious claim to the empty space in his life.

3 FURNACE HEAD

IN the hectic dreams that came to him, bunked down in the stokehold of the tramp steamer that bore him from Ragusa, Lionel Robertson set out once again in an oarless rowing boat into the darkening current of the Stour. On the eddying currents of the river was etched a fabulous world of lions and griffins and billowing castles. As the little craft came into open water, and the blackness of night stretched from end to end of the sea, it began to bounce most uncomfortably at the mercy of the waves. Unsure by now of the difference between sleeping and waking, as the hulk to which he had entrusted his safety rose and fell, shuddering and groaning, in the choppy Adriatic, Lionel knew only with terrible certainty that he had embarked at last upon the adventure of a lifetime.

His promise to work his passage had degenerated into farce almost at once. The ship was scarcely out of sight of Ragusa before he was hanging limply over the rail, his limbs turned to indiarubber; with all the will in the world, Lionel could not muster the strength to raise his head from the swishing water below, or do more than cling on while his whole body seemed to turn itself inside out, again and again without mercy, emptying God knew what into the inky depths. Lionel, it will be remembered, was not a good sailor.

'Got a touch of fever back there in Ragusa,' was his shamefaced attempt at explanation as the first blue-grey dawn came up over the Adriatic. And it was true that he was still soaked to the skin and covered with coaldust.

For that reason, no doubt, the skipper had consigned him to the stokehold, where the heat of the furnaces must, he supposed, eventually have dried him out and the ingrained grime that was upon him would not transfer itself to the ship's living quarters.

In his present state, Lionel was grateful even for this. When the sacking he slept on was lit up with the glow of the open furnaces, and the stokers noisily went about their business, he would clutch the smooth surface of those few gems that had remained to him from the payment of his passage and find comfort in the touch of their finely chiselled lines on his fingers. If he held one up to the light it was translucent in the fiery glare. Lionel, at these moments, craved nothing so much as to pass through the glowing, opaque looking-glass of rock crystal into that rare vanished world of beauty and grace.

If ever he got out of this alive, if ever the bunch of shuddering rags in the stokehold became a human being again, Lionel would not forget these moments. As he shivered and retched and dreamed, Lionel knew that nothing would ever be the same again. Sarajevo had been a mission, an adventure if you like, but there could be little doubt now of its abysmal failure. In any case, it had not been of his own choosing. Now, sunk about as low as he considered it was possible for anyone to sink, the enchantment of his days in Ragusa solidified into a ferocious determination. In his own way, in that darkness, he prayed. 'If there is a god who watches over washed-up, seasick explorers, I promise him anything, anything at all, just to find that bright world, that must still be there, for one who knows how to look, to uncover the lost civilization of these master craftsmen, and bring it back to the light of day.'

What further indignities Lionel may have suffered before abandoning the horrors of his passage at the first sight of Corfu, history does not record. But as he worked his way on coastal steamers round the western side of Greece before at last reaching the limit of the narrow-gauge railway that would take him to Athens, Lionel mercilessly examined his life so far. He had always been a dabbler in the past, a seeker after adventure. But the adventure that deep down he craved had always eluded him. Now that he had found it, Lionel was ready to devote his remaining years and all his energies to the one grand project that as he travelled at a sedate pace past the mountains and seas of Greece took firmer and firmer shape within him.

Dimly, he had begun to realize that the world of the gemstones that had so entranced him and (as he continued to believe) sustained him through his escape from Ragusa and his ordeal on the tramp steamer, was not totally unknown to archaeological science. In Athens, where he spent that winter, Lionel regained his Edwardian whites, his cane and his monocle, and furnished as he soon was with introductions to the best houses and all the learned societies of the Greek capital, he made good use of his time. Here he pored carefully over the erudite journals and the archaeological reports that had largely passed him by in the pre-war world. From time to time, on his earlier travels, the ripples of the archaeological sensation emanating from Crete had attracted his notice. But only now did he begin to study systematically what was known of the ancient civilization that had so unexpectedly and irrevocably laid its hold on him and had already been christened Minoan, after the legendary King Minos. Lionel would not, after all, be the first to tread this particular path that he had marked out for himself. Arthur Evans, the discoverer of Knossos, he had encountered once or twice during forays to the Ashmolean Museum in Oxford. He had found the older man distant and irascible, and the subject of their meetings in any case had had nothing to do with Crete. But the reports he now read of the Palace of Minos uncovered by Evans, and of other ancient palaces beneath the soil of Crete, gave a solid assurance to the next stage of his quest. He had much more to go on than a hunch and the word of the skipper of a Greek tramp steamer in Ragusa. Although it meant another day and a night at sea, there was no question about Lionel's next (and, as he already felt in his bones, his final) destination.

It was the spring of 1915 when Lionel Robertson arrived in Crete. His first thought, as he clambered out on the deck of the ship that brought him, was that he had sailed into the heart of landlocked Bosnia. This first sight of a strange land was touchingly familiar: the ring of mountains, minarets pointing towards the dawn sky, the sound of the muezzin as the anchor chain rattled and the bum boats came out from behind the cardboard cutout of the Venetian fortress of Kastro to ferry the passengers ashore. The strong offshore wind blew dust in clouds far out over the harbour.

'Laska!' The steamer from Piraeus was ready for disembarkation. This proved to be a hazardous proceeding, as the passengers queued on the gangway above the choppy water and flying spray, waiting to be hustled into the boats by happy-go-lucky stevedores. When it came to Lionel's turn to jump he was alarmed to see the gap widen by several yards before the crest of a wave brought the gunwale almost to his feet and a rough hand closed round his elbow, tugging him into space. The short ride to shore brought back all Lionel's seasickness of the past twenty-four hours. The southerly gale had made itself felt almost immediately on leaving the shelter of Piraeus, and Lionel had abandoned himself abjectly to the misery he knew there was no escaping.

Kastro was already, in those days, the largest town on Crete. But Lionel had no eyes on that first morning for the engaging jumble of Turkish-style houses, with their wooden upper storeys jutting out over the street, crammed cheek by jowl with the crumbling monuments of a more distant European past, the whole huddled within the massive fortifications built by the Venetians in a vain attempt to keep the Turks at bay. He glanced idly at the dry bowl of a fountain guarded by stone lions, half silted up with dust. The streets smelt powerfully of horse dung and roasting coffee. In sheltered angles, under flapping awnings, the men of the town, with black tasselled kerchiefs on their heads and baggy breeches of the same colour, sat stolidly sucking the amber mouthpieces of hookahs. Even the wailing, wistful music that floated by Lionel from one of these establishments, as the horse and trap that bore him rattled past, transported him achingly back to the lost Balkans of his innocence.

40

Establishing himself with as much ceremony as he could at the Hotel Excelsior, where the palm trees crown the highest part of the fortifications, looking down over the harbour and the rough coastline to the east, Lionel could not rid himself of the melancholy thought that the new and unfamiliar sense of purpose that now guided his life had been won at the cost of that innocence. And the saddest thing was that he had never known he had it. In a nomadic life that had taken him from Constantinople to Durazzo and up into some of the wildest country in the Balkan peninsula, Lionel had not infrequently been taken for a spy. But absolute confidence had always enabled him to bluff it out. Spies, at least in that part of the world, were paid agents. Lionel, although he had always had a keen sense of the political niceties of the region and had often taken it upon himself to inform and advise people he knew in government service in London, had never in those days been in anyone's pay. But Sarajevo had been different. In Athens he had visited his sense of waste and betrayal upon a bewildered Minister at the Legation. It had been indiscreet of him to do so; that he had so far forgotten himself was the proof of how thoroughly he had already put his abortive mission to Serbia and Bosnia behind him. The Minister had affected total surprise at Lionel's injured tirade, and afterwards he had had to reflect that this was probably genuine. It was difficult, in any case, to explain rationally why in 1915, at the age of forty, and with his escape from Sarajevo behind him, Lionel Robertson should have felt his estimation of himself for the first time tarnished.

But before his departure for Crete he had been invited again to the Minister's residence. The Minister had quizzed him about his plans, the unusual circumstance of a British subject, and a prominent one at that, devoting his energies to archaeological fieldwork at such a time. There was always the possibility, of course, that Lionel was already in contact with Whitehall through different channels, in which case he, the Minister, would not wish to put his oar in, far be it from me, my dear fellow. On the other hand, if this were not the case, there was, the Minister now bethought himself, a small service for his country which Lionel would be ideally placed to perform. Greece's continued neutrality was by no means assured, as he was no doubt aware. German submarines were rumoured to be refuelling in Souda Bay, other movements of enemy shipping could usefully be reported. The actions of the German and Austrian vice-consuls on the island ought to be monitored by someone on the spot.

Lionel transfixed the other with a basilisk stare, his monocle in place in his right eye. 'Something quite incredible is going to happen in Crete,' he said quietly. 'Of that I assure you. *And you want me to play wise man to your Herod?*'

'Sir,' replied the other with icy charm, 'England is at war. Surely you realize that a great deal more is at stake than whatever it is you plan to dig up in Crete when, as every trueborn Englishman must hope and pray, this war is concluded in victory?'

'I'm afraid I don't see it that way,' said Lionel levelly, for the first time recognizing within himself the fire of obsession.

'Then I shall have to put it to you another way.' The Minister was breathing heavily now, there was no mistaking the truth of the threat: 'How long do you think you will last in Crete without the support of this Legation – the support, that is, of His Majesty's Government?'

Lionel had left the Minister's residence in a towering rage, that had still, more than a week later, not fully abated. One day he would be free of this, he promised himself, but that day was not yet. He stood, six foot three in his socks, on the somewhat threadbare oriental carpeting of the Hotel Excelsior in Kastro, and drew from an inner pocket of his coat the one Minoan gemstone – as he now knew it to be – that remained to him from the fiasco of his passage from Ragusa. It was the agate on which the carved impression of a charging bull was invisible to the naked eye. It had become, for Lionel, a talisman. Holding it to the light of the window, he pressed its surface hard against the heel of his hand. Sure enough, the strong delicate outline of the bull, its head lowered, all four hooves drawn up to suggest speed rather than anatomical accuracy, appeared superimposed on the lines of his hand. The image faded almost at once. He would be true to his purpose. He was already beginning to pay the price he had promised to the god who watches over explorers down on their luck. So be it, then. But one thing was certain: nothing and nobody was going to stop him. And he closed his fist fiercely this time around the tiny gem, with all his strength forcing its imprint into the flat of his palm, until his arm began to tremble from the effort and tears stood out in his eyes. It was a promise sealed.

Lionel had taken care that his arrival should not go unannounced. Already, by the end of that first afternoon, several calling cards had collected in his room. When he strode downstairs for dinner he found a reception committee gathered to welcome him. Magnesium flares flashed as he allowed himself to be photographed for the local paper, *Patris*. With fastidious reluctance he even consented to pose in a threefold embrace with the mayor, in old-fashioned evening dress and bright red Cretan cummerbund, and the Bishop of Kastro, whose one fiery eye disconcerted Lionel more than the patch that covered the other one. His Grace had been wounded fighting against the Turks back in '96. It was not for nothing, Lionel learned, that the Bishop of Kastro had earned the nickname 'the gunpowder priest'. He supposed that the least he could do in return was invite them to dinner and was taken aback by the vehemence of their refusal.

The mayor, whose balding head reached only half way up Lionel's shoulder, was adamant. Lionel was a guest on Cretan soil. It was the first time in Crete that Lionel heard himself addressed as *xenos*, which ambiguously means both stranger and guest. Even used, as it clearly was now, as a term of respect, Lionel would never cease to be irked by this. And thirty-six years later, when he came to be buried with full civic honours in that same Cretan soil, among the flowering oleanders on the highest point of the now restored Venetian ramparts not far from the spot where the Hotel Excelsior had once stood, Lionel Robertson would still be revered and remembered as 'our *xenos*' – guest and stranger.

Untroubled by such prescient thoughts, Lionel did not insist. For this first evening, he would be their guest. By the time the evening was over, he supposed he must have met all of Kastro 'society' and several of the town's licensed eccentrics. It was past midnight before he was returned to the Excelsior – in a carriage that seemed to his fuddled senses to have been adorned with sleighbells. Descending from the carriage, he stopped outside the darkened entrance to the hotel to clear his head. The wind had dropped and the sky was clear. Among the curved sabres of the palm branches arching high above him, the stars seemed to hang in bunches. The night glistened with a metallic blackness. Lighting a cigarette, Lionel dismissed the coachman who had delivered him and took a turn slowly among the boles of the trees, towards the edge of the ruined ramparts. The hospitality of his hosts had begun soberly enough at the hotel. But at the point where he had thought it would be polite to embark on a speech of thanks and retire, it had transpired that the evening was only just beginning.

Since Easter, by the Orthodox calendar, was not far away, the choice of food offered him, both at the hotel and later, was severely restricted. He had been treated in several different venues to *mezédes* consisting of stewed greens, a soft soapy cheese and large quantities of snails, which his hosts assured him were a delicacy of the island. No less obligatory than the observance of this convivial fast was the consumption of large quantities of the local raki, which they called *tsikoudiá*. It was considered manly, he was told, to down a squat, flat-bottomed glassful in a single gulp. And his hosts had been all of them men. He had lost count of the number of times he had been called upon to raise his glass during the evening. Lionel, although constitutionally strong, had been unprepared for the rigours of this exercise, which was why he now needed so badly to let the cool night air restore some clarity to his senses.

He had already dismissed from his mind the vainglorious vice-consuls of the Great Powers, all of them Cretans got up like patriarchs in swelling cummerbunds and *braggadocio* moustaches. The bishop, with his keen eye, had given his blessing and left early. The others besides the mayor had been notables of various sorts, former revolutionaries many of them, who had made good under the protectorate of '97 and now seemed to be honing their political connections in Athens, since Crete had at last been united with Greece. They were mostly a good deal older than Lionel. An exception was a clean-shaven doctor called Veniamin whom he had taken the opportunity to cross-question about the incidence of malaria on the island.

'They won't take pills and they won't touch infusions unless they've been made with mountain herbs gathered on moonless nights and blessed with the unspeaking water. Holy water, that is; nobody's allowed to speak in its presence. Anything else they call devil's medicine. I don't try to persuade them otherwise, it's a waste of breath. I just mix up some quinine and mutter some mumbo-jumbo to impress them – actually it's not mumbo-jumbo, I say a Talmudic prayer, it can't do any harm, can it, but it's mumbo-jumbo to them – and bless the concoction with a little charm I always carry around for the purpose. An exquisite thing. A lot of the peasants have them too, you may have seen them?'

To Lionel's lively expression of interest the doctor drew from his waistcoat pocket a tiny oval of blood-red haematite which had been pierced and threaded with a fine chain. Screwing his monocle into his right eye, Lionel squinted carefully at the object proffered for his inspection. Its carved surface had been much worn, so that the outline of the working was all but lost. 'You know what this is, of course?' queried Lionel.

The doctor nodded eagerly. 'Minoan, I thought so. Before the war started in Europe, everybody was very excited about the discoveries. Now it has all fallen flat. Nothing is happening any more. What they call the Palace of Minos has been abandoned since the English went home, there's nothing much to see. Have you met our Director of Antiquities?'

And so Lionel had shaken the hand of the great Xanthoudidis, who greeted him effusively and discoursed at length about the newly discovered civilization of the Minoans, that had been hailed as the oldest in Europe.

'The divine Homer tells us in the *Odyssey*,' Xanthoudidis intoned majestically into his ear, 'that Crete, in what we must now think of as Minoan times, boasted a hundred cities. Today we have begun to uncover four of them. There is much work to be done. And you, Sir Lionel, are an archaeologist of some fame, are you not?'

Lionel felt constrained to disavow the title that was not yet his, but tacitly acknowledged the praise. With the loss of innocence, he had also learnt a new caution. Lionel had determined not to reveal too much about his plans, to prepare the ground carefully. Gone was the serendipity of the antiquarian that had carried him round the Balkans, on the adventures he had been happy to recount for the benefit of the patriarchal vice-consuls tonight. The purpose that now drove Lionel with the force of an obsession was well on the way to becoming a reality. All that was needed was the determination, which was not a quality Lionel lacked, and above all the patience, which he would have to learn. Already it was clear to Lionel that it would not be enough to be another archaeologist uncovering another Minoan palace. He had to find *the* site, he had to possess the key to that lost civilization, to unlock the secrets of the earth and astonish the world with the freshness and the brilliance that he had already divined in the carving of the Minoan sealstones. To make the past live again. It was a vast ambition, he acknowledged that. And a very personal one, too. The discovery was to be his, Lionel Robertson's. In that way he would invest, he would own, he would set his stamp on a segment of human history that lay beneath the soil here in Crete. None of this could he confide, at least not yet, to the Director of Antiquities, and Lionel fell silent.

From somewhere there appeared at his elbow a tall, sallow-faced man who might have been ten years younger than himself. 'Varvatakis,' the newcomer introduced himself with shy insistence. One of the patriarchs who was passing slapped the younger man loudly on the back, making him wince, and said to Lionel: 'Our greatest poet since Homer: Nikos Varvatakis. In these hard times, now turned miner and capitalist.'

The young man turned anxious eyes on Lionel and said, in excellent French, 'I came here to talk to you. May I?' Despite the diffidence of manner, the politeness was purely ornamental. Lionel nodded his assent, but allowed his gaze to wander round the room. Varvatakis had a great deal to talk about. He was a poet and writer of plays, he said. He had written a play about a master builder. But he hadn't been able to get it performed. Someone had already written a play about a master builder, it seemed. Lionel smiled indulgently: 'Ibsen, wasn't it?' But no, no, this was someone *else*; it had nothing to do with Ibsen, whom he, Varvatakis, greatly admired. *His* master builder was quite different from Ibsen's. No, Varvatakis' master builder was of the purest, most indigenous and ancient Greek stock. His dilemma came from the folksongs of the people. His task: to build a bridge. His problem: the foundations of the bridge keep falling down. Lionel knew that he had heard this story before, but his comparative folklore days were over, he was impatient to be rid of Varvatakis. But he was held by a look in the latter's eye that reminded him of Coleridge's Ancient Mariner, and on attempting to disengage himself discovered that his interlocutor had hooked the second and third fingers of his left hand around the middle button of Lionel's waistcoat, thus making flight impossible. Perhaps, indeed, he had not heard the story before: *and now*, Varvatakis was telling him, in that same obsessive monotone, *the stage is set for the Woman to enter . . .*

There was something about going down into the foundations of the bridge. Lionel reasserted himself. 'Is that what attracted you to mining?'

The other was momentarily put out, then switched track, abandoning the wife of his master builder where he had left her, deep in the foundations. Well no, he didn't think so, the point was, all his life he'd lived a life of the mind, a life of pen and ink. He felt as though (if you'll excuse me) he was excreting ink. He'd scaled the Olympian heights of philosophy and poetry already by the age of thirty, and surveying the world from the top, what did he see? A world in tatters, a world in turmoil, in disarray, a world given over to ease and luxury, in short (Varvatakis almost spat out the word) a *bourgeois* world. What was needed was a Saviour, but the only salvation mankind could expect was a savage one indeed. Anti-Christ and Christ in one, the cloven-hoofed shepherd. Armageddon was coming. From which quarter the destruction would come, he, Varvatakis, did not yet know. From the traditional enemy, the Turk? From world war? Or perhaps from the powers of the earth itself and the strong bond that binds the simple people of a place to the place that nurtures them. Perhaps from the vigorous upsurge of alienated labour, from the toil and guts of the proletariat. Varvatakis took a deep breath. It was not true that he was a capitalist. He and some friends had put some small capital into a venture to mine lignite. There was no coal in Greece, and the fear of international blockade meant that the government was granting special licences to find and extract substitutes. Personally he, Varvatakis, wasn't much interested in lignite. Lignite was a pretext. He wanted to work with his hands. To be a worker among workers. To see for himself the nature of the bond that binds these hardened natures to the earth.

Snatches of these and a pot-pourri of other conversations in French, Italian and Cretan Greek came back to Lionel now as he filled his lungs with the pure air of the night. From somewhere below him a cock crowed and then another, although it would be several hours till dawn. Now and then a dog barked in the distance. There had been something missing ever since he landed on this island. The somehow cynical arching of the young poet's eyebrows as he had talked of the Woman, who had clearly fared badly in his ill-fated play, came back to Lionel now with a jolt. He had not yet seen a female face here. Used as he was to trekking through remote places, he was accustomed to rationing the pleasures of female society. But here he was in a town of some size, and what was more, one which he intended to make his base of operations for some time to come. He became conscious of an emptiness that was almost physical.

And despite everything, he recognized the contours, the shape of that emptiness there beside him.

Hermione was dead; Hermione whom he had seen for the last time almost two years ago on his last visit to Upland Grange – and he could still all too vividly remember what a relief it had been to depart. If these were tears pricking behind Lionel's eyes in the solitude of the Cretan night, they had no business there, he knew that. He had failed Hermione. Quite consciously, often impatiently; perhaps, though without willing it, cruelly.

The news had taken a month to reach him. He had been summoned to the Legation in Athens in the first days of the New Year. The Minister himself had shown him the telegram: 'Sorry, old chap,' and left him to his grief.

It was as though somebody had taken a hatchet to his life and sliced it cleanly through. Hermione had not occupied a large place in his thoughts for

46

some time. Perhaps that was why it hurt so much, now. It was hard for him to recall her face, harder still to summon up some memory of real happiness in which she had played a part. But the pain was like the clean blow of a knife. Something of him had been severed. And because everything in Lionel's mind just now was bound up with his grand project, he had come to see Hermione as the last bridge back to his former, relatively carefree life. The last bridge was down, there was no going back. There was nothing there to go back to.

It was now that Lionel remembered he had a son, as he was wont to do at unexpected moments. Daniel, born with the century, must now be fifteen. Lionel had brought himself to write to the boy after his mother's death: a long, as he remembered it, uncharacteristically confiding letter. Lionel had a huge circle of acquaintance – much of it scattered across the embattled parts of Europe and cut off from him now – but there was no one to whom he would have been ready to entrust his new sense of purpose in the way he found himself writing to the son he scarcely knew. After the shock of Hermione's death, there was someone after all, at the other end of Europe, to whom he might unburden himself. And the curious thing was that he had never felt the slightest impulse to confide like this in his wife. It was a tenuous thread indeed, but it was there.

Before leaving Athens he had received a reply: painfully formal, written in a small stiff hand that looked as though it had been carefully copied. He wondered under what beady eye of starched school matron such a missive must have been composed or worse, perhaps, dictated. And he wondered, too, what depths of reproach or even loathing lay beneath the dutiful endearments.

Dearest Father,

Thank you for yours of the 15th inst. Yr condolences most gratefully received. We beat the Lancers 6–3 at hockey on Wednesday. House master gave us a spiffing tea. Hope you are in good health, as is

Your ever affectionate son
Daniel

Why on earth *hockey*? Lionel asked himself, with a spasm of irritation. He had last seen the boy two years ago, an unrecognizable, already gangling youth in blazer and shorts. His son seemed set to inherit his physique, at any rate. Would he recognize him if they were to come unexpectedly face to face?

Because it was not just Hermione he had, as he now saw all too clearly, wilfully neglected. And from this distance, with the shape of his future life, as it seemed to him now, already sealed, and the assurance of eventual success there, in his pocket, in the shape of the last Minoan sealstone from the jeweller's attic in Ragusa, there was no denying what a waste those years had been. Could he not have forced himself, while they lasted, to live the kind of life Hermione had wanted? As it had turned out, the years would not have been too many. Could he not have played the part of tender husband and father to his son as she had begged him then? 'Even if you cannot, in your heart of hearts, love me,' she had said, 'can you not at least be a proper father to your son? Can you not live with us until he is grown up and can go his own way? And then, oh yes, I am resigned, I promise you, I *promise* you, Lionel, I too will be content and never again come between you and whatever it is that matters so much to you. Never.' And the tears had stood out in her eyes but she had not wept. If she had wept and clung to him he could have lost his temper, he could have braced himself in an icy tantrum, all cold and untouchable, until she had left the room, and gradually his breathing and his heartbeat would have returned to normal and life could have been resumed. But that had been her unthinking, her always unrealized, cruelty. To leave him no way out. And so the dreadful words had been spoken: calmly, even cordially, and irrevocably. And Lionel had turned away from her, to return only twice in the space of a decade, leaving his estranged wife and his son, as he grew up, to wander among the huge rooms of Upland Grange, and make do as best they might while basements, attics and finally living quarters had to be cleared to make way for Lionel's plunder, crated and shipped from the Balkans via Harwich. And what piddling expeditions and discoveries these had been, by comparison with the project on which he now was ready to stake so much. Now, it seemed to Lionel that he could have sacrificed some of the freedom he had craved then, for her sake and his son's. And that was the worst thing: that it was only now. While Hermione lived, he could not – he would not – have acted differently.

With the thought, Lionel was abruptly returned to the present. A rough voice called out behind him and, turning, he had just time to take in, in the light of an approaching storm lantern, an astrakhan cap pulled low over the eyes, the impression of a uniform and the gleaming butt of a revolver. His reflexes were faster than his thoughts. Before he had had time to remember that he was in Crete, in a neutral country, he had dropped on all fours, scuttled behind the bole of a palm tree and from there broken through a hedge of oleander bushes. Gathering his wits, he looked back as the puzzled gendarme called out once again in Greek, raised his lantern all around, then shrugged and resumed his beat. Lionel wiped the sweat from his brow, and made his way, somewhat shamefaced, back to his hotel.

Lionel's purpose in coming to Crete soon became a matter of intense speculation in the small world of Kastro society. It was generally felt that the pleasantries and camaraderie of his first evening had made a good impression, but when that impression had come to be analysed in the days that followed, as it was hour after hour in the Christian and Muslim coffee shops of the town, it had to be conceded that the English *milord* (for so they christened him at first, finding his name too much of a mouthful) had proved remarkably successful at keeping his own counsel.

The story had passed like wildfire through the poorer quarters of the town, and was already reaching new heights of elaboration in the country districts. The *milord* had found a treasure in a faraway land, and made a secret deal with the captain of a ship, to bring it home with him. But the ship's crew became suspicious and one night they opened their mysterious passenger's trunk and found: *treasure*, more gold and silver than you could ever hope to see in a lifetime. The ship and its crew were Greek: word of honour, that's true. They began to argue amongst themselves. Some wanted to cut the *milord's* throat there and then; others suggested cutting the captain's throat, too. But then, how would they sail the ship safely to their home port? They started to shout in whispers, they nearly came to blows, and the *milord* woke up. He offers to resolve their dispute for them, but of course he can only do that if they spare his life. Is it a promise? Word of honour? They solemnly promise. Well, he says, you take a stout rope, as wide as the deck. That's right. Now, half of you pull that way on the rope; the other half pull this way. Like that. Whichever side pulls the other side across to the opposite side of the ship, wins the argument. But the *milord* had tied both ends of the rope to the rail, and in the confusion jumped into the sea himself. So the ship sailed on, carrying the *milord's* treasure. But the *milord* still carried round his neck one small charm, and this is what saved his life. A dolphin lifted him on its back and carried him straight here, to Crete. When the ship's crew came to land, they were ashamed of what they had done. So they'd buried the treasure, you see, and now the *milord* was looking for it all over again.

There was some dispute about where the *milord* had come ashore, and whether the dolphin had really brought him all the way to Crete. Hadn't he stepped into *yero*-Pandelis' bum boat from the Piraeus steamer and been sick as a dog over the side?

In polite society other, superficially more plausible, hypotheses were contested. According to one faction Lionel was (of course) an English spy, sent to make trouble on the island and so (it wasn't very clear how) to bring Greece into the war on the side of the Anglo–French. Another thought that he was a great capitalist (undoubtedly he was wealthy) sent to nose out the possibility of some rich commercial concession. It was hotly debated, among the proponents of this theory, whether such a concession would benefit the island or not, and a vociferous minority was determined to resist a humiliation that might or might not bring profit. It turned out that Varvatakis, who was one of the few people in Crete at this time to know what Bolshevism was, and at this time hated it, had singled Lionel out as a fifth-columnist of international communism.

Lionel was dreaming. In his dream soldiers were digging trenches in the mud. So many of them wielding spades and shovels with a curious, jerky motion, too many to count. The trenches got deeper and deeper and the mud slid back into them. It was night and there was silence, except for the unnatural sound of a man crying. No one, it seemed, could find him in the darkness to make him shut up. In his dream Lionel knew that the night was full of waiting men. Fear crept through the silent mass and coiled round his guts, colder than steel. He knew these men were afraid; the fear that bound them together in silence was his fear, too. And he knew the disgust and the vicious, mindless rage that fear inspires. Oh yes, he was ready to kill. In the darkness a terrible power was coiled taut, ready to spring.

And suddenly the barrage began and Lionel hurled himself forward, up, up, out of the trench, into no-man's-land, into the glare of rockets and searchlights, into the pandemonium of sound that assaulted his senses from every side. Only to find himself spreadeagled on the faded Oriental carpet of his hotel room. He struggled to free himself from the bedclothes that had followed him in his leap from the bed. The noise and the flares beyond his window were real. Guns were firing and what might have been heavy artillery was bursting not far away. And through all these sounds the insistent, hysterical crashing of bells. Could the war have come to Crete while he had been asleep? He remembered now, a sort of expectant calm had reigned all day. And the day had begun badly. He had been awake early and gone out of the hotel through the kitchen entrance, not to wake the hall porter. Just outside the door he had slipped and nearly fallen in a pool of blood. The *maître d'hôtel* had come up as he cried out involuntarily, and steadied him with a firm hand under the elbow. There was blood all over the man's apron and his forearms, which were bare and covered with dark hair.

'It is the blood of the lamb,' the *maître* had said reassuringly to Lionel. 'For the Resurrection.'

And now, as this scene flashed through Lionel's mind, understanding dawned. Tomorrow was Easter in the Orthodox calendar. Still reeling from the continuing assault on his senses, Lionel went to the window and threw the casement open. Below, the square was packed with people. There was no streetlighting, but a tide of flickering light seemed to pour from the door of the church opposite and spread through the crowd as he watched. By now there were a thousand lighted candles below him, eddying and swaying like the current of a river. A dull murmur came from the crowd, but the sounds of gunfire were not coming from below. As his eyes got used to the strange half-light, Lionel saw on the other side of the square human figures swarming up the outside of the belfry, crouched among the domes of the church, leaning dangerously over the parapets of the adjacent buildings. Some held rifles or old-fashioned muskets and kept firing furiously in the air as fast as they could reload. Others threw fireworks out into space, and Lionel watched in horror as a sputtering catherine wheel was tossed in a lighted arc into the crowd, which made way for it with screams of fear and delight. Rockets fired from the densest part of the crowd soared in showers of sparks into the air and star bursts exploded high above the palm trees. For an instant everything in the square stood out, sharply etched in a brilliant silver light. A posse of policemen galloped without any semblance of order close under Lionel's window, firing their revolvers in fast succession into the air. He had time to see the moustachioed faces triumphant with childlike happiness, before he perceived his danger. A roof tile shattered above his head and he heard a vicious ricochet not far from his right ear. The gendarmerie were celebrating the Resurrection with live ammunition.

At last the shooting and the fireworks began to die down, the crowd and their candles began to disperse. One by one the churches across the town fell silent as the people of Kastro retired to their homes, to break their six weeks' fast from meat with the stringy stew cooked from the intestines of the lambs they had slaughtered on their doorsteps that morning. For a long time Lionel lay awake, thinking of the war in Flanders and the newsreels he had seen in Athens: blackened, cheerful faces peering up out of trenches as smoke billowed silently from fieldguns manned by grinning tommies. It had not been quite believable, that silent, celluloid war.

The tall Englishman was by now a common sight in the bazaars in the centre of town, and particularly in the jewellery quarter, where the news soon spread that he had a special interest in lucky charms and would pay good prices. He bought a horse from a Muslim *bey* who still discreetly kept his harem behind the barred windows of his house in town but found it safer and quieter, as he explained to Lionel, to live on his estate in the foothills two hours' ride to the south. Hassan Bey spoke little Turkish, it turned out, but became effusive on discovering that Lionel could hold his own in Cretan Greek.

'The *giaoúrides* have got it all their own way now,' he sighed. '*Ach*, Yunanistan. If it had gone otherwise, you and I might have been blowing each other to pieces instead of haggling over a horse. England at war, Turkey at war. The great empires fight like giants, the earth shakes and the sky thunders. And the little country of Yunanistan is at peace because the *Rum* cannot agree whose side to fight on and fight instead among themselves. God is great, long may this peace last.'

The purchase was a protracted business, beginning in the coffee shop and continuing through two visits to the *bey*'s large, rambling townhouse, where Lionel was obliged to drink more strong dark coffee, and discourse as lucidly as he could on the world situation before the matter that brought him there could be broached at all. When it was done he was proud of his purchase, a dappled grey whose dark colouring, Hassan Bey assured him, was proof that its grandsire had been of pure Arab stock. Lionel politely disbelieved him, paid half the price originally asked, and the two parted with protestations of undying friendship.

From then on Lionel was frequently seen about the hillsides and the rough tracks between vineyards and olive groves that crisscrossed the Kastro district of Crete. Riding with his long back perpendicular in the saddle, a white pith helmet on his head, and a saddlebag full of instruments for measuring and recording that had rarely been seen before in those parts, he cut a conspicuous figure.

One of his first expeditions, now that he could roam further afield, was to Knossos.

A straggle of Mediterranean pines below the track heralded the low mound of Kefala, which Arthur Evans had begun to dig with such spectacular success in 1900. At the far end of the mound Lionel spotted the watchtower that the excavators had built, to gain an aerial view of the site. The whole place was abandoned and overgrown with weeds and wild flowers that were already beginning to turn yellow and brittle at the approach of summer. The place was deserted, and Lionel was able to wander for hours undisturbed with only the lizards and the darting swallows for company. Here and there walls stood up to about knee-height, and on the steep eastern side of the mound the controversial reconstruction of the grand staircase had already begun before the excavators left. A low pitched roof covered King Minos' throne and its gypsum-floored antechamber. Trying to follow the intricate groundplan, Lionel could well understand how the legends of the labyrinth had grown up. But he was unprepared, after unearthing the enthusiastic press reports of a decade before, and sifting through the more scholarly literature that had accumulated since, for the emptiness and desolation of the place itself. A warm south wind moaned through the pines on the edge of the site and rustled through the dry grass. On half-submerged doorjambs and flaking plaster the signs of burning could still be seen. Following the traces, Lionel could see that on the day of the fire the wind had been blowing strongly from the south. It would have been a day like the day he landed at Kastro. Instead of dust from the quayside, the smoke from the burning palace would have streamed above the pines and the hills and far out to sea, a signal to the world, if anyone was there to watch, that the dominion of King Minos was at an end. This was what you found if you dug up the past, Lionel told himself irritably: ruins. There had to be *people* to bring the place to life, but the excavators had vanished, leaving behind their conical spoil heaps, overgrown now too, a rusty, overturned wheelbarrow, and the incongruous, spindly watchtower.

Idly, Lionel picked a wild poppy and put it in his buttonhole. He scrabbled among the thorny weeds to pocket a few sherds. He knew he would not find what he was looking for here. But this was his first meeting with Minoan civilization on its own ground. As he turned his steps towards the tree by the roadside where he had tethered his horse, Lionel had to admit to himself that he was disappointed. There was nothing here of the zest, the vibrancy, the sheer concentrated craftsmanship and love of life that had captivated him in the tiny gems he had found in Ragusa. What had been, three thousand and more years ago, a thriving, bustling palace of the Minoan priest-kings, was already half-way returned to the earth and the blazing, blood-red scatter of the Cretan spring. And mercifully so. It was a derelict thing that had been wrested from the soil.

He came up the hill, somewhat oppressed by these thoughts, to find two boys patting his horse and gently, and only half in jest, questioning it about its master. They jumped to attention at the sound of Lionel's approach, but made no move to run away. Youths, rather than boys, Lionel corrected his first impression as he came up to them and saw the incipiently bushy dark moustache of the one he took to be the elder, and the scrawny down on the upper lip of the other. He greeted them in Greek and their expressions relaxed into wary smiles.

'Are you the English archaeologist?' they wanted to know.

Lionel wondered if he was being mistaken for the legendary Evans. 'No,' he admitted. 'But I *am* English.'

'And you are interested in archaeology? All the *milordi* are interested in archaeology. Aren't they?'

'I suppose so,' said Lionel. 'Where do you live?'

The younger one waved a hand vaguely towards the west. 'Over there. My brother's got something to show you if you're an archaeologist.'

It was not the first time Lionel had been approached in this way since coming to Crete. People picked up things in their fields and backyards. Despite the coming of scientific archaeology, and stiff new regulations since the island had become part of Greece, there was still, Lionel knew, a brisk trade in unofficial excavation and the robbing of ancient tombs, which brought to light finds of considerable market value. Usually, when people came to him like this in the country districts, they had a grossly exaggerated idea of what a bronze coin or a broken potsherd would fetch. Lionel was more interested in trying to locate the sources of their finds than in the finds themselves, but this information was often jealously guarded. So he first asked the youths their names.

'Manolis,' said the elder. Everyone in Crete was called Manolis, that Lionel knew.

'Yannis,' said the younger.

'Manolis and Yannis who? Do you have another name?' More often than not they didn't, they were simply sons of so-and-so, or their father or grandfather had a nickname that had stuck and become a kind of family name, like Skatovergis, which means Shitrod or Baroutoyoryis, which means Gunpowder George.

The brothers seemed silently to tussle over this one. The younger drew himself up to his full height (a good deal lower than Lionel's) and declared, 'Laskaris. Descended from the emperors of Constantinople, the Queen of Cities. We are *milordi* too, except that we have lost our capital city to the Turk and our family has become poor and scattered here and there, and we have only a little land that our uncle is keeping for us when we are of age.' It all came out in a rush, and it touched Lionel deeply.

'Well, you young Laskarids,' he said kindly. 'And what have you got to show me?'

The brothers began unwrapping a cloth that the younger was carrying. 'Careful,' said Manolis. The cloth was slightly damp; whatever was wrapped in it seemed to be flat and irregular in shape. With a thrill of excitement, Lionel recognized the boys' skill in preserving something that, carelessly handled, would already have crumbled into dust.

The object inside the cloth was about nine inches long and four or five wide. As it came free of its wrappings Yannis could not repress a lewd giggle. 'How much for *her*, mister archaeologist?'

Lionel found himself staring at a fragment of white plaster. On the cracked, brittle surface a girl's head had been painted, with long hair banked up in ringlets and secured by jewelled pins, with pouting full lips: the original crimson had scarcely faded with the passage of time. It was an exquisite, delicate thing, sharply drawn in profile. The strong, proud nose was infinitesimally upturned at the end, the visible eye was huge, elongated and dark. This was what Lionel had so missed this afternoon, prowling disconsolately around the abandoned ruins of the Palace of Minos. Here, in this precarious fragment of plaster, Lionel recognized at once the lines and life and lightness that had so attracted him to the Minoans in the first place. Here, too, were the female grace and subtle charm that had so eluded him since coming to Crete.

And Lionel knew at once that what the boys had found was in a class of its own. For one thing, it was far better preserved than most of what had so far been uncovered of Minoan wallpainting. But it was more than that. Out of the hieratic lines and colours before him came an almost living, physical presence. The slightly parted lips spoke to Lionel in a language he had almost forgotten: of the pleasures of the flesh. The girl painted here, though young and perhaps inexperienced, was not, it seemed to Lionel, quite innocent of these pleasures. The hand of the long-dead painter certainly could not have been: Lionel felt a frisson of complicity, of a naughtiness that captured the fashions and affectations of his own youth, as he contemplated the pose, the dab of high colour on the cheekbone, the droop of a jet-black eyelash drawn with the finest of brushes.

With an abrupt and yet gentle movement, one of the brothers, he didn't notice which, snatched the fragment of plaster back and began to wrap it again. 'You don't like her?' It was as though they were embarrassed, or impatient, at his long contemplation.

'Where did you find this?'

Manolis now took charge. 'Ten drachmas. You don't have the money now, we come to your hotel. Tonight? Is it agreed?'

'But don't you realize what this is *worth*?' The words were out before Lionel could stop himself. The brothers exchanged glances.

'Listen,' Lionel ploughed on, 'I will give you a hundred drachmas for this, but only if you show me where you found it. Is it agreed?'

'Two hundred,' said Manolis at once.

Lionel laughed. 'All right, a hundred and fifty it is. Come to my hotel tomorrow morning and you can take me to the spot.'

But the brothers had gone into a huddle and were conferring in urgent whispers. Affecting to ignore them, Lionel untied his horse and began to mount.

'Till tomorrow morning, then,' he shouted, as he prepared to ride off.

'No. Wait.' There were, of course, a dozen reasons why the boys could not show him the site of their find. Already he regretted taking them so far into his confidence. He might waste days in their company if they laid a false trail for him. They could tempt his curiosity for long enough with absurdly inexpensive treasures and by the time he found their source, the site might have been so plundered as to be archaeologically almost worthless.

He listen impassively to the boys' improvised excuses, drawing every inch of authority he could from the distance that separated him, mounted, from their anxiously upturned faces. At last, although it hurt his collector's vanity to do it, he said curtly, 'Then I'm afraid the only advice I can give is to take it to the Archaeological Museum in Kastro. If you can satisfy them it's legally yours, I daresay they'll give you something for it. Now good day to you.' And he rode off.

'*Barba*, we're back.'

'Where the hell have you two boys been? Your mother's been looking for you since yesterday morning. The vineyard's only half dug over and you two—'

'Leave it, *barba*. The vineyard can wait. We're going to be rich.'

'What do you mean, rich? You own ten *stremmata* of land between you, the house is almost falling down, the vines are blighted, the currant market has collapsed because of this damned war, there's only you two to work the land and instead of working you disappear off for days at a time. You're not going to get rich, word of honour you're not, you're going to leave your mother in her old age like stubble on the plain. Rich, indeed.'

'But uncle—'

The older man's heavy dark features gathered into a frown. '*Have you been to the foreign milord, after I told you—*'

'Uncle, listen. We're saved, and mother too. You won't believe it. We took him something we'd found. Like you said we weren't to, I know, but listen to what he said. He said it was worth *three hundred drachmas*. That's enough to—'

'How much did you say?'

'Well, we didn't agree a price. But he offered a hundred and fifty there and then. But he'll pay more, I'm sure of it.'

'So what happened? Didn't you get the money?'

'Well, no – but he's going to, when we go to him in Kastro.'

'But Manolis, you've forgotten – how he got sort of cold and nasty and told us to go to the Museum.'

'Shut up, you fool,' Manolis hissed loudly in his brother's ear, but it was too late.

'What, and have our own *milordi* come up here, Mr Archaeologist this, Mr Archaeologist that, and for this you need a permit, for that you need the beneficence of his grace the prefect of the region, and for everything you need bloody money and the right connections. I know what would happen. It's been done before, I've heard about it. It's called expropriation. The foreigners come here and take over our land and dig up what's ours that's buried there. And our own lackeys – archaeologists, museum people, they're all the same, they're all in the pockets of the foreigners, they even dress like Europeans, they're trying to be like them and make no mistake, you two, the said Europeans just laugh up their sleeves at the way our toadies carry on, toadying up to them, and take all their flattery. You mark my words, they're after one thing and one thing only, all those rich *milordi*. They're treasure-hunters, freebooters. And if there's any treasure here, by Christ and the saints it belongs to us. So no more *milordi*, no more toadying, you two, do you understand?'

'But *barba*, what about the money he's going to give us?'

'Laskarids are *honest* men, Manolis. Never forget that. I've said: no more *milordi*.'

In Europe the Great War continued to rage. By that summer, news of the Anzac disaster at Gallipoli had travelled to Crete. The war had suddenly come close. After Gallipoli, Lionel found the Cretans treated him with a new sympathy. Well, you people certainly tried to give the Turk a bloody nose, they seemed to be saying; and, like us, you've found it isn't easy. A hard nut to crack, the Turk – even, it seems, for the biggest empire in the world. Lionel detected a note of grim smugness in all this. The Cretans, even many of the Muslims he met, were patriotic to a degree that frightened him. They would never comprehend the lively disgust that bound him, Lionel, to his country. And bound he continued to be, as he dutifully filed his despatches for the confidential courier who would convey them to the Legation in

Athens. Lionel had accepted the price to be paid, and was punctilious in paying it. But it did not instil in him much love for his native land – or, indeed, for himself.

As summer gave way to autumn rains and winter gales, Lionel adapted to the slow rhythms of the place. He continued to roam on horseback over the island in all weathers; he asked questions in bazaars. Everywhere he went he talked to local schoolmasters, many of whom were enthusiastic antiquarians. By the time he had been in Crete a year Lionel had walked and ridden over hundreds of square miles. He had prodded over and cursorily mapped all the known ancient sites, he had developed a keen eye for the pottery that could often be found lying scattered on the surface of ploughed fields. He knew as well as anyone the lie of the inhabited lowlands where, in ancient times much as today, the centres of population must have clustered. In summer the mountain bulk of Psiloriti receded into the heat-haze, but in winter when the clouds lifted, its dazzling white in the clear air seemed to hang over the old ramparts of Kastro and the snow would descend almost to the edge of the plain. He could well believe the claim that Crete in its heyday had boasted a hundred cities. He had spotted more than fifty sites which would yield, he was sure, secrets of the same lost civilization as the Palace of Minos at Knossos. But even Lionel's ambitions were not so extensive. He was in search of the one site that would rival Knossos in the richness and artistry of the finds. It was the ancient Minoans as a living people who by now held him in their grip: their art, their sense of beauty that he had first glimpsed in the sealstones in Ragusa, that had spoken to him of his own youth in the painted figure the two Laskaris boys had shown him at Knossos.

The Cretans, in their way, were not so far wrong in identifying him with the treasure-seekers of local legend. It was treasure of a kind that Lionel was seeking, though its value, for him, would not be dependent on the gold or silver or precious metals discovered. His goal was nothing less than a civilization.

And by the end of 1916 he was convinced that he had found it: on a hilltop not far from Kastro with a commanding view of the whole sweep of the bay, from the conical peak of Stroumboulas that guards the mountain road westwards, to the sharply-etched ridge of Iouktas to the east. The nearest village was half a mile away. It was farming land, with smallholdings of vines and olives among a scatter of low white-painted houses of mudbrick. The local, Turkish name for the place was Kulhantepe: Furnace Head, as it was enigmatically explained to him. Lionel had all the antiquarian's faith in the hidden clues preserved by placenames. From a distance the outline of the long escarpment might be reminiscent, he supposed, of a recumbent human figure with the head slightly raised. Someone he asked thought he remembered the place being used by gipsy charcoal burners 'a long time ago, fifty years, a hundred, how should I know?' Lionel could see in his imagination, a long way off, the sinister red glow of braziers on a winter night. It must have looked as though the hilltop itself were smouldering with fire.

Lionel did not come on Kulhantepe by chance. He had made enquiries about the Laskaris brothers after they had failed to turn up at his hotel more than a year ago. They were well known in the bazaar. Hard facts were difficult to come by, but Lionel became convinced over a period of months that Manolis Laskaris was carrying on a brisk clandestine trade in Minoan antiquities. And clearly, in these straitened times, there were buyers who could be discreet, even in the tiny world of the relatively well-to-do in Kastro. Some may have been agents for collectors abroad, though Lionel supposed that the times could not be very propitious for them. Others, he strongly suspected, were making a canny investment as the value of the drachma plummeted and the certainty loomed that Venizelos would prevail and take Greece into the war. The painted head of the young girl that could have been his for ten drachmas, he never saw again, and for this he never quite forgave the brothers.

More than once he thought he saw Manolis. But all the young men from the country who crowded the streets and cafés of Kastro during the day wore the same black tasselled kerchief and baggy black breeches; he could easily have been mistaken. If it was Manolis, then Lionel could be sure he was avoiding him, since he himself was conspicuous enough. In due course he learnt the name of the village. When he went there, on a day in late autumn, it was a cluster of white-daubed hovels where dust and straw blew round his horse's head. The faces of the houses were blank as tombs. Inside, they seemed to be as empty of life. Everyone was at the olive harvest. From here to the hilltop of Kulhantepe he needed no other guide than his practised eye for the terrain. As he rode on, he waved to groups of olive-pickers who stared at him stonily in return. On that first day he must have spent less than an hour at the place that within a few years would become known throughout the world as Ariadne's Summer Palace.

It was a commanding position, with a gentle gradient to the north, but falling steeply away to a now-dry riverbed to the southwest. Stepping over the vines and the tangled weeds that were beginning to grow again now that summer had ceased to scorch them, he mapped out the outcrops of masonry that broke through the soil. He examined carefully what might have been field terraces on the steeper western side, but were not, although they served that function well enough today. With mounting excitement he realized that the outer, retaining walls of the palace still stood in places to a height of more than ten feet. Inside, where the roots of the Laskaris' vines would have crept to find nourishment through the centuries, there must be deep and, with any luck, undisturbed deposits. In the preface to the first volume of *Ariadne's Summer Palace*, which appeared on the eve of the Second World War, Lionel Robertson would describe the discovery of that day:

58

The wind was again blowing strongly from the South, as it had been blowing on the day that I first landed at Kastro, and as we now know that it was blowing on the day that Knossos and Ariadne's Summer Palace, too, were destroyed. So great was my conviction, which seemed to emanate from the very ground on which I trod, that beneath my feet lay some of the most important treasures of the Minoan civilization yet to be unearthed, that I formed the resolution there and then, and without further preliminary investigation, to purchase the land of Kulhantepe and begin to excavate as soon as circumstances would permit.

'Of course,' as Rex Prebble will remark confidingly to Dan half a century on, 'it says nothing in *Ariadne's Summer Palace* about how he did it. You've got to admire your grandfather's nerve. But it's not a pretty story.'

With the wind at his back now, Lionel rode his horse slowly down the slope that led to the village. His eyes were fixed on the distant curve of the shoreline and the white-flecked sea beyond. But the chances are that he saw none of these things. In his mind's eye the future must have begun to unroll inexorably from this fateful here and now. Whether the triumphs to come, or any inkling of the price yet to be paid, passed before his eyes at that moment, is not recorded. But abstracted Lionel certainly was as, almost without noticing it, he entered the village.

Here he found his way barred by half a dozen men carrying long-handled rifles from the last century. They wore crossed bandoliers on their chests, and each carried a heavy knife at his waist. Still scarcely comprehending, Lionel reined in his horse. As he did so, he sensed a movement behind him. He turned to see more men, similarly armed, moving into the spaces between the houses, blocking his retreat. Others had now appeared, looking down from the flat roofs. Somewhere outside the village a donkey was braying as though in pain. Dogs barked here and there. The wind moaned past the houses, whipping up dust devils in the open space between them. The circle of men, their black kerchiefs drawn down low over their eyes, was intently silent.

Then the silence was cut by a sound that Lionel could not at first recognize but by some atavistic instinct made the blood freeze in his veins. A hard, grating, whining sound. And then he knew. The sound of steel being sharpened on stone. His horse whinnied and pawed the ground. Lionel tightened his grip on the reins.

Two of the men now came forward and grasped his horse by the bridle. Still in total silence, the invitation to dismount was unmistakable. Slowly, Lionel got down from his horse, realizing as he did so that any tactical advantage that had remained to him was now lost. He allowed himself to be escorted between the houses, to the edge of the open ground beyond. Here a man was standing under a plane tree. Not far away was a wooden wellhead. The man was huge: not as tall as Lionel, it's true, but much, much broader. A bull of a man, Lionel could not help thinking at once. His head rose tall out of his shoulders with scarcely any neck at all. He had a steep forehead and high hairline; his sharply chiselled features and pride of bearing reminded Lionel of photographs he had seen of desert Arabs. Beside him, miniature caricatures of himself by comparison, their faces set in an imitation of the severity of their elders that to Lionel seemed rather touchingly vulnerable, stood the two young men whom he recognized from Knossos.

The man's voice, when at last it broke the silence, seemed to come from deep within his chest.

'Do Englishmen fight with fists, or with knives?'

'Why should I fight at all? I am — ' (Lionel had learnt to exploit this one) ' — a stranger in your country. I haven't come here to fight.'

'Then what have you come here for? To dig up treasure? To pick up our land by the handles and carry it off?' It was almost a growl.

Lionel was impressed by the man's intensity. Also by the silent, armed throng that he could sense at his back. He stepped forward and stiffly held out his hand, introducing himself. 'I have had the pleasure of meeting these two young men,' he went on, enunciating carefully, 'whose name if I remember right is Laskaris. I don't think I—'

But the other ignored the ritual of greeting, and remained obstinately anonymous.

'These two young men are not yet of age. They are poor men, but honest. All they have is the vineyards up there. Their father gave his life, fighting the Turk.' Here he spat on the ground close to Lionel's feet. 'They have a mother who is a widow, and sick. They should work hard, but they don't. They waste time, they wander about. Here and there they pick things up in the fields. Perhaps they dig for treasure, it doesn't matter. They are poor, but honest, do you understand? They find small things, they take them to the bazaar. Some *milord* comes and pays money. A little money – a little treasure. It pays for the doctor to come from Kastro for their mother. But they don't find any treasure here. They have to go far away, looking for it. That's why their vineyards are so bad.' The man was suddenly bellowing. 'There isn't any treasure here. Understood?'

Lionel's confidence began to return as this tirade continued. It was the silence, so uncharacteristic of the Cretans as he knew them, that he feared most. He could sense the coiled-up violence beginning to dissipate in the group behind him, too.

In his mildest manner he said, 'I am not looking for – treasure, as you call it. But I am interested in buying land. I have a good reason for wanting to buy part of the land that you say belongs to these two young men. You will see that I will pay a good price for it. Now, to whom shall I send my lawyer tomorrow?'

The mention of a profession that, Lionel should by now have known, is not much loved in the villages, was a tactical error. The other flared up at once. 'No lawyers, no *milordi*. I have said. Now go. Go with God. And never come back.'

Lionel wasted no time on his return to Kastro, somewhat shaken after the emotional switchback of the day. He established a reasonable price at which to begin negotiations for the purchase of the land. Even without the hostility he had encountered at Kulhantepe, he knew, the process could be expected to take months, perhaps even years. Lionel was prepared to sit it out. At first nothing happened. His lawyer's emissaries were turned back at the entrance to the village. But he had allowed word to spread of the generous, though not excessive, sum he was prepared to pay. This was a price that could have been commanded by more fertile and accessible farming land than Kulhantepe, in the relatively prosperous years before the outbreak of war in Europe. Now, and particularly given the dilapidated state of the vines and the field drainage system that Lionel had had confirmed, it was an offer that could not be refused. It was just a question of waiting.

But when, after an impasse that lasted into early spring, Lionel did receive a response, it incensed him even more than the previous silence. The document had been drawn up by a lawyer in Kastro, but beneath the pompous legalese Lionel had no difficulty in discerning the intemperate bluster that had been directed at his head on the edge of the village that windy afternoon. It was signed Manolis Laskaris, uncle and guardian of the legal owners, Manolis and Yannis Laskaris. Confusingly, but not improbably, uncle and nephew had the same name. There were a great many flourishes about the two under-age boys and their sick mother. The right to retain their home as the inalienable possession of the family was reiterated in several paragraphs. Lionel read irritably on. He had no intention of paying good money to evict those people from their wretched hovel, nor did he want to be burdened with collecting rents. He had already decided where on the site he would build a dig-house for himself and the team that would gather at Kulhantepe once excavations began. The Laskaris' home had no part in his plan. Finally, having a view to the undoubted natural advantages of the site and its unbroken seigniority by a family of ancient and distinguished lineage, Manolis Laskaris proposed to settle, on behalf of his young protégés, for a sum four times what Lionel had offered.

It was only two days after this that the English *milord* was reported to have embarked for Piraeus. True, he had kept on his suite at the Excelsior. Heads nodded sagely, knowingly. That was just for the look of the thing. No doubt someone would be sent from Athens or wherever the *milord* ended up next, hunting for buried treasure, to collect his things. Yes, some said more cynically, and pay his bills, too. Varvatakis who, when not mining, was

61

often seen about the better houses of Kastro, offered some wisecrack about the Trojan Horse, but nobody took much notice. Weighty matters were being deliberated that spring in the offices of the municipality of Kastro and of the prefect of the region. Turkish names for villages and local landmarks, now that the island was part of the Greek motherland, were to be abolished. Even the name of Kastro itself was to be changed – although it would be several generations before the new name would be used without self-consciousness by many of the inhabitants. On the new maps that were being prepared in the offices of the prefecture, the hilltop of Kulhantepe had already disappeared. Since the place had never been known by any other name within historical memory, the civil servants of the prefecture rechristened it, no one knows whether prompted by the imagination of their profession or the prescient hint of the English *milord*, 'Upper Land'. When Lionel returned, as return he did, in the summer of 1917, the title deeds he signed were to 'ten *stremmata* of cultivated land at Ano Meri'.

The deeds were signed in the presence of lawyers and, for an appropriately high fee, countersigned and authorized by the prefect of the region. The price was a good deal less than Lionel had originally offered. Attached to the deeds was a florid document bearing several seals and the signature of Venizelos himself. To the Englishman Lionel Robertson was conceded on behalf of the Provisional Government in Salonika the right of compulsory purchase of land for the purpose of excavation to extract lignite, in the national interest.

No one seemed much concerned whether lignite in fact existed at Ano Meri. It had been enough to invoke the traces left behind, in the last century, by the gipsy charcoal burners of Kulhantepe.

4 FIRST BLOOD

ON the day after Venizelos' victory at the polls, which would ensure at long last Greece's entry into the carnage of the European war, Lionel rode out at the head of a detachment of gendarmes to claim his prize.

The day was white-hot and still. Dust lay everywhere, coating the leaves of the vines they passed, even lying in a thin film over the water in the troughs where the horses drank noisily and gratefully at each village on the way. The water was cool though, from a local spring, and the trough would be shaded, more often than not, by a giant plane tree whose already browning leaves would drift down lazily to mingle with the dust and the trampled mud where the water had overflowed. The men all wore sweat rags under their forage caps. Lionel was glad to have his pith helmet, but the perspiration ran into his eyes and he was acutely conscious of his reddened northern skin alongside the hardened, swarthy faces of his companions.

Around him, as they rode uphill into the midday glare, the talk was all of the war. Their hero (for he was a Cretan), Venizelos, was sure now to commit troops to the Salonika front. They would volunteer, of course, every man of them. It was all very well guarding the fields of the rich and keeping order on public holidays, but it wasn't real men's work. Some were old enough to have taken part in the fighting of '96 and '97, and had bloodcurdling tales to tell. The younger among them were more enthusiastic still. No one seemed quite sure who the enemy were this time: some said the Turks, others the Bulgars. The *kapetanios* wanted to know, as others had done since his arrival in Crete, why Lionel was not in uniform fighting for his own country. Not to be outdone by the spirit of manly boasting around him, Lionel gave a somewhat lurid account of his escape from behind enemy lines in Bosnia. England, he explained, was a staunch friend of Venizelos. He himself had come to Crete to find lignite, that would be needed to power ships and factories, to help Greece win the war. The men looked doubtfully at one another. Wars in their book were won with muskets and knives and the heady, infectious, irresistible cry of *Ayera!* That was how they had driven the hated Turkish rulers out of Crete in '97. That was how they would drive these Bulgars or Turks or whoever they were on the Salonika front into the sea. And they wouldn't stop there. In a year, two years at most, Constantinople would be theirs once more, the interrupted Mass would be resumed in the cathedral of Saint Sophia and who knew, even perhaps the emperor himself, who had lain frozen into marble in a secret hiding place within the walls, ever since that fateful day hundreds of years ago when the Queen of Cities fell, would come riding miraculously into the fray to reclaim his own. There would be no stopping them then. With the cry of *Ayera* echoing from mountains and plains, the Greek army would sweep through Asia Minor, liberating their brethren who had remained slaves to the Turk, setting fire to villages and cutting off the heads of their enemies as their enemies had so often done to them. Ayvali, Smyrna, who knew, perhaps even Antioch. The younger ones stared moist-eyed into the haze and dust of the road, touchingly transported to fields of glory. Their elders were more reticent, gruffly tolerant of the dreams of youth.

But on one thing all were equally sceptical, although deference to the distinguished foreigner in their midst forbade their saying so outright: what was this about lignite? Surely nobody ever won a war digging for coal?

It was early afternoon and the sun was almost overhead when the little group of horsemen passed through the village. By now they had fallen silent, and were riding close together, with Lionel, the reason for their expedition, in their midst. The houses were as still and apparently uninhabited as before. Even the animals seemed to have gone. The *kapetanios* at their head confided to Lionel with a worried frown, 'This is what they would do in the days of the Turks. When the Turks sent out the *zaptiedes* our people would lock up their houses and take to the hills.' The man's voice trailed off, clearly disconcerted by the comparison his words had evoked.

At a slow canter they advanced through the village. Some of the men had unslung their rifles, and fixed bayonets. The olive trees shimmered in the heat. Where they grew close to the track, the men would rein in and inspect them carefully for any hint of an ambush. The horses were becoming fretful, Lionel noticed. At last they saw them, ranged in the open in front of the vines where the Laskaris' fields began. There were about a dozen of them, all in black, from tasselled kerchief to boots, standing out against the white hillside. As before, they carried a mixture of rifles and muskets, some of which must have been very old indeed and Lionel wondered how seriously they were to be feared as weapons. He was more worried to notice that several of them had fixed bayonets.

The gendarmes, as they approached, fanned out a little, carelessly trampling the unstaked vines. The two sides faced one another at a distance of ten yards. Lionel had spotted the elder Manolis in the centre of the line, conspicuous by his bulk and his bull neck. He wasn't sure at this distance which of the flanking figures were the nephews whose land he now legally owned. Perhaps Manolis had hustled them away for safety. As though a signal had been given, Lionel handed the *kapetanios* the bundle of official papers he had brought with him, tied with the seal of the prefect. The *kapetanios* and three of his men dismounted, and went towards Manolis, whom they seemed to recognize by instinct. At the distance where he sat on his horse, Lionel could not hear what was said, but he noted the exaggerated gestures of parley, the unfurling of the papers, the back of the hand imperiously tapping the unfolding sheets to proclaim their authority, though Lionel doubted whether either man could read what was written on them. Again with large-scale, almost hieratic gestures, the papers were rolled up again and replaced in the officer's tunic. Now was the moment of confrontation. The air was thick with the whirring of cicadas, the buzzing of flies that kept settling on the horses' flanks; from time to time one of the horses whinnied restively. The heat was appalling. While the men on either side of them stared one another out over the tips of their bayonets, the leaders, their weapons still slung, conversed eloquently with their hands. The *kapetanios* half turned with an outstretched arm pointing to Lionel, then wheeled round to point emphatically towards the hillside beyond the line of armed men. Manolis stood with his legs apart, like thick trees rooted in the ground, and waved his upturned palms up and down. There was nothing doing. No doubt he was appealing to the gendarmes' patriotism: the lawyers and prefects could write what they liked, the Laskaris weren't giving up their land without a fight.

It seemed to Lionel that he was watching a deadly pantomime. Any moment now, the fund of words and gestures would be exhausted. The legal niceties had already been forgotten. Blood was going to be shed here today, everyone sensed it, even the horses seemed to sense it. And blood could not be shed without anger. The gestures he was watching spoke of anger; he could see the knotted veins in Manolis' throat, his darkened face. The lust for blood was rising on either side, the impatience of the mounted men beside him to push forward and beat this impudent human obstacle out of their path. But facing them were men who for generations had clung to the stony fields that gave them a living, whose forefathers' blood had soaked into this very soil, defending what was theirs against Turks, Venetians, Arabs. Whatever happened next, it came to Lionel with a surge of melancholy, he would never, for the rest of his life, be able to live down this moment. He had the sensation of being lashed to a giant wheel that he had himself set in motion, helpless now to stop what he had started. But even his cold, English veins were not immune to the rising of the blood. The tension was unendurable.

And then suddenly it was all over. It was one of Manolis' henchmen who made the first and only move. Almost before Lionel had time to take in what had happened, the rifle held in the man's hands had jerked upwards and outwards, thrusting the blade of the bayonet deep into the body of the gendarme opposite. The only sound was a powerful grunt from the attacker. The wounded man fell back into the arms of two of his comrades. Both sides froze, all eyes seemed mesmerized by the spreading stain on the military tunic. The man's eyes were half-closed, he seemed not to know what had happened to him. Blood was pulsing now from below the armpit. Dark drops splashed on the ground and were quickly soaked up by the stony soil. One of the gendarmes tore the garment back from the wound and tried to staunch the bleeding. The bayonet had entered just below the shoulder; the arm was all but severed. It hung with the fingers limply bent, a dead weight, useless, like a branch lopped clumsily from a tree. The skin had already begun to curl back from the wound. Pain was starting to creep into the severed nerve-ends as the gendarme now began to moan rapidly, insistently, tossing his head from side to side in the arms of his comrades.

No one had the stomach to continue the fight. Already Manolis' henchmen had begun melting away among the vines. The *kapetanios* had shifted his attention from Manolis, who faced him defiantly for only a moment longer before he too turned his back and silently faded into the rocks and trees of the landscape. All the attention of those who remained was on the wounded gendarme. With much dithering and muttering the would-be heroes of the morning bound up the torn flesh as best they could, although the blood continued to pump through whatever thickness of makeshift bandages they could apply. The victim began to whimper as they tried to manhandle him into the saddle. Eventually he was there, slumped forward over his horse's neck, his good arm clinging to the reins, and a comrade riding close on either side to see he didn't fall off. No one paid any attention to Lionel.

At last the *kapetanios*, remounted, rode up to him and with curt formality handed him back the roll of papers. He had done his duty, and now he had a wounded man to get back to Kastro before he died from loss of blood. He hoped the Englishman would understand. In any case, Lionel was now master of his property.

With a hasty salute the *kapetanios* wheeled his horse round and set off downhill at the head of his detachment.

Alone now, Lionel slowly dismounted and surveyed the stony ground and the straggling vines that were now his. He walked, not quite steadily, past the dull stain that was already turning brown. The flies had found it and were buzzing noisily.

Suddenly the buzzing was inside his head. Feeling faint, he fell to his knees. Lionel Robertson's first action on gaining possession of Ano Meri was to be violently, and repeatedly, sick.

★

Lionel's victory was in any case a Pyrrhic one. During the months that followed, the countryside round Kastro was drained of men of working age to fight in the war. From his vantage point at the Excelsior, overlooking the harbour below, Lionel could only watch and wonder as day after day the young men, with more enthusiasm than order, marched down to the quay and overcrowded the bum boats and caïques that had been commandeered to take them to the waiting troopships. Bands played in the heat and dust, but there were more spontaneous celebrations too, with impromptu displays of fierce dancing in the tradition of the mountain villages, and itinerant bagpipe players weaving in and out of the throng, lending a joyous, frenetic heterophony to the occasion.

So Lionel's plans were frustrated by a lack of manpower. He had also known that he would need to gather a team of experts – architects, draughtsmen, archaeologists – from England. And while the war lasted there was no chance of that. During the last year of the war Lionel's anxiety and impatience grew. Gone were the poise and the control that had enabled him to locate his goal at Ano Meri, prepare the ground and pounce when the time was ripe. Now he fretted and fumed. He even thought, in despair, of joining up himself. But Lionel had always believed, as a rational man, that this war was avoidable, although he had not believed that it would be avoided. When it came down to it, he was simply *irritated* by his fellow men, that they could perpetrate such a thing, month after month, against one another. Precious little seemed to have been gained or lost, so far as he could make out, on either side. It began to look as though the war would go on for ever, nation after nation hurling its youth into the trenches to be consumed like coal in a furnace. And when it was all used up, what would be left?

Even the Laskaris brothers, Manolis and Yannis, he learnt, had gone off to the war: too young to have had a say in the disposal of their property but not too young to lay down their lives for their country (though surely Yannis must be under age?). But these thoughts, and the impatient irritability that marked all Lionel's dealings at this time, were fuelled by a single anxiety. His son, Daniel, was in his last year at school. A new ardour had crept into the dutiful letters that arrived in Crete often after a delay of months. Daniel had distinguished himself in classical languages. He had immersed himself in ancient history. He would, he assured his father, be taking up the place at Oxford he was certain to be offered. But not yet. It would be humiliating to be conscripted. He and a group of fellow sixth-formers were going to enlist at the earliest opportunity. If possible, even before the end of the school year. He would be eighteen in April, he reminded his father.

Lionel was guilty of many things in his treatment of his wife and son but one thing he would never forget: the day his son had been born.

It had been a windy April dawn at Upland Grange. Below the long french windows with their elegantly swagged lace curtains, the spring tide had breached the sea wall in several places, and angry white horses whipped against ploughed fields. In time-honoured fashion Lionel paced up and down the parquet. It had been going on all night. All night the to-ing and fro-ing from the kitchen to Hermione's bedroom; all night the urgent whispers at the corner of the stairs that he had neither deigned nor dared to hear. Soames, the housekeeper, had interrupted the almost military order of the operation only to bring him hourly cups of tea. To his silent interrogation she would reply each time, cocking her head to one side in a way she had: 'Not yet, sir. Midwife says we're doing fine.'

The closest he had allowed himself to come to the sickroom (as he thought of it) was the landing where the little window of pre-Raphaelite stained glass was at this hour of the night mute. He had been ashamed of his curiosity and returned hastily to the drawing room. He hated Hermione's pain and knew that whatever was going on behind the bedroom door would disgust him. The early months of her pregnancy had been the worst, sufficient even to dislodge him from his beloved Ragusa as none of her earlier entreaties had been able to do. Since then, as her skirts had become wider and she had begun to waddle in that curiously serene gait, feet well apart and her tall shoulders angled backwards, he had come to feel that she was leaning somehow consciously away from him. Lionel had tried, but he couldn't help feeling caged at Upland Grange, and doubly so with a pregnant wife and the extra servants and precautions that entailed. And Hermione had glowed with the bloom of ripe fruit, until he had wished he could shake her out of that damn' blissful composure of hers and remind her that, well, she was the only company he had. What Hermione thought during those months he never knew; perhaps, he wondered bitterly, even thought was unnecessary to her. And now – because he couldn't, by the later stages of that night, disguise from himself the sounds escaping past the closed door and the knowledge that without a doubt his wife was in very great pain – he felt a savage bitterness that she was paying the price for her earlier serenity. The thought brought him no satisfaction. What his wife must be enduring was beyond his imagination. More than ever, whatever it was, it left no place for him.

So Lionel had watched the grey dawn and the silent, inexorable flooding of the fields as the tide rose and rose on that spring morning. His eyes were bloodshot, his hair wild. He had never before felt so lonely. Behind him the door opened and he spun round. Soames was standing in the doorway, tears unashamedly pouring down her cheeks. 'Sir,' she could hardly speak, she was so overcome. 'Sir, you have a—' Her bosom heaved as she ushered in a woman in nurse's uniform whom Lionel had never seen before. From a bundle in this woman's arms, that he had failed to take in at first glance, came a sound he could not place. A choking, gurgling sound. Something was moving in the bundle. And then Soames got the word out – 'son' – and the midwife was handing the wrapped bundle into his outstretched hands and the three heads came together to pore over the puckered red face and stubby waving red fingers that were all that could be seen of the Robertson heir. For Lionel it was a moment of recognition and unexpected possessiveness. He forgot Hermione and all her pain; he forgot the frustrations of the last few months. All of him was consumed by love for this tiny human being that was his, *his* son. Nothing, in the elation of that moment, would ever take that moment away from him so long as he might live. 'We'll call him Daniel,' he murmured impetuously. His voice broke and he turned it into a laugh. 'Daniel in the lions' den.' And he laughed until the tears forced him to stop. 'And may God deliver you, little Robertson,' he added when he had control of himself again, almost too quietly for the others to hear.

Suddenly he felt awkward with the living bundle in his arms. He handed his son back to the midwife and said, with an abrupt change of tone, 'And my wife? Is she well?'

'Sleeping soundly, sir. A terrible night she's had. She needs to sleep, poor thing.'

And so began Lionel's guilt about Hermione that would lead him, in the years that followed, to forsake both wife and son.

The sole heir to Lionel's name and fortune had a lonely childhood. It was a fortune founded on the wool trade. Both family and fortune could be traced back to the seventeenth century, when religious persecution had driven skilled Protestant weavers from Flanders. The earliest recorded Robertsons had washed and carded wool on the rich grazing land of the Vale of Dedham. The industrial revolution had seen the first woollen mills go up along the banks of the Stour. By the time that Lionel was born, Robertson Mills had the biggest turnover on the Essex-Suffolk border, extending inland as far as Sudbury and exporting vigorously to the far corners of the Empire through the docks at Harwich. Lionel's father had run the business with ferocious rectitude but had spent his time, and no small part of his fortune, subscribing to learned Victorian societies and taking part in geological expeditions to far corners of the globe. In his dotage he had returned to Upland Grange and, while still nominally in charge of the business, had set himself the task, with only two unpaid assistants, of mapping the known geological composition of the counties of East Anglia. The *Robertson Gazetteer* and the generously illustrated, fold-out maps on thick parchment are still prized by local geologists and from time to time since Grandfather Robertson's day have been eagerly seized on by the emissaries of American oil companies. It came as a shock to Grandfather Robertson when Lionel declined absolutely to take his hereditary seat on the Board of Directors. By the time that Lionel was twenty-five, and embarking on his third university degree, this time at Tübingen or was it Göttingen – the old man was in his eighties and names and things tended to run into one another so – it had become clear that the running of the business would have to pass out of the family. To the old man, whose prime had coincided with the middle part of the century, amassing a fortune had been little more than a pleasant diversion from the real business of life. He simply couldn't understand Lionel's reluctance – his refusal, alas – to saddle himself with the family business on the grounds that it would leave him precious little opportunity for anything else. But there it was: Lionel, in a series of stormy scenes, had refused. Almost the last act of Grandfather Robertson's long life had been to sign over control of Robertson Mills to a talented overseer who had won his way inch by inch on to the Board and whom he distrusted. That done, the old man had closed his eyes with a sigh. He could not be too hard on his son. Had he himself not travelled, studied (on his own, though, this business of collecting university degrees was pretty queer), conferred with learned men in London while the millwheels effortlessly turned by the power of great Nature herself, needing only the occasional guidance of his controlling hand and the judiciously administered whiplash of his tongue? Grandfather Robertson had died at the age of eighty-seven, as happy, surely, as it is possible to be in these circumstances. A man of his century, he had left something solid behind him.

Daniel hardly knew the old man. The nearest to a playmate he had for much of his childhood was Trudgill, who lived in the Lodge by the gate and had charge of the grounds. Trudgill had a gruff voice and would thrash you if he caught you out in the woods after dark. There were mantraps in the woods, he said, set to catch poachers. Daniel never saw a mantrap, but he soon found that the way to get to the remoter parts of the grounds without having Mummy or more likely Nanny Bodger calling you back before you could even get your knees decently dirty, was to offer to help Trudgill do his rounds. If he was badly dishevelled by the time they got back to the Lodge, or had lost a shoe, and legs and arms had got plastered with the strong-smelling mud of the estuary, Trudgill would beat him before returning him to the kitchen door with a laconic, 'Found this 'ere lad up to 'is tricks again, Miss. Gave 'im a bit of a 'iding, I did.' Daniel subjected himself readily enough to this punishment; it set the seal on the unspoken pact that allowed him to go out with Trudgill again.

It was with Trudgill that he first penetrated the locked East Wing, where the windows were shuttered and darkness reigned. He knew that even to mention these rooms in front of Mummy was to send her into a towering rage; Nanny Bodger was soothing as always, but told you nothing. His mother always seemed a long way away, even when she was sitting there in the room with you, crossly telling Nanny Bodger off, or putting on those rather frightful spectacles without rims that made her look a hundred, and going through the household accounts with Soames.

He was fourteen when she died.

He had been at school then, of course. Uncle Henry had come: Major Stephenson, that is. He hadn't been wearing his uniform this time, and Daniel knew at once, when Matron fetched him just as the bell rang for tea, and led him with a hushed air towards the Headmaster's study, that something awful had happened. At the study door she turned to him at last, and unexpectedly took his hand in hers. 'I'm afraid there is some bad news from home. You'll be a brave boy, won't you?'

And with a final squeeze of his hand she led him into the study. Here, muffled by the beautifully bound books that lined the walls, punishment had been meted out to generations of boys. Daniel, like any of his peers, had eyes only for the threadbare spot in the carpet in front of the Headmaster's desk. To the outside observer it must have appeared a delightful sanctum; the boys approached it with the dragging steps and fear-glazed eyes of calves going to the slaughter. So it was with relief that he stood to hear the Headmaster's kindly words, and felt Uncle Henry's arm fall comfortingly around his shoulders. He was to go home that night. He was to stay at home until after the funeral. And nothing could dent his joy as Major Stephenson led him out to the drive under the eyes of half the school and there, drawn up beneath the gaslight, was a gleaming, green motorcar. Daniel had never ridden in a motorcar before. 'We'll need to keep you warm somehow, young man,' Major Stephenson said as Daniel, his eyes wide, climbed eagerly over the door and settled himself in the passenger seat.

It seemed to Daniel that they drove half the night. Except for a few shouted exchanges as they started off, it proved impossible to talk above the roaring of the engine and the rushing wind that took Daniel's breath away. As the lights of the school receded down the drive, and the lit streets of the town flashed by and disappeared, his excitement was terrific. He kept jumping up and turning in his seat, breathlessly trying to focus on familiar landmarks as they shot by from this new and superior angle. Soon they were out in the country, and the bleak East Anglian wind began to chap the exposed parts of his face and his hands. Sitting quietly now, he gazed out at the darkness on either side; they might have been flying through space. Only the narrow, jumping beam of the headlights showed that they were on land, and within minutes the monotony of road and verge and a hint of ditch beyond, with here and there a startled rabbit darting into the beam, had changed his mood completely. Shivering now with his school coat notched up round his ears, and Uncle Henry's travelling rug tucked round his bare knees, he felt the cold and damp creep round him and knew with the terrible knowledge of the young that the wonderful moment was over and the cold and the pain were just beginning. He looked over at Uncle Henry, whose broad, firm-set features were just visible in the weird glow that came from the dashboard. Sensing Daniel's eyes on him, Major Stephenson reached over and gave his knee a comradely squeeze through the rug. In that light, the older man's eyes looked funny. It came to Daniel with a shock that perhaps he had been crying. But *he* could not cry. Crying was for the lonely silence of the dorm, long after lights out, when the jokes and dirty stories had stopped, when you burrowed deep under the blankets with your knees drawn up to your chin and your arms over your face, for that single refuge of solitude where no one could see you or hear you, not even God, and you could let it all out in hot tears, all the weakness and self-pity that you knew they'd kill you for if they ever suspected it was there inside you, in their midst.

So Mummy was gone. Gone where?

But as the car buffeted and plunged through the rain-filled darkness of the Fens, Daniel knew where.

Those things were your *Father's*, you see. And your Father, Daniel knew even before he was sent away to school, was not much spoken of. 'Your dad now, 'e's an explorer. You know what that means? 'E goes all over the world – British Empire mind, there ain't a corner of the globe you don't find men like your dad, English gents, like you'll grow up to be, young Daniel. Finds things, he does. And sends 'em home so we can all be proud of 'im.'

What things, Daniel wanted to know. But here Trudgill became vague. 'Tell you what,' he said, 'next time 'e sends a consignment' (Trudgill made it sound like raw wool; he had been invalided out of one of Grandfather Robertson's factories after an accident with a machine) 'you can come and help me, see. See for yourself.'

Daniel had not long to wait. Something indefinable had been in the air for days. Now suddenly the house was in uproar. Extra servants had been drafted in. A special goods train from Harwich was due at the halt. Carts and horses had been all but commandeered from the farms around. Trudgill, unshaven as usual and his limp more pronounced from all the excitement, was in his element, giving orders, contradicting them, and shouting crossly when no one knew what to do. Inside the house, rooms that Daniel had never seen open were aired, dust sheets taken off furniture and the furniture, some of it smelling horribly old and dusty, brought in to clutter the inhabited part of the house. Into Daniel's bedroom was moved an ancient grandfather clock with a metal spike on top and what looked like angel's wings of dark wood sweeping upwards above the face. No one ever wound this clock, it never ticked or chimed like the clocks downstairs, solidly, comfortably. In the darkness, as he lay awake in bed, its bulky, brooding presence seemed to breathe out dust and silence. On a summer afternoon when he plucked up the courage to unlock the door and peer inside, the weights hung low, unevenly, like the udders of the cow Mrs Trudgill milked each evening. Above him the cords vanished into the piebald darkness where shafts of sunlight penetrated the clockface, creating a chiaroscuro of cogs and gears. The old wood creaked at his touch. His breath disturbed a million particles that poured out into the room and streamed in a golden dance towards the window: the hours and minutes of long ago, turned to dust.

There was pandemonium in the drive. Daniel had given Nanny Bodger the slip early and ensconced himself next to Mrs Trudgill's skirt in the cosy sanctuary of the Lodge. At the crash and furious whinnying he was outside before anyone could stop him and racing to the scene. His life almost ended there and then under the hooves of Poldark, the gentle drayhorse from Tattersall Farm, who had broken out of his shafts and was bolting in the opposite direction. Somebody screamed. Daniel, perceiving just in time the danger coming hurtling towards him, flung himself flat before the flying hooves and somehow escaped unhurt. Picking himself up, and probably less frightened by his narrow escape than any of those who had witnessed it, he raced on. Half way down the drive, Farmer Tattersall's cart had come to a dead stop and now seemed immovable. The iron-bound boxes that had been Poldark's load had proved too much for the agricultural vehicle to bear and had fallen through the floor. They lay now in a scatter of splintered wood between the wheels. Red-faced, his mouth opening and shutting in futile expostulation, the drayman stood waving his arms about in the ruins of his cart.

What, everybody wanted to know as order was gradually restored to the scene – considerably hampered by Trudgill losing his temper and sending a message up to the house that the young master had been damn' near killed by a runaway horse, and the ensuing intervention of Mummy, Nanny Bodger and a bottle of smelling salts – what, everybody wanted to know, could possibly be in the boxes?

After that, Daniel's adventures were over for the day. In the way of adults, they gave thanks for his escape from death by tanning him within an inch of his life and sending him early to bed.

It was to make amends for this treachery that Trudgill finally allowed him, once the boxes and trunks and huge shapeless objects wrapped in tarpaulins had been safely stowed, into the forbidden territory of the East Wing. It was daytime but the shutters were closed and Trudgill carried a candle. Its small flame cast leaping shadows over walls and ceilings and the strange shrouded shapes that cluttered the rooms. At first Daniel was almost frozen with fear. Several times the candle guttered out and he could not stop himself clutching at his companion in the darkness. Trudgill would swear and light a match, and the little flame would be restored. Gradually Daniel's eyes became accustomed to the gloom, his nerves began to relax. 'Them there are boxes of treasure, see? I don't rightly know what they got inside, these 'ere ones took six men to lift. Your father's the only one has a key.'

Plucking up courage, he began to move out of the little circle of light that came from Trudgill's candle and away from the reassuring warmth of his voice. His eyes were becoming used to the darkness. It was not, after all, quite dark in the rooms. Through chinks and cracks in the shutters came here and there a shaft of grey light; he could see his way, just. Barking his shins frequently against objects barely distinguishable from the darkness, but with the joy of discovery in his heart, Daniel forged ahead.

He was in a high hall, with a cold stone floor like in church. Above his head were stained glass windows. The colours were lifeless – he remembered the overcast sky outside – but he could make out the figures. In one a soldier was holding up a woman's severed head, his hand wound round and round her long auburn hair and the blood a bright splash of scarlet against green grass and flowers. His eye travelled downwards into the gloom, and then he caught his breath sharply. People were standing, in absolute silence, all round him, hemming him in. The silhouette of a half-turned head loomed suddenly against a window far above. Figures without shadows were crowding him in the semi-darkness. He reached out and his fingers touched something colder than stone, harder, it seemed, than metal. Concentrating his gaze, in growing terror, he made out men and women, many of them not wearing any clothes, standing in ghostly stillness in strange attitudes. One was bent down as though to throw something, another had his arms outstretched as though to bear the weight of the world. Here was one who wore a long tunic down to his ankles; Daniel ran his hands in wonder and awe over the moulded veins in the feet, the fluted pleats of the tunic, so cold, so icy cold and still. He peered upwards to find the face. The chin was firm, the lips slightly parted; on his head he wore a diadem, the curls of his hair peeped from below it. And now Daniel froze. These eyes were not sightless like all the others. A flame gleamed in their depths, their whites flickered, a dancing light was reflected in the jet-black pupils. Before Trudgill and his candle could get to him, Daniel had begun to scream, flinging himself in terror against the bases of the statues, striking out with his seven-year-old's fists at marble and bronze, crying over and over again, hysterically, rhythmically, 'Let me go, let me go, let me go.'

But of course the wonders and the terrors of the East Wing did not let him go. Sometimes accompanied by Trudgill, more often, as he grew older and more confident, on his own, Daniel went back to the forbidden rooms. By the light of a carriage lantern he would spend hours in the cold half-light, drawing. He drew gorgons' heads and armless, broken torsos. He tiptoed close behind polished marble buttocks and scrutinized them for signs of orifices. He considered the evidence for the different shapes of the adult anatomy, male and female. The female especially. It seemed to be true: girls didn't have a thingy. He wondered how they managed. Standing on a box dragged into the hall of statues, he allowed his fingers to explore their crevices. The marble was quite smooth; there was nothing missing. The mystery remained.

With the lamp and the precarious courage it brought him, he penetrated deeper into the rooms than he had ever done with Trudgill. Here were animal skins, thick with dust and a smell he didn't quite like. The heads of deer, their antlers spreading to incredible dimensions as the lamp threw their reflections on the ceiling, stared sorrowfully down at him. It took him several visits, and a tussle with his fear that years later would still come back to trouble his dreams, to pass safely beyond the doorway where a stuffed brown bear reared up on its hind legs, a savage paw raised to strike.

The whole of the East Wing was an Aladdin's cave, and the mystery of the locked boxes was more exciting to Daniel's seven-year-old imagination than any possible discovery of what they contained. His greatest treasure was at the same time one of the least remarkable. He came upon it in an upstairs room, along with a baby's crib, a broken doll's house and a one-eyed rocking horse. They were scattered higgledy-piggledy about the floor, and he began to pick them up. Then he found more in a metal bin with BREAD written on it in large, bold lettering. They were tiny lead soldiers: infantrymen with their red coats gaily painted, Cossacks with funny hats, Turks with turbans and curved swords. The cavalry were there too, the men with sabres drawn came apart from the horses, but their legs remained splayed so that they fell down helplessly. They could neither walk nor sit. There were cannons and beautifully made little wooden gun carriages, the gun crews moulded in their allotted tasks: bending to place wedges under the wheels, poised to thrust a ramrod down the barrel still-smoking from the last volley, the officer with his sword raised, ready to give the order to fire.

Daniel was enchanted by his find. For years his greatest pleasure when he came home for the holidays was to retreat into his private domain, quickly and familiarly slipping past the landmarks of his former terrors, to settle himself in the semi-darkness of this upstairs room. By now, he had begun to read history. Painstakingly, he reconstructed the battlefields that sounded so dull in lessons at school: Balaclava, Blenheim, Ramillies. With dramatic licence with regard to period and costume, he began to extend his range: Agincourt, Crécy, Flodden. And, dispensing with the artillery and most of the cavalry, and mentally kitting out his forces with the short tunics, shining breastplates and plumed helmets of a time more distant still, his favourite battle of them all: Trasimene. From sunrise to sunset men hacked and speared each other to death by the shore of the still, green lake. It was Hannibal's last throw: victory would lay open the way to Rome and the boys of the Lower Second would in centuries to come be drilled in Phoenician verbs instead of Latin; in place of the laborious construing of Livy, some prosy Punic historian who never was born would hold sway now in schoolrooms the world over. Hannibal, who had led an army of elephants over the Alps in winter, was one of Daniel's heroes. But the glamour of ancient Rome, that Hannibal had been determined to extinguish, had also captured his adolescent heart. Not many of Daniel's troops on either side came away unscathed from the carnage of Lake Trasimene.

By comparison with all this, his father, when he appeared unannounced and became a seemingly permanent and unwelcome guest in the house, was a terrific disappointment. Daniel was thirteen then, and nothing was explained to him. He could barely remember what his father looked like, he had been a child when the old rogue, as Daniel would never, ever, learn to call him, had set out to explore the Balkans. Daniel was told to address his father as 'sir', and did so dutifully. He looked up at Lionel's leonine head with awe. Once when his father reached out to ruffle his hair in a rare gesture of affection, Daniel could not stop himself from flinching. Late at night, when he was supposed to be asleep, he could hear voices raised in the drawing room. Although he tiptoed to the edge of the landing, he could make out little, and what he could he didn't understand. In the morning his mother's eyes would be red, and his father would go out riding early, saying curtly that he would be back for supper.

For once, he could get nothing out of Trudgill, who only blew smoke rings from his pipe and looked sadly towards the estuary, avoiding Daniel's questioning gaze.

But Daniel's greatest anxiety throughout that long summer was for the treasures of the East Wing. It never occurred to him to confide in his father. So thoroughly had he learnt his lesson that those rooms should never be spoken of, let alone entered in secret, that to confess his trespass to their incontestable and unapproachable owner was to risk worse even than the certainty of a beating: what Daniel feared was exile from his domain. And so he quickly became the jealous but impotent guardian of a treasure that was his by right of conquest. Several times that summer Lionel visited the East Wing, marching loudly through the rooms and throwing the shutters wide to let in the forbidden daylight. As a matter of fact, on at least one of these occasions, Lionel looked round for his son; the boy might have been interested, he was far too taciturn, Lionel thought, he needed drawing out. But on the days when Lionel went through the inventory of the East Wing his son was nowhere to be found. Little did he know that Daniel was watching his every move in an agony of apprehension, flitting noiselessly from bush to bush and hedge to hedge, always keeping the windows of the East Wing in his sights. It was as though Hannibal had reached the gates of Rome and held the keys of every house and every coffer in the land. Daniel's puny thirteen-year-old frame was powerless to stop the desecration. Tears pricked at his eyes: his father had no *right*, no right at all, after all these years, to come back and take away from him what was rightfully his.

And suddenly, as the autumn mists began to rise from the estuary in the evenings and it would soon be time to pack Daniel's trunk again for school, there came a change. There was a quietness about the house. His mother's eyes stopped being red in the morning; instead her face was so pale it was as though you could see through it, her thin lips had almost disappeared. There was no more shouting downstairs after Daniel had gone to bed. Something terrible was going to happen. Or had already happened.

It came with the rattle of a pony trap on the gravel. His father's trunks were packed, everything was ready. It remained only to say goodbye, and his leavetaking was as unexpected as his arrival. The servants were lined up in the hall; Daniel was summoned to the drawing room. His father was standing with the long french window behind him, his hands clasped behind his back.

'Daniel,' he said, and stopped. The older man's embarrassment was infuriating to Daniel. Couldn't he just come out with it – and go, if he was going? 'You are a young man now. I'm sorry we haven't been very good friends, so far. But I'd like to tell you a secret. You mustn't let on to anyone: not your mother, not even Trudgill. Will you promise?'

Daniel nodded dumbly.

'Where I'm going, Daniel, is a country far away. This time it won't be exploring, finding treasures, writing the stories of my adventures. This will be a secret adventure, and only you and I and a certain Colonel in London, whose real name even I don't know, will ever know it. I didn't want to leave on this adventure without saying goodbye to you and your mother. I don't know when I will be back. It's very very important, you see.'

Daniel looked up, his eyes shining, 'You mean, you're going to be a *spy*?'

'Ssh,' Lionel put his finger to his lips. 'That's not a very polite word, is it? Let's just say, a very important mission. But that's our secret, agreed? And now I've a present for you. You may be too old for it already, but it's something I used to play with when I was a boy, and I'd like you to have it.'

His father reached behind him and brought something large from the table. He squatted down in front of Daniel and placed it on the floor between them. With a sinking heart Daniel recognized the metal bin with the high black lettering: BREAD, and knew what was coming next.

'Open it,' his father urged.

Masking his emotions as best he could, Daniel knelt down and prised off the lid of the bread bin. The gasp that came from him as he did so was involuntary and genuine. The chipped and faded colours of the little lead soldiers that had given him so much pleasure were gone. The whole set had been repaired and repainted with a gay, gaudy brightness that dazzled him.

'They're almost as old as I am,' his father explained apologetically. 'But I had Trudgill touch them up. They look as good as new, don't they?'

Daniel gazed up at his father with tears that might have been of gratitude. 'Thank you, sir,' he said, hardly able to control the surge in his heart.

In the hall he clasped his father's hand firmly. He joined the little party waving at the top of the steps as the pony trap drove off, bearing Lionel

Robertson on the first leg of the journey that would bring him, ten months later, to the riverside quay at Sarajevo.

Daniel could feel only relief at the removal of a threat.

He never touched the toy soldiers again.

And now, while in France the war ground inexorably on towards its first Christmas, and at the other end of Europe Lionel Robertson, recently escaped from Ragusa, was establishing himself in the archaeological seminaries of Athens, in the darkest time of winter Daniel stood bareheaded in the blustery rain at his mother's funeral. Beside him stood Major Stephenson. The magic and melancholy of the car ride had set up a kind of complicity with Uncle Henry. Now shared grief was deepening the bond. After the relatives and the directors of Robertson Mills had left the house, and the decanters of brown, sticky sherry had been tidied away, the two faced one another in companionable silence on either side of the fire. The fires had been laid but not lit before the funeral, so that the room was still draughty. The wind moaned in the chimney and as the kindling caught and the smaller lumps of coal began to glow, the smoke at first came billowing back into the room and made Daniel's eyes water. For a long time Major Stephenson seemed content to stare, with Daniel, at the shifting shapes of the flames licking round the coals and the spreading glow at their centre. A numbing warmth unfolded from the grate, enveloping them and insulating them from the cold expanse of the room.

At last, as there seemed to be no prescribed behaviour for this moment, Daniel found it surprisingly easy to ask, 'What did my mother die of, Uncle Henry?'

Still looking at the fire Major Stephenson said carefully, flatly, as though he had rehearsed the words many times, 'She had something growing inside her that killed her. I arranged for her to come to London, to see doctors. They took her into the hospital. They did everything they could for her. She didn't suffer much pain. But they couldn't save her. It was all over very quickly.'

'Was she too ill to write? Could you not have written to tell me? I don't understand. Mother was lying there in London dying, and she never wrote a thing. Couldn't I have seen her before she—?'

'Your mother didn't know she was dying. Nobody was sure until the end, but – I'm sorry Daniel, you could say it was my fault, but I didn't want your mother to know how ill she was. The doctors agreed. She died still hoping, you see. I think she believed up till the end that she would get better, come back to Upland Grange, she would see you and be with you again. And that helped her to fight for her life. Hermione Robertson wasn't someone to give up without a fight.'

'Did you love my mother very much, Uncle Henry?'

Major Stephenson's face reflected the glow of the fire; there was perspiration on his forehead. 'I do love your mother very much.'

'Even though she – isn't there any more?' Daniel felt very adult saying this. He had decided, as he watched Uncle Henry, that he had a better grip on his emotions than a man more than twice his age, and was young enough to take a certain pride in this.

'Even though – as you say. You can't stop loving all at once, you know.'

'You're not a real uncle, Uncle Henry, are you?'

For the first time Major Stephenson looked up from the fire. From the quick jerk of his head it seemed for a moment as though he was going to find the question impertinent, though he had never once so far talked to Daniel the way adults talked to children. This was one of the things Daniel liked about Major Stephenson: he talked to you as though you were both the same age. Then he seemed to shake himself, and stared levelly at Daniel's face. With a stiffness that Daniel could not understand, he said, 'No, I am not your "real" uncle. Your mother has been a dear friend and an exceptional comfort to me. I should like you to know that in other circumstances – and possibly, had she lived, these circumstances would not have been entirely unforeseeable – I would have married your mother.'

Daniel returned the stare; he could feel a vein throbbing in his temple, but he kept his face under tight control. 'And – she, would she have married you?'

Major Stephenson dropped his gaze. 'Yes, Daniel. In other circumstances, of course. But yes, I do believe she would.'

Impulsively Daniel flung himself on his knees beside the other's chair and took hold of his arm. 'I want to be friends with you. But I'm not going to call you Uncle Henry any more. I'm going to call you plain Henry. I'm glad you're not a real uncle, and we can be proper friends. But only if you'll let me call you Henry. Shake on it?'

Daniel had never spoken like this to an adult before, not even to Trudgill. But he couldn't remember an adult ever sharing a confidence with him, and certainly not in the simple but deeply-felt way that Major Stephenson just had. He admired Major Stephenson much as he had earlier admired his motorcar. What he had said was soppy but sincere; obscurely, Daniel thought it put his idol in his power.

So they solemnly shook hands on it.

There followed a lonelier time than ever for Daniel. Henry, when he delivered him back to school a week after his mother's funeral, had been very smart in his uniform. His buttons shone, his boots were polished, his broad handsome face had seemed to Daniel at once infinitely knowing and boyish. As he turned to get back in the car, Henry grinned and saluted. Bursting with pride, Daniel shyly tried to salute back. Then he stumbled over the threshold and was at once absorbed into the familiar mêlée and smells of carbolic soap, boiled cabbage and chalk dust. Henry, as a regular soldier, was in charge of a training course for new recruits on Salisbury Plain. This war turned a soldier's life upside down, he had told Daniel. You wouldn't believe what the raw recruits were like. And the show wasn't going to be over by Christmas. They were going to need real soldiers at the front, and Henry had applied for a transfer to France.

It was soon after this, after a joyless Christmas at Upland Grange with only Soames, the chinless tutor who had succeeded Nanny Bodger and was engaged only for the hols and, when he could escape to the Lodge, the Trudgills for company, that Daniel received the first letter from his father. It was the first sign Daniel had had that Lionel Robertson was still alive, and his feelings, as he studied the superscription on the envelope and examined the unfamiliar stamp, were more mixed than he would have cared to admit. He had found a hero to worship in Henry, who had loved his mother and wore uniform and would soon be off to France to fight. He was unprepared to face the ambiguities of his father's absence. It came back to him all of a sudden that he had confronted his mother's death with a resolute certainty. She had been that kind of person, it was true: you always knew where you were with Mother; things were not to be doubted, things were as they were. And a chasm had opened up where scarcely a chink of affection had apparently existed before. It seemed unfair that he should notice his mother so much more now she was dead than he had when she was alive. But the finality of death seemed somehow to suit her. That, without a doubt, was as it was. He had never been able to think of his father with the same certainty, and still less since that over-dramatized, almost conspiratorial parting of a year and a half ago. Had it been his father whose death had been tenderly, firmly announced to him in the Headmaster's study, it would not have come as a shock. Alive or dead, he couldn't visualize his father anywhere. And if he had once felt his absence as pain, that time had been so long ago that time and memory had already healed over the scars.

So he opened this letter, that came quite literally out of the blue, with trembling fingers. It was several pages long, written out in an elegant, large hand. Lionel had learnt of the sudden death of his wife, and sent his son his condolences. That over, the letter unexpectedly took wing. It was an adventure story his father told, of having to hide in enemy territory, of escaping over the rooftops to stow away on a tramp ship. Even the fourteen-year-old Daniel's scepticism was aroused, but you had to give him his due, his father told a rattling good yarn. He'd never have thought such a thing. Daniel read the last part of the letter with shining eyes:

The captain of the ship, however, was not to be trusted and before long I began to fear for my life. It was only by the greatest good fortune that I was able to save but one of the precious gems from the rapacity of that pirate and his crew. One night I heard them whispering together in the stokehold which had become my berth. The ship had been sailing down the Adriatic coast for some days, Corfu was to be the first landfall. In the darkness I went up on deck. The night was clear and moonless; dawn was not far away. There were mountains close in on the starboard side; I recognized the Corfu channel. We would make the port by midday. At that moment I made up my mind. The shore, I estimated, was less than half a mile distant. I would never have a better chance. So – overboard I went and swam for it. From Corfu I made my way very slowly by ship and by train (this is rough country) to Athens, from where I write.

To this missive, and a good many more which followed in the course of the next three years, Daniel wrote dutiful replies. But he kept his father's letters in the safest place he knew at school, under his mattress, and treasured them ever afterwards. They are very worn and brittle now, neatly docketed in a green binder in the Public Record Office, which will not long ago have moved out of London to a mausoleum of concrete, glass, and civil service haircord near Kew Gardens, when Dan Robertson will gingerly unfold them in pursuit of what is, beyond doubt, an archaeological scandal.

Daniel spent the last summer of his schooldays not at Upland Grange but in London. He was relieved at the change – the place had somehow shrunk since his mother's death. No more consignments of archaeological specimens had arrived at the halt on the Harwich branch line. Even so, most of the inhabited rooms had had to be closed up. The staff had melted away in the early months of the war, to volunteer for the front or to work in the munitions factories. The austere, portly figure of Soames haunted the empty rooms and imperiously maintained order over the inevitable decay. The only haven of warmth and life was the Lodge. Trudgill, because of his foot, was not fit for service, and a new cosiness and domesticity had reigned at the Lodge since the arrival of Sarah Jane, as round and chubby-cheeked a little creature as Daniel had ever seen. She smelt of apples when Mrs Trudgill presented her baby daughter to him, her own cheeks dimpling with rosy pride. Daniel had vaguely supposed that Mrs Trudgill must be too old to have children. On the way back to the house Trudgill confided that Sarah Jane was adopted, but he tried not to mention it in front of the missus, it had been the dream of their lives to have children of their own, he'd agreed to the adoption when it became clear that their dream was never to be fulfilled, but the missus you see, it's as though she'd had that baby inside her own body, she really feels as though she laboured to bring it into the world, it's hers you see, Daniel, she feels it really is hers, and it's for the best, there's no sense in keeping reminding her, surely there's no harm?

Daniel had politely agreed, but deep down felt cheated. His place at the fireside in the Lodge, enjoying the easy-going warmth of Mrs Trudgill's frustrated motherhood, had been taken from him; and now as never before he had nowhere else to turn. Of all the little betrayals, tactical or involuntary, that had punctuated his childhood devotion to the Trudgills, this was the one that struck the deepest. From Mrs Trudgill, and from her only, it irked him to be told that he was a grown man, to see the way she simpered at him when he paraded before them in his army cadet uniform from school. They took it for granted he would enlist as soon as he was eighteen. His childhood fell from him very quickly in an afternoon at the Lodge at Upland Grange. There was no going back now.

So it was a relief, as well as a surprise, when a letter arrived at school inviting him to an address in Kensington for the whole of the summer holidays. He could bring a friend if he wished. Major Stephenson was due home on leave and had particularly asked . . . The letter was signed 'Joanna Stephenson (Mrs)'. Daniel tried this conundrum every way he could think of. Joanna Stephenson was Henry's mother (he supposed that even a handsome infantry officer must have a mother); she was Henry's brother's wife, possibly widowed; she was his unmarried sister who had reached a certain age and taken a decorous refuge behind the title. It couldn't be that Henry . . .? All these possible solutions, even the last, which for some reason he found it difficult to utter, he discussed endlessly with James Firkin, the chosen friend who had agreed, after some parley and exchange of letters with his parents, to come to Kensington for a month. Firkin was adamant. 'Why, she's his mistress, of course. Your uncle Henry's got everything, you say: money, good looks, promotion – it sounds as though he'll be in charge of a division before this scrap is over. Don't tell me he's not a success with women!'

Daniel resisted this line of attack as best he could. But the mystery was only resolved when the two young men, very self-conscious in blazers and boaters and surrounded by trunks, tennis rackets and butterfly nets, decanted from an electric brougham not far from South Kensington underground station. Mrs Stephenson herself came out to the top of the steps to greet them, and stood in the shadow of the white-painted portico with a hand outstretched in welcome. She was wearing white, with a large bonnet tipped well back from her face. Daniel was at once struck by the eggshell beauty of her appearance, a hint of blue about the delicately formed temples that reminded him of a Wedgwood bowl he had once been thrashed for breaking. And with the memory, the pavement on which he stood seemed suddenly to tilt away from him, the solid earth beneath his feet to wobble in its orbit like a small boat caught in short water. The gap of yards that separated him from the top step extended to an enormous distance; he was staring through the wrong end of a telescope but he could still see with absolute precision the clear penetrating blue of her eyes and the mistiness of a smile that was meant to be formal and welcoming but couldn't help also being indefinably seductive. He saw a memory of something that might never have been: sea mist and sunlight on a field of cornflowers, and at last the jolting stopped and a cold weight settled at the bottom of his stomach. He was looking into the eyes of his mother, as she had rounded on him for breaking the plate. His mother's eyes had had the same piercing blue, the same etched dark lashes. Sometime, somewhere, these eyes had smiled in welcome, seeming to promise an inaccessible depth of love and tenderness there to be unlocked by one who had the key. And Daniel had broken the plate. He never found the key. Perhaps those depths were never there. For a further dizzying moment, as he stood stupidly staring, this woman with her hand outstretched to take him into her house both was and was not his mother. Then, as he still made no move, and Firkin, awaiting his cue, remained beside him on the pavement, she came forward into the sunlight, and time and distance became themselves again. 'The second Mrs Stephenson,' she introduced herself in crisp tones that echoed, though now only distantly, in Daniel's memory. 'Do come in. Potts will take your things and can show you to your room later. We'll have some tea in the conservatory.'

'Everybody says that the second Mrs Stephenson is uncommonly like the first,' Henry confided jovially to Daniel in one of his rare expansive moments when at last he came home on leave.

He never found out whether Major Stephenson had been married before, or had represented himself to his new wife as a widower in deference to the memory of Daniel's mother.

Or, as Lucy will more than half a century later explain, with a hint of scorn, to her father Dan, 'Men always fall for the same women again and again. It makes a kind of pattern, you see: nothing new ever really happens.'

'What about women, then?' Dan will want to know.

'Oh, they make just the same mistakes.'

At the time of this conversation Lucy will be twenty-one, unattached, and soon to embark on her training as a psychoanalyst.

When Henry did come home on leave, Daniel found him indefinably changed. He and Firkin were beside themselves to hear at first hand about the war. But Henry didn't seem to hear their questions; something funny had happened to his eyes, there were times when they seemed to look through the spot where you were standing, not even as if you were a ghost, as if you just weren't there at all. When he talked to you, it was as though he were doggedly trying to pick up the thread of conversations from the time before he went away. There was often a stumbling concentration in his voice as he accompanied Daniel and Firkin on butterfly-catching expeditions among the allotments in Hyde Park. It was like watching a blind man trying to find his bearings in a place he had known before he lost his sight. Firkin found this disconcerting, too. Before Henry came they had talked late into the night about the war and morals, and sometimes also about girls. Now they talked about Henry. Most of the time he was disarming, affable, bluff, much as Daniel had described him to his friend. But he seemed also somehow smaller – not just thinner, which was to be expected after more than a year living in trenches at the front, but shrunk. They noticed that he flinched easily. He spent a lot of time in the evenings with the whisky decanter; he snapped irritably at Mrs Stephenson.

The boys sensed a private silence in him. At first they thought he was deliberately holding back some secret that they might, with cunning or tact, be able to worm out of him. But then they began to realize that his evasions were not simply a matter of will. His broad, open face would look pained, his forehead would pucker in a way Daniel had never seen before. He seemed not to understand their questions.

There was one evening, towards the end of Henry's leave, when the mask slipped. Neither of them was sure afterwards what had triggered it, perhaps he had just had more whisky than usual. Mrs Stephenson had retired, the house was silent. Without warning, Henry began talking fast, in a low monotone. At first the boys couldn't make out what he was saying; he talked too fast and he was looking away from them, at a worn point in the carpet on the other side of the room. 'Did you hear that one, sergeant? That was close. Coal box, always tell from the crump, can't you? Fifty yards, maybe less, been a lot of damage down the line tonight . . . But no, sarge,' this with a leering lurch into cockney that was quite unlike the Henry they knew, 'you ain't 'earing nuffink tonight, know why, sarge, 'cos you've blown your bloody brains out, that's why.' Another long muttering and a change of voice. 'It's not the first time, sir, they *will* do it. Haven't been in the line long, sir, have you? You'll get used to it.

'Don't,' suddenly Henry seemed to register the presence of the two youngsters, 'don't be in a hurry to get out there, lads. I've seen things I'll never tell to a living soul. I wouldn't know how to, they don't make the kind of words to describe it. Truly. Believe an old soldier. You're not eighteen yet, Daniel, are you? You, Firkin? Pray to the good God who watches over battlefields just as long as you can believe there is one. Pray this war is over before you reach the age.' And then, to their astonishment, he began to nod his head rhythmically and repeat again and again, 'Shit shit shit shit.'

That night they helped Henry to bed, and retired themselves in an awkward silence, not looking at one another.

'Got a touch of the old war nerves, your uncle Henry,' Firkin ventured next morning.

Daniel agreed.

Mrs Stephenson was more robustly disposed. She talked at length of the wickedness of the Kaiser, of the butchery of children and wholesale rape of women in Belgium in 1914. It was still going on in France, she said, whenever the Hun pushed our gallant lads temporarily back, there were always terrible tales of atrocities against the helpless local population. 'England looks to you, my dears,' she dimpled irresistibly at Daniel and Firkin, 'to make sure that sort of barbarism never reaches Kensington.'

'I think your aunt's a peach,' Firkin confided to Daniel later. 'How old do you think she is?'

Daniel had never been able to think of the second Mrs Stephenson as his aunt. 'Too old for you, you old lecher,' he retorted, but beneath his banter he had guessed at the way his friend's mind must be running and was disturbed to feel similar stirrings in himself. Henry's new wife no longer reminded him of his mother, or if she did, it was of a mother too young for him to have known. She took the two of them to concerts at the Royal Albert Hall and one afternoon they all went down to Buckingham Palace and waved little flags as the guard changed and the great and good of the land rode past in horse carriages and shining motorcars, even grander than Uncle Henry's. And the sun shone and Mrs Stephenson always wore white and indefatigably organized collections and bazaars and tea parties, all to raise money to help 'our poor dear soldiers out there'. And whatever the news shouted by the newsboy who was always outside South Kensington underground station from morning till night, her eye might often be misty but was invariably dry.

Once after a visit to the British Museum, when they had found most of the collections mothballed because of the Zeppelin raids, as they were riding westwards in the gathering dusk and the food queues were lengthening outside the shops, Daniel impetuously took Firkin and Mrs Stephenson into his confidence about his secret domain at Upland Grange. Distance, childhood memory and his vividly fresh disappointment with the greatest collection in England now multiplied the magnificence of the shuttered East Wing, and he was surprised by his own eloquence as he described its treasures.

Mrs Stephenson listened with her head held aloft; he detected an intentness (maybe excitement, even?) in her eye. 'I'll tell you what. First leave we get, I'll invite you both to be my guests, and you can see for yourselves. Will you come?'

There was not the slightest doubt in any of their minds that before the year was out Daniel and Firkin would have followed in Henry's footsteps and gone to the war. Each of them, in a different way, savoured a delicious certitude in planning ahead for the resumption of a life that, they also already sensed, would never be the same again.

'I'll come,' said Firkin and shook hands firmly on it.

'I'll come – and Henry, of course?'

'And Henry, of *course*.' Fleetingly, in the dusk, he held her warm fingers in his hand and felt those cornflower-blue eyes upon him.

On that balmy evening Daniel felt the presence of barbarism riding into Kensington in the depths of his own tremulous heart.

Before he returned to school Daniel had written a long letter to his father. He would not be completing his final year at school. He and Firkin would be volunteering early. He did not mention Henry, of course, nor did he question his father's aloofness from the great struggle of our time. Daniel knew where his duty lay, but it wasn't only duty. In London, among the uniforms and so few men in the streets, he had felt trapped. On the battlefield he expected to find freedom, he could feel a great cry rising in his breast; it had no words as yet but in the heat of battle he knew it would burst from him and he would know its sound, already he could feel his lungs expanding: *air*, he needed more air.

The letter, which in due course will bring a lump to Dan Robertson's throat as he leafs through the boxes in the Public Record Office, ends simply, 'Pray for me, father.'

5 SOLDIERS

'THE element of surprise was the greater for the morning mist . . . lying thickly on the low ground . . . Fighting began in front and on their flanks before the men could take their battle formations or make ready their weapons . . . The pandemonium of battle was so great that no word of command or exhortation could be heard by the troops. In that chaos not one of them could recognize his own unit or knew his place in the ranks. Enveloped in the mist, they did better to trust their ears than their eyes . . . Some, as they turned to flee, were encumbered by the throng of their own side still holding their ground; others, as they still tried to press forward, were driven back by their fleeing comrades . . . Military discipline, the training of the barrack square, all went for nought . . . If units existed at all, it was chance alone that formed them . . .'

The close-spaced print of the book danced in front of Daniel's eyes. His pocket Livy was his steady consolation in the trenches. The ponderous rhythms of the ancient language brought comfort by the light of a stubby candle-end, on nights when he was not on patrol and the random thud of artillery shells made sleep a matter of fitful snatches. In the pages of Livy he relived the glorious battles of his adolescence, and wondered all over again about the devious entanglements that had thrown so many millions of men face down in the mud to fight to the death over a ruined land. Now and then the ground would heave from a particularly near explosion, earth would drop from the roof of his dugout. As he read he skipped lines, he missed main verbs, but it didn't matter, he kept the book held close to his face; he knew if he lost concentration the waking nightmares of the trench would come pouring in from the darkness, pressing into that undefended space behind his eyes from which one day, he felt sure, he would be unable to dislodge them and then he would lose his reason altogether. Reading in this disjointed way the two-thousand-year-old sentences of Livy, he found himself recognizing without surprise the measured narrative, as it would be preserved for all time, of yesterday's battle and tomorrow's.

It was in that same morning mist, not ten days ago, that Uncle Henry had, in the euphemism of trench warfare, 'ceased to reign'.

Daniel's unit – which he knew was contemptuously referred to in the line as the 'children's crusade' – had not been involved in that particular show. But word had spread fast along the line. From the Ancre to the Somme British troops had gone over the top, helped by the summer ground mist, and won a great victory. Already this victory had a name: the 'Battle of Amiens', and there was much excited talk among the young officers and NCOs with whom Daniel shared his trench: the march to the Rhine had begun. There was nervousness, too. The children's crusade had been in trenches now for several weeks. If the line was really pushing forward, it would be their turn any day now. The older hands were sceptical, particularly those who had survived the German offensive in April, when they had been forced back to their present positions. Victory, a seasoned NCO assured Daniel, didn't mean much in this war. What you won today you'd lose again tomorrow, next week, maybe not till next year but you'd lose it all right. Sure as eggs is eggs. And you might have lost ten, maybe fifteen thousand men in the process. That had been the total number of the Roman dead at Trasimene. Daniel remembered an importunate questioner in the Latin class: surely Livy had exaggerated?

And among those dead, on the morning of 8th August, on the north bank of the Ancre, had been Henry Stephenson.

Daniel's war so far had been an exhilarating extension of summer holidays. He and Firkin and some other enthusiasts from the sixth form had been accepted for training that winter, and learned to bivouac on the hard, frozen ground of Salisbury Plain. Training at first had been a desultory affair; the sergeant majors and drill instructors weren't much interested in boys their age. Even when they were eighteen and technically fit for commissions, they would not be sent overseas for at least a year. That was Policy, that was, and Daniel had his nose rubbed in it. In the red dawns, as he warmed his frozen hands for a few seconds round a mug of tepid tea – all the warmth his body would get that day – he chafed at the delay, at the pettifogging arms drill, at the trivial complaints of the conscripts who didn't want to be there but were taken much more seriously than the young volunteers. Then in April, with the frosts gone and a cold grey wind scouring the plain, the great day came: he was eighteen. All around him men cursed and swore and he had his first taste of mud in the dummy trenches that crisscrossed the Wiltshire landscape; but the sap was rising in the trees, buds were bursting; he had never before that winter lain on the bare earth and felt its deadness seeping through the pores of his skin, invading his body, numbing his senses, and now he felt with a peculiar joy the energy bursting out all around him, and that energy was pulsing through his veins and tingling in his nerve-ends. He was eighteen, he was just in time, surely the war could not be over before he got to France; the greatest adventure in human history lay waiting for him across the Channel, and he was ready for it. *Bliss was it in that dawn to be alive.* Secretly he wrote poems and dedicated them to the second Mrs Stephenson. Later he tore them up.

Then suddenly everything changed. New faces appeared in the training camp; tents and barrack rooms were filled to overflowing. Grim-faced instructors yelled themselves hoarse. Orders were posted and countermanded. The young volunteers were treated the same as everybody else and discovered too late how privileged they had been before. Tempers flared; fights broke out. Someone had prodded the hornets' nest.

It wasn't long before Daniel discovered the reason. The Germans had made a series of surprise attacks all along the British-held part of the line in France. The names of St Quentin, the Lys, Chemin-des-Dames suddenly were being bandied about. Nobody seemed quite certain what had happened at these places, but there was a frightful flap on. Almost before he knew it, Daniel found himself hustled along with a batch of half-trained recruits and entraining for Dover.

There followed a confused succession of days and nights, the fetid smells of cramped humanity aboard a troopship bound for Boulogne, and Daniel's first sight of France amid the chaos of a depot where nobody seemed to be expecting the new recruits. But even here the warm sunshine and the shining sea kept up the illusion that it was all a great holiday.

It was not until he was assigned a platoon and summoned to a briefing addressed by a comic-opera colonel in a field above Cap Gris Nez that Daniel learned that Policy had changed. This was an emergency, the Army needed men as it never had before. The children's crusade, although the colonel didn't call it that, was on its way to relieve our flagging forces. Daniel and his young cohort would be joining the Third Army in front of Arras. They would be the spearhead of the march to the Rhine.

Now, instead of the iron-hard ground of the Salisbury Plain, Daniel and his platoon camped out in fields of waist-high corn with poppies flowering in the ditches. They were shunted this way and that in stiflingly hot, overcrowded trains; they spent whole days and nights inexplicably motionless in railway sidings. They passed through training camps and base camps. Senior officers bawled at Daniel or demolished him with crisp sarcasm; he learned to bawl at the men under his command, though his voice would sometimes crack. They were older than he was, most of them, but not by much. And in the faces of all the officers he confronted he saw at first, above the shining buttons of the army tunic, the broad handsome face of Henry. It seemed to Daniel the most natural thing that they should meet on the battlefield, that he should march up to the idol of his adolescence and return the salute Henry had given him when they parted on the school steps four years ago. That he should silently, because no words would be necessary, be accepted into the confraternity of men willing and worthy to be entrusted by such as Mrs Stephenson with preserving the summer peace of Kensington.

He had been sent into Arras on an errand. All the way he fretted about being away from his post and his men. What if the offensive should begin without him? It was a hot, sticky afternoon, and all around him the harvest was going on, as no doubt it had always done, as though the war was on another planet. Now and then a heavy shell would burst – the bombardment was lazy and apparently random these days. The farmhands and women working in the fields never turned their heads. Daniel, feeling himself out of his element, and lightheaded from lack of food and sleep since he had been at the front, took a perverse comfort from these distant, stray sounds of battle. And all the while he chafed to return to his trench.

The town, when he got there, had been badly damaged by shelling. It was a surprise to see people in civilian clothes among the uniforms that jostled about the streets. There were even women doing their shopping and children running about. All this seemed unreal, scarcely possible, so close to the battlefield. He had finished his business early, when he heard shouts and the breaking of glass from a narrow side street. Without thinking, he dashed towards the sounds. There was a house and a woman screaming at the door and a tangled brawl of soldiers in the uniforms of several nations. At school Daniel had always been one to keep out of fights, but now he had been trained for battle and this was his first taste of it. Blowing his whistle he pushed his way inside and upstairs, laying about him with his cane. For his pains he got a black eye and a series of blows that thrust him backwards against a mirror which splintered at his feet. There were lots of women now, some of them half undressed, and all of them screaming in French. In the mêlée he recognized a single tommy who seemed to be being worsted by a group of Canadians. Tribal instinct prevailed. Hurling himself on the backs of two of the Canadians he threw them off balance long enough for his compatriot to struggle to his feet. In the heat of the moment he was neither surprised nor embarrassed to discover the man was an officer, and that he was without his trousers.

'Let's get out of here,' the officer muttered, grasping Daniel firmly by the arm.

By the time they reached the bottom of the stairs the officer had struggled into the rest of his clothes, though he still looked badly dishevelled and his tunic was torn.

'Are you all right, sir?'

For the first time the officer looked at his rescuer.

'What's a young man like you doing in a place like that?'

'You don't mean . . .?'

Outside in the street there was no mistaking the red light above the door of the house they had just left. Daniel was eighteen and the only naked women he had touched had been made of marble and hidden away in the East Wing of Upland Grange. His eyes grew very wide. He had had his first experience of battle, and already it left a tawdry taste in his mouth; he felt his colour rising. He was glad he had been able to help a comrade-in-arms; but he felt dirtied. He wanted to be rid of this brother officer.

But his brother officer clapped him cheerfully on the shoulder and offered to buy him a drink. 'It's the least I owe you, young man,' he said and led Daniel down another side street.

'Actually,' he confided as they sat over stale beer that made Daniel's head swim, 'there's one more thing you could do for me, if you would.'

By now Daniel would hardly have been surprised by anything. 'I'm going to have to have this tunic sewn up before I go back to my regiment tonight. I've got some papers in the pockets, chap I used to know bought it in the last show, I promised to take them to his wife, last rites you might say, but I gave him my word. Could you give them safe keeping for an hour or two? I've nowhere else to put them.'

Daniel was in an agony of impatience to get back where he belonged. All this brawling and beer drinking wasn't at all his idea of war. And what if he missed the offensive? On the other hand, it didn't sound the sort of request that could decently be refused. Reluctantly he nodded, and stretched out a hand to receive the bulky envelope that the other passed across the table. He almost put it in his own tunic pocket without glancing at it. But as he made to do so his eye fell on the superscription, and the blood froze in his veins.

'Is something wrong?'

But Daniel could not speak at all. Eventually he managed to say, 'Not – not Henry? Henry Stephenson?'

And so, in that cramped *estaminet* in Arras, Daniel heard how his idol Henry had 'ceased to reign', shot through the neck by a stray bullet just minutes before the attack had begun on the north bank of the Ancre.

And after some haggling it was agreed that he, and not Major Dowell, would be the one to hand over – 'in person, mind you, he asked me that several times before this last show, it's as if he kind of knew' – Henry's last letter to his wife.

From then on events held Daniel in their grip. The iron wheels of war were turning and as they turned carried Daniel and the children's crusade inexorably with them. That same night, as the ground mist crept silently across the trenches, so thin that you could see the waning moon above it but so thick at ground level that even the sentries at the end of your own trench were invisible, the whistles were blown in earnest and Daniel waved his men

91

over the crest of sandbags and pressed forward with them into no-man's-land, easing aside the barbed wire where it had already been cut by the forward parties. It was 4.45 am. After that there were no more days and nights, there was no more sleep, or if he slept, his dreams were, if anything, more vivid and more violent than his waking impressions. The noise never stopped, the children's crusade had rarely time to make itself at home in new positions – captured German trenches now – before the order would be given to move on. Daniel could not have said if the ground gained was only a few hundred yards, or if beyond the next set of concrete defences they could expect to come upon the Rhine. Time and distance meant nothing. Distance was as far as the line of his own platoon stretched, as far as the next bare, shattered tree or stump of wall. His horizon was marked by enemy machine-gun posts. These he had some success in pinpointing, and several times led a group of his men in an outflanking manoeuvre, to take out the gunners from the rear. It was like smoking out wasps at Upland Grange. Sometimes the Germans tried to surrender. At that range it was easier to bayonet a man than to shoot him with a rifle. The wheels of war were turning and nobody knew what to do with prisoners. There was the night when their attack was covered by drenching rain, and the gun barrels steamed and officers and men went forward floundering in deep mud. There were the dead and, worse, the dying men they found in the German trenches they overran. Once they came upon the remnants of a platoon that had been caught in their trench by a gas attack. There had been no gas warning that day and Daniel and his men quickly wrestled with the cumbersome equipment that made them look like ghosts of the damned. They gave the doomed trench a wide berth. When they were safely past, one of the men lobbed a couple of grenades in, 'to put the buggers out of their misery'.

And strangest of all, to Daniel's eyes, in the kaleidoscope of battle, were the tanks. He had never seen a tank during his training. Now, with a roaring, clanking noise these great metal monsters would emerge ponderously through the cloud of mud thrown up by their treads, crushing whatever lay in their path, the machine-guns mounted on either side viciously punching the air. They passed many broken-down tanks, too, abandoned by their crews, immovable iron monuments to the battle that still raged ahead.

Perhaps by now he had lost the sense of hearing. Or maybe there really was a lull. But this scene, as it stretches remorselessly into the future, infinitely and exactly repeated in Daniel's dreams and waking hallucinations, takes place in silence. It is a warm autumn afternoon; before him lies the curve of a river and on the far bank a silver birch wood, the leaves already brown and beginning to drop. On this side a meadow of long grass with the mist beginning to rise, already up to waist height. He and his men are keeping cover, surveying the meadow for any sign of the enemy positions they know are not far ahead. Behind him, in the trees on this bank, are hundreds, perhaps thousands of men, waiting for darkness to advance across the open ground. The silence is complete. Then out of the mist comes a sound, a rhythmic drumming sound that gathers momentum as it comes closer. It is the sound of horses' hooves, galloping all together. Breasting the mist as though floating on air, comes a troop of French hussars in perfect formation, their helmets gleaming in the setting sun, sabres drawn and held perfectly at the vertical. A bugle sounds, and the formation wheels to the right, following the river, only a few yards ahead of where Daniel and his men lie hidden in the trees. No one can believe his eyes. Not even, it seems, the enemy. At first there come only a few hesitant cracks of rifle fire. No one can want this thing to happen. The drumming of hooves is deafening now, a wave of exhilaration passes through the watching ranks. And now at last the guns start up in earnest. In twos, in threes, in tens the horses and riders go down under the devastating fire of the concealed machine-gunners and riflemen on the opposite bank. The dead and wounded sink soundlessly into the mist, a few riderless horses have turned tail and are bolting back across the meadow, foam flying from their mouths, no doubt trampling the bodies of their former riders as they go. Only a handful of those brave hussars, still in control of their horses, wheel about and manage to leave the field with the sorry semblance of an organized retreat. The firing continues sporadically for some time. 'Fucking bastards,' Daniel hears several shocked voices break the silence round him. 'Fucking bastards.' A glance at the men's faces is sufficient to tell him that they are not referring only to the enemy.

And finally – because this was the last act of Daniel's war, the ineluctable point to which all these turnings of the wheel were, for him, leading – there was the village. For an immeasurable time they had been building roads across what seemed to be swamps, laying down wire netting, duckboards, debris from wrecked trees and buildings. Working more like navvies than soldiers, the men complained, and Daniel had not disagreed. The village was on a canal bank. Everywhere there were bridges down, the main street was full of rubble. Not a house had been left untouched. The afternoon sun lay heavy on the ruins; Daniel knew, as he crossed the canal by the makeshift arrangement of girders that did duty as a bridge and led his platoon into the main street, that something terrible had happened here. Soldiers of different regiments stood about at corners as though dazed and not knowing where they were. The fighting seemed for once to have stopped. Again, Daniel's ear registered nothing. A pall of silence lay over the scene. Furniture and clothing lay about the streets; when he looked more closely Daniel could make out unburied bodies too. Whole walls of houses had been demolished, dowdy wallpaper flapped limply where the outside air met the intimate space of a living room, a bedroom. Here and there smoke drifted lazily from blackened joists and plaster. His platoon was detailed, without much ceremony, to join a burial party, and as they picked through the rubble and gathered the dead to bury them in a mass grave on the edge of the town under the expressionless gaze of the survivors, Daniel found himself shaking with an anger and nausea that he knew he could not much longer control. He found one of the senior officers who seemed to be in charge. Was this what armies did in retreat, he wanted to know? Surely somebody was recording all this, the Huns could be made to pay for what they'd done here, surely? People back home must be told. He'd heard enough stories already before he came out; now he was seeing it with his own eyes, and far worse than anyone had known in Kensington. For reply he was told curtly that he could carry on.

He tried again with another officer. His buttons, he was told, were a disgrace to his regiment. Some allowance had to be made in combat conditions, the officer conceded, but the battle had ended several hours before. Daniel was to look to his buttons. And, it seemed, his men's, too. He felt a tug at his sleeve. 'Listen, mate' – it was a sergeant lying sprawled under a hedge, a bottle of wine in his hand – 'you don't want to talk like that. Not here. The way the story goes, Gerry pulled out of this village more than a week ago. Nobody knows who got here first. And nobody's ever going to fucking know. Get my meaning? That's war, see. It makes yer sick. Have a drink,' and he waved the nearly empty bottle in Daniel's face before rolling over and belching loudly. 'Got to get some shut-eye now. All be gone in the morning.'

He found the little girl in a garden. Her eyes were open and as blue as the sky. Her fingers clutched a shapeless rag doll – protectively, it seemed to Daniel. Daniel wasn't good at telling children's ages. She might have been five; she might have been seven. Her face was smudged with dirt as though she had been playing. Her clothes were torn and had been pulled up to her middle. Blood had flowed from between her legs and covered the ground. Her fingers had found it before she died and some of it was smeared on the doll too. The body was quite stiff when Daniel gave the order to his men to lift it.

Daniel watched the girl's long pale hair out of the garden. He found himself unable to follow. His legs would not obey him. The world took a lurch beneath his feet, as it had done once in Kensington, but time and distance did not, this time, comfortingly reassert themselves. As his perspective shifted, out of control, he found himself looking up at the sky that was a bowl of light and round the edges were the tops of trees, the broken-off outlines of walls, plaster blackened by fire; and as he watched, the light began to thicken and it was as though the whole of human time was pouring through his body in a cascade of light, and all through history the scene he saw before his eyes was there, not repeated but the same moment, eternally there, before his eyes. As he watched, the light seemed to splinter into fine lines like fibres, he could almost touch them; he reached out with his hand to ward off the gathering brightness, to ease the fibres apart, and as he did so terror gripped him because there were gaps between the lines of light, he could see behind the light. In that moment he recognized with a terrible familiarity what he could never afterwards describe: *the machinery out there.*

It was a vision vouchsafed, surely, to few who survived. Daniel remained out of time, in a darkened room in a military hospital, for many months. He heeded no one, he scarcely ate or drank, and all the time, monotonously, without inflection, his lips formed the same word over and over again: *shit.*

In due course the armistice would be signed and the children's crusade would reach the banks of the Rhine. But Daniel would not be among them. The war was over for him on that October afternoon by the canal. But he had seen what he had seen, and knew that for him this war would never be over, so long as he might live.

This was not an easy thing to explain to Joanna Stephenson. Daniel's convalescence left him mentally exhausted. He had no real memories of that period to hold on to, but was left with the sense of an arduous climb upwards, through a dark tunnel, towards the light of day. Now, back in England, first of all at an Army convalescent home near Southend and latterly in the neglected but peaceful rooms of Upland Grange, he was alive again. The ordinary, cold light of an English day had never seemed so precious. With quiet thankfulness he found he could breathe as once he must have done without ever realizing what a rare and inexplicable gift it is to draw the living air into your lungs and feel its nourishment expand through your whole body. How he had existed through those intervening months was a mystery to him. He felt, as many returning soldiers must have done, as though he'd come back from the dead. Only: in fifty-one days of more or less continuous fighting he had suffered barely a scratch. If he had been wounded, it was in a place where no searing astringent could cauterize the damaged flesh, where no gently plied needle could knit the torn membranes back together. His scars, he supposed, had had to mend by themselves. *Battle fatigue*, his discharge papers, when finally they came through, had declared. And he felt a fraud, being so physically fit and well. Afraid too, because the scar that might yet fester and gape when he least expected it was not in any part of his body but in the fabric of the air and the light that pressed against him, giving him life.

There had never been any doubt in his mind that his first action, when the doctors pronounced him well enough, would be to deliver Henry's package. He was not yet free to strike out into the new post-war world that everyone was talking about. The second Mrs Stephenson drew him like a magnet. He had written to her already, they had exchanged several letters. But he could not discharge his duty to Henry by post. It was a close, warm day in June when he paid off a cab at the door of the white-painted house in Kensington, ran up the steps and pulled the bell. She opened the door to him herself. She was wearing black, with a thin veil pulled over her face that only seemed to emphasize the high-bridged nose, the small, prettily pursed mouth, the dimples of her cheeks that always gave her a quizzical, perhaps a faintly ironic, air. Almost two years had passed since he had first entered this drawing room. Then, with Firkin, they had taken tea in the conservatory, served by the lugubrious Potts, and the two boys had sat on the edge of their chairs in embarrassment.

'It seems like yesterday,' he ventured now, as she continued to stand, silently facing him.

'Yes,' she said. At last she seemed to recollect herself and invited him to sit down. There was a tray prepared, he noticed. Deftly she whisked away the muslin cloth that covered it. 'I'll just fetch the tea,' she said, and left him alone.

'I'm afraid I have no servants now,' she explained when she returned. She poured his tea with a hand that shook slightly. She was left-handed, and it jolted him to notice that her hand was bare of rings. Surely, when Henry was alive, she'd worn a wedding ring? 'I can't tell you how ghastly it's been. Coal has been almost unobtainable since the strikes; all one's friends have gone down with influenza and it's catching, you daren't even visit them. You, I trust, have been spared the influenza?'

She talked in this way, with a brightness that seemed to Daniel forced, for some time. He assured her that he had been spared the Spanish influenza that had laid so many households low that spring. He conceded that the war had indeed been 'ghastly'. He supposed mentally that put his experiences on a par with the frustrations of securing regular coal deliveries in Kensington. He felt the room, and the first beautiful woman he had ever talked to entirely alone (for such she was), receding to a great distance. The room from this perspective was much smaller than he had remembered it; beyond the lace curtains the portico of the house across the street was almost close enough to touch. There were bare patches on the walls where pieces of furniture had stood that he only vaguely remembered. The distemper on the walls was slightly yellowing. *Was it for this . . . ?*

He wasn't thinking of himself. He wished she would speak of Henry. That had been the whole purpose of his visit; to pick up what remained of the severed threads, to bring back something of Henry by talking about him with the only other person living who could have loved him, Daniel supposed, as he himself had loved him. All over England memorials were going up to commemorate the names of those who had made 'the supreme sacrifice'. Henry had made that sacrifice. Why did this woman not want to talk about him?

At last, feeling himself little more than an onlooker, now, but determined to play the scene to the end, he drew from his pocket the bulky package that

96

Major Dowell had given him in Arras. He watched her face, in an agony of apprehension, for any sign of emotion. As her outstretched hand closed round the package, and in the second before he relinquished it, her eyes flickered upwards to meet the intensity of his gaze. The cornflower blue of the irises grew suddenly to enormous proportions, he could see nothing else but the liquid promise of those eyes framed by their unblinking black lashes. In spite of himself he felt his pulse beginning to race, before he tore his eyes away. He forced himself to follow the envelope, as she put it down quite casually among the tea things.

'Won't you open it?' he managed to say.

'Would you like me to?'

So she busied herself with finding a paper knife; at last she slit open the outer envelope. From it she drew a pocket watch which Daniel supposed he had seen many times but actually he couldn't remember at all – it was just a pocket watch like any other – and a lock of jet-black hair. 'My hair, you see,' she said expressionlessly. 'In all his travails, I was with him. I'm glad of that.' It was so commonplace; not a trace of Henry remained in these trivial keepsakes. But Daniel's agony was mounting. Why could she give no outward sign of gladness or sorrow? Could she really, after just a year, not feel anything? He had no thought that he might be needlessly, vicariously stirring up feelings which by rights belonged to her alone. He wanted her to be distraught, to weep in front of him. Could it be that he wanted to see her suffer? That he wanted to be sure of her pain? Surely it was for those cornflower-blue eyes, that etched, pointed chin, the imperious calm of that voice, that Henry had laid down his life? The supreme sacrifice, as Daniel saw it, had been made for her.

'There's a letter too,' she went on, still without expression. 'You must forgive me, but I shall read it later. And now,' with a return to something of her earlier animation, 'you must tell me about yourself.'

So Daniel talked, obediently, sadly, in jerky, disconnected snatches, about his convalescence; about his plans to go up to Oxford in the autumn. Firkin would be joining him there, if he got demobbed and home from Mesopotamia in time. There would be lots of veterans, his College tutor-to-be had written to tell him, among the new students. He would be sure to find Oxford congenial.

Suddenly, on an impulse, he said, 'Do you remember that time when we went to the British Museum and it was such a sell. I invited you all to Upland Grange – Firkin and you, and – and—' He plunged on, appalled now at the risk he was taking. 'It won't be the same, of course. Firkin's not here, and – and—'

'Henry's dead,' she interposed, almost sharply.

That stopped him in his tracks, but only for a moment. Daniel gulped. 'Yes. Yes, that's right . . . Well, I'd like to repeat the invitation. Just for you.

Will you visit me at Upland Grange? We can open all the shutters in the East Wing and you'll be the first person ever, I suppose, to see the whole collection. A private view. Would you come? Would you really?'

'Yes,' she said, 'I'd like that. I'd like that very much.'

In the event she came for luncheon. It was a long way in those days to travel for such a short visit but it would not, she declared, be quite proper for a lady in her situation to spend longer in the company of a young man at his home. This constraint, which had not at first occurred to him, only increased the turmoil of Daniel's feelings.

The day was overcast but warm. Lunch was served by the now elderly Soames on the terrace overlooking the estuary. The tide was far out and the mudbanks gleamed with a grey wetness that always reminded Daniel of the scales of dead fish. He felt shyly proud to be offering her chilled Chablis as she exclaimed with unaffected enthusiasm about the house and the grounds and the view. She had never been to Upland Grange; this had been part of Henry's life, not hers. Henry was not mentioned during the meal, but Daniel felt his presence more strongly than he had done since that day in Arras when he had learnt of his idol's death; a benign presence hovering beyond the terrace where the gnats hung in clouds and thistledown drifted past in the heavy, warm air. He was not used to drinking wine, and it seemed they had both drunk quite a lot. When the dessert came – glass bowls piled high with fresh-picked raspberries and topped with syllabub – she suggested pouring more of the wine over the fruit and Soames, with lips pursed, was sent to fetch another bottle. That was the high point of the day, sitting back without embarrassment on chaises longues that had been drawn up at the end of the terrace, cornucopia in hand for all the world like ancient Roman banqueters. She laughed heartily at this comparison. He had never seen her laugh before: the corners of her mouth turned upwards, a flush came into her cheeks.

But with the coffee the conversation took an unexpected turn. 'I brought you his letter to read,' she said suddenly. No need to say whose. 'It contains news that might possibly mean more to you than it does to me.'

Her face had puckered and for a fleeting instant seemed to Daniel almost ugly all of a sudden. He had never suspected such bitterness under her cool poise. 'You see,' she went on, and the afternoon temperature on the terrace seemed to plunge by several degrees, 'he had a child that he now wants to recognize. You understand what I'm saying? A child born out of wedlock. Henry's bastard.'

Daniel was thrown as much by the change of tense as by the venom with which she spat out this last word. There was something pathetic, and rather frightening, about her reaction: Henry, a year dead, had done this to her *now*. And he could not be scolded, or reasoned with, or called to account. Henry's ghost was an almost tangible presence where the gnats still hovered over the box hedge, and no longer benign.

With trembling hands he read the letter. It was a long letter, rather florid in style. Daniel didn't think it had been written in the forward trench where Uncle Henry had 'bought it'. The handwriting was too careful, the sentences too long. Daniel knew how, even on a quiet night, some explosion, the squelch of duckboards as a heavy tread went past along the trench, or just the sheer discomfort of constantly scratching for lice, would force itself upon your shaky concentration. His own letters had been scrappily written, not very coherent missives. This one had been carefully composed; Henry must have thought long and hard, finally not stinting on the heartrending expressions of affection, but also not flinching from the revelation that he had never been able to make to his wife – or for that matter to Daniel – face to face: he had a daughter. Born, as Joanna said, out of wedlock. A daughter that he now (the letter was undated and the writer dead, but 'now' means now, the moment when you read, the moment there's no escaping from) wished to recognize with due form.

Silently he folded the letter and handed it back to her. 'I won't do it, Daniel,' she said. 'I've been to his lawyers, ages ago, all that sordid business is over and done with. I refuse – I refuse to go into it all again.' She turned away from him to stare across the estuary, that was now beginning to fill with the rising tide. 'It's horrible, isn't it, the hold the dead still have over us?' she murmured, more than half to herself.

Her look when she turned back to him was hard, accusing. 'I wanted you to see that. To see your reaction. You didn't have a hand in this, I suppose? Have you been in cahoots with Henry?' Her eyes continued to bore into him, a delicate blue vein throbbed in her temple. 'It says nothing here about where this child might be, who she is. Even if I wanted to, I can do nothing to fulfil his last request. Unless *you* know who this child is.' She held up a hand. 'No, I don't want you to tell me. His last wish, I'm afraid, will never be fulfilled by me. But I wanted to know if you *knew* – his horrid little secret.' And she slammed the letter down angrily on the chaise longue beside her.

Daniel felt his body turned to stone. There was a roaring like a great wind inside his head. The luncheon, the afternoon he had mentally prepared with such trepidation, had shattered and fallen in sharp fragments at his feet. Henry had been deserted in death by those who had most cause to love him. It was a pitiful, reproachful ghost that now began to fade forever into the oppressive green of that overcast June day. It seemed to Daniel as cruel as anything he had seen done in battle. Hadn't it been his adoration of Henry that had bound him in the first place to this woman that, come to think of it, he hardly knew? If the news of Henry's secret had come to him in some other way, it might have acted very differently on his emotions. But now, in his fury at Joanna's rejection of his idol, he saw only what Joanna saw: the disgrace of his having fathered a bastard, and the perhaps more damning disgrace of now (that treacherous word again) trying to foist that shame on those who had loved him and whom he had deceived.

The afternoon was suddenly stifling, the lustreless green of the meadow and the woods beyond, the seeds and pollen hanging heavy in the air, pressed in on him with the weight of uncontrollable, overcrowded growth. He jumped to his feet, tugging at his collar. 'Air,' he muttered, 'more air.' Then, collecting himself a little, he turned and offered her his hand. 'I promised to show you the secrets of the East Wing, remember? Shall we go?'

If she noticed the change in his voice and the wild, distant look that had come into his eyes, she gave no sign of it. The hand that she allowed him to take in his, as he led her into the cool of the house, trembled slightly.

She gasped as one after another Daniel threw wide the shutters and casements that for years had protected Lionel Robertson's treasures from the light and air. She could hardly have known that for Daniel this was an act of desecration. The stifling afternoon, the gnats and the thistledown invaded the rooms; the onyx and enamel eyes of the statues, that had been sightless for so long, sparked into sudden life. The naked bodies – of athletes, of warriors, of truncated women – were shockingly present in the light of day. These figures still aroused in him something of the prurience with which his seven-year-old self had sought for orifices in the semi-darkness. Daniel felt his own body as cold and as remote from him as the marble and bronze he diffidently showed her, pointing out the astonishingly lifelike detail of the veins beneath the taut skin here, the almost living softness of a highly polished marble torso there. He scarcely noticed her exclamations of surprise and delight as he led her unresistingly from one room to another. It was upstairs, in a room full of dancing dustmotes, as for the fortieth or fiftieth time he flung the shutters wide, that he suddenly took her, with all his strength, in his arms.

She let out a cry of surprise. Those cornflower-blue eyes once again filled his entire field of vision as he forced his lips against her, tilted back her head, and kissed her again and again. At first her body gave way limply to his embrace. Then, struggling for breath, she fought to free herself. When she could speak she whispered fiercely, 'What are you doing?' but he thought it was not a question that demanded an answer and the blue depths of her eyes still drew him on. He tore inexpertly at her clothes. 'Daniel, stop it.' Her voice might have been sharper this time but to his aroused senses it lacked all conviction. He hardly knew what he was doing. His body was in the grip of a power he had never before experienced; beyond the stillness of the rooms his ears were filled with the rushing of an invisible wind. The room was piled high with antique furniture. They fell together across an old four-poster bed whose canopy was sagging at one end. The aged bedsprings screeched furiously in protest. 'Yes,' she cried out breathlessly, but he couldn't tell if the violent movements of her body beneath his were of resistance or pleasure. Out of the silence of time the violated springs shrieked rhythmically in Daniel's ears. He was pounding into her, he had eyes only for her eyes, and as it went on he saw, mirrored in her contorted face, all the passionate anger he had felt down below on the terrace, and even before that, in Kensington. So the war must have been 'ghastly', must it? So she no longer wore Henry's ring. So she had contemptuously refused Henry's posthumous last wish. It was for you, it came to him now with savage clarity, it was for *you* – *you* – *you* that Henry died and so many like him, and he himself, a creature of stone and air, not flesh and blood, was in that moment Henry, Joanna's rightful husband, and for the second time in his life the light became a torrent, pouring through the desecrated darkness of these rooms, in the moment of violent climax emptying out of his body into hers, as the dust of generations rose slowly and thickly to blend with the thistledown hanging in the air.

He came to; she was shouting at him from the far side of the room. Her hair and clothes were awry, her cheeks blazing. He was oblivious to her words; the terrible power of the light was ebbing from him. And then, as the colours and shapes of the day began to re-form around him and the intoxicated beating of his heart began to slow, came shame. He began to recognize the words she hurled at his head. He was vile, he had betrayed her. Why had so many better men had to lay down their lives, so that the likes of him could crawl upon the earth and do this to her? No woman could feel safe in England again. And she flung at him the word that he had never heard used outside the Ancient History class where it had raised suppressed titters among the boys and a studied vagueness on the part of the Latin master. The word was *rape*.

With this she turned and ran from the room. Daniel, adjusting his clothes as he went, followed more slowly. He no longer felt his body like stone; the hard serenity of the statues had left him. He felt soft and limp and (her word) vile. He was ready to curl up like a foetus or a slug. Disgust crawled like a physical sensation on his skin.

He stood at the door, watching her plunge, half walking, half running, across the gravel sweep towards the drive. As he watched, a small figure launched itself into her path. It was Sarah Jane, who had picked up her parasol and whatever else she had left behind on the terrace after lunch. Daniel saw her swerve instinctively out of the child's path, hesitate, then grab the parasol before resuming her headlong flight. God knows what the child must have thought. Sarah Jane turned in evident puzzlement towards the house. Seeing Daniel she began to run towards him; he recognized the sheaf of papers she still clutched in her hand. Sarah Jane would be five this winter.

And as he stared into the smudged face that he had grown used to seeing about the Lodge and the grounds, where she seemed to run wild as he had once done, it was as though he saw Sarah Jane for the first time.

Out of the upturned face of the child, the truth stared back at Daniel and struck him with the force of a whiplash.

6 SARAH JANE

'OF course,' Dan explains to his daughter Lucy, now twenty-two and about to embark on a career as a trainee psychoanalyst, 'we can't be certain it happened quite like that. But Joanna Stephenson disappears completely from the family papers after that visit to Robertson Grange in June seventy years ago.'

'I think you rather enjoyed the story, the way you told it. It's a typical male fantasy.'

Dan returns his attention to the road. The traffic is bad this close to Christmas. All Dan's Christmases have been snowless. Everywhere he goes these days, electronic imitations of the voice of Bing Crosby come at him to wish him otherwise. But Christmas 1989, on the road to Suffolk, promises to be no exception. Rain is spattering on the windscreen. Ahead, the traffic has slowed almost to a standstill: the carriageway has been blocked off with red and white cones. *Repairing worn-out road*, the signs proclaim. Lucy, curled up in the passenger seat beside him, turns up the heating.

As a single-line tailback stops and starts and overheats on the hard shoulder, Dan glances idly across the empty, coned-off lanes. Here and there some heavy machinery has been parked. Nobody is repairing the worn-out road today. To begin with he had some qualms about revealing the results of his researches at the Public Record Office to Lucy and her friend Milica, whose long legs are uncoiled so far as is practicable along the cramped back seat of his Citroën 2CV. But he no longers feels quite *in loco parentis* towards his daughter, and rather enjoys the frankness that she, first, has brought into their relationship. Dan has always felt more comfortable in female company than in male, but is curiously reassured by the lack of ambivalence in his feelings towards his daughter. She is short, with straggling mouse-coloured hair that she might wash more often, a freckled face and upturned nose, and green eyes. He finds her femininity soothing, at the same time that her professed feminism keeps him intellectually on his mettle. Lucy at twenty-two is formidably committed to a future career as a psychoanalyst, and her knowledge of the works of Sigmund Freud, Melanie Klein and Jacques Lacan is already prodigious. 'Of course, psychoanalysis is still terribly patriarchal. Old Freud with his fantasies about Moses and penis envy is old hat, but it's still the dominant mode. The point,' Lucy has more than once confidently explained to Dan, 'is to change it.'

She has accused him only this morning, not for the first time, of seeking out her company as a screen for stalking her friends. 'It's called displacement,' she has told him, but without elaborating, and, so far as he can tell, without censure. He has hotly rejected the suggestion, but as he wonders now if Milica has fallen asleep in the back or has been following the story as it unfolded over the whirring of the engine and the swishing of the tyres on the wet road, he cannot hide from himself the jolt of anticipation that ran through him when Lucy phoned him, only yesterday, to say that yes, Milica was coming, was he sure that was OK, and he'd replied with a breeziness he feared must be transparent to his precociously psychoanalytical daughter, that that was fine, just tell her to bring a toothbrush.

'But it still doesn't explain why we're going all this way to Upland Grange to spend Christmas with an old witch you say is half ga-ga,' Lucy breaks in on these thoughts. 'If you ask me, Dan, I think it's perfectly daft.'

His daughter has called him by his Christian name for almost as long as he can remember.

'Sarah Jane is the only one of the whole bunch who's still alive,' Dan now explains patiently. 'The scandal isn't going to go away. It's not just a professional matter, it's my family after all – and yours. You and I are going to get to the bottom of it before the international investigation starts up. We need Sarah Jane. And not to put too fine a point on it, the old lady's not going to be around for ever.'

'But is it so that there will be an international investigation?'

Dan turns round at this point to acknowledge the hitherto silent but not unfelt presence of Milica in the back. 'I'm afraid it's virtually certain. We know now what bits of the site at Ano Meri were dug and filled in again. We know it happened in the summer of 1939. That last season was actually interrupted by the declaration of war. In the chaos that followed, the excavation records went missing. That's the charitable view. It doesn't explain why the same people who hadn't time to gather up their notebooks in the scramble to get on a destroyer to Alexandria did have time to fill in several square metres of trenches, and do it carefully enough that nobody spotted it for more than forty years. No, it looks as though the old rogue has a case to answer, all right.'

'But how,' Milica's slightly guttural voice demands, 'will this old lady help us?'

Dan sighs. Actually, he has rather enjoyed prolonging the mystification of his passengers. He has by now about exhausted the resources of the Public Record Office and the family papers deposited with the Fitzwilliam Museum in Cambridge. He has read, sometimes with a lump in his throat, the correspondence between father and son. He has recognized, with feelings of tender surprise, the spidery neat hand of his mother on faded papers that seem now very remote through being docketed in official folders in the public domain. Among them have been the citation for Lionel's knighthood, his parents' marriage certificate issued in 1926 by the British consulate in Milan: solid, documentary proof of his own existence. But now he is following a new lead, which he has not so far confided to Lucy and Milica.

'My mother kept a diary, you see. It was mentioned in her will when she died.' The close atmosphere of the little car suddenly seems unbearably hot. It has taken Dan several years, and the provocation of his less than sensitive archaeological peers, to reach this point. His mother's presence has never entirely left him. To talk of her life as something complete and over is still painful to Dan, so much of his mother still remains to watch over him even now. 'I've never seen those diaries.' He does not add that even to have searched for them would have seemed a kind of sacrilege, then. 'But now, if I don't find them, I'm afraid the excellent and thorough Horst Wesenthal will get his paws on them first. They're not in London, they're not with the Robertson papers at the Public Record Office or the Fitzwilliam. I've a hunch they got left behind at Upland Grange.'

'You didn't say anything about that when you got me to write to the old dear!' Lucy reproaches him now.

'I think seasonal goodwill is a much better line, don't you?' says Dan serenely, and silence falls once more in the little car.

Dan has wondered if it is not her silences that he values most about Milica. There is much about her that he doesn't understand. In her succinct way she has let it be known that Christmas in a Socialist country, even one as progressive as Yugoslavia, is apt to be duller than a wet English weekend and, to make matters worse, if she goes home she will be at the mercy of competing relatives who are widely scattered, which would make for an expensive and physically tiring trip. Dan has noticed that Milica does not like things to be tiring.

So far as he can make out, her family belongs to the ruling caste that emerged under Tito's brand of Communism. But she shows no desire to return home, and despite the continued plunge of the dinar seems confident that her family can continue to fund her in higher education in England. The last time he met her was just over a month ago, at an all-night disco to celebrate the breaching of the Berlin Wall. Milica then threw herself about on the dance floor, took off her hairband and let her long, thick hair swing wildly about her face and shoulders, joining in the jubilation with the best of them.

But over a maudlin *slivovic* with Dan at a corner table, while getting her breath between dances, she confided some misgivings in a way he found touching: 'You see, *we* were brought up to believe the wall was put there to protect us from the capitalist wolves outside. It's wonderful that it's gone. Really. And East Germany, anyway, is not like my country. The East Germans have a real police state and you can see on the television how unhappy the people have been. But now who stops to ask, when they pick up bits of that horrible wall to sell as souvenirs – and maybe how else will people in the East find enough money to live? – *who will protect us from the wolves?*' And who exactly are 'we', Dan wanted to know. 'Oh, you know,' she waved a dismissive hand. It was the first time that he caught himself wondering what her father did for a living, and felt immediately ashamed of himself. This is the age of winners and losers, he reflects now; and if he can afford to be cynical about Milica's anxieties, has he the right to be any less so about his own knee-jerk compulsion to protect the privileges of his 'job for life' at the Institute?

For a new broom has been sweeping through the Institute of Chronometry in London. Now boastfully dubbed, on all external correspondence and internal memos, 'An Institute for our Time', Leo Spengler's gift to the nation has been under new management these past eighteen months. One of the first edicts to be issued from the designer-furnished suite on the top floor, as part of a new proactive managerial strategy, has decreed that from October 1989, students shall be admitted to the Institute. This has caused understandable consternation. Students for the time being are to be postgraduate only, which means that fears of being jostled in the corridors by long-haired louts, and the risk of sitting down on a used hypodermic in the loo (for such seems to be the perception of contemporary students among the denizens of the Institute) are at least not immediately realized. But further brisk memos have been issued concerning 'recruitment'. Students, to be cost-effective, are so far as possible to be recruited from outside the European Community. A mission has been sent to the Far East, with instructions to trawl the trainee schools of the watchmaking industry in Japan and Korea. Yet more memos have expanded in almost lyrical terms upon the advantages of 'industrial sponsorship' and 'inward investment'. On the ground floor, heads have shaken slowly and the gloom has steadily deepened. There might possibly be a bright future for black holes in space; surely there will be for Nanosecond Technology and Computational Chronometrics, all more happily placed on the upper levels of the building. But archaeology students are already well served in the capital; it will not be easy for Dan and his colleagues. And by now the bottom line of the new policy has gradually become explicit. *No students: no dough*, as Lucy has succinctly summed up Dan's longwinded attempt at explanation.

Dan, faced with this imperative, has thought of Milica.

It is, he suspects, an insidious alibi for feelings that have no place in the new austerity watched over by Foucault's silent pendulum. But Milica, in addition to the qualifications which appeal to Dan, has a B.A. in Arch. and Anth., is not eligible for the subsidized fees paid by nationals of the European Community, and has no visible financial worries. Her application has been seized upon with some relief by Dan's colleagues on the ground floor of the Institute.

Suddenly, Milica taps him quite firmly on the shoulder. Understanding, Dan turns on the car radio. Another jingle and it will be time for the half-hourly news bulletin. The silence in the car is now expectant. One by one this autumn the Communist regimes in eastern Europe have been going down like ninepins: Hungary, East Germany, Poland, Czechoslovakia, Bulgaria. Now it is the turn of Romania. And here, for the first time, the worm has turned. In Bucharest and in Timişoara, a town little heard of before or since, but now under virtual siege, Ceauşescu has turned his élite troops and tanks against unarmed civilians. Hardly any news is getting directly out of Romania. Word of the fighting is being filtered through the Tanjug News Agency in Belgrade. Refugees and journalists with horror stories for the world's media are pouring over the country's western border into Yugoslavia. Milica listens to the bulletin wide-eyed. All this is very close to home, for her.

Even while they have been on the road and the darkness of the shortest day has gathered around the little warm cocoon of the long-suffering 2CV, events have been unravelling with breathtaking speed. Ceauşescu, appearing on a balcony to reassert the authority of his forty-year rule, has been openly shouted down. Now, since the last bulletin – *WYVO this is Radio Wivenhoe, bringing you independent radio news* (with what relentless cheerfulness, Dan can't help himself from marvelling) *from North East Essex and around the world* – Ceauşescu and his wife have been arrested trying to flee the country. Mob rule has overtaken Bucharest. In the car the two girls are talking at once. Milica is holding forth volubly, proud of the diplomatic and humanitarian stand taken by her country, faced with the imminent collapse into civil war of a neighbouring state and the threat of mass exodus across its borders. Lucy wonders if the sudden fall of the dictator will calm the crisis or merely make things worse. Dan is struck all at once by the unfamiliarity of these events taking place, hour by hour, at the far end of Europe. This is history *happening*, it's a one-way ride, and it gives Dan an unaccustomed, uncomfortable sensation. Dan belongs to a generation that without knowing it has learnt to stop worrying and love the Bomb. Dan is unused to history *happening*.

He tries to explain this intuition to his passengers. Milica, who has been well schooled in history, is sceptical. With her slightly American intonation, she says, 'Sure, but didn't you have the Cuban missile crisis, the Vietnam war? What about when Kennedy was assassinated?' All of them, he thinks wistfully, events that for her and Lucy will never be more than paragraphs in textbooks, old newsreel footage, the increasingly introverted memories of people like himself as they grow older.

'Well, yes, of course things *happened* back then. Of course they did. But when they happened they didn't *change* anything.' Floundering now, Dan finds himself almost wistful for the certainties he has grown up with. Was this what Milica meant that night in the discotheque? What was it she said: with the Berlin Wall gone, *who will protect us from the wolves?*

Annoyed with himself Dan snaps out, only half in jest, 'And if I hear that *rat-a-tat tat* drummer boy again this Christmas I shall throw the radio out the window and we'll have no more news. For God's sake, Lucy, can't you turn it off?'

Silence falls once more inside the little car.

Ahead of them in the darkness lies Upland Grange, where Sarah Jane, bedridden, waits to welcome them. As he turns off the dual carriageway and heads into the treacherous lanes of the Essex-Suffolk border, Dan's thoughts flit uneasily across the years. He has reason to fear for the welcome that Sarah Jane will even now be making ready for them.

Lionel had come back here, to Upland Grange, in October 1919. It had been almost a full year since the Armistice. Already, from his lonely outpost in Crete, he had given thanks to the god who watches over washed-up explorers and who had not let him down. His son had been invalided out. Facts about what had happened to Daniel were still sparse. Lionel's imagination failed completely before the experiences his son must have gone through. He supposed it must have been a kind of harrowing of hell. But his son had been luckier than so many.

Throughout the spring and summer of 1919, Lionel in Crete had been assembling his team for the assault on the hill of Kulhantepe. It had taken some time for his former mood of irritable anxiety to clear. But when the island gathered itself to burst out in the almost violent green and wild colours of the short-lived Cretan spring, and the clouds began to lift from the mountains of the interior, Lionel felt at last a lightening of his whole being. The war was over, his son was safe. The seaways were open again.

There was much to be done. And Lionel set himself to work, his former energy at last restored. The undersea cables linking Crete to the mainland of Europe carried a brisk traffic that spring and summer. The telegraphists of Kastro were taxed to the limits of their patience and abilities, transcribing telegrams in several languages, to and from destinations they had scarcely heard of.

Lionel was assembling his team. Then, in the summer, when the seas were quiet, he had set out on his travels: to Egypt first, then to Piraeus where he boarded a train that would carry him haltingly through the wreckage of Europe: to Munich, to Paris, and finally to England which he had not visited since before the war. He planned only the briefest of visits, before he would be off again, impatient as always to be on the spot, to have everything ready for the start of digging, which had already been scheduled for March, 1920.

By the time Lionel reached Upland Grange in October, Daniel had left for his first term at Oxford. Lionel descended like a whirlwind on the place. In less than a week he had made arrangements for Soames' retirement, which was overdue, ordered some redecoration and rebuilding, rejected out of hand Mrs Trudgill's suit to be promoted to housekeeper and move with her family into the servants' quarters in the West Wing (living was very cramped for them in the Lodge, with Sarah Jane now a growing girl), appointed new staff and left a trail of consternation behind him. So far as Dan can discover, Lionel did not think it necessary before taking these steps to consult his son, whose home, when all was said and done, it also was.

Lionel found the place gloomy. He had determined he would move to London for the remainder of his stay. At the Athenaeum there would be company, and he might learn something from the latest archaeological gossip, now that almost everybody was back in civilian clothes and trying to pick up the pieces. But first, it seemed, Trudgill had something urgent to communicate to him. The poor man was standing on one leg, or so it appeared (Trudgill's limp had got worse with the years, he stooped a little now too), by the back door, holding a paper in his hand. Making little effort to conceal his impatience, Lionel lit the gas. It was cold in the kitchen, but he was not minded to invite his groundsman to take off his boots. Surely Trudgill's business would not take long.

But Trudgill was slow to come to the point. He hoped his master would not mind him taking the liberty. He said this several times. And tapped the papers in his hand with deep if inarticulate significance against his knee.

It was a rambling story Trudgill told.

'I know nothing of these people,' Lionel interjected once.

But Trudgill held up his hand. 'Wait, sir, I beg of you.'

And before the tale was told, Trudgill had penetrated, still in his boots, from the kitchen into the wide living room overlooking the Stour. He stood there like a squat stork on one leg, holding the thumbed sheaf of papers in his hand, gesturing with it, but Lionel was still none the wiser.

Then, as darkness fell outside the great window, Lionel suddenly found himself giving his full attention to his groundsman.

He did, after all, know the people in this story. Mrs Trudgill had brought that little girl of hers – what was her name, he had forgotten – up to the house, a snivelling, pert little thing with red hair and freckles. He hadn't noticed anything else about her except the whining way she held on to her mother's skirts; a spiritless creature, Lionel had supposed then and curtly turned down Mrs Trudgill's request. But now, as he came to the point, Trudgill was investing this harmless nuisance with the stench of betrayal.

The mistress, you see, sir, had died in childbirth.

Lionel felt his face hot as though he had been struck. He took a step forward. 'How *dare* you . . .?'

But he had known Trudgill for more than twenty years. He couldn't imagine how the man dared; nevertheless, he knew he could not be lying.

Lionel took a firm grip on himself, clasping his hands behind him, standing straight and tall with his back to the fading light that was still reflected from the estuary beyond the window. 'Tell me,' he said. 'Since you have gone so far, you will have to tell me everything.'

So Trudgill's moment came, and he confided to the master all that he knew – had guessed about Sarah Jane, whose name now thundered in his head, never to be forgotten again. Major Stephenson's letter was there as corroboration of a kind. Lionel ran an eye over it and handed it back to Trudgill with a snort of disgust.

'Is this all the evidence you have to support your story?'

Dumbly, Trudgill nodded.

'It would never stand up in a court of law.'

Trudgill bowed his head.

'In fact, it's the purest nonsense. Why have you come to me with this fairytale?'

'Sir, it's true. As sure as I am standing here, it's true sir. I've turned it over in my mind every way, I get no peace, can't sleep o' nights. Mrs Trudgill never wanted anything said, for her that child is hers, all hers see, she loves Sarah Jane as her own. I feel for her like a father, can't believe sometimes she's not my own flesh and blood. But that's a fact, sir. I want the world for my daughter, sir – in a manner of speaking, if you understand me, sir. 'Course I know she's not my daughter, not really, but I got to see her right all the same. Her father now – her real father, who's dead now of course, God rest him – he wanted her recognized. It says so in that letter.'

There was a beseeching tone in Trudgill's voice now, he must have rehearsed every word, lying awake torturing himself night after night in the cramped quarters of the Lodge, listening to the little girl's even breathing or staring into the darkness as his wife got up to nurse her through the coughs and colds of infancy, and all the while nerving himself, preparing himself for this moment. He owed it to the little girl he thought of as his daughter, and now here he was, braving the legendary wrath of the master.

'It's in your power to help Sarah Jane any way you would, sir. Surely there's room in the big house? There might be something you could do for her, more than simple folk like us can do that love her just the same as if we was her real parents.' And drawing himself up as straight as he could, Trudgill delivered his peroration: 'She's your own flesh and blood, sir. Well, in a manner of speaking. It ain't right her growin' up a skivvy.'

And Lionel, as he listened, became calm again as the pounding in his ears subsided; a terrible stillness possessed him. As he listened, he was ready to forget the wretched figure in front of him, it was something else he saw as he stood against the light, his features invisible to Trudgill. Lionel understood. It was this war, of course. This war had shaken everything loose. He should not have been so surprised. It was no more and no worse than he should have expected. He had only himself to blame if, after all, he had failed to anticipate it: from Trudgill's boots on his carpet, 'taking the liberty', to the shocking betrayal that probably, had he stooped to look for it, had already lurked in Hermione's poisoned entreaties the last time he had set foot in this place. Had she, even then, been warning him, threatening him even? At the time it had seemed to him simply ridiculous that she might take a lover, he hadn't given it a thought. But now, out of the darkness of the war, had come this bastard. This monstrosity.

Lionel's hands were clenched tightly behind his back. He would, if he could, have plucked the unfortunate Trudgill from him like a leech and crushed him under his heel.

He said only, 'Does my son know anything of this?'

Trudgill was sure he did not.

'Then I charge you, if you are to remain in my employment, to see to it that he never does. What has passed between us will not be spoken of again.'

But it will be spoken of on this, the shortest day of 1989.

Dan slows up the car at last as the headlights catch a brick pillar where a rusted signboard has come adrift. 'Upland Grange,' he announces with a cheerfulness he doesn't feel. He turns the car sharply, past the shadow of an abandoned lodge, into the drive. Here the darkness seems to be absolute. The car bumps over the gravel surface, and at last swings to a stop in the semi-circular sweep in front of the house. Suddenly the security lights come on, dazzling them, and a furious barking of dogs starts up.

'What's this, the headquarters of the Gestapo?' Lucy sounds uncharacteristically intimidated.

A small dumpy woman is heading towards the car, a plastic cape held over her head against the rain. At her feet is a seething mass of dogs, some of them, to Dan's untrained eye, potentially dangerous.

'Come on, come on, don't sit there in the car on a night like this. The old lady said you was expected. In you come, dear,' this with a conspiratorial leer at a frightened Milica who has just emerged from the car and shows signs of jumping back in as a yapping terrier threatens to attach itself to her calf, 'you'll have to take us as you find us, I'm afraid. But you won't mind that, will you – seeing as how you're *family*.'

These last words are spoken with a depth of mistrust that almost freezes Dan in his tracks. He is grateful for the comforting presence of his daughter and Milica. This is going to be every bit as bad as he has feared.

Indoors, the small woman shakes the rain from her cape, despatches the dogs back where they came from, and bustles across the hall. 'I'm Pat, by the way. In case you didn't know. Joe can take your things. If I can find him.' Suddenly she has gone, and the same stentorian voice that a moment ago quelled the tide of dogs can be heard echoing through the ground floor of the house.

'Joe's the husband, I think,' Dan whispers to the others. 'Sarah Jane's younger son. The other one, Sidney, is in business in Ipswich.'

There is nothing that anyone can say to that. In the uncomfortable silence Dan glances round him. The oak panelling has been overzealously hung with hunting prints and horse brasses. The green threadbare carpet he surely doesn't really remember from his childhood. Pat's reappearance is almost a relief. Now she snaps on a lighted signboard hanging in a corner, which spells in green letters the word RECEPTION. *Welcome to Upland Grange Hotel. Prop. Mrs S. J. Lambert. Closed Christmas and New Year,* Dan reads on a card that has been imprisoned under perspex, along with some local maps and announcements of last summer's car boot sales, on the formica-topped desk beneath it.

Once again, Dan wonders about the one-way ride of history.

Lucy is whispering in his ear, aghast. 'You didn't tell me they'd turned it into a *hotel.*'

But Dan is miles away. 'Didn't I? Sorry. I think it's always been one. Since she took it over, I mean. Obviously, it's fallen on hard times.'

Over the Reception Desk, there is a pantomime of filling in the register, and some quiet parley at the end of which Dan wearily but patiently brings out his cheque book.

As they follow Pat's directions ('First floor, past the TV room, the last three rooms before the fire escape'), Lucy furiously tugs her father by the sleeve. 'We're not *paying* to stay in this dosshouse, are we? Honestly Dan, the old witch *invited* us, it was me she wrote back to, remember? "Seasonal goodwill" and all that crap. We had that conversation. Dan,' Lucy stops at the bend in the stairs, barring his way. '*What is going on here?*'

But Dan merely shrugs. 'They're business people, Lucy. They're running a business, and don't forget times are hard. If it helps, we're paying the "trade" rate. And anyway, it's me that's paying. OK?'

'I just hope you know what you're doing,' says Lucy darkly as they continue to the top of the stairs. Milica, who has gone ahead, has pressed a knob on the wall and half a dozen dim bulbs in the shape of candles have come on in the corridor. Even more dimly, at the far end, another green illuminated sign announces: EMERGENCY EXIT. There is a smell of dust and old polish everywhere, a country smell of dogs and an institutional smell of underdone bacon. The heavy tread of Joe approaches down the corridor. It's the sort of house where the floorboards make their own familiar noises and here at last, as Joe looms in the doorway, is something from those long gone years that even Sarah Jane, her huge son Joe (unshaven with a crewcut, check shirt and overalls, over six feet and broad with it) and the formica revolution of the fifties have not been able to extinguish from Upland Grange: Dan *knows* the sounds of the old wooden floors with an intimacy that takes his breath away.

As he unpacks, he shakes his head sadly. It is forty years, give or take, since he last set foot in this house, and he had never thought to do so again. Damn Horst and his suspicions. Damn Rex and his well-meaning advice. Damn his own perverse determination to pre-empt the lot of them and be the first to probe the scandal at the heart of his family. Nothing good will come of this, he is now bleakly certain. They shouldn't have come. For the first time it strikes him that he too has a past, there must be buried memories waiting to jump out at him from the very fabric of this place. The old rogue and Daniel, the legendary father he never knew, may be one thing. The mystery that is no doubt merely a tiresome obstacle to Horst, for Dan has its own teasing fascination. But his own past life is another matter. He hasn't thought about that. Somewhere hereabouts is a child in shorts with grubby knees whose grandpa has been telling him the most marvellous stories. And he doesn't want to turn a corner of the landing and find himself face to face with that child.

Pat has promised to 'rustle them up something cold' in the Dining Room. The huge high-ceilinged room is in semi-darkness. The tables, all but one in the corner by the door, are bare of linen, with chairs stacked upside down on top of them. Tinsel Christmas trees have been set up in the alcoves round the room, streamers of coloured crêpe paper stretch above their heads into obscurity. Most of the available light in this corner comes from a huge illuminated tank. Inside this oasis of light, blue lobsters with tied claws and large red-shelled crabs lumber past one another desultorily amid a stream of air bubbles. From hidden speakers wafts insidiously, at subliminal volume, a funereal medley of seasonal musak arranged for electronic keyboard. It seems to be on a loop: *rat-a-tat tat*, Dan crossly drums his fingers on the table. Balefully he returns the stares of the captive crabs in the tank.

'The staff's all gone home for Christmas, see,' Pat explains with defiant apology as she brings them plates of cold ham and undressed lettuce. 'It's just family over Christmas as a rule. Can't afford to keep the staff, not worth the overtime, Sid says. Seeing as you was coming of course, well, that's different. But then I was forgetting, you're family, aren't you? So just you enjoy your meal now.' Pat's roly-poly features loom briefly close to Dan's face, as though daring him to relish the unappetizing fare she has plonked down in front of him. The eyes that stare into his are cloudy with something worse than mistrust.

'*Dan*,' whispers Milica urgently (somehow it is unthinkable to speak loudly in the sepulchral gloom), 'why is it these people are afraid of you?'

'I don't know.'

But it is not this that is preoccupying Dan as the sorry meal drags on. Surreptitiously he is watching Milica's face. To have brought Lucy into this is perhaps excusable – she is at least, in Pat's heavily sarcastic phrase, 'family', and anyway, without Lucy he wouldn't have got even this far, of that he is quite sure. But Milica is different. Whatever her expectations might have been of an English Christmas, she can hardly have been prepared for anything like this. He is ashamed now of the boyish enthusiasm with which, in that subterranean discotheque a month ago, he had first held out to her the prospect of this visit. Then, as now, her expression had been guarded, impassive. Milica wears no visible makeup and her features are large. Handsome perhaps, striking, with her straight dark hair that reaches thickly to her shoulders. But not beautiful. He is ashamed of being attracted to someone hardly older than his daughter. It worries him that he cannot read what is in those stoical, ox-like eyes.

It's time she joined the Institute and became his student. That at least will put the relationship on a proper footing.

Pat has cleared away the drab remains of the evening meal. There is a bar in the corner of the billiard room and here she has poured them lavish glasses of brandy and ginger wine. 'I suppose all this goes on the bill?' Lucy whispers but Dan's answer is pre-empted by a commotion outside. The dogs have started up again, there is a long slither of wheels on gravel, then the bang of a car door. Pat's voice can be heard, from the distance of several rooms away, quelling the uproar.

The door of the billiard room opens and closes with a bang. 'I won't waste time with preliminaries,' the newcomer declares as he strides into the pool of dim light around the bar, his hand outstretched towards Dan in no-nonsense fashion. Though he is dressed in a golfing sweater and baggy corduroys, everything about him seems to Dan to spell businessman. Dan takes the proffered hand, which is clammy and almost instantly withdrawn, with some alarm. 'I'd better introduce myself. Sidney Lambert. I don't believe we've met.'

'No, that's right,' stammers Dan, caught off balance by the abruptness of this meeting and an indefinable sense of threat that puts him instantly on the defensive. With an awkwardness that brings a flush to his cheeks, he introduces himself and his companions. The name Robertson can hardly fail to mean something to Sidney Lambert, but he gives no immediate sign of it.

'Mrs Lambert invited us to spend Christmas with her,' Dan volunteers, to fill the silence that threatens to engulf them.

'Oh God, don't I know it.' Sidney runs a well-manicured hand through his hair in a gesture that even to Dan's strained senses seems contrived. 'But why, man, *why*? That's what we all want to know. I don't suppose *you* do, do you?'

But before Dan can think of an answer, the other has turned to run an appraising eye over the two girls. As though recollecting himself, Sidney Lambert draws a stool up to the bar. 'Can I get you young ladies a drink? And you, what will you have?' There is something about the way this is said that makes it seem to Dan less than convivial.

Drinks gurgle into glasses. Sidney pours himself a large bourbon. 'Cheers,' he raises his glass. 'On the house.'

There is a pause. Dan can feel Lucy and Milica beside him settling into their places to watch whatever is coming next. Suddenly he's on camera, in the starring role. And inwardly he is panicking. It's a recurring dream he has, he's on the stage, he's a talking extra in a film, he's to read a paper at a conference, it's always at short notice and he hasn't had time to learn his lines, he's standing up before an audience and – *there's no script*. Dan licks dry lips and takes a gulp of ginger wine.

'D'you mind if I talk to you frankly?'

Dan doesn't think this is really a question and mutters something indistinct.

'Mother's not in good health. I presume you knew that?'

Dan nods silently.

'*Physically*, there doesn't seem to be much the matter with her. Apart from age, of course. It's her mind that's going: *senile dementia*.' He pronounces the words very slowly, as though Dan and his companions might have some difficulty assimilating them. 'It's not easy to live with, I can tell you. And as you can see there's a business to be run, though that's not really my department, thank Christ.' Sidney takes a long breath. 'The fact is, the old girl's got some damn silly ideas into her head.'

Dan considers the socially sanctioned reply of polite solicitude and rejects it. 'What ideas?' he asks, rather sharply, instead.

'Oh – oh, just ideas. Things about her family, a whole lot of people who've been dead for years. When people get old and their minds come a bit loose, that's where they wander back to often enough, isn't it? Second childhood and all that. Listen: *I don't want her given any encouragement.* You can't have any idea what it's like. It might seem just quaint to an outsider, dear old lady, such a character, half way off her trolley of course, but it's vintage stuff, takes you back half a century. None of it can make any difference nowadays, so what's the harm, you may well think. I'll tell you what's the harm.' Sidney approaches his face very close to Dan's. 'I have to live with the old dear, and so has Pat and so has my brother. It isn't *fair*, do you hear?'

'I really don't understand,' says Dan as blandly as possible. 'If you must know, there are some things about my own family I think your mother could help me with. I grew up in this house, I assume you knew that? Some things that belonged to my mother might still be here.'

Sidney's knuckles have whitened on the edge of the bar. Now he smashes down his half-finished glass so that bourbon slops over his hand and he shakes it impatiently over the floor. 'See here, Mister Robertson or whatever it is you're called. It was my father's money bought this place from the Robertsons when they were bankrupt. Never mind the way they treated my mother all those years; she hadn't a lot to thank them for, as you probably know. When she dies, she's going to leave it to her own flesh and blood. Joe and me. Who d'you suppose has been running the place these past five years, you tell me that? It belongs to *us*. And I'm not having any long-nosed Robertson sneaking back to tickle the old girl's fancy with whatever dreams of grandeur have got into her scrambled brains. She's daft, have you got that? Dotty. Out to lunch. She doesn't know what year she's in half the time. Thinks it's the General Strike she's watching on the telly. Boer War, I shouldn't wonder. God knows how old she is. But I warn you, Mister Robertson, if I catch you or anyone whispering a word of that nonsense near the old lady I'll have an injunction out so fast you'll be through that door and back where you came from before you can say Santa Claus. Christmas or no Christmas, I know a lot of people in the law.' At the end of this speech Sidney raises his brandy balloon, empties it swiftly, and storms out of the bar.

'So much for the season of goodwill,' says Dan grimly.

'And you've *paid* these ghastly people,' protests Lucy.

Milica is silent and thoughtful, twisting the stem of her glass in her hands. There are sounds of an altercation in the kitchen; the dogs are beside themselves. 'I think we should find the old lady now,' says Milica practically. 'It may be our only chance.' They have already slipped off the bar stools and are silently making their way upstairs, Dan unsure whether he fears making a fool of himself as much as he fears Sidney's officious wrath.

The upper floors are in darkness, and some time is wasted in pressing knobs on the walls to bring the lights on for a few seconds and then groping their way back to the stairwell in the dark. Sarah Jane must be in the suite at the top of the West Wing, the one Dan remembers as his mother's.

'You go in first,' he says to Lucy. Milica knocks and the two of them go in. After an interminable interval Milica comes to the door and beckons to him. He realizes he is perspiring with relief. Now, at least, Sidney will be unable to eject them until he has said his piece to Sarah Jane. Neither of the sons, he is certain, will dare to make a scene in front of the old lady. He advances now across the room which was once his mother's. Once again, to his alarm, memory springs momentarily alive before his eyes. He sees the tall lattice window in the gable, which is dark and curtained now, thrown wide open and the sunlight streaming in to catch his mother's face where she sat up in bed, a white embroidered bedgown pulled up to her throat. On her face is a slightly admiring, slightly alarmed smile of greeting as he carries the tea-tray proudly in and sets it down without spilling anything, the triangular pieces of toast buttered the way she likes them, the tea and the strainer and the little jug of milk all in place. She looks at him and looks at the tray, and laughs and hugs him and says, 'Oh Dan, how wonderful. But – what about a *cup*?' and the flush of shame rises from his ankles through his middle, and his cheeks and hair seem to flame, perspiration stands out on his forehead just as it does now. That must have been, he can't place it exactly, during their last summer at Upland Grange, the year the old rogue died. His mother's eyes had been red that summer, though she tried to hide it from him that she had been crying. 'Why do we have to leave, mum?' To the nine-year-old Dan it was one of those things. Only later did he miss the meadow and the boats and the morning light on the river, but by then Upland Grange was already a memory, at once remote and painful to the touch.

The room has the smell of a sickroom now, and the small body perched among a pile of pillows on the bed has none of the contours of his mother. Sarah Jane Lambert has a broad sunken face on which the traces of freckles can still be seen. Her chin tapers almost to a point and her nose is a little flat and a little upturned in a way that might still be cheeky, mischievous. Her hair lies in long flaxen strands about her. But it is her eyes that hold Dan's attention as he advances hesitantly towards the bed. They are the deep dark blue of a newborn child's. Lucy's eyes were like that once, though you'd never believe it now. But no, Sarah Jane's are a bit lighter, it's the intensity and the indrawn shape of the sockets that gives them that colour. These are not, Dan thinks with a shudder, the eyes of innocence.

A curved hand is extended from beneath the bedcovers. He takes it briefly, never taking his eyes off her face. The skin of her hand is dry and hard, he can feel the twisted shape of the bones inside. He sits down and listens to her voice. Having got here, he has all the time in the world. Until she tires and her voice runs out. But Sarah Jane, it seems, has much to say.

'So you're Daniel,' she concludes a long, silent appraisal of him. 'Sit there, dear boy. Sit there and talk to me. Nobody talks to me nowadays. They think I'm batty, that's why. Yes, you've the look of *her* all right. Stuck up old bitch she is too. Dead I s'pose poor dear by now, is she?' This is said in an entirely friendly way. Her eyes continue to scrutinize him critically as she goes on. 'Dead the lot of them, the Robertsons. But listen 'ere young man. I've got Robertsons in under my skin. Nobody knows it, but you're looking at the last of the Robertsons right here. Don't matter much that Bud came along when all them toffee-noses said I was on the shelf for good. Sid and Joe's papa that was. During the war, you never saw so many Americans. But Bud was special, see. Bud married me. Only he's dead too, of course, Bud is. Funny thing though, *he* doesn't come back like the others do. *You've* come back, I can tell. There's no use denying it, I could see it from the way you walked, the minute you came in the room. They all walk like that. As though they've forgotten how. It's from being under the ground. They're all under the ground now, which don't stop them coming back to talk to Sarah Jane and telling her things. The last of the Robertsons, you see. I don't count Sid and Joe. I done my best but Bud wasn't that kind of man. Nice he was, in a beefy American sort of way. 'E was good to me. Gave me those two boys. But 'e didn't have class, Bud didn't, and no more do they. No, when I go, that'll be an end to the Robertsons. They'll stop coming back then, I shouldn't wonder. Won't be nobody left for them to talk to.

'So you're Daniel. Well, you've changed, that's all I can say. Well well. It's a funny thing, they always used to be older than me. That was in the old days. Now when they come back, I'm the oldest of the lot. Anyway,' this in quite a brisk, almost businesslike tone, 'what have you come to tell me?' And she cocks her head on one side as though to listen to no earthly words.

Dan tries patiently, carefully, to explain himself.

'Papers, eh?' Sarah Jane seems greatly amused. 'I don't know what you want with *papers* in your state,' and she laughs harshly. 'But if it's *papers* you're interested in – well, I've something to show you, young man. *Sid!*' The voice is suddenly shrill, imperious and, to Dan's consternation, Sidney Lambert steps silently forward from behind him. Both the sons, he now realizes, are in the room, though he hasn't heard them come in. 'Sid, show the gentleman my birthright.' There is a crafty look in her eye. 'Mind he don't touch it, but see he reads it, every last word. And rub his nose in it.'

'Mother, really, I—' Sidney's protest is purely token, though his discomfiture is real and visible. His mother fixes him with a look, and he takes a key, opens a locked drawer in the cabinet beside the bed, and takes out a sheaf of yellowed papers. One by one the pages are spread on the coverlet in front of Dan for him to read, the twisted brown hands holding down the corners, under the wary, mortified gaze of Sidney Lambert.

My dearest, dearest Joanna, (Dan reads)
If this letter ever reaches the hands of the one I love, it will be because it's all up with me. I am arranging for it to be brought to you by a brother officer. This must be a letter in which there are no more secrets between us. I must write to you of things which are not for the prying eyes of the Army censors. I am, as you know, a practical man and have not the turns of phrase that the solemnity of the moment, shd this letter ever have to be delivered to you, ought to warrant. But the time has come for me to make my confession. And there is no other soul in all the world to whom my confession could be made than to you, my dearest angel. May I, in this moment of dread, count upon that supreme virtue of charity in you, without which, as the Scriptures tell us, we are all but sounding cymbals and tinkling brass? . . .

A lump comes into Dan's throat as he reads. As he reaches the end, and the sheets are jealously, impatiently gathered away by Sidney, he dares to lean forward and take Sarah Jane's crooked hands in his. 'Let me tell you,' he says. 'You were not quite five years old. A lady came to visit. It was a warm sunny day. They argued. Perhaps they behaved a bit strangely. I'll bet you spied on them, did you? And she left this behind. You've kept it all these years. And, oh God, you guessed what it means?'

A look of terror passes over the shrunken face before him, but she doesn't withdraw her hands. '*How do you know?*'

Dan is embarrassed at the reaction he has caused. How can he explain about the Public Record Office, the more mundane letters and documents of the Robertson papers that have been neatly docketed in civil service binders and tagged with electronic bleepers? As he remains silent, her features begin to relax and for the first time she shows signs of tiring.

'So it's true, then,' she murmurs, as much to herself as to anyone else in the room. 'You see,' she seems to be appealing to her sons, but they are almost out of earshot. Tears well up in the parched sockets of her eyes. 'It's true. I always said as how I was a lady, and nobody ever believed me. Then along comes Bud and sweeps me off me feet and there's an end to it. Couldn't be no lady, not married to a GI, could I? But Bud got rich robbing the PX, no questions asked, he got demobbed before they found out. Wouldn't do to go back to the States, so here we stayed and Bud went into the grocery business and made a packet and when this place came up for sale Sarah Jane *got her own back*. For bein' a skivvy all her life when by rights she should have been a lady and rich. For them Robertsons looking down their noses at her just as though she didn't exist and them knowing perfectly well all the time. Oh that was a day, that was. You're too young to remember, boys, the first time I set foot inside this house, and it was all mine. Least, it was Bud's, and Bud was mine so everything was mine, after bein' a nobody and going short for all those years. That was when we made the hotel, and it did well enough till Bud went and died. Still, we don't do too badly. But there's the funny thing.' Her gaze begins to wander and settles on Dan. 'Bud doesn't come back. *You* do. The Robertsons come back. And my sons ain't Robertsons. *Not got class*,' she almost spits out the words. 'There's no more Robertsons after Sarah Jane. The letter proves it.'

With a renewed spasm of fear she pulls her hands clear of Dan's. '*But you ain't gettin' it back, Mister. If you was the Devil hisself you ain't takin' that letter back. It's Sarah Jane's birthright, see.*'

Dan does his best to set her fears to rest. 'The papers I want to see would have belonged to my mother. They didn't turn up with my mother's things when she died, so they may still be here. I'd like your permission to look.'

The old woman's joy and gratitude are painful to Dan. '*Sid! Joe!* You're to let this young man look through the lofts. He's to come as often as he likes. And his daughters, they're nice and they don't cause trouble. Just so long as he don't lay a finger on my birthright. You've got that locked away, have you?'

'But Dan,' Lucy is still puzzled. 'even if that letter means what you and she both think it means, that doesn't make her a *Robertson*. Why d'you think she's so hung up about the Robertsons, anyway?'

It is a grey, drab Christmas morning. Dan has insisted that the girls should solemnly hang up stockings outside their rooms, and has quietly filled them, before going to bed, with the presents he has brought. Lucy has given him what she calls a phallogocentric tiepin. Tastefully designed, it might, depending how you looked at it, represent either a pen or a penis. Milica is embarrassed at having come empty-handed.

'Well, as to the why, you're the analyst,' Dan rebuffs the question amiably. 'Strictly speaking, of course you're right. She's not a Robertson. But her mother was surely Hermione, Lionel's wife. The legal evidence may not survive – you'd never make a case in law on the basis of that letter, as Sidney must realize – but I don't think there's much doubt. That makes Sarah Jane my father's half-sister, and your and my something-or-other that's too complicated to work out. But it's blood-is-thicker-than-water, and more than a touch of *folie de grandeur*, that's my reading of your patient, Ms Psychoanalyst.'

'I think you have left something out.' Milica is trying hard to make up for her gaffe in not having come armed with Christmas presents. 'If I understand correctly, your famous father and grandfather were quite horrible to her for years. For all her life, no one recognizes this that she calls her birthright. And what use is it to her now?'

But Dan is excited to be on the trail. The few trappings of Christmas at Upland Grange are bleak indeed, and outside the ground is sodden, the outbuildings overgrown with moss. Rain sweeps across the mudflats of the estuary. Only the dogs, to judge by the riotous barking from the hidden depths of the ground floor, seem to be having a good time. By afternoon, Dan is festooned with cobwebs from the spacious attics of the Grange, and his thick archaeologist's cord trousers are ingrained with dust. At first, Sidney Lambert insisted on standing over the three of them, guiding their eager scrabbling by the light of his torch. But soon, as Dan had been hoping, he has tired of this, and by now Dan and the girls have the spaces of the attic to themselves. Sidney has pointedly marked off certain areas. Outside these, he has shrugged with a hint of crossness, God alone knows what might be lying around. But there's no treasure trove here, see. Anything Dan finds and wants to take away, he's to show it to Sidney first, got that?

It has been an unsystematic business from the start. If his mother's diaries *have* been left behind here, Dan has no way of guessing what they might look like, how many there might be, or how they might have been packed.

Stooping under the eaves, and taking turns to hold the single torch that Sidney has been gracious enough to leave them, they have sifted through more issues of the *National Geographic, Reader's Digest* and assorted East Anglian periodical publications than Dan had ever imagined could have been printed. Boxes of paper, boxes of crockery, junk that must go back, surely, to the time of the Robertsons, all these confront Dan and his helpers in the attic.

'This could go on for weeks, Dan,' says Lucy despondently, sitting down on a packing case whose contents are spilling through its frayed corners. 'How long before we all go raving bonkers?'

'I thought you didn't use words like that in your chosen profession?' Dan teases, but Milica breaks in on this exchange with her characteristic urgency.

'Who has the radio?'

Eastern Europe is still with them, this Christmas Day. Milica has brought her transistor into the attic, and placed it high up for best reception. Dan refuses to listen to the seasonal entertainment, however, so Milica is only allowed to turn it on for the hourly news bulletins. Alerted by the sound of chimes below, Milica now diverts the torch to pick out the latest resting place of the radio, on a shelf between two roofbeams. Outside it must already be dark. The sound of rain has started up again on the slates above their heads. It is cold in the attic.

All of them stop what they are doing as the irrepressible good cheer of Radio Wivenhoe crackles into explosive life around them. They are just in time to catch the end of the familiar jingle. In Romania the deposed Nicolai Ceauşescu and his wife have been summarily tried and shot.

There is a shocked silence in the attic. *Rat-a-tat tat*, is still going on in Dan's head. The rhythm of their search has been broken. *A one-way ride*: Dan is forcibly reminded of his intuition in the car on the way up here. In the moment of stillness that follows, Dan finds time to feel a pang for the elderly Mrs Ceauşescu: mightn't she have married the miner's son next door and never missed the Swiss bank accounts and the palace as big as Versailles? Half-forgotten history lessons crowd vividly upon him. The French Revolution (this year has seen much razzmatazz to celebrate its bicentenary) and the fearful symbol of Enlightenment run amok: the guillotine.

He is aware that Milica and Lucy are looking at him. He is aware too that something else has been happening to him while he has stood transfixed, unseeing at first, his eyes simply following the beam of the torch in Milica's hand. Something has begun to happen that will affect him far more deeply than the violent end of the Ceauşescus, something that ever afterwards will be inseparable in Dan's mind from his private obituary for the Cold War in this moment with the rain drumming on the eaves of Upland Grange and the callow voice of WYVO Radio Wivenhoe.

The girls have turned to follow the direction of Dan's gaze. The radio, where Milica had hastily parked it earlier, is resting on a tattered bundle of brown paper. On the outside of the bundle, Dan's consciousness has at last registered the delicate, faded lettering that he has been staring at all this while. The handwriting is almost as familiar to him as his own. Dan has scarcely any need to trace out the well-known curves, drawn with a fine nib: still less does it matter in this moment of discovery what words they spell. It is as though his mother's voice has come upon him out of the darkness under the eaves. Trembling, he moves towards the package.

It must once have been a square parcel, tied with string, but the string has long since snapped, the paper is blotched and torn, several of the uniform notebooks have spilled out across the shelf. Dan picks up one at random. Lucy brings the torch close. Nobody has thought to switch off the radio, but for once Dan is oblivious. The notebook in his hand has stiff covers and a sewn binding like the exercise books he can remember from school. The paper is brittle, the small, neat script faded. The handwriting, though dated in style, is so clear, it is as though the laconic words he reads are ringing aloud in his head. It is suddenly an intoxicating sensation, to be holding the past in his hand.

Still without a word, he exchanges glances with Lucy and Milica.

'Journey's end,' breathes Lucy at his side, with barely disguised relief.

Before they depart on Boxing Day, Dan nerves himself for a final encounter with Sidney Lambert. It is mercifully brief. Sidney's inspection of his precious booty is cursory, almost insolent, but Dan is too mindful of its value to himself and the investigation into the scandal of Ano Meri to risk protesting. He has already gathered the notebooks, carefully re-packaged in a large cardboard box, into the back of the 2CV, the three of them are in the hall saying their farewells to Pat, when the summons comes. Dan is not to depart, after all, without paying his respects once more to Sarah Jane.

Today it seems, embarrassingly, that Sarah Jane is wearing makeup. Her manner is more distraught than before, but her words are more lucid.

'So you found those *papers*, then?'

Dan nods. 'My mother kept a diary. Did you know?'

Sarah Jane tosses her head. 'I don't pry. Shouldn't have been left here, should it?'

'I should like to take it with me.'

Now it is the old woman's turn to take Dan's hand in hers. She draws him close to her and he can feel those seeing blue eyes raking his features. 'You're good, you are. I'm glad you came. You know about my birthright and you can tell those sons of mine. Come again. I don't get much company. Don't mind Sid, he's prickly but he don't mean no harm. Joey now, he's a sweetie. Takes after his father. Beefy, bit of a crook maybe, only his dad had more brains. I think Joe'll stay out of trouble. Don't you mind them. Come and see me again.'

Impulsively Dan kisses her on the cheek. Her skin feels brittle against his lips, the smell of dried sweat and bedpans almost makes him gag, but the sheer, helpless sadness of it all is stronger still. With a heavy heart he turns to leave Sarah Jane to her ghosts and the emptiness of the Upland Grange Hotel.

As he turns in the doorway he hears her chuckle, with little mirth but without malice. 'Of course, I knew at once. You're an impostor.'

7 EUROPA

LIONEL Robertson returned to Crete in the last of the halcyon days of autumn, before the winter gales set in. A date had already been set for the start of excavations at Ano Meri: along with the swallows, when they came flying back from Africa, bringing with them the first warmth of the Sahara, from the corners of Europe and the Empire would come Lionel's handpicked team of specialists to oversee and direct the work.

Lionel's arrival this time was little short of sensational. Under his fastidious direction was unloaded – by crane on to a lighter and ferried thence to be winched up on to the quay – a brand-new Hispano-Suiza motorcar, with flashing mudguards, shiny leather upholstery, and a klaxon that was the envy of the townspeople of Kastro who gathered round on the quayside to inspect this wonder of the modern world. Some time later Lionel, donning cap and goggles, showed a series of moustachioed willing helpers how to crank up the engine, jumped into the driving seat, and began a triumphant progress through the narrow streets of the town. At the old Venetian portal, that no one in those days had thought to rebuild to the gauge of modern traffic, he nearly came to grief. But after some anxious moments he was through and facing open country and the road to Ano Meri.

And here his triumphal progress changed character once more. Whether or not Lionel had foreseen this, there was no possibility of negotiating the stony horse-tracks of the interior of the Kastro prefecture in anything more mechanized than the large-wheeled wooden carts that brought the farm produce into town and were used by the peddlars to take their wares around the villages. Lionel's triumph could so easily have ended in ignominy. But while he continued to sit, imperturbable behind the wheel, good-naturedly sounding the klaxon to the delight of the throng that still surged around him, the youth of the town came to his rescue. More than a dozen young men in the ubiquitous black breeches, with black tasselled kerchiefs on their heads, attacked the telegraph poles which had recently been set up to connect Kastro to the other towns to westward. Swarming up the poles, in minutes they had torn them free of wires. In another moment, half a dozen poles had been pulled to the ground and were being inserted, to enthusiastic cheers from the crowd, under the chassis of the Hispano-Suiza. In this way Lionel and his motorcar came to be carried shoulder-high over the stony tracks to Ano Meri, as he returned to his fief like a conquering hero, ready at last to begin the dig on which he had already staked so much.

It was the last day of March, 1920. The vines had been uprooted from the long flat summit of Kulhantepe, a swathe cut through the olive groves. In the darkness before dawn the workmen that Lionel had recruited from the surrounding villages began arriving with their picks, shovels and wicker zembils in which the day's finds would be collected. The workmen numbered almost a hundred, evenly divided between Muslims and Christians. Lionel had been punctilious about this, despite the remonstrances of the Bishop of Kastro who had expounded to him the dream of all Greeks, to liberate their brothers in Smyrna and Constantinople from Muslim tyranny. But Lionel had been adamant: in Crete, so far as he could see, the two faiths had lived side by side for centuries, and everyone who lived in the island was to have a stake in the discoveries of Ano Meri. Lionel was determined to see fair play.

The wages the *milord* was offering were not inconsiderable in those post-war days of uncertainty. Crete had not seen a dig on such a scale since the early excavations of Evans at Knossos, twenty years before. The eyes of the islanders – and, Lionel had seen to it, of the world – were on Ano Meri this windy March day of 1920.

The men were singing in a ragged chorus as they trudged up the track from the village. Lionel and his team had pitched tents below the summit of the hill, and one by one the Europeans emerged from the tentflaps into the gale. In years to come the number of overseers and and specialists working on the site would fluctuate with the fortunes of the excavation, but was never more than a small fraction of the number of Cretan workmen employed. On this day in March there were but four of them: Bertie Shaw, a sandy-haired, softly-spoken archaeologist from Nottingham whom Lionel had poached the previous summer from the Valley of the Kings; Angus Cramond, a rugged architect from the west coast of Scotland whom Lionel had known for years and knew to be, among other things, a superb draughtsman; Reinhard Kreuzenberger, who still smarted from the insult of having been picked out as a restorer of Minoan frescoes from among the unemployed avant-garde artists of Munich; and Lionel himself. The wind that was rising as the light grew around them took their breath away. Following the example of the workmen, who were by now standing around in groups, all but Lionel wound handkerchiefs over their mouths and noses. Before the day was over the dust was going to be frightful.

As the sun broke from behind the serrated crags of Iouktas across the plain, the assault was ready to begin. Trenches and baulks had been measured and marked out with string and tentpegs. Rings of stones marked the sites where the earth dug from the trenches was to be heaped. Lionel, poised like a general on the commanding centre of the site, summoned his foreman to him. Manolis Laskaris, who together with his brother Yannis had been dispossessed of the hilltop of Kulhantepe, now stepped forward, a bright new whistle hanging round his neck. Manolis, who had long been pilfering from the site and had, Lionel was generous enough to recognize, an unsurpassed eye for the terrain and for the most delicate objects that might be found beneath it, had been Lionel's first choice for foreman. At first Manolis had gruffly refused to consider it, would not so much as speak to the intermediaries that Lionel sent. But even Manolis, hardened and taciturn as he had returned from the Macedonian front, had been won over in the end. Bertie Shaw had been sceptical of the arrangement: set a thief to catch a thief, was that it? But Lionel had been adamant, and now no one, it seemed, was more deeply under the *milord*'s spell than Manolis who, while his uncle squandered what remained of the family holdings, month after month, in a futile lawsuit to overturn the purchase of the land and evict the hated conqueror, had already begun to win the respect of his fellow villagers for the fairness with which he exercised the authority invested in him by Lionel.

Now, as Lionel raised his hand in what might have been a familiar greeting to the risen sun, Manolis' whistle blew. With military precision the assault began, in several parts of the site at once. Dust streamed in clouds from the summit of Kulhantepe. Bodies bent and straightened, many of them, as the day wore on, stripped to the waist; zembils filled and were carted off to the finds tent for sorting later; hugely overloaded wheelbarrows negotiated the narrow baulks and lines of duckboards leading to the spoilheaps that rose all round the site. Such activity had surely not been seen on this spot, Lionel reflected during the morning, since the time when the first builders came up here, with their dressed stone blocks and teams of slaves, to begin the construction of the palace that now, after three millennia, was beginning to re-emerge into the light of day.

Lionel had already briefed the representatives of the world's press, a week ago in the lobby of the Hotel Excelsior in Kastro: what the expedition hoped to find was a small palace of the Minoan dynasty of priest-kings, exceptionally rich, according to preliminary indications, in artwork of a quality and state of preservation not yet found on the island. His confident optimism, as he had expected, found favour with the gentlemen of the press, and had been rewarded today: some of them, he was pleased to see, had endured the rigours of the trek out to Ano Meri, and were eagerly ensconced, with notebooks and cameras, in the branches of the olive trees on the edge of the site. When the men broke for *kolatsó*, a simple breakfast of dried bread, olives and cheese, and handed round *tsikoudiá* in old wineskins that smelt of goat, Lionel made sure that some was handed up into the olive trees. The press liked their sensations to come quickly. As an archaeologist, Lionel knew he had all the time in the world. Temperamentally, and as the publicist he also was, he understood the impatience of the journalists. A spectacular find today was worth four or five of the same find tomorrow or in a week's time. And propelled by these thoughts, Lionel strode about the site during the enforced interval of *kolatsó*, his hands clenching and unclenching, his nails biting deep into the skin of his palms.

As the day wore on, and the bones and convulsed sinews of the prehistoric fabric began to emerge gaunt and stark from the bald summit of Kulhantepe, it became clear to the excavators that the ancient palace they were uncovering had ended its life violently. Doorways had been overthrown, giant millwheels overturned. The pottery, which came up in abundance and filled relays of zembils to overflowing, had been scattered in wide arcs across the ancient floors. Where plaster still adhered to broken doorjambs it was cracked and often blackened by fire, just as Lionel had seen at Knossos. Here and there Lionel pointed out to his team how the tongues of flame had leapt along the walls, traceable by the undulating marks of blackening, driven by the same south wind that today whipped up the dust from around their ankles and carried it far away over the fertile rolling plain towards the sea. Even in the excitement of that first morning, Lionel again felt a touch of the melancholy he had experienced years before at Knossos. A frustration, an anger almost: who could have done this, three thousand years ago or more? And why?

But before that first morning's digging was over, Lionel's impatience had found its reward. It was (of course) Manolis who spotted the different colour and texture of an object protruding from the blackened deposit in the cross-section of the trench, Manolis who expertly picked round it with a pointing trowel until, surely like a midwife bringing a child into the world, Lionel thought, he was able to draw an irregularly shaped object, about six inches long, and grey-black from the half-burnt clay in which it had lain, out of the hole he had made and hand it to Lionel.

In the surrounding trenches work had stopped, everyone was craning round to look. 'Back to work!' roared Lionel in his effective, if unidiomatic, Cretan Greek; and Manolis, on cue, once again blew his whistle. While the workmen began to drift back to their trenches, Lionel muttered to Bertie Shaw, who happened to be standing nearest, 'Get those apes down from the trees, Shaw, will you? This should open their eyes.'

Water was brought from the well and the object washed clean of the remaining clay. Lionel and the tight knot of archaeologists and pressmen who now gathered round him had eyes only for the discoloured female figure that had emerged into the light. She was made of fine porcelain that had once been painted. The colours had run, and mingled with the earth in which she had lain buried. The huge bell-like skirt with seven flounces, the impossibly narrow waist and the full, bare breasts were already familiar to Lionel from similar figures that he had seen in photographs and in the Kastro museum. On her head she wore a flat cap or tiara that had the effect of angling her features slightly downwards. What captured the attention of the onlookers was the exquisite moulding of the face. Her chin was pointed and her mouth set in a firm, straight line. Under arching eyebrows her eyes were enormous, with sharply painted pupils that seemed both dilated and gazing with a peculiar intensity. Lionel gently ran a finger over the tiny features. It was the face of a young girl. Here again was the promise of feminine beauty and style and laughter that he had briefly and tantalizingly glimpsed in the bundle Manolis and Yannis had unwrapped before him and whisked away again on that distant afternoon at Knossos that had set him on the trail to Ano Meri. The eyes of this porcelain figure held something else as well: these were the eyes of a priestess or a goddess, privileged to see into the mystery of things.

But she had been damaged, this goddess, during her long sojourn under the earth. Her arms, that must once have been outstretched, were missing, truncated just below the shoulder. Time had left her appealingly, sadly vulnerable. He felt the possessive tenderness of a father as he picked up the figure and cradled it in his hand, feeling its slight weight in his palm.

Then, remembering himself, Lionel held the figure up to the jostling journalists. 'Gentlemen, let me introduce you. This is Ariadne, virgin priestess and daughter of King Minos. Ariadne, who gave Theseus the thread to find his way in the Labyrinth. Without Ariadne, Theseus would never have slain the Minotaur to come out of the Labyrinth alive. Without Ariadne, no outsider would ever have penetrated its secret. Ariadne, meet the gentlemen of the press. You are welcome, sirs: to Ariadne's Summer Palace!'

There was a cheer and much scribbling in notebooks. Cameras whirred and clicked. In that March gale of 1920, something had been born into the light of day and duly christened. Ariadne and her summer palace were once again a part of history.

But this was only the beginning of the series of discoveries that rocked and delighted a jaded world in that second post-war spring. In the heady success of those days, the newspaper headlines and the stories in the illustrated magazines reached around the world and were seized on everywhere. 'The Best of British!' was how the popular press trumpeted the undeniable combination of luck and flair that were the hallmark of that first triumphant season, while the *Morning Post* more lyrically reflected that the sun would never set on the Empire so long as its gifted sons continued to roam the world, with confidence and with fierce independence of mind and means, still following in the footsteps of the great British pioneers and explorers of the previous century.

And Lionel, it must be said, basked in all this glory. He had brought down the portcullis sharply on his own truncated past life. Lionel, in these first triumphant months, lived only for a past that had ended three thousand years before; the future for him was the future of the excavation. His excavation. It was Lionel Robertson's stamp that guaranteed the finds that were now being transported by the cartload to the museum in Kastro for further study and eventual exhibition – where they are still, today, among the greatest treasures of that austere edifice of painted concrete with its surly guardians and sanitation that would doubtless have disgusted any Minoan. And it was Lionel's quick mind and determined imagination that imposed order on the jumble of broken walls and foundations, on the labyrinthine complexity of storerooms and workshops, corridors and stairways, and interpreted Ariadne's Summer Palace to the world. It was Lionel too, reckless of danger, who was the first to enter the sealed throne room in the lower storey of the west wing that would be found to contain, as he believed unshakably until his dying day, the secret of the oldest civilization in Europe.

The throne room owed its preservation to a chance combination of circumstances. It belonged to a terraced series of rooms that had been built into the steep westward slope of the hillside, and held in place throughout the centuries by the massive retaining wall that had attracted Lionel's attention when he first visited the site. The collapse of the rooms above, probably at the time of the fire that swept through much of the rest of the palace, had sealed the room almost intact. Although its contents had been badly damaged by damp, and the roof had been penetrated at some time by the twisted roots of olive trees that were probably already hundreds of years old, this room had at least escaped the devastation of the fire.

The narrow hole, where a workman's pick had unexpectedly gone through to reveal the space behind, was quickly enlarged. Wooden props were sawn to size, and an aperture created, large enough for a man to crawl through. Grasping a powerful electric torch in his teeth – he would need both hands to scramble through and ward off the debris that looked as though it would fall from the ceiling at any moment – Lionel rejected all protest and inserted his head and shoulders into the darkness.

As he stood up in the enclosed space and transferred the torch to his hand, shining it around him, Lionel could not repress a cry of wonder. It was what he had always dreamed of. No living being could have stood here since the day of the catastrophe. Greedily, curiously, he drew the musty air of the chamber into his lungs. It smelt of damp, of earth and decay, but he fancied there was a faint aroma too he could not place and would not have known how to describe. It reminded him of the smell – no, smell was too strong a word, the air rather – in a French café in the early hours of the morning, of stale wine and the reminiscence of cigar smoke. It reminded him of the sooty smell mingled with roasting coffee he associated with Europe's great railway termini; of the lingering aroma of fried bacon and lard at the top of the backstairs of his club in London. The air he drew in and savoured with these conflicting sensations was not like any of the memories it prompted in him. It came to him as a cinder-smell of long-lost sweetness, of honey and wine as thick and black as treacle, and female fragrance. All that was imagination of course: he could not have said, then or later, what might have been its actual ingredients. But he knew as he breathed out (and wondered, belatedly, what baleful bacilli might have bred unhindered down here to wreak revenge on the violator of their sanctuary) that he had touched with his senses the last preserved breath of a vanished civilization, before it dissipated into the circumambient air of today.

His feet crunched on the debris that littered the floor. The unique evidence that would have proved once and for all the purpose of this room, something that in Dan's time will still be hotly disputed among professional archaeologists, was almost certainly destroyed beyond recall in these first few minutes of Lionel's wonder.

Because Lionel's attention was fully taken up with the walls.

In the middle of the side wall of the chamber was a low seat of polished gypsum. Ariadne's Throne, he immediately dubbed it. But what he could scarcely believe, as he ran his torch back and forth to either side of it, were the frescoes that ran round three sides of the room. The fourth side was open above a balustrade where stone bases were all that remained of a colonnade holding up the roof. Beyond, Lionel divined one of the sunken rectangular pits, that before the upper storeys collapsed would have been open through a lightwell to the outer air and were known to the archaeology of the time as 'lustral basins'. It was not this that held his attention, as he once again raked the remaining three walls of the chamber, this time more slowly, with the beam of his torch. The frescoes reached from the floor to the low ceiling. In the light of his torch, the Minoans leapt into life in front of Lionel's dazzled eyes. On a rocky seashore young girls in tight-fitting tunics and skirts with pointed flounces danced and played. The rocks, brightly-coloured, rose out of the floor in conical, convoluted shapes. The girls, it seemed to Lionel, were gazing anxiously out to sea, one even had a delicately drawn foot raised as though to enter the water. With rising excitement, Lionel followed the story on to the next wall. Here, far out in the pale turquoise, was the bull, not so much swimming as skimming the water, its powerful haunches clear of the stylized foam of its passage. On its back, riding the bull and clinging to the horns, her full breasts bare and an expression ón her face that might have been of religious awe, sat the girl who seemed to be the focus of the whole intricate composition: a princess, a priestess, a goddess? And on the final wall, badly damaged by damp but recognizable in all its outline to Lionel's excited imagination, was Crete, a pastoral landscape with wild flowers and birds, the snow-capped back of Mount Ida, the Psiloriti of today, and here in the lowlands the downward-tapering columns of a palace, Ariadne's Summer Palace itself perhaps, its flat roofs surmounted triumphantly by stylized horns, the horns of the sea-bull.

Lionel's excitement, as he scrambled back into the daylight, was almost beyond coherent speech. 'It's the story of Europa,' he gasped, pointing back in the direction that he had come. 'Europa and the Bull. In there, painted on the walls. Europa carried over the sea to Crete. It's the beginning, don't you see? The beginning of everything!'

Later that same day, in a slightly more composed frame of mind, Lionel sat down to write his despatch for the *Morning Post* that would be syndicated round the world. In the immediate aftermath of the discovery, he had almost come to blows with gentle, softly-spoken Bertie Shaw. He had given orders at once for workmen to be sent in to shore up the roof, so that a proper examination of the painting could be made. But Shaw had been adamant. First, the finds on the floor must be recorded and removed. 'How much damage do you think you've done in there already?' Bertie had reproved him with uncharacteristic asperity, and Lionel had exploded.

'In there, Shaw, is the find of the century. The roof may collapse, the colours may fade now it's open to the air. And all you can think of is *stratigraphy!*'

But Bertie had had his way, volunteering himself to go in with Manolis and record the position of at least the most important objects on the floor. As a result, it would not be until tomorrow at the earliest that Lionel could revisit his find, and satisfy his gnawing anxiety lest the intervening hours of unguarded exposure to the air should expunge the lines and colours that had leapt with such vitality in the beam of his torch. So Lionel contented himself, sitting up late by the light of an oil lamp in his tent, with describing what he had seen and interpreting it, as was his wont, for lay readers around the world:

The myth of Europa, ravished by Zeus in the guise of a seaborne bull to whom she bore Minos, the first ruler of Crete, has long been considered one of those less-than-edifying tales by which the sophisticates of classical antiquity chose to while away an idle hour, and so been relegated to the realm of elegant fairytale. But archaeological science has made great leaps in discerning the lineaments of true history behind the web and woof of legends handed down from before the days of writing: behind the legends of Homer's Troy lies a real citadel, whose riches have been laid bare by archaeology; behind the legend of King Minos and his labyrinth, lie the maze-like palaces of Crete, of which Ariadne's Summer Palace is but the latest, and perhaps the richest, to come to light.

The significance of today's find is that it proves the enormous antiquity of the Europa legend. Knowing as we now do, thanks to the discovery at Ano Meri, that the Minoans themselves told this story about their civilization and its origins, we may once again set the improbable world of fairytale to work alongside the spade and the hard-headed science of the archaeologist. Carefully analysed, what may these frescoes have to tell us about the real historical origins of the bright civilization that was the first to grace a European shore? The key to the Minoan labyrinths, and perhaps to so much more of significant human development since, lies now within our grasp.

Or, as Lionel would more succinctly, if cryptically, express it the next day in a telegram to Venizelos, who had not yet lost the election that would precipitate a new Trojan War in Anatolia: *I have looked upon the oldest ancestress of us all.*

Lionel flicked the amber beads he affected only in the bazaars and the houses of the more well-to-do-citizens of Kastro where he was often nowadays invited to dine or take part in some excruciating *soirée*. The night outside was dark and windy; he had arrived in a cape pulled up to his ears, his hat pulled well down over his eyes. Lionel had long known of the tall narrow house by the harbour, which smelt of damp and sesame cakes and the charcoal braziers that kept hookahs bubbling in the curtained rooms. It had been Varvatakis who, on learning of his enforced celibacy, had first proposed a visit here, and that in itself had been reason enough for Lionel to refuse. Now the discoverer of Ariadne's Summer Palace sat awkwardly in the little sitting-room among the ludicrously draped curtains and the tawdry pictures, chewing moodily on the tiny sweetmeat he had been brought in a bowl of rosewater. A bald, bullet-headed servant offered to light a hookah for him. Catching from the open door a distantly familiar tang that reminded him of burnt thyme and here suggested something else, Lionel discreetly enquired and was offered the finest black from Proussa. It might, for once, help if his senses were dulled a little.

He had always supposed that sooner or later he would come to the tall house by the harbour. Why now? And why, at the pinnacle of his life's achievement, this melancholy? The Europa frescoes, it was true, *had* lost some of their initial brightness before they could be fully photographed and Kreuzenberger could complete his initial drawings. But the German artist had shared every bit of Lionel's excitement, had warmly endorsed his interpretation of the scene, and had already set to work with easel and paint, while the workmen shored up the roof around him, to recapture and restore the former glory of Europa and the Bull. The roof was now secure, and Angus Cramond was working on the drawings for an ambitious reconstruction in concrete that would shore up the throne room and the floor above it, and restore the broad gypsum staircase that must once have led down to this wing of the palace from the open space at its centre. It was perhaps nothing less than an uncontainable excitement that had brought Lionel here tonight. He was, he half ruefully supposed, as the long-unfamiliar soothing aroma of hashish warmed his lungs, in love with his Minoans; there was no one living to whom he could offer the love and allegiance he had bestowed on Ariadne and the glittering denizens of her summer palace, on the priestly, maidenly Europa and the exaltation with which, in the fresco, she rode the white bull over the waves to meet her destiny in Crete.

And so, alongside his excitement, Lionel was conscious of a powerful pang of shame.

He sensed a presence behind him, a scent of mastic and honeycakes. He hadn't seen where she came from. Now he was obediently following her through the heavily swagged curtains. This new, tiny room could only, he supposed, be called a boudoir. The bed was strewn with freshly picked roses. The bald-headed servant carried in the hookah after him and laid it down with a deep bow. For the first time Lionel brought himself to look at his prize.

She was, he realized with a shock, probably not more than fifteen: a tall, skinny creature in a pleated gown that left her bony shoulders bare and then fell straight to the floor with the lines of a Doric column. Lionel's senses were swimming. The scents of the room and the intimate presence of this female body after so long were licking along his arteries, the blood was pulsing in his head. But there was another Lionel in the room, one he hadn't had to reckon with in earlier escapades. This Lionel, with the benefit of wisdom, no doubt aided too by hashish, was able to look down from a little way above the two figures in the room, and was appalled by the pale thin shoulders, the gawky shyness and shocking youth of the one, by the pathetic greying loneliness of the other who sat bolt upright on the bed drawing, for something to do, on the amber mouthpiece of the hookah, and was himself.

'What's your name?' It was something, to break the silence.

'Eminé,' she said, looking at him with a puzzled expression, as though she had not been warned to expect this. Lionel wondered if it was her real name, but then reflected that she would not be sophisticated enough to lie.

'Your first time, Eminé?' Lionel meant it to sound brusque, but heard something else in his voice that only increased the aura of shame that was growing more strongly around him with every moment.

She nodded silently. Her voice was a soft lisp, he liked it. He studied her long, painted fingernails, the bright red hole that was her mouth. Who had done this to her?

Lionel came to a decision. He stood up from the bed. 'Listen, Eminé. I'm afraid not tonight. I'm sorry.'

The small face crumpled at once, tears stood out in her eyes. She went down on her knees in front of him, hugging his knees. 'Please, please don't say that. Don't go. My father will kill me.'

'*What?*'

Slowly the girl was rising to her feet again, caressing his body as she did so. But the tears on her cheeks, and the pitiful look of terror in her eyes, were real enough. It came out in a rush. 'My father is a Muslim *bey*. Our house is falling down, we have no money. My brothers have left for America. Who knows if they are alive or dead? There are Christian men in Kastro who will spend a lot of money on a young mistress if she knows how to please them. But first, you see, she must be broken in.'

It was all terribly matter-of-fact. Lionel couldn't help remembering the *bey* who had sold him his horse: the languorous, world-weary conversation, the fierce pride, the enthusiasm that lit up only for the points of an Arab mare.

'If I don't go with you, he will say it is my fault.' She looked at the floor, 'My father will whip me.'

Lionel ground the heel of both hands into his eyes. When he looked up, she hadn't moved, but the garment she wore had noiselessly slipped from her shoulders, and slumped into a little pile round her ankles, like a snakeskin or the discarded tail of a lizard. He found himself staring at her nakedness. The bottom of her ribcage stood out further than her tiny breasts, her stomach was flat and smooth, her whole frame spoke of undernourishment. The tuft of hair between her thighs was either not fully grown, or had been inexpertly shaved.

Gently, he extended his arms to her and sat her on his knee. The cloying smell of mastic was overpowering. 'Listen, Eminé,' he said. 'I will give you all the money you would have earned here tonight. Surely that will satisfy your father?'

The girl's sobbing only redoubled. 'You don't understand,' she kept repeating, 'you don't understand.'

But the conqueror of Ano Meri understood only that something of himself he had always taken for granted was no longer there to be given. Lionel at forty-five, as he tried in vain to soothe the trembling, naked figure who kept pulling with something like desperation at his buttons and muttering endearments in Greek and Turkish through her sobs, came face to face with the absolute loneliness of his obsession.

That night the lamp burned until dawn in the Englishman's suite at the Excelsior. Lionel Robertson had once again bethought himself that he had a son, at the other end of Europe. It was time he wrote to the boy again. God knew, there was enough to tell.

And already as he wrote, the words that brought to life again the triumphant discoveries of the past weeks took wing; as they poured out to fill the empty paper Lionel felt himself slowly cleansed of the folly and shame of the night. Dawn found him staring sightlessly over the wild shoreline that stretches eastwards from Kastro, a new and unexpectedly comforting resolution forming in his breast.

Lionel had learnt patience while he had been in Crete. Daniel would be still in his first year at Oxford. Hardly pausing to reflect that he scarcely knew this son of his, Lionel began to lay his own plans for Daniel's future.

8 THE GRAND TOUR

DANIEL at Oxford was one of the many young men at that time whose careers had been interrupted by the war, and who were therefore by no means uniformly young. On the other hand, he made one of the youngest of this cohort, and never quite got used to being numbered, as he was by dons and scouts alike, many of whom had a manifestly better claim to the title, among the 'veterans'. He quickly discovered the advantages of this status, however, and after a first year spent coughing almost incessantly in a damp and draughty college room, was granted permission to join the growing colony of shell-shocked poets who lived out of town, in the more wholesome air of Boar's Hill. Here, at evening gatherings and on weekend country walks, he learnt to gaze with more curiosity than awe at such as Robert Graves and Edmund Blunden (with whom, although they were a good five years his senior, he also went to lectures in town) and listen to their verses. All of them in turn, these younger veterans, sat with varying degrees of respect at the feet of John Masefield, who was also shell-shocked and not yet Poet Laureate, and whose wife kept hospitably open house on Boar's Hill.

Higher up the hill, and socially remote from Daniel and his like, stood Youlbury, home of the legendary first discoverer of the Minoan civilization beneath the soil of Crete: Sir Arthur Evans.

But Daniel was not much moved in those days by the glories of the past. He had returned to Upland Grange for his first Christmas vacation to find Lionel's changes little to his liking, and had much sympathy with Mrs Trudgill's continuing grievance at being turned down to replace Soames up at the house. On a freezing January morning the new housekeeper, alerted by a thick pall of smoke curling round the door of his room had come barging in and thrown a ewer of water over him as he sat in a trance, puffing on Balkan Sobranie tobacco as he often did all night to keep the terrors of sleep at bay. After that he had caught a cold that turned to bronchitis, but insisted on travelling back to Oxford with a fever and was laid low for most of the following term.

The absence, all that winter, of any word or explanation from his father irked him. Perhaps, secretly, he felt wounded by it. Mixed with those feelings, undoubtedly, was a dose of guilt: was it possible that the reverberations of that terrible June day in 1919 could have reached Lionel, and if so, was the thunderbolt at this very moment hanging over his head? But more to be feared than even the explosion of his father's wrath was the possibility, always very real in Daniel's eyes, that his father would simply and quietly forget him. To belong nowhere: Daniel knew that he didn't belong easily, and those things that had given him a sense of belonging in earlier years – Mrs Trudgill's hearthside, the secrets of the East Wing, the toy soldiers that had been his pride and joy, his sleep, above all the ability to sleep without terror – had one by one been taken from him. So it was with feelings of terrified dismay that he seized on the letter that arrived at the start of his first Trinity Term. While in the college garden the fallen cherry blossom blew into drifts like unseasonable snow, Daniel began to read:

My dear Daniel,
   You may perhaps have asked yourself, in the intervals of the momentous events which, as I understand, have recently played such a harrowing part in your own young life, with what excuse your father has chosen to remain at a distance from the tumult of battle and doggedly, 'roguishly' some say (I am well aware of that!) fought and won a campaign of his own. Here, at the edge of what we are pleased to call (and with what justice I leave it to you to determine) civilization, I have set myself the most daunting task of all: to uncover beneath the vineyards of an uncomprehending local populace, whose intransigence and avarice I have only lately overcome, the foundation stone, the fons et origo, of the said civilization. And I have found it. Daniel, I have found it.
   'Ariadne's Summer Palace', as I have named it, has proved to be the richest in finds of all the Minoan sites so far known. Sealstones (those tiny objects of such wonderful craftsmanship which, you will remember, first drew me to Crete) have turned up in abundance. We have found decorated cups and vases with patterns of finely stylized flowers (saffron crocuses and arum lilies are expecially frequent) and all the abundant creatures of the sea (octopus, starfish, dolphins). There is gold, too, and precious stones, which have necessitated our maintaining a guard over the rudimentary shed which for the time being must serve to house all our finds. Then there are carved gold cups, with filigree work so fine that a powerful eyeglass is required if one is to perceive all the intricacy of the design. How were such things made? The goldsmiths of Kastro today, who in the general way are not modest of their prowess, admit frankly that they could not reproduce such work.
   And now to the discovery of the season, or as I venture to think it may not unworthily be called in times to come, the discovery of our still-young century: Ariadne's throne room with its painted frescoes . . .

But Daniel was no longer reading the lines that danced in front of his eyes. The wonders that fell tumbling from the tightly-packed pages of the letter were as nothing compared to the reassurance that came from the very fact of the letter's existence, from the – it suddenly seemed to him – extraordinary fact of its being addressed, out of the blue, to *him*. For others to whom Lionel Robertson was no more than a name, the tale of discovery told in this letter was nothing short of sensational. Excerpts from it have frequently been printed in popular archaeology books, so much so that Dan, when he comes upon it in the neutrally-lit anonymity of the reading room in the Public Record Office at Kew will be surprised, and moved, to find its contents so familiar. To Daniel, at the start of his first Trinity Term, it meant only one thing: that however far away he might be, and however little he, Daniel, could comprehend him, *he had a father.*

To this and subsequent letters from Crete that continued to arrive at sporadic intervals during his time at Oxford, Daniel responded only a little less laconically than during his school days. Daniel could think of no words in which he could describe his own recent experiences to his father. And what else was there to say? He wrote instead about his studies and his spectacular success in Mods, but without confiding how little they engaged his mind; he even copied out his prize-winning compositions in Greek verse for Lionel's approval. But despite the cuttings from the papers and the illustrated weeklies with which friends and acquaintances kept him steadily supplied (Daniel never regularly read a newspaper) and the unmistakable aura of vicarious admiration with which they did so, Daniel proved unresponsive to the single, all-consuming passion which fired his father's letters. In his replies, he expressed enthusiasm, instead, for Lionel's purchase of a motorcar, and as time went on came to take a lively interest in the building of the Villa Europa that was by then beginning to rise among the olive groves below Ariadne's Summer Palace.

Lionel had selected the best and most durable materials locally available, with the addition of reinforced steel struts to be built into the walls. These were being specially imported on the advice of Angus Cramond, his architect, as experimental protection against the earthquakes that still, according to the available records, laid low this part of Crete two or three times a century. The villa was to house the members of the excavation team, the distinguished guests that were already beginning to arrive as news of the finds at Ano Meri travelled round the world, and a suitable staff. It did not, from his father's accounts, conform very well to the futurist dreams that by then were beginning to haunt Daniel's imagination. Why not put the steel struts on the *outside*? But he had to concede that the building, for all its evidently lavish scale and furnishings, served a utilitarian purpose and was anyway in the back of beyond, where only archaeologists were likely to see it.

At Oxford, Daniel wrote poetry which was dubiously received by the genteel veterans of Boar's Hill. Futurism, the Vortex, all those gritty machines and hard-edged verses that didn't connect with one another: all that was *passé* now, surely? The war had put paid to the anarchic poetry of progress and violence, they soothingly advised him. But Daniel took no notice. With his friend Firkin he went to Cubist exhibitions in London and carefully scrutinized their frenzied lines and geometrical shapes for any hint that these painters of the future might have glimpsed something of the exhilarating terror of lines and light that had made his own present life seem so provisional and precarious. On the whole he thought not. Those people were playing games. But the poetry he wrote at this time he did not destroy, although little of it was ever published.

To Daniel, poetry was not a game. In his mind's eye, as he looked towards Oxford from the serenity of Boar's Hill, he erased every trace of human activity from the landscape, levelling farmhouses and steeples and especially the softly golden stone of college spires and domes, the proud neoclassical pediment of the Ashmolean Museum, the neo-Gothic casements of the Bodleian Library. Not that Daniel's fantasies were of a pastoral disposition. As his daydream advanced there would usually come a moment when a brown swathe of mud advanced across the scene, the no-man's-land that was never far from the inner horizon behind his eyes, the ruined space contested by armies more mechanized and more ruthless than any yet seen in battle, and it was on that devastation that Daniel set about laying in his mind the foundations of the cities of the future. Monstrous constructions of iron and glass sprang up from end to end of the Oxfordshire landscape, high-speed electric railways crisscrossed the view while external lifts whizzed up and down the corners of buildings, conveying their passengers at dizzying speed towards the topmost layers where they were lost to sight among the drifting summer clouds.

Nothing of this, of course, found its way into his letters to his father.

By the time of Daniel's final term at Oxford, the future had become a matter of more mundane concern to the shell-shocked poets of Boar's Hill. Many, it seemed, had gradually made their peace with the post-war world: there was a place in the family firm, now sadly depleted of manpower, to look forward to, or a tidy income and a comfortable job in the City. Further afield, there was an Empire that needed men well drilled in the rigours of Latin verbs to run it; for a few committed souls the League of Nations beckoned. Daniel could not tell at what inner cost to his fellows this peace had been achieved. But he didn't think it was for him.

'Why don't you follow in the footsteps of all those artists and poets in the last century?' Firkin would chaff him. 'You know: the Grand Tour. *In Rome I saw the gladiator die. The mountains look on Marathon and Marathon looks on the sea.* It's the obvious thing for a Greats man, with all that Latin and Greek in your head.'

Firkin had by this time turned aside from the regular path trodden by Oxford undergraduates and was beginning to immerse himself in the new and somewhat suspect science of Anthropology. Daniel secretly envied his friend the solidity of his family, in particular his three younger sisters, and the roast leg of mutton with lavish helpings of potatoes and freshly chopped mint soaked in vinegar to which the whole family would sit down after James' father had preached the late morning sermon in the village church. Daniel had been invited to join them on many occasions, and was the more impressed by the feeling that nothing of this was being especially provided for his benefit: this was how it must be *every* Sunday. And if James and his plump, twinkling mother nourished hopes for himself and Lavinia, the eldest sister, and for that reason conspired to invite that awkward but so interesting young man whose father was a famous archaeologist more often, and to ensure that the table was on those occasions laid to the highest standards and the girls turned out better than usual, Daniel never suspected it. Mrs Firkin reminded him of photographs of Queen Victoria in middle age and set him wondering whether the course of history would have been at all different if the Empress of India had possessed a sense of humour. The Reverend Firkin took a lively interest in Lionel Robertson's discoveries and assured the assembled company that archaeology in the Holy Land had already confirmed the truth of much that was in Scripture and that an enlightened Church had nothing to fear, in his opinion, from the march of Science. 'Provided only,' the Reverend continued, waving a podgy finger at his son before absently licking off a trickle of gravy, 'that the masters of Science are themselves enlightened and have not forgotten the lesson of the one tree in the garden: *thou shalt not eat of it.*'

Firkin's differences with his father were amicable, Daniel understood, but profound. And it was as though James had deliberately chosen to study the skulls of primates (there were several upstairs in his bedroom that his mother dusted daily) and, his most recent enthusiasm, the history of primitive religion, for no better reason than to provoke the Reverend Firkin. This vicarious domesticity came to an end for Daniel when the first batch of 'veterans' graduated in the summer of 1922. Firkin, determined to follow the primitive to the ends of the earth if necessary, found it convenient on several counts to carry out his planned research into cannibalism in the South Pacific by donning the frock of a trainee missionary – thereby securing his father's blessing and a modest stipend for a mission that was far from godly.

That autumn found Daniel back at Upland Grange, listlessly wondering whether to wait for a letter from his father or to set out on his travels at once. At the opposite end of the continent, the newly formed armies of Kemal

Atatürk smashed their way through the embattled Greek enclave of Smyrna. While Smyrna burned and the dream and hope of the fiery Bishop of Kastro collapsed into ashes, the new state of Turkey was defying geography to declare itself part of Europe. Firkin, who before his departure had seen this coming, had assured Daniel that the Greeks had asked for it, sending an army into Anatolia. 'That's what comes of putting all your trust in ancient glories, you mark my words.'

It was in keeping with the bohemian ways he intended to adopt that he insisted on staying at the Lodge with the Trudgills, who were the only living link left with his childhood in the place, thus making their cramped living quarters even more cramped, and their grumbles about the new order 'up at the house' more tiresome than he remembered them. He made a point of playing with Sarah Jane, now an engaging tomboy of nearly eight, and wondered at the sense of jealousy he had experienced so strongly at her first, unexpected arrival. He had a deeper motive, too, for taking serious notice of the child. As she climbed trees in the park and swung perilously from branches above his head, as they ran races down to the mudflats of the estuary, or while they sat companionably for hours together at high tide to catch the river crabs with line and bait, he would anxiously scan her features, strain to catch the hidden intonations of her voice, for any trace of her parentage. If his intuition of three years ago had been correct, it now rested with him to right the wrong that had been done to Sarah Jane. But he had no proof, family likenesses are notoriously unreliable and there was really nothing in the teasingly open face with its cheeky upturned nose, the close-cropped pale hair, the broad East Anglian vowels, that he could honestly recognize as a resemblance. Only her eyes disturbed him when he looked her full in the face. But how many people in the world have blue eyes? Then there was what Trudgill had told him about Mrs Trudgill, how she thought of her adopted daughter as her own; and indeed it touched Daniel's heart to see beneath the daily bickering and scolding between mother and daughter the tender anxiety that Mrs Trudgill had once lavished on himself at Sarah Jane's age. The girl seemed happy enough in all conscience, for all her parents' grumbling. What good would it do to raise suspicions that would surely shatter this little domestic trio, whatever the eventual outcome? If he spoke to Trudgill now, as he had more than once found himself on the brink of doing, there could be no going back.

'Coo, Mister, what a whopper!'

Trudgill, to his continuing embarrassment, had been unable to stop his daughter from addressing Daniel in this way. It was high tide at the dilapidated little landing stage at the bottom of the meadow. The bucket of crabs was almost full. Usually, when the session was over, Sarah Jane would empty them over the landing stage and watch gleefully as they scuttled this way and that and got stuck in the cracks between the planks in their panic to get back in the water.

'That's the king crab, Mister, you watch out for him. Grab him, can you? He's letting go.'

Daniel obligingly detached the furious crab from the bait, grasping the shell just above the pincers. He held it in front of Sarah Jane's face for her to admire. She eyed their catch critically for some time.

With a sideways look at him she said, 'Put him down, will you?'

Daniel obeyed. This time, before the crab had more than begun its frantic scuttle back to its element, Sarah Jane had brought the metal heel of the bucket sharply down on its back. With a crunch the crab broke open. Daniel winced and looked away. It was some minutes before the claws had ceased scratching against the wooden pier.

'What did you do that for?' he demanded, quite angrily.

Sarah Jane set her jaw. 'Just 'cos,' she said.

As there was still no word from Lionel, and Daniel found himself incapable of setting the next stage of his life irrevocably into motion, he took pity at last on the Trudgills and his own comfort, and moved instead into the more spacious quarters of the Grange. Here he had his trunks sent on from Oxford and surrounded himself, as autumn lengthened into winter, with his books and the smoke of strong Balkan tobacco.

It was only the imminent threat of his father's arrival that finally precipitated him, in the early summer of 1923, on the first stage of his Grand Tour. Crete, his father wrote him from the now completed Villa Europa, was in an uproar after the shambles in Anatolia. The order had gone out that spring for the entire Muslim population of the island to be deported, to make way for a tide of Greek refugees uprooted from Turkey, who were already sweeping through the mainland and now beginning to arrive in boatloads along the shores of Crete. Everybody, Lionel wrote, blamed somebody for the disaster, but its true scale was as yet untold. It had seemed wise in the circumstances to opt for a study season this year, and Lionel would be setting up his headquarters for the duration at Upland Grange. He hoped earnestly, with this opportunity, to renew his acquaintance with the son he had not seen since Daniel had become a man. Moreover, it seemed a good time to take stock and consider the future, both for Daniel and the excavations at Ano Meri, given that he, Lionel, could not expect to live for ever.

Daniel panicked.

Gone was the reassurance, the sense of vicarious strength he had been able to draw from earlier letters arriving from distant Crete. The shadow of his father had once again fallen over the seclusion he had created for himself in the West Wing of Upland Grange. For the riches that Lionel had unstintingly bestowed on him through his letters (though it had scarcely been their contents that had so much moved Daniel), his father now demanded a return.

142

And this return meant yielding up to his father all these things that Daniel, in spite of himself, had again begun to think of as his own. It meant the sacrifice, it was all too plain now, of his long-cherished but still unformed plans for travel. Not for him the afterglow of a completed civilization: that he had been determined to leave to his father, who was welcome to it. Daniel's goal would rather be the still crude, primitive mainsprings of one yet to be built. But how could he explain all this to the most famous archaeologist of the time? How evade the trap that had just been revealed to him and already had all but sprung shut?

Once upon a time, in the turmoil that now descended upon Daniel's emotions, he would have turned instinctively to Trudgill. All of a sudden, faced with the imminence of his father's arrival, Daniel's lonely childhood in this place came back to him: the conspiratorial companionship of his escapades with the groundsman, the unresented beatings, the warm evenings in the cramped quarters of the Lodge that to him in those days had been merely cosy, the log fires in winter and Mrs Trudgill's plump cheeks and plum jam. A childhood that had ended with the unlooked-for arrival of Sarah Jane, who had displaced Daniel, not just from his cherished place at the Lodge, but also from a whole world of affection he had not until then realized had already passed him by. Faced, for the first time in his adult life, with the imminent appearance of his father, it struck Daniel with the force of revelation that the Trudgills had been the nearest to *real* parents he had known in all those years. Was it perhaps *that* that he still could not in his heart forgive the usurper Sarah Jane? *She* had never had to creep out illicitly to find the companionship and the easy-going, gruff tenderness that were not to be had at home but he had known and now glimpsed again, with what touching longing, at the Lodge.

It was in this way, full of the bitterness of a lost childhood, that Daniel set out at last, on his own version of the Grand Tour.

In the event, after an obligatory stay on the fringes of bohemian Paris, which he found rather drab, he got no further than Milan. Here, in the home town of Marinetti and the capital of pre-war Futurism, he fell in with a more or less violent and frustrated crowd of *arditi*, shell-shocked, many of them, like himself, and kept company with a shifting population of painters, cabaret singers, poets. Everywhere were the fascists in their black shirts and black boots. There was much fighting talk of breaking heads, and scuffles on the streets after dark were not uncommon. The very atmosphere of Milan in those years was brittle, and if Daniel found it in one way stifling, in another it was well adapted to his own frame of mind. Many of his acquaintances admired Mussolini. They wrote bad poems in his honour, comparing him to a masterful projectile, a head full of gunpowder, a great bull with teeth of steel. Daniel had little interest in the politics of Fascism; it was enough for him to be living in a country that could at a stroke sweep away nineteen hundred and twenty-five years of pious history and start its calendar over again, with the slate wiped clean, from the year one.

For two years, he shared the upper floor of a ramshackle tenement facing the railway station. The grand swagger of Stacchini's all-marble façade which was beginning to rise amid cranes and scaffolding appealed to Daniel's imagination. On sleepless nights he would stare out at the unwinking, mysterious lights of signals, red, green and yellow, where the tracks curved out of his line of sight into the darkness. He thrilled to the sight of the great locomotives, before they were swallowed under the cavernous roof of the station, their massive bodies hardly distinct from the darkness, the driver leaning out of the cab, etched against the orange glare from the stokehole. Though he had quickly tired of travelling himself, Daniel loved the anonymity, the flux of mass travel. Soot from the trains settled in every corner of his home, settled in his hair and under his nails. The smell of soot, and the sharp tang of roasting coffee as it was wafted up three floors from the bar on the street below, would ever afterwards for Daniel bring back all the longing and all the loneliness of Milan.

Not that he lacked for company; indeed, his years in Milan were the most gregarious of his life. He shared the flat with Enzo, who was a racing driver, and a journalist called Massimo, as well as an assortment of friends the two of them brought back to talk and smoke with long into the night, and a bewildering variety of girls who would turn up for breakfast and at odd hours of the afternoon. He quickly became fluent in Italian, although he never spoke it really well – he would often admit that he had never had his father's flair for languages. A lot of his time he spent reading. He tried to write poetry in the Dada mode and some of it was published in a short-lived magazine called *Minotaure*. He bought a sports car and learned to drive; some of his happiest hours at that time were spent tearing at dangerous speeds down the still unmetalled roads of Lombardy, disdaining hat and goggles, the wind rushing past his face and lifting his hair, exhilarated by the roaring beast under the bonnet and the plume of white dust that he knew would hang above the road behind him long after he had gone, while in the distance, high above the haze that hid the distant Alps, giant towers of cumulus gathered in the upper air.

His nights would be spent in crowded underground dives, where Negro jazz bands were much sought after and absinthe and grappa were expensive but *de rigueur*. The women in those places were rather smart, and smoked cigarettes in long holders; the men, their slicked-down hair uniformly parted in the middle, played with knives. Once, to impress an improbable blonde in a shimmering pearl dress, Daniel had skewered his left hand, palm upwards, to the table. There had been a brief commotion as blood flowed across the rough-hewn table-top; a girl – a different one – had obligingly screamed, and

144

for a few delirious minutes Daniel became the centre of attention, until his hand was bound up and he and his friends were asked to leave. He couldn't afterwards remember the girl's name, but he had severed a tendon in the back of his hand and never regained the full movement of his third and fourth fingers.

It was Daniel's second spring in Milan, though there was little in the universal stone and grime of the city to suggest a change of season. But the stove in the flat remained unlit during the day, and the swallows were back nesting under the eaves. Daniel had come face to face at last with the failure of his Grand Tour. His correspondence with his father had languished and left a gap behind. He felt no inclination for further travel, but the way back to Upland Grange was blocked by the quizzical, cheeky, cornflower-blue eyes of Sarah Jane who in his dreams would challenge him: 'Mister, ain't you goin' to give us them keys to the house, then? I'm a lady now, you know', and with that look of open innocence would bring down the heel of her bucket with all her strength on his poor, upturned palm ('Just 'cos,' she would say in the dream and shrug) and he would wake, months afterwards, with the pain of his self-inflicted wound.

It was Massimo, recently promoted to a staff job on the *Popolo d'Italia*, who first heralded the change that was about to come over Daniel's life that spring. He had a box for the next opening night at La Scala. Daniel was at first unwilling to join the party. He had been to the opera a couple of times before. He was no musician, but the loud brash tunes and ham performances on stage, the over-dressed and mostly middle-aged opera-goers who eyed one another critically across the auditorium through opera glasses and lorgnettes at the interval, all these were redolent for Daniel of the kind of stuffy tradition he had come to Milan to escape. But this was to be a special opening night. The opera was to be the swansong of a composer whom all Italy had mourned and whose funeral cortège Daniel had followed – mostly out of curiosity, it must be said – along with half of Milan in the pouring rain soon after his first arrival in the city. It was said that *Il Duce* himself would be in the audience. This opening night was going to be news, and on the strength of it Massimo had a box and was not short of offers to fill it.

In the event Massimo's box was occupied by a rowdy crew who put their feet up on the red plush parapet and had several times to be admonished by the *màschere*, those sombre denizens of La Scala who reminded Daniel of papal nuncios, with their chains of office round their necks, and whose task it is to glide with silent authority through the densest parts of the crowded theatre and escort the faithful to their seats. In the foyer the hubbub was intense. The traditional *carabiniere* in full dress uniform, an erect feather standing a good eighteen inches above his helmet, had been reinforced by several of his comrades tonight. Nobody seemed to know whether *Il Duce* was coming or not. Everybody was determined to crowd the doors to catch sight of him if he did. *Viva Il Duce!* a few ragged voices struck up at the far end of the foyer. A hush fell, followed by a great roar of acclamation, but the atmosphere of boisterous reverence was quickly dispelled. *Il Duce* would not be coming after all, the whisper ran round beneath the bright chandeliers. Had something happened? Nobody knew, but by the time the *màschere*, showing at last some signs of impatience, had done their work and every seat and every box was occupied, there was an atmosphere of electric anticipation in the audience.

The lights were beginning to go down when Enzo, who had been scrutinizing the row of boxes opposite for some minutes, nudged Daniel sharply in the ribs. 'That's the most beautiful girl in the house. Have a vote on it at the interval, if you like. But you mark my words.'

Disdaining the proffered opera glasses, Daniel followed the direction of Enzo's eyes. All he saw was the blur of a plain white dress, a cloche hat pushed rakishly backwards in the latest London fashion. He had eyes only for the much older gentleman sitting next to her. He would have been tall, standing; his greying hair was brushed backwards from his temples, and he rested his chin on a stick held between his knees. Across the distance of the auditorium his features were indistinct; Daniel could not rationally have said that he recognized him, but an emotional charge ran through his whole body and left him momentarily breathless. It wasn't possible, surely? But by now the lights had gone down and a wave of excited applause greeted the appearance on the podium of Arturo Toscanini.

Daniel was in an agony of impatience for the first act to be over so that he could look properly at the box opposite. He even thought, wildly, of going out now, during the performance, of making his way round, knocking gently on the doors of the boxes until, surely – he could count fairly exactly how many doors – he could pinpoint which box . . . But he thought better of it. 'After all, he tried to reason with himself, he was probably wrong and would only end up looking ridiculous. So Daniel sat on his hands and tried to concentrate on the spectacle on stage.

This was not hard to do. The curtain went up on a scene of blank towers and glittering pagodas; an exotic crowd swaying to the quicksilver modulations of mass hysteria, now baying for blood, now tender in supplication for mercy. The savage, inexorable beating of gongs and a restless, brittle flitting of xylophones; lush vocal melodies and soaring strings and brass, this was the stuff of opera as Daniel knew it, but now edged with strangeness and danger. Evening in Peking, and a sentence of death is pronounced. The blood-stained executioners turn the whetstone to prepare the two-handed sword; the crowd in its excitement tramples an old man who has fallen; a slender girl, her head in a cowl, begs mercy. And here, tubbily striding across the stage, rising on tiptoe to hit his top notes, comes the hero of the evening, Miguel Fleta, in the first public creation of the role of Puccini's Unknown Prince. The old man turns out to be his father, an exiled king without a kingdom. And the girl? The girl is Liù, a slavegirl on whom the prince had once smiled in happier times and now, for the sake of that smile, devoted body and soul to the old man. The prince, though, has eyes only for Turandot, the princess whose heart is of ice, who now appears in solemn silence in the moonlight. To love the princess Turandot is death. Daniel is unmoved by the inhuman apparition of the princess. But his heart goes out to the little triangle at the front of the stage, to the joy of the old man reunited with his son, to the heartrending, simple melody with which the slavegirl begs the prince not to throw away his life and the smile that has sustained her through so many trials. The act ends with the tumultuous crash of the gong, stage right, by the palace door. The prince must follow his destiny, and in this way gives notice of his suit to Turandot.

As the curtain fell the audience was on its feet, the applause went on and on, stentorian shouts of *bravo!* came from every part of the house, flowers and streamers were thrown at the stage. By the time the commotion had begun to die down and the lights had come up, Daniel, good manners forgotten, had snatched the opera glasses from Enzo and begun scanning the boxes opposite. He raked them once, he raked them twice; he tried the upper levels, in increasing agitation. But no, the box where he had seen the man and the girl was empty. As though in a trance he kept his eyes trained on it all through the interval. One by one the boxes facing him filled up once more. Across the auditorium he now found himself staring at a clutch of débutantes in old-fashioned crinolines. What had happened to the man and the girl? Had he imagined them?

He nudged Enzo. 'What's become of the *bellezza della Scala* then?' he demanded.

But Enzo had forgotten his bet and merely shrugged.

He too, it seemed, had lost his heart to Turandot.

Daniel's sense of frustrated anticipation redoubled during the second act. By now he was no longer concentrating on the stage. The princess's riddles, which the hero must answer in order to win her and save his head, were tedious and sparely orchestrated. Looking more and more from the stage to the half-circle of boxes visible to him from where he sat, Daniel detected a restlessness in the audience as well. The sumptuous steps of the pagoda, that had drawn gasps of admiration when the curtain first went up, the huge crowd gathered on the temple steps and the glittering costumes (Turandot's robes embroidered with gold, the feathers of her headdress standing even taller than the one worn by the *carabiniere* on the door outside) were beginning to pall for Daniel. The prince, he had no doubt, would solve the riddles. But the puzzle of the man and the girl opposite remained. There was no sign of them, so far as he could tell in the light reflected from the stage. And now, as a new, soft, vibrant tune entered the score, one he knew instinctively he would hear again, the plot on stage took a new twist. The prince proposes a riddle of his own to his reluctant prize: you don't know my name, he says. Tell me my name before dawn and at dawn I shall consent to die. The crowd thunderously wishes ten thousand years of life to the reedy, ageless emperor who has ineffectually presided over the whole long ritual of this act. Mussolini, where are you? Daniel irreverently thought as the curtain once again came down, to applause that was only slightly less tumultuous than before.

It was now, in the downstairs crush bar with its wall-mirrors and chandeliers, that Daniel came face to face, after thirteen years, with his father. During this interval he had been determined to comb the house, to make sure. And he had not been wrong. The girl that had so excited Enzo's admiration was talking animatedly in Italian to the crowd of débutantes who had taken over their box. Lionel stood slightly aloof and behind them, a head taller than most of the crowd. His eyes, which might have been searching too, met Daniel's where he stood at the door. Daniel elbowed his way forward, suddenly suffused with a warmth and sense of relief he would not have known to expect, at the sight of the broad grin of welcome that spread across his father's face.

'Do you know,' said Lionel, 'I think you are quite surprised to see me!' – and for the first and last time in his life seized him by the shoulders and kissed him, in the continental fashion, on both cheeks, to Daniel's intense embarrassment. Disengaging himself, Daniel stood back to survey this father whom he had only ever really known during one short period of his life, when he had been half the age he was now. Lionel's streaked grey hair and expansive waistcoat gave him a more distinguished appearance than Daniel remembered from those pre-war schooldays. He was still tall, but not, Daniel thought, taller than he was himself, which was why his father now seemed shorter and, oddly enough, more knowable. Lionel, too, stood back to eye his son critically, and seemed not displeased with what he saw.

As Daniel had not yet found his voice, Lionel placed a fatherly arm around the shoulder of the girl who had been his companion earlier, and drew her into the space between father and son. 'Laura, my dear,' he said, 'meet the Prodigal. I told you I had a son in Milan, but he's a bohemian and doesn't answer letters.'

Daniel blushed, and shook hands. 'Laura Middleton,' she said. Her voice was primly musical. 'Your father does tease. But he's a dear man, aren't you Lionel?' She arched her head over her shoulder to flash him a radiant smile. Daniel was rather shocked at this familiarity. She could hardly be more than twenty, but was modishly dressed, even by the proverbial standards of an opening night at La Scala. From beneath the rim of her cloche hat curled a wisp of dark hair. Her dress was white and tight and shone under the chandeliers. She played unselfconsciously with the boa round her throat.

To Laura rather than to Lionel, since politeness seemed to require it, he said at last, 'I had no idea my father was here. My father is an archaeologist, he lives in Crete – but of course,' he ended in confusion, 'you must know that already.'

'Indeed Laura does.' Lionel's voice was reassuringly strong. 'Her great-aunt is the Contessa Mondadori, the widow of one of the finest Italian archaeologists of pre-war days. The Contessa is my hostess and Laura's. Between us, we have the honour of chaperoning the Contessa's six granddaughters tonight.'

The girls in crinoline were pretending to talk excitedly among themselves, as they watched this scene unfold before them in a strange language and did their best to make sense of it.

Doggedly, Daniel tried to pursue the thread that had kept him on tenterhooks all evening. 'I saw you before the performance started. In your box. But then – when I looked at the interval, I couldn't find you.'

'The girls wanted to change round. There's the bell for the next act – there *are* only three acts, aren't there? – we'll have to go. I've *no* idea which box your father and I will be in. Perhaps he ought to have some of the girls to himself, what do you think?'

The bells were indeed ringing for the next act. As the rush began to eddy towards the door and a wrangle seemed to have broken out among the granddaughters about who was to sit with whom for the final act, Daniel hastily shook hands with his father and Laura, and promised to join them afterwards.

He returned breathless and elated to his box, and was somewhat disconcerted to find himself staring across the auditorium once again into the eyes of the *bellezza della Scala*, whom he now knew as Laura Middleton. She seemed to be admonishing the girls in her charge. Daniel's father must indeed have got the remainder to himself, somewhere out of his line of sight.

Daniel was prepared for his interest in the final act of *Turandot* to be little more than perfunctory. But the intensity and the turmoil of his emotions seemed instead to overflow into the orchestra pit and on to the darkened stage, as though the music and the drama, the tenderness and cruelty of the plot, were but the gigantic echo of what was already happening in his own heart. In Peking it is now night, lanterns have been lit and, beyond a low balustrade, a backcloth depicts swirling clouds and a distant craggy hill. *None shall sleep in Peking tonight*, the heralds proclaim through streets near and far. The name of the Unknown Prince must be known before dawn. If not, all shall die. Such is the edict of Turandot. None shall sleep. *Nessun dorma*, the prince himself is alone on stage, and here again comes the warmth of that melody uncoiling upwards through the strings, the melody with which the prince has issued, in the previous act, his rash challenge. *Then let none sleep* (Daniel, whose nights have for so long been visited by insomnia, is appalled): *my secret lies locked within me and, come the dawn, victory shall be mine!* The tenor holds the climactic high note for longer than it seems possible for human breath to endure, then the whole scene collapses into a vicious pantomime. The music is now brash and brittle, and Daniel is sitting on the edge of his seat. The old man and the girl from Act One have been brought on, bound. They, the torturers triumphantly declare to Turandot, who is watching all the while in icy silence, can tell the prince's name. *Torture them, kill them,* the hysterical crowd demands. And now tears spring up in Daniel's eyes, for it is Liù, the little slavegirl, who comes forward. She, she alone possesses the secret, she declares. And for love of the prince who once smiled on her, she will die under torture rather than reveal it. For love. And at the end of her swansong, as the torturers begin their work in earnest and she cannot help crying out in agony, Liù snatches up a dagger from one of the guards and kills herself. It is the old man, not the prince, who mourns her death, and at his reproaches even the hysterical crowd is softened with pity for her sacrifice. Softly, sombrely, Liù's body is carried off stage. Dawn is coming, and the victorious prince must confront the princess alone.

It was at this moment, on 25th April 1926, as is well known, that maestro Toscanini laid down his baton, bowed deeply to the audience, and announced that here the performance would end. It had been at this point that Puccini, too, had been taken from us.

There was uproar in the house: an almost hysterical mingling of sentiment for the composer who was already a national idol, of fury at the interrupted performance, of shock at the flagrant violation of operatic tradition. Daniel was caught out when the lights came up: his face was wet with tears. Still too full with the drama he had witnessed on the stage and the brutal irruption of real life in the form of death into the score, he blundered past his companions in the box and made for the outer doors. By the time that his father and Laura had assembled the Contessa's brood and joined him, he had managed to pull himself together somewhat. Social niceties came to the rescue of father and son. How many cabs would be needed? Surely it would be an intrusion upon the Contessa's hospitality? No, Daniel was to rest assured. The Contessa was a wonderful old lady who would like nothing better than to . . . And in no time they were there, and getting out of the cabs in a narrow cobbled street, with a great deal of noise and bustle. Daniel was ushered through a door in what seemed to be a towering blank wall and hustled through a courtyard where the spring night smelt of bleach and freshly baked dough.

The Contessa who rose with outstretched hand to greet him was tiny; her pale, powdered face seemed permanently gathered into a smile, her hair tightly packed into a bun of the purest silver and, at this time of night, held in by a hairnet. She wore a kimono of what looked to Daniel like Chinese silk, bright red with dragons emblazoned on it. By contrast, the fire burning low in the grate looked merely tepid.

'You must excuse my receiving you *en déshabillé*,' she crinkled at Daniel as she pumped his hand up and down. 'Your father tells me you are the Prodigal Son returned. Any son of *il leone* is welcome in my house, prodigal or not.' She made him sit on a three-legged stool by her rocking chair and, as she questioned him, it seemed at random, about his life and habits, her fingertips moved as though absently over his hair, his clothes, even his face and throat. Her touch was almost imperceptible, like moths' wings, and Daniel, who as a rule hated to be touched, found this tactile inquisition strangely soothing.

'Of course, you realize,' said Laura quietly when the old lady had finally bestowed a beaming benediction and retired to bed, 'that the Contessa is blind.'

'And now: Lionel,' this with a relaxation of both tone and attitude, as she fell into an angular pose leaning against the mantelpiece, 'please may I have a cigarette?'

Soon the room was full of comradely tobacco smoke, Laura holding a long cigarette holder with an air of bravado that, for the first time in his brief acquaintance with her, struck Daniel as forced.

'You'll ruin your voice if you go on like that,' Lionel admonished her. His manner was teasing rather than severe, but seemed to Daniel's hypercritical senses to mask a real affection for the girl. 'Laura is one of our most talented young mezzo sopranos,' he turned to Daniel to explain. 'She has a great future in opera, don't you, my dear?'

And so, as strangers will who suddenly find themselves drawn into one another's company but are not yet ready to face, in words, what it is that has brought them together, they fell to discussing the neutral topic of the opera they had just seen. Laura had nothing but admiration for the silver-voiced Maria Zamboni who had sung the slavegirl Liù. Raisa, on the other hand, had been too harsh on her top notes. But what a gruelling, what a thankless part was Turandot! Opera in Italy had gone to the dogs if you asked him, was Lionel's irritable verdict. Italian opera, for Lionel, meant Verdi, the grandeur of the *Risorgimento*, an open-hearted nobility of sentiment. Tonight's spectacle was vulgar sentimentality, pandering to the tawdry instincts of a crowd that was no better than the crowd on stage. 'It's a stark fact,' Lionel concluded: 'Puccini died before Fascism became what Fascism is now. But what he left us was an opera that glorifies the dangerous dreams and petty sadism of the blackshirts. And where that road will lead, none of us knows.'

Inwardly Daniel cringed. He made a half-hearted attempt to defend the opera, but felt it was his own deepest, inexpressible emotions that were on trial, and became instantly ashamed of them. This in turn only made him defiant and inarticulate. In desperation, to change the subject, he asked Laura what she sang. 'Everything,' she said simply, and he realized he was listening

151

to the sound of her voice as much to her words, 'but opera is my first love. Mozart, Rossini, Verdi of course. I'm only in my first year of training,' she added with a sudden access of shyness.

'Go on,' Lionel prompted, 'tell this son of mine how you learn to be a *diva* in post-war Europe.'

So Laura, still standing by the fireplace, told anecdotes of her training in Milan, of her life before that in England, of her father who was an English diplomat, of growing up with her Italian mother in a huge house off the Bayswater Road, and as she talked and laughed, her small, mobile face and the unaffected, dancelike movements of her slender body seemed to draw up every nuance of her words, to mimic the absurdity or the sadness or the plain joy of the moment she was describing. Standing as she was between father and son, the light cascade of her voice seemed to exercise a soothing power over both as they sat and looked up at her.

When at last Laura left them, kissing Lionel full on the face, offering Daniel her hand with a formality and a slightly mocking smile that aroused him spontaneously to kiss her on both cheeks, the fire in the grate was almost out. Daniel wondered if he too should take his leave.

'No, no, dear boy.' *Il leone* waved a great paw in the air, and sat back expansively in his chair. 'Laura is an exquisite creature, don't you think so? How the Spartan life of the excavation would be transformed by a girl like that! But there you are, she has her own life. That's a girl with a future, a career. Her determination is wonderful. I shouldn't wonder if the next time you and I find ourselves together in Milan, it won't be Laura Mondadori we're jumping to our feet to applaud on the boards of La Scala.'

To Daniel's puzzled look he added, 'Her mother is a Mondadori. It's the name she means to use, as a singer.' Lionel's large features softened as he spoke. Daniel could not miss the wistfulness in his father's eyes. Why, even now, did he feel a stab of envy? 'Laura's completely bilingual, you know,' Lionel went on. 'She can pass for Italian among Italians, but she came out in London last year and I'm quite sure no one there was any the wiser.'

'Is that what brought you to Milan?' Daniel's tone was almost resentful now.

There was no mistaking Lionel's astonishment, whether at the question or the manner of it. 'Surely you know why I am here?'

Miserably, wonderingly, Daniel shook his head.

'Listen, Daniel.' Lionel sat hunched forward now, his large hands placed squarely on his knees. 'There are a great many things that might have been expected of a father that, it cannot have escaped you, I have not fulfilled. I mean, as a father. I will offer you now only one excuse. By the time I was your age, *my* father had my whole future mapped out. It wasn't the future that I wanted, and I turned it down. I think it was the greatest disappointment of the old man's life. He tried, after a time, to hide it, but he could only see it his way: I should have carried on his life's work and I failed him, threw it all away, forced him to hand over control of Robertson Mills to strangers. I was the sole surviving heir, you see. Don't you think it's depressing to think of those upright, hardworking Victorians and all their dead children? We forget too easily. I refused him, and he never forgave me. He couldn't forgive what he could never have understood.'

'But Father, what you wrote to me about at Upland Grange, about carrying on your work in Crete. Surely you were putting *me* in that very position? Would you have expected *me* to give up my plans for the future when you yourself—?'

Lionel raised a hand to stop the uneasy flow. 'And especially for a father who had so little claim on your life thus far. Daniel, I know it. I said I would offer only one excuse and now you have it. It has always been my belief,' Lionel's tone became brusque and teasing, 'that a father's true work is already done before his child is born. Forgive me if I shock you, but I think frankness is best between us. The male of the species wasn't made for monogamy and child-rearing. We try, of course, it's only civilized. But in other than the most crudely and uninterestingly practical ways, we must, I think, expect to fail.'

Daniel was perched awkwardly, leaning foward out of his seat, his long legs twisted uncomfortably under him. 'So why *did* you come to Milan? You owe me nothing, you've said it. Though I appreciate the arrangements you've made, even if you never wrote to explain, sometimes it would have helped, you know, if you had. And, of course, I'm not short of money, I assume it's you I've to thank for that too. But—' suddenly Daniel's voice rose almost to a shout, 'but surely after all these years I owe you nothing either!'

'I don't believe you do,' said Lionel mildly. 'You and I have met on perhaps no more than two occasions in as many decades. There is no debt on either side, I accept that. Though I have thought to offer you some apology for my own failings.' This with a grin that transformed the older man's face, making it seem almost boyish, impish and at the same time rueful. It was a side of his father that Daniel would never have guessed at.

To his own surprise Daniel found himself grinning back.

'Now,' Lionel pressed on in a more bantering tone, 'why don't you tell me something about this bohemian son of mine I hardly know?'

'*Please*, Father.' Daniel spoke now with a nervous edge to his voice. To his fury he could feel his face going scarlet. 'I am *not* a bohemian. That sort of thing went out before the war. All right, I haven't much to show for twenty-six years, I admit that. I'll try to explain. I'd like to explain, actually.' It was all tumbling out in a rush, Daniel felt his control of his words slipping from him. 'You see, Father, all this time I've been looking for something. Maybe that's a family failing.' This was said without humour, though Daniel did look his father in the eye as he spoke. 'If you must know – perhaps I wrote to you about this, did I? – a world in the making. The future, finding the future, building the future. I'm a war veteran, remember – doesn't that sound grand! I daresay all it means is I shan't ever grow up. Not properly. Not like you and – and – other people who were grown up before the war started. Maybe, when you've been through the war, even just a few months of it as I did, all you're really looking for is an antidote. And the best antidote is the one whose symptoms most closely shadow the disease. I don't know if this makes sense, does it? No, I don't suppose I *can* explain after all, not properly. But it was not frivolous, Father, not – *bohemian.*

'And there's something else, since you ask. It's over. *Finished.* I realized that tonight.' And once more, in his imagination, Daniel heard that warm melody coiling upward through the strings and the bright top note held by Puccini's Unknown Prince for longer than human breath, surely, can possibly endure, and sensed in the darkness of the auditorium the gossamer shimmer of a tight-fitting white dress and a cloche cap set at a rakish angle, a single wisp of brown hair curling loose beneath it.

Very quietly, Lionel said, 'You see, Daniel, you and I owe each other nothing. That is understood. But I have believed for many years now that when you were ready you would come to me of your own free will. Am I wrong?'

Lionel's voice came to Daniel as a deep, soothing rumble, as though it were only the articulate tip of the speaking sounds that come through the silence of the house, the slight hiss from the embers in the grate, the draught blowing down the chimney.

'I have come to Milan for no other reason, I assure you, than to tell you this: that there is a place for you at Ano Meri, if you want it. A place for you – you may find this hard to credit – in a father's affections.'

Daniel stared at his father transfixed. And suddenly the defences that had built up over the years, the prickly protection round the heart of his loneliness, were breached and the collapse was as total as it was unexpected. For the second time that night Daniel found himself overcome by unaccustomed tears, and buried his face in his hands. He looked up at last to see his father bending over him, for a brief dizzying second he was in a blue-painted room, the windows were open wide and the white lace curtains were full like sails in the warm summer breeze, birds were singing and pots and pans were clashing; this must be home and this was his father bending solicitously over the child he must then have been. If such a scene had ever taken place, he experienced it only now in the sudden recollection.

He stared into those pale-blue eyes, then rose to his feet. Lionel opened his arms to his son and clasped him to his breast. Flooding through Daniel's emotion-wracked body was all the solidity and reassurance he had once felt when his father's letters began to arrive from the excavation in Crete. And all the horror that had precipitated his flight from Upland Grange on the fragile, will-o'-the-wisp quest of his Grand Tour.

Disengaging himself without another word, Daniel collected his hat and coat, and fled into the drizzling rain and the sounds of a city already gathering itself for the dawn.

Throughout the next two weeks, until his father set out once again for Crete, Daniel became a daily visitor at the Palazzo Mondadori. Although nothing as coldly premeditated as a decision could be said to have been taken, he was visibly a changed man. His Italian friends noticed the lightening of his mood and joked about it genially. He responded in kind, but already found it extraordinary that what was no more, when all was said and done, than a circle of fairly chance acquaintances, should have circumscribed his life and his ambitions for so long. In that spring of 1926 Daniel Robertson was up and away; in the hazy sunshine and spring downpours of late April he felt change working through him, he hardly knew the new self that was forming in him but he knew there was no going back and he had faith in whatever was to come. All at once he stopped talking about the Future. The world could go its own way; but the future for him, Daniel Robertson, was upon him, was now.

With his father he pored over the proofs, maps and illustrations that many years later would go to make the first volume of *Ariadne's Summer Palace*. He allowed the resonant, authoritative voice of his father to guide him through the labyrinth of ruined foundations, of storerooms and pillared shrines, of sophisticated drainage such as had barely yet been seen in Crete in modern times, of sinister double-headed axes of blackened bronze, of the dozens of scenes depicted on walls and vases where dolphins leaped and lithe acrobats perilously, incredibly grasped a charging bull by the horns and vaulted over its back, of the miraculously preserved throne room with its frescoes of Europa and the Bull, and the restorative genius of Reinhard Kreuzenberger. Daniel followed carefully the drawings and plans of the site architect, Angus Cramond; he made notes and calculations and here and there added a suggestion of his own. Perhaps, in view of the steep slope at this point, the upper floors also fell away in a tiered effect? Surely the foundations at the bottom of the slope would not have borne the weight of five storeys? Long into the night, under the benign eye of the Contessa, father and son discussed, debated, argued. Day by day, while Laura came and went, and sometimes joked and sometimes scolded, always, to Daniel's consciousness, an evanescent presence in flickering white, the scattered notebooks, drawings and photographs were sifted and arranged. By the time that Lionel left Milan the first *Excavation Report on the Minoan Site of Ano Meri* had substantially taken shape. Although, when it appeared, this report would bear only Lionel's name, it was very largely the work of Daniel. In this way the foundations were laid for an archaeological partnership that in years to come would go through strange extremes, but nonetheless would seamlessly outlive both men to baffle Dan and the later excavators of Ano Meri.

The old rogue left Milan well pleased with the latest recruit to his team.

After Lionel's departure, quiet descended on the Palazzo Mondadori. Daniel continued his visits as frequently as before. Soon Laura's course of studies would be over for the long summer break. Daniel was not sure afterwards who first suggested that he join the household when it decamped to the Mondadori summer residence on Lake Como. It must have been the Contessa, but it was done with tact, and no outward sign of the collusion that must, however delicately, have taken place with Laura, so that in his consciousness it only gradually became an established fact, without anything ever being said. In the meantime he continued to work on the papers from Ano Meri that his father had left him. Often now he would stay at the Contessa's late into the evening; Laura had grown used to finding him there when she got home and he didn't, he told himself, want to disappoint her. She would come into the room and stand just behind his chair, looking over his shoulder at his work. A delicious glow would spread around him but he wouldn't look up, so as to prolong the moment. Sometimes she would stab a sudden finger at the plan he was working on. 'Look,' she might say, 'that wall here is the continuation of this one. Don't you see? Part of it's gone completely, or something else has been built over it. But the line's the same.' And he would align them with his set square and more often than not she would be right. Or if he seemed unduly stubborn in refusing to acknowledge her presence she would cup her hands over his eyes and say, 'Guess what I'm wearing today.' Then he would let his head tilt limply against the high back of the chair and draw the soft scent of her presence into his nostrils listening for the imperceptible but different rustlings of silk or lace or wool before making his guess. And more often than not he would be wrong. Then she would uncover his eyes with a tinkling laugh and his head would tilt even further to look up at her and the wayward curl would have come adrift from her short crimped hair. With laughter in her voice – 'You're a hopeless prince, do you know that?' – she would tease, and he'd turn round, as though angrily, and pinion her wrist to the table, bringing her face close to his. But they didn't, at the Palazzo Mondadori, kiss.

He bought her, for his first present, the score of *Turandot*. She tried to get him to accompany her on the piano but his sightreading was clumsy, she said he was ruining the rhythm when he stopped to look for the right notes. In the end she accompanied herself, and he was delighted to sit back and let the light touch of her fingers on the keys wrap him round. And as she began to sing, the voice that was already so musical when she spoke was transported into a different realm. The sheer concentration and power of the sound that came out of her slender throat thrilled him. *Liù non regge più*, she sang, and when she came to the final aria, willingly offering up her secret love of the prince to the princess bound in ice, Daniel found the emotion that had burst through him to engulf the orchestra and the stage at La Scala trembling once again around the slim white figure perched at the keys. The aria came to its plangent end: . . . *per non vederlo più* . . . *and never see him more.* She sat in the same position, her fingers over the keys, for several seconds before she turned to him, flushed, and said almost formally, 'Thank you, *thank you*, Daniel. It's a wonderful gift.' And he wondered fancifully for a moment whether she meant his present to her or the gift of a voice that was truly wonderful beyond anything in his experience.

In the railway carriage travelling north from Milan, Daniel cautiously took Laura's gloved hand in his. As it was not withdrawn, he held on. Hatboxes and a chattering assortment of the Contessa's granddaughters were strewn around them. They took no notice, spoke little and for much of the short journey stared together through the misted glass of the window at the rain outside. When after an hour the train stopped at Como and Laura disengaged her hand from Daniel's, he found that his arm had gone to sleep, and it required some minutes' painful pummelling to get the circulation going again. She, it seemed, had suffered similarly. As they got down from the train under the leaking umbrellas that an importunate crowd of porters jostled to hold over the steps, both were laughing and neither, much to the annoyance of the granddaughters, would tell what was so funny. There followed a long drive up the lakeside in old-fashioned covered carriages. The clouds had come down low and Daniel could see nothing of the scenery that the Contessa and the girls had so effusively praised. Even the house when they reached it seemed drab, despite its fairytale turrets steeply roofed with tiles of yellow and green, the long balustraded walk under the plane trees giving immediately on to the lake and the private jetty, the orangery where Daniel first drew into his lungs the full-bodied scent of lemon blossom (*Kennst du das Land*, Laura sang for him that first evening as the rain still beat down, *wo die Zitronen blühn?*)

It rained for a week. The Contessa apologized cheerfully to Daniel at least once a day. 'Never mind,' she would say, 'the sun is still shining – above the clouds.' The maids lit log fires in all the rooms, and the pungent scent of woodsmoke and the smell of freshly polished hardwood floors mingled in the stairwell. There was no question of going out, so Daniel spread his papers from Ano Meri all over an attic room the Contessa had opened up expressly for him, and set to work. With him, more often than not, sat Laura.

Laura, it turned out, knew a lot of things about the excavation that had not found their way into Lionel's letters to Daniel. She told him that Angus Cramond liked to be known as Gus and drank a lot of whisky. When the nearby villages celebrated their saints' days, the drinking and dancing would go on day and night and Gus would come back haggard and staggering, to sleep for forty-eight hours. Reinhard Kreuzenberger – they called him Kreuz

157

and he didn't seem to mind – was a gentleman at heart. But he had his moods, you had to be careful with Kreuz. He always wore a red polka-dot kerchief round his neck. He said he was a Communist. Sometimes he would rant long into the night about the alienation of the masses. It sounded terrific fun, Laura thought. Then there was this lawsuit that had been going on, even longer than the excavation, it seemed. But the funniest part was this. Who had Lionel chosen as his foreman and put in charge of the site? Manolis, an expert antiquities thief! But Manolis was good. Because he knew every inch of the site, and he'd been handling ancient objects ever since he was so high, he knew exactly what to look for, there wasn't much that escaped him. 'Poor Manolis, though, the land belonged to him and his brother before Lionel moved in. That's what the lawsuit's about, apparently. There's an uncle in the background, he's the one that keeps it going. A perfectly horrible man. The Bull of Minos, Lionel calls him. He hasn't a hope, of course, but it seems he's sold the rest of the family's land to pay for the lawyers. Lionel feels quite sorry for the boys – well, they're grown up now, of course, but that's what he calls them, "the boys" – he says if the uncle succeeds in bankrupting them he'll be honour bound to up Manolis' wages. But, of course, the lawyers are costing *him* money too.'

'It's funny,' she said on another occasion, 'I've never met any of these people – except your father, of course. But it sounds so wonderful – I feel as if I'd known them for years!'

After a week the weather changed. Daniel awoke one morning to find his room ablaze with sunlight. Rubbing his eyes he went out on to the balcony that overlooked the lake. The water was bright turquoise; the sky pale blue. The lake was quite narrow at this point, in the angle between steep rocky walls that shut out any wider view. There were boats out, their sails flapping idly; here and there a column of woodsmoke rose lazily, vertically into the air. The girls were playing quoits under the palm trees; their voices came to him quite clearly in the stillness.

Laura, when she came downstairs, put a hand under his elbow. 'No work today. Agreed?'

He nodded.

'We could take a boat,' she suggested.

So they packed a hamper and set off from the jetty – Daniel rowing, as there wasn't enough wind to fill the sails. And as he rowed, Daniel, for almost the first time in his life, began to talk about himself. She sat in the stern, nodding now and then, or asking him a question. Her face seemed to mould itself to the mood of the tale so that watching her he felt himself drawn on easily to tell what came next. He told her about his childhood, about his absentee father. He told her that he had been in the war, but neither of them wanted to talk about that. He told her about his student days on Boar's Hill. It turned out she had relatives there, whom she had last visited – now, when could that have been? They tried to work out if they could have passed each other in the Oxfordshire woods and not known about it.

'And now?' she asked him gently, but he thought there was a wistfulness in her voice.

'Now – well I suppose the next stop is bound to be Crete. I have to send the excavation report to my father. I expect he'll want to change things, bring it quite up to date. To be honest, for years I thought that was the last place on earth I'd want to go.'

'Really? I wonder why?'

'Oh, it's difficult to explain. There's a sort of certainty about my father – well, you must know what I mean. I've never been able to see things the same way. I'd have liked to, I suppose. Maybe that's it, maybe I envy him his certainties. His success, too. But now I feel quite differently about the excavation – oh, you know, involved. Excited. I feel there's a future for me there after all. What do you think?'

She was gazing at him intently, almost askance. 'How I'd love to come with you!'

Daniel stopped rowing.

'Why don't you?' he said.

'You can't be serious.'

He leaned forward and took both her hands in his. 'I am, Laura. I'm deadly serious. Why do you think I told you all that just now? I've told you things I've never told anyone. I don't think I quite knew, myself, as I was saying it. But there had to be a reason and this is it. Surely you've noticed? Something has happened since I met you. I could never have got so hooked up on my father's ideas, on the whole business of Ano Meri, if it hadn't been for you. It's alive for you, you see, you bring it alive. You make it seem worth doing. But don't you see, Laura? It's for *you* it's worth doing, because you believe in it and tell such wonderful stories about a place you've never been; maybe you're a little bit under my father's spell, but that's the point. It's thanks to you I can take my father seriously and at the same time not feel – well, overwhelmed by him. I don't know if this makes any sense, does it? Laura, listen. We could get married. Now, at once. We could go to Crete together, we could be archaeologists in the summer months and you can come back and sing in the winter. It's perfect. You said yourself you'd like to go to Ano Meri. My father wouldn't mind. In fact, my father would welcome us with open arms.'

Her chin trembled as she whispered, 'Yes, Daniel. If that was a proposal then yes. I mean, I will.' Her features had never seemed to him so pale, so tenderly pointed. Her face was suddenly radiant in the afternoon sunlight and the flickering reflections from the water all around, that now broke into little creaming waves as a breeze at last began to blow from the surrounding heights. As though in a dream she slid forward into the bottom of the boat to receive his long, deep kiss. He touched her almost with reverence, their fingers explored one another's faces, hair. Her eyes were wide, it was as though she was seeing him for the first time, her future husband. And a tremor ran through her whole body. With all the certainty of her nineteen years Laura knew that she was in love. She would have given herself freely, gladly, there and then in the boat as the breeze began to blow more strongly and little bursts of spray began to break against the side.

But Daniel had already left her, to busy himself with ropes and pulleys. Just so short, he would be shocked to realize in years to come, is the moment of complete and perfect happiness that comes once in a lifetime. What was it his father had said about Laura, that first night after *Turandot*? What had he himself meant, in the heat of his excitement only a few moments ago: *a little bit under my father's spell?* With a touch of the chill wind that lifted the hairs on the nape of his neck came the anguish of suspicion, of doubt. Would this wonderful girl who had just now promised herself to him ever be truly, absolutely his? The sun had disappeared, the choppy water now reflected the green-black clouds that all of a sudden shut out its light from the valley.

Laura ducked only just in time: Daniel had the sail aloft and the boom swung over, tilting the boat so far that the creaming water was lapping the rowlocks and she had to cling on quite grimly to prevent herself falling out. Daniel's face, as he crouched by the tiller, was impassive. She could see the light of excitement in his eyes, focussed on the distant point of the Mondadori jetty. He seemed to be calculating distance and speed, in a wager with the elements. Feeling her eyes upon him, he looked up. His face was wet with spray, and he grinned at her, like nothing so much, she thought, as a small boy showing off a wonderful toy. She grinned back. He shouted something, but it was drowned out by the rushing wind and water. Neither of them seemed to care. Then his hand was on her shoulder, pointing. She nodded that she understood. With a loud slap of canvas the boom swung over; she felt the power of it grazing her hair, and Laura scrambled, quite wet, to the other side of the boat. They had tacked, and now Laura followed the line of Daniel's outstretched arm. Dead ahead of them was the jetty.

The rain came down just before they reached it. The little boat bumped up against the wooden piers, Laura leapt ashore first and tied the painter. Daniel scrambled up after her. They stood for a moment, clinging to one another, laughing with relief, with excitement, with something that needed no name, soaked to the skin, their drenched clothes tight about them. And as the rain streamed down and the palm leaves thrashed in the wind, they kissed once more, deeply, hungrily. Then, with the strange unison of two people in love, they separated, looked simultaneously up at the sodden sky, shrugged with comic exaggeration, and broke into a run towards the house.

★

That night a solemn series of interviews took place in front of the Contessa. At last, rising to place a hand on each of their heads as they knelt before her in front of the fire, the old lady pronounced her blessing. It was agreed that telegrams would be sent in the morning – to Bayswater and to Crete. If Laura's parents would give their consent, they would be married at the consulate in Milan.

9 PAX MINOICA

LAURA Robertson lay between sleeping and waking. Outside, she could tell from the raucous chorus of cocks and donkeys from near and far, day must be beginning to dawn. When she opened her eyes, she knew, the first sight to greet her would be the ghostly shimmer of the mosquito net hung like a tent over the bed. The windows of the Cabin were uncurtained. The stars would already be fading. It was only at this hour, when the sky turned an infinitely fragile shade of the palest blue, and shafts of yellow and orange drove upwards into the air from behind the ragged cliffs of Iouktas across the plain, like trumpets heralding the coming sun, it was only then that the soles of her feet would tingle with the short-lived dew of the night, if she were to brave the scorpions and Manolis' sullen chiding and go out barefoot to the stone trough that miraculously would have filled up with spring water since the drought of yesterday, and would, if she were in time, catch the last of the stars taking refuge in the deep translucent stillness of the water, until the gentlest, most cautious touch of a hand would send them scurrying like tadpoles this way and that, diving and sliding in long broken lines between her fingers, always eluding her delighted grasp. It had been a game she and Daniel played in the first months. To catch a star.

It had been at this hour, too, that she had first set eyes on the land that in her excited imagination had already taken on, for her, the unknown contours of her future. Her first sight of Crete had been, like Lionel's, from the deck of the Piraeus steamer. But she and Daniel had had a calm passage. The night scents of the sleeping town and the mysterious country beyond had drifted out to meet the ship as the anchor went down with a tremendous rattle, breaking the early morning stillness. From somewhere on the still-darkened shore a factory hooted as though in answer, and then another. The ruined Venetian fortress, with its crenellated top, seemed close enough she need only lean out over the rail to pluck the dry weeds that choked the upper ramparts. Throughout the whirlwind that had begun with her marriage to

162

Daniel – their journey together briefly to England, then with hardly an interval to draw breath setting out once again by train – Laura had felt herself borne serenely by an invisible wind. An ethereal wind that carried her unresisting before it; but to this wind her body and her whole being were transparent and permeable. It must be love, so new and so unexpected, that had so opened up the pores of her soul, she didn't know how else to describe it. As though the passion that rose in her with the hard physical closeness of Daniel's body was too big to spend itself in even the most deeply felt embraces but spilled out to the long horizons of their travels. In that openness she was ready to embrace the world, it was as though the rhythm of the world was inside her and her heart was wide open to receive the wind of the world blowing through her.

At Victoria Station, as the Orient Express was announced, the names of the destinations were resonant for Laura with the longings of her childhood. Tales of far-flung service and adventure came back to her now, that her diplomat father had used to tell during those intervals when he was at home in Bayswater. As the train got up steam and her gloved hand was parted from her parents' who stood, still waving, on the platform, Laura felt herself launching upon the role that all her tentative, stage-struck rehearsal of the operatic repertory had really been preparing her for. The heart in her body beat time to the groundswell of a vast orchestral score beyond the range of human hearing. In everything she did and said and thought it was as though a melody was unfolding in a rhythm not of seconds but of months and years, a melody more tenderly beautiful and, yes, more dangerous than any yet conceived and executed by man. And Laura was content to be carried forward by this inaudible music: whether it turned out to be *opera buffa* or high tragedy or what her teacher at Milan had called *melodramma*, she would willingly play her part to the end. In the train out from England she surrendered herself to the tranquil, reassuring presence of this music in the rhythm of the wheels, day and night: Calais, Cologne, Vienna, Budapest, Belgrade. And here they left the great train, to take the southern spur and after another, slower day and night on winding tracks, with the haunting whistle of the steam engine punctuating their lovemaking and their dreams, Laura and Daniel at last reached Athens.

She felt this music again now as she stood with Daniel at the rail of the ship, watching the light of her first Cretan dawn grow around them. She was scarcely conscious of Daniel's arm around her waist, so much had he become a part of her. No need to look at his face in the half-light; she already fancied that she saw with his eyes, she could feel them equally straining to catch each detail of the scene as it emerged from the gloom with a slowness and an abundance that no lighting director or audience would ever tolerate in the theatre. She knew that this land was as strange to him as it was to her; and both of them knew, even from that moment, that whatever else might come in their lives and whatever plans they had already discussed for their future, it would be here, on this long thin island at the edge of Europe, that their real home would be from now on. The mountains that ringed the horizon, in sharp silhouette, had the most extraordinary, abrupt shapes. Daniel silently pointed out the crags of what must be Iouktas, behind the town, that was said by some to resemble a dead god sprawled across the plain. From here it looked more like the cruel beak of a bird of prey. And now the light came flooding from the east, the wisps of high cirrus cloud, that had begun to glow pale pink when they first came on deck, dispersing in a blaze of yellow and gold. In the west, where a mountain peak rose in the shape of a perfect cone and below it the outline of the land was rent by a deep ravine, the full moon was already paling into the surrounding sky. Dead opposite, the rim of the sun appeared; for a split second Laura was able to look at it, at the stream of fire that flashed across the tops of the waves; she felt herself pulled taut as though the string of a celestial musical instrument, stretched between the two horizons, were being finely tuned to play. For an exquisite moment she felt the opposing forces of gravity, of sun and moon on either side of the sea, joined through her body. As the sun struck her fully in the eyes and her vision was momentarily shattered, it was as though the string was touched into sound and in the pure harmony of that music she herself was dismembered, scattered, the atoms of her being falling evenly like rain to baptize every field and growing thing, every cliff and inaccessible mountain top, every hidden silent pool of precious water, of this land that was now by this miracle given to her.

'So that's what they mean by the music of the spheres.' Laura turned to Daniel a face full of delighted laughter, as she blinked the spots of darkness from her eyes. From the tightening of his arm around her and the affectionate way his lips brushed the ringlet that always came loose under whatever hat she wore, she was sure he understood.

And Daniel, as he sensed the strangeness of this land that he too was seeing for the first time, and the delight radiating from his wife's features, was in his own way scarcely less moved. For him too the sight of this jagged landscape that stood out ever more sharply in the growing light was inexplicably also the culmination of something that had been growing silently, darkly within him all those years. He had ended up, after all, at the furthest apogee of the old Grand Tour. Europe and civilization extended no further than this, its extreme edge. And he was unaccustomedly content that after all, despite the very different intentions with which he had set out, he should have wound up here, on this foreign shore which his father had made, to such public acclaim, his own. It was Laura who had shown him the way, of that there could be no doubt. Laura who had drawn him out of his nightmares, of that lingering life below the earth that still had not quite let go of his dreams. If he was whole now, standing with his arm unselfconsciously placed round his wife's middle, in the warm still air between sun and moon in perfect balance on either hand of the sea – what was it she had said? the music of the spheres? – as the ship swung at anchor and the bum boats came swarming out of the little harbour below the Venetian ramparts, he owed to Laura. She had made him whole. She would make him whole. He need never revisit those years again. It was a resolution made, solemnly, facing the full pale disk of the moon where it hung above the conical peak that in years to come he would know as Stroumboulas. Thanks to Laura, he had come through.

The Cabin, where Laura lay now between sleeping and waking, had been Lionel's wedding present, newly built and still smelling of freshly cut and planed wood when they arrived at Ano Meri from the Piraeus steamer on that summer morning. She had remarked then about the absence of curtains. For answer Lionel had unhooked the sturdy shutter of as yet unpainted cypress wood and showed her how it could be barred and fastened. Later she confided to Daniel that lying here with the shutters closed made her feel like one of Noah's animals in the ark, and thereafter invariably slept with them open, even when the spring rains beat against the Cabin and Aspasia, the housekeeper at the Villa, would shuffle across the intervening space of mud, her black headscarf plastered against her cheek, gingerly carrying a covered brazier of glowing charcoal and muttering in tones of solicitous admonition, '*Zésti. Kaló.*'

But on that first morning the sun was already hot, and Ariadne's Summer Palace beckoned. Outside the Cabin, Lionel had been waiting, like a cat with two tails, she couldn't help thinking in the euphoria born of the early hour and the strangeness of everything around her. It was the most natural thing in the world for her father-in-law to offer her his arm as, with Daniel ambling more awkwardly on her other side, the three of them set off up the slope. More even than her first sight of Ano Meri, Laura would never forget from that morning the smell of fresh earth, a heady combination of withered thyme and aniseed, of mule dung and the ground itself closing its pores that had been open to the night dew, before the onslaught of the sun.

Screwing up her eyes against the dust and glare, Laura recognized from the descriptions, plans and photographs that had lately become so much a part of her life the broad-backed ridge of what was once Kulhantepe, where the vines had been cleared and the olive trees felled. It was here that Ariadne's Summer Palace was being wrested, season by season, from the earth that had overlain it for three thousand years. Already an impressive grid of rectangular trenches and baulks had been laid out. Laura was able to recognize without being told the open rectangle of the Great Court that had once, according to Lionel, been the centre of the bustling palace. Here the activity appeared to be particularly intense this morning. As they skirted the open space, Laura thought she caught sight of a smirk in Lionel's eyes and wondered.

On the other side of the court, the maze of broken walls and passageways ran on beneath the baulks and into the unexplored hillside. It gave Laura a thrill to see how the lines and strange, complex pattern of the labyrinth had become through the centuries part of the living earth. She asked Lionel how long he thought it would take to uncover the entire palace.

Lionel laughed easily. 'A lifetime, I shouldn't wonder, quite likely more than one. You never know, that may be why you two are here!'

Laura didn't think she would ever want the excavation to finish. Even while she watched the bustle of the workmen, who stopped what they were doing and wiped sweating foreheads with the backs of their hands as the little party went past, she sensed how the excitement must dissipate once the sun began to dry the newly excavated walls, the turned earth was sieved as she saw happening by the spoilheaps now, and the finds removed for safekeeping and cataloguing. It was the sense of the unknown that Laura found most moving, not the careful piecing together of fragments severed from the earth.

It may have been for this reason that Lionel's pride and joy, which he kept till last, was such a disappointment to her. The throne room, where six years ago the panels of the Europa fresco had been found, had now been shored up in concrete, and was reached by a wide and shallow staircase that Gus Cramond had reconstructed from mostly original blocks of dressed limestone. Under the guiding hand of Lionel's architect this steep part of the site, on its western flank, had begun to rise above ground again. Laura marvelled at the height of walls and staircases and the strange proportions of the downward-tapering columns that had been vividly painted in reds, blues and black. The frescoes from the throne room had long been removed to the safety of the Kastro museum, where Lionel assured the new arrivals they were well exhibited, side by side with Kreuzenberger's brilliant reconstructions. The gypsum throne, with its high rounded back and narrow seat, was still in position. Lionel was most pressing that Laura and Daniel should take turns to sit on it. For some reason Laura found the experience unpleasant: the cold stone and the shortness of the seat imposed a rigid, hieratic posture. The darkness of the room, which was lit only dimly through the colonnaded lightwell facing her, and the smell of damp and earth subdued her spirits. It was a relief to climb back up the staircase into the sunshine.

They now found themselves in the centre of the Great Court and the activity Laura had observed earlier. On two sides of the court groups of workmen were erecting wooden scaffolding; a long ramp of duckboards was being constructed over the partly uncovered foundations of what Lionel explained were granaries and storage magazines.

'Somewhere down there,' Lionel waved a hand to where the olive trees began, fifty yards or so down the incline, and went on, apparently oblivious to the hammering and shouting going on around the little group, 'must be the grand entrance used by the princess Ariadne when her court retired here from

166

the heat of Knossos in summer. We haven't got that far yet, but never fear, we will, we will. In the meantime,' he went on, 'that's the way the procession will come.'

Laura and Daniel turned to him blankly.

But Lionel was enjoying himself. The bigwigs from Kastro were all expected, he explained mysteriously. A cinematograph crew had been booked to come out from Athens and catch the event on celluloid for the world's cinemas. An American billionaire, several generals from Athens, the Minister from the British Legation; there might even be a representative of Royalty. The Press of several nations. And, of course: archaeologists from all over the Aegean and the Near East.

'But what for?' Laura wanted to know. 'What's going to happen?'

'You two are going to be married, of course.'

'But Father,' Daniel sounded genuinely irked, 'surely that's going a bit too far? We're married already, and anyway, don't you think all this publicity is a bit, well, *vulgar?*'

'Nonsense,' retorted Lionel and turned to Laura. 'My dear,' he said, taking her by the elbow, 'you are now among the Minoans, a people who to judge from their painting and their jewellery loved beauty and fine spectacle more than any in the world. They would have had no truck with a consular *office*. Their princes and princesses were married in style, before the whole court. There would have been a sacrifice of bulls to the Lord of the Earth, the Earth-Shaker that these people had, believe me, good cause to fear. And before the bulls were sacrificed young acrobats would dance the dance of death, grappling a charging bull by the horns, and when the creature tossed its head, up they would go to turn a perfect somersault and land on its back. What you might call *taking the bull by the horns.* You'll see the frescoes and the little seal-engravings later. But it must have been a dangerous sport, and the Minoans, being a happy people, chose not to immortalize the many mishaps that must have befallen these acrobats. Ah well, I was wandering from the point. No, Laura, here in Crete there are strange gods to be appeased. And the greatest of these are the Press and Public Opinion. Not forgetting the pompous old bigwigs of Kastro, who also expect to receive their libations. Yours will be the first Minoan wedding to be celebrated in three thousand years – here, at Ariadne's Summer Palace.'

By the time the day came even Laura had been caught up in the momentum of the event, though she noticed with concern that Daniel was still fretting with annoyance. It only made matters worse when Aspasia, at the head of a group of the village women, came to the Cabin with the robes they had to wear. Lionel had provided the material – fine Egyptian linen – and Kreuz had quickly doodled the designs. The women had then embroidered them over a period of weeks and here they were, proudly displayed before the bride and groom. They were simple white tunics, hemmed with red and blue whorl patterns, stylized Minoan arum lilies picked out on front and back. Later Laura learnt that the village women had refused absolutely Lionel's suggestion that they form a solemn procession in flounced skirts, wearing only their men's zouave jackets on top, in a passable imitation of the bare-breasted Minoan priestesses. The bridal garments were at least more modest, though Daniel protested that he felt like an advertizement for an old-fashioned barber's shop.

The town band had been brought bumping up the rutted track to Ano Meri in a charabanc and had taken their places in the ruins. The visiting dignitaries had been assembled under parasols on the makeshift scaffolding. Laura was amused at the patriarchal array of heavy dark suits and gold watch-chains. Several had stowed top hats between their knees. Nobody seemed to be very young. There were one or two ladies from Kastro, dressed and made up for the grand opera stage but who sat together and chatted and never stopped giggling. It wasn't the first time, but it made the deepest and most lasting impression on Laura then: she had been catapulted into a world of men. As the village women formed up behind her into a sullen train, it struck her forcibly that the only members of her own sex she was ever likely to come in contact with here were either peasants whose language and whose world she would never understand, or those giggling old snobs on the stand. As the sun beat down on the Great Court, and the band struck up with the Greek national anthem, Laura felt a sudden surge of loneliness. She glanced sideways to where Daniel was standing, his head, like hers, crowned by a freshly woven wreath of laurel leaves. The band played some more that was discordant in the extreme. Clearly their hearts were not in it. Kreuz had apparently been trying to initiate them into *The Rite of Spring*, but the result was more modern and atonal by far than Stravinsky's score. At the far end of the court, under a canopy, two huge double axeheads of blackened bronze, with curved blades, had been set up on new shafts to flank a trestle table which served as an altar. Branches of palm and myrtle had been laid across it, and as Daniel and Laura came nearer, a white-robed hierophant began pouring a red liquid into a long ceremonial goblet shaped like an ice-cream cone. The cone, it seemed, had a hole in the bottom, and through this hole a slow red stream was poured over the altar and surrounding earth. The hierophant spoke a few incomprehensible words.

Lionel stood up at this point and made a ringing speech about the blood of the sacrificial victims being mingled with wine. 'In this ceremony you are witnessing now,' he went on, and the clear grandiloquence of his voice seemed to carry, over the heads of the assembled spectators, above the shimmering leaves of the olive trees on the slope, and away over the plain to the distant, ringing crags of Iouktas where the great god Zeus, some say, lies buried, 'the past that lies beneath your feet is restored once again to the vibrant life of so many centuries ago. The spectacle of a young man and a young woman brought together in mutual devotion, and so destined, God willing, to sow the seed of generations to come, is one that evokes awe in the heart of each one of us, regardless of faith or custom or the age we live in. It must have been just so when the kings of the dynasty of Minos brought their court here in the summer months, to escape the greater heat of the plain. You can easily imagine, on such a day, the princess Ariadne gazing out from this very spot over the vineyards and farms tilled peacefully under the watchful guardianship of Minos. You can imagine her staring out across the blue, secure in the knowledge that the ships of Minos ruled the seas. Yes, ladies and gentlemen, in those days there was no need for castles and fortifications. Archaeology has taught us that the priest-kings of the dynasty of Minos for many centuries held peaceful sway over land and sea . . .'

There was more, then ragged applause. The cinematograph cameras whirred, the Press clambered about the ruins taking notes, cameras clicked. Laura and Daniel were handed shallow bowls with the same red liquid. The hierophant then poured from one into the other and back again. Finally both were bidden to drink. To Laura's relief it seemed to be nothing worse than the local *rozakí* wine. She fancied Daniel's eyelid moved in a wink over the rim of his bowl and a tremor of laughter and relief ran through them both. As the moment came for them to embrace before the crowd Laura thankfully flung her arms around her husband's neck, oblivious to the eyes of strangers on all sides, and burying her face in his shoulder burst out laughing. 'Oh thank God, Daniel, thank God,' she said over and over again. When they both straightened up and adjusted their features once more, she assured herself that he too had been laughing silently. Even in the midst of this alien charade, at the ends of the earth, they were at one in laughter. Laura felt suddenly exhilarated. If they could survive this and share intact their deep, private laughter at the very centre of the alien crowd, then yes, she had chosen well; the bond that united her with Daniel was strong and well made – sealed and made fast, it seemed to Laura now, by the absolute absurdity of these proceedings.

But it was not yet over. Laura throughout the rest of the celebrations felt herself uplifted by the tide of reflected laughter that she had sensed in that very public embrace, radiating from Daniel's body through her own. There were mock combats by some of the workmen who stirred up the dust in the middle of the court. The band played military music and ended up with *God Save the King*. Suddenly everyone was crowding on to the court and stumbling, in a tightly-pressed group, back over the uneven ground towards the Villa. And then came not the least of the day's surprises. As they left the boundary of the site and surged all together towards the head of the track between the olive trees and vines, all at once the crowd parted to make way for the diminutive figure of a Greek priest with tile hat and beard who advanced stockily up the track, swinging his censer and chanting continuously. The locals crossed themselves and those nearest to him leant forward to kiss his hand. But Papa Nestoras was not to be deflected from his course. Before the astonished eyes of the assembled company he tramped three times round the perimeter of the site, and at every vigorous swing of the censer a cloud of incense dissipated slowly over the ruins. Only once this impromptu exorcism had been performed did the priest stride purposefully up to the newly-married pair and pronounce his blessing in what, Laura realized with a little thrill, must be the unadulterated language of the Gospels.

In the grounds of the Villa, lambs were being roasted over spits. Freshly baked bread was being divided. Wine and *tsikoudiá* were flowing freely. 'Have you noticed' – Daniel had been buttonholed by a thin, long-faced man in a threadbare suit and without a hat in the midday sun – 'that the people of the village have become the servants of the distinguished guests?' Laura noted, without surprise in this polyglot company, that this conversation was being conducted in Italian.

'They're paid to work for the excavation,' Daniel was explaining with a touch of asperity. 'We're not living in the Middle Ages, you know.'

'That's just what I was wondering. Varvatakis, by the way. Nikos Varvatakis. Profession: poet, *poète maudit*, alas. But we live, you see, in a transitional age and there are few who have yet woken up to the fact.'

Daniel sounded interested. Laura allowed her attention to wander, but remained within earshot. 'What do you mean, a "transitional age"?'

'An age without direction. An age of luxury and despair. An age that hopelessly waits for the coming of a Messiah. History has many such ages. Think how it must have been in Ariadne's Summer Palace when the ships of the blonde-haired Dorians first appeared on the horizon. For decades, perhaps for centuries, sunk in idleness and lethargy, summer and winter cocooned against the elements, in the sumptuous surroundings of a palace built for them by the labour of the peasants who were shut out as soon as their work was done. Performing ever more complicated rituals to appease gods they no longer believed in. A priestly caste for generations watching, waiting for the deathblow that would set them free. Perhaps the Dorian invaders never came, perhaps they were only ever an excuse. But you can imagine the surge of triumph when those huge walls up there were finally overturned, when the frenzied crowd swept through the palace magazines, seizing everything they could carry and putting the rest to the torch, defacing the frescoes, throwing down the wooden effigies of the old gods. Maybe the long-awaited Messiah came in the form of those blonde-haired invaders from the north, maybe the transitional age dragged on throughout centuries of darkness. Maybe, even, some gifted leader emerged from the downtrodden people, who had risen up at last to put a stop to this civilization that was as ready to die as an apple rotting on the branch. In that age without writing and without monuments, nothing of him would have outlived his own lifetime. That's the kind of age we're living in now – like a rotting apple that the forces of putrefaction and gravity will inevitably, maybe sooner maybe later, prise loose from the tree to scatter the seeds of new life on fertile ground. And that's the kind of Messiah we all await.'

Laura now entered the conversation, 'You mean, you're a revolutionary? Are you a Communist?'

Varvatakis seemed visibly to shrink backwards as though he had trodden on something dangerous. Daniel, to ease a moment of sudden tension, introduced his wife. 'A *chanteuse*, how delightful.' But Varvatakis had no smalltalk, and the kind of talk he had just been having was clearly not judged suitable for Laura's sex. Turning back to Daniel, as though it were he who had asked the question, but still obviously ill at ease, Varvatakis went on urgently, lowering his voice, 'I should not say in Crete, in Greece, in 1926, that I am a Communist. The generals and chiefs of police who are here might send their bravos after me one dark night. Actually, my views are well known. I have written letters to the head of every government we have had since Venizelos left us (and we have had many governments, one after the other, each more transitional than the last). I am a newspaper correspondent, private teacher, poet. I do not hide my ideas. But no one in authority has the courage to act on them. Now,' without seeming to notice it Varvatakis had taken Daniel by the arm and was leading him away towards the edge of the group, 'perhaps I shocked you with my poetic evocation of the glorious days of Ano Meri? Your father talks of the peaceful exercise of power by the priest-kings of Ariadne's Summer Palace. But the exercise of power is never peaceful, is it? *Rule King Minos, King Minos rule the waves.* A delusion, is it not? And a very English one . . .' At this point they passed out of earshot and Laura, in some annoyance, decided not to follow them.

That night the earth moved.

('No, Lucy,' Dan will chidingly explain, now that he has his mother's diaries in his possession, 'it didn't mean that in those days and even if it did, she wouldn't have put it in her *diary*, now would she?')

The last of the guests had gone, the bravest of them hitching a ride on the Hispano-Suiza motorcar that had stood under a rough shelter of brushwood ever since Lionel's triumphal arrival with it six years ago. Daniel had been allowed to prepare the car for use and, now that there was a road of sorts up to Ano Meri, to show off his skill in negotiating it for the benefit of the wedding guests. The villagers had become quite lit up with the singing and dancing of the late afternoon. A small pear-shaped viol perched on the player's knee produced an astonishing, insistent, swirling volume of sound, backed up by the strumming of the local lute, and the villagers had danced in a decorous circle, until one of their number got carried away and began leaping higher and higher, slapping his boots with his hands and turning somersaults in the air, all in perfect time to the music.

Now most of the debris had been cleared away, Aspasia had cooked and served dinner at the Villa. Laura had already got used to these subdued evenings by the lamplight. Cramond, gaunt and angular, was still offering round the demijohn of raki, though no one else ever seemed to touch the stuff. Laura had tasted it once and the room had gone black around her as she retched uncontrollably, the sour taste like rancid butter gagging in her throat. Gus called it contemptuously the 'natives' firewater', but Laura had noticed that of all the company he was the only one to spend time among the Cretan villagers and in return, it seemed to her, was treated with respect rather than the deference that she herself found both reassuring and infuriating. For Bertie Shaw, lighting his pipe in a cane chair in the corner, the attitude of the Cretans was at the best of times no more than a technical problem, she knew, but clearly not one that was engaging his attention tonight. He gave every appearance of trying to follow Gus in an interminable anecdote about fly fishing on Loch Lomond, but as neither was sober the story seemed to keep going back to the beginning. Daniel, meanwhile, was telling his father enthusiastically about his new acquaintance ('a dangerous buffoon' was Lionel's comment).

On the other side of the room sat Kreuz, strumming listlessly at the old upright piano that Lionel had bought in Laura's honour. Dear, impossible Kreuz with his large hands and large enthusiasms, his guttural consonants and broad licence with English idiom that the others smiled at; he didn't seem to mind, even went out of his way, Laura suspected, to convey by the liberties he took with it his profound but genial disdain for the language of his fellows. It was hard to imagine how those hands and Kreuz's curiously top-heavy frame could produce the fine brushwork and sharply minute detail of his painting. Kreuz had not forgiven the world for according him the fame, as a reconstructor of ancient frescoes, it had denied him as an original artist. In following Lionel to Crete he had left behind, apparently, a tempestuous career experimenting with Expressionism and Cubism. Daniel had expressed great interest in Kreuz's past work, but Kreuz would not be drawn further. If his own paintings existed anywhere, he had none of them with him in Crete. Once he had told Daniel that he had destroyed them. But to Laura he had confided that he paid rent on a garret in Munich where more than a hundred canvases were stored. 'And of those the world has not even seen the half,' he concluded with lugubrious pride. 'I am sorry for the world.' Laura never knew how to respond to Kreuz in these confessional moods. If she expressed sympathy, more likely than not he would roar with laughter, slap his hands noisily against his pink, almost hairless thighs, and abruptly change the subject. If she took his self-deprecating mockery at face value he would stare at her with those cow's eyes of his as though he had been struck a mortal blow but still could not find it in him to voice his reproach. Then he would nod several times in quick succession and say, 'So. Is it then so, Frau Robertson?' and it would be all she could do to stop herself from bursting out laughing.

Laura often sang for them at this time of day, with Kreuz a flamboyant if not always reliable accompanist. She had just got up to ask if he would do so now.

Suddenly the solid floor under her feet bucked violently, making her overbalance. Furiously she whirled round; in that first split second she actually thought someone had tried, for a silly prank, to kick the legs from under her. But it was the floor that was moving, undulating like the waves of the sea; it was like walking up to her waist in sand, nothing was firm, there was nothing to hold on to; all of them were on their feet swaying about ('like the Tron Square on Hogmanay,' as Gus said afterwards); the oil lamp suspended from the ceiling was swinging in a huge arc, the flame guttering perilously. With one of the oldest instincts of man the members of the excavation team stumbled one by one into the safety of the open air. Only Lionel, amid the rattling of glass and china, as the fabric of the Villa creaked violently like the bulwarks of a ship in a storm, and from the ground beneath rose a dull rumble that Laura couldn't pinpoint – was it coming from near or far? it seemed to be resonating in the very air and inside her eardrums, she was inside the sound, she couldn't escape it – only Lionel stayed indoors, his commanding voice rising above the tumult: 'The basement! Into the basement!'

Outside in the darkness pandemonium had been let loose. Every chained-up dog, every cockerel, every sheep and goat, donkey and mule for miles around was giving tongue, the air was whirring with the panic of birds normally sleeping at this hour. The hierarchy of creation seemed suddenly fragile, unbelievable. The terror and the powerlessness of Laura Robertson, *née* Middleton, of the family of Mondadori, of Bayswater and Milan, daughter-in-law of a world-famous archaeologist and would-be star of international opera, were in no way different, it seemed to her at the centre of that cacophony of nature, from the universal terror of all these created beings. She clung (another primeval instinct, she thought afterwards, with little pride) to Daniel. But Daniel, too, was shaking like a leaf. He held her though, and slowly the rocking of the earth began to subside. There came a few more shocks (like someone tapping crossly with a hammer from beneath her feet, she described it later), but the ground was becoming solid once more. The rumble had died away, to be replaced by the dry rattling sound of sliding scree. Here and there in the distance the red glare of fires began to glow. The few lights that burned this late in distant Kastro had all gone out. Apart from the fires, and the distant stars that alone seemed to have been untouched by the catastrophe, the darkness was absolute.

173

'Father,' whispered Daniel to Laura. 'Where is he?'

'He stayed inside.'

'Oh God. We'll have to get him out. Gus, Bertie, are you there?'
Cautiously the men groped their way back to the door of the Villa. The oil
light in the living room had gone out. The house was silent. 'Lionel! Are you
in there? Are you all right?'

Lionel's voice seemed to emanate from the very ground. 'Of course I am.
Come in. It's quite safe down here.'

A light appeared. Lionel had kept an oil lamp with him. Now he emerged
from the stairs. Even Lionel had not escaped the awe of the moment, yet in
almost his normal voice he said quite jovially, 'It's been our first real test of
the earthquake-proof frame. We'll have to have a thorough examination in
the morning, of course, but I think we can say that the Villa Europa has stood
the test.'

Hesitantly, almost reluctantly, they trooped back indoors. The suspended
lamp was relit; it had almost stopped swaying now. The shadows revolved
more slowly and at last were still. The pitcher of raki had fallen on the floor
smashed; the rancid odour of the liquor pinched Laura's nostrils. She
made her way through to the kitchen, to fetch a mop and clean it up. But she
was unprepared for the sight that met her eyes in Aspasia's domain. The
contents of every cupboard had been hurled to the floor by the violence of the
earthquake, every piece of crockery and glassware in the Villa seemed to be
smashed. It would take for ever to clear it all up. Suddenly, out of sight of
the men and faced with this destruction, the moment of crisis over, Laura felt
the last of her resistance give way. She sank her head between her elbows on
the cooking range, mercifully unlit that night, and wept.

'The remarkable thing,' she heard Bertie's voice saying at a great distance,
'is the way it repeats the finds scatter in the North Magazines. It's as though a
giant hand had simply swept everything on to the floor. Only there we've got
masonry as well.'

'Amazing confirmation of your hunch, Lionel,' Cramond's voice said. She
never quite knew when Gus was being Scottish and when sarcastic.

'I think we may confidently say,' this was Lionel's voice now, 'that the
final devastation that befell Ariadne's Summer Palace was due to no human
agency or malice. Earthquake must have thrown down those walls and
tipped over the oil lamps that set the magazines ablaze. The bull beneath the
earth. No wonder the Minoans revered the bull so much. We all heard him
bellowing tonight.'

And now (*only now*) Daniel: 'Oughtn't we to find out what's happened
down at the village?'

Gus and Kreuz agreed with alacrity to form themselves into a rescue party.
There might be people hurt, or worse, down there. They shouldered shovels
and picks ('we won't need much, they're mostly only mudbrick, the village

houses') and prepared to set off. *And all the while here am I in the midst of this mess crying my heart out and I might as well not be here. Not one of you have even noticed me.* Laura looked up to find Daniel anxiously leaning over her. 'It's been a shock to us all. In more senses than one,' and he tried to laugh wryly. 'Would you mind if I went down to the village with Gus and Kreuz? I'll take you back to the Cabin first, of course, see you're OK. They may need help down there.'

Can't you see I bloody well need help right here? The words were screaming inside her but Laura had not lost all her self-control: pride would never let her utter them. Dumbly she nodded, and dabbed at her eyes. 'Sorry,' she tried to grin. 'I don't know what came over me. Of course go to the village. Best take some brandy. Bandages. Iodine, if you can find a bottle that hasn't broken. And Daniel – take care, will you? Promise me you'll take care.'

She had got up, by now, her arms were round his chest. 'Let's go now,' she said. 'I don't think I can take any more.'

As he helped her spread the mosquito net and kissed her tenderly on the lips, hair and eyelids, she cradled the back of his head in her hands. She was utterly exhausted, she had no strength left, but she knew there could be no sleep for her while Daniel remained out there in the darkness, amid the devastation that must be waiting down in the village.

'And this was our wedding day.' She managed a rueful grin as she waved him on his way, every tautened nerve in her body calling out for him to divine her need and stay, but at the same time knowing her craving to be selfish and ashamed of it.

Slowly, as the oil lamp shed its warm glow, the solitude and comforting, Spartan simplicity of the Cabin began to assert themselves. Before settling herself for sleep she would always read from her little pocket Dante, and she forced herself to do so now. The book was dog-eared from her convent days. Little else had remained to Laura of her education in her mother's religion, but to her Dante she clung tenaciously. Not just the *Inferno*. Among the torments and the grand passions of the damned she would tiptoe with awe. But she found great comfort in the inexorable, gentle justice of the *Purgatorio* and the milky, gem-studded realms of Paradise where the greatest mysteries of all are made lucid in the love of a simple child whose name is a blessing.

Laura wasn't sure, as she thumbed the well-loved pages tonight, if she still believed in God. But she believed in love, and allowed herself to be transported by the musical rhythms of the Italian language back to the earliest memories of her childhood. Accompanying Dante through the circles of the empyrean, Laura found she could once again surrender her will to the music of the spheres that she had heard almost palpably shaping her destiny on the journey to Crete. As the hours ticked by and still Daniel did not return, this poetry with its hidden music calmed the fluttering of her heart and brought a troubled peace to her mind. And in that state of grace, before finally turning out the lamp and preparing after all for sleep – Daniel could not be much longer now, he would have spent a harrowing night, but he himself would be restored to her unharmed, she was sure of it – Laura, as was her habit, jotted down in a few dry words in her diary the momentous events of the day.

And now at last, in the darkness, she heard the stealthy, steady sounds of Daniel's return. Daniel was all right. And Laura, with infinite gentleness, sank into sleep.

10 THE OLD MAN OF CRETE

LAURA relished this early hour, lying adrift between sleeping and waking. Often in those first months, as she lay under the mosquito net and let the sounds and sensations of early morning wash over her, Daniel used to come to her, gently parting the netting and snuggling under the sheet beside her, and without opening her eyes she would receive him surging into her body and the sweat of a summer day would break out early before at last they would roll, still clasped together, out of the rumpled sheets and on to the floor where she would open her eyes and kiss him all over his face, and without a word they would pick themselves up and dress and hand in hand go out to the stone trough to catch a star.

Now, with the passing of years, she had grown accustomed to the quiet sounds of Daniel getting out of bed in the next room. She could feel his tread on the wooden floor of the Cabin, moving softly so as not to wake her. She always listened for those sounds. If, by the time the glow of day had begun to penetrate her closed eyelids, she had not heard them, the old anxiety would tug at her heart and wearily she would force herself out of bed and tiptoe through to knock on the door of his room. If he was still asleep she knew she had to wake him now, but so carefully and gently as to dispel any return of the nightmares that must have disturbed his sleep earlier. Often on these occasions he would spring bolt upright on the bed and bark out an order in a voice she scarcely recognized; his eyes would spring open, wide-awake, but their fixed pale-blue glare would be oblivious to her presence, to the room and the walls of the Cabin; he would babble something, usually it made no sense. It was at one of these turbulent awakenings that she had heard, for the first time since she had heard it as a child, in the street, the word *shit* and she knew what it meant, and felt, in the midst of her consternation, a stab of pride. She was a woman now, she had become an adult.

But the fear that gripped her on those mornings when no sounds came to her through the flimsy wall of the Cabin, was that Daniel wouldn't be there.

She would knock and pause and then gently peer round the door. It had been a shock that first time: the mosquito net had not been hung, the room was empty.

Her first instinct had been blind panic. He'd brought her here to the ends of the earth, where the dust got under her hair and nails and parched her throat; where taciturn Manolis had suddenly slammed down the flat of his spade on the earth only inches from her sandalled foot and without apology bent down to pick up a flattened grey object, that was still twitching, and held it close to her face, not to frighten her, let's be fair, although it seemed like it at the time, to warn her in the only language he could know she would understand, before he tossed the object carelessly over his shoulder and said very earnestly staring into her face, '*Skorpiós*', and she had understood and shuddered. Daniel had brought her to this desert outpost only to abandon her. The thought, born of panic, she quickly suppressed, but remembering it now as she lay deliciously between the sheets and relished the last moments before the prickly sweating heat of day would strike, she was able to reflect with a degree of contentment on Daniel's helplessness and her own. Daniel had not seen that moment of weakness, of crowding terror, and once she had recognized it for what it was she had taken care to hide those moments from him when they came again, though whether from her own pride or from anxiety not to add to his burden, Laura could not now be sure.

That first time, Laura had forced herself to think calmly. Daniel must have stayed late at the Villa last night. He and his father and Gus had been deep in some argument when she left them. He may simply have fallen asleep where he was. Fighting her fears, and a sudden urge to cry that she knew she could not give in to, at least not yet, Laura imagined herself going up to the Villa in her nightdress. 'Did my husband sleep here last night?' Looks of surprise, some embarrassment, the men would not be properly dressed. Then Cramond's darkly sarcastic guffaw, some guttural explosion from Kreuz, Bertie Shaw would cock a sandy eyebrow, Lionel towering in the shadows with a knowing smile on his face. No, if Daniel *was* at the Villa, he would reappear soon enough. But she didn't think he was. And in that case, there was not the shadow of a doubt in Laura's mind: it was up to her to find him.

The pre-dawn glare from behind the crags of Iouktas was already intense; in the distance the white-washed sprawl of Kastro was by now in sunshine. She could hear the bustle of men and mules beginning to arrive from the village, the clatter of implements and the soft swishing as the wicker zembils were unloaded from the store. Work would start at sun-up, Lionel was always punctilious about that. If her hunch was right, Laura had not much time. Throwing a coat over her nightdress, she left the Cabin and set off quickly through the olive trees, skirting the track used by the workmen. The site, when she reached it, was still deserted. Groundsheets and here and there a makeshift roof of corrugated iron protected those parts of the excavation that were still in progress. No point in searching there. Laura made her way perilously along the narrow maze of baulks towards the steepest part of the site, where the trenches were deeper than the height of a man.

'*Password!*' a hoarse voice rasped out of the darkness just below her ankles. Laura froze. She peered downwards into the deep trench. He had taken some of the long fine netting that the villagers had left under the olive trees after the spring harvest and anchored it with stones over the top of the trench. Through a hole in the netting the end of one of Cramond's theodolites poked up into the sunlight. Using it in this way he could surely see nothing through it but sky, but as Laura's heart turned over, the figure below her in the trench swivelled the instrument cautiously round. The same voice, which she barely recognized, came back at her harshly from below. 'Tonight's password is *shit*. Say the password.' As Laura still stood paralysed, the voice came again, angrily now, 'Say the password or I bloody well shoot.' And now Laura's eyes, as they grew accustomed to the gloom of the trench, opened wider still. The muzzle of an old-fashioned musket was aimed straight at her out of the darkness; she heard the click of the lock. He must have taken it from one of the workmen. As Cramond was fond of pointing out, the natives in this place seemed to sleep with firearms under their mattresses. She had never feared the trigger-happy workmen, who had let off volley after volley to celebrate the Dormition of the Virgin and would let fly from time to time, even under the firm eye of Lionel and his team up at the site, for no better reason than out of sheer exuberance, as much as she feared her husband now. There was no telling if the weapon was loaded.

'PASSWORD!' the voice roared.

Under the chill weight of her fear, time slowed almost to a stop; there was time to think of what must happen if she fled, if she turned up breathless and dishevelled at the Villa. She saw herself in the dazzle of the early morning sun gesticulating, pointing, gasping for breath, and the disbelieving faces: Cramond, Bertie, would Kreuz have a sneer? the dark shadow of concern on the face of Lionel, then the stealthy mustering of the workmen, a cautious encircling of the trench, a sign from Lionel, sudden movement, a scuffle, maybe, oh God, a shot fired, an answering shot, and here they were bringing him out, they would bring him out unharmed, they would, wouldn't they? And in the split second that she saw these things Laura understood too what they would mean.

Laura gave the password.

Then, kneeling down on the baulk to bring her face close to his she added, in as military a voice as she could muster: 'Come to relieve you.'

'Pass.'

'How do I get down?'

The voice was sounding confused now. 'Here, it's quite easy.' The net was parted and a voice that was Daniel's again was guiding her anxiously; she felt the touch of his hand that was ice-cold and trembling, as he helped her down. At the bottom of the trench, husband and wife faced each other. Daniel was shaking all over, his eyes blinking furiously. 'Laura?' he muttered wonderingly. 'What are *you*—?'

With an effort, keeping her voice crisp and impersonal, she said, 'You've been on watch all night. Here, I'll take over. You need to get some sleep.'

'What time is it?' She could see his body begin to relax; if she hadn't caught him he would have slumped against the side of the trench. She cradled his head in her lap. 'Now,' she said, in a voice that was at last her own, 'sleep.' And with a huge yawn that racked his entire body, Daniel was instantly, deeply asleep.

These days Laura was content to hear from the sounds in the next room that he had slept and so she could relax her watch. This was what made the first hour of the day such an oasis of peace and solitude. If Daniel had slept, she need not wake up just yet, and the tapestries of fading dreams and fleeting thoughts she would weave during those hours before *kolatsó* became ever richer and more precious to her. Here, as the Cretan sun warmed the outer walls of the Cabin and the smell of freshly-planed cypress wood faded with the passing years, she retraversed in her mind the cool, sometimes stormy pilgrimages she had made, each year so far, with Daniel to Milan and London when the excavation season was over. During those wet winters in Milan she still laboriously put her voice through its paces under the bad-tempered guidance of her teacher, who chided her for lack of concentration and a tightness in her throat that privately she blamed on the dust of her Cretan summers.

But although they went back each year, and Laura still sang and still for a month each autumn took Daniel to stay with her parents in the house in Bayswater, she had come by now to realize something else. Something that instinctively she had known, and even welcomed, on that day seven years ago when the Orient Express pulled out of Victoria Station. From that journey, no matter how many times they might come back and try to pretend they were picking up the threads of the lives they had each left behind, there could be no true return. Her life now was with Daniel, and Daniel's life was here. It was here in Crete, fired by his father's obsession, that Daniel truly lived; the rest was marking time. And so, despite herself, Laura found that it was for her too.

It would only ever be in those unfettered hours, her eyes half-closed under the white blur of the mosquito net, that Laura would graduate with the highest honours from the Milan Conservatoire, she knew that now. While the mules fretted and stamped in the growing heat outside, Laura trod the stages of La Scala, Covent Garden, the Met, and bowed again and again to the rapture of full houses drumming their feet and throwing flowers and bouquets. In those morning hours she lived the lives it would never, in the nature of things, be given to her to live in the waking world. Whole operatic roles ran effortlessly through her head. And Liù, the slavegirl in *Turandot*, would come back to her then, the exquisite tenderness of her pleading and her wistful, distant love for a prince who once smiled at her but will be forever deaf to her pleas and her self-sacrifice.

But soon enough would come Aspasia, padding over in her slippers to bring her a tepid boiled egg and a mug of steaming camomile tea: Laura had tried and found she detested the intensely strong, sweet coffee of the island. Later, when the archaeologists were all up at the site and Aspasia would have gone down to the village to cook for her children, who had been unharmed, praise be to God, in the earthquake, and to see that Spinalonga, her youngest and the village idiot, hadn't got into mischief, Laura would go quietly over to the Villa and sit down at the piano. Of all Lionel's kindnesses to her, it was this tinny, upright piano that never ceased to evoke her silent gratitude. To Laura it was a last thread linking her to the world she had left behind. And if she was sure there was no one about, she would rifle through the vocal scores that she had had sent out from England, running her voice thrillingly up and down the octaves.

But sooner or later there *would* be someone to hear her. Kreuz would have prowled silently down from the site to refill his bottle of turps and would clap her heartily round the shoulders at the end of an aria, making her jump with surprise and embarrassment. Or one of the workmen, coming up late after *kolatsó* on his way to a scolding from Lionel, would stop with his mouth open in the glare of the sun, and stare through the window of the veranda as though bewitched. They were a trial to Laura, the workmen. One in particular, one of the cohort of refugees from Smyrna that Lionel had co-opted, seemed to worship her from afar. He was a barrow boy (they were all called boys, though this one was sixty if he was a day), the others called him Hadzi–Aga and teased him, apparently, because he spoke only Turkish. She had seen him standing quite still, his bald, perfectly spherical head bare and glistening in the sun, in an attitude of deep devotion, just beyond the veranda of the Villa, day after day always at this same time. Shyly she had mentioned this to Lionel, and the old man had disappeared. But she never quite believed she was alone after that. The stoical features of the old barrow boy who for all she knew had lost a family, everything, in the fires of Smyrna, haunted her while she sang, she imagined his gaze burning through her light cotton dress, unseen, but not out of earshot.

Yet as time went on she found it more and more difficult to sit down at the piano. Her throat felt constricted, she made excuses to herself. And the Mondadori voice that had shown such promise began to wither like the weeds of the Cretan spring under the onslaught of the summer sun.

Now, even on those mornings when Laura could assure herself that her husband had indeed slept, a part of her was always on the watch. And as the years had gone by, this wakeful, watchful anxiety for him had taken root without her noticing, and begun to grow and spread out shoots and branches, to put out strange growths that were not the Laura she knew and recognized. It was something of *him* that was growing within her, imperceptibly changing the chemistry of her body, insidiously altering the contours of her thoughts. She was thinking, as she often did in that blissful anticipatory hour of the early morning, of the child they would surely one day have, but that day, it seemed, was not yet. She had pinned her hopes on this child, that obstinately refused to be conceived. Last winter, in London, she had plucked up the courage to see a specialist, but Daniel had been sceptical. 'You can't force these things,' he was wont to say. 'You have to let them happen.' But she couldn't help noticing that he seemed less and less inclined, himself, to help them along. And in the meantime what her love for Daniel had implanted in her was something monstrous, like the giant prickly agaves that lined the tracks between neighbouring fields, with their fleshy leaves the size of soup plates that turned grey and rotted but still kept their spikes and gave off a stench of decay – and somehow for all her love and all her watching, by the spring season of 1933, Daniel was out there on the other side of the barrier.

To Laura ever afterwards, this monstrous growth took form in the shape of Daniel's varsity friend, James Firkin. He arrived on a stormy night in late March. Everybody had gone to bed. Rain was thudding on the wooden roof and walls of the Cabin, an evil wind was howling under the doors. Daniel had returned with the car after a daylong vigil at the port of Kastro. Last night's steamer had put back into Piraeus. Distrustful at the best of times, Daniel had hung on, interrogating officials, demanding to see the telegraph operator in person; finally the harbourmaster had deigned to post a typewritten notice outside his beleaguered office. There would be no steamer until tomorrow evening at the earliest. Fretful and wet from his harbourside vigil, Daniel had driven through the rain and the ruts that had turned to mud, to return to Ano Meri without his guest.

And then, out of the buffeting of the rain and the wind, had come another sound, indistinguishable at first from the storm. The sound of horses' hooves. Laura was sitting up writing in her diary. She stopped and looked up. The sound didn't go away, so it wasn't inside her head. She felt an unreasoning terror brush her with its wings. She had heard, translated by Lionel or Gus Cramond, some of the tales that the villagers told of the spirits of streams and trees that could take on human form and lie in wait for the unwary to steal from them their shadow, their voice, or their wits. She had heard of the daybreak riders, the figments of the morning dew who could be summoned by the blast of a conch shell; of the grim horseman all in black, astride a black horse, who would turn up unannounced, seize young men by the arm and girls by their hair, drag infants wailing from their mothers' breast and tie them to his saddlebow, and deaf to all pleas, set out with his grisly chain of captives for the kingdom of snakes and mud, the kingdom of the dead.

Daniel had heard the sound too. He reached the outer door of the Cabin before her, she felt the blast as it opened. 'Firkin!' she heard him cry, and he had dashed out into the mud, carrying a storm lantern. Three horses had reined in before the veranda of the Villa. From one of them a small figure, draped in an unmistakably English sou'wester, clambered down with simian agility. Daniel was in time to clasp him as he reached the shelter of the veranda and the two men embraced with long whoops of delight. Laura arrived breathless a few moments later. The horses were already wheeling away into the night, their guest's shadowy escort almost instantly swallowed up in the blackness. Indoors James Firkin stepped out of his rain-proofing, shaking raindrops all over the room. Stripped of his carapace, her husband's friend seemed to Laura's eyes even smaller and uglier. His face was broad and his eyes, which were somehow not quite symmetrically placed, bulged like a frog's. His shoulders were broad too and, again, there was something disconcerting about their lack of symmetry. His head and body were built to large proportions, she now realized; it was the short legs that gave the overall impression of smallness. Laura didn't disguise the fact from herself – or from her diary: she disliked James Firkin from the first.

'But how on earth did you get here? You look as though you'd dropped from the clouds. You know there's no steamer until tomorrow?'

Again Laura felt that supernatural shiver, although she had to admit that his voice when he spoke was disarmingly urbane: 'Very nearly right. What does the apostle of the primitive do when he finds the seaways closed to him? He takes to the skies. Imperial Airways, my dear chap: if you've been as far round the globe as I have you learn the advantages of travelling in a manner that may not yet be fashionable, but is indisputably fast. Didn't you know the flying boat for Alexandria touches down to refuel at Spinalonga? From there only insistent persuasion and a few coins stamped with the image of his Britannic Majesty were necessary to secure a passage to shore. And once on shore what, my dear Robertson, would keep me from you and the pleasure of making the acquaintance of your lovely wife?'

Lionel was away in England for nearly the whole of that ill-fated season of 1933, being knighted at Buckingham Palace. Without his invisibly firm guiding hand, the smooth-running machine of the excavation seemed to lurch and grind. Laura had no doubt that the grit in the well-oiled wheels was Firkin. He stayed for two months, but had no role in the excavation. He was unfailingly charming, an unceasing conversationalist. It was Firkin who proposed expeditions to different parts of the island; Firkin to whom the others began, as people will, to defer. Even the workmen began coming to him for instructions, although he conceded blandly that he didn't know the first thing about the dig, while Gus translated and Daniel, who was supposed to be in charge, stood ganglingly by. The life of the Villa was beyond dispute more fun. But all this Laura observed with a grieving heart. The king had handed over his court to his jester.

It had been a last-minute decision of Lionel's that the excavation should go ahead this spring without him, and whatever Daniel thought, Laura resented it bitterly. She had been looking forward more than she could say to spending a complete year in England. Now she had had to abandon a series of tests she had begun at the Royal Free Hospital. She had expected Daniel to stand up to the old rogue. Father and son had been getting on one another's nerves lately; it didn't take much to send Daniel off into one of his white-hot silences, and Lionel had become more irascible with the passing years.

But instead, Daniel had been ecstatic. He had broken the news to her, standing pale and proud on the threshold of their hotel suite in Mayfair. In his moment of triumph he looked taller and more gangling, above all more vulnerable, than ever. His father had shown such great confidence in him. At his age, to have charge of the excavation. His father trusted him. Didn't she see, this was the acid test, the opportunity of a lifetime?

Now, back in Crete, as the summer heat began to flare, Laura could not help the frustration of seven years from boiling to the surface. In Lionel's absence, for the first time, they quarrelled. And it was over him they quarrelled.

They were driving up the rutted track to Ano Meri in the Hispano-Suiza, at the end of a long day spent ordering supplies in Kastro. Laura, dreading the new licence that reigned these days at the Villa, was hot and edgy. The jolting of the car made things worse.

'Can't you slow down?' she snapped.

Daniel said nothing, but she glanced across and saw his jaw set firm in the failing light. The car was bouncing more than ever across the ruts left behind where the ground had hardened after the spring rains.

'Daniel! Stop it. Slow down, I tell you.'

The Hispano-Suiza took a bad-tempered swerve, she was flung against Daniel, there was a screeching grind of brakes, and suddenly she was choking in a cloud of dust.

'What's the matter with you?' he muttered crossly. 'At this rate we'll never get home.'

The engine roared, the dust rose to envelop them where they sat in the open car, but nothing happened. He glared at her furiously before flinging himself out of the car to inspect the damage.

He got back in, slamming the door, and turned to her where she sat very still, staring forwards. 'Well now you'll bloody well have to get out and help me push, that's all.'

Laura was still staring straight ahead. There were tears in her eyes, but she held them back. Her throat was full of dust, she could hardly speak. 'Daniel, what's happened?'

'Bloody car's slewed into the ditch, that's what's happened. And now will you please get down off your high horse and help me push it back into the road?'

'I don't mean to the car. To hell with the car. To hell with getting back to the Villa. I mean, what's happened to *us*, Daniel?'

Only now did he hear the desperate appeal in her voice. But by now he was beside himself. His hands clenched tight on the wheel of the immobilized car. Quietly, almost under his breath, he said, 'It's my father, isn't it? You didn't want to do this season, I know. You don't trust me, you don't think I can manage on my own. You're waiting for me to make a mess of things, aren't you? Just like all of them. Except James. James is the only one's got any faith in me. I thought you'd got faith in me. But no, you keep carping all the time. I thought you might trust me at a time like this. Especially at a time like this. But oh no. And I know why, Laura, I'll tell you what it is that's really the matter with you. I'll tell you why you didn't want to come out to Crete without my father, why you're so determined this season's going to go wrong. You're a little bit in love with my father, aren't you? More than a little bit, if some people are to be believed.'

She rounded on him hotly. 'Who? If *what* is to be believed?'

But she knew perfectly well who, and inwardly she cringed.

'Well at least you don't deny it.' And she hadn't, she couldn't, although it was not true in the vile, hurtful sense he seemed to mean.

'Listen, Daniel,' Laura forced herself to be calm. 'Your father's like no one else in the world. You know that as well as I do. Yes, I suppose I do miss him. But, oh, Daniel, not in the way you said, never in a million years. How could you think such a thing?'

But his voice carried on as though he hadn't heard her, it held a suppressed bitterness, his eyes had taken on a hidden expression she had begun to recognize lately. 'That's why you married me, isn't it? You were ready even then to follow my father to the ends of the earth, he as good as told me so himself. And now he's not here it's brought you face to face with the man you did marry, with what it's really like spending month after month here at the butt end of civilization. And you'd rather be in London, simpering when the old man collects his gong or whatever it is. The magic's gone with the old man, that's what's biting you, isn't it?'

'*Daniel!*' She gripped his arm furiously and shook it. 'For God's sake, will you listen to me? Have you any idea how perfectly bloody I feel about this season – and the way your father dropped it on you without so much as asking first? Oh yes, I know what a responsibility it is and I take it seriously all right, believe me I do. But he had no *right* to do it, can't you see? That's what's "biting" me as you put it, if you really want to know. No, I didn't want to come out to Crete this season, absolutely right. But you're quite wrong about the reason. I'm angry at your father, if you must know. You'd think nothing and nobody but Lionel Robertson and the excavation existed. I don't think it's ever crossed his mind that you and I have a life of our own. I love *you*, Daniel, you and no one else in the world. And that's just the point. I want to have a child. I want to have *your* child. And I was supposed to be seeing—'

She felt tears coming now, tears of suppressed anger, of built-up frustrations she dared not put into words. Bitterly she fought against them. Unable to control the muscles of her face any longer, she threw open the car door. Over her shoulder she flung at him, 'I love you, Daniel. And, oh God, you don't make it easy,' and ran among the olive trees.

She hadn't gone far. He would come for her now and it would be over. She could hear the brittle weeds of early summer breaking under his footsteps as he came nearer. She kept her back to him. Now he held her by the shoulders. His body was hard. She loved its angular awkwardness. This was the man she loved. No, he didn't make it easy for her. But the world had prepared a host of platitudes ready for a moment such as this. The deeper hurt, the deeper gulf, could not be cured, that she could see, but for the moment the world's platitudes could suffice.

'I'm sorry, Laura,' he said, and with relief flooding through her she allowed her body to go limp. She turned to see the anxious tenderness in those pale-blue eyes – his father's eyes, she thought with an involuntary shudder. It was a hateful thing he had accused her of. Lionel, who had brought them together, must not be allowed to break them apart, not now, not ever. In that moment, with Daniel's hands upon her and the anxious tenderness still making his eyes beautiful, she was resolved upon that.

She put up her hands on either side of his face, drew him to her and kissed him on the mouth, on the eyes; he lowered his head and she kissed his lank hair. 'Oh Daniel,' she whispered, and relief that they had stepped so near the brink and yet stepped back from it coursed through her. 'Yes, oh yes,' she whispered a moment later as his hands grasped her strongly, as his breathing became short and urgent against her breast.

It was almost dark by the time they returned to the stranded Hispano-Suiza, holding hands and laughing inexplicably.

'And now,' said Daniel as they stood together contemplating the car, 'will you help me push this rattletrap back on the road?'

Daniel's first season in charge of the excavation ended in the havoc that Laura had feared. Firkin was, of course, well over the horizon before the thunderbolt fell. Lionel, now Sir Lionel Robertson, descended on Ano Meri

186

out of a clear blue sky – also, like Firkin, by way of the Imperial Airways flying boat and the refuelling station at Spinalonga, a mode of travel he much preferred to the sea on which he had suffered so much in earlier years. Father and son were closeted in the Villa for the best part of a day. The workmen hung listlessly round the site all morning; halfheartedly Bertie tried to direct them in cleaning some newly-uncovered foundations, in brushing down the cross-sections in the side of a trench. Nobody looked at anyone else.

The explosion, when it came, could be heard up at the site. Nobody, afterwards, could remember what words had been spoken, but the excoriation was public and spared no one. To Laura, it was as frightening in its way as the earthquake. The solidity of a world she was beginning to resent but which, when all was said and done, had at least the advantage of being firm beneath her feet, was suddenly taken from her. Weeks were to pass before Daniel would even exchange a civil greeting with his father; a ghastly pall fell over the team. He wouldn't talk to Laura either, or only in clipped monosyllables. She could see it and she hated it: Daniel was retreating, his proud sallow features pinched and wounded, into the shadows that, she alone knew, lay in wait for him. His nights were disturbed. He blamed the nightingales – 'The nightingales won't let you sleep at Ano Meri' became his trance-like refrain – and one night awakened everyone in the Villa by blasting off with a shotgun into the 2 am darkness. Lionel only rubbed salt in the wound by assuring him crossly that the most wakeful nightingale had tucked its head under its wing several hours ago and couldn't everyone damn' well have some peace to sleep. Afterwards, through the wall of the Cabin, she heard Daniel tunelessly intoning the words of the prince in *Turandot: Nessun dorma. Let no one sleep. No one sleep in Peking. Come the dawn, victory will be mine.* Her heart went out to him, but she dared not go to him. Daniel, among his shadows and the frozen anger of his heart, was becoming almost daily more of a stranger to her: an unknown prince indeed, and Laura's love knew no bounds.

But Laura with the passing years had gathered shadows of her own about her, and the toneless murmur through the wall brought them rushing in. Even had she known how to comfort Daniel in his despair, she might at that moment have held back from going to him. If at twenty-six her life was already condemned to failure, to an unending routine of cleaning and repairing bones and pots, and sometimes those exquisite pieces of jewellery or painted plaster that Lionel would swoop down on with a boyish delight that gladdened her heart and then whisk away from her to receive the more expert attention of himself or Kreuz, if her life was a failure, was not this in large part the fault of her husband? But Laura was not by temperament one to blame others, and she was an assiduous reader of Dante. Like the heroic figures condemned to eternal punishment in the circles of Hell, she had made her choice freely.

★

It was on Firkin's second visit, in the year of the Berlin Olympics, that he brought his specimens. If Firkin himself was loathsome to her, the 'gear' that travelled with him, which he was wont to exhibit, with some panache, after dinner at the Villa, was infinitely more so. The shrunken heads were the worst. He had an assortment of these, with wrinkled black skin on top and frizzy tufts of hair that fell out over the fruitbowl that Aspasia had not yet had time to clear from the table. In his dry, urbane way, Firkin gave latitude and longitude, described tribes as endogamous or exogamous. Johnny here had fallen as a trophy to a neighbouring tribe only last year. Expensive and prolonged barter had been required in order to obtain him. What there was of him. The Muratoans were not very specific in their accounts of how they dealt with their victims. Wherever you went, the *enemy* tribes were invariably the cannibals. He had seen human flesh consumed only once. So far as he was aware he had not tasted it. Laura shuddered. You couldn't ever be sure, it seemed, what morsels were ceremonially handed round on plantain leaves. Johnny had undoubtedly died unpleasantly. His flesh may well have been consumed. Firkin was collating the narratives of flesh-eating he had collected, and intended, once he reached England, to publish a monograph on the subject. It would, he assured his spellbound if somewhat queasy audience, be of considerable interest.

But what was most frightful about Johnny was what had happened to his face. Giant mother-of-pearl had been forced into his empty eyesockets. The translucent silver, streaked with grey, gave the skull an electrifying stare but also, to Laura's mind, conjured up great pools of tears that were condemned never to flow, the silent suffering of eyes that had no lids and would never, so long as the hideous thing existed, find refuge in sleep. A coconut mask, with grotesque features, had been fastened over the lower part of the face and garishly painted. In life, Firkin explained, Johnny had been an enemy, to be feared, hated, and killed without mercy. But once safely despatched (so Firkin's Muratoan informants had explained) he had become an object of reverence and atonement. In preserving a part of him in this way, the tribesmen had performed their own act of contrition. Living by violence (it was kill or be killed in those beautiful islands that the early missionaries had likened to paradise), it seemed that even their savage hearts were not insensitive to feelings of remorse, a religious awe in contemplation of a life violently extinguished by their own hands. The manner of it might seem to us primitive and brutal, Firkin ended his impromptu lecture, but was this veneration for the victim of collective violence so different in essence from some of the most fundamental rites and practices of the Christian Church: the act of Communion, for instance, or the collection and veneration of the relics of martyrs?

Firkin was travelling north this time, on his way to deposit his specimens at the British Museum. During the weeks of his stay, the piano at the Villa fell silent. Laura was more often than not content to retire early. Lionel had by now handed over most of the daily running of the excavation to Daniel and was absent for long periods in England, overseeing the final stages of his lifework, *Ariadne's Summer Palace*, which would run to at least three massive volumes. But for the last weeks of Firkin's visit Lionel was back in Crete and was present at some of these late-evening performances. He sat well back in his chair, his eyes half closed; sometimes Laura wondered if he was even awake. Often only a grunt would signify that he was giving his attention. When he took Firkin to task, it was with a genial restraint that set Laura's teeth on edge. Didn't the king see the poisoned chalice that his jester was passing round his court? If he did, Lionel gave no sign of it. 'But after all, my dear fellow,' he was content to chaff, 'these people are savages, as you say yourself. Our most distant ancestors may have been little better, that I grant you. But in Europe there were no *missionaries* or anthropologists to teach the natives higher ways. We now know that between three and four thousand years ago people lived here in beautifully constructed palaces, with paintings, jewellery, running water and drainage, all the trappings, in short, of Civilization as we know it today. If you want to find where *we* began, my friend, you need not travel to the ends of the earth, where civilized order is but a gleam in the petrified eye of such as your poor Johnny. Look beneath your feet, here, at Ano Meri and the other sites in Crete. And you'll see that our rapidly deteriorating century has some catching up to do.'

But Firkin was not, after all, to escape Lionel's wrath. One day Lionel found him up at the site, wielding a handpick borrowed from one of the workmen. He had been burrowing into the side of a trench, in the new section south of the Great Court where the baulks were being marked out for next season's digging. Lionel promised him he would flay him alive and throw his carcase to the wolves if ever he found him meddling with the excavation again. Afterwards Firkin claimed that his real offence had not been disturbing the stratigraphy (surely such a small investment of personal enterprise could not be so heinous?) but in violating the white man's taboo on manual labour. A dangerous precedent to set for the natives, that was it, old boy. Of course, an anthropologist has to go quite native himself, live like the tribesmen he is studying. Otherwise where would be the point? You couldn't study human society through the wrong end of a pair of binoculars. You had to get your hands dirty. That was the way you got results. Firkin's huff lasted a week, and during that time he kept well away from the site.

But Firkin, unlike Daniel, seemed disinclined to bear a grudge for long. It was he, towards the end of June, who proposed one of his expeditions. And surprisingly, Lionel agreed. The workmen were laid off for a week, all except Manolis, his brother Yannis and two or three others who were to be in charge of the muletrain. All of the excavation team were going. It was some time since Laura had explored the mountainous interior of the island and her spirits lifted at the prospect, even if the life and soul of the party was to be the unspeakable Firkin. In her diary she noted laconically: *Tomorrow to Mount Ida: Nida Plateau and Cave of Zeus. What joy!*

It was a slow trek through the winding foothills to the mountain village of Anoyia. The earth smelt of hot pine resin, on the higher slopes came wafts of wild thyme. Where smallholders had terraced narrow strips of cultivable land out of the hillsides, cocks crowed and donkeys brayed. Higher up came the evanescent sound of bells where invisible flocks were perhaps even now on the move, on the way to their summer pastures. Everywhere, from near and far, a million cicadas rasped and chirped, perfectly camouflaged against the bark of trees, the stems of shrubs, triumphantly, deafeningly, filling the day with their sound. In the distance the mountains swam in the heat. The excavation team were mounted on horses, but their pace was slowed by the state of the mountain tracks and the plodding progress of the mules that Manolis and half a dozen of the villagers were leading on foot, never seeming to tire, hour after hour. Daniel and Firkin had disappeared ahead, but Laura, who was an inexperienced rider, was content to get the measure of the chestnut mare that snorted between her knees.

She had never quite overcome a shrinking fear of the foreman whom Lionel would still, as a sign of familiarity, call a thief to his face, but who had never been known to flout his boss. Laura had watched him grow in stature, from the sullen, awkward youth who had killed the scorpion to the stolid, leathery-skinned, broad-shouldered foreman of the excavations who had earned the grudging respect of both the excavation team and the workmen in his charge. There was no job too large, too small, or too delicate to be entrusted to Manolis Laskaris. And under, of all people, Lionel's patient tutelage the former thief and petty dealer in antiquities had become one of the finest practical archaeologists in the Aegean. No one, not even Bertie, was as quickly alert to the minutest change in the colour or texture of the soil, the first hint of a burnt layer beneath which a sealed floor deposit ought to be found. No one had a more deft touch with the point of a trowel to prise intact out of the soil the wafer-thin fragments of painted plaster from which Kreuzenberger's reconstructed frescoes would grow to astonish the world. And when it came to recognizing and rescuing the often tiny precious sealstones, those gems that had captivated Lionel's heart before ever he came to Crete, as they emerged as dull as the most insignificant pebble from the earth, Manolis was unrivalled.

Contemplating him now as he plodded companionably enough beside her, uphill at the head of the muletrain, she felt almost sorry for the foreman. If he expected anything else from life he gave no sign of it. But she knew from Lionel how Manolis and his uncle had squandered all they possessed in a futile legal battle to oust the usurping archaeologists from their land; a battle that,

190

Lionel had assured her, had been doomed from the start, in a country where victory at law went to him who could delve most deeply into his pocket and enjoyed the familiarity of the highest powers in the land. Laura didn't think Manolis was badly paid, by comparison with the other workmen on the excavation. But assuming, as she also believed, that he was honest, it must be a bitter irony to him that all he had in the world was the wages paid to him by the usurper.

Communication with Manolis wasn't easy. He took his orders from Lionel and Lionel alone. Gus, who spoke good Greek, he largely ignored though sometimes he would burst into a loud roaring guffaw at something Gus had said, even if no one else seemed to be laughing. These bouts would cease as abruptly as they began, and nothing Gus or Lionel could say would draw him out again. Daniel – and this Laura could neither help noticing nor forgive – he treated with contemptuous deference. Daniel could make himself understood perfectly well in Greek, of that Laura had no doubt, but Manolis would always screw up his face in puzzlement when Daniel addressed him. When comprehension was at last assured he would seem about to remonstrate, then he would shrug and turn away without a word – though so far as Laura could see he was as punctilious in following Daniel's instructions as he was his father's.

And yet she trusted Manolis. Come earthquake, come flood, he would risk his life if necessary to ensure the safety of the mules and the cargo entrusted to him. Why else did she keep her horse browsing at a walking pace along the sides of the track while Manolis plodded beside her? Was it not that she too, who felt so much her fragile vulnerability in this remote world of men, wanted to place herself in Manolis' charge, to be protected by his fierce, forbidding pride?

After a while she broke the silence. She talked to him, as perhaps Lionel had never bothered to do, about Ariadne's Summer Palace. How extraordinary it was that, at a time when most Europeans were still savages, on this island had lived a people who were as rich and had as fine houses as any who lived in London or Paris or the great cities of today. A people who had no need of castles and fortified walls because they had learnt to live at peace under a king more benign and enlightened than many present-day governments. She wasn't sure how much of what she said Manolis was following. But suddenly he interrupted her. In his halting way, in a gruff mixture of English and Greek, he embarked on a story of his own. At first she was baffled. Then it dawned on her that the story of the ancient Cretans was, for Manolis, the story of his own family.

Once upon a time, when Constantinople was the Queen of Cities and Crete had been won back from the pirates, there were twelve noble families which ruled here. One of these had been the family of Laskaris, which had also ruled in Constantinople. Then had come the hated Turks, and laid

191

Constantinople waste. Only in Crete were the Laskarids still free men. Came wars, came invasions: Venetians, Turks, Barbary pirates, the Laskarids lost their wealth and their fine houses, they fell to tilling the earth. In every revolution Laskarids had fought and distinguished themselves, taking to the hills with their women and children, their chickens and goats, to escape the plundering Turks. Each time the revolution was over they would come back to find their houses burnt, their crops destroyed. Each time they would build again, plant again. So it went on. Till one day freedom came. The Turk was defeated, Crete was united with the Greek motherland. But in the hour of freedom had come for the Laskarids the greatest bitterness of all, excuse me, *kyrá*, but that's how it was. The land that had been theirs from the dawn of history was theirs no longer. And then had come the disaster in Smyrna and all the refugees, the shanty-town, poverty. His damnfool of a kid brother, Yannis, was mixed up with those people, there would be revolution, Yannis seemed to think, but that was dangerous talk. Revolution was for Cretans, and those wretched people – you had to feel sorry for them, how could you not, but they weren't Cretan. They didn't understand the *land*.

During the hottest part of the day they rested at the side of a ravine where a giant plane tree offered piebald shade and there was water, ice-cold and crystal-clear, pouring from the rock. Later, as the shadows lengthened and they resumed their trek, Manolis, now unstoppable, resumed his tale. The excavations, for him, were proof positive of his family's ancient pedigree. The teacher at primary school, where he and Yannis had each attended for all of two years, had told them of the glorious civilization that lay beneath their crumbling, mudbrick houses and broken-down sheep pens. Under the ground, he had told them, they would find the proof of a noble ancestry, proof that Greeks had lived in happier times; and what could be done once, could be done again. He exhorted them, said Manolis with a contemptuous snort, to rebuild the flower of the Hellenic nation. Well, we saw what happened to that when Smyrna burned. But as Manolis talked on, Laura began to glimpse beneath his broken words a vision, a yearning laden with poignant nostalgia, whose existence she had never in all those years suspected. In the ruins of Ano Meri, this rough brigand saw not just the glories of a past from which he and his ancestors had been many times dispossessed. Even in the act of uncovering its treasures, he found himself scrupulously bound to hand over every one of them, first into the unfeeling, clean white hands of the archaeologists, and then for good into that hated temple of Authority, the Museum. '*Signómi, e* – excuse me for talking like this. But none of these people can *feel* the objects they take from the ground. None of them *feel* the ground itself. Cretan ground. Laskaris ground. I feel them, *kyrá*. When I touch the soil, every object I touch, I know what I am touching. It speaks to me. It has its music, like the *lýra*.' Laura remembered the pear-shaped viol and its swirling, never-ending strains at her Minoan wedding, an age ago. 'These are my fathers,' he ended simply. 'I understand them.'

That evening they stayed at a stone-built, whitewashed inn in the village of Anoyia. Tomorrow, when Lionel's furious haggling with the local guides had reached a solution, they would set off into the unmapped foothills of Psiloriti. Following, so Lionel proclaimed, the itinerary of the processions that at nine-year intervals would accompany the reigning king of the dynasty of Minos to the sacred cave in the flank of the mountain, there to renew his covenant with Zeus, king of the gods. Before she turned out the light, resigned to the fleas and cockroaches that she had learnt to expect in such places, Laura thumbed through her pocket Dante, her constant companion. No, she had not been wrong, though she had begun looking in the *Paradiso* and was obscurely saddened to find the lines she was seeking in the *Inferno* instead. Never mind, she had a story to tell Manolis in the morning. She thought it would appeal to him.

In her dream that night she saw a monstrous creature, hideously deformed. She could not describe it or say what it was about it that was so horrible, but even in her sleep she felt her skin crawl and only later remembered the rough straw palliasse and the sightless bedbugs that must have visited her sleeping body. It was perhaps a giant scarab standing on two legs, a stag beetle with curving horns but no eyes, it was going to kill her, there was no doubt of that, she was ready to scream, only, as is the way in dreams, no sound would come, her legs were paralysed, she could feel the creature's hot breath on the nape of her neck and at the last minute she turned, she must know, even if it was going to devour her, what this abomination looked like and she saw only that it was weeping, tears were welling from where its eyes should have been, weeping for its own blindness, its own deformity and she thought, as though it were the most natural thing in the world, *of course, the scapegoat* and she woke up to find her own face wet with tears.

Their way the next day lay across a wilderness such as she had never before seen. Everywhere grey, broken rocks lay jumbled around them. The dense sound of the cicadas, that after a while you only noticed when suddenly and for no particular reason they would stop all at once, and all together, was left behind. Here only the wind sighed lightly across the rocks; the dark birds of prey that circled overhead, she realized with a thrill, were mountain eagles. In this shattered world of rock nothing seemed to grow, not even the dry brittle weeds that littered the lower slopes. Except that here and there the guides would point out an unsuspected dell, where soil had collected and a hidden spring or subterranean trickle had made an oasis of brilliant green with even some tiny alpine flowers or sometimes a stunted tree. It was here, their guides explained, that the local shepherds brought their sheep and goats for high pasturing in the summer. And sure enough, Laura's ears caught from time to time the distant, strangely comforting sound of sheep bells. Why pasture at all in such inhospitable terrain, Gus wanted to know? The guides winked at one another. In a place like that you could cook stolen meat, the best kind. And the party was regaled for some time with tall tales of raids and counter-raids on each other's flocks by the shepherds of Anoyia and the rival mountain villages.

The sun was sinking once again when they crossed the final ridge and there below them, like a dusty emerald, like a green lake in the middle of a desert, lay the round plateau of Nida. Opposite, the guides pointed out their destination, still some miles away, an almost invisible dark gash in the flank of the mountain. And above it, in all its glory in the setting sun, rose unencumbered at last by foothills, the terrific bulk of Psiloriti, the highest mountain in Crete, the Ida of the ancients. Its humped back was still streaked with snow. The haze that from the coast blanked out its features was now left far behind; in the chill of the evening air every muscular ripple, every bony ridge stood up in strong relief. 'Look!' cried Laura, unable to stop herself. 'Don't you see? It's a great sleeping bull! That saddle at the far end above the plain is the horns, then there's the thick neck. Follow the ridge to the right, and as far as you can see it's the flank of a sleeping bull. Do you see? Facing away from us, its haunches curved in. You can even make out the line of the ribs with the snow in between. It's a giant, sleeping bull!'

A silence fell on the party. Lionel reined in his horse close to Laura's, squinting into the glare of the setting sun. 'By Jove, you're right. Do you see, Kreuz? Could you bring it out in a painting? The sleeping bull. The bull god who shakes the earth. No wonder the bull was sacred in ancient Crete.'

They pitched camp below the ridge, overlooking the green plateau. Laura was glad they had brought sleeping bags, though it had seemed scarcely credible, back at Ano Meri, that they would be needed. Here, as darkness fell, the air was thin and cold. The guides scavenged some firewood and lit a fire. Lionel extemporized on Laura's discovery. 'The cave in the flank of the Earth-Bull. The place where Minos, like Moses, received the god's commandments. You can imagine the preparations, the climax of a nine-year cycle, when the king and court and all their retinue of priests and retainers came up here, perhaps the whole populace pitching their tents in the fertile plain. The solemn procession of the chosen few, escorting the king to the sanctum. The king going alone into the darkness. It must have been a kind of initiation, of purification. Then the shouts of joy. The king has come back out of the darkness. Long live the king!'

Daniel interposed petulantly. 'Of course, it wouldn't be the same man who came out of the cave. That was the secret of Minos' eternal youth, don't you see? At the end of nine years the priest-king would be killed and his body and his blood scattered over the fields. Minos' pact with Zeus was founded on sacrifice. There are parallels in other cultures: the king sacrificing himself for his people.'

194

But Lionel paid no attention, and continued to sit by the embers staring towards the dark mountain, his chin resting on his stick.

It was the next day, as the little party made its way across the soft, perfectly circular plateau towards the cave, that Laura found herself once again riding alongside Manolis. 'In the middle of the sea,' she told him, having rehearsed this all through the previous day, 'there lies a wasted land. Its name is Crete and in it are the ruins of many cities. Here in olden times men lived together in peace and perfect justice. Beneath the great mountain Ida – Psiloriti, there in front of us – stands an ancient man, a giant. His head is made of gold, to remind us of that golden age when men were not jealous of one another and lived in harmony together. The top of his body is made of silver, the lower part of bronze, his legs are iron except that one foot, the one he leans on, is made of clay. The whole of this giant body, all except the golden head, is split and cracked. Throughout the centuries the Old Man of Crete has wept bitter tears for that lost age of gold. His tears have welled up through the fissures of his body and run beneath the earth to make rivers.' The rivers of Hell, Laura did not add.

Manolis nodded slowly, and gave a short laugh. 'So the *milordi* have fairytales too?'

'Oh yes, lots of them.' She hadn't quite seen her Dante in this light, but no matter, she seemed to have scored a success.

All the way across the plateau she swopped fairytales with Manolis.

It wasn't until the going again became steep, on the final ascent to the cave, where Daniel and Firkin must already have vanished inside, that Laura was struck all at once by the depth of her loneliness. Swopping fairytales in pidgin Greek with Lionel's foreman. Like stubble on the plain.

The cave was dark and dripping. The men had brought powerful torches; she could hear their voices magnified and distorted. Lionel pointed out the altar at the entrance that had been cleared in recent excavations. So the archaeologists had reached even here – fellow Britons too, according to Lionel. Laura declined to go any further. She could feel the open wound in the mountain. If the huge slopes above her were the flanks of a sleeping bull, then this must be the way to its heart. She fancied she heard the giant heart of the mountain beating, then realized it was only her own heartbeat pulsing in her ears.

Suddenly she stiffened, involuntarily a stifled scream broke from her. '*What's that?*' she cried out.

Lionel was at her side first, his arm was round her. 'What is it, my dear?'

'*Look!*'

Lionel looked. From a dim ledge a little above head height came a faintly translucent gleam. His eyes, like Laura's, were still accustoming themselves to the darkness. Then he, too, saw. The shrunken skull, the grotesquely built-up face, the glassy mother-of-pearl eyes. Laura was sobbing quietly. It had given her a shock, that was all. Seeing that thing here, of all places. She turned imploringly to Lionel: it was a practical joke, wasn't it? A perfectly harmless practical joke. The shock over, it was his rage she feared, she could already see Daniel biting his thin lower lip till it bled, she saw another fatal wedge thrust into the tottering structure that held the three of them, she and Daniel and his father, in a sort of precarious equilibrium. And his rage, when sure enough it came, was like a whirlwind gathering from the depths of the cave, a rising sibilant sound until all at once it was upon them, the voice of the *liondari* amplified to a roar by the cavern. The acoustics tore away the words and amplified only the brute sound, and it was enough. Laura heard, '. . . bounder, sir . . . mindless, childish prank . . . a gentleman and a scientist . . . you abuse the hospitality of . . .' and then the sentence of execration, '. . . remove those horrible relics from Ano Meri and never, I repeat never, return to Crete again.'

One by one the archaeologists scrambled into the sunlight. Laura couldn't look at Daniel. The expedition lay in ruins.

It was a silent train of horses and mules that re-traversed the green plateau. Overhead the sun struck mercilessly through the thin air. Laura wished she had brought her parasol. The rocky ridge at the far end of the plain kept shifting in the heat, the ground beneath her horse's feet seemed to be floating free, adrift. For a panic-stricken moment she wondered if it were another earthquake, but no, animals and men plodded steadily; the ground must be firm then. She felt the blood bursting inside her head, pounding like a red-hot torrent through her veins. The sun was directly overhead. Something was happening to her, something that had never happened to her before. Her body was at boiling point, the explosion must come, it could not be averted. For a moment she saw the little group as though from a great height, a pathetic clutch of ant-like creatures in the vastness of the plain. It was a giant arena, they themselves were the puny spectacle watched with indifference or even wry amusement by all-seeing, inhuman eyes. The frustrations and the betrayal and, yes, the hot anger, long suppressed, of ten years could not be stopped up much longer. Laura looked straight ahead at Daniel's upright back, lifting easily up and down to the rhythm of his horse's hooves. And beside him the squat, self-satisfied frame of Firkin, the practical joker. At one time, it came to her now, after an incident like this she and Daniel would have come together in private laughter. It had been the *liondari* who was made a fool of after all, and the perpetrator had copped it as he deserved. Quietly, their arms twined about one another, with no one there to watch and censure, they could have laughed and hugged one another and kissed before returning with suitably grave faces to join the sombre homeward trek. But Daniel was deep in earnest conversation with his friend, the friend who, as Laura would have it, had turned her husband's wits and set him at odds with the father he would never, now, stand up to either. Her head was on fire. At the bottom of her stomach she felt the icy claw of despair.

And then time stopped. The rocky outcrop that marked the end of the plateau was not far away, but the shifting mirage was now frozen as though etched on glass. The horses and their riders still pressed forward, but riding now on air, without movement. The wiry grass beneath their feet was the same, the distant rocks came no closer. Manolis and the mules, still doggedly trudging, were motionless on the spot, transfixed by the barb of the noonday sun. And Laura, out of time, felt her body light as air. Freed from the spell that held the others rooted where they were, she wheeled her horse easily round. Before making off at a gallop across the plain she came abreast of Daniel and Firkin, prodding each of them teasingly with her riding crop. Now she was digging her bare heels into the horse's sides. The green plain was level before her. Far away, where the midday haze had gathered about the lower flank of the mountain, was the dark gash of the cave, its coolness, its moist secrecy. Faster and faster she galloped. She had never ridden like this before. The wind of her passage lifted her hair, caressed her breasts. Her trembling knees kneaded the flanks of the beast that rose and fell between them, carrying her onward. Behind her she could hear the thundering hooves of the pursuit, but she dared not turn her head to see who would shortly catch up with her. And now the plateau was at an end, the rush of her speed checked as her horse began to slither on the scree path that led uphill to the cave.

In the shadow of the opening in the mountain she dismounted and turned to her pursuer. It was as she had thought. Daniel, if he had followed her at all, had long since turned back. It was Firkin, grinning teasing laughing James, who jumped down from his horse and goosed her lightly with his riding crop in retaliation for her challenge. The only sound was the delicious trickle of water, invisible in the blackness behind them. For an eternity they stared at one another, drinking deeply of what they saw. Laura appraised anew the lopsided, beetle-like features and saw again the scarab-monster of her dream. But she was beyond fear. He was ugly and she loathed him but he was smiling. His hands when he took her were white and soft: a priest's hands.

As though in a trance she spoke aloud the unspeakable words: 'Give me Daniel's child. Give me Daniel's monster child.'

And the cave shuddered to its depths.

She was lying on the ground, in the green of the plain. She fought with the blackness, nausea overpowered her, she must have been sick.

'What's happened?'

'Indá 'pathe i kyrá?'

'Daniel.' It was the Daniel she knew, his long pale face bending anxiously over her. 'Where am I? What happened?'

Lionel was there too. Everyone had dismounted, it seemed. Time had resumed its course with scarcely an interruption. 'The cave?'

'We all left the cave an hour ago. You must have fainted. Keeled over out of the saddle. Are you hurt?'

Nausea and shame and understanding flooded in together. In a loud voice Laura gasped out, 'Daniel. I'm going to have a child. Our child. Isn't it wonderful?'

And then the blackness returned.

11 A JOB FOR LIFE

IT is January, 1990, the day when policemen are blown over in the Strand and lifeboat crews are lost at sea, as Dan will learn in the evening from the television news. On the ground floor of the Institute of Chronometry ('An Institute for our Time') the sounds of the tempest outside are subdued. Bursts of rain pelt against the small barred window of Dan's office. Across the narrow street the electric-blue glass of the latest office block has been ingeniously angled by its architect to reflect from street level a portion of the distant sky. The giant letters, TO LET, painted across the upward-reflecting surface in the hope, Dan supposes, of attracting the attention of low-flying executive helicopters on their way to London City Airport, are dulled almost to invisibility. The ruins of his umbrella are dripping quietly in a corner. His trouser legs from the calf down are soaked; he has taken off his socks and shoes and put them on the radiator where he hopes they will have dried before his first meeting of the day. He rubs his numbed feet against the carpet under his desk. He's bound to catch a cold. Dan catches colds easily. He is of an age to fret about such things.

He has collected a bulky stack of mail from his pigeonhole in the pharaonic hall where Foucault's pendulum gloomily marks time. Brown internal transit envelopes predominate. The flow of memos from the upper levels of the building is reaching the proportions of a cataract. These he will leave till last, by which time his feet, if not his socks, will perhaps be dry. Much of the rest, he notices as he quickly scans the envelopes before setting them down in a neat pile on his desk between computer screens, is postmarked before Christmas. Before the bleak epiphany of his visit with Lucy and Milica to Upland Grange. Before the one-way ride of change had swept away the last bastion of the Cold War in Europe. Before Dan had begun gingerly to decipher the neat, faded script of Laura Robertson's diaries.

He has left off abruptly in his reading of the diaries, seized with a sort of panic. What he has read so far makes no sense when set beside the meagre facts, such as he knows them, about his own beginnings. But he fears, beneath their drily telegraphic surface, to come upon the first stirrings of himself in embryo. Never mind the old rogue and the scandal that now seems set to rock his own life, Dan is afraid to interrogate too close the *fons et origo*, as his grandfather might have put it, of his very existence upon the planet.

He has broached this subject with Lucy, who is bracing, if also, to Dan's way of thinking, abrasive. 'It's well known,' Lucy has assured him, 'men don't like to contemplate their place of origin because it's also, for most of them, the object of desire.'

Dan raised his eyebrows.

'The vagina, of course.' Dan winced. 'There, you see.' His daughter is capable of pursuing her theme relentlessly. 'You don't like to hear the word. But so much of male desire is actually the pursuit of the origin, you know. Sex is all about getting back to the place you came from. And the fear of death is the fear of actually getting there.'

'Oh come off it,' chides Dan. 'What about women's sexuality then?'

'A woman's sex organ,' says Lucy looking him straight in the eye, 'is binary and that's all there is to it.'

He has tried to grapple with that one. 'So doesn't it matter to women where they came from?'

'Women *know* where they come from, silly.'

And Dan finds himself wondering, not for the first time, what this precocious daughter of his does know. He assumes that she is sexually experienced, but is, if anything, relieved to know almost nothing of her private life. She remains, so far as he is aware, unattached. She can have no inkling, surely, of those thirty-six hours he spent at Margaret's side in a whitewashed delivery suite shut away from day and night, those hours of pain under the merciless light when time was measured in contractions, the terror and joy of that moment when he was allowed to peer between his wife's grotesquely parted legs and first glimpsed the bald dome the size of a tennis ball, streaked with blood and mucus, his first sight of the Ms Robertson who twenty-two years and nine months later would sit demurely cross-legged on the flokati rug in front of the gas fire in his South London home, assuring him calmly that women *know* where they come from. He has stared with awe into that place of origin as she, he supposes, unless she abandons psychoanalysis to become a midwife or a doctor, is unlikely ever to do. And respectfully, horrified, overwhelmed by love for the tiny creature being squeezed through that aperture on waves of such pain as he can scarcely now imagine, he has clung with all his might to Margaret's sweating, clenched hand gripped in his, and watched with wonder Lucy Anne Robertson's progress down the birth canal and into the world. He has helped the midwife place the baby in Margaret's arms and heard for the first time that peculiar cracked cry of the newly-born human, the most compelling, the most imperative sound in the world he has always thought since.

From this reverie Dan is roused by a knock on his half-open door. Looking up, he sees Rex Prebble already inside the room. The knock has been a considerate afterthought.

'Oh, sorry Dan, have you just got in? I don't suppose you've seen this yet then?'

Rex waves one of the hated internal transit envelopes.

Dan gives it a wary glance, then shakes his head. 'I've only just started on these,' he murmurs apologetically.

'Well I'll spare you the trouble with this one. Cathcart's been made Head of Level. I haven't seen any sign of the famous consultation that's supposed to happen first. Have you?'

Dan sighs wearily, his mind still elsewhere. 'Are you surprised?'

The new broom that has been sweeping through the Institute for our Time has brought many changes. A strategy document that would have swept away the time-honoured chronological hierarchy of the building was surprisingly thrown out after intensive lobbying of the Trustees. But the new Director, in finally accepting the idiosyncratic deployment of specialisms in the horizontal plane, has now appointed to each floor, or 'level', its own line manager. The terminology is unfamiliar to the denizens of the Institute, still reeling from budgetary crackdowns and the steady trickle of earnest, lost, desperately serious young men and women who have turned out to be the much-feared students. From top to bottom the institution has been stirred like an antheap. For as long as anyone can remember, staff in their different disciplines have cooperated as equals. If decisions have not been taken, as one sexagenarian protested furiously at a full session of the Institute's Academic Council, that is because the time and expertise of highly specialized academics are not necessarily best spent on such trivial day-to-day matters. 'Precisely,' the velvety feline voice of Lady Ottoline Tussaud, chairing her first such meeting as Director, cut in with unerring aim, 'and that is why the Trustees and I shall be making a series of executive appointments. To see that decisions *are* made.'

The shudder that ran round the chairs, specially ranged for the occasion on four sides with Foucault's pendulum at the centre, was almost audible. Lady Ottoline (Madame Tussaud as she is inevitably, and without affection, known) is widely believed to have a 'hidden agenda'. Friends of the Institute have asked questions in the House of Lords, where the oracular responses of government spokesmen have tended to confirm their worst fears. Nowadays, the public spaces of the Institute are deserted. People who have not spoken to one another for years, sometimes who have not even known of each other's existence, have been coming together in twos and threes in offices and the backs of seminar rooms. *Have you heard . . . ? Is it true that . . . ? You too . . . ?* There has been hushed, heady talk of resignations, either singly or *en masse*. But the more experienced among the Institute's staff know that this is only a way of letting off steam. The few resignations that have reached the Director's desk have been accepted with alacrity, and as though to ram the message home Lady Ottoline has refused to rule out compulsory redundancies. It's a long way down to the gutter outside where the one-legged mendicant has long ago disappeared giving place to a less submissive crew. *Can you spare us a bit of change?* seems set to become the litany of the London streets for the new decade.

Cost cutting, and its human cost which has become so visible and disquieting to all who work at the Institute, have come almost to be taken for granted after the dreary chipping away of the eighties. Now a new notion appears to be blowing down from the higher levels of the building: that rather than being gradually whittled away into insignificance as one by one its staff succumb to unremitting pressure and opt for the obscurity of an early pension, the Institute of Chronometry should instead be reformed 'from the ground up'. Briefly, hope has flickered in many breasts, including Dan's, only to turn to a more insidious fear. The Institute is to become a vibrant new flagship for the nineties – but of what nobody seems to know, the admen are still believed to be working on that. Certainly, the specialists who have been beavering away on their several planes for all their working lives are not being consulted. And a new round of jitters has spread rapidly through the building in the first weeks of the new year.

According to press reports only last week, it is Lady Ottoline's view that the Institute has for too long occupied itself with 'a lot of hieroglyphs'. 'It just shows how much they know about what we actually do down here', was Rex's comment to Dan then. 'But decoded, that means us.'

And now even Dan, whose tendency is to shun the innuendo and the intellectual *mise en abîme* which is academic politics, can see how Rex's latest announcement fits into the suspect agenda. Dingle ('call me Dingo') Cathcart is the most recent recruit to the groundfloor level which is the domain of the ancient world, an arrival which raised a number of eyebrows when it took place less than a year ago. For one thing, the recruitment of new staff, in all the long years of retrenchment, has been almost unheard of. For years, Dan's colleagues have been leaving and not being replaced. More seriously still, Cathcart comes from what is contemptuously known in the trade as the 'high street'. He is not an archaeologist at all, but an apparently successful antiquities dealer. 'Set a thief to catch an honest man,' was the shocked verdict of Rex and most of their colleagues at the time. Cathcart's elevation now, to the newly-created managerial post of 'Head of Level', merely confirms their worst suspicions.

'The new broom is sweeping fast, Dan,' Rex warns him now, 'and I prophesy it will sweep exceeding small. I've an appointment with our new leader in half an hour. Compare notes at lunchtime?'

Left alone once more, Dan turns his attention back to the piles of mail. Is he, too, about to be summoned to the presence? He ought to check. But in the heaped-up external mail he catches sight of Paola's handwriting. His heart leaps, then with a kind of sideways lurch slips back almost into its normal course. It is only a Christmas card. She has mislaid his home address again. And the envelope is not one of the ones with a pre-Christmas postmark. He scrutinizes it carefully to see.

Paola, did Lucy but know it, was also a beginning. Paola it was who once handed him, almost like a gift tossed carelessly in his lap, the life that Dan has obediently – and not without satisfactions, happinesses, above all not without the continuing miracle that is Lucy herself – lived for close on thirty years. Dan would not wish his daughter to be burdened with this knowledge, but neither can he himself escape it.

It had been Dan's first time abroad: in 1961, the first of two summer seasons that constituted his initiation into practical archaeology. His mother, who bore her widowhood with such serenity, seemed more than usually apprehensive about his going. All the way to Crete. On his own.

'Why, I was born there wasn't I? It'll be like going home.'

But there had been a grim twist to his mother's mouth, a look almost of fear in her eyes, a look that only gradually in later years began to fade away whenever he mentioned Ano Meri and the fabulous time he'd had there. His father, he knew, had died in Crete. And Laura's way to keep her husband's memory alive, throughout Dan's childhood, had been never to speak of him. The name of Dan's father was never spoken in the house while his mother lived.

She had never gone back to Crete herself, after the war. She hadn't wanted him to go either. It is clear to him only now, in hindsight, how deeply she must have hated the idea of his going. And yet, when she saw how set he was on the trip – it was a marvellous opportunity, he'd assured her, things like that don't come along every day of the week (and they didn't, not for first-year Chemistry students in 1961) – she hadn't tried to prevent him. A shiver runs through him now. The diaries come to an end early in the war, he has checked forward to see. It seems they will offer no clue to the fears she had for him then, returning to his birthplace in his twentieth year. And Dan, as he stares absently at the grey world beyond the bars of his groundfloor window, experiences again that disturbing sensation that troubled him at Upland Grange Hotel, only a few short weeks ago: whatever it was had made him, had brought him, Dan, into the world, must in some way, even in 1961, have still lingered in the dust and thick heat of Ano Meri, in the wooden walls and uncurtained windows of the Cabin, in the purple splash of bougainvillea that all but hid Lionel's Villa Europa with its open roof-terrace and earthquake-proof basement. At nineteen, he could have had no inkling of such a thing. Whatever had been lying in wait for him, that his mother had so much feared, had not materialized.

Until perhaps now, faced with the scandal and the evidence of his mother's still only half-read diaries.

So while Dan still holds the envelope that contained Paola's Christmas card in his hand, and storm-force winds lash the upper floors of the Institute of Chronometry, whirling debris from the street past the bars of his groundfloor window, his thoughts roll back across the years to the unfinished concrete and dusty streets of Kastro, where once a week, if you were lucky, you could hitch a lift in the excavation Land Rover, have a hot shower and sip ice-cold *Tam-tam*, a now forgotten brandname approximating to Coca Cola, in the fountain square with Paola and Margaret, the two of them freshly changed into the familiar one 'best' dress they each had for the summer, their hair still wet from the shower. Margaret and Paola were the only two girls on the excavation (you couldn't count Doreen who went everywhere with Garel Thomas, and of course from time to time there was Mrs Hummingbird who was rumoured quite to like men younger than her husband but held no attraction for nineteen-year-old Dan). Apart from Paola, Dan was the youngest member of the excavation and his role, he soon learnt, was vaguely that of untrained apprentice. He could be asked to do almost anything (except for the taboo on manual work, of course) but without any expectation that he would be able to do it or that it was worth anyone's time to try to show him how. As a result Dan mooched around. Once he tried to show off the smattering he had learnt ('That's an LM II pot, isn't it, with the octopus designs?'). Doreen, who 'did' the pots, turned a dazzling smile on him: 'Oh, are you an expert on pot sequences then?' But Dan had shot his bolt, and if Doreen, whose knowledge of Minoan pottery he assumed to be prodigious, was at all interested in the subject, she was not going to share that interest with a novice.

(Of course, he wonders now, as the tempest continues outside, if Doreen had been more forthcoming, had opened the door a chink upon the apathy which, he has learnt since, is by no means incompatible with a vast knowledge, would he ever have been goaded to become the expert he is on the clay composition of Mediterranean pots?)

Margaret was a rung above him in the undeclared hierarchy of the excavation. She had explained to him early on, her brow slightly furrowing, gazing intently at him out of her green eyes (Lucy's eyes), that she was beginning a doctorate in archaeology. 'A Reassessment of Furumark's Aegean Chronology: the Evidence from West-Central Crete', she rolled the title off her tongue with satisfaction. Dan had never before met someone who was engaged on a doctorate, and was impressed. Margaret lived and worked under Doreen's thumb. Presumably with her Doreen would share something, at least, of her fabled knowledge of LM II pottery sequences in the privacy of the potshed, under the roof of corrugated yellow perspex where everyone and everything had a look of perpetual jaundice and the temperatures soared into the hundreds. But Dan was shy of asking Margaret too much about her work. It was not so much her work, in any case, that interested him. That summer Dan was interested in sex.

Paola's status was harder to gauge. Where he, as the second youngest, could be asked to do anything, Paola, who was even younger, never seemed to have any duties at all. All the men of the excavation (except Dr Hummingbird who had his wife to keep an eye on him) flirted with Paola, which annoyed Dan because he did too and thought it ought to be something special to himself. But then, she was strikingly beautiful, her body long and smooth as though her olive-dark skin had been turned on a lathe. Her jet-black hair hung down below her shoulders and was cut square to frame her small face with the disconcertingly Roman nose – and those eyes, deep, dark and almond-shaped that drew every man's gaze as she went past. Dan, innocent in those days of the artifices of kohl and mascara, had lost his heart to Paola's eyes. Late at night, while the frogs croaked in the distance and only the young bloods of the excavation were still up, desultorily drinking ouzo out of tin mugs, the charms of the female members of the team would be lubriciously dissected. Did Paola, in particular, have 'any tits'? Dan felt miserable at such times. Virginity, the lot of an only child living at home, weighed heavily on him. When he took part in these conversations he felt his private longings cheapened by the vocabulary of gregarious lust. But the alternative was a loneliness the sociable Dan dared not contemplate.

The other thing he learnt, that puzzled him at first, during these late-night sessions, was how much his peers who vied for Paola's favours by day, in the fellowship of nighttime seemed to resent her presence on the excavation. What was she doing here, so inexperienced? Why didn't somebody give her something to do, while they were all slaving away? And there was much speculation, some of it surprisingly malicious, it seemed to Dan then, about Paola's origins. Too young to be anyone's mistress, what were the chances she was Hummingbird's illegitimate daughter? Well, old Ralph would have had to have got going pretty sharpish in that case. Anyone know what Ralphy was up to before the war, eh? Before long the fantasy would peter out. Nobody could imagine anyone as blandly English as Ralph Hummingbird fathering a bird like Paola. That, in 1961, seemed hilariously funny. And inwardly Dan writhed. His eyes used to follow Paola about the excavation, and once a week, in the fountain square in Kastro, would feast surreptitiously on the contours of her best dress across the little metal-topped table, while he brightly made conversation with the two girls whom, with any luck, he'd have to himself for the next hour until the others got back from spear-fishing. He didn't, at this time, know what women looked like naked.

Margaret's bust stood out solidly before her. He badly wanted to know about Paola's.

Work was suspended at the excavation over the mid-August holiday. Garel and Doreen and some of the younger members of the excavation had been allowed to take the Land Rover and drive westwards over the mountains, for three days of swimming and sightseeing. Dan and the two girls were of the party. It was the hour of the afternoon siesta, the sun still high in the sky. Dan, not without ulterior motive, had challenged Margaret and Paola to a race along the beach. The white strip of sand was said to be twenty miles long. Perhaps it was. As they ran, it seemed to vanish in either direction into the shimmering distance. At last the three of them flung themselves down, breathless.

For a long time they talked – about the privations of life on the excavation, about Dan's grandfather, about Cambridge where Margaret was doing her doctorate, and Dan aspired more than anything to follow in her footsteps. Paola, usually more reticent, began to talk about herself too. The mystery that had aroused the imagination of Dan's peers was no mystery at all. Her father was quite a well-known Italian archaeologist, who had been excavating for years in the south of the island. Ever since she could remember she had spent her summers with her father in Crete (Dan noticed that she never mentioned her mother). This year there was no digging, but her father hadn't wanted her hanging round in Milan, and had hit upon a way for her to improve her English in relatively familiar surroundings. She had, as she somewhat bitterly put it, been 'stationed' with the English at Ano Meri. But they didn't seem to like her and she wished she could go home.

Only a faint ripple of breeze disturbed the sea and sand. Margaret had begun to snore gently. Dan in his swimming trunks, his unnaturally white body exposed to the full force of the sun, felt light-headed in the light. It seemed to be probing the mouldy corners of his being and flushing them out, he could feel the residue of London smogs and cold dark rain, of the proprieties of home and the solid expectations of his grammar school, rising like vapour into the air and dispersing. No wonder, he can even now remember thinking, under all this heat the Greeks believed in metamorphosis. He could feel it happening to him. He was not the Dan he knew. The pulsing brilliance of this light was awakening something in himself that had long lain in the dark. He was not, deep down, a stranger to this place, a spark of this light that now seared him was stirring into life within him, ready to burst, exploding to the surface and – well, that was the difficult part: and what?

Dan raised himself on his elbow. Margaret, her face pillowed on her arms, was sleeping gently, the sweat standing out in fat beads all down her arms and legs and on the exposed part of her back. She had eased the straps of her swimsuit down over her shoulders, leaving exposed the bulge where her right breast began. Turning the other way, his eyes met Paola's, full on him. The bikini was still a relatively exotic article of swimware then, and Paola's was minimalist. Two triangles of bright red material, connected by string, concealed the goal of Dan's now considerably goaded curiosity. There was a lot of smooth-tanned, lithely-slim Paola to look at, and Dan looked. He couldn't help himself. Those almond-shaped eyes, black as the best Greek olives, were moist as though she had been crying. The talk had drifted away, but she had been telling them (if Margaret had still been awake then) about how lonely she was. Dan turned over on his side and experimentally, comfortingly, he hoped, laid a hand on her stomach. Paola continued to look at him intently, then snuggled closer, bringing her face very close to his. Her eyes, her dark hair, the Roman nose, it was all a blur now, the nose was somehow burrowing into his face, her lips were open, his own had met hers, his tongue touched hers and a kind of electric shock ran through him to the navel. He drew back, and she giggled. They both giggled. Then they tried again, and stayed that way for some time. At last she gently disengaged her mouth from his and lay back on the sand. Her eyes were almost closed, the lids just flickering, and the whites very white under the lashes. Her breathing was different, somehow fast and shallow. She clasped his hand, that was still, a little awkwardly, stranded on her stomach, and stroked it. He held his eyes, as though hypnotized, on her face. With his heart in his mouth he felt her moving his hand downwards over her body, past the navel, and – this must be a dream, it can't really be happening, not to me – beneath the band of her bikini bottom, into that region that in his previous, inconclusive explorations with girls has always been out of bounds and that now turns out to be unbelievably soft and moist and – yes, there is no other word for it – *nice*. A sigh escapes from Paola's lips, her mouth comes slightly open, he tries to kiss her again but no, that's not what is wanted. With infinite caution, still half expecting the cross smack on the wrist or the impatient laughter that a false step on this perilous ground must surely provoke, he allows his fingers gently to move over the forbidden contours. And as he does so something stranger still, and indefinably exciting, happens to Paola's breathing. *Sì, o sì* she half gasps for the first of how many times in his ear, and all of a sudden her thighs clench tightly and her whole body jerks to leftward, away from him. Has he done something wrong? But the instincts so recently awakened in him tell him no, and he tenderly withdraws his hand and wipes it on the sand.

'And now,' says Paola, opening her eyes very wide again, and casting a quick glance at the still somnolent form of Margaret, sprawled blissfully under the sun, 'your turn.'

As the three of them walked back to the beach to where they had left the others, Paola and Margaret went together, paddling at the water's edge, leaving Dan to follow some way behind. Their heads were close together in what seemed to be earnest, animated conversation.

That night they camped on the beach. They made a fire of driftwood and warmed up tins brought from the excavation. As the embers died down they unrolled sleeping bags – a protection more against insects or stray scorpions than against the cool of the August night – and lay down to sleep round the fire. Dan lay awake looking up at the stars. He had never seen so many and as his ears filled with the comfortable sound of the sea nestling against the land, he sensed his body taut with longing, with expectation. He was on the brink of something momentous in his life, something quite other, it seemed to him now, than the smutty talk of Ano Meri late at night or the furtive infatuations and fumblings of his adolescence. Resigning himself willingly to this nameless power that had him in its grip, Dan fell into a deep and blissful sleep. He dreamt he was getting into a hot-air balloon, in the midday heat of this same beach, with a shadowy companion. The ropes were undone and the balloon took off with tremendous speed, skimming over the sea. The balloon, he somehow knew, was headed for the North Pole, and the blue Aegean gave way to the grey wastes of the Atlantic. Under fogs and past icebergs the balloon unerringly steered its way to the North Pole, where an igloo would be waiting and warm; there he would take his companion, who was Paola of course, but all the way she stood in shadow, with her back to him, he held her diffidently around the waist, there he would take Paola in his arms and she would be his, all his. But now the balloon was descending, everywhere about them was dripping ice, there was no igloo to be seen with its welcoming light and warmth. Paola turned indignantly to face him. Only, the face that stared aghast into his own was not Paola's.

Dan awoke with a jump to find his sleeping bag unzipped and the night dew cold on the sand.

Once the sun rose it was again unbearably hot, and the little party breakfasted early on porridge and fried bacon brought from home. Before the sun was far above the mountains they had doused the fire and scoured the cooking utensils in the sea, ready to strike camp. All that day the engine of the Land Rover growled up and down precipitous slopes, its wheels bounced over unmade roads while its passengers with more or less fatigue and discomfort bounced on the hard metal seats in the back. They stopped to explore a Minoan peak sanctuary that took hours to find; later in the day a tiny, whitewashed monastery. In the afternoon they strolled through a seaside town with Turkish minarets and the crumbling remains of a Venetian castle. It all seemed rather flyblown. Sand had invaded the streets and even got into the huge tasteless red watermelon they bought and divided up on the seafront. All this passed by Dan in a haze. To talk intimately with Paola was not easy in these circumstances. With a myriad interruptions, he told her his strange dream of the night before. And, through the course of the day, plotted what they were to do that night.

In the evening when they made camp Dan was scarcely aware of his surroundings. There was an orange grove, with only a few half-withered oranges left on the trees at this time of year, and the cool sound of irrigation channels. The water was cold and clear to drink, Dan preferred it to wine or ouzo and settled into his sleeping bag to wait for the appointed time, with a clearer head than had been usual since he came to Crete. The stars were further away tonight, screened by the gently stirring, silvered leaves of the orange trees. There was no moon; it was by the light of the stars alone that he picked his way among the trunks, carrying his sleeping bag to the place he had pointed out to Paola earlier.

She was there, waiting for him. He couldn't see the dial of his watch in the illusory glimmer of the stars, but she couldn't have had long to wait. He could sense the excitement of her naked body as she responded to the touch of his fingers, his lips. There was no need for words, there was no time to lose, it must be now; impatience, a power beyond him, drove him on. And all at once there was all the time in the universe, all the light years of eternity came together in the silence of the stars that were witness to the act, the moment of total possession stretched out in an infinite dilation to the beginning and end of time, here and now and always. 'I love you,' gasped Dan into the silence, and it seemed the whole universe sighed back in the exultation of his lost virginity.

'A strange dream indeed, was it not?' said Paola knowingly – mockingly? certainly teasingly but not unkindly – as the sunshine of a new day warmed the orange grove and the steep cliffs that towered behind it. And he stared at Paola with horror and admiration. It came to him suddenly that he must hate Paola but it wasn't that, it wasn't the treachery, it wasn't the humiliation, more than these the aura still surrounded him of something that Paola, whatever she had done, could not have given him and could not now take away. Last night in the darkness, the touch that met his finger-ends, that responded to his lips, the body-smell so close and eager, the short fast breathing in the rhythm of his own impetuous excitement, all of them had even then cried out to him the truth, could he have but heeded it. But the spell of last night had been too strong, the world could have ended (as in a way it had) and Dan would not have turned aside. And now, knowing and admitting that knowledge into his thoughts for the first time, in the all-seeing, inexorable but strangely gentle light of day, Dan could not find it in himself to wish what was done undone. He knew. There was no need for words.

It had not been Paola in the orange grove last night.

And up from the water channel, a clutch of dripping aluminium pans in her hand, wearing a sleeveless dress Dan hadn't seen before, her breasts swinging unhindered beneath it, a glow, the freshness of dew, the warmth of the finest, invisible down on her skin, an expression of serene calm on her face, came Margaret. And Dan stood up at her approach, and oblivious to Paola and the others, who were watching curiously, opened his arms to her and held her close, and heard again the sharply indrawn breath that had mingled with his in the silence of the stars and the orange trees. And he said again, quite loudly, with no regrets and no shame, 'I love you.'

Dan and Margaret returned to Ano Meri intertwined, and remained so for the rest of that summer. Sometimes he caught Paola eyeing them together, and he couldn't make out if in the depths of those almond eyes lay disinterested mischief, wistfulness, or even a malicious design. Nor, as time went on, could he quite lay the ghost of a desire that had not, after all, been slaked on that extraordinary night beneath the stars.

It is the ghost of that desire that Dan imagines he can still detect, now, lingering in the depths of the airmail envelope held in his hand. But it is Paola's perfidy that he feels most strongly on this tempestuous day at the Institute of Chronometry. The life she once high-handedly gave him, at the start of his twentieth year, is unravelling fast. Paola is well past forty now. Does she remember, he wonders, her threat to become a nun?

And the ghost of a longing, a desire that has been consummated so many times and so tumultuously between the mirrored planes of Paola's hotel suite still lingers to haunt Dan, to tease him with its passing. What, he asks himself angrily now, is there left for *him* beyond Paola's fortieth birthday?

It is at this moment, when Dan's thoughts are far away and his nose is still buried in an airmail envelope, that there comes a sharp tap at the door of his office. A managerially-groomed blonde head pokes peremptorily into the room.

'Head of Level's expecting you, Dr Robertson.'

Dan extracts his features smartly from the envelope that takes with it the last of Paola's belated seasonal greeting, and of so much else that has no place any more in Dan's life in the first weeks of 1990.

'Oh, sorry,' he mumbles grumpily. 'I was just on my way.'

'Head of Level does appreciate punctuality, Dr Robertson. OK?'

Dan pulls his steaming socks over his feet and squelches unshod along the corridor.

'Of course I don't hold with all this "no hieroglyphs" business, myself.' Dingo's secretary, the owner of the managerially-groomed blonde head, makes real decaffeinated coffee. She hands Dan a cup now and retires. Dan has not been in this office since it has been refurbished. Everything has been finished in a light-coloured, softwood veneer. In contrast to the threadbare carpets and metal furniture he is used to, it gives a soothing impression. Deceptively so, it turns out, as the interview proceeds.

'But we have to keep up with the times. No doubt about that. No doubt at all.'

Cathcart is probably younger than Dan himself, but he doesn't look it. Dark-rimmed spectacles with flat lenses that catch the light give his face a seemingly fixed expression of petulance. His hair is wiry, dark and thinning, and he sports a red patterned kerchief at his throat. He has dark hairs, too, on the backs of his hands, Dan notices now, as his Head of Level fiddles with the empty cup and saucer in front of him on the desk.

With some firmness, Dan says, 'Hieroglyphs, as I assume the Director is aware, are ancient writing systems. My own work deals exclusively with prehistory. Writing plays no part in it.'

'So you don't feel your own particular field is under any threat?'

'Well, no,' lies Dan, trapped. Round one to Dingo.

Cathcart pushes the empty cup and saucer away from him. 'We have to tread carefully here, as I'm sure you're aware. Very carefully. Relevance is the criterion in education and research these days, and the Director is concerned that not all of the groundfloor activities can properly be described as relevant.'

'Relevant to what?' Dan snaps back. It is against his better judgement, but he knows he will have to give an account of himself to Lucy afterwards.

'Honestly now, I don't think people in a position of responsibility like ourselves should be filling our heads with questions of semantics. Relevant to today, of course. Now, my role as I see it is to stand up for the academic activities I've been, for my sins, put in charge of. But I haven't been appointed just to rubber-stamp everything that goes on – and put my own head on the block. There's going to have to be some give and take. I want you to tell me about your neck of the woods – in simple, layman's language if you wouldn't mind – and then we can chat a bit about how it might fit into the way things are shaping up on this level. What might change, what might, at a pinch, have to go. OK?'

Dan nods miserably. It's going to be a horrible morning.

'I should go for a secondment if I were you,' is Rex's gloomy advice later that day. 'Even short term, that way you get a foot in more than one camp. No news about that EC business I suppose, is there? What have they decided to go for, an international committee of enquiry into Ano Meri? You're bound to be co-opted, I'll bet they even pay well. That's the sort of thing might come in quite handy at a time like this. Tide you over, if you see what I mean.'

But Dan's sense of alarm is only increased by mention of what to him will always be simply the 'scandal'. To his jaundiced mind, on this day when the gale seems set to rock the Institute of Chronometry to its solid foundations, the prospect Rex holds out offers scant refuge.

Alone again while the January day darkens outside the barred window of his groundfloor retreat, Dan inspects his shoes which are stuffed full of computer print-out and still soaking wet. The socks he has worn all morning are still not dry; thankfully he takes them off again, hiding his naked feet under the desk. A comforting, whirring sound fills the room as he turns on the larger of the two computers with which he shares the restricted space. As the screen comes to life, Dan embarks on a familiar voyage of discovery, tracing lines of order against background chaos, manipulating the huge databanks that are his pride and joy, with confident ease.

The ancient world in Dan's hands does not come to life, its stones do not speak. What emerges from Dan's computer screens instead is a vast silent pattern, a conceptual crisscrossing of lines across the Mediterranean from natural clay deposits to the grave goods of kings and the middens of troglodytes. On his screens Dan gathers up the scattered threads of human activity over centuries and across thousands of square miles. Powerful software, and his own skill honed through twenty years that have seen unimagined developments from punched cards and magnetic tape (it was all in the mind in those days, those were the testing times) to the 3-D graphics of today, enable Dan in 1990 to trace some of the earliest signals of purposeful human activity amidst the background noise of random distribution. Lucy has demanded to know before now why anybody should want to do this. 'OK, so you can prove that pots from site A end up shipped to X, Y, Z and God knows where else. Have pot, will travel. So what?'

Dan on such occasions has sighed. 'It's not where this or that pot went that matters,' he insists, but even as he speaks he is alert to the boredom factor inherent in trying to explain. Even with Lucy, who cares about him if not about his work, for all her callow cavilling, he knows from experience he has about forty-five seconds. 'We're dealing with millions of sherds and thousands of sites. What you can see – you can even display it graphically on the screen nowadays – is the *pattern*. Look.' He presses a button, and against a shadowy outline of the Mediterranean basin a forest of glowing lines shoots out, it seems in all directions. 'That's distribution in space, mapped at 2000 BC. Just an example. But you can also introduce the third dimension, and that's where it really gets interesting. No, since the map only needs two dimensions, the third dimension isn't depth. It's time. Now watch this.' And with the change of perspective on the screen the lines that a moment ago looked, in Lucy's irreverent words, like nothing so much as a packet of dried spaghetti broken open over the floor, have acquired the edges and contours of a modernist sculpture, a Surrealist collage. The third dimension reveals scrolling, spiral shapes, thick blocks of light that emerge from pinpoints and recede back into pinpoints. 'It's like a musical score,' Dan breathes, unable to suppress the note of wonder that has crept into his voice. Dan is in his element. 'More complicated than any music yet played. But to play the music you have first to learn to read it. That's our job. And it'll take a lot more data and a few more lifetimes, I shouldn't wonder.'

Lucy's green eyes are aglow with the light reflected from the screen. 'The still sad music of humanity,' she quotes wistfully. Then she tears herself from the mesmerizing screen. 'OK, Dan, great. It's a wonder of technology and hard work. I know how hard you work.' She manages to make it sound like a reproach in Dan's ears. 'But *why*? Can you tell me that?'

And faced with the bland green stare of his daughter's questioning eyes, Dan has been alarmed to find that he does not know why. It wasn't a question people asked at the time he embarked on his career. Lucy at twenty-two has been asking it of herself ad nauseam. Prior to accepting Milica finally as his student he will have to interrogate her too, fairly exhaustively, about her motives and expectations. How did he himself escape? He doesn't know that either, now. Scientific research was something one did if one jolly well got the chance. In those confusing days of the mid sixties, not long out of university, his doctorate not yet finished, Dan had landed a plum. Everybody said so. And on the strength of it – he can still remember the wave of euphoria that carried him up to Cambridge that day with the letter from the Institute in his pocket – had tied the knot with Margaret. Lucy would never have been born but for the timely godsend of that letter of appointment.

It wasn't very well paid, of course. But in those days, it had been a job for life.

Now his daughter's question tugs at his attention, since it has this morning been put to him again, in almost identical words, but with a more pressing edge to them, by Dingo Cathcart. It must be a sign of the times that he has not thought it sufficient answer to confess, either to his daughter or to his new superior, that some of his happiest hours have been spent in that not quite imaginary, not quite real either, intricate, flickering labyrinth of lines and shapes.

But Dan cannot concentrate this afternoon. His glance keeps slipping sideways to the filing cabinet where his mother's diaries are stashed away under lock and key. For the first time he sees his professional life as an evasion. It seems to him suddenly that the life he has lived for – well, it's close on thirty years since that first summer at Ano Meri – has almost unravelled. The trouble is, his life is unravelling backwards as well as forwards, and it isn't a comfortable feeling. Like being adrift on a raft in the midst of the ocean, without horizons. Or like standing on the peak of a high mountain and suffering, as Dan is apt to do, from vertigo. That feeling of there being nowhere to turn, nowhere safe to look. There can be no excuse for continuing to dodge the truth to which he alone has access in his mother's diaries. Though he acknowledges to himself the terror with which he

213

contemplates discovery. It isn't just his distaste for the scandal that will not now go away, still less the dubious temptation aroused by Rex's comradely advice – to take his place amid the bureaucratic pack hunting down the past wiles of his father and grandfather. It's something much more intimate and dangerous that Dan fears to touch, something for which as yet he can find no name.

Involuntarily he looks down at his bare feet under the desk, and notices the knotted veins beginning to stand out.

Time is staring Dan in the face, and it scares him.

As week gives way to week and month to month the havoc wreaked throughout southern Britain on that January day is tidied up. Power lines are restored, trains start running again, the wreckage of cars and lorries is gathered up from motorway verges. The pain of randomly-wrecked lives recedes to the inside pages of the tabloids, to disappear altogether within a few more days. The storm has touched us all in its passing. Attempts to sue the Met Office, it is reported, are likely to fail. Insurance companies mutter about 'acts of God' but pay out anyway. Nobody knows what to do with a disaster, even a minor one, that can't be blamed on someone.

Dan wishes his own life could be put back together so seamlessly. But Rex has prophesied correctly: a bulky envelope bearing a Luxembourg postmark and the insignia of EC Directorate General XLI (Archaeology and Heritage) has arrived in Dan's pigeonhole at the Institute. *Professor Daniel Robertson is hereby invited . . .*

The terms of reference of the enquiry into previous excavations at the site of Ano Meri, Crete, enclosed with the letter, run to seventy-five closely typed pages. Owing, presumably, to a clerical blunder, the copy enclosed for him is in Dutch. But the covering letter is expansive in the inducements it sets out, undreamt of in the chronically straitened circumstances of the Institute of Chronometry. A part-time salary is offered for the estimated twelve months that the enquiry will take. It is expressed and may only be paid in ecus, but a quick conversion suggests it is still a princely sum, almost as much as Dan earns from his full-time job. Allowable expenses are listed and at a first glance seem almost limitless. As he will shortly put it, incredulously, to Rex, 'It seems you can claim for using the Paris *pissoirs*, just so long as you send in your claim in ecus.' But at the bottom of the second page comes the final inducement, the one that brings him up short. He is entitled to apply (in ecus of course) for the costs of appointing a research assistant on a part-time basis, subject to limits which again seem by the standards around him highly generous.

It will not be the first time in recent months that Dan's thoughts have turned to his newly-recruited student, Milica.

Dan has read this letter over several times, has spent what seems like hours staring at it – in what Cathcart jovially, but without humour, has taken to calling 'the firm's time'. Guiltily he has taken it home and pored over it some more. It is evident that things do not happen with great despatch in Directorate General XLI. A response is requested by mid June.

'So you see my dilemma,' Dan has put it helplessly to Lucy. 'As a dedicated professional, I should put everything I know at the disposal of the committee and hope this thing will be properly cleared up. As *me* on the other hand, I'd far rather keep my head down, so that when the axe falls – as it's bound to, Lucy, you can feel it in the air – it isn't me it falls on. And then there's this other thing. The Europa Exhibition's going ahead this June in Cambridge. To commemorate seventy years of digging at Ano Meri. Anyone would think it's the worst possible time, but I suppose it would look even worse if they cancelled it. Anyway, Rex reckons it's part of a cover-up.'

Lucy looks shocked. 'How so?'

'Well, strictly speaking it's guesswork. But I think Rex is right. It's the establishment, you see, the old-guard Brits in other words, who see the old rogue as one of their own. They're going to gather round to show the world what a good old rogue he was really and how much he selflessly gave to archaeology, Crete and the world. (Anyone who doubts *that*, should be made to spend a night at Upland Grange Hotel!) I rather think the same establishment had a way of looking down the wrong end of their noses at Lionel Robertson when he was alive, but when the chips are down the British upper classes close ranks.

'Then on the other side come the Greeks bearing gifts, in this case the original Europa fragments from the Kastro museum; they've never allowed them out of the country before. It's supposed to be a gesture of goodwill, sending them here, but there's no such thing in archaeology. It's a chance for them to remind the world where European civilization came from, and at the same time up the stakes for the enquiry. The Greeks suspect the worst, that's natural enough, though I must say I don't believe it. From the records I've been looking at, the Robertsons were pretty scrupulous. All that ever found its way back to the Fitz was plaster casts and copies of Kreuzenberger's reconstructions.'

'So you get to choose: join the cops or join the robbers, is that it?'

'I'm damned if I even know which is which,' says Dan crossly. 'Cathcart keeps banging on at me to come off the fence. Make up my mind. National interest, some crap like that. But all Cathcart cares about is "relevance", and I don't know if he's got me lined up with the hieroglyphs for the high jump or finds me just too damn relevant for comfort. From his point of view, if I take part in the enquiry, I suppose he can shave a few bob off my salary, and it ought to put the Institute in a good light with the profession. On the other hand, he's a bit of a crawler is Dingo. Must be, to have got where he is. The old guard may feel it's worth their while to lean on him.'

*

But matters, it seems, are not to be left in Dingo's hands. It is in the second week of May, with less than a month to go before the opening of the exhibition in Cambridge, that an embossed invitation from the Institute's Director, for an 'informal dinner' at the home of one of the Trustees, arrives in Dan's letter box. Cautiously he tries it out on Rex, who shakes his head in wonder. Nobody has seen one of these before. 'They don't invite you to dinner "At Home" in order to sack you,' are Rex's cheerful parting words. But Dan is not reassured. Promising Rex a full report, he buys a new suit at half price from one of the shabby retailers in Oxford Street, and sets out on the appointed evening for Bayswater. The genial camaraderie of his closest colleagues, in the face of shared adversity, will be of no help to him here. This one Dan knows he must face alone.

He has some difficulty finding the address. It is smart enough to be in a square whose house numbers run half way up the neighbouring side streets. The plane trees are just coming into leaf. Tired botanical smells waft across the railings from the tiny locked garden in the centre of the square. His heart in his mouth, Dan rings the bell. A Filipino servant in livery invites him wordlessly to place his invitation on a silver tray, before spiriting it away. Another divests him of coat and briefcase. Dan wonders for a moment if he is to be searched as well but no, he is ushered upstairs. Either he is inexcusably early, or the party is to be a very small one. Lady Ottoline rises, takes him by the elbow and introduces him to their host. He has never met the new Director of the Institute, other than at a distance at meetings. He has no reason to suppose she could pick him out in a crowd or even knows his name, other than as an item to be ticked off on the staff list of the Institute. Now she guides him into the centre of the room. 'Daniel,' she simpers, 'I'd like you to meet the Chairman of our Trustees. George, may I introduce Daniel Robertson.' A blinking Dan finds himself shaking hands with a very large man indeed. A watch-chain hanging from his waistcoat pocket seems purposefully to advertise his protruding bulk. His hair, which is perfectly white, stands thickly upright on his head, making him look even taller than he is. His tortoiseshell glasses and upward slanting eyebrows have been lampooned by all the best-known cartoonists and animated on television in latex caricature. Dan has the presence of mind to recognize 'George', who is not otherwise introduced, as the Marquis of Peterloo. A Labour peer, obviously: Dan cannot for the life of him remember the man's real name, or what he is famous for. A career of potential political notoriety cut short by elevation to the Upper House, he seems to remember. George pats him on the back. 'Glad to have you aboard, Daniel,' he booms in a Mancunian accent that has by no means been overlaid.

The only other guest is a thin, restless man whose name Dan does not catch, only that he is 'an under-secretary at the Ministry'.

'Well,' booms George, as orders for drinks are unobtrusively taken, 'we may as well get down to brass tacks. Who's going to start the ball rolling?'

And the ball, so far as Dan can see, is none other than his own head. It is an evening, as he will relate to his daughter when it is safely over, injecting a degree of comedy that was far from his mind at the time, of the most refined torture. 'A most distinguished family, the Robertsons . . .' he hears. 'In the forefront of British archaeology in its pioneering days . . .'

'Well, of course, I . . .' But they are performing for each other as much as for Dan. His turn will come, two gins and tonic and half a dozen glasses of Chablis later. The momentum has not been lost over the 'intimate' dinner table (it has been a working supper), and now, faced with an exquisitely sculpted mountain of fresh fruit of every season and half the countries of the world, a veritable ziggurat of colours and shapes, all of them stolen from nature, the barrage has stopped and Dan feels three pairs of eyes at last upon him, three pairs of ears waiting, with not unlimited patience, to hear what he has to say. He feels himself falling, his lips are tight and trembling, his tongue is in the wrong place. He has bitten the inside of his cheek and he can taste the blood salty on top of the ripe fruit. He shouldn't have drunk so much. He only did it to steady his nerves. But his nerves have gone to pieces anyway. Worse, he cannot now remember the determined sallies that one after another rose up in him unbidden earlier in the evening, without the chance of being spoken.

'Can we get one thing straight?' Dan begins, hearing his voice thick and not quite focussing on the faces around him. '*You've got the wrong guy.*'

Dan glares at the shocked faces round the table.

'I beg your pardon?' The Marquis of Peterloo's eyebrows have risen higher than even their latex image has ever been seen to do on television.

'Don't you see, you've been talking all this time as though I were Lionel's son or somehow in his confidence and knew something about this whole sorry business. You keep calling me by my father's name, it's as though you're accusing *me* of something that was done before I was even born. It's not *my* name, don't you see? I'm Dan. And if that's too plebeian for you, you can call me Dr Robertson.' Dan pinches himself below the table. His discomfiture is embarrassing them. He will have to do better than this.

The man from the Ministry leans forward. 'Very well then, Dr Robertson,' he says, thereby freezing the social pretensions of the occasion beneath a bed of ice for which Dan has only himself to blame, 'we ask of you certain guarantees. It would scarcely be an exaggeration if I were to invoke the national interest.'

The beaming round face of Dingo Cathcart swims into Dan's mind, the glint of his flat lenses against the softwood veneer cabinet behind him. The very same words. And Cathcart's voice superimposes itself on the drily official tones of the man from the Ministry, to grate like sandpaper in Dan's inner ear.

'Let me see if I've got this right.' Dan is breathing heavily now. 'What you're suggesting is that if I give evidence, or take part in this enquiry, basically I'm letting the side down. The cat out of the bag. Our European partners into the tawdry secrets of good old British archaeology. I'm a kind of one-man, one-way Channel Tunnel, that's how you see it, isn't it? But there's another side to it too, can't you see that? I'm a professional working in an international field. There's no uniquely British fief in archaeology any more, not in the kind of advanced, theoretical archaeology I do, anyway. If I don't cooperate with this investigation, for one thing it will look as though *I'm* hiding something, which believe me I'm not.'

'No?' Lady Ottoline fixes him with the full hypnotic splendour of her gaze. 'I understand that you have been spending time at the Public Record Office, that you have examined the excavation notebooks from Ano Meri that are housed at the Fitzwilliam Museum. It has also not escaped my attention that certain papers of your late mother's were recently removed from the Robertson family home in Suffolk. You are not a disinterested party, Dan.'

'Of course I'm not disinterested, I never said I was. Yes, if you must know, it matters to me a great deal what skeletons may be lurking in the family cupboard and I've exercised a perfectly legitimate curiosity to try to find out. I've already told you, I haven't turned up any facts that aren't already publicly available. I'm as much in the dark as you are.'

Dan wishes he could clear his head of the Chablis. Three pairs of eyes are staring at him with an intensity that is almost tangible. He tries to order his thoughts. 'I don't see how I—' he stammers.

Lady Ottoline is leaning forward across the table, her forefinger moving up and down as it points towards him. 'Very well, Dan,' she breathes in her silky tones, 'we shall take you at your word. But, as we've explained to you tonight, there's more at stake than skeletons in your family cupboard. Now, what we ask of you is your cooperation in protecting the memory of your grandfather and your father.'

'And,' the Marquis's face is bright red by this stage of the evening, his voice hoarse with benevolent urgency, 'you must also consider your own feelings. If this enquiry goes ahead, you can't help attracting your share of the limelight. I don't think any of us round this table meant to accuse you of anything, Dan,' (George's eyes have almost disappeared behind the genial pouches of his face) 'but I can understand how you feel. That's what happens when the spotlight's on you. Believe me, I know,' and the Marquis casts mock-rueful glances at his companions to either side of him.

Dan looks down at his plate. 'All very well, but I don't see how. You can't just stop these things in their tracks. Maybe six years ago, when the discrepancy with the records was first noticed. But it's taken this long to get the enquiry off the ground. You can't just ring up Luxembourg and tell them to call the whole thing off. For one thing, why should they?'

218

'The simplest way to deal with a committee of enquiry,' Lady Ottoline's voice is deeper and huskier now, 'is to provide it with what it wants. No further investigation is then necessary, and the committee will have no choice but to disband itself.'

All heads have turned towards Lady Ottoline. The Marquis has twisted his features into an expression of polite puzzlement; the man from the Ministry merely looks expectant, giving the game away.

'I don't understand,' says Dan, the only one who doesn't.

Lady Ottoline's hair is rigidly permed, Dan cannot tell if the streaks of grey that are discernible this close are natural or not. There are tiny wrinkles round her mouth and her eyes, but they do not seem to Dan kindly. 'The possibility we have to consider,' she says carefully, 'is quite simply that nothing was suppressed at all. If there were some perfectly innocent explanation . . . ?' The question is left hanging, its suggestiveness coils round Dan with a force that is almost irresistible.

'But surely, we know already—' Dan tries to protest, but Lady Ottoline's look is enough to dry the words in his throat.

With a brilliant smile, she sweeps on, 'On the face of it, it is perfectly possible that the records were mislaid for no better reason than that there was nothing of importance in them. Intuitively, the unbiased observer will surely see it that way. All that is lacking is the proof.' Lady Ottoline pauses long enough for the significance of her words to sink in. 'Harold?' She beams suddenly towards the no longer nameless man from the Ministry, who seems to brighten under her gaze.

'Yes, quite so, Lady Ottoline.' He coughs before continuing. 'Documentary proof, obviously. Not a full excavation record. It would be a miracle if that turned up now. No harm in looking for it, of course, but I gather that has been done already.' Dan looks down hastily towards his plate to avoid the appraising glance directed at him. 'No, I think something more informal would fit the bill. A document of the time, whose authenticity no one can doubt. I think such a document might be found.'

'And this document,' George interposes loudly, 'supposing of course such a document existed – you would submit it to the enquiry?'

The man from the Ministry, almost animated now under the continuing radiance of Lady Ottoline's eyes, raises his hands from the table. 'Good lord, no. That would be tantamount to recognizing that the constitution of the enquiry was necessary in the first place. Certainly not.' His voice drops. 'Ministerial channels, George. A quiet word from the Minister to the EC Commissioner for Arts and Heritage. A little bombshell,' Harold permits himself a deprecating smile, 'dropped from a great height.'

'The point is, Dan,' Lady Ottoline's voice is pure velvet now, 'if you have in your possession evidence that could be used to support this – intuition, I should be grateful if you would bring it to me without delay. Harold will be responsible for the rest.'

Dan can feel the room begin to sway around him. The absolute reasonableness of Lady Ottoline's voice, the seductive ease of the solution held out to him, the prospect of release it offers from an uncertain future and a dizzying past, is almost more than he can bear. Relief spreads through him, beginning at his toes and ending at the tips of his ears, which are burning, which must be the colour of beetroot. This was how it used to be when he'd got into some scrape at school. And as he stares at the rock-like, grainy features of Lady Ottoline confronting him across the table, other things come back to him too. Dan, as a child, had never been able to lie to his mother.

There is a leadweight at the bottom of his stomach. 'I would like to help you,' he says now. 'But I'm not sure I can.'

'It's a matter of loyalty, Dan. You owe it to your family, and the Institute. If this information, whatever it turns out to contain, were to find its way to the committee of enquiry, if you yourself were to take part in what is, after all, a form of witch hunt – well, you do see, don't you? You must recognize where your loyalties lie.'

'And if I don't?'

Lady Ottoline's voice is sharper than the silver fork that stops halfway to her mouth. 'You have a job, Dan – *a job for life.*'

12 THE SCANDAL

THE exhibition is to be a retrospect and an appreciation of the life and career of the old rogue, Dan's grandfather. When the Robertson Collection was sold off after Lionel's death, many of the better pieces found their way into the basement of the Fitzwilliam, where they have remained unseen, except by a few experts, ever since. Some of the sculptures collected on Lionel's Balkan travels are to be brought up for the occasion. Several of the letters and notebooks Dan has unearthed in the Public Record Office will also be on show. Firmly placed under glass, to prevent the curious from leafing through in search of further scandal, the excavation notebooks from Ano Meri, which have long been in the possession of the museum, will also be displayed, opened at carefully selected pages. There will be photos of the excavation, beginning with that first triumphant season in 1920, and continuing intermittently until the very eve of the Second World War, blown-up colour pictures from the sixties (Dan himself appears in some, in shorts and tee-shirt) and the whole thing will round off with the EC dig that has now, in its turn, dragged to a halt for lack of agreement on how to spend the budget.

Dan can feel his daughter's attention flagging as she sits curled up in the passenger seat of his much-travelled 2CV. The motorway to Cambridge is crowded on this hot June day, and Dan is in sombre mood. His attendance at the opening of the exhibition is obligatory, he has been dreading it for months. There has even been an invitation for Lucy ('unto the *n*th generation,' she whistled with disbelief when it came), but as it happens it is the night of the May Ball at her old college. Since she has asked him his opinion frankly, Dan has without hesitation taken the unselfish course and assured her that of the two the May Ball is bound to be the more fun. But he is glad to have her company on the drive. To be honest, it's Milica, who might have been curled up in the back seat, her hair blowing in the wind from the open roof on this hot day in early June, that he misses most.

'I thought it was all about this painting of a woman bonking with a bull.'

Lucy's slightly petulant tone brings Dan abruptly back to the present.

'I don't know what they teach you in psychoanalysis,' Dan laughs. 'But yes, it's to be the Europa Exhibition, and pride of place goes to the fresco from the throne room, Europa and the Bull.'

'Sounds like just another myth of origins, and a typically male one too. Don't tell me archaeologists still go in for that kind of crap?'

'Don't *you* start,' Dan protests. 'That was the way they did archaeology in those days. Don't forget these people had the classics drilled into them at school. I told you, my father read Livy in the trenches, in the First World War. *My* kind of archaeologist doesn't take much notice of that kind of crap, as you put it; and the old rogue's been pilloried for it anyway in all the specialist journals. So what, he found the fresco. *And* it's not pornographic. I don't know where you got that idea from.'

'Anyway,' says Lucy, with a change of tack but not, he suspects, of subject, 'when are you going to get down to those diaries Milica's looking after for you? I must say it all sounds a bit over the top to me, whisking them away from the Institute before Cathcart and his mob can prise open your filing cabinet. You still haven't read them through, have you, Dan?'

It is to Milica, who has modestly confided that she has some experience of such things, and Dan wonders with some concern what she can mean, that he has entrusted the safekeeping of his mother's diaries, since the dinner in Bayswater. He trusts Milica. But beneath that trust lurks a real reluctance to read them to the end. It won't do, and Dan knows it.

The traffic grinds slowly past coned-off stretches of motorway. 'No,' he confesses miserably. 'Let's get the exhibition over with first. I don't know if those people will have given up or will come back to put more pressure on. I think I'll find that out tonight. Then I've still got another week before I have to reply to Luxembourg, remember? I've got it worked out, Lucy. After tonight, I'll know what to do. I'm sure of it.'

But his daughter can be remorseless. He has had the feeling lately that she is practising on him without his knowledge. What *do* trainee psychoanalysts do to train? She has always been much better at extracting information from him than he has from her.

'There's something you're afraid you're going to find in those diaries, Dan, isn't there? All this elaborate business of hiding them, wicked Madame Tussaud and her fraudulent plot, it's not really them you're afraid of. More often than not these things turn out to be alibis for our deepest—'

'I know, I know,' Dan interrupts crossly. 'Freud and the Id. ID parades of the mind. What was that awful stuff you were so excited about last week, the "mirror stage"? Parent holds up child to mirror, the physog looking out at you is *you*, your *self*, but what's the shadowy form behind you, holding you up, giving you that self and taking it away again? Something like that, wasn't it?'

'Hey, that's good, Dan! We'll get you on to Lacan yet. Next lesson is the *nom-du-père*.'

'The *what*?"

'It's French, Dan.' Lucy can be infuriatingly reasonable at times.

'I know it's French. The name of the father. But what does it mean?'

He shouldn't have asked of course. But at least it deflects Lucy from probing the secrets of his unconscious that he can only wish were buried more deeply. Dan finds the explanation hard to follow. It's nothing to do with anyone's real father, she assures him. Rather it's a shorthand expression, like a function in mathematics. It isn't a name and it isn't a person. So far as Dan can see it's a kind of shadow, a deprivation, a provocation to desire. 'An inevitable consequence of patriarchy, Dan,' Lucy consoles him now. Dan has never seen himself as much of a patriarch, and banteringly denies the charge. 'It's not something you or I can help, Dan, we're all part of it. It's a system, and it determines the way we are.'

But beneath the easy banter with his daughter, Dan cannot help thinking of the forbidden name of Lionel's son, his father, that has lain like a shadow over so much of his life. He has always taken a deep pleasure in his daughter's lack of inhibition, even when he also finds it disturbing. He wonders anew at the ease with which the tender 'daddy' he can still remember first became 'dad' and imperceptibly slipped to 'Dan'. But a shadow there has been over Lucy's life too, and its outline, its contours, Dan knows full well, are his own.

He doesn't deserve Lucy, he reflects, not for the first time.

As he drives at last into a tourist-packed Cambridge, disdaining the 'Park and Ride' facilities blazoned on signposts on the way in, and drops Lucy off at a gated portal on Trumpington Street, Dan's thoughts are still troubled by twenty-year-old memories of this city. Almost as old as Lucy herself. Dan always feels uncomfortable on the rare occasions he comes here. The sense of guilt that Cambridge brings back to him, and that has been heightened, though Lucy could not have known it, by the conversation in the car, will not help him tonight.

Dan has more than an hour to kill before the evening reception which will mark the start of the exhibition. Prompted by some instinct that Lucy would doubtless have been able to find a word for, he parks the car and heads not for the Edwardian tranquillity of King's Backs but out towards the railway, where he quickly loses himself in a maze of two-storey terraced houses of yellowish-grey Cambridgeshire brick fronting directly on the street.

The front door in Gwydir Street has been painted maroon, there are pot plants behind lace curtains in the front window, the inevitable shabby bicycle padlocked against the wall. He has taken many twists and turns through these identical, interlocking streets, many of them cul-de-sacs, to find himself here. Now in memory Dan passes through the front door that was not maroon then, but a pale, rather bilious green. Inside, in the tiny sitting room playing by the gas fire, his daughter Lucy is almost three. She it is who leaps up, as a flurry of wintry fenland air sweeps through the room before he can shut the door against it, and leads him forward excitedly to show him the tower she is building out of bricks. Margaret is there and for the first time, after six years of marriage, Dan finds it necessary to avoid her eyes. He chucks his daughter under the chin, Lucy grabs firm hold of his finger and starts to tell him about the tower and about Johnnie who came to play. Dan squats down to listen, with a wink over his shoulder to Margaret. He is absorbed all at once by his daughter's small features, by the friendly popping of the gas fire. Coming in from the outside world there is an aroma here that he hasn't consciously noticed before because it is part of him, an aroma of soapflakes and starch and slightly fusty carpets; the kettle is whistling from the kitchen.

In those days Margaret was working part-time at Sainsbury's, her doctorate on Bronze Age Cretan pottery successfully completed. Dan had been commuting for some time to the Institute of Chronometry in London. It was only a matter of time before they moved to London, but Margaret wasn't keen. Cambridge – even the Sainsbury's check-out, where some of the most intelligent people in the world smiled at you benignly as you pointed out the year on the cheque should now be 1970, and you could hug the autograph to yourself for a precious second before stashing the cheque away in the till – was synonymous for Margaret with civilization. Dan, whose own doctorate has been more modestly acquired in London, still feels an outsider here. It is the first home they have bought together, in a terrace put up more than a century ago to house college servants and now much sought after by the latest generation of hopefuls trying to secure a foothold on the academic ladder, and poorly protected against the winds of the Fens. What's more, Dan's mother has not been in good health recently; the house in South London, small though it was after Upland Grange, is not easy for her to manage just now. The suggestion has been made that they should sell up in Cambridge and move in with Dan's mother. Margaret has always been a little overawed by Dan's mother, which is another reason she is reluctant to make the move.

As a result Dan has more than once had to stay away overnight lately, spending the night at his mother's. He can understand Margaret's feelings. There is a serene rectitude about his mother in her mid sixties, an unflappable grandeur that is, so far as he can see, entirely benign, untarnished by anything so base as competitiveness or disapproval, but he can see how these qualities might seem offputting to someone who had not known her, as he has, since childhood. He has always had the feeling that his mother's life was complete and finished before ever he was born. The years of Upland Grange, the trauma of what she first, and then imperceptibly he too, began to call his 'exile', the gaze of her eye as it fell on him and he could only ever think of it with love, as the gaze of love, but not love in the way the word is used, in the way he has got into the habit of using it himself, all these things came out of a life that had already known all the joy and perhaps all the grief too that can be allotted to a single human span. Dan understood this in his mother's grey eyes. Once he had sat on her knee and she read to him. Later, before he was married and Lucy was born, she scolded him and would exclude him sometimes from her house for weeks at a time until he apologized for some thoughtlessness, which eventually, cringing with a shame that only she could induce in him, he would do and only then be allowed back into the calm oasis of his South London bolt-hole. Much later still, when she lay dying, her austerely combed head propped on white pillows, she could no longer speak, only stared up at him out of those grey eyes. This time there was nothing she could do, no miracle she could perform to set things right for him, but even then her eyes had held a depth of love that he knew would shore him up even beyond the finality of death, and so, he supposes now, confronting a maroon front door in Gwydir Street in June 1990, there are still after a whole decade tears yet to be shed that can unman him without warning, if he isn't careful it's going to happen to him now . . .

So it was both an anxiety and a relief to spend the occasional night in London when Lucy was three. His mother wouldn't let him do anything for her; he was more worried than he would have admitted, even to Margaret, about her recent illness. Even then, he couldn't contemplate the hole in his life that her death would one day leave. And all this – he could understand it, but it irked him too – Margaret saw as a threat, almost as a rival affection. Which made moving to London more difficult.

On these occasions he would invariably ring up night and morning. *Are you all right darling? And the baby?* Lucy is hardly a baby any more, but this is the form Dan's solicitude takes. And it is at his mother's, on a night when the wind lifts slates from the roof and he is more than usually anxious about the state of things in Gwydir Street, that the telephone wakes him, something past midnight. He leaps to the phone, his heart in his mouth. He hears the pips of a coinbox. What can have happened? 'Margaret, darling—' he almost gasps out before he registers the unfamiliar voice on the line. As he listens he blinks stupidly, then turns on the light on the upstairs landing. His mother appears, majestic and dishevelled, in the door of her room; he waves her back to bed, with a nod that all is well. In spite of himself, he feels his pulses racing. It can't be, after all those years. But Paola – where have you *been*? Why didn't you—?

According to Paola her plane from Rome to New York has been blown off course. Surely such things don't happen nowadays? The voice at the other end sounds hurt, then urgent. She has not many coins left. Until eight o'clock tomorrow she will be at the Airport Hotel, Heathrow. She knows no one in

London and it is a terrible night. Dan, will you come to me? You will come, do say you will come.

There is something mesmeric in the voice, even as distorted by the phone. He feels his insides turning over as he glances wildly about the familiar ornaments, the threadbare carpet of his mother's landing. 'How did you know where to—?' But there is a sharp click at the other end of the line. Paola has run out of coins.

For several minutes he stares stupidly at his feet, his thoughts in turmoil. *Do you drop everything in the middle of the night*–and Paola is right, it is a terrible night, he can hear the rain beating on the skylight – to drive half way across London to Heathrow because someone phones you up that you can't have seen more than half a dozen times in as many years? There are any number of things he could have said to her, from *send me a postcard from New York*, to—. But this is just the trouble, he can't think of any way he could have said no to that mesmeric voice, so commanding; but it wasn't that, she didn't know anyone in London she said, the voice sounded so *lost*. Seemingly without any conscious control over his actions at all, Dan finds himself stumbling back to his room, groping for his clothes. Surely this is worse than folly?

He leaves a note for his mother, explaining that he has taken her car and will be back in the afternoon. Something's happened at the Institute, but no need to worry, I'll phone. With terrifying lucidity he realizes the purpose of the note isn't reassurance at all, it's just so his mother won't ring up Margaret. And Dan has been an exemplary husband for six years now. As he drives, hunched over the wheel, through torrential rain, losing his way a couple of times on the South Circular, his heart is still pounding and his thoughts are all of Paola. Paola in the blazing sun of Crete, Paola in the red bikini, Paola deep in conversation with Margaret, the wistful look of mischief in those olive-dark, almond eyes. Paola at his and Margaret's wedding. Teasing flirtations that were never more than that, on the fringe of august gatherings of archaeologists – Dan was engaged to be married, wasn't he, and Paola had more than once placed a reproving finger on his lips when despite everything, Dan felt himself capable of throwing away all that he had been so painstakingly, so lovingly building around him in those years. The gushingly ornate card that popped through the letter box one day and for a short time only punctured the easygoing equilibrium of Dan's present life: Paola was announcing her forthcoming marriage. And a cryptic postcard from the Caribbean on her honeymoon. That was the last he has heard of Paola, until now.

Her summons has come through the rain from another life; it is not the Dan he knows who is hastening now to answer it, it is that other Dan whose life split off from his in the orange grove under the stars, the Dan who was lifted out of himself by the heat and light of a Cretan beach, who entered then, in the sleeping presence of Margaret, the forbidden territory he has been banished from ever since, and that other Dan has lain dormant as his own life has unfolded, has lain unsuspected, waiting, waiting for the phone to ring, poised to spring back into full existence, to pick up the thread that has lain underground for so long, to set the interrupted story into motion once more.

It is this other, hidden Dan, who leaps from the car under the arc lights of the Airport Hotel and stands blinking in the lobby, trying to shake the rain from his clothes. Without embarrassment he asks for Paola's room. In an airport hotel, it seems, nothing is unusual. Moments later Paola has flung herself into his arms. She is largely, but not completely, undressed.

'You came! I can't believe it. How wonderful you are,' and Dan is unexpectedly ready to bask in the reflected glow of her wonder. It has not occurred to him that she might have doubted his coming. He *feels* wonderful. He tells her so and she cavorts around him, waving her arms and laughing. He has never in his life felt so relaxed as now in her presence. He has never felt so much at home as here and now, in this place of transit where he has never been before.

Dan sits, fully clothed and still damp from the rain, on the edge of her wide double bed. They are on the tenth floor and the sounds of the tempest outside are magnified here. Every so often a jet plane goes by overhead, sounding very close, and the whole room shakes. Paola is talking and laughing all at once, remembering past meetings, things they have done together, people in the archaeological world they both know. Something she says reminds Dan, with a sudden surge of chagrin and anxiety, that Paola is married now.

'So are you, had you forgotten?' she chides him.

In panic Dan looks round for signs of male occupancy in the room. He couldn't at that moment have told whether his panic was lest Franco (all Dan will ever know of Paola's husband is his name) should suddenly turn out to be with her after all, and the night's drama is going to end in farcical anti-climax, or that he isn't, and the fantasy that has sustained him all the way here from South London is about to turn into reality, with consequences his more sober self can already see stretching without hope of disentanglement into the future. It is a moment, he can see in hindsight, when his life was balanced on a knife-edge.

There comes a knock at the door. Almost with relief Dan jumps off the bed, but Paola has already swept a startlingly bright kimono over her shoulders and gone to answer it. Laughter is bubbling up in her face, her eyes are brimful of happy anticipation as she returns to him. She has ordered champagne.

A long while later, as he lies awake in the darkness with her head cradled in the hollow of his shoulder, he asks her dreamily, reflectively, 'Why did you do it, all these years ago? A strange dream you called it, remember? I don't know what you meant to do but you gave me something terribly precious. And took away something too.'

Paola is coiled into the darkness at his side, he can hear her breathing lightly, she is not asleep. But she doesn't answer.

'Some men would say it was a pretty mean trick to play,' he insists, but still gently.

'Dan, Dan, you don't understand. I wasn't married then.'

Dan is almost shocked. 'I should think not.'

He can feel her propping her face on her elbow to search for his features in the darkness. Puzzlement and irritation are in her voice. 'Dan, I am a Catholic. It was expected I would make a good marriage. In Italy you don't make a good marriage unless you are a virgin.'

'And—' the name is difficult to say, but despite everything he is indignant now on her behalf '—and Margaret?'

'We talked it over,' says Paola simply. 'Margaret didn't want to be a virgin.'

'And now you're married – you can do what you like. Is that it?'

'My husband,' says Paola with audible relish, 'is rich enough he can buy himself women anywhere. And he goes – because he is rich – of course everywhere. I think he is in Buenos Aires now. Perhaps it is Manila. And I am travelling to New York, via London. And we can drink champagne and make as much love as we like in the best suite in this a little bit shabby hotel. You see?'

Dan feels wakefulness returning. 'Hey wait a minute. You said your plane had been diverted, you didn't *expect*—'

'Do you wish I hadn't come?'

And the only answer to that, of course, is to make love again.

It is not a happy Dan who gets off the train at Cambridge station a little more than twelve hours later. He has concocted his cover story. There really has been damage at the Institute caused by the storm last night. For only the second time in its history, Foucault's pendulum has had to be stopped and taken down, for repairs to be made to the roof. It will make a narrative to tide him over the shameful crossing of the threshold back into his old, his present life. It will be like waking from a dream, he has insisted to himself all through the bleariness of the day, and even while his head nodded forward half-asleep on the train. A strange dream, in all conscience. And one, he is absolutely clear about this, that will never be repeated. The unfinished business of his Cretan summers, the unfulfilled desire that had lain dormant for so long, has reached its appointed end and that is that. All that matters now is to fit himself back inside the draughty house in Gwydir Street, back inside the familiar, comforting contours of his marriage. If asked at this time, did he love his wife, Dan might have been a shade puzzled by the question, but would assuredly have answered: yes.

But in the event, his tale of Foucault's pendulum turns out to be superfluous.

228

'So what a surprise,' Margaret greets him, as he pushes the door shut against the flurry of wintry fenland air that sweeps through the room. 'Paola being in town,' she prompts, responding to a look that he hopes is blank. But already Lucy has taken him by the hand and is leading him forward toward the gas fire where she has been building a tower of bricks. He allows himself to be absorbed all at once by his daughter's small features, by the brightness of her chatter. The homely aroma of the room envelopes him. The kettle is whistling from the kitchen. How could he have forgotten the strong warmth of Margaret's voice offering to make the tea, the reassuring firmness of her shoulders and buttocks as she moves towards the kitchen? Last night took place on another planet. Last night never happened.

With a pat on the head to Lucy, he moves after Margaret, coming up behind her as she pours the water from the kettle. Kissing her chastely on the back of the neck, he says softly, 'So you know about Paola?'

Disengaging herself, Margaret half turns to face him. There are blue veins round her eyes, but that is nothing unusual. Margaret is often tired these days. He discovers in a panic that he cannot read her face. Disappointments he has not thought to ask about have moulded the palely-freckled cheeks, have etched lines beneath the fringe of mouse-ginger hair. The eyes she turns on him seem suddenly to have suffered their share of pain, the anxieties of motherhood, and to accept them with a stoical, almost a placid resignation. She fits the tea cosy over the pot. 'Get a couple of mugs, will you, darling?' she says, and leads the way back to the sitting room and the fire. 'Of course I know about Paola. She rang up – oh, not long after lunch, Lucy was just waking from her nap.'

Dan stares into the gas fire. At eight o'clock that morning Paola was supposed to be leaving the hotel to catch her flight on to New York.

'It was quite like old times with Paola. Didn't you think so? She doesn't sound as though she's changed a bit.'

Dan doesn't know what to think. Dan for the moment is incapable of thinking. He nods miserably and stares into the gas fire. Dumbly he says, 'I'll get the milk for the tea, shall I?'

'Are you all right, darling?' she calls after him.

He stumbles back with the milk. Margaret doesn't seem to mind not talking about Paola. And he cannot bring himself to ask, certainly not in front of little Lucy, what Paola can have said. Later perhaps, in bed – assuming, that is, she will still share her bed with him – he will try to explain. But already he knows he will do no such thing. What has been can be neither defended nor explained, it simply *is*. And since Margaret in her own stoical way seems able to live with it, then so must he. His marriage has been saved, though not in the way he had planned. There will be no lies and no evasions, no tall tales (even if this one, coincidentally, happens to be true) about Foucault's pendulum.

As he drifts off to sleep, an arm round Margaret's shoulder and her broad buttock comfortably curled against him, he feels the beginning of a deep gratitude to Margaret. Trust her not to make a fuss. He still loves her as he has always loved her since that night in the orange grove under the meteors. Margaret is someone you can rely on. Which is more than he can say for Paola.

And as sleep takes him, comes the last insidious twist of the day's composite act of cowardice. Bless you most especially and above all, Margaret: this way, it can happen again. And Dan's sleep is, for the time being, blissful.

It's like what they say about murder, Dan mused to himself as he packed his sponge bag: it gets easier each time. They were living in London now, at his mother's house. His mother was much better, but the arrangement suited everybody, and Lucy had just started at the same South London primary school he had once gone to himself.

'You didn't tell me you were going to be away, darling,' Margaret loomed with mild reproach in the bathroom door.

'Didn't I say, darling? Paola's in town. We—'

And in the look of utter horror that suddenly transforms Margaret's blandly long-suffering face he sees mirrored the sinking feeling that goes right through the bottom of his stomach and leaves him cold and trembling inside. It is a moment that is fixed, like a cinema still, in his memory. Himself with sponge bag in one hand, toothbrush in the other. Margaret, her eyes like holes bored deep through her face, one hand on the doorjamb, perhaps for support, the other clenched, knuckles white, in front of her mouth.

Years later, when they were amicably, sensibly planning the divorce, she said to him, 'It was the casual way you let it drop. As though I was always supposed to know I was part of a *ménage à trois*. Suddenly it stripped away everything that had been up until that moment, I saw our marriage as something completely different. And I suppose I just sort of assumed it'd always been like that. That you'd been – carrying on with Paola from the beginning and I'd been so obtuse not to notice.'

Now, as the bathroom floor seems to buck and dip beneath his feet and he wishes for nothing so much as to be able to sink through it and never be seen again, Dan can do no more than stammer, 'I thought – oh God, Margaret, I thought – you and Paola—' And suddenly he knows what it is he wants to say and only just manages to hold back the words, even as he stands there facing the horror in her face, with toothbrush in one hand and sponge bag in the other, he feels nothing but disgust at his own pathetic cowardice: you and Paola made it all right between you, somehow, woman to woman, I don't understand, but you made it all right, didn't you, like you did that first time?

But Margaret's mind too, it seems, has gone back to that extraordinary night in the orange grove, and it is only now, slightly over a decade later, that that scene is played through to the devastating emptiness of its final line: 'That night, in Crete. *You thought I was Paola, didn't you?*'

In the sensible accord that has taken the best part of another decade to build, Dan can spread his hands helplessly and remind her of these words. 'You didn't exactly go out of your way to disabuse me, now did you? What did you and she cook up between you that night?'

But Margaret's long-suffering resignation has by this time given way to bitter fatalism. There are lines among the pale freckles of her cheeks, a new hardness in the blue shadows beneath her eyes. 'I suppose the truth is, we both deceived you a little bit, Dan. It took me a long time to learn how much I'd also deceived myself. I suppose deep down I believed it was me you loved really, not her. I believed it because I wanted to believe it. I wanted to very badly, you know. Can you imagine that, now? But I did.' She laughs shortly. They are (it has been a conscious decision, they have worked hard at this) friends. 'I must have seen an awful lot in you, Dan Robertson.' And at the comical, rueful, desolate look on her face it is all Dan can do to stop himself coming over to sit beside her on the sofa, put his arms round her and draw her to him to comfort her and laugh together at the foolish mess they have made of twenty years of adult life. It isn't so easy, this business of being friends. And because he knows that, and they are both determined to be sensible, he stays where he is and the moment passes.

Back in the bathroom, it seemed to Dan the frozen moment would never end. And then the noise came from her throat. A tearing, ugly noise, not the sound of crying, not a shout, there were no words behind this noise, it was the naked, brute sound of grief, no words of his could ever reach to where that sound came from, involuntarily her fingers pulled at her cheeks, it was an inhuman face that faced him across the bathroom, it was as though he had indeed done a murder and was watching the degradation of a mortally wounded human being into something hideous and inert before his eyes.

'Stop it,' he shouted. In terror he leapt forward and slapped her face. The sound stopped, but she continued looking at him with eyes that held no recognition in them. She took a step into the room.

'Margaret. Darling.' It was an appeal of helplessness.

Suddenly she sat down on the side of the bath and the tears came. He moved close to her and tried to put an arm across her shoulders, but she shook him off furiously.

'How long has this been going on?' she hissed at him, her face still buried in her hands.

'Darling, it's only since—' he could hear his own voice start to break '—you see, I thought you *knew*. It's got nothing to do with – us.' But this already sounded hollow. 'I promise you, I'll stop it this very night.'

She dropped her hands from her eyes and stared at him. Her face had turned into wet, streaked putty, it seemed to have no shape. 'You can look at me and talk of – going to *her*? And *tonight*?'

'I tell you, I'll break it off. Any way you like. But I can't just—'

'What, you can't just walk out on her casually like you've done on me, is that what you mean? "Oh just packing my bag, Paola's in town you see." "Sorry Paola, can't come fucking with you tonight, the wife's been making a scene." Can't you, by God.'

And she stares at him, neither of them seeming to believe what is happening.

'All right, all right.' Dan finds this anger preferable to what has gone before. The awful, never-ending moment is over. It will all, in a sense, be downhill from here. The world is not quite where it was, in relation to his feet, but at least he is standing on something. He can pick up the pieces, put something back together. 'I'm sorry,' he offers lamely.

But Margaret has now stopped crying. 'Sorry. You're sorry. You bust up my whole life oh so casually, "Paola's in town, you see" – and God knows what this is going to mean for Lucy, I suppose you hadn't even thought of that, had you? – and then turn round as easy as anything: "Sorry".' She is shouting at him now. 'I don't even think you *are* sorry. Not for what you've done. You're sorry because it never seems to have occurred to you I'd mind. That's what it is, isn't it? What do you mean, *thought I knew*? How was I going to bloody know if you didn't bloody tell me? So you just drop it in ever so casually, "That bitch is in town", and see how I take it, I suppose? Well I'm not taking it. Now go on, pack your bloody sponge bag and clear out. Off you go, have a good fuck. How many fucks do you get in a night, with *her*? Make the most of it, they're all the fucks you're getting in a long while, make no mistake of that. And when that bitch is no longer in town,' Margaret stands up, arms on her sides, 'you can come back with your tail between your legs and we'll talk about what happens next.'

And so Dan finds himself thrown out of his mother's house, with nowhere to go but Paola's hotel, with the mirrored suite and, he has no doubt, champagne on ice all night. He has never felt less like sex in his whole life.

But neither is he so certain, any more, of his promise to break with Paola.

The Cambridge evening air is still and balmy. The streets are full of young people dressed up in the glittering fashions of fifty, a hundred years ago. The May Ball season is at its height. Dan has re-traversed the populous arteries at the centre of the city, leaving behind the maze of streets that has once again swallowed up the maroon front door and the sealed memories of twenty years ago. Soon, beneath its massive classical pediment, the Fitzwilliam Museum will be opening its portals to the great and good who have been invited here tonight, to honour the tarnished memory of Lionel Robertson, CBE.

232

Dan has known for some time that Paola is fading out of his life. Almost literally: with every postcard, every late-night phone call out of the blue, he can feel her presence getting fainter. Paola belongs in the past now. Over the years, she has slipped away from him between the refracting planes, leaving only the mirrors of her hotel suite behind, dull and empty, and even now, as his imagination returns to that room of so many tumultuous lovemakings, the bright surfaces have misted over, the ghost of a landscape begins to show through, a real landscape with trees and roads and hills, he can't place it, it doesn't matter, but it means there *is* life out there after all, there *is* life for Dan beyond Paola's fortieth birthday. Beyond the surprise party in the flat in Milan when for the first and only time in her life, it seems, Paola invited all her friends and, it was thoroughly suspected among the gathering, her lovers past and present – only to bunk out at the last minute. Or more likely that, too, had been carefully planned as part of the entertainment. Like the champagne in the jacuzzi and the fatally compromising message left by a well-known senator that somebody discovered on the answering machine, as the search for any clue to their hostess's whereabouts degenerated into a party game of some sophistication. The message, once found, was played over and over, plugged into the amplifier and played again, as the nuances of the senator's breathing drew whoops of riotous applause and the sexes mingled freely in the bubbling jacuzzi until someone started off a tasteless whisper about AIDS, those had been the early days of AIDS, no one quite knew, but it put a dampener on the party, where Dan found himself in any case a disconsolate loner. He had only come to see Paola, and help tide her over the watershed of forty that he knew she had been dreading so much.

And rather as she herself seemed to have wanted, now that she has left his life, it is as though she no longer exists. He is quite incurious about what she is doing now. Can she really have entered a nunnery? He doesn't think it likely. The thought of Paola, the real person, out there somewhere, hardly stirs him at all. But Paola's entrances and exits, the visits to the opera, to experimental theatre, the hotel suite with the mirrors, that have punctuated his life, are still indelibly part of him. He imagines her presence infinitely dissolving like a homeopathic medicine: never vanishing (Paola is in his hair, his nails, Paola is a taste, a smell, a writhing warmness that surely even old age will not take from him), but no longer there, no longer occupying space in his life, to prompt words, action, above all the evasions and the half-lies that for two decades of his life were second nature to him – and he has still not fully kicked the habit.

The Fitz have certainly pushed the boat out tonight, Dan thinks to himself as he waves his invitation card under the nose of a flunkey who tries to bar his entrance. He has disdained the formal dress that seems to be ubiquitous around him. If he had hoped to be inconspicuous, turning up in a loose-fitting suit of brown corduroy with patches on the elbows and cuffs, and the light haversack that goes everywhere with him, the last vestige of his field training as an archaeologist, he has to admit to himself that he has failed. Before penetrating the august austerity of the galleries he has been obliged, for security reasons, to submit his inoffensive haversack for examination, then to exchange it at the cloakroom for a metal tag with a number on it. Now, wearing an identifying badge that another flunkey has laboriously matched up with the name on his invitation, Dan enters at last the company of the great and good.

There is a loud murmur in the galleries. Only a few people seem to be looking at the objects in cases and placed around the walls. Dan feels suddenly lonely and exposed. A glass of wine is pressed into his hand. Someone whose name he ought to remember is at his elbow. He takes a deep breath. There is no escape. The exhibition is about to be opened.

The gallery is full of people. There are the ambassadors of at least two countries whose soil the old rogue has probed in his time and whose treasures have found their way, by one route or another, to Cambridge and the exhibition now being mounted. HMG has even contributed a transient Minister for the Arts and a couple of burly minders who stand out in this company almost as much as Dan himself. Greek high society is also well represented, recognizable by the skin-tight gold lamé mini-dresses of the women. Dan vaguely recognizes one or two of the richest patrons of modern archaeological science, the unassuming and surprisingly friendly scions of families whose names enter daily every household in the land, branded on packets of detergent or supermarket carrier bags. But overwhelmingly this is a gathering of archaeologists, amateurs as well as professionals, historians of art as well as prehistorians. And what is being talked among the largely ignored exhibits, as at all such tribal gatherings, is shop.

But not all the exhibits are being ignored. An animated group has gathered in front of the fresco panels which have been reproduced on the covers of so many archaeological textbooks and tourist guides to Crete. It is the modern reconstruction of this fresco by Reinhard Kreuzenberger that everybody, including Dan, is familiar with. He has seen the original only once before, in the museum in Kastro, and remembers his disappointment with the jigsaw of plaster fragments, blackened by damp and cracked by the passage of more than three thousand years. The vibrant colours, the hint of *art nouveau* in the starkly drawn lines, many details of the composition, as it has become famous throughout the world since that momentous discovery in 1920, can only be guessed at from the original fragments. It is in front of these fragments, which have been specially loaned by the Greek government for the occasion – the 'real thing' as one of them expresses it with plump satis-

234

faction – that the group now stands in reverential awe.

A post-structuralist historian of art is explaining in a braying voice how Kreuzenberger got it wrong. The young girls gathering saffron on the shore, who are supposed to be Europa's handmaids, are really monkeys. It was only the ideology of late capitalism, especially as manifested in the quasi-fascistic subtext of the Munich school where Kreuzenberger had studied before the First World War, that dictated a hermeneutic strategy that . . .

Dan moves away to the other side of the gallery, where the reconstruction, that has been reproduced so often, has its permanent place in the museum. Here he finds more congenial company. The ground floor of the Institute of Chronometry is well represented: Rex is there and Jennifer Southern, who seem to be sparring amicably in front of Kreuzenberger's handiwork.

Jennifer is well launched upon her current theory of lustral basins, those mysterious sunken areas in the Minoan palaces. Dan has heard it many times before. His nerves need steadying. Pointing to the reconstructed fresco behind them, he recounts his conversation with Lucy in the car. Even Jennifer smiles. 'God knows,' Rex chortles, 'if Kreuzenberger had been making his reconstruction today, *what* the figures in that bucolic meadow might have turned out to be doing!'

'So how come a nice gal like this Europa goes riding on a bull anyhow? They sure don't do that in the midwest.' It is a softly spoken drawl which Dan places vaguely in the southern states of America. The newcomer is perhaps a journalist, but no. Embassy, he introduces himself: cultural side.

'You didn't do classics at high school, I suppose?'

'I guess not.'

Dan is about to explain once more, as he has done for Lucy in the car, but Jennifer has fixed the enquirer with the steady glare of obsession. She is about to instruct him, in her soft, patient voice that once started will not easily let go. All the most seemingly innocent stories of our early childhood, and all the myths and legends left over from the childhood of our civilization, she will inform him, preserve the memory of primeval terrors and, correctly understood, can help us to unravel the ritual practices of our ancestors from a time long before written records began. Jennifer has a convoluted theory of the use for which the so-called palaces of Minoan Crete were built, and as Dan remembers it, it involves the mixing behind closed doors of prodigious quantities of wine and blood. He reckons the Embassy, cultural side, deserves this, and turns to Rex.

'Is Horst here?' he asks.

'He should be. I haven't seen him though.' Rex glances at him curiously. 'Are you looking for him, or avoiding him?'

'Both,' says Dan promptly and they both laugh.

'I should tread carefully among this lot if I were you. There's a lot of veneration for the old rogue still around – just look about you. But the real archaeologists are here too, the people like you and me, they could hardly keep us out. And let's face it, Dan, even the grey professionals can't resist the whiff of scandal in the air tonight!'

Dan turns away from Europa and the Bull and looks towards the entrance to the gallery, where the bronze bust of the discoverer and first excavator of Ano Meri, also on generous loan from the Greek authorities, sightlessly outstares the approaching visitor.

The transient Minister for the Arts, it seems, is about to make a speech. 'What the hell—?' Dan's mouth has fallen open. 'Sorry, see you later,' he mutters as he squeezes urgently through the crowd that is turning all one way to face the speaker.

Dan has not been wrong. Unbelievably, incredibly in this gathering, it is Milica, dazzling in a sleeveless ankle-length black dress with silver braid and a silver band in her hair. 'What on earth are *you* doing here?' He sounds quite cross as he grasps her by the elbow and moves with her to the edge of the crowd.

He peers suspiciously at the name-badge she is wearing. *Ms L. Robertson*, he reads.

Dan begins to laugh. Heads turn in his direction. The Minister's discourse is raising polite titters round the gallery, but nothing like this. Is something the matter? Tears come into Dan's eyes: wordlessly he steers Milica round the corner of a display case and lets the sensation of ridiculous delight and relief wash over him. He has been so keyed up. Milica, a mere research student, has no business gatecrashing such a distinguished gathering. But there is no one in the world that he would rather see right here than Milica.

'But good God,' he has a strange way of showing his pleasure, it occurs to him even as he speaks, an anxious scowl on his face, 'there are people here who *know* Lucy, some of them used to pick her up from her cradle. What are they going to think?'

'They will think she's changed since then.'

This is said with a completely straight face. Dan is once again convulsed by nervous laughter, he cannot help himself. It is Milica's turn to reprove him. 'People are looking at us, Dan.'

'I should bloody well think they are.' Dan wipes the tears from his eyes, and looks up at a round of applause. The Minister has concluded his speech. The hum of conversation rises once again. 'OK, now you're here, what am I going to do with you?'

She taps him lightly, but not disrespectfully, on the shoulder. 'Don't worry about me, Dan. I'll look after myself. And remember, Lucy's a grown-up girl now. And she spends her holidays on the Mediterranean!'

It is with an inexplicable feeling of lightness that Dan forays out once more into the throng, quite jauntily picking up a fresh glass as he goes. He is no longer trying to be inconspicuous. He is in search of Horst Wesenthal. He needs to talk to Horst, find out what sort of a man he is, what he knows and what he expects to find out. And now Dan has the courage to do it.

He has no difficulty in recognizing the close-shaven grey head, the narrow shoulders in a dapper suit, standing by the bronze bust of Lionel Robertson. Horst shakes his hand warmly, easily detaching himself, at Dan's unspoken invitation, from the group he is with. '*Prosit,*' Horst raises his glass, his gently probing grey eyes appraising, it seems to Dan, a potential adversary with an almost equal mixture of calculation and warmth.

An expectant silence follows. Then both begin to speak at once. Horst's English is fluent, slightly American, his manners impeccable. It is unexpectedly easy to talk to Horst about the tangible things of archaeology. Soil resistance and the composition of potter's clay, this is neutral ground, a natural meeting-place of minds. Horst, Dan quickly decides, is sound. And unbidden, Dan finds himself talking about his researches in the Public Record Office. What is there is open to all; Horst is welcome to it. To anyone who is interested it explains a good deal about the early excavations at Ano Meri, the kind of people Sir Lionel and his son – Dan's father – were. 'You have to see it in perspective. English amateurs in the Aegean between the wars. They didn't see things the way we do. They were looking for the dawn of their civilization, and they believed they'd found it. My grandfather certainly did, anyway. That's the *context* for whatever happened at Ano Meri. It doesn't make sense outside that context.'

'But there is a truth to be discovered, is there not? That is why we have the enquiry.'

This is the crux that has been tormenting Dan since the evening of the dinner in Bayswater. *Is* there a case to answer? In the clear grey light of Horst's eyes upon him, Dan has no doubt that there is. Or if by any chance there isn't, then Horst's committee will establish that too. Dan's gaze slips past the Prussian to the bronze bust of his grandfather. He stares into the blank eye sockets, as though willing himself to bore through the sculpted contours of the head and wrest its secrets from the cavity within. Horst notices the shift in Dan's attention and turns too. Together the two men silently confront the enigma that has brought them together. And as he does so, Dan knows with devastating finality that no matter what he says to Horst now, no matter whether he opts in the end for the intellectual rigour of the professional archaeologist that he shares with Horst or submits instead to the velvet-sheathed stiletto of Lady Ottoline, the two of them could stare for a lifetime into the bronze features of Lionel Robertson and the one will see only a cussed impediment on the road to truth, while Dan can still recognize, beneath the frozen likeness of a time before he was born, the mobile face of his grandfather, wizard teller of stories and constant consolation in the trivial sorrows of childhood. Under that gaze there can be no true meeting of minds.

'Your contribution will be invaluable to the enquiry,' says Horst now. 'Is there, do you know, evidence? Family papers perhaps?'

As he listens to the even, not unsympathetic tones, Dan feels a distance opening up. It is one thing to chat, the way he would to a colleague anywhere in the world, about soil composition and the resistivity of fired clay. But the dispassionately held trowel of the archaeologist is intruding where it has no business to intrude. It is an almost physical encroachment, and he recoils from it.

'I don't know,' he snaps curtly, registering as he does so the hurt surprise in the other's eyes. 'I haven't replied to the invitation yet. I've got to think.'

And this is suddenly an urgent, an immediate need. Abruptly he turns his back on Horst and the bronze simulacrum of Lionel Robertson in his heyday before the war, and pushes out into the crowd, as though in search of somebody or something. *Milica, where are you?* He recognizes the voice of helplessness inside himself and tries to suppress it. Milica is in animated conversation in front of the original Europa fresco, she seems to have found soulmates among the post-structuralists. He finds time to be pleased she is enjoying herself. Dan wishes he could leave, but the reception is in full swing, it would look like flight. And he can't leave Milica unprotected in her fragile disguise. He may yet have to vouch for Ms Lucy Robertson.

'Dr Robertson, I presume?' To Dan's alarm it is the transient Minister for the Arts. He finds himself staring at close range into a pair of round schoolboy spectacles on a rubicund face that looked younger at a distance. The minders have imperceptibly moved into position to isolate Dan and their charge from the surrounding throng. Dan feels a tightening in his throat, and gulps nervously from his glass.

The Minister chats pleasantly for some minutes, in the way that Dan assumes such people have been trained to do. Like Royalty, he supposes. And wonders if the man is wearing makeup. The television cameras were here earlier, it's quite likely.

'Of course,' the Minister laughs heartily, revealing prognathous, and not quite matching, front teeth, 'it's a shame those EC wallahs trying to poke their nose in. Must be a bit uncomfortable, *I* should think it was, for you I mean. Your own family and all that. Now I hear from Madame Tuss—, tut tut, Lady Ottoline I should say,' this with a conspiratorial leer at Dan, the lapse has not been accidental, he is sure of it, 'that there may be a way out of this mess. Such a shame, when you look round a glittering international gathering like this, and all these splendid things on show – this is a great country, Dan, it's at times like this I'm always reminded of it, we've got too accustomed to saying we're sorry all the time and talking ourselves down, don't you think? – I'll take a wager your grandfather never did anything you or any of us ought to be ashamed of. There's so much mean-minded bureaucracy – and of course a lot of it's to do with envy, who won the war, there's all that mixed up in it too, I shouldn't wonder.' The Minister claps Dan powerfully on the back. The minders are ready to move on. 'Have a word with Madame T., will you? There's a good chap. And don't for God's sake tell her I said so!'

And with that it's over, Dan is released back into the throng, which is beginning to thin out now. He recognizes the sculpted grey-blonde perm of the Institute's Director bearing down on him. Without pausing to think he flees for cover, surfacing just in time in a group containing Rex, Jennifer and a couple of Cambridge archaeologists he has never before seen in suits. Their Director takes them in at a glance. 'Glad to see the Institute of Chronometry so well represented,' Lady Ottoline's benevolence sweeps the faces before her like the desert khamsin. 'Enjoying ourselves, are we?' Dan nods dutifully with the rest, feeling his boss's eyes fixed particularly on him and willing himself to resist. There is an awkward pause.

'Hi there, Lucy, great you could make it.' Rex has risen to the occasion and greets Milica with a broad wink and a frantic gesture of his hand, invisible to Lady Ottoline, to warn her off.

Taking her cue, Milica heads down the gallery, raising her glass to Rex and Dan. But before she can turn away Lady Ottoline's gimlet eyes have taken in the badge on her shoulder. 'Your daughter, Dan?'

Dan, frozen to the spot, makes an infinitesimal movement of his head.

'A lovely girl. Well, I hope there are going to be no thick heads back in London in the morning. Good night, all.' And with that Lady Ottoline sweeps majestically towards the exit, carrying along, Dan now notices, Cathcart and Harold, the man from the Ministry, in her wake.

For the moment, he has escaped.

But at a price. He has caught the look of puzzled recognition in Lady Ottoline's eyes as she followed the broad line of Milica's retreating back. And Lady Ottoline, everyone is agreed on this, never forgets. Milica's harmless deception will be stored up against him, he is certain of it.

The reception is winding down at last. Desultorily, the well-dressed groups are breaking up, farewells are being said. Half-meant promises are being exchanged: to meet in Mauritius, in Fiji, in Indonesia. From the improbable trajectories on which these people seem to be bound one might be forgiven, Dan thinks, not quite soberly, for imagining Cambridge and England still to be the centre of the world. He has had a good deal to drink and eaten little. It is not too late to catch Rex and Jennifer, who have gathered up a contrite Milica and headed off with an indeterminately large crowd for the city's most famous Greek restaurant. Dan has promised to join them, but he won't. He needs more than ever to be alone.

Nothing has been changed by tonight, Dan tells himself. But of course it has. Tonight is the night he has to take the reins of his life in his hands. For longer than Dan can remember he has set out to please others, or at least not to annoy them unnecessarily. He has lived the life allotted to him on a crowded planet. Tears of shock come to his eyes at the audacity that has been forced on him. He can evade no longer. The look in Lady Ottoline's eyes has convinced him of that. The anarchic common sense, the forbidden presence, of Milica (who was indeed stunning tonight, it's not too late to catch her up; the Eros, Rex had said, they'd be at the Eros, till pretty late no doubt) has been the catalyst of a chain reaction whose end result he cannot at this moment imagine.

Without noticing, he has been clutching the metal cloakroom tag in his pocket tightly. As he lets go, he can feel the number on it imprinted on his palm.

Attendants are busily clearing away glasses. As the temporary denizens recede, the gallery is given back to the ghosts who will inhabit it for the three months of the exhibition. Filled with the strangeness of his new-found resolve, Dan is curiously reluctant to leave. He tops up his glass from an opened bottle just before it is snatched away. They are starting to turn out the lights in the far corners. Beyond the high barred windows the June dusk has at last fallen. The thud of disco drums in the distance has been audible for some time. A steam organ starting up in the college grounds beyond the windows takes him back, just, to the fairgrounds of his childhood. It is Lucy's college out there (the last, she never tires of reminding him, to have admitted women students). He thinks of her now preparing for her May Ball, and for a moment experiences an almost overwhelming urge to sweep up Milica and crash the party together. Lucy has told him about the all-night open-air discos, the black velvet, and champagne breakfast in the dew of early morning. At her age he would have hated it. Now, he wouldn't last half the night; he hasn't the stamina. But for the first time in his life, he longs briefly, absurdly to dance and shout and sing and drink black velvet at an all-night party.

Almost everyone has gone now. He hasn't any excuse to stay longer. Draining his glass, Dan runs his eye lingeringly along the painted panels to which his grandfather once gave the title, with what degree of poetic licence is now evident, 'Europa and the Bull'. Not the brilliant, bright reconstruction that bears the old rogue's stamp of approval, with its strong colours and *art nouveau* lines, but the fragments of the original that have so disappointed Dan twice in his life already. His gaze flits past the young girls in tight-fitting tunics and skirts playing on the seashore, to the bull, far out in the pale turquoise, not so much swimming as skimming the sea, its powerful haunches clear of the stylized foam of its passage. On its back the girl, riding the bull and clinging to the horns, her full breasts bare, an expression of awe on her face. As his eye follows the damaged images, Dan now watches a scene unfold that, if it is there at all, has escaped even the boisterous genius of Kreuzenberger, and many more sober commentators since. In a field of purple lilies, flowering papyrus and saffron crocuses, where a river winds in and out and a wildcat stalks a sitting duck in the reeds and blue swallows dart about overhead, the girl bends far forward, her breasts dangling like a cow's udders, the nipples bright and erect, the expression of radiant devotion unchanged upon her face, ready to receive the bull that, trans-figured, advances on her from behind.

Outside where the May Ball is preparing to hot up, the steam organ whistles once, twice, in the gathering darkness. Dan shakes himself impa-tiently, hands back his cloakroom tag and is ushered, the last to leave, out into Trumpington Street and the night.

It has been a feverish week, but Dan has not dared slacken pace for fear his resolution should desert him.

His mother's diaries he has read to the end, only to comment enigmatic-ally to Lucy, whose full attention he has captured at last, 'The solution to one mystery is simply another mystery.'

Playing on her disappointment, as he refuses to divulge more, Dan will say only, 'Surely your devious post-Freudians have taught you that?'

She accuses him of dodging the issue, of being devious himself. But Dan is adamant. 'Don't you see, it gives me an alibi. Who could I possibly tell what I now know?'

'How should I know, since you won't give me a clue what it is?' complains Lucy reasonably.

'That's just the point. I've got an answer that isn't *the* answer. It won't help Horst much – and his Lordship and his ilk will be hopping mad if it ever comes to light.'

Dan has been positively gleeful all week. The diaries have been only the beginning. The firm sense of purpose that came to him all at once in the darkening gallery of the Fitzwilliam has now been reinforced tenfold. What he has to do now is no longer, in his mind, any business of Horst Wesenthal and the impartial legal and scientific minds of the EC enquiry. And it is certainly no business of Lady Ottoline and her establishment cronies. There is indeed a mystery to be unravelled, and this mystery concerns Dan alone.

A plague on both your houses, he almost cries aloud as he types his letter of acceptance to Luxembourg. The means have been given into his hands. Watch out, Horst, watch out, grey Luxembourgeois bureaucrats: here I come!

Dan pulls himself together. One step at a time. A carefully worded letter to the Director, copy to Head of Level. That will take a little longer, but must also be done this afternoon, before his nerve breaks.

241

Before closing the letter to Luxembourg he makes a brief foray down the corridor to the photocopying room. He has ticked the box requesting the appointment of a research assistant. A copy of Milica's *curriculum vitae* tucked inside the envelope, he now seals it. The die is cast.

13 THE HEART OF THE LABYRINTH

Y ES, Laura reflected, as she savoured the few moments that these days remained between sleep and waking in the delicious cool of early morning, that had been the turning point. The Nida Plain and Cave of Zeus. How much had changed since then! This year's season, everybody knew, had been wrested from the jaws of the international crisis. Daniel had ordered a wireless set from London, and since Lionel refused to have it in the Villa, he had rigged it up in his bedroom. Now, to Laura's daily annoyance, at any moment the whole troop of them would come over to the Cabin and crowd round Daniel's door, while he fiddled with knobs, and the whines and hisses of the short wave drove out the last of her daydreams.

Nowadays she sat bolt upright as soon as she heard it. If it was war, Daniel would not sit twiddling for long. The continued burble of the wireless meant that, at the end of another night, the world was still, precariously, at peace.

And with each day that war did not come, the digging continued. Already it was high summer and the villagers were starting to complain and go missing: their vines had to be pruned and tied in preparation for the grape harvest. The season had never before gone on beyond the first days of July. Now July had come and gone; August, and all over the island the flags were out and the villagers gathered in their best clothes in village squares in the evening to dance and drink *tsikoudiá*, and the men fired off their ancient muskets to honour the Dormition of the Virgin. And still Lionel kept up punctiliously the routines of almost twenty years. On the face of it, the 1939 season was uncannily, almost eerily, like so many seasons past. Up at the site, the activity was more frantic than ever. But imperceptibly a hush had descended on the Villa Europa. It was as though nobody dared speak up, for fear of dislodging an entire world.

And reassured by the burble of the wireless, as August moved gently and inexorably towards September, Laura would find that the habit of day-dreaming had not altogether left her. As she lay listening to the sounds through the wall, her mind would often go back to that ill-fated expedition of three summers ago. For Laura at least, that had been the turning point.

And even now she would wonder, with a wistfulness that hurt, whether she could really have been with child at the moment when the world seemed to stop around her and she had come to her senses to find herself fallen from her horse. What was sadly and irrevocably true was what Dr Veniamin had explained to her with kindly patience much later, when she was again well enough to take things in: that no human embryo could have survived the violence of the fever that had then lain hold of her.

There had been no visible warning of her collapse. One moment, as Bertie Shaw put it, there she'd been, riding along in front of him, maybe she was swaying a bit in the saddle, but they were all of them suffering from the heat, each moodily withdrawn into his own thoughts after the fiasco of the cave. Bertie had been biting the ends of his sandy moustache, wondering disconsolately, even then, how far the ramifications of this rift between father and son might be expected to colour the future of the excavation, which was for the time being his own future too. Then without warning, far too quickly for him to ride up alongside her and steady her or break her fall, she had let out a little cry, let go of the reins, and slid 'all of a piece', that was how Bertie described it afterwards, out of the saddle.

And now here they all were, crowding round Laura where she lay on the ground, her eyelids quivering spasmodically, deathly pale. Her sun hat had rolled away and her hair, which she was beginning to grow long that year, had come undone and seemed to flow in glowing brown waves across the ground. Daniel was holding his water bottle to her lips. Lionel and Gus between them raised her shoulders, but her head lolled forward and they had to ease her backwards again. Manolis came up and stood respectfully, stolidly, behind the little group. 'Fever,' someone said. A moment later everybody was saying it at once. And, indeed, Laura's unnaturally white skin was brittle and hot to the touch. It was then that the sickness came. She had to be held, like a little child. It was Lionel who held her, as the spasms went on and on. At last there came a lull. And it was then that Laura, briefly regaining consciousness, made her unexpected and already poignant announcement.

Daniel flung his arms round his wife's neck. Lionel wondered if he were sobbing; he was capable of it.

They set up a makeshift camp at the edge of the rocks, and made Laura as comfortable as they could in the deepest part of the shade. Manolis and the villagers filled up water bottles in relays from a nearby spring. Daniel and his father took it in turns alternately to douse her with cold water and to try to force a little between her lips. Sometimes she stirred and tossed. Once or twice Laura's eyes opened very wide, she seemed to take in where she was and what was happening to her. Once she apologized, enunciating slowly and carefully like a child on its best behaviour or a habitual drunkard who cannot be sure he is sober, for being such a trouble to her companions. Towards sunset, Daniel, whose fingernails were bitten to the quick, set off on horseback with Firkin, carrying a couple of buckets. In the chill before dawn they returned exhausted, their horses winded and fretful. They had been up to the snowline and brought back bucketfuls of dirty brown ice that even as they applied it to Laura's face and shoulders was turning to slush.

Only Manolis and the villagers slept that night.

The next day Laura was strong enough to be lifted on to a mule, where she sat side-saddle with a villager at the animal's head and Daniel and his father – he would let no one else touch her – walking on either side to hold her upright. Some of the way, she babbled; her lips formed words, sound came out, but none of it made sense. Occasionally, just like the night before, she would straighten and seem to know where she was, and make some perfectly coherent remark in a weak voice. For long stretches she seemed to be singing; it was a cruel, mumbling parody of the clear mezzo soprano of Laura Middleton, a kind of obsessive repetition. Like a phonograph needle that's got stuck, as Bertie commented afterwards.

Of them all it was perhaps Lionel who was the most affected by Laura's illness. While she lay day after day, white between the sheets in Dr Veniamin's clinic in Kastro, poised, so the doctor had frankly confessed, on a knife-edge between life and death, Lionel kept watch at her bedside, his chin resting on his hands, his hands firmly, solidly, without tremor or movement resting on the stick propped between his knees. Daniel, during that interminable summer of 1936, found he had to keep himself busy; the excavation over, he worked as never before on the finds up at the site, driving down in the afternoons to look in at the clinic. Lionel's heart went out to his son too; the fretful impatience, the nervous edge in his voice as he talked too loudly to doctors and nurses, the way he fidgeted at the bedside and kept looking away from the inert form of Laura who could neither speak nor recognize him, all these Lionel could understand, it could have been his own younger self. Lionel had lost nothing of his energy with the years, but he had steadied, he had slowed down. It was the most natural thing in the world for him to sit like that, hour after hour, for once not thinking, not planning, just watching and waiting.

Laura was the good angel of the excavation. It was Laura, Lionel was in no doubt of this, who had brought him back his errant, bohemian son. Laura who held the invisible threads in her hand that kept his life's work going, whose serenely beautiful presence somehow held the team and the workmen and the bigwigs of Kastro and even the now distant gentlemen of the world's press together. Dear god who watches over washed-up travellers, who has not let me down in all these years, let her not die. Let Laura not die.

And Laura did not die, although as inch by painful inch she was dragged at the hands of softly-spoken, clean-shaven Dr Veniamin back from the threshold of death, it became clear that something had changed in her. Daniel could see this too. Dr Veniamin had performed his miracle. Only, the Laura who had been restored to him was not the Laura he had loved on Lake Como. For his part, he loved her no less, he was sure of that. But now as she sat up in bed and was able to talk again, and express astonishment at how long she had been oblivious to the passing world, she would look past him, her eyes would avoid his, her forehead would pucker. Her laughter had gone. Something had gone out of her life that day at the Cave of Zeus.

And Daniel knew that his father blamed his friend James Firkin. More than ever he found himself hating the unshakable convictions by which his father lived his life. It was ridiculous to blame James, though it was clear that everyone else did, and Firkin had long since left under a cloud.

To Daniel it was quite clear where the true blame lay. It was his father who had once, as though miraculously, brought Laura into his life. And it was Lionel, whose shadow the passing hours had traced upon her sickbed, who now, in Daniel's mind, came to part them.

Summer was declining at last into autumn. Laura was well enough to be discharged from the clinic. Veniamin thought the cooler, clearer air of Ano Meri would do her good.

Lionel had slept deeply. Now he was wide awake and dawn was still several hours off. Since he had passed sixty he seemed to have less need of sleep. Often at this hour he would light the lamp and pore over the plans of the site. Sometimes in the silence when even the darting geckoes were still and only the occasional dog in the distance would stir in its sleep and bark to scare away the night, inspiration would come to him. The pace of the excavation had slowed in the last few seasons. Lionel was gestating his lifework: the three massive volumes of *Ariadne's Summer Palace* would soon be completed.

But tonight he felt confined within the earthquake-proof walls of the Villa's basement. Grasping his stick firmly, Lionel set out into the darkness. The moon had set but the stars were brilliant and clear, he knew every step of the track, every loose stone, between the Villa and the site. The gaunt, broken outline of Angus Cramond's reconstructed portico flanking the ceremonial north entrance to the palace, whose downward-tapering columns had risen again in red and black painted concrete, looked much larger and more poignantly unfinished in the light of the stars. Lionel picked his way carefully up the ramp. Looking down from the top he could make out the shape of the truncated walls quite clearly in the darkness. Beyond lay the darker line of the olive trees and far in the distance, across the plain, a silver haze rose above the sea. The night smells of the place filled Lionel's nostrils,

246

and he gratefully drew them into his lungs. It was only now that the earth seemed to breathe, and the thyme, verbena and wild aniseed, that in the daytime shrivelled under the onslaught of the sun, had their hour. Lionel sometimes thought he liked Ariadne's Summer Palace best at night. He had peopled this darkness, the shades who slept in the corners of these broken-down walls were his familiars, they must surely be grateful to him for their even partial resurrection.

Lionel plodded on across the open space of the Great Court. He fancied a shadow followed him in the starlight, palely diffused around him. The shadow of an old man more stooped than he liked to think, walking with a stick. On the whole Lionel Robertson was content. He would not live forever. But Ano Meri would be his monument.

He stopped for a moment at the far edge of the court, where the baulk began. Here the regularity of the paved lines ran in under the crumbling pebbles and topsoil that had been the natural hillside of Ano Meri before Lionel and his team had set to work. Who knew what mysteries still remained in there, beneath the living earth, to tease his mortality?

And with a spasm of irritation Lionel remembered his son's irreverent friend, Firkin. It had been hereabouts that he had come upon the scoundrel dabbling at the side of the trench. The thought of Firkin's insect-like features, and the loathsome relics that had had such a devastating effect on Laura, crawled across the back of his neck with a physical sensation of repulsion. There was something evil and primitive about Firkin. The thought of him meddling here of all places, of his fingers that had in all probability, on his own admission, touched human flesh cooked to be eaten, probing into the soil here at the heart of Ariadne's Summer Palace, made Lionel shiver with disgust and indignation. The shades who still rested under that soil, protected by the centuries, awaiting the benign resurrection that Lionel alone could give them, deserved better than that.

Lionel understood his Minoans, and with the thought his earlier feeling of satisfaction began to return.

Retracing his steps down the track towards the Villa, Lionel turned, as he often did, a benevolent eye towards the uncurtained and unlighted windows of the Cabin, where it nestled in the curve of the olive trees. He was still, though at a respectful distance, keeping watch over his beloved Laura. And he was startled to see, as he was about to turn away, a movement in the darkness by the stone water-trough.

'Who's there?' he called out sharply in Greek.

For answer there came only a tiny yelp, and, incongruously, a crunch of heavy footfalls on the pebbles.

For only a second the hairs on the nape of Lionel's neck rose. He knew well enough the villagers' stories about the Nereids and demons that lie in wait for the unwary at the darkest time of night. Lionel had never lost the rational scepticism of his exploring days in the Balkans.

'Come.' Lionel beckoned peremptorily towards the veranda of the Villa, where a lamp burned all night. Turning in the pale circle of light he recognized the bullet-shaped, perfectly bald head of the old barrow-boy from Smyrna.

Lionel prided himself on knowing the names of all the workmen in his service. 'Why here, at this time of night, Hadzi-Aga?' He spoke sharply, still fearing some harm. It came back to him now that this was the geezer who had taken such a crush on Laura, the workmen all teased him about it and none of them could understand what he said because he came from Smyrna and most of it was Turkish. 'What have you got there?'

All he took in at first was the slither of something soft. With a deep bow, Hadzi-Aga opened his arms to reveal what he was holding. '*Ya kyrá,*' he said. '*Skyli-yavrí.*'

Not much the wiser, Lionel accepted the wriggling bundle into his arms. Hadzi-Aga was suddenly voluble, explaining. Lionel forced himself to pick out the few words he recognized. The tiny, button-eyed puppy he was holding was a present to Laura, to get well. Word had quickly got round the village. He, Lionel, was please to give the puppy to Laura, with the deepest respects of Hadzi-Aga.

At last understanding dawned, and his anxious suspicions seemed now only foolish. It was the most unorthodox, but it was by no means the first, such proof of the villagers' solicitude. Deputations had already been bringing medicinal herbs to the kitchen door of the Villa, drams of thrice-distilled *tsikoudiá*, lamb's testicles which even this late in the season were a great delicacy, and all of these, Lionel knew, had been gravely accepted by Aspasia on Laura's behalf, and their restorative properties garrulously extolled to Lionel himself. Poor old Hadzi-Aga must have been standing there half the night.

Lionel laughed genially and patted the old man on the shoulder. 'There there,' he said, 'it's a splendid present and just the thing for the *kyrá* for her convalescence. I thank you on her behalf.'

And with that Lionel turned on his heel, wondering what to do with this latest addition to the excavation team until morning, and what Laura would think of this unlooked-for gift.

He need not have worried. Laura was enchanted with the mongrel sheepdog, Jack, as she called him, which quickly became Tzak, in the pronunciation of the villagers, and Tzak he remained. Laura was convinced that Tzak had escaped being turned out to die, as she had often seen done with unwanted animals in Crete, only for her sake. She too had had a brush with death, and it made a bond between them.

In 1938, the year of the Munich crisis, with war already in the air, Lionel was back in England. *Ariadne's Summer Palace* was in proof when Neville Chamberlain stood on the steps of an aeroplane at Heston and waved a white piece of paper at the waiting reporters. There would be peace in our time. Herr Hitler had given his word.

The presses rolled and a thousand copies of *Ariadne's Summer Palace* were duly bound in three handsome volumes of almost a thousand pages each, with maps, diagrams, and photographs, many of them the work of Daniel, who is acknowledged along with the other members of the excavation team and 'the charming and unfailingly obliging Mrs Laura Robertson'. Daniel, more touchy than ever by this time, was not best pleased and sent his father a curt note of congratulation to Upland Grange, where Lionel was staying at the time.

The nightingales won't let you sleep at Ano Meri. The nightingales won't let you sleep at Ano Meri. When it wasn't the nightingales, there was the tintinnabulation in his ears. Daniel's sleep was more disturbed than ever. Laura, who was still far from fully well herself, had begged him that winter to go to England, to come with her to England, to see a doctor. 'What kind of a doctor?' he would respond stiffly. 'Are you suggesting I'm going mad or something?'

'No, of course I'm not,' she retorted. 'But can't you see, you've been at Ano Meri too long, we both have. You're so involved in the work now. You're wearing yourself out.' And it was true, Daniel had shouldered nearly all the burden of the dig for the last five years. It was too much for anyone.

For a moment it even looked to Laura as though he might agree. They could set off once again by ship and train across Europe as they had done for the first time on that extraordinary, whirlwind honeymoon twelve years ago. Once again the rhythm of the train and its haunting whistle would punctuate their lovemaking and their dreams. There really was no reason to stay on at Ano Meri. It was only obstinacy in the face of Laura's entreaties, and a loyalty born of resentment that made Daniel feel bound to the post his father had entrusted to him.

But there was something else too. The news from Upland Grange had revived old memories. Trudgill was dead, carried off by a coronary the summer before. Sarah Jane continued at the Lodge – 'a sprightly yokel in her mid twenties', according to Lionel's letter – where she looked after her invalid mother. No one now need know what Daniel had willed (from cowardice – *per viltà*, Laura would have said) not to know. But he couldn't trust himself, in his present frame of mind. Returning to the place of his lost childhood, where Lionel reigned supreme, to bask in the glory of his three volumes just published, a landmark in British archaeology, as the *Times* had just enthusiastically hailed them, oblivious for all he knew to the sprightly and no doubt still cheeky yokel in her mid twenties who looked after her widowed mother at the Lodge – how could Daniel stop himself from shouting the tawdry truth from the rooftops, screaming it in his father's ear, with a savage delight flinging in his father's face the treasonable, shameful fact of Sarah Jane's parentage that he had concealed from him, for very pity, for nearly twenty years?

And now here was Laura, who knew nothing of this, begging him, for his own good as well as hers, to go with her to England. Daniel, as he still faced her silently, found himself aching to say yes.

But then, as though to seal matters, came from the recesses of his mind the poisoned words of Varvatakis – Varvatakis, who had divorced his own wife years ago and was known even in the dour society of Kastro as a misogynist, who had cast his spell over Daniel and preached international Communism at him and found fertile ground, but not so much as to blind him utterly to the man's excesses and absurdities, which he saw quite clearly: 'man's destiny is the upward path; a woman cannot help but drag him down, towards the dust and clay he came from.' At the same moment as he rejected his mentor's words as foolish and untrue – was it not Laura who for the last twelve years had enabled him to rise above the ruins of his wartime experiences and do something with his life? – Daniel could not erase them from his mind. It was not only to his father that he now felt an obstinate sense of duty. With Varvatakis for guide, Daniel had visited the low hovels of the shanty-town with their corrugated-iron roofs, the damp basements dug out of the earth in a desperate bid to make room for growing families, the eye disease, the tuberculosis, the rickets; he had heard so many tales of corrupt bureaucracy, of the complacency of the authorities and the well-to-do of Kastro, of the tangled responsibilities of the Great Powers who had, at the very least, stood back while Smyrna burned, of the failures of the now discredited League of Nations. Now as he confronted Laura and his heart was ready to melt with tenderness, Varvatakis' words seemed strangely not so inappropriate after all.

And Laura felt the finality of those lowered eyes, the hunching of the shoulders, the infinitesimal shake of the head. 'I can't, Laura,' he said.

His explanations passed her by, she knew the arguments. Anyone can think of arguments. What mattered to her was that moment of decision she had witnessed. A door had been open and it had closed in front of her eyes. It was not a matter of argument. The subterranean bull, that the Minoans perhaps believed in, had turned over in its sleep. Something in Daniel had turned away from her. And it hurt. God, how it hurt.

Laura's gift to him on parting was the two-year-old Tzak, the mongrel sheepdog, who by this time had begun to show some aptitude as a gundog.

'I know you'll take care of him as though he were me,' she said. They were her last words to him as she turned with dry eyes to clamber into the bum boat that would take her to the waiting steamer. She had made no firm promise to come back.

It was only then, alone at Ano Meri that winter, one dark December day, when the clouds bulged low over Psiloriti and the cold wind blew through the crevices of the Cabin, that Daniel's thoughts reached out once again to Upland Grange and he acknowledged to himself the passing of Trudgill, the friend and confidant of his earliest years. Daniel took the rifle that he had recently bought for the occasional hunting expedition, some rounds of ammunition and the dog Tzak, of indeterminate breed, who was now his only companion, and climbed without stopping, half way up the conical peak of Stroumboulas. Here, in his newfound loneliness, he bade farewell to his childhood friend according to the Cretan custom, banging off round after round into the empty air until his head and ears were ringing and his heart was at last empty too.

So it was not just the worsening international situation that made that final season's digging, in the summer of 1939, so uncannily, and so precariously, like the reprise of an earlier time. Laura had come back, of course. In Milan she had seen, in all its cruel finality, the last fading of her hopes as a singer. The relatives who had once been pillars of stability in her life – her dear Contessa Mondadori, for instance – were dead, her chattering cousins married to industrialists, to rather frightening officials of the Fascist Party, to strutting military men. While she had been immersed, with Daniel, in the secrets of the remotest past, time had swept across the face of the planet. Home was no longer Milan, was no longer London, where her parents had turned into old people; they needed comfort themselves, they had none left to give. The world Laura had known had somehow run dry on her. There had come a time, in the wake of her illness, in the terrible emptiness it had left behind, when freedom had seemed a necessity. But it had cost her dear, and Daniel too. And the emptiness, away from Daniel, had been even harder to bear.

It had been more of a relief than she could have imagined, to come back. To find the mongrel sheepdog Tzak grown up into a gundog and Daniel's inseparable companion. To find the heads of the villagers, of the burghers of Kastro where they sat hour after hour at little metal tables ranged outside the town's coffeeshops, turning unashamedly like sunflowers to stare at her as she passed by. Nobody had noticed her in Milan; amid a crowd, made and dressed in her own image, obedient to the manners that she, too, had been brought up in, she had been invisible, a ghost haunting her own past. The music of destiny, that she had pledged herself all these years ago to follow to the end, still sounded in her dreams. But now it was the discordant music of the age, a music evocative of shivered glass and tortured metal, a music of dissolution, tonality dismembered; gone were the great operatic sonorities that had launched her into adult life.

And Daniel had accepted her quietly, without fuss or sign of emotion, back into his life as though it had been the most natural thing in the world that she should have gone away and, now she was back, that was that. It was to protect himself, she saw with anguish. But she no longer knew how to reach him.

Now Lionel too was back. He returned to Ano Meri in May, to find the season well advanced. It was a relief to him to be in one place again. The one place, he supposed irritably, as he found himself coughing from the dust and suffering from the heat within hours of descending from the flying boat at Spinalonga, that he could truly claim to have made his own. The bougainvillea had taken well round the Villa Europa, the deep purple cascade was a balm to the eye seared by the jagged light and the hot wind that blew down from Stroumboulas in the afternoons. Lionel at sixty-four was feeling his years upon him. He was troubled by shortness of breath; the Cretan dust had finally settled on his chest.

The team at the Villa was once again the same as it had been that very first season: Gus Cramond, Bertie Shaw, and of course Kreuz, faithful to the last. That seemed to be fitting, for Lionel knew there would be no more seasons after this one. For the first time in his life, with so much to be done before the new catastrophe that threatened to overwhelm everything, Lionel Robertson felt his strength beginning to fail him. For Lionel the coming war was nothing more nor less than a personal affront. If a man's span is three score years and ten, then no matter what Neville Chamberlain said, it was all too likely that there would never again be peace in his, Lionel's time. And this he resented, with a deep, unforgiving rancour.

With every day like a gift from heaven, the excavation went ahead that season at a furious pace. On the steep west side of the Great Court, beyond the reconstructed throne room and the broad staircase leading down to it, the outer retaining walls of the palace had been uncovered, still standing, to a depth of nearly twenty feet. A series of soundings here showed that Ano Meri had been inhabited for at least two millennia before the final destruction of the Summer Palace. The Minoans themselves, it seemed, had dug deep circular pits into these deposits, which they had then lined with plaster. 'Wells', had been Lionel's first description of them in the excavation notebooks, but any water that might once have come to the surface here would have been more easily tapped lower down the slope. And the pits, so far as they had been able to excavate any of them, were chock-full of debris. Failing satisfactory explanation, Lionel could find no more evocative designation for them than the standard archaeological term for such things, *bothros*. Bothros 2 seemed the largest, more than five feet across. By the time the decision was taken to abandon it – there were more interesting things than middens to occupy the excavators in what must surely now be the last few weeks of digging –

Bothros 2 was deep enough to stand up in. If the soundings were right, there must be, as Bertie cheerfully put it, tons more rubbish down there.

Before defections from the workforce and a creeping combination of fatalism and exhaustion began to take their toll on the excavating team, Lionel ordered the long-delayed assault on the maze of small rooms that flanked the southern side of the Great Court. Plans for this part of the excavation had been drawn up several years ago, and the outline trenches marked out on the ground, but the sheer richness of the finds from trenches that had already been opened up meant there had always been more pressing work elsewhere. Now, faced with the prospect of having to leave Crete with no certainty of when, if ever, he would return, Lionel was determined to leave as little as possible of the palace untouched. Small finds were unearthed at an unprecedented rate. 'Who's going to keep a proper record of all this?' Bertie wailed, quite literally wringing his hands. But Lionel and Daniel were working simultaneously on keeping the notebooks up to date. Laura would catalogue the small finds. Lionel had learnt to respect Bertie's professional horror of the unstratified find, although he still fumed at some of his archaeologist's 'pernickety ways'. Wicker zembils piled up in the corrugated-iron shed, all of them duly labelled. There was no time now, but there would be once the season ended . . .

It was in the hottest days of summer that the desertions began. The first to go was Gus, and his departure was almost furtive. Something was said about going home to receive a commission. Bertie was more open. Within a matter of days after Gus's sudden departure, he confessed that he too had been in touch with some people in London – his father's regiment – surely Lionel would understand, in the circumstances . . . Actually, there was a chance he'd be back in Crete before long. It was top secret, of course, mustn't say a word to a soul, but he'd volunteered for something special. Lionel let his lieutenants go more sorrowfully than in anger. He had seen it all before, but this time had no confidence in his own power to ride out the storm.

On the day that German troops invaded Poland, Reinhard Kreuzenberger made his farewells. His pathetically small trunk was already packed. But the artist had waited till the last possible moment. He presented himself stiffly to Lionel on the veranda of the Villa. 'In a few days maybe, my country and your country will be at war. My paintings are left behind in a garret in München. For them I go back, not for the Führer. I hate – you know this – what the Nationalsozialisten have done to Germany. But I will go back. And when this war is over will come, do not doubt, that bright day for the peoples of the world that always I am dreaming of.'

Lionel rose to the occasion and the two men embraced. Lionel had no time for Kreuz's egalitarian dreams, as the artist well knew. For Lionel the bright days were to be found in the past, in the traces beneath the soil of Ano Meri, in the successes of a life that had seen its share and more of excitement. But for a fleeting moment he envied Kreuz the jovial, wistful faith in a future – any kind of future – that he might live to see. And then he remembered what Kreuzenberger was going back to, and could only wonder what tortured nightmares lay behind that self-deprecating pomposity, the gleaming pink cheeks that never tanned in the Cretan sun, the gentle, twinkling mockery, what reserves of unspoken courage, what bedrock of conviction. After almost twenty years, the people Lionel had worked with most closely, who had shared his own dream and made it a reality, were becoming strangers again. Gus and Bertie, recalled to the service of King and Country. Reinhard, who it suddenly dawned on Lionel had not the slightest doubt he was going to his death. It was all coming to an end. As the workmen drifted away and the excavation team disbanded, it was as though the ruins of Ariadne's Summer Palace had already begun to be reclaimed by the earth. The Minoans of Lionel's sealstones, of Kreuz's brilliant fresco restorations, those peaceable, life-loving rulers of the sea were vanishing into the air from which they had been conjured.

It was high noon in Crete when Chamberlain's broadcast words echoed eerily in the silence of the Cabin. *This country is at war with Germany.* Only Lionel, Daniel and Laura were left.

The 'phoney war' that lasted until the spring of 1940 was nowhere more phoney than in Crete. And even as the drily rounded voice of the BBC came through the crackles and the hiss of the short wave on the wireless with news of Denmark and Norway invaded, of Dunkirk and the fall of France, the Battle of Britain and latterly, when the clouds returned once more to Psiloriti and the weeds and wild flowers began pricking through the soil with the first autumn rains, with more sombre accounts of the Blitz, life at Ano Meri entered upon an unexpected, and protracted, Indian summer. In the evenings the sun sank behind the pass that leads up to Anoyia, leaving behind a sky the colour of molten brass and the air still thick as honey with the day's heat. It was at moments like these that Lionel was wont to compare their tenuous, shadowy occupation of the Villa with the final phase of the civilization they had been excavating all these years. After the catastrophe, after the walls had been shaken down and the oiljars overturned, setting light to Ano Meri and all the other known palaces of Minoan Crete, the remnants of the inhabitants had crept back. They had lived a squatters' life among the ruins, rebuilding here and there, making shelters out of the debris, even reopening some of the derelict workshops, but only to produce pots and artefacts of much inferior quality. Until after only a few generations even these survivors had melted away, leaving the ruined palace to sink into the earth and oblivion.

And Lionel himself, during those months, sank into a kind of hectic reverie, reliving the last days of Ariadne's Summer Palace. Minos no longer ruled the waves: *pax minoica* was no more. The flaxen-haired invaders from the north, whom Varvatakis had once so vividly invoked, regularly raided the coasts. The inhabitants lived in fear, and retreated to the hills, leaving behind the bright, ordered life of the palaces that had endured for two thousand years. Even the memory of that splendour, in the darkness and fear of those later generations, was turned into something monstrous. It was out of that darkness that the legends of the man-eating Minotaur were born. In an age when no one living could any longer remember the palaces in their heyday, or even imagine how they could have been built, their ruins must have seemed like nothing so much as sinister mazes. And at the heart of the maze, at the heart of the labyrinth, the imagination of those evil times had placed the Minotaur, half-man, half-bull, the issue of a queen's bestial passion. The whole story was nothing but the reworking, in a time of despair, of that other legend, in which the Minoan dynasty itself had sprung from the union of Europa with the bull-god, Zeus.

In Crete, unbelievably, the phoney war continued into its second year, even beyond the excitement of Mussolini's attack on Greece at the end of October, and the jubilant riots in Kastro that threatened to demolish the last dusty vestiges of the town's glory in the days of the Venetians.

On the mainland, the Greek army had begun to push the invading Italians back through the snow, and was pursuing them across the mountains of Albania. It was the only victory the Allies had won in this whole war. But the jubilation in Kastro was muted. As Daniel explained, the Cretans had had all their fighting men called up in the first days after the Italian attack on Greece, and shipped to the mainland. His friends, he said, but he wouldn't tell Laura, when she pressed him, who exactly they were, expected an encircling move by the Germans, perhaps through Bulgaria. Hitler's stormtroops were of a different stamp from the *macaroni-eaters* (he must have learnt the word from Varvatakis, thought Laura grimly). If the Greek army in Albania were surrounded, and the Germans launched an attack on Crete across the Aegean, the island would be defenceless.

And yet even now, with winter over, down in Kastro people went about their business. Everywhere in the surrounding farmlands, women and old men ploughed, sowed and planted. Here at Ano Meri it was time to gather the olives, the second harvest that would produce the crop for olive oil, and all around the site the women had spread nets on the ground under the trees, and the village children scrambled up into the branches with sticks to beat the bitter black fruit into the nets. All the men of military age were away at the front. And at the Villa, while the lull still lasted, archaeology continued too.

Day after day Laura unpacked zembils in the corrugated-iron shed, while the gentle spring rains coaxed a cosy, companionable sound from the metal roof. Aspasia, who had welcomed them back from the long winter in Kastro like returning heroes, often came up to help when she had washed up breakfast at the Villa. Only half a dozen of the village women came to the site now, and their wages, Laura knew, had been pitifully reduced. But the water pump still worked, the women's chatter was as loud as ever, and the finds of that final, hectic season's digging were beginning to be cleaned, sorted and catalogued.

Sometimes Spinalonga, Aspasia's last and idiot son, would come along. So far as Laura could make out, the women ribbed him mercilessly about his lack of sexual prowess and manly courage, and he would growl and threaten to chase them, which made them all laugh shrilly. Spinalonga wasn't his real name. The villagers called him that because he was simple and didn't walk properly. They'd used to tease Aspasia in the beginning that she'd stolen him from the leper colony at Spinalonga, and the name had stuck. Lionel had assured Laura that the leper colony had closed down years ago. Spinalonga, as he well knew, since he had used it often in these latter years, was where you caught the flying boat for Athens. But to Laura, who had watched the misshapen youth grow up, and had learnt enough Greek to follow Aspasia's never-ending stream of worry about him while she brought her her egg in the morning, while she dusted in the Villa or helped with the potsherds, Spinalonga was first and foremost Aspasia's youngest, the apple of her eye and a source of increasing torment as old age began to leave its mark upon her.

Spinalonga seemed to take the women's jokes, which Laura thought must be pretty coarse, in good part. He had a fine set of teeth, and laughed a lot: a happy, open, vacant laugh. His body, though it had not grown straight, had most certainly grown since Laura had first known him. His shoulders and hands were huge. It was his legs which were crooked, making him unfit, as the women never tired of pointing out, for you-know-what. Laura felt sorry for him, and would sometimes give him shelter in the shed if she felt that things were getting out of hand outside. In return, he would fix his huge black eyes on her face, as though carefully and wisely reading something invisible to everyone else, and nod and grin and bare his teeth. Laura never knew how much he could understand. Certainly nothing that anybody could recognize as speech had ever come from his lips. But he took an evident pleasure in pleasing her. She had only to point to a particularly heavy zembil, and he would have tugged it out into the middle of the floor before she'd had time to think where he was to put it. And so they would work together. She pointing, and sometimes enunciating very carefully the Greek words she knew, which were the daily currency of the excavation, and he seeming to read her wishes in her face, grinning and bending, nodding, anything to oblige the *kyrá*.

Between him and Tzak, thought Laura sadly, what was it about dumb creatures that so drew out her love?

But those who had the power of speech, in the extraordinary atmosphere of secrecy and anticipation of that time, were not to be trusted with it; could not, perhaps, trust themselves. In Kastro that winter, the staff at the British consulate, which had been increased to implausible levels while Greece was still neutral, had suddenly donned the uniforms of the regiments from which they had been secretly seconded the year before. 'Liaison officer', 'Military Mission', were terms that soon came to be bandied about, without too much precision.

'Guess who I saw in the Fountain Square today?' Laura had once tried to catch Daniel by surprise. 'Bertie! . . . Bertie Shaw, silly, who else? I hardly recognized him. He was there in uniform drinking with a group of officers, there were some Greeks with them too. I waved, but I don't think he wanted to see me, so I went on . . . Did you know he was in Crete?'

'Uh-huh, I'd heard.'

'You haven't seen him then?'

But Daniel had refused to be drawn. As the months went by, Laura had kept watch over him as best she could. And learnt, too, to keep secrets of her own.

That was how it was in the early spring of 1941. While the three of them still lived in the same house, ate the same meals, listened twice a day to the same news broadcasts on the wireless, each one of them had retreated into an inner world. Lionel had never been so single-mindedly engrossed with his Minoans; he seemed to bear a grudge against the war and avoided speaking of it. Daniel: the prisoner of apocalyptic ideals she barely understood and instinctively mistrusted, of the nightingales that wouldn't let him sleep. Even her own work among the bones, beneath the gentle drizzle, surrounded everywhere by the rampant green of the short-lived Cretan spring, was a refuge. And a prison. And she herself was scarcely to be trusted either. Was it not she, who through two winters in Kastro, without telling anyone, not even Daniel, had quietly resumed her acquaintance with softly-spoken, always exasperated Dr Veniamin who had saved her life when she was ill, and had trained as a nurse to enrol in the Greek Red Cross? Could she, in this new world where 'civilian clothes' meant only another kind of uniform, hope to step out of her prison with a mere change of dress? Could she, at the same moment as she cheered the latest news from the front and was briefly buoyed by the shared sense of victory, could she fail to think of her own Italian dead, piled in heaps in the snow? Could she completely forget or disown her own trivial, harmless act of treason in this momentous conflict: the passport in her mother's name of Mondadori, among the mothballs at the bottom of her wardrobe?

At night she still read from her beloved Dante. The *Inferno*, when you got down far enough, was not the boiling fiery pit of popular imagination. The damned were condemned to relive their crimes for all eternity and the lowest of all were the traitors. In the pit of Hell was a lake of ice. That was where the

257

old man's tears ended up, the Old Man of Crete, in the frozen lake of Cocytus. And who could be indifferent to the fate of the treacherous Ugolino, whose earthly punishment had already been so terrible? Locked in the tower with his sons. The silent, gnawing days of hunger. Waiting for the key to turn in the lock. And at last, instead, the hammering that would seal the tower forever. Laura wasn't sure whether the dying Ugolino, already blind from famine, had tasted the flesh of his beloved sons in this world. But in Hell, where he shares for all eternity a crevasse in the frozen lake with the traitor he once betrayed, his teeth are savagely embedded in his enemy's head, just where the spinal marrow joins the brain. It is from that savage repast that the immortal soul of Ugolino will raise his eyes to tell his tale to Dante and the world.

Laura's back ached continuously from standing by the workbench, stooping to the zembils. All at once she put down the skull she had been examining, trembling all over. It was more than a daydream. There had been a reason for this story to force its way, from all the debris down there, to the surface of her memory. She had already cleaned this skull and laconically recorded it in her notebook. It belonged to a deposit of human bones that had not been recognized at the time. An underfloor burial, no doubt. Such things were not unknown, though it was the first at Ano Meri. She would have to tell Lionel about it. She was almost finished with the zembils from that hastily-excavated room just south of the Great Court. She had already described and drawn this skull. What had made her go back to it? Her hand was shaking now too much to write. She willed herself to put the skull back with the other bones that she had neatly tagged, ready to be transported to the museum in Kastro. It was an undistinguished, an incomplete burial. The bones would probably be thrown out. For a dizzying moment it was still possible not to look again, not to check, not to confirm the horrible suspicion that had entered her mind. But the teetering moment was already collapsing into the next, she was reaching down to the tray beneath her feet to pick up the skull again. She was rummaging among the tibia and femurs that surrounded it. She hadn't the expertise to tell if they all belonged to the same individual. The light, brittle, only slightly discoloured calcium danced in her hands. She stood up straight, breathing deeply, to get a grip on herself. Then she looked again.

She had not been mistaken. The longer bones were marked with fine little incisions, in groups of twos and threes, near their ends. There was no doubting it, now she examined them carefully. And Laura had handled, and learnt to identify, enough discarded bones of sheep and goats, even sometimes of ox or bull, from the Minoan midden in Bothros 2 and elsewhere around the site, not to recognize the marks she now saw before her eyes. But it was the skull that, even as she was still taking in this information, continued to fascinate Laura. It was somehow misshapen, strangely

258

deformed. Something was missing. Gingerly, she turned it upside down. The hollow part was still full of the white, stony clay of the site. Suddenly she couldn't bring herself to scoop it out, anyway it was quite hard, but even as she gingerly prodded at it with the point of a trowel she felt herself re-enacting a hideous memory inherited with the flesh and blood, the instincts and the fears, that made up her own self, and she broke down entirely. Still clutching the dreadful relic in her hands above the workbench, she sank to her knees, and her body was convulsed by sobbing.

It was late afternoon outside. The women had all gone home at lunch time. Laura was alone at the site, there was no one to hear her. Gradually she felt the hysteria ebbing from her, leaving her body colder than a stone. She got to her feet, and putting down the skull on the bench, began quietly to retch. Somebody, while Ano Meri had been at the height of its exotic glory, had carefully cut away the base of this skull where once the spinal cord would have connected with the brain, and emptied out the soft matter through the aperture. And since the other bones in the collection had been hacked clean of flesh with cleavers, there could be little doubt, in Laura's feverish but at the same time coldly rational mind, that she was looking at the remains of a feast no less grisly than that imagined by Dante, but with the awesome difference that it was real, and she had touched the evidence with her hands.

Daniel came. She had had no idea of the passing of time. Now it seemed she had been missed down at the Villa. Daniel didn't ask what the matter was, not at first. His arms were round her, he was calling her his gentle little princess, his Liù, as he had not done, it seemed to Laura, for ages, his presence was solid, enfolding her. Whatever she might have persuaded herself over the years, all that she knew, and had set herself to protect, of Daniel's weakness throughout their marriage, he was at that moment the stronger of the two and waves of gratitude washed over her. She cried over him unashamedly. And as she cried – without reason now, in the moment of comfort it no longer mattered what had started it, how she had got into this state – as she cried she felt her tears begin to breach and wash away the barriers of dusty prickly pear that years before she had imagined separating her love for Daniel from the Daniel whom she loved. As she let it all, absurdly, meaninglessly pour out, she recognized the fierce pride in herself that had, all unnoticed, appointed her Daniel's guardian angel, and she was content, while the drizzling rain resumed its drumming on the metal roof, to feel her angelic wings dissolve in unabashed humility.

At last she raised her head and laughed a little, sheepishly, through her tears. 'Oh Daniel, the most dreadful thing . . .'

There was a new energy in the air between them. Daniel was at once impressed by her discovery. To him, as he turned over the bones she showed him, they were merely bones. Human bones, that had been cut and hacked by a butcher's cleaver: the notched incisions told their unmistakable tale. But still, to Daniel this was Archaeology, this was Evidence. It conjured up none of the horror that had so taken hold of Laura, alone in the shed with her thoughts hour after hour. But he could see, with a kind of angry remorse, what it had meant to her. Could he not at least have shielded her from this? It was irrational, but he couldn't help it: what could his father have been thinking of, to assign her such a task?

'By Jove,' said Daniel, getting a grip on his thoughts once more and lighting his pipe in unaccustomed good humour, 'I shouldn't wonder if we haven't strayed into the Minotaur's lair. It lends a certain something to the legend, doesn't it?'

Laura was still shaken. 'Don't, Daniel . . .'

Daniel continued to muse. 'If there didn't happen to be a war on, and rather more pressing things to occupy us all, I rather fancy Ano Meri would be hitting the headlines with this. The old man would love it.'

But Laura's thoughts had already run ahead of him. Her hand had slowly gone to her mouth. 'Do you really suppose he would? Your father I mean? *What in the name of God are we going to tell him?*'

Daniel shrugged. 'Better let him see for himself. In present circumstances the Minotaur's dinner is deader than a dodo, in news terms. But he'll have something to say about it all right. This is going to have to fit somewhere into the scheme of things.'

Laura gripped his shoulders tightly. The strong tobacco made a cloud about her face, drawing her closer to him. 'Don't you see? What price now Ariadne's Summer Palace as a paragon of old-world civilization? In fact,' Laura felt her chin trembling and fought to control herself, 'in its way this is just as beastly as Hitler and this whole beastly war. It's all over, there's nowhere left.' She was sobbing quietly now, leaning on his shoulder. 'There's nothing beautiful or noble or happy left in all the world. Just beastliness. Oh Daniel, we'll have to break it to your father gently.'

They said nothing to Lionel that night. And in the Cabin very late, after writing in her diary, Laura crept through to Daniel's bed and he made room for her under the mosquito net. He may have been surprised at how passionately she made love. But when later they slept, still huddled together in the narrow bed, no nightingale intruded on his sleep, not that night nor any of the nights that followed.

And this even though the days were some of the most difficult and painful of Daniel's life.

Lionel listened patiently and calmly while they broke the news. Then, gathering up his stick and his aged sou'wester (it was drizzling again outside), he set off ahead of them up the track to the site. The weather brought out his cough, and several times he had to stop to catch his breath, blinking and apologizing for holding them back. Lionel was beginning to show his years. Like an acanthus stalk at the end of the spring rains, Laura now incongruously thought, his long spine was beginning to droop at the top. She felt sorry for him as they stopped for the second time in the rain and he tried to dislodge the phlegm that had settled somewhere deep in his lungs.

Their first goal was the finds shed, where Lionel was unfailing in his lordly attentions to Aspasia and the group of women, who fell silent at his approach. Inside, he took out his magnifying glass, and pored for some time over the relics that Laura showed him.

'Is there anything else?' he demanded, sharply now. Something of the old irritability was beginning to return.

'Well, I don't know. I haven't got to all those yet,' stammered Laura, pointing to the as yet untouched zembils on the floor.

'Tip them out. Come on. All of them.'

Bertie Shaw would never have forgiven such an act. Even Laura was horrified. 'What, all together, on the floor? You'll mix up the deposits . . .'

'Let's get on with it,' said Lionel gruffly, and before the others could react he was on his hands and knees in the little shed, scattering the contents of one zembil after another, and sifting quickly, expertly through their contents with his fingers. Hesitantly, slowly, Daniel and Laura joined him.

At last they straightened. 'I think you'll agree, Father,' Daniel hazarded, 'that what Laura has found is quite unique.'

'Just as I expected,' Lionel snapped back. 'Now let's see the notebooks.'

Laura watched uncomfortably as he flipped back through the records she had been keeping day after day, seeing the spidery writing and the neat ink drawings with critical, outsider's eyes.

'And there's nothing in any of the deposits you've already described?'

Laura shook her head.

'Let's make sure.'

But this time Lionel didn't demand to rifle through the finds, he was content to skim the pages of the notebooks, trench by trench.

When he locked up the shed to leave, Laura noticed that the notebook she had been working on yesterday was tucked firmly under his arm.

The clouds were beginning to lift and a shaft of wan sunshine lit up the site as they traversed the Great Court. Here, Laura and Daniel had celebrated their marriage, in the bizarre Minoan style of Lionel's devising. She remembered the makeshift altar that had been set up at the south end of the court, the libation and Lionel's flamboyant speech for the cinematograph cameras about the blood of sacrificial bulls being mixed with wine. Only a few feet away, in the as yet unexcavated baulk, the grisly remains of a much more savage rite had even then been lurking, awaiting the day of their discovery.

It was as she had thought. The remains had come from one of the little rooms opening off the court. Daniel, still inclined to joke, he was in excellent spirits, pointed out the arrangement of outer and inner doors – 'like a gents' lavatory, so you can't see into the holy of holies from outside in the court'. But Lionel was in no mood for joking and pressed on.

The room told them nothing. It had been fully cleared in that final assault nearly two years before. It was just one of a series of small rooms, with broken-down walls surviving up to only knee-height, and remains of a doorway and a gypsum threshold with dowel holes for heavy doors. No trace of any window survived.

'There was a large amount of rough pottery in the deposit,' Laura reeled off the facts from memory. 'Two bronze tripods, up-ended bronze cauldron, much unglazed ware, possibly fallen from the floor above. The bones were lower down, either on the floor or sealed beneath it. Scattered just inside the door. This whole suite of rooms may have been kitchens.'

Lionel straightened suddenly and banged his stick. 'That's enough. This whole business has gone too far. Laura, you found something that startled you and you've let your imagination run away with you. Daniel,' there was a new and powerful contempt in the old man's voice now, 'I don't know whether my son is a knave or a fool. I will speak to you both later, at the Villa, and then this matter is to be considered closed. Is that understood?'

Daniel nodded dumbly, miserably. He had nothing to say.

Later that day Lionel summed up in his most judicial manner. The evidence they had uncovered was the crudest form of practical joke, easily unmasked. Lionel could only assume that his son and daughter-in-law had been taken in. Anything else was unthinkable, but his tone made it clear that he had thought it nonetheless, and judgement was merely suspended. Did they not remember that friend of Daniel's whom he, Lionel, had had to ban from the site, and his stupid, vulgar prank at the Cave of Zeus? Did they not remember how this man had been found burrowing into the baulk, venturing an amateur little excavation on his own? It had been, Lionel now clearly recalled, at the very spot where the doorway to the little room had since been uncovered. At the time Lionel had suspected Firkin of attempted theft. Now it turned out his purpose had been more cunning – and more sinister. What might he not have planted on the site, from the atrocious trophies he was then transporting back to England and took such heartless delight in showing off to his long-suffering hosts?

Daniel listened to this tirade, his head in his hands. With weary resignation he said finally, 'How can you be so sure of where it was you found Firkin that day? Could he even have reached the spot where—?'

But Lionel swept magisterially on. 'There can, I'm afraid, be no doubt about it. We have all been abused, and scientific archaeology has been tweaked by the nose.' And suddenly, swiftly, with the old terrible intensity that those who had known Lionel in his heyday would never forget, he

262

pronounced sentence. 'I want every trace of this disgraceful episode removed from the site. At once. And from today, the excavation is suspended. I shall be in touch with the Military Mission in Kastro to determine how soon we can all leave Crete.'

Laura was watching Daniel closely; she flinched for him, for both of them, at every whiplash of Lionel's tongue. She had waited, it seemed for a lifetime, to see him stand up to his father. It only now came back to her how much she had also dreaded that moment, should it ever come.

His voice when he spoke was calm. There was no sign of the white, pinched look of suppressed fury that had so often before awakened Laura's sense of pity and anger on his behalf, but also, as she knew to her cost, shut her out of his thoughts. Daniel's long, gangling frame had broadened out lately; as he faced his father across the huge study desk in the basement of the Villa, Laura saw in him suddenly the image of Lionel himself as he must have been before she ever knew him, the poised, assured, above all the determined conqueror of Kulhantepe.

'No,' said Daniel quietly.

'Whatever do you mean, no?'

'What I say, Father: no. I will not do as you ask. You accuse my friend, and by strong implication you accuse me too, of fraud. Without proof. And on the strength of that accusation you now ask me to perpetrate a much greater fraud. I see you have already taken possession of Laura's notes. Now you want to destroy evidence which is unique in the entire prehistory of Europe. That I will not do.'

'Then by God, Daniel, it shall be done without you.' The blood had come up in Lionel's face, there was no holding back the storm now.

'Listen, Father.' Daniel spoke quietly, urgently, his voice punctuated by a high cracked laugh Laura had never heard from him before. 'It's quite obvious these bones haven't been pitched into the trench recently. They're as old as Ano Meri itself, and you won't explain them away by casting a stain on Firkin's character or mine. But all right then, suppose I do connive at this fraud – because, make no mistake, that's what it will be – you must see clearly what it means. If you're determined to throw away your reputation and the scientific value of everything you've done here, all right then, I shan't stand in your way. But how long do you think you can cover up the truth? For one generation, for two? It's lain here undisturbed for three thousand years. Suppose it has to rest another three thousand, it won't be any less true for that. Don't you see, History is on the move and what you're trying to stop is History itself. But it won't be stopped. Not for you, not for Hitler, not for all the might of His Britannic Majesty's precious Empire!'

'Fiddlesticks. You're a dreamer, Daniel, you've never had your feet properly on the ground. And you've some damn' fine friends, I must say. People like that rascal from the South Seas; that crackpot poet Varvatakis;

Kreuz, damn him and bless him, he was a brilliant artist for the job, and for that I forgave him everything else, but as for the notions he'd got in his head . . .'

Daniel plunged straight on. 'Father, I would never have wanted to say this, but you force me to it. If there's a dreamer among us, feet not properly on the ground and so on, that's you. You've *created* Ano Meri and your Minoans in your own image, haven't you? That's what's wrong with this dig, with us, with everything about it. It's not science, it's not real. It's *you*. Lionel Robertson, the *liondari*, the Boss. Wonderful. But then something turns up that knocks your elaborate dreams for six, forces you, if you were honest, to think again. And all you can do is accuse the real scientists, people like Firkin, God help him, of playing silly practical jokes.'

'Your friend did play practical jokes – a very silly and a very tasteless one. He didn't deny it.'

'Then you might at least find out whether he denies this one, mightn't you? You refuse to look evidence in the face. So your Minoans weren't such lovable people after all. It isn't the end of the world. But to stoop to the cheap tricks you accuse others of – no, Father, that I will not do.'

Lionel sat forward facing Daniel intently, his large hands placed squarely on his knees. 'Daniel,' he said, his voice almost breaking, 'my mind is made up. If you dare to defy me in this, then as God is my witness I have no son.'

And into the stunned silence that followed these words Daniel was appalled to hear himself pouring, quite calmly, deliberately, with vicious sarcasm, the poison that had been stored up for twenty years. 'But you have a daughter, haven't you?' It was his own voice, and this was hateful, what it was saying, but he couldn't hold it back. 'Not yours, of course, oh no not yours. The bastard daughter of Hermione, your wife, my mother. But after me, the nearest to an heir you'll ever have. Maybe you'll be better served by *her*. Back you go to England and embrace your bastard daughter. Yes, I'll even tell you her name, you know it, of course—'

But Lionel had held up a hand as though to ward off a blow. 'Stop,' he cried out, white and shaking. 'There is no need to mention that name here. I know it well enough. But if it was Trudgill told you this, I'll have him out of his place in Hell to answer for it.'

'No, Father, not Trudgill. A little bird told me.'

Laura clung horrified to Daniel's arm, feeling herself cast aside in the duel to the death of the two men's self-esteem. Lionel fell back in his chair, as though winded, and wiped his brow. 'Then it is truly finished,' he seemed to be muttering.

Daniel stepped forward, biting his lip, as the realization caught up with him that somehow even now, in this supreme moment of crisis, he had miscalculated. 'You *knew*?'

'Oh yes.' Lionel's voice sounded diminished, as he sat collapsed in his chair, shrunk in on himself. 'Oh yes, Daniel, I knew. And it has been my care and duty to keep you, and dear Laura also, untainted by knowledge of the betrayal you now so heartlessly fling in my face.'

With a visible effort he pulled himself upright. 'Very well, everything is finished now. There is nothing to keep any of us here any longer, and every reason to leave before it is too late. I ask you to do as I say only until we reach Alexandria. Tonight we leave Ano Meri. The motorcar will serve, I trust, as far as Kastro. Crete we leave by the next available means. If you value your life, and, Daniel, if you value your wife's safety as you ought, you will obey me in this. Stay behind, and I have no doubt they will crucify you when I am gone.'

Rising now unsteadily to his feet, gaunt and uncharacteristically bent, Lionel held up his stick towards Daniel. 'Now you listen to me. This is my last wish to you as a father. Before nightfall these disgraceful relics are to be disposed of. After that, whatever you may choose to do is no concern of mine.' Suddenly Lionel raised his voice to shout at the pitch of his dust-laden lungs, '*I have no son!*'

Later that day, as Laura was packing up their few belongings in the Cabin, her eyes pricked by tears of frustration, of injustice, of sadness, she heard the sounds that had not been heard at Ano Meri for many months, sounds that neither she nor Daniel would ever hear again, the sounds of workmen coming up the road from the village, the banging of picks and shovels, the snorting of the mules, a raucous, tuneless snatch of song. She started up in dismay and went to the uncurtained window. But she knew why they came, and for very shame she didn't want to see.

Later again, Daniel came sheepishly in, shaking the light down of drizzle from his clothes. A glance at his face told her what he had been doing. They avoided looking at one another.

'How did you . . . ?'

Again that uneasy laugh. Something was happening to Daniel that she could barely comprehend. His voice when he spoke sounded flat, resigned. 'How *do* you destroy bones? I did what I'll bet the Minoans would have done if the roof hadn't fallen in on the remains of their dinner. You remember Bertie's middens? God knows what else might be down there. Anyway, that's what I did with them.'

Laura cocked an eyebrow. 'Bothros 2?'

'Bothros 2.'

It is in this telegraphic form that the answer to Dan's riddle has come down across the decades, drily preserved without comment in Laura's diary entry of a few days later, to be imparted in due course, and in the very strictest confidence, to Milica, now salaried as Dan's research assistant, on a day when

England fans are running wild in Sardinia and World Cup mania has taken over the television screens, to the strains of a warm melody uncoiling upwards through the strings and the triumphant voice of Luciano Pavarotti holding, for longer than human breath, it seems, can possibly endure, the climactic final note from *Turandot*: *vincerò. I shall win.*

Darkness was falling on that day in early April 1941. The engine of the aged Hispano-Suiza roared as, for the last time with Lionel at the wheel, it took the rutted track that led to the metalled coast road and the flickering lights of Kastro. Laura sat in front; Daniel perched behind, on top of the luggage.

Behind the car, almost leaping on the running board at the bends, ran Tzak, the abandoned gundog, barking and whimpering. Daniel had promised Laura curtly that he would be taken care of. Laura couldn't see how, and stared straight ahead, dry-eyed, into the gathering darkness.

Lionel dined at the Marine Club, which had been taken over as a temporary officers' mess by the Military Mission. When Laura and Daniel met him later, as agreed, at the Excelsior, they were unprepared to be hustled through the blackout to the port. They were, Lionel curtly assured them, only just in time. There was a destroyer standing out in the bay. Civilian personnel were being evacuated. Perhaps, Lionel even twisted the knife, they had reason to be grateful to that blackguard friend of Daniel's after all. Hadn't they heard the day's news? Hitler's armies were even now sweeping south through Yugoslavia towards Greece. It might be their last chance to reach Alexandria in safety.

The harbour was in darkness. Only Lionel carried a torch. Out of the almost tangible blackness they saw an answering flash from the boatman who was to take them to the destroyer. Only the minimum of luggage had been allowed, just what each of them could carry. The single-cylinder engine of the little boat started up with a popping, hammering noise that seemed to violate the night. Laura sat at the prow, feeling the warm black air stirring her hair, listening to the swish of water past the keel. The ruined Venetian fortress was a patch of thicker darkness as they passed under its walls and out into the slight swell of the bay. The destroyer seemed to be a long way out. For what seemed an age she sat all alone in her space of darkness, between an invisible sea and an invisible, starless sky, while the night scents of the land receded, and the evil-smelling engine pounded in her ears.

She had seen no light, but suddenly the darkness to port solidified into the plates of a ship's side.

'All aboard, please. Next stop Alex,' came a cheerful voice from far above. The only way up, Laura realized with a sinking feeling in her stomach, was by rope ladder. Laura had not been on a rope ladder since she and her classmates had been put through their paces in the rudimentary convent gym. She dreaded the height, and trying to find the writhing steps with her feet, and not knowing how far it was to go.

The boat's engine had all but died, at last she could hear herself think. Their travelling suitcases were expertly hoisted away, knotted by the boatman to the end of an invisible rope. Daniel was meanwhile insisting that his father should be first up the ladder. Huffily, ill at ease, perhaps sensing even then that his son's capitulation, after the terrible words of the morning, had not been all it seemed, Lionel set off into the blackness. Laura was next. Daniel grasped her with both arms from behind, to steady her as she stood up to take hold of the first wooden rungs. Surprisingly, he kissed her full on the cheek and patted her bottom almost jovially. Laura launched herself into space, and felt the whole ladder dancing with the weight of Lionel's progress above her. Almost at once the little boat was lost to sight. She had to concentrate hard to keep her footing, to stop herself from panicking. It couldn't be so very much further. The jerking above her had stopped. Lionel must have reached the deck.

She felt her progress slowing before she could have told herself why. Daniel should by now be grasping the bottom of the ladder in his turn, to begin his ascent. She stopped, and the ladder was still.

'Daniel!' she hissed in a loud whisper. But the sound was drowned out by the banging of the single-cylinder engine. Surely it was louder than a moment ago.

"Urry along there, please. Both sides now. 'Ow tight.' It was the voice of a Cockney bus conductor. But beneath the blithe humour Laura could detect a note of real impatience. The Navy, they had been warned, were anxious to be clear of the Italian airfields on Scarpanto before dawn.

For a moment she swung in mid air against the cold metal plates of the ship. Then, in a rush of sudden, terrible emptiness, the truth dawned upon her. The embrace disguised as a helping hand, the kiss, the pat on the bottom. It had been more of a valediction than Lionel got, at least.

There was no mistaking, now, the sounds of the engine below. This wasn't Daniel dithering, a last-minute crisis of conscience. This had been *planned*, even perhaps from that morning, certainly by the time he had come in from disposing of the evidence in Bothros 2, and been unable to look her in the eye. Tzak, it came to her now, in a bitter flash, would be well cared for. He had foreseen even that. But what about her? Already Laura had begun, slowly at first, to climb back down the ladder towards the boat.

'Wait! Wait for me!' she had finally to cry out in alarm as she slithered the last few rungs and flung herself from the side of the destroyer, into the blackness where the thumping of the boat's engine seemed already to be starting to move.

As the boat drew towards the shore, and the rumble of the destroyer's engines told her that it, too, was under way, with Lionel aboard and all alone (like stubble on the plain), Laura grasped Daniel's face between both her hands. This close, she could almost see his features, as a grey blur. 'Daniel Robertson, I have one word to say to you, and you will find it very shocking. *Shit!*' she shouted at him above the pounding of the engine, and she felt his body relax in the laughter of horrified complicity that enveloped them both.

Much later that same night, back at Ano Meri, in the Cabin that was now for good or ill the only place of refuge left for Laura and Daniel, they talked and talked in a way they had never done since the first months after they met, and perhaps not even then with such frankness. In the course of that long night, Laura confided her secret of the past winter, her nurse's training. And another secret, that she had been longing to break to Daniel ever since the long winter she had spent apart from him in Milan: 'We can have a child,' she told him through sudden tears. 'Yes, really. I never told you, but I went to see a specialist. He assured me. It's as certain as these things can ever be, he said. Now I've told you, it'll be all right, won't it? Whatever happens to the rest of the world, we'll have a child. Right?'

And Daniel buried his face in her hair, that she now wore loose and long and that smelt somehow of the wild thyme that grew among the olive groves. Had they really been so far apart? And inwardly Daniel could only nod to himself in sadness, because he knew they had, and the rain began to fall again steadily, comfortingly, everlastingly on the wooden roof of the Cabin, as he cupped his hands round the living warmth of Laura's hair and raised her lips to his and kissed her full on the mouth.

'Right,' he said with a grin, and she grinned back.

That same night Daniel opened up to her a stranger secret still. At the bottom of his trunk in his room, freshly pressed, no doubt by Aspasia, its brass buttons polished and gleaming, lay the uniform he had last worn into battle.

She gasped. 'How on earth . . . ? You never told me!'

Daniel shrugged, and smirked conspiratorially. 'It just happened to be there. I'm not signed up as a regular soldier, you see. But I think it'll come in handy, don't you?'

Laura stared down at the neatly folded trouser legs and tunic, the sleeves reverentially crossed over the lapels, and felt the flesh crawl on the back of her neck.

He was inviting her to look into his grave.

14 THE SACRIFICE

DURING April the skies cleared over Crete. The hot weather came early that year, and with it came the first bombing raids on Kastro. Helplessly, Laura watched from the terrace of the Villa as the dark specks grew on the northern horizon, the undulating drone of heavy aero engines grew to a roar, and a squadron of bombers, sometimes as many as a dozen of them, banked steeply over the coast, to run in almost lazily, low over the roofs of the distant town, and unload their cargo of death on the harbour and the gun emplacements that had been hastily set up on its far side, towards the airfield. Sometimes the explosions sent shockwaves through the ground even as far as where she stood. Often, when the breeze was from the south, no sound came to her at all, the puffs of black smoke sprouted silently from behind the tight-packed roofs. On other days the explosions sounded like a relentless, rhythmic percussion, syncopated by the erratic and sharper cracks of the ack-ack batteries, the few that there were. They never seemed to have the slightest effect on the attackers.

On the second day Laura donned the uniform that she had kept a secret from Daniel for so long. She could stand it no longer, she said. She couldn't sit idly by. There were bound to be civilian casualties. Veniamin must need all the help he could get. She had promised him.

Daniel folded her in his arms, in the bright sunlight of the terrace, and gazed at her seriously. No more words were necessary. In the two weeks since Lionel's departure they had reached a new understanding. Archaeology was behind them. Daniel was now openly recruiting Cretan civilians to fight in the event of a German attack, busy putting his local knowledge to use, talking to the British and Australian officers who had now begun moving in, with their regiments, to the environs of the town. Some listened sympathetically to his passionate talk of liberating the oppressed of the shanty-towns and educating the backward peasants of the villages, of the germ of a new political order to come, beyond the present conflict. But among

269

everyone he spoke to, British, Antipodean or Greek, there was agreement on one thing: there had been a bloody balls-up. Something for Chrissake, should have been done to make up for the Cretan regiment that had been whisked away to fight in Albania and was even now being rounded up and disarmed by Hitler's stormtroopers. Where was the military planning? Where were the installations, the reinforcements that were so badly needed? Troops were now arriving, as Daniel could see for himself, although in pitifully small numbers. At the other end of the island Souda Bay was being turned into a fortress, that was where the brunt of the action was going to be. Daniel appealed again and again for weapons to arm his Cretan irregulars. The response he got from the C-in-C was a sardonic reminder of the Duke of Wellington's words: 'I don't know what they will do to the enemy, Robertson, but by God they frighten me.' Regular soldiers viewed his efforts with more or less suspicion. Officers with service in the colonies could recognize all too well the signs of the *good man half gone native*, which was synonymous in clubrooms the world over with *unreliable type*. Daniel was dimly aware of this, but it only added to the superiority he felt. They were just doing their duty in an unfamiliar corner of the globe. He was on home ground, or so he believed. And when the chips were down, the difference would show.

So Laura donned her new identity as a Red Cross nurse, and Daniel drove her into Kastro. There was an unaccustomed silence in the town, it felt like the time of the afternoon siesta, but it was mid morning, the metal shutters had been raised on half the shop fronts, others stayed obstinately closed. There were few people in the streets.

The town itself had so far been largely untouched by the raids, which were concentrated on the harbour. But Veniamin's clinic had been taken over, and Laura quickly found there was work to do: British, Australian, some Greek gunners from the remnants of the Greek army who had escaped being rounded up in Albania. There was a new atmosphere in the place, Veniamin and his staff were run off their feet.

She parted from Daniel at the door of the clinic, in the dusty side street. 'Whatever happens,' she said quite gaily, 'I'll see you back at the Villa. Trust me.'

'I do, Laura. Absolutely.' He looked briefly up into her eyes as she stood above him by the door of the car; he didn't get out. That unruly ringlet had come loose even beneath the rim of her starched cap. He grinned up at her, it was a grin full of confidence, full of a childlike trust, of his deep, undogmatic conviction in Laura's love. She looked almost pert in her uniform as she trotted briskly up the steps away from him; he caught himself watching the movement of her buttocks as though he were eyeing a stranger. After how many years? – good God, it must be fifteen to the very day – he felt with a great surge of happiness and promise, that he was only now truly getting to

270

know the most beautiful girl in the opera house in Milan on that distant April night, to see beneath her poise and the quicksilver anxieties it concealed, even beneath that headstrong determination, when she would set her nose and chin in a way she had: he felt he had unlocked a mystery. If he had failed to understand her, if he had never properly tried to understand her, it wasn't, after all, because she had locked away her deeper, truer self beyond his reach, it was because she truly *was* all of the inexhaustible selves he saw in her daily. It was like starting all over again, he felt buoyed up. With Laura, it was unthinkable that they should ever come to the end.

She turned at the top of the steps, and with a little wave was gone. As he eased the car expertly out of the narrow street, Daniel's mind ran on into the future. He was not sanguine about the hastily-organized defence of Crete. That last week had seen the trickle of evacuees from mainland Greece swell to a tide – high-ranking civilians, and now increasingly also military personnel. The Greek king and (so Varvatakis informed him) his English mistress were on the island. So was his government and a skeleton civil service. At the Marine Club in the harbour, and at the headquarters of the Military Mission in the town, Daniel talked to officers in whose restless eyes and stumbling narratives he recognized, like a deeply buried memory, the recent experience of being under continuous and heavy fire.

The collapse in Greece had been a shambles.

In the harbour lay several naval ships with jagged holes in their plates, some listing badly, others with their superstructure blackened and twisted. The caïques in the inner harbour, that Daniel had often enough watched peacefully towing their string of little boats out to sea in the evening, their acetylene lamps already lit for night fishing, were many of them in no better shape. Their numbers had been swelled by those that had survived the hazardous voyage, under continuous dive-bombing by Stukas, across the open sea from Greece. Many more, it was clear from the harrowing accounts of those who survived the crossing, had been sunk on the way.

It happened, as evil things do in Greek belief, on a Tuesday. Rumours had been flying all over the island since the weekend. Even some of the military men Daniel met, on his increasingly hectic rides on horseback round the prefecture of Kastro, had the jitters. All along the coast, from the harbour, past the old Greek army barracks, to the airfield on the cliffs to the east, the heavy guns were trained out to sea. And day after day, thousands of pairs of binoculars were anxiously trained the same way, scanning the empty pale blue sea where it met the sky. The temperature soared. Summer came early to Crete in 1941.

Daniel had not been idle. His 'home guard' was already beginning to earn the respect of the professionals. At a string of key points surrounding Kastro, Daniel had his local militias primed and ready. Thanks no doubt in part to

Varvatakis, he had known unerringly where to find 'sleeping' opponents of the former oppressive regime whose writ still ran in Crete, and in particular those likely to have ignored or evaded the systematic efforts of the authorities to disarm an unruly population. Weapon stores were dug up, antiquated uniforms more bizarre, in those times, even than Daniel's were dusted down. It was an army, as many of its impromptu lieutenants were wont to call it, of grandfathers and young boys. But women came forward to bear arms as well. And some of the most bloodthirsty of Daniel's recruits were the priests. Not that any of these people needed much urging. Daniel did not attempt to disguise from himself that his role was at most that of catalyst.

On that fateful Tuesday Daniel was back at Ano Meri. Of the younger village men only Yannis, on account of his weak chest, and Spinalonga were left. There had been no word of Manolis, who with the rest had been fighting in Albania, for more than three months. Yannis had always treated the Robertsons with reserve, but whatever his personal feelings he and Daniel were comrades in arms, in their different ways even fellow idealists. Under Daniel's tireless direction he and Spinalonga, the now tottering Hadzi-Aga and some of the older men, had spent the previous day carrying sandbags up to the flat roof of the Villa Europa. The position chosen by the Minoans, overlooking as it did the pass to the west, would be of strategic importance in any battle, now as then. With half a dozen gunners on the roof of the Villa, and as many more concealed in the olive groves below, Daniel had no doubt that the pass could be held. And if it could not be held, the way lay open for a tactical retreat to the wild uplands behind. In the mountains, the possibilities for guerrilla warfare were unlimited. None of the island's many conquerors in its history, he was assured with equal confidence by educated and unlettered alike, had ever been able to subdue the mountainous interior. No more would the Germans, if they came.

It was the hour of the afternoon siesta. Despite the rumours, the morning had brought nothing more than the daily 'hate' down at the harbour in Kastro. The bombers had done their work and swung away out to sea again. The sea was empty to the horizon. It had been another false alarm.

Daniel had made up his bed in the earthquake-proof basement room that had been his father's. He was awoken from a deep sleep quite late in the afternoon.

'Archangels with umbrellas are falling from the sky!'

He knew Aspasia's voice, but she seemed to have lost her wits. Frantically she shook him by the shoulders, repeating her message and jabbing her finger aloft. In a moment he was awake. There was no mistaking, even through the thick walls of the Villa, the heavy drone of aero engines. Yannis Laskaris was already on the roof, staring towards Kastro through a pair of binoculars with a single cracked lens. Below, Daniel could see other, more or less familiar forms running among the trees. Without a word, and avoiding his eyes,

Yannis handed him the binoculars. They were hardly necessary. Daniel had never seen so many aeroplanes; to his eyes the Junkers transports were huge. Beneath them, towards the coast, the sky was thick with parachutes. Above the sound of the engines the crackle of small arms could be clearly heard, though none of the parachutists seemed to be heading as far inland as Ano Meri. Several of the planes had been hit – at last the batteries dug in on the far side of the town seemed to be doing something; the heavy sound of the Bofors guns at the airfield carried quite clearly over the din. He watched unbelieving as a Junkers, trailing black smoke from the wing, cartwheeled into the sea and disappeared in a spout of white water. A few seconds later another blew up in mid air.

Yannis was already moving towards the stairs. 'We'll get the bastards,' Daniel thought he heard him spit between his teeth, before he was gone. The others he had seen in the olive groves were all heading in the same direction. With mingled satisfaction and chagrin he saw his carefully nurtured 'home guard' slipping into action, but out of his control. He would need men here, the strategic advantage was here, not down in the plain where the parachutists were falling. But his hot-headed warriors had no thought for strategy. By the time he was lost to view among the trees, Yannis had already unsheathed a long heavy knife. '. . . be back!' Daniel thought he heard, in Greek, flung over his shoulder. *Bloody well better be*, he thought.

And while the battle raged in the countryside below, and at the western gate of the town, Daniel remained alone at his post, to savour the anti-climax and his diminished authority.

With the faithful Spinalonga, whose bent legs prevented him from following the others to the brutal game of hide-and-seek that was even now going on in the darkness that covered the plain, Daniel alternated watches on the roof throughout that night. In the hot weather, Tzak spent the whole night there, only occasionally stirring to scratch for fleas. Daniel's improvised military network had not given way entirely; throughout the hours of darkness, runners came and went. By midnight Daniel knew that Kastro was in German hands. But many of the parachutists had been killed, most of the survivors were still holed up in vineyards and olive groves, cut off from the spearhead that had taken the town. They would be mopped up by the Cretan irregulars tomorrow. The Allied troops dug in round the airfield had given a good account of themselves too, it seemed. The invaders would be wiped out.

Although he scarcely admitted it to himself, Daniel's sense of anti-climax was only deepened by this news. He had put everything of himself into preparing for this moment. Now it looked as though the long-dreaded German attack was going to end in fiasco. By the time dawn appeared as a faint pencil line of greenish yellow above the serrated top of Mount Iouktas, Daniel was beginning to wish he too had broken ranks and joined in the bloodthirsty manhunt for paratroopers. The men he thought of as his own would presumably today be pressing forward to the walls of Kastro. The thought never for a moment left him that Laura was in there, in a town in enemy hands. But he kept his image of her at bay, he forced himself to think coolly. It was part of the self-imposed training of the past months. Still, before the Stukas reappeared over the seaward horizon and began dive-bombing with their hideous shrill whine at what seemed to be indiscriminate targets in the plain, Daniel had been ready to abandon his post and follow the victors towards Kastro.

By the end of that day he learnt that the Germans had withdrawn from the town into the surrounding countryside. There had been running battles all day. The roads were unsafe, with re-formed units of paratroopers dug in on hilltops, in farmhouses and abandoned buildings, while smaller groups lay hidden in ditches and olive groves. Towards sunset he got his first glimpse of the invaders: two motorcyclists with sidecars, the riders stripped to the waist but recognizable by the shape of their helmets and the swastika pennants they flew. They were far below him, on the winding dust road leading up to the westward pass. From his vantage point on the roof of the Villa, Daniel squinnied at them through the sights of his rifle. He was confident he could have picked them off, even at that distance, but prudence suggested it was better not to give away his position too soon. Ano Meri might yet come into its own. That night Daniel felt strange emotions, all but forgotten, begin to curdle within him. The classic German helmet had not changed since he had been in battle before. He found himself shaken by a terrible excitement. He had thought to be cool and precise this time around; rationally, almost coldly, dedicated to a cause that he knew to be just. Men like Reinhard Kreuzenberger would die for such a cause. For him, Daniel, it was the testing time.

Dr Veniamin was all but asleep on his feet. He stood beside Laura at the deep stone sink. He had removed his surgical gloves but his pale bronze arms were streaked with blood up to the elbow. Only an intermittent trickle of water came from the open tap.

'Without water we'll be finished,' said Veniamin grimly. 'I'm trying to organize some of the walking wounded to carry water from wells about the town. It's what they say the people of Kastro did when they held out against the Turks for twenty-four years. Just think of it, twenty-four years, shut in within these walls! We're only into the fourth day.'

'Get some rest, do. There won't be another raid before dawn. I'll manage, really I will.'

Veniamin looked at her with an expression that could have been tenderness, could have been condescension. 'The battle won't go on for ever, Laura. They don't do sieges any more like they did in the seventeenth

274

century. This one will be decided one way or the other in the next few days. We'll all just have to carry on till then.'

Since the shortlived German occupation of the town and the withdrawal of the invaders to the vineyards outside the walls, the daily 'hate' had been stepped up. Now bombs fell not just over the harbour area but all over the town, as though at random. Bombers came over night and morning. Each day, in the scorching heat, the streets were filled with rubble and the dust of centuries of human habitation slowly rising, dispersing in the quivering air. On the few occasions Laura had been outside the clinic she had been awestruck by the silence. The Cretans she knew to be an emotional people, ready to give vent immediately to the slightest stimulus of joy or grief. Now, the only sounds were the rasping of spades, the occasional oath, a single, distant woman's voice sobbing without control, sometimes the sharper, more intermittent crying of victims trapped beneath the rubble.

Since the bombing of the town proper had begun, the nature of Laura's work had changed dramatically. The military had largely left Kastro, and Laura assumed they must have their own field hospitals in the outskirts, beyond the walls. Into Dr Veniamin's clinic were carried the helpless civilian victims of the bombing, sometimes terribly damaged, to be treated as best they could be by the handful of staff available. It was the children, hideously torn by shrapnel wounds, that most affected Laura. There had been a five-year-old boy with a fragment of bomb casing embedded in his spine. His legs and arms dangled uselessly. Before and after Veniamin operated on him he lay staring straight ahead of him, unblinking, never crying. The only word he ever spoke was *Mamá*. His mother was dead under the rubble. He had other injuries too. Laura often tried to talk to him. Sometimes he would turn his head to look at her, not so much uncomprehending, but as though comprehending too much. On the second day after his arrival, Laura followed Veniamin to the foot of the bed, out of earshot. Tears in her eyes (it was the only time), she glanced at him interrogatively. With a slight click of the tongue, he shifted his head imperceptibly upwards. It was the Greek gesture that says 'no'. There was no hope.

Paschalis (that was his name) died the next day, and his body was hastily covered up and removed to make space for more victims of the latest raid. He had seen his death approaching with those wide-open, unblinking eyes, had stared into it without hope and without fear, only from time to time opening his mouth to utter, tonelessly, without inflection, the word *Mamá*.

It came to Laura then that if she had indeed been with child at the time of the abortive expedition to the Cave of Zeus, her child would have been Paschalis' age now.

She once found time to ask Veniamin if he believed in God.

'I was brought up to believe in the God of the Jews,' he replied. 'It's a harsh faith: no rewards, no – forgive me – Christian sentimentality. History teaches that my people have seen all this before, and worse. Now, I wouldn't say that I believe all that, the way I was taught it, no. I am for one thing a Socialist. I believe in suffering, and evil. As a doctor I believe in pain. Those are the real things in the world. And perhaps from the Jewish faith I have also learnt never, never to give up in the fight against them.'

The climax of the bombing came on the Sunday. As darkness fell, Daniel watched impotently from his vantage point on the roof of the Villa Europa while distant Kastro erupted into flame. The familiar rising and falling drone of aero engines filled the air; the bombers themselves were invisible, except where a searchlight from the airfield caught a fuselage like a tiny, silver fish. It was a hot, still night; the thud of exploding bombs was carried clearly to Daniel's ears. It went on and on; he could feel the distant explosions jarring the ground beneath his feet, he felt them like pounding, unrelenting punches to his own body. Would it never stop?

By midnight, long after the last sound of aircraft had faded into the darkness, the fires were still raging down in Kastro. Laura was somewhere in that maelstrom. Seeing the destruction as he had, he could scarcely imagine how anyone could have survived. Instinct told him that Laura could not be among them. She would not have left her wounded to go down into the shelter.

It was the last run of the aged Hispano-Suiza. The order had gone round during the afternoon to evacuate as many of the wounded as possible from Kastro. No one seemed to know where the order had come from. Some said the Mayor's office: the German Commandant had given notice, before withdrawing, that the Luftwaffe would now destroy the town. There was also a rumour that German reinforcements were on their way by sea. By morning the town would be bombarded to make way for seaborne landings. Veniamin was adamant. He himself would stay behind with the most severely wounded who could not be moved. Whatever happened, somebody had to stay. Several refuges had been considered for the evacuees. One, inevitably, was the Villa Europa at Ano Meri, since the house was known to be one of the most strongly built in Crete, and its earthquake-proof basement would provide ideal shelter. Laura , with only one other nurse and a nervous junior doctor, was to guide them there.

When she had demurred about going, Veniamin was uncharacteristically stern with her. She should not delude herself that she was avoiding danger by leaving the town at such a time. The countryside was bristling with paratroopers, no one knew for certain if the roads were still open, or when the Stukas would be back to resume their indiscriminate dive-bombing. Once at the Villa, her wounded, who were after all the prime concern, would be much safer than in Kastro. To evacuate them, with their accompanying staff, including Laura, was a calculated risk. If she, Laura, didn't wish to take that risk for herself, then no doubt another volunteer could be found . . .

Stung, she left the tiny, hot office on the second floor of the clinic without a word. She never saw Veniamin again.

A battered truck, with a Greek military driver, would carry the wounded and a stock of medical supplies. There was some uncertainty at first about how Laura herself and her companions were to travel. Transport was scarce, and the truck was already full. It was Laura who came upon the motorcar she knew so well, abandoned near the western gate of the town. A tightness came into her throat as she recognized it, but she fought the feeling down. Daniel wouldn't have had any use for the car since the start of the invasion. He would have far greater freedom riding on horseback round the foothills, with Tzak loyally loping along in his wake, perhaps pausing to bark from time to time at the scent of a rabbit, then scampering, paws flying, to catch up with his inflexible master. In due course, in the heat and the generally panicky air of that afternoon, a driver was found for the Hispano-Suiza, and the little convoy set off westwards. A sheet daubed with paint in the insignia of the Red Cross had been stretched across the roof of the truck. Similar banners, equally improvised, had been added to its bonnet and sides, and now to the motorcar as well.

The road, as they headed out of town along the coast, was pitted with small craters from bombs and shells. Burnt-out vehicles had been pushed to one side, sometimes there was only just room to pass. The driver was evidently nervous about booby-traps, and several times got out to reconnoitre before edging past these wrecks. Some of the scattered houses had been abandoned, a few had been destroyed by fire. The rest had their shutters obstinately closed. Intermittently in the glazed heat the sound of firing came from the fields. As they neared the turn-off for Ano Meri, where the shanty-town sprawled along the edge of the sea, a group of people who must have heard them coming suddenly rushed out into the road, carrying a door as a makeshift stretcher and on it an old man, the stumps of his crudely bandaged legs already giving off a strong whiff of gangrene. The two drivers and the doctor argued with the group. There was no room in the truck. Orders were not to pick up stragglers. No, there was no reason. Kastro was full of terribly wounded people, that was how it was, and now, for God's sake, would they get out of the way? Laura was able to follow less than half of this altercation, but it shocked her to hear the doctor spell out quite brutally, in the hearing of the old man, who was fully conscious and moaning, turning his head from side to side, as the argument raged back and forth, a bright, fierce hope in his sunken eyes, that he wouldn't last forty-eight hours, even if they took him. It's not on, *bárba*, we're only taking curables.

Suddenly Laura became aware of a new sound. The shadow of the Stuka, flying at treetop height, had flashed across the little group almost before anyone had registered its presence. The slipstream whipped up the white dust of the road as its engine roared in a steep turn. Quickest off the mark was the driver of the truck, who leapt into his cab and drove his vehicle, with a force that raised screams from the wounded in the back, into the deepest shade between two tall eucalyptus trees. Almost as quickly, the knot of people in the roadway had disappeared, leaving only the old man helpless under the sun on his makeshift stretcher. Laura, seeing herself abandoned, made a half-hearted attempt to tug the heavy door, but somebody ran from the shadows to pull her away. She was only just in time. The Stuka had begun its dive, coming in along the line of the road, its wings tipped with black and yellow stripes – like a wasp, Laura thought incongruously. The hideous howling that had been devised by Hitler's engineers to strike terror into the hearts of the world's lesser races seemed to pierce her through and through. She had heard Stukas before, in Kastro, but never this close, never so low; for a moment it seemed certain the pilot was as determined on his own destruction as on that of his victims. Laura could already imagine the ball of fire that must engulf them as the plane hit the road and its ammunition and fuel tanks exploded, but no, with deadly precision the Stuka pulled out of its dive. Laura covered her face with her hands as the howling stopped and a stream of machine-gun bullets punched into the roadway. It seemed to go on for ever, the clatter, the raucous blare of the engine, the loud mosquito-whine of the ricochets.

When at last Laura raised her head the space above the road was filled with white dust. The Hispano-Suiza was on its side and blazing furiously. As she watched, the windscreen cracked in the heat and fell with a pathetic tinkle on the roadway. The flames were already licking round the edge of the wooden doorway on which the body of the old man still lay. Laura found her limbs paralysed, the way it happens in nightmares. It was somebody else inside her, someone quite unconnected with the horror in front of her, but in there, thinking inside her own head, that told her it was just the lens of superheated air through which she saw him that made the old man seem to move in the fire. He was dead, of course. Even if she had had the power of motion, there was nothing she could have done.

The sheet with the insignia of the Red Cross had been blown from the car by the slipstream and hung now as though in mockery from the branches of the eucalyptus trees by the roadside.

In slow motion, life returned to the scene, and Laura gingerly, cautiously, reclaimed the use of her limbs. The truck driver's prompt action had saved the day. None of their party had been hurt. But the truck itself was bogged down with a broken axle. They would have to spend the night here. The two drivers between them reckoned they could manage a running repair. There were enough wrecked vehicles lying about, they could find the parts they needed, and work all night if necessary.

No one paid any attention to the blazing wreck in the middle of the road, that had become, within minutes, the funeral pyre of an unknown refugee from the burning of Smyrna.

To the end of her days Laura could never smell eucalyptus without feeling in her nostrils again the acrid fumes of burning tyres and upholstery, and the sickly-sweet basting odour of human flesh consumed by fire.

Daniel was incensed, next morning, at the arrival of the truck which now, in addition to its intended human cargo, carried Laura, the two nurses, a doctor and an extra driver who had insisted he had nowhere else to go. Grasping Laura almost roughly by the shoulders, he shouted, 'But weren't there any *plans*, for God's sake? Does no one down there understand that Ano Meri is a military position? What do you think I've been doing these last weeks?' – and he waved wildly towards the sandbagged roof of the Villa. 'Don't you see? You've brought all these bloody wounded into a battle zone.'

Laura was tired. She could have done without Daniel's shouting, but it didn't matter, really it didn't. With a tremendous effort, she said, 'Well, they're here now, and our orders are to care for them in the basement of the Villa. You can hardly refuse us that. If there's to be fighting here, we'll just have to take our chance. There's fighting everywhere. Oh Daniel —' and she told him about the end of the motorcar.

In front of the anxious stares of the little group from the truck, who were watching this scene, Daniel touched her cheek. 'You poor thing,' he said, 'you've really been through it, haven't you?'

Laura nodded and took his hands in hers. She hadn't seen him wearing his uniform before. It was a tight, almost an ungainly fit, its stiff lines so different from the officers' uniforms she had got used to seeing in Kastro. She could have laughed from sheer love at the seriousness of it. But he was staring at her, blinking furiously. 'I saw the bombing,' he said unevenly, 'I thought you were gone.'

'We'll talk later, there'll be time. As you see, I'm here – and to hear you talk anyone would think you didn't want me to be!'

Daniel had regained his composure and was already striding briskly over to the little group. He made an incongruous little speech of welcome, his legs and arms looking to Laura very long as he gesticulated, showing the way to the stretcher bearers and the walking wounded, down to the earthquake-proof basement. 'The whole of the Villa could be destroyed over your heads,' he told them cheerfully, 'and you would be quite untouched down there. Of course, you might run out of air before anybody found you.'

Laura already had her private nightmares of Lionel's earthquake-proof basement. She remembered very vividly the terror of the night the earthquake struck. Only Lionel had risked putting the structure to the test. Laura had been haunted ever afterwards by the fear of being caught down there like a rat in a trap. Now she would have to do what she could to calm the fears of those in her charge.

There was no time to confide any of these anxieties to Daniel. Already she had realized that he was by no means alone at Ano Meri. His lieutenants had returned; the roof of the Villa and the olive groves below were bristling with weapons. She recognized the sallow features of Yannis Laskaris peering over the sandbagged parapet of the roof. In the black breeches they always wore, the men were a sinister, silent presence. She realized too that they were not here idly. They were waiting, it was a silence of anticipation. And it had not been she and her wounded that they were waiting for.

With a breezy promise over his shoulder to Laura that 'he'd be back', Daniel bounded up the outside staircase to the roof, Tzak at his heels. It would be today, he was in no doubt of it. Day by day his Cretan irregulars, who had rushed off at the start of the invasion to make short work of the paratroopers in the plain, had been falling back on the Villa. The Germans had by now consolidated their positions around Kastro, and were already beginning harsh reprisals against the local population for their resistance. An order had gone out, Daniel was informed from many quarters, that civilians killed bearing arms were not to be buried, and this had struck the Cretans as particularly barbarous, with their strong sense of respect for the dead, and especially since it was their own country they were defending. With the destruction of Kastro in last night's bombing raid, and the failure of the heavily armed British, Australian and Greek enclave round the airfield to break out and dislodge the invaders from their positions, Daniel sensed the mood of his Cretan fighters changing almost hourly. Gone was the fierce compulsion to launch themselves at the enemy wherever and whenever he was to be found. They had come back to the Villa – local men he knew, some whom he had recruited from further afield, others again with the wiry toughness of the mountain villagers, whom he had never seen before – as though instinctively recognizing that the plains were now in enemy hands. These men, Daniel knew with pride, were born guerrilla fighters, with tactics learnt over centuries. Ano Meri would be held for a time but would not, unless the fortunes of war changed elsewhere, be the turning point of the battle. It wasn't infantry tactics in the rudimentary form that he had learnt all those years ago on Salisbury Plain. Most of the men under his still (it had to be admitted) loose command would have been court martialled and shot if they had behaved like this in France in 1918. But Daniel learnt a lot since then. He had learnt, above all, about his fellow human beings. And he saw nothing incongruous in his new-found determination to set them free.

Now, at his post on the roof of the Villa, Daniel saw the first vehicles come into view below on the winding road that heads up to the westward pass. There were motorcycles with sidecars, like the ones he had seen before, but this time they were followed by a column of light armoured cars. Even as he felt the muscles tighten in his throat, and his eye began to water with the concentration of aiming through the sights of his rifle, Daniel had time to wonder where they had come from. Had they too been dropped from the air? And now there was no more time for thinking. Ano Meri had come into its own, as he had foreseen. Rifles and old-fashioned muskets cracked from the roof of the Villa and the surrounding woods. The motorcycles swerved and ran off the road, one burst into flames. Soldiers in helmets jumped out of the armoured vehicles and ran for cover. The turrets of the vehicles swivelled uncertainly, they couldn't know where the attack was coming from, they were firing wildly. Daniel saw, with a terrible satisfaction, men falling as they sprinted from bush to bush. In a few minutes it was over. It had been the first skirmish. The armoured column turned back and disappeared.

Later that day they were visited by a lone Stuka that dived repeatedly over the hilltop of Ano Meri. Its bombs dropped harmlessly in the vineyards below the Cabin. It didn't return.

It was towards evening that the attack began in earnest. The men hidden in the trees reported an infantry patrol and at least two armoured cars approaching up the steep rutted track. They were thorough, the Germans. Rather than risk exposing a whole column on the road below, they had delayed to flush out the commanding position of Ano Meri. This was the success of guerrilla tactics, Daniel reflected with unalloyed delight. Even as he began firing at the first sight of the attackers, he found himself transported back to the march to the Rhine all those years ago. He had had some success, he remembered now, in flushing out such positions himself. Like smoking out wasps, it had been. Undeterred, he settled himself more comfortably behind the sandbags; his shoulder was already bruised from the kick of his rifle. The thing now was to keep on firing. To fire and to keep firing. All around him the firing was going on; he had been here before, it was strange that he could have forgotten, the intervening years became telescoped, then shrank to a pinpoint of light and were lost. He was back where he had always been, in the trenches, in the mud, and he knew what was going to happen, it had happened before, but this time he was ready for it, expecting it; his body would open up to the terrifying cascade of the light, he would see once again what he had glimpsed before, there was no mystery about it, this much he had learnt in his forty-one years: the machinery out there.

The battle was now fast and furious. Daniel no longer looked round to assure himself that his troops were in place. There would be time to take to the mountains and regroup . . . It would have to be soon. But for the moment Daniel was, for perhaps only the second time in his life – savagely, utterly, with his whole being – happy.

15 THE UNVEILING

'MANY happy returns, Dan!' Lucy has remembered his birthday and come down to South London with Milica and a bottle of *vin mousseux*. It is the night of the World Cup semi-final. The England fans have finished with Sardinia and are now seething in a noisy, televised mass outside the stadium in Turin. Dan has the television on with the volume low – partly for Milica's benefit (she says she played in a women's football team back home), and also to catch the operatic strains of Pavarotti with which the programme began and will as surely end. The boast of the prince in *Turandot* is on everyone's lips this summer: *Nessun dorma. Let no one sleep.* The soundbite doesn't extend beyond the final bars: *vincerò. I will win.* Dan can see that this is apposite enough to a football spectacular mounted in Italy. To Lucy and Milica, who do not share his love of opera, he explains his objections. 'He does win, yes. But at an inhuman cost.'

Milica, with an eye still on the screen, demands details. Dan is content to oblige with the plot of *Turandot*.

'So hang on,' Lucy demands, when he has finished, 'why does this, what d'you call her, ice princess, ask these riddles? Why's she so keen to cut off the heads of all her suitors?'

Dan smiles benignly. 'Well, it's straight out of Freud, isn't it? Turandot sees herself as a castrated male and revenges herself by a symbolic act of castration. Cutting off heads equals cutting off penises, isn't that so?'

Milica has looked away at this point. 'Yes, of course I know that,' says Lucy, quite seriously. 'But is it in the opera?'

'No, it isn't.' It is Dan's turn to be serious, now. 'There *is* a reason in the opera, and it's a much better one than that hoary old Freudian chestnut. Listen to this. It's quite short, and the game's got half an hour still to go.'

Dan gets up, turns off the television volume, leaving the picture, and selects, from long practice, the right track on the CD. The long accompanied recitative is somewhat shrill, the voice and the music hard, strident. It is difficult for the girls to concentrate on the tiny print in the booklet with the libretto, in four languages, that Dan enthusiastically holds out to them. Generations ago, so legend has it, in time of war, a princess of the royal blood was dragged from her chaste bed, raped and murdered. Her blood calls down the centuries. Turandot, whose forefathers were begotten from that foul act, will never submit to a man, to the image of that primal violation. Her riddles, and the sentence of death on all who fail to answer them, are the revenge of her sex. The recitative builds up to a terrific climax, the voice now leaping the octaves, the centuries-old humiliation rising to an incandescent pinnacle of pride: pride in that infinitely old, infinitely lost purity of a distant time.

Dan turns off the CD. Lucy is visibly impressed; he isn't sure about Milica. 'Of course,' he can't resist adding, 'it's the myth of the Amazons really, transplanted to ancient China. But I thought it might appeal to the feminist in you?'

'Unfair,' protests Lucy at once. 'Still, it makes a change from Pavarotti and the lager louts.'

Attention has now reverted to the screen, and even Dan will shortly be sitting on the edge of his chair, as the semi-final, after extra time, is to be decided by a penalty shoot-out. The volume is turned up, a hush falls in the Turin stadium. As the penalty kicks go into the goal mouth, or not as the case may be, Dan is wryly reminded of the coconut shies of his youth. What kind of a sport is this? But there is no denying the solemnity of the occasion, and as England comes up to take the last kick that will decide the fate of nations, in the world of football, even he is biting his fingers.

It is all over very quickly. There is something shocking about the finality of it. A muffed kick, and England is out. Germany is through to the final.

This was the night when Paul Gascoigne wept in front of the world and thirty million viewers in England loved him for it.

And then the credits come up and the blazing voice of Pavarotti, holding his top note for longer than it seems that human breath can possibly endure: *vincerò.*

Dan hates birthdays, and the one just gone has been no exception. It was nice of Lucy to remember the day. But he had known she was going to ask him about the diaries. Since he has told Milica (and bound her to secrecy) it would hardly have been fair to keep Lucy in the dark. But, as he reflects on the talk that lasted long into the night after the drama of the World Cup was safely over, he knows what it is he had been dreading about confiding in his daughter. It is her questions. *Yes, but what happened after that?* And the question, he couldn't imagine how she would phrase it, but Lucy was never stuck for words, she would find a way and however she asked it, he knew in advance it would shock him to hear it expressed out loud. Which all goes to show, as Lucy did indeed point out, that unconsciously the question is not new to him at all. He has been asking it perhaps all his life – well, ever since he was old enough to understand where people come from.

How did he, Dan, ever get to be born?

Here, he has to admit, his mother's diaries are of no help. With the secret evacuation of all Allied troops from the vicinity of Kastro, under cover of darkness, in the early hours of 28th May 1941, reliable, confirmed reports of the Robertsons who stayed behind come to an end. What emerged from Crete during the years that followed – years of clandestine resistance, undercover missions from Alexandria to the Cretan mountains, of merciless German reprisals against the local people – is the stuff of legend. And out of these legends, Dan has long ago conceded ruefully to himself, came I. The story of the resistance in *Festung Kreta* – Fortress Crete, as the Germans dubbed it soon after their victory – and the individual, hair-raising stories of the British officers infiltrated to organize it, have been told and retold many times. Many solid facts have come to light after half a century. But much will probably always be surmise. Some of the tales that have circulated since may well be too good to be true, and yet in another way they *are* true: true to the legendary, heroic spirit of that time. Among these are several stories of Daniel's exploits after the fall of Crete, stories that for Dan are part of that marvellous tapestry of tales woven by his grandfather, in the big room overlooking the estuary at Upland Grange.

Daniel had organized a break-out by British POWs here, destroyed a munitions dump there. His headquarters was in the Nida Plateau, near the Cave of Zeus, some said actually inside the cave; and certainly that cave, like many others less famous all over the Cretan mountains, was used by the resistance. Daniel had been seen at various times practically all over the island. In Kastro itself, where he had nonchalantly gone to take a bath one hot afternoon, he had been stopped by a patrol of Germans who had with them some Cretan stooges from the local gendarmerie. Under questioning, he had convinced even the gendarmes that he was a Cretan shepherd from the neighbourhood of Ierapetra, and they let him go. All the British officers in occupied Crete adopted Cretan dress, which makes them difficult to identify in photographs. Dan has by now sifted through hundreds of published and unpublished photographs from the time. There are some passing likenesses to his father as Dan knew him throughout his childhood, from the enlarged photograph that stood on his mother's dressing table in the top-floor room at Upland Grange – in whites and spats, leaning back with long bare arms against a low wall or balustrade, his hair quite long with a slight lift at the front as though a breeze is blowing; it appears he is laughing. Ever since the move to South London this photograph has kept its place on the tiled mantelpiece above the gas fire, in this room where a couple of nights ago Dan celebrated his birthday with Lucy and Milica. But which of those blurred, unshaven faces, framed by the tasselled Cretan kerchief, is his father's?

And the stories are not only of Daniel. The dangerous double game played by Laura has often been praised in published accounts, although she herself would hardly ever speak of it in later years. By day the Italian housekeeper for the German divisional commander and his entourage who moved in swiftly after the conquest to take over the Villa Europa; by night in secret touch with British and Cretan partisans, risking her life to pass on the contents of Lieutenant Colonel Meyerhof's safe, through a network of intermediaries, to the British military authorities in Egypt. And chief among these intermediaries, in the legendary lore that has grown up around these years, was none other than Daniel himself. That Daniel returned to visit the Cabin, at dead of night, after the German takeover is proved by numerous accounts, many of them romantically embroidered. Laura herself, after the war, was characteristically – and understandably – reticent about this. But the living proof of some, at least, of these tales is Dan himself. He has often thought that his own begetting may have been the last act of his father's life. There is no firm evidence, but rumours have always persisted that Daniel was killed, not in the mountains which were his base of operations, but somewhere near Ano Meri, some say even in Kastro itself. It seems all too likely that he was ambushed on one of those moonless nights when, with the recklessness that is his hallmark in all these stories, he had fulfilled his promise to Laura: that he would be back. Nikos Varvatakis, who survived the war, later gave it as his opinion that his English friend and fellow idealist had been lured to his death by the chthonic charms of Woman and had died, moreover, *apáno sti glýka* – in the moment of sweetness.

Dan finds himself wavering between wanting to accept this story and being revolted by its mawkishness. Somewhere at the back of his mind – and trust Lucy to have wormed it out of him the other day – has lain unacknowledged the suspicion that his father's death must have been his, Dan's, fault. From things that were said, or more often not said, in his childhood; from the prohibition, amounting almost to a taboo, on the name of Dan's father that is also, disturbingly, his own name, has grown an obscure sense of guilt. Perhaps this helps to explain Dan's self-effacing character, his anxiety not to claim too much room for himself on the planet. But Dan has changed a good deal recently. He has begun to look back on his acquiescent self and wonder. His researches have brought him closer and closer to the moment which few of us, probably, can contemplate with total equanimity – the moment of our own beginning. And at forty-eight the childhood question is once again ringing loudly, even frighteningly, in his ears: *where did I come from?*

If he could only know how his father had died, the shadow of that guilt might be laid to rest. Of course, it isn't very likely now. But Dan has embarked upon a lonely and no doubt dangerous path – between the feline Lady Ottoline and the machinations of her establishment cronies on the one hand, and Horst Wesenthal and the magic ecu on the other. These seasonal, birthday thoughts if anything strengthen his resolve. Only by returning to Ano Meri – with Milica endorsed by the bureaucrats of Luxembourg as his research assistant – can he hope to delve further into this mystery which by now, in his mind, concerns him alone. He must speak to Milica, arrange a period of leave from the Institute. He must take up the trail in Crete. Treading, if necessary, as quietly as his father must have done on that fateful, moonless night almost half a century ago.

It was not until the autumn of 1943, when Laura Robertson and her fifteen-month-old son arrived in Alexandria aboard a Royal Navy submarine carrying high-ranking defectors from the Italian garrison in the eastern sector of Crete, that Lionel accepted the truth of his son's death. Reported sightings of Daniel in the mountains had begun to tail off after the end of 1941. Although Lionel used all his influence in Alexandria and Cairo and was able to check on the debriefings of almost all the service personnel coming back from secret missions to Crete, he had had no positive identification for more than a year. The sightings that were reported were now invariably at second-hand. And even Lionel had had to notice that when his son had been seen at all, it was quite likely to be on the same day in widely separated parts of the island. Daniel, by 1943, was already a local legend. There was no firm news of his death, but only the most tenuous of rumours to keep hope for him alive. Certainty, and the terrible finality of the immutable, came with the arrival of Laura, although she too could give no definite information about where and when Daniel had died. And with the news came the unlooked-for present of a grandson, at the last possible minute and long after Lionel, who had never consciously nurtured dynastic ambitions, had ceased to wonder why his son was so long about begetting an heir.

For a long time after that Lionel allowed himself to become a semi-invalid. Laura looked after him, as well as the baby. This he didn't question. It was better not to question, not to think at all. Lionel Robertson was seventy when the war ended. In his seventy-first year, with the seas at last clear of U-boats, he returned to England and Upland Grange with Laura and this new, ineffably distant, tiny piece of life who, Laura calmly informed him, had already been christened, under the Greek rite, with the name of his dead son. This new Daniel Robertson was already growing through the years that Lionel had missed in his own son's early life, and he doted on the boy, though he sometimes forgot that this was not the child he had taken from the arms of the midwife under the moist eyes of Soames on that April morning forty-five years ago, and when he did remember he would have what Laura brightly referred to as 'one of his dizzy turns'.

The war was over. But Lionel had refused to rouse himself to take much interest in its progress. At worst, while Rommel had been advancing, seemingly invincibly, along the North African coast, it would have been inconvenient to be displaced again. For Lionel, the rise of Hitler, the Rhineland, the annexation of Austria, the Sudetenland, had all been so many noises off. It was simply the Kaiser and the armament race all over again. Nations were in the habit of going to war over such things, and he had been privileged to see in advance of most of his contemporaries the futility of that in 1914. A strong Balkan sun still shone on those years; through the gathering darkness that Lionel was now, in part wilfully, drawing about himself, those memories were still bright and clear. In those days he had carried his fate in his own two hands. Now, with this new war, the modern world had come out in arms; the chubby, morose face of Kreuz swam before him. Kreuz had hated the Nazis and the British Empire evenhandedly. Lionel could never be a hater, but this of Kreuz he could understand. Whatever had happened to Kreuz? And then, in the way of his memory during those years, the mists parted and he remembered. What was it Laura had told him? Believed taken prisoner at Stalingrad. There was no reason to think the Soviets had treated Reinhard Kreuzenberger differently from all the other German prisoners, just because all his life he had been a Communist, and been punished for it by being sent as a non-combatant driver to the Eastern Front. Kreuz might, Laura had explained carefully, still be alive somewhere in a Soviet labour camp. From what she had heard, for his own sake she hoped he was not.

This was a world that Lionel could not, or would not, understand. Gus Cramond, captured during the evacuation from Crete, had spent the rest of the war in a series of prison camps, only to be shot for allegedly trying to escape, two days before American troops liberated the stalag where he was being held. Bertie Shaw was dead too. In the Sicily landings? Lionel could not remember. *All my sad captains.* And Laura had told him, too – her composure for once breaking down and it had been his turn to comfort her – about long-faced, pale Dr Veniamin in Kastro, with his wife whom no one ever saw and his two daughters who had grown up to be beauties. They must have been about twenty the last time he remembered seeing them; Lionel thought them featherbrains, but they had turned more than their share of young heads in Kastro and were always very politely spoken. The small Jewish community of Kastro had been taken from their homes in the night and put aboard a large caïque. The caïque had been torpedoed, possibly by the Germans, more likely by an Allied submarine commander ignorant of its cargo. An eyewitness to the embarkation had confirmed that all those put aboard were tied together hand and foot. There had been no survivors.

And so Lionel allowed himself to become old, and took refuge with his medicine bottles and the plaid rug drawn up round his knees in the long drawing room overlooking the river at Upland Grange. Most of the house was shut up now – Laura found she could only afford coal and electricity for a few rooms. The house was a shambles too. The US airforce had been billeted in it for much of the war and had just moved out. Sarah Jane, who still looked after her ailing mother in the Lodge, had apparently married one of them. Although Bud Lambert was rarely to be found at home, Laura discovered that he too had moved into the cramped quarters of the Lodge, and having been used to the run of the Grange in his uniformed days (what was he still doing here if he'd been demobbed? – could it all be for insolent-eyed, freckled Sarah Jane?) was said to be grumbling dreadfully, and, to Laura's intense annoyance, continued to shoot in the grounds without so much as asking permission.

Sarah Jane herself Laura found she could not contemplate without a shudder. It wasn't the poor woman's fault. But Laura could never pass by Mrs Lambert with her headscarf and her flat, freckled features at the end of the drive without hearing again the strangled tones of Daniel's voice sawing into the umbilical cord that still bound him, and her, to his father. Laura could not escape the conviction that if those terrible words had remained unspoken in the earthquake-proof basement of the Villa Europa, her husband might still have been alive today.

Lionel's only consolation at this time was to tell stories to his little grandson. Even his Minoans had been largely abandoned to gather dust, since he had laid down his pen on that fateful day in Alexandria. Now and then he would be dragged and coaxed to give a lecture, to inaugurate an exhibition, but he did it with a bad grace; the lecture was the same that he had given before the war, and he was rarely invited twice. All the passion and verve of the life of an old rogue came to be distilled, in these last years, into the deep brew of tales which in their turn would become Dan's earliest memories. And after little Daniel had gone off to bed, Lionel would sit in his rocking chair staring out at the darkening waters of the estuary, as the tide ebbed to expose the mudflats briefly glistening before the ruins of the sunset collapsed into night.

As there appeared to be no servants at Upland Grange, Ralph Hummingbird announced himself. Nice pile, he thought appreciatively, as he mounted the steps and pulled the antiquated bell; pity it's in such a state. Ralph, whose own background was modest, was a connoisseur of country houses. His specialism was conservation, a discipline still in its infancy in those first post-war years, and he felt for the buildings he examined, and sometimes for their occupants too when they were still extant, all the affection that an eohippus, privileged with foresight of its place in the evolutionary tree, might have felt for the last of the dinosaurs. Ralph Hummingbird had had a good war, blowing up bridges. In these years of limbo following the peace, he was assiduously laying the foundations for a long and successful career in public service.

The dinosaur he had come to visit, when at length he ran him to earth in his rocking chair, plaid rug drawn up over his knees, tea tray at his elbow, was not at first sight untypical of the species as Ralph had come to know it. But for Sir Lionel Roberston he had long nurtured a special reverence. And his mission was an unusually delicate one. How to begin?

There was some preliminary scuffling as Lionel rifled testily through the formidable letters of introduction which Ralph had brought with him. Then, putting down his spectacles, 'Well, hrmph, Dr Hummingbird . . . Or is it Mr Hummingbird?'

'Oh, Ralph will do,' said Ralph.

'Well . . . er.' (Later, to Laura: 'Did you see, when he left, the fellow had no *hat*?')

Dr Hummingbird turned out to be a young man in his late twenties, a Cambridge archaeologist, with special interests in conservation. The term was new to Lionel, who questioned his visitor closely. Conservation was allied to restoration, Lionel now learnt. And he himself (he had never been averse to being flattered) was responsible for one of the most spectacular, some would say even daring, restorations of an archaeological site anywhere in Europe.

'Ah, you mean Ano Meri.' And the shutters came down, suddenly and with seeming finality, over Lionel's gaunt features.

But these were only the preliminaries. It was known that Sir Lionel had not interested himself in pursuing further excavations at Ano Meri in the five years since the war ended. Now peacetime pursuits, such as archaeology, were beginning to come back on the agenda. Was Sir Lionel – Ralph had to use all his tact here – by any chance considering resuming operations in Crete? Or if not, might he be open to discussion with other parties . . .?

Unexpectedly (to Laura, who was present) the shutters had risen again. Lionel was giving this young man his full attention. And it was clear to Laura, at least, that Hummingbird was concealing more than he revealed, and was indeed in some anxiety.

Now Lionel began to interrupt. 'The conditions laid down by the Greek authorities are what, precisely? . . . And your Department proposes . . . ?'

Under this sharp interrogation, so different from what he had been led to expect from the appearance of the old dinosaur in his chair, Ralph was beginning to stammer. Acutely miserable, he said at last (this was what he had been told to avoid at all costs), 'I'd better tell you straight out, sir. The Greek government has passed a law by which all archaeological sites become the property of the state. My university has good contacts with the Antiquities Ministry in Athens; with your approval and support we can secure future excavation rights at Ano Meri, and a long lease on the Villa Europa, so that British excavations can continue.'

Lionel appeared to be breathing with difficulty. 'With *my* approval – *you* can secure – lease – from the *Greeks*?'

'I'm afraid it all belongs to them now, sir. We have to negotiate with the Ministry of Antiquities in Athens. The point is, everybody knows the Greeks haven't the resources to dig all these sites, it'll be as much as they can do to maintain them. The Ministry doesn't quite advertise the fact, but they still need foreigners to come in and run the excavations. If we don't offer a deal now, Ano Meri could go to the French, or the Americans. You wouldn't want that, would you, sir?'

Lionel's hands were twitching on the arms of the rocking chair. 'And what compensation did you say was being offered?'

Ralph shook his head miserably.

'No compensation?'

'Don't shoot the messenger!' appealed Ralph, helpless now.

'I don't see why not. Do you?'

Lionel's eyes bored into his. In the presence of that all but silent rage, a fury that was now almost wholly turned inward against Lionel himself, Ralph felt his hair and face singed as though by a fiery breath. The lion did not roar, instead Ralph imagined a fierce beast biting its wounds in hot silence, knowing the cause of its pain and for the moment too full of it to lash out and crush its puny assailant. Ralph would never, in all the modest triumphs of his future career, forget that moment. Where an older generation – Lionel himself, Ralph shouldn't wonder – had proved its manhood by shooting ferocious beasts in distant corners of the Empire, he, Ralph, had had to bag his first trophy nearer home. It wasn't pride he felt, and it certainly wasn't sorrow for the old man who, from his look, would have had him horse-whipped if only he could.

In his own unassuming way, without a trace of malice and more by bungling than by design, Ralph Hummingbird had done his bit to inch open the door to the post-war world.

He had also, although he never knew it, done more than Laura and even little Dan had been able to do in seven years to rouse Lionel from his torpor. Within days, Upland Grange was thrust back into the bustling activity that had not been seen there since the final stages of preparation of *Ariadne's Summer Palace* more than a decade before. Telegrams were sent, letters drafted and re-drafted. The telephone was in constant use. Lawyers came from Ipswich, from Cambridge, even from London. The Vice Chancellor of Ralph's university was summoned to Upland Grange – and came. Lionel bought new clothes and went up to London, renewed membership of his club, that had lapsed since before the war, spoke to cabinet ministers and peers of the realm. He came back from London almost asphyxiated. The place had been bombed so you couldn't recognize it, he complained, pink willow-herb grew among piles of bricks. And the fog – the famous London fog that smelt of soot and coaldust, tickling memories long forgotten, of

290

invisible ships hooting on the river, of longings that drew him on to embark on voyages he had never made and never would make now – the fog had crept inside his weakened lungs and deposited its evil, airborne effluent, blocking up his breathing.

But all to no avail. No longer a willed invalid, Lionel had regained, in his mind, much of his former strength, only to discover that the dissolution of the body was real. Seeing, in his clear-sighted way, no possibility of comfort, he impatiently threw away the petulance and gloom and the illusory refuge they had sustained. For all his efforts, Ano Meri – the site, the Villa Europa, and the Cabin – had been irrevocably taken from him. Just as his son had been taken from him. Just as even now, day by day, the powers of his body and the light of day were inexorably ebbing away. In the pale winter light of the first months of 1951, that hid nothing and disguised nothing, Lionel found himself able to think at last about his son. A piece of himself, that had been violently severed. In advance of his death, he was precisely conscious of his own flesh piece by piece dissolving away, cut cleanly from the bone with scarcely, now, any pain. Could this be the meaning of the terrible ritual that, so Daniel and Laura had been convinced, was once enacted in Minoan Crete? The son that he had disowned – that he had provoked by his rash act of temper into unforgivable rebellion – had perhaps seen further into the truth of things than he, Lionel, ever had, fully clothed as he had been in the flesh and blood of an era that time had all but picked clean. Then, he had found the idea of such a sacrifice, at the heart of the life-affirming civilization of the Minoans, too grotesque to contemplate. It was only now that he saw this clearly: whether Daniel had been right or wrong, had not he himself, unwittingly, made no less terrible a sacrifice, of his own son?

Lionel's last visit to Crete coincided with the opening in London of the long-heralded Festival of Britain. No, he testily fended off reporters as he boarded the aeroplane at London's tawdry-new Airport, it was nothing to do with any premonition. He had announced this visit as his last, for the simple reason that he proposed to return to Crete once and once only. Yes, it was true that it was ten years since his son had been killed there ('yes yes, absolutely, a hero's death, yes, you may say that'). He had not been back since. At his age was he going to take up archaeology again? Definitely not.

His travelling companion was Ralph Hummingbird. (Laura had absolutely refused to come, pleading Dan's schooling and tender years as excuse. Lionel did not insist. Laura would never set foot in Crete again.) With Ralph, as he had brought himself, with some grimacing at first, to call the young conservationist, Lionel had developed a mutually patronizing relationship that suited both of them well enough. Faced with the expropriation of Ano Meri by the Greek authorities, Lionel had had no choice but to co-operate with Ralph's university. This had brought considerable kudos to Ralph himself, who was not so insensitive as to fail to recognize what it must have cost the old man to come round to the idea. As the negotiations proceeded Ralph had become a kind of chaperone to Lionel, and had had nothing to lose by championing his interests such as they still were. It was, Ralph ruefully thought, a little like the relationship between the collector of big game and the prize specimen it will require all his ingenuity to bring back home alive and well to breed in captivity. In his own way Lionel seems to have sensed this too. With Ralph he would divert himself with fits of temper and peevishness, as though to keep the young man on his mettle. But deep down he was glad to have a cicerone to steer him through a world he no longer knew, and he accepted, most of the time, the price. If he was an exotic, famous beast in Ralph's charge, then Ralph was welcome to the reflected glory, provided he didn't preen himself too shamelessly in front of Lionel. It was also, of course, Ralph who kept the keys of the cage. So be it.

There was another reason for returning to Crete at this time. And here, too, Lionel suspected that Ralph had played his part of invisible intermediary. A bronze bust of the discoverer of Ano Meri had been commissioned. The sculptor had worked from photographs, apparently; Lionel had known nothing of the project until the unveiling, which was to happen that summer, was announced to him (this too by way of Ralph). Lionel had laughed cynically at the news. 'They take away my land and my discoveries with one hand, then they flatter me with the other. What do they take me for? Bronze bust my arse.' But a spark of the old vanity had remained: secretly Lionel was pleased. And he agreed to be present at the unveiling ceremony, when, Ralph confided to him only now, on the aeroplane, he was also to be given the freedom of the city of Kastro.

Two days later the daily flight from Athens touched down on the airfield that had been hastily built on the cliffs to the east of Kastro during the war. Lionel stood blinking at the top of the steps as the cabin door opened and the heat of the Cretan summer hit him like a wave. They had laid on a hero's welcome. The town band, that he remembered playing on dusty Sunday afternoons down by the harbour, was drawn up on the tarmac. A red carpet stretched out towards the Nissen hut that still served as the terminal building. Girls in a passable, but decent, imitation of Minoan dress were lined up with bunches of flowers. The Mayor of Kastro, a younger man whom Lionel did not recognize, shook him by the hand and kissed him on both cheeks. Press photographers flocked round. As he walked up the red carpet towards the Nissen hut and felt the heat of the day thrown upwards from the tarmac and the crumbly earth that was reddish here, Lionel saw the years unrolling before his eyes like the jerky cinema films of his youth. In the same moment, he was being welcomed, half a lifetime earlier, by the Mayor, the one-eyed Bishop, and the consuls of the Great Powers self-conscious in their cummerbunds; in the same moment the cinematograph cameras whirred once again to celebrate Laura's and Daniel's Minoan wedding. He lived again the spring rains of so many excavation seasons, the deep heat of summer, that after ten years' absence he felt now seeping into his bones, bringing back life to the worn-out membranes. Lionel put his hand to his eyes. For a moment the brightness, the lightness of his tread on the carpet, were too much for him, he seemed to be floating on air. He was vaguely aware that the band had stopped playing, anxious faces crowded round him. Was he all right? Should a doctor be called?

'Never felt better,' snapped Lionel, steadying himself on Ralph's arm. And the procession continued.

For a week Lionel was lionized in Kastro. He was appalled at the changes he saw in the town. The bombing had been terrible, everyone told him, and indeed much of the town as he knew it had disappeared. But the rebuilding seemed to be going ahead much faster than in London. Inside the walls, the devastated narrow streets that had been overhung by wooden balconies had been cleared and widened, the Turkish-style houses replaced with blocks of grey concrete, already streaked from the winter rains, and all over the town optimistically left with rusty iron rods, like a forest of bamboo canes, waving out of their flat roofs – in case, it was explained to him, fortune should smile sufficiently for the owners to add more storeys later. There were daughters to be married, and these days it was the height of fashion to live in an apartment. When the daughters married, they would each need an apartment of their own as dowry. The daughters of Kastro seemed to have multiplied tenfold since he had last been here. Building was going on even outside the old Venetian walls. You could no longer tell where Kastro ended and the outlying farming villages began.

After the unveiling at Ano Meri was over, Lionel managed to give Ralph the slip and pottered up on to the site. They had built a perimeter wire round Ariadne's Summer Palace now. Just outside it, dominating the car park that had been roughly levelled on the ground below the Villa, the hollow bronze features of Sir Lionel Robertson still, to this day, gaze with sightless penetration from this plinth, seeming to see right through the approaching visitor. (It is the same bust that, in 1990, would dominate the entrance to the commemorative exhibition at the Fitzwilliam Museum in Cambridge.) Lionel had found this face-to-face meeting with the empty effigy of himself unexpectedly disconcerting. It was, he supposed, a good likeness. This bronze Lionel was ten, fifteen years younger; it was as though the face he knew but had lost from the mirror each morning had inexplicably been returned to him. Yet there was something frightening about the gleaming, chiselled features that both were and were not his own. A stranger had made this; Lionel had forgotten his name, but he had only a few moments ago shaken him warmly by the hand. Someone who could have no inkling of the living, tangled world within Lionel's head. Inside this head of bronze was only empty air; its gaze that seemed to challenge all comers was a gaze out of nothingness. It was like coming on an abandoned snakeskin. The life that he had already, before this, felt beginning to desert him, had never filled these features, put light behind these eyes. Lionel was reminded of his disappointment when he had first visited the ruined palace of Knossos: the Minoans had departed, and left only debris behind. It was disconcerting to see in his own monument, the provocative likeness of a man whom everyone present could see, surely, no longer existed. An empty husk.

So when at last it was over Lionel was glad to elude the dispersing crowds, the shouting and the dust where cars and charabancs were revving up to depart, and wander slowly, leaning from time to time on his stick, over the site. The first thing he came to was the fence. The gate was open, and inside was a little wooden hut with a glass window and some postcards, already bleached and curled from the sun. On a wooden chair that must have been borrowed from the village café, one black-booted foot propped up on the crossbar, sat the *phýlax*, whose monotonous job it would be to open the site each morning and lock it up each evening, and now and then take five drachmas from the stray visitor who had wandered so far off the beaten track. Lionel paused before him, fumbling in his pocket. Humbly, before this guardian of the state to which all this now belonged, he held out a coin.

The other turned in a half circle on his chair, to indicate generous refusal, and began coughing. When the paroxysms had begun to ease, he stretched out a shaking hand to Lionel, but without attempting to get up.

'Haven't you recognized me yet?'

And only then, as the figure before him was again racked with coughing, and as he coughed it seemed that his body had somehow become twisted, crooked, Lionel recognized his sometime foreman, Manolis. 'Wound from the war,' Manolis explained morosely. 'Pierced the lung. Haven't known a moment's peace since. You must excuse me. Sitting here's all I'm fit for.'

A phrase he remembered Laura using came back to Lionel now. 'Like stubble on the plain, eh?'

Manolis stared long and deeply at him. Then slowly he nodded. 'Like stubble—' his voice broke, '—on the plain. Is your lordship well?'

But the old relationship was gone. 'Oh Manolis, how much we have both lost, you and I!' Lionel looked round for another chair, but there was none, so he remained standing. 'When I first met you and your brother, you were heirs to a kingdom, do you remember?'

'Yannis is dead now.'

'How did he die? In the resistance?'

Manolis spat. 'No, after. Our own people killed him. My brother was a Communist. Left a young widow and two children. The little one was hardly weaned when they got him. I help them as best I can. But I'm lucky to have even this job. The brother of a Communist, you see.'

'So what do you do here all day?'

'Exist, what else? I've got a *briki* and I make my coffee. Clear the weeds from the ruins. On my own, with half a man's breath. *Ftou*,' and he spat again in the dust. 'There's no more digging, of course, all that's over. Go on, see for yourself. Your lordship is welcome.'

As he turned to plod on up the slope, Lionel couldn't tell whether the sound that came from behind him was of coughing or of mirthless laughter.

Lionel inspected the site carefully. The painted reconstructions, the work of Gus Cramond, had begun to peel; there was a smell of stale urine in the semi-darkness of the throne room. Truly, what kind of a princess could have kept court so far from the living daylight, cramped beneath a low ceiling in a basement room? The scene of his triumph so long ago now seemed drab and somehow sinister. Ano Meri he had long ago determined would be his monument. But what kind of a monument, in all conscience, would he one day be leaving to the world?

Out in the sunlight, as he painfully ascended Cramond's broad staircase back to the Great Court, the foundations and the massive retaining wall that had kept the palace from sliding down into the ravine for thousands of years, reminded Lionel of nothing so much as bleached bones. It was all there, of course. What was left of the vanished civilization of the Minoans would still be there, generations hence, for other archaeologists to discover. Once he had thought he understood these Minoans, his imagination had peopled these rooms, this broad paved court, with queenly, chattering women, with lithe-waisted princes, with musicians, acrobats, a solemn-faced priesthood, a corps of ingenious engineers and architects, with painters as talented as Kreuz and not half so lugubrious – it had been a world that made sense. Now, taking in with new eyes those gaunt ruins, the straight lines and once-level floors now made crooked by the earthquakes of centuries, Lionel wondered.

In his pocket he still kept the tiny seal of polished agate, engraved with the bull and the leaping acrobat, the sole survivor of his treasure trove from Ragusa. He sat down on a low wall on the southern side of the court and took it out to examine it. The late afternoon sun struck fire from its surface; the engraving was lost. Carefully, as he had done so many times before, Lionel pressed the warm shiny stone into the heel of his hand. Sure enough, the magic was still there. The skin on the hand had become loose and blotched. But the bull was unchanged, its horns still lowered in a proud charge, the slender figure of the acrobat still arched in a flying handstand over the animal's back, legs bent backwards from the knee, already poised to steady himself from the shock of landing, the flailing ankles effortlessly etched by the unknown artist to conform to the oval contour of the stone. And as he watched, the impressed lines faded from his hand.

He looked up as he saw someone coming towards him. It was a girl, or a woman, it was difficult to tell in the light. His first thought was that Laura had come to Crete after all, it seemed so natural that she should be here. He half rose to greet her, but it was not Laura. She took his hand with easy familiarity. He couldn't put a name to her, though surely he had met her before. It was pleasant to be chatting like this, as the day began to cool, still holding her hand in his. And as he talked, she listened, and prompted. Her voice was warm and matter-of-fact, memory began to drift back to him. Of Sarajevo, and the mountains, and the mill. He had not spoken Serbian for many years, but it seemed he was doing so now, and understanding it, with none of the hesitancy that had hampered him then. It was the most natural thing in the world for him to be telling this woman, or girl – she was a Muslim of course, he remembered that, she wore a white veil that left only her bright black eyes visible – what he had never breathed to a living soul: how it was that this particular Englishman, then six foot three in his socks, had come to be in Sarajevo on the morning of the archduke's assassination. It was a relief to talk like this, to feel her hand in his, to gaze into those ageless eyes. It had all been perhaps for nothing more than this. They fell silent. The sun was almost gone.

'Won't you,' Lionel said, understanding now and feeling no fear, 'won't you show me your face?'

It was Manolis who found him, as he did his rounds at sunset before locking up: sitting back on the low wall at the south side of the court, his stick propped between his knees. His face was slightly upturned, his eyes open. As empty as the eyes of the statue by the gate.

16 BOTHROS 2

AIR fares to the eastern Mediterranean are ridiculously cheap this spring. It is not long since the outbreak of the Gulf War sent a shudder round the world and overnight made Saddam Hussein and the American television network CNN into household words. The shock waves have lasted longest, perhaps, in the travel industry. No one had quite been able to believe that Saddam and the forces ranged against him would go all the way to the brink, but once the missiles started landing and top hospitals around the world were very publicly put on standby to receive the casualties from chemical and biological weapons, it hardly seemed possible it could all be over in a couple of months. In the event, the casualty units have remained unused, the promised campaign of international terrorism in support of Saddam has failed to materialize. It was the IRA, not the long arm of the Iraqi Ba'ath Party, that scored a direct hit on Downing Street at the height of a snowstorm back in February. Here in Athens, where the orange trees are beginning to blossom all along the bright, broad boulevards, it is the home-grown '17th November' organization that has been booby-trapping official cars, driving the diplomatic community behind steel barricades, manned by shifty-looking policemen swinging machine carbines in a manner that does nothing for Dan's sense of personal security now, as he waits to be body-searched before being admitted to the concrete monstrosity on which is emblazoned the familiar shield and the words, *Dieu et mon droit.*

It has seemed better, after all, to register his presence and call on some official help while he is in Greece. He is amused but not surprised to learn that UK consular facilities cannot be extended to his research assistant, as she is a Yugoslav national. There is in any case no anticipated threat to British citizens and interests in Greece, especially away from the capital. Dr Robertson may find there is more practical assistance that can be given him by the British Council just around the corner (and similarly barricaded against entry, he discovers). In the meantime, just in case, here is the number

297

to call in an emergency.

Dan has spent the winter furiously, and uncharacteristically, impatient. Had it not been for Saddam Hussein and the panic that has stricken the airways he might have got here sooner. As it is, there is no time to lose. The EC enquiry is moving slowly but surely, the moment cannot be far off when Dan will have to put his cards on the table. Either, as he has explained to Milica, he will have to come clean about his mother's diaries and their inconclusive revelation, or it will be time to call it a day, plead conflict of interest and resign after all from the enquiry. But before that, Dan, egged on, it must be said, by Milica, is determined to probe the scandal to the end. It will not be difficult, with modern techniques, to establish beyond all possible doubt the age of the relics that were, according to his mother's diary, bundled unceremoniously into the Minoan midden of Bothros 2 on a drizzling afternoon in early April 1941. Before he shares his knowledge, Dan wants to be sure. But it is more than that. Horst and his colleagues will be content with an explanation. Dan needs to *understand*. And for that he knows he must re-traverse the ground on which his father lived and died, he must try to recapture from the place itself whatever trace might be left of the shadowy, tormented father he never knew.

Obscurely bound up with this quest has been the arcane psychoanalytical algebra with which Lucy has sought by turns to bemuse and enlighten him. The Name of the Father, that isn't a name and isn't a person, but whose utterance in his own case has so long been prohibited – he can no longer remember where the prohibition came from, it's no doubt to do with his aversion to being called by it himself – the phrase has haunted him ever since that day last summer driving Lucy to Cambridge for the Europa Exhibition. Can this be the shadow, the deprivation, the provocation to desire, the elusive object that he now feels drawing him relentlessly onward? Dan, whose constant companion has become the ever-practical, the innocent-wise, the (ever since the exhibition he has recognized with a mixture of admiration and alarm) fundamentally anarchic Milica, has a problem with desire.

As March has given way to April the clouds have come down from the north and settled like cotton wool on the mountains that hem in this packed metropolis. It is raining when Dan and Milica make their way over shiny, uneven pavements to the recommended travel agent. Nowadays everyone flies to Crete, Dan has been assured. He has put it to Milica. It is thirty years since he first visited Ano Meri, and then, as a penniless student with only what he could carry in a frame rucksack on his back, the only way to get there had been deck class on the overnight ferry. The ferries must be a sight more civilized now. They wouldn't go deck class of course, not at this time of year. Milica has shrugged in a way she has, 'Why not?' and smiles.

The travel agent's is full of umbrellas and wall-size posters emphasizing the ease of travel to Katmandu and Bangkok. To secure a couple of first-class cabins on the evening sailing to Kastro proves more difficult. The foreign tourists may have all but disappeared, but Easter is approaching, the boats are always full at this time of year. Then it turns out there are no single cabins on the ship. They will have to share. There follows a brief, huddled parley. There has recently been a spate of memos at the Institute on the subject of sexual harassment in the workplace. As the father of a liberated daughter, Dan likes to see himself as a 'new man' of the nineties, relaxed and at ease in the company of colleagues of the opposite gender, which in any case is the one he has always found the more congenial. With Milica he is acutely conscious of his double professional responsibilities: to his student and his assistant. Milica is in that respect quite unlike the other women he has been close to in his life. So Dan examines his conscience now, as he carefully folds up the long document of perforated paper that turns out to be their travel ticket. None of Lady Ottoline's memos seems quite applicable to this situation. *Where two employees of the opposite sex are travelling on business together it is expected that . . .* That what? Surely the Institute, if the Institute were paying, would want to save money?

And so, that evening, Dan embarks, for what will be the third time in his life, for Crete. The ship is not a bit like the rusty old converted oil tanker that did the trip back in the early sixties. Getting on board, he and Milica have to run the gauntlet of the huge lorries that are backing up the ramp on to the vehicle deck, with a roaring of engines and a medley of shouted instructions, all seeming to contradict one another, from the crew. Everything on board is made of metal or plastic, even the bright red uniforms of the stewards who are lined up at the purser's office and seemingly outnumber the first-class passengers. But on the way up through the lower decks Dan has caught a glimpse of the past he remembers, still travelling with them: a huddle of old women in black settling themselves down on a linoleum floor that has been almost completely eaten away by cigarette butts, surrounding their makeshift encampment with a rampart of plastic bags, surely more than among them they could possibly have carried on board. And a certain cackling intonation of voices all squawking at once. Yes, he has been here before.

Listening now to the regular, gentle breathing of Milica above him in the upper bunk, Dan wishes he could sleep so easily. He has given Milica a head start, while he moodily downed a last ouzo in the bar. Now, in the cramped space and with the presence of Milica so close and yet so chastely beyond his reach (there is an indefinable scent in the cabin that at once soothes and excites him), Dan's senses are only partially lulled by the swishing of water past the porthole. There is a precarious comfort in the creaking of the furnishings, the rattle of the toothbrush glass next door in the bathroom, the rhythmic pulse of the engines. Whatever Lady Ottoline's code of practice for sexual harassment (well, for the avoidance of it rather, he knows what he means) might have laid down for a situation such as this, Dan is glumly satisfied that his conduct has been exemplary.

Twisting and turning in his bunk, Dan has the sensation of being asleep but still in the grip of the waking thoughts that continue to jangle in his brain. This voyage across the Cretan Sea is for Dan fraught with danger, a perilous course he has elected to steer. Even in coming so far, Dan has put his professional career on the line. Surely it's been misguided from the start, he panics now: a pathological symptom resulting from the paranoia of the Institute and the theme music for the World Cup, *vincerò*. But it's only in the managed make-believe of sport there's such a thing as winning, the rest of us have to make do; that had been his grandfather's most terrible mistake, not to realize that, and he paid for it, didn't he? But the narrow bunk is rising and falling beneath him, Dan can hear the bursts of spray crashing past his porthole, hurled by the solid shape of the hull carving a passage through the waves; he is wrapped up by the motion, he is part of it, the ship will not turn back and no more will Dan.

He must have slept after all. The ship is shuddering and rattling, there are bright orange lights outside the porthole. Milica is up and dressed, practical as always in jeans that make the most of her long legs, a short-sleeved jumper and a headband that sweeps her long thick hair back from her face. Her eyes, rather wide apart, are on him now, gently interrogative. 'Strange dreams, Dan?' she asks him.

Dan nods. (Oh God, he hasn't been talking in his sleep, has he?)

Outside, doors are banging, an unintelligible public address system is booming. 'Go and see if you can find some breakfast, will you?'

A short while later Dan and Milica are whisked by taxi along the quayside and up into the town to the car-hire office. Beyond the bright sodium lights of the port area, Dan only just catches a glimpse of the conical peak of Stroumboulas that he remembers from all those years ago, standing out against the grey of dawn. To his right, as the taxi swishes along the waterfront – a light drizzle is falling – the Venetian fort still guards the inner harbour with its caïques and luxury yachts, a cardboard cut-out. So this is Kastro.

Having negotiated the terms of a week's car hire, in an air-conditioned office manned by politely-spoken spivs in the livery of a multinational company, he takes Milica for breakfast of yoghurt and honey in the fountain square. Where thirty years ago half-naked children played and shouted, climbing on the backs of the stone lions and dodging, at great risk, it had always seemed to Dan, the motorbikes and three-wheeled trucks that crowded the little square with a great deal of hooting and shouting and dust, now the whole area has been pedestrianized and paved with smart new slabs, the bowl of the fountain has been cleared of rubbish and wire railings protect what is, after all, a monument of some distinction. True, there is no water in the fountain, but the sheen of prosperity is everywhere to be seen. Milica slowly sips a *café viennois*, served with ice cream in a long sundae glass, through a straw. Dan is annoyed to find they don't serve Greek coffee, as he remembers it, in tiny cups full of grounds.

The clouds are down on the mountains as they drive out of Kastro. The coastline is built up now almost all the way, it isn't until the turn-off, where the shanty-town, built in the 1920s, is now a prospering suburb, that the road rises through the vineyards and olive groves along the back of the ridge that leads to the site. Although close to Kastro, Ano Meri lies off the main tourist itineraries, Dan is glad to discover. The road has been widened a little since the early sixties, but there are still cuttings through the white, chalky soil that would not be easily negotiated by the tourist coaches, and the last part has yet to be asphalted. The car park, beneath the empty gaze of Lionel's bronze features, now returned from loan to the Fitzwilliam Museum, has remained small. There is no sign at Ano Meri of the *tavernas* and boutiques, that have taken shallow root round many of the prestige archaeological sites on the island. The fame of Ano Meri derives more from the quality of the finds it has contributed to the Kastro museum than from the remains on the ground. The reconstructions of Lionel's day, as Dan and Milica will shortly discover, are in poor repair, and some have had to be demolished to make way for new excavations.

The Cabin, now enlarged and fitted out with a fridge and indoor washing facilities, has long been established as the dig-house for foreign archaeologists. The larger Villa, almost completely submerged in a surging wave of bougainvillea, is the local outpost of the Ministry of Antiquities, and kept locked and empty for much of the time. It is not empty now, however. Dan's arrival has been announced in advance, and his declared mission – a survey of the site and re-examination of the recent finds on behalf of the EC committee of enquiry – meets with the approval of the authorities. The Mayor of the local suburb, the one-time shanty-town, is at the head of the reception committee; also the village president, who has turned out in the Cretan costume of an earlier time, black-tasselled kerchief on his head, baggy black *vráka* and ceremonial white boots, and with them, in modern dress but ranged with stiff formality under the rampant bougainvillea, the senior archaeologists of the prefecture.

'This is going to be rather ghastly,' Dan whispers to Milica, as they get out of the car and go to meet their hosts.

The Mayor is the first to be introduced: Manolis Laskaris, and a startled Dan finds himself shaking hands with a man of about his own age and height, who bears little resemblance to the morose, coughing *phýlax* he remembers. This Manolis Laskaris has his family's dark, Cretan colouring, but his features are small, his fawn suit and gold tie-pin draw attention to themselves, the stubble of a fast-growing beard is perhaps modelled on the 'designer' look of the previous decade, his eyes are grey and seem to focus on a point just below Dan's left ear, though the smile that lights up his face seems open and eager. The rituals of greeting are soon over. Dan and Milica are shown to their accommodation in the Cabin. Returning to the Villa, their itinerary for the next week is explained to them.

To the Mayor, Dan says, 'You must be related to—?'

The Mayor slaps him heartily on the back and laughs his easy laugh. One of the young archaeologists intervenes to interpret. 'He explains his father was Yannis Laskaris, who was the brother of Manolis, who worked at Ano Meri as *phýlax*.' The Mayor continues with a long tirade, which sounds to Dan's ears jovial and insistent. He notices the Mayor has a gold eye-tooth. 'He explains,' the archaeologist continues in a dead-pan voice, 'that his father Yannis was killed in the white terror. We can talk of these things now, thanks to the new political reality that has swept away the outworn apparatus of the rightwing para-state. The Mayor wishes you to know that the efforts of his father, and of his uncle Manolis Laskaris, in the anti-fascist struggle, have only now been commemorated in a sculpture and a plaque which he invites you to visit in the town square. This is true, he informs you, also of many other Cretan patriots who could not be remembered after the war because of the white terror inspired by the imperialism of – the Mayor begs you excuse him – the British and the Americans.'

As the translation draws to a close, Dan observes the Mayor beaming at him with evident pride in the torrent of his words being delivered in a foreign language. 'The Mayor hopes you will be welcome in the municipality.'

Dan hopes so too, but acknowledges this gracefully. Milica, he notices, is nodding as though sympathetically at his side. They haven't talked much about politics, he and Milica, but he supposes this sort of thing must be second nature to her, from back home.

Dan wonders what reaction the name of his own father will provoke. But on this subject the Mayor, it seems, has less to say. 'Some people collaborated with the British, yes. A few even collaborated with the Germans. Unfortunately, they were incorrectly educated in the political reality. Only the rightwing para-state pretends the British were the friends of Crete. The struggle of the Cretan people is the same as the struggle of the German people under the fascist tyranny, and of exploited peoples everywhere. Perhaps,' the Mayor adds as an afterthought, doubtfully, 'also of the English people.'

Dan can take only so much of this. 'My father was killed here, in Crete, fighting with your people against the Nazis. Part of my investigation here is to find out how he died.'

302

Milica looks at him sharply.

The Mayor shrugs. 'There are many tales of the occupation. I myself was not born in the time of the *milordi*. Your father has the name of a brave man, it is true.'

'And this – commemorative plaque you were talking about. Is my father mentioned there?'

The Mayor clicks his tongue, jerking his head peremptorily upwards. 'Only Cretans – and patriots.'

'Dan, you are giving away the baby with the bathwater,' Milica whispers urgently to him later. And then, seeing the look on his face, 'Oh God, my English again.'

'I wish you could be my interpreter with these awful people. I thought you understood Greek?'

'Only a little. And here the dialect is quite different. Listen, there is a storeroom at the back of the Villa. If the time comes, I think it will have all that we need.'

'You're a brick, do you know that?'

Milica's eyes are wide. 'A *what*?'

Standing well inside the perimeter wire, facing the blank north wall of Ariadne's Summer Palace, with its narrow ceremonial ramp that leads – but not directly – into the Great Court, Dan explains the site to Milica.

'Of course, modern archaeology doesn't think of it as a palace any more.' (Dan is mindful, if intermittently, of the teacher-pupil relationship.) 'It all comes down to economics. One of the first centres for storage and redistribution in Europe. The country people brought their produce here. The priests and priestesses with their robes and rituals were actually the managers of a rural economy. You can see how difficult it would be to break in here, and if you did you'd soon be lost. But you can get an idea of how it would have functioned: goods in, that way; goods out – you wait here for the black bronze doors to open and bowing low to the priest you receive your daily bread. No doubt it needs a tremendous atmosphere of awe to work. But think of the way English people talk about the Stock Exchange, the balance of payments. No Milica, you are looking at the Canary Wharf of the Aegean Bronze Age. With the difference, I suppose, that it worked – for hundreds of years.'

'My teachers at the Karl Marx Institute would say the same, perhaps,' reflects Milica. 'But they would also say: Ano Meri was the first step on the road to our national people's economy. Everybody can see what is wrong with our national people's economy today, but who would say so, especially if they had a job at the Karl Marx Institute? Why do the English always make themselves less?'

'Because we're so damn conceited,' snaps back Dan at once.

'There you go again, you see?'

'We just can't help it, can we?'

So Dan guides Milica over the site, hiding from himself as he goes an irrational sense of anti-climax, of disappointment. Palace or warehouse, it is a smaller thing than he remembers. The Great Court is surely not as big as the gravel sweep at the end of the drive at Upland Grange, the whole excavated extent of the site equivalent perhaps to the street of terraced houses where he lives in South London. The resurrected columns, tapering downwards and painted in strong black and red, although now badly peeling, and Gus Cramond's concrete struts, with a grain painted into them to make them look like the long-decayed original cypress wood, are the only features that lend any atmosphere to the site. The throne room has been fenced off. The Europa frescoes, in a much cruder copy of Kreuzenberger's reconstruction, have been stuck back on the walls but are badly stained by limestone deposits dripping from the concrete roof. In the dim light that filters through the lightwell, the images are hard to make out. For the rest, the maze of foundations, crumbling walls and broken-off porticoes seem to Dan stripped bare of history. And of course, for him, they are barren, too, of the kind of data that can feed his computer maps and make them glow with meaning. The rough pottery thrown out on the spoilheaps, that he turns over with his foot, has for him a potentially greater richness. Even the great retaining walls, still intact to an impressive height in the south-west corner, now that they have been fully exposed and cleared, stir Dan's emotions with what can be no more than the faintest echo of his grandfather's excitement, when once he had stood on this very spot on a windy November day, and come to the momentous decision that would determine the course of the rest of his life, and Dan's very existence. Looking round these tidied-up ruins now, Dan wishes with a sudden, long pent-up rage, that he could exchange all this for the comforts and the modest grandeur and, yes, the safety of Upland Grange as he knew it in his earliest years.

Returning to the Great Court, he points out to Milica the spot where the old rogue was found on the evening after the statue had been unveiled. That had been the beginning of Dan's exile. He had cried tears for the old rogue, the teller of stories, when the news came to Upland Grange; but death in the magical world that grandpa had loved to create for the infant Dan was surely nothing but another adventure. And the life of an old rogue, as Dan could see it by the age of nine, with its medicine bottles of different colours, the plaid rug and that indefinable but not quite pleasant smell, was something so unlike living as he himself joyously experienced it, running wild in the grounds, playing hide and seek and romping with his village friends through the empty parts of the house, that death, by comparison, might not be so very different or so very terrible. So Dan did not grieve much for Lionel. It was his mother's choked-back tears, her fraught expression, her frequently bitten lip, that scared him. And gradually it was borne in on Dan that these were not the signs of grief and mourning, but of something more pressing and more terrible.

All he understood then was that they must leave Upland Grange and go to live in London. His mother's eyes had been dry in the cold dew of that September morning. A new school awaited Dan in London; she had timed the forced move, he has long since realized, with care. Dan's new life in the cramped bustle of South London was to get off to a flying start. She had primed him well, talking to him softly in the long light evenings as the Stour and the woods and the estuary melted each night a little bit more irrevocably into the surrounding darkness. She had talked of the fun they would have, of the great city Dan had never seen, of the new friends they would both make. At nine he would still sometimes sit on her knee in confiding moments and she would hug him to her. And at last she would scold him off to bed with mock threats that made him laugh, though he knew that if he listened at the top of the stairs he would hear the sobs she had constrained all day breaking painfully from her. And he would curl up with the blankets over his head not to hear.

Once, though, she had taken him on her knee and breathed over him, like an incantation, the words, half spoken, half sung, of that other language that was private to him and to her, that he didn't really understand but that brought him close to her; to him it was the language of song, the language she sang in, as she still did, though mostly now to herself; it seemed to Dan he had never heard words more beautiful, and she cried then and he didn't know what they meant: *Tu proverai sí come sa di sale lo pane altrui . . .*

In these words, he knows now, Dante amid the unearthly joys of Paradise learns of the exile that will await him on his return to the world.

It was something to do with a Mortgage, that he knew, though he had no idea what a Mortgage was. The house had been mortgaged all those years ago, when the old rogue had needed the money for his wonderful discoveries in Crete. Someone in a suit and carrying one of those round hats had come to the house: 'But surely you can understand,' his mother's prim, anguished words have been printed on his memory ever since, '*I never knew*. Sir Lionel never discussed such things. Nobody had the slightest idea.'

There had been more men in suits that summer. Men with clipboards and measuring tapes. Men in overalls who, while Dan was desultorily squelching about the mudflats, took away the furniture. Most of it he never saw again. And there had been a tall, tubby fellow in a red check shirt who had chucked him under the chin, called him a cute guy, and had given him a packet of chewing gum which he resignedly surrendered when the visitor had gone. His mother could be really cross at times, he knew these moods, it was better to give in quietly.

And then the bright cold morning in the dew, and his mother calling that the taxi was ready. His nine-year-old self was suddenly overwhelmed by the knowledge that his mother's cheery anticipation was nothing but a sham for his benefit, he *knew*, without even looking at her, that for her there was nothing left in the whole world to look forward to, that their eviction was somehow ignominious; he saw her for a moment stripped of the enormous, all-encompassing power of a mother to spread her wings and protect him from hurt. His mother, his real mother who cried at nights and he knew without false pride that it was for him she cried, didn't want to do this. Then neither would he.

And suddenly Dan at the top of the wide staircase, seeing his mother handing the last of their suitcases to the taxi driver, turned and ran. Breathlessly he hurtled down the long carpeted corridor, throwing wide all the doors of the rooms as he did so. There was a little stairway at the end of the corridor. At its top was a passageway that led into the locked East Wing. The forbidden rooms of the upper storey had been emptied now, like the rest of the house. Beside himself Dan ran from room to room, hurling wide the casements and shutters, sobbing wildly, running faster and faster to catch the sunlight on the grass and the estuary, to imprint on his memory those sights that he would never see again, and all the while shouting absurdly, because there was no one there to hear, *No, no, I won't go, I won't.*

Clattering furiously downstairs into the great hall of the East Wing he skidded to a stop and stared in terror at the naked giants that looked down at him from their plinths, at the upraised hands of stone and metal that seemed poised to strike, to punish. Dan had never before penetrated the gloom where his grandfather's trophies from the tombs of Upper Moesia still stood with the dust of forty years on them, awaiting collection to be transported to their final resting place in the basement of the Fitzwilliam Museum.

It was here, huddled against a cold marble base, his face in his hands and his shoulders shaking uncontrollably, that his mother at last ran Dan to earth, and her warmth enfolded him and took him away forever from that horror that had suddenly stopped him in his tracks.

In this way Sarah Jane became mistress of Upland Grange, and Dan's exile had begun.

'Of course,' the Ephor of Antiquities is helpfulness itself, 'you had only to let us know and a permit would have been issued as a matter of course. Unfortunately, the request from Luxembourg was for a surface survey only. For myself, I should be only too happy to assist you in any exploratory work you may find necessary for your investigation. Of that my colleagues at the Ministry fully approve, as you can imagine. But a permit has to come from Athens. And the request, really, should come from Luxembourg. You see my difficulty?'

Dan is doing his best to keep his newfound impatience under control. 'And how long will that take?'

The Ephor shrugs. 'Three to six months.'

'So look here, then. Your Ministry is all for an enquiry being conducted into possibly missing finds from Ano Meri, you promise full support to the EC committee. But rather than let us *find* what *you're* more anxious than anybody else to have found, you're going to send me back to London empty-handed, hold up the whole work of the committee, for *three to six months*. You can't be serious.'

The Ephor spreads his hands across his large desk. 'I am sorry, *kyrie* Robertson. It is the law in this country. Conduct surface surveys as much as you like. To go beneath the surface you have to have an excavation permit.'

'And the request *can't* come through Luxembourg,' Dan will furiously explain to Milica in the car a short while later, 'because Horst isn't going to entrust a delicate thing like that to me, at least not on my *own*. And that's the whole point: to get there ahead of Horst.'

Milica smiles happily. 'Then we take the law into our own hands?'

Dan stares at the road ahead. 'You realize we could both end up in prison? If we were caught it would be the end of my career. And a bad blot on yours.'

'I know,' says Milica with none of the solemnity Dan feels. 'But only if we are caught. And why should we be caught?'

It is one thing for Milica, Dan feels with a stab of petulant envy, brought up in a country where everything is theoretically controlled. Dan is hemmed in by a much heavier baggage of awe, an instinctive terror of putting himself outside the pale. For Milica the law means nothing more than a set of rules to be circumvented. She has explained it to him before: there are some rules you can't break because if you do you'll be found out. The rest you *can*, if you know how to go about it. Fools are the ones who keep to the rules, or who get caught when they break them. But how do you know which rules are which?

'That,' it seems so obvious, so ineluctably commonsensical in Milica's squarely uttered, guttural consonants, 'is the secret of success in my country.'

It is their last full day in Crete. Tomorrow evening, after a final round of handshakes and farewells in Kastro, Dan and Milica have their return passage booked to Piraeus. It's now or never, Milica has warned him.

The week has passed in a switchback of formal receptions by archaeologists and local dignitaries, alternating with rather desultory hours spent alone with Milica poking about the site, conducting the surface surveys that Dan knows perfectly well will reveal nothing, at least nothing of what he himself so badly needs to know, and filling up the notebooks that in due course he will assiduously convert into a report to which his and Milica's various travel and expenses claims can be attached. Whatever else he does, Dan intends to convince the committee of enquiry of the meticulousness of his methods.

Dutifully, Dan has stood in the dull sunshine outside the municipal offices where the bronze plaque stands to commemorate the fallen patriots of the National Resistance. Above the inscription, Dan has taken in the torrent of tiny figures marching in low relief towards the future, some holding banners, others rifles or pitchforks, the square-domed hat of the Greek priest conspicuous among the multitude. There are no facial features on the stylized relief, no heroes stand out of the crowd. It is, the Mayor's interpreter has had no need to explain, the People that is on the march. Now, with strangely mixed feelings, Dan leads Milica to the highest point of the old Venetian walls of the city, to an elegantly landscaped vantage point where a simple cross stands in the centre of a close-cropped square of grass, a well-meant approximation to an English lawn, and below the cross the words have been simply carved: LIONEL ALGERNON ROBERTSON, 1875–1951.

In summer, Dan knows, the oleander bushes will be in full flower, pink and white, and the sea below will be whipped to an intensity of blue by the afternoon wind. Now beneath a ceiling of high, thin clouds, in the damp stillness of spring, before the tourists have arrived, it is unnaturally, almost uncannily, quiet. From this spot the whole rugged coastline stretches out beyond the harbour to the east, past the chimneys of long-abandoned factories, along the cliffs and broken spurs of rock towards the new international airport. Behind, over the massive fortifications that withstood a twenty-four-year siege before finally succumbing to the might of the Turkish Sultan, the flat roofs and television aerials of the post-war suburbs sprawl towards the jagged crags of Iouktas that dominate the town. And in the other direction, to the southwest, where the bulk of Psiloriti is lost in cloud, beyond the roofs and the white concrete towers of the new University hospital, somewhere in the green haze, amid the rolling vineyards and olive groves, even Ano Meri is probably visible if you know where to look. Higher up, the bare flank of Stroumboulas is marred today by the rust-red gash of an enormous quarry. A thread of smoke hangs in the still air above the westward shoreline. In the bend of the coast, where the new road cuts a level swathe, nestles a power station whose tall red and white chimneys stand out even at this distance, among the cluster of oil tanks where a tanker is unloading.

'Here lies,' Dan murmurs softly to Milica, 'the conqueror of Kulhantepe, who squandered a fortune.' He half-laughs ruefully. 'You've got to hand it to him, you know. Everybody else always did. And he hasn't ended up too badly, either.'

But Dan is all at once overcome with melancholy: what place now on the planet for an old rogue of Lionel's stamp? The turning world, like a kaleidoscope, has dissolved the frame in which Lionel's hopes and achievements and failures could ever have happened. As well try to set your seal upon the water, Dan concludes morosely.

No, there is no trace here, any more than there has been all week at Ano

Meri, where he and Milica must now return to resume their surface survey, of those vanished generations. Dan has had his fill of memorials. Each of them, to his jaded imagination, a saddening reminder of a past placed by the very act of remembering more than ever out of reach.

'It sort of makes archaeology rather pointless, if you think about it.' He tries to explain his silent train of thought to Milica, as they arrive back at the Cabin.

But Milica's thoughts have been following a very different track. 'I think, before we do anything else, Dan, we should look at the fence. Tonight's our last chance, remember.'

'I know.' Now that the moment for action is almost upon them Dan feels his senses dulled, his enthusiasm gone; there is a brackish taste on his tongue, a dryness in his throat. He has slept badly all week.

Milica clicks her tongue. 'For God's sake don't *look* so like a thief!'

But Dan cannot help feeling furtive as he follows Milica to the edge of the car park, skirting the fence that protects the site. Nobody has taken much interest in their doings so far. The *phýlax*'s hut by the gate is pulsating with the sound of rock music as they pass. They are unlikely to be disturbed from that quarter.

The ground beneath the olive trees is carpeted with a blaze of weeds and wild flowers in yellow and purple. Dan recognizes the grey-white bells of asphodels nodding with simple dignity above the exuberant tangle. It is all so different now from those blazing, burnt-up summers of memory.

The fence is a good six feet in height, with barbed wire on the top, and carried on concrete posts. 'Can't go over,' Milica throws the words in clipped fashion over her shoulder. 'Either we go under, or we cut.'

'Here.' Dan's voice is barely above a whisper, although they have the hilltop of Ano Meri to themselves. A couple of the concrete posts, well out of sight of the car park or the *phýlax*'s hut, are loose. He shows Milica how, when the time comes, they will be able to hitch up the wire and crawl under.

The night is clear, with a moon, which adds to Dan's unease. His shadow and Milica's are all too clear in the moonlight. The archaeologists from the Villa have locked up and gone home. No one lives there now, except occasionally during the excavation season. The elderly woman from the village who came in to dust and clean each morning has long departed. The nearest houses are nearly half a mile away. Still, Dan urges extreme caution. There might be a poacher about, or a zealous agricultural field guard might conceivably be doing his rounds this late. Someone taking a short cut home from a party . . .

'Oh come *on*, Dan.' Milica, quite impatient now, leads him boldly over the open ground to the storeroom at the back of the Villa, whose key she has already purloined and will replace tomorrow before they leave.

'Here,' she says, flashing her torch around the interior of the store. 'Spade, pointing trowel, one for you and one for me, hand pick. Tarpaulin – we don't want to leave any traces, do we. Zembils? No need.' She places the implements into his nerveless hands, and turns off the flashlight.

Dan stumbles in the entrance, pick and spade fall to the stony ground with a crash that sounds like an explosion in the still night. They both freeze. Somewhere a long way off a dog is barking. A cock, nearer at hand, seems to scent the coming of summer and crows long and lustily. There is a mistiness in the air, which has formed into a gigantic halo round the moon. As the moments pass Dan cannot believe they haven't been accosted, that their suspicious presence hasn't been observed. As he picks himself up, thankful that Milica cannot see his expression in the darkness, Dan experiences a sudden surge of hope. What is this terrible invitation to go on, this newfound glow of confidence, now that the die is cast? Shaking with relief, Dan puts the moment of weakness behind him.

They barely make an effort to conceal themselves, as they skirt the deserted car park where the bronze bust of Lionel Robertson casts a gleam in the moonlight. Past the open ground, they enter the softly-carpeted olive grove; the crushed stems of the asphodels will be a dead giveaway in the morning, should anyone think to look. And now to the weak point in the fence that they marked down this afternoon.

Crouching down instinctively, they make a dash through the open moonlight, flitting through the wasteland of broken walls and passageways. Again by instinct, with no words spoken, they avoid the glaring expanse of the Great Court, threading the maze of the northern magazines instead. There has been recent rain; puddles have collected on the uneven surface of the court. From the forbidding bulk of the throne-room complex, with its covered corridors and stairs that break off, it seems to Dan, more abruptly than ever in the moonlight, comes the sound of water dripping. Dan's feet, he has realized, are soaking wet. It is going to be an uncomfortable night.

From the level terrace where the Minoans dug their middens through the accumulated debris of two thousand years, the slope falls away sharply to the west. The bones of the land, piled higher and higher in ridges and dark valleys, are silver and black in the moonlight. From the distant haze the snows of Psiloriti have a ghostly sheen. Near at hand the smell of the wet earth that has still not closed its pores from drawing in the evening rain, is overpowering. From the invisible lemon groves below the wall comes a waft of cool, waxy fragrance. A farmyard cock, oblivious to the hour, crows with a long drawn-out note. From further away another answers. There are clumps of weeds growing in corners of the site. Dan fancies he hears a sliding movement: a gecko perhaps, or a late-night lizard? Yesterday he found a baby tortoise wedged in an impossible niche above the Great Court. He had lifted it down and watched with satisfaction as it lumbered off to the shelter of some overhanging bougainvillea.

310

Dan is more comforted than otherwise by these reminders that he and Milica are not quite all alone on the hilltop of Kulhantepe.

Bothros 2 is distinguishable by the well-like circle of dressed stones on the surface. It is marked as unexcavated on the latest plan of the site Dan has acquired from the European team that was working here in the eighties.

But Dan knows better. Horst has cleared out the neighbouring Minoan midden, Bothros 1, down to subsoil level. There is now a grating over it, for safety, and Dan has noticed, in daylight, how it is already filling up again with Coca-Cola cans and cigarette packets.

Dan finds himself talking at first in whispers. 'Well, this is it, Milica. Who's going to turn the first sod?'

The rasp of the spade as it penetrates the damp earth is like a violation of the darkness. Once again, Dan feels waves of panic approaching. It's like vertigo; he can't bring himself to look up, to take in the shapes of the land and the mountains that look taller and starker in the moonlight; he experiences a buzzing in his ears and his knees go weak. The chill has risen from his soaked feet to his knees, he feels his strength as well as his precarious courage ebbing away into the soil beneath him. He finds the only way to keep these terrors at bay is to look down, to watch carefully as his spade carves out the shadow of a semi-circle inside the ring of stones, to pile the stony earth neatly on the tarpaulin they have brought for the purpose. Milica's shadow as she carves an answering semi-circle half a dozen feet away overlaps with his own, as though the two of them are grappling together in the deepening pit that is opening at their feet.

From time to time he can hear Milica grunt as her spade hits something hard; her breathing is fast and shallow. Neither of them is accustomed to the exertion. Dan needs to stop quite often to catch his breath and wipe the sweat from his forehead. He has never before heard his own heartbeat so loud; the urgency of the blood pumping through his arteries frightens him. His efforts have banished the chill from his legs, his feet feel as though they are being slowly boiled. He will have blisters tomorrow.

As the moon rises higher and the pile of earth on the tarpaulin grows, Dan and Milica find themselves standing up to their waists in the pit. The going is more difficult now. The space is cramped, they have to take it in turns to dig, while the other holds the torch. The pace of work has slowed too.

'Not much further I reckon,' gasps Dan, when at last his chest is level with the ring of stones on the ground. His feet are lost in the deeper darkness below.

Above them the moon has become smaller and more distant, its light has hardened.

'Let's stop a moment, Milica.' He straightens slowly, his back aching from effort and anxiety. The moonlight, as it pours into the narrow funnel of the pit, strikes tiny cold fires from the crystalline gypsum lining that remains intact in many places. But the bottom remains in darkness; they have only the feeble ring of the torchbeam to help them. Everything is in black and white, like a silent film.

The damp has barely reached this far down, the earth they are turning out is light and friable. It makes digging a little easier, but by now fatigue is beginning to take its toll. Dan knows he won't be able to keep it up much longer.

Milica has been crouching with the torch at the lowest point of the darkness. 'This is bone,' she announces laconically at last, her voice hoarse with suppressed excitement.

Dan bends down painfully to follow the thin beam of the torch. These layers have not been disturbed since Laura's ghastly secret was unceremoniously dumped here half a century ago. Whatever it was she had really discovered, these bones that are pitifully, starkly breaking the surface of the soil now must be the bones that she held in her hand on that rainy afternoon in the finds shed. The bones that sparked the final, fatal rift between Lionel and his son. Dan takes a deep breath. This is his moment of triumph. His nerve has not failed him. He has been the first, after all, to probe to its heart the scandal that has rocked his whole life to its foundations. Whatever the truth, the evidence is now in his hands. His earlier anxieties forgotten, Dan falls to his knees, scrabbling through the loose earth with his trowel in the beam of the torch that Milica holds not quite steadily for him. Her uncomplicated excitement has infected him fully at last.

There seem to be a lot of bones. 'We should have brought a brush. I'd forgotten how crumbly this soil is,' Dan mutters as the point of his trowel quickly, deftly probes, dislodging stones and clods of earth, neatly scraping back the soil to reveal the angular knobbed shapes that before his eyes emerge into the unmistakable contours, oddly disturbing despite his years of archaeological training, of human remains. *Membra disiecta.* This is what they've been looking for, isn't it? But Dan is trembling all over. This is archaeology in the raw, it's a far cry from the elegant patterns of data he can bring to life on his computer screens back in London. The light, stony, slightly clinging soil is under his fingernails, his knuckles are scraped, his forehead and hair are crusted with it. His knees are sore and his trousers torn. The fusty smell of ancient, damp earth is all around him in the close space, mingled with his and Milica's sweat. Milica, a shadow behind the quivering torchbeam, must be in the same state. The hard reality of it is under his skin, the bones that he is expertly disinterring are brittle beneath his fingers. He feels a sudden revulsion at handling them, the relics of his own mortality. He is in the presence of someone – quite possibly, if the diaries are correct, of several people – who were once alive. And who near this spot died a terrible death.

'Dan, look out!'

The torchbeam has yawed violently away, leaving him in darkness. Milica has thrown herself against him, winding him, pinning him to the side of the trench. Now she tugs at him frantically, hauling him behind her towards the surface.

'What on earth—?' Dan looks round dazed, half expecting to find the archaeologists of the prefecture drawn up to witness their arrest, and the prefect himself with two pairs of handcuffs and a sardonic smile of triumph in the moonlight.

But the moonlight is as silent and empty as before. Only the deep pit they have dug, with the thick, tangible blackness in its depths, is new in the night. Nothing else has changed.

'Listen,' Milica hisses, gripping his arm tightly.

'I can't hear anything.' The water has stopped dripping. The land below the wall breathes out only silence.

Milica snaps the torch back on and shines it into the darkness from which they have come. The beam searches for a moment, then comes to rest.

'You see?'

Dan shudders. A snake about a foot long is slithering among the remains he was uncovering only a few seconds ago.

'How did it get there?'

Milica's grip on his arm has scarcely relaxed. 'I think it fell in. Just now. It's all right, Dan, it couldn't have been there all along.'

'What kind is it?'

He can feel Milica shrug in the darkness. 'Better safe than sorry.'

Dan grasps the handle of his spade firmly. He is oddly reluctant to do the deed. 'The Minoans had a thing about snakes, didn't they?' He laughs uneasily, trying to recover his equilibrium. 'Jennifer goes on about it, at the Institute, remember? The goddess with the snakes twined around her arms. *Holding in her hand the key to the life eternal,* isn't that it?'

In the nervous tension of the moment, the rich Scottish timbre of Jennifer's speech comes uncannily to life. They both laugh wildly. Recognizing the rising hysteria that threatens to grip them both, Dan tightens his grasp on the handle of the spade.

'Sorry, mate,' he mutters as he drives the blade with quite unnecessary force through the uncoiled body of the snake, severing it into two almost equal halves. It is some moments before the two parts are still, and jumping down into the trench Dan ejects them on the end of his spade. The small stain of blood on the metal is jet-black in the moonlight.

'Won't be a minute.' Dan is out of the trench again and doubled up behind a broken wall, out of sight of Milica. The sweat stands out cold on his forehead, there is a roaring in his ears, his stomach contracts in agonizing dry retching.

Now Milica is calling him.

'OK,' Dan calls back softly. 'Business as usual,' he says to her with a wan grin as he rejoins her in the trench. But he notices the sharply worried look she gives him, though she says nothing.

During his absence she has continued the work of clearing. Silently she guides the lightbeam over the floor of the pit.

'Dan, *look!*' she says now, in an awed whisper. In the dancing light Dan follows the embryonic outline of a spinal column, the dome of a skull, the straight lines of thigh bones vanishing beneath where he and Milica squat crouched together in the narrow space.

'Dan, I'm sorry.' Her voice comes to him as though from a great distance, but there is a quality in it he has never heard before. 'These aren't loose bones, Dan. Not the bones that Laura found.'

More cautiously now they scrape for some minutes in silence. And now as Dan and Milica stand back from their discovery their giant shadows recede with them and the moon that, unnoticed by either of them, has risen high enough to shine directly into the open grave that is Bothros 2, picks out in sharp relief the complete skeleton of a man, something over six feet in height, lying on his back with his knees slightly drawn up, and tucked round his feet the curled remains of a dog.

As Dan moves to try to dispel the numbness that has overcome him, a spark of moonlight flashes among the bones. Gingerly, almost reluctantly, hardly knowing what he is doing, Dan eases the point of his trowel into the space inside the ribcage, and picks out something round and gleaming. He places it on the palm of his hand and shows it wordlessly to Milica.

Dieu et mon droit. The words come unbidden, under the pitiless light of the moon, to clamour inside Dan's head.

He hears his own voice, but all the while Dan is someone else, looking down from the impartial moon on the strange antics of two renegade archaeologists below the surface of the planet.

'So that,' says Dan with simple, desolate finality, 'is where I come from.'

17 BEYOND THE PALE

OUTSIDE the small windows of the Cabin, with their frames of polished cypress wood that remain, after all these years, uncurtained, dawn is lightening the sky. Washed but unslept, Dan lies on his back, his eyes wide open. Milica, who is as fatigued by the night's exertions as he is, has gone to her room, as she says, to catch some sleep.

Cocks are crowing, donkeys braying. Everywhere there's a sound of birdsong, swallows are swooping past the casement, still with its 1920s lattice-work, nesting under the eaves. Dan can smell the coming of summer, that won't reach England for another couple of months. He can smell the sunlight already beginning to strike heat from the ground outside, it's as though a door has been opened into that long-ago double summer under the Cretan sun. He imagines time wheeling about, to deposit him back on the threshold of that door. This time, knowing what he now knows, will he go quietly back to England when the summer ends, to take his degree and go on to do research (in London, Cambridge will still be too expensive), will he marry Margaret and settle down to the comfortable obscurity of the Institute of Chronometry? All those years, with the grand passions of the Robertsons before him as a constant example of what to avoid and yes, until now he has avoided it quite well.

But now and only now is he beginning to understand what it was his mother feared for him, a callow nineteen-year-old setting out for Crete where he had been born. His mother, he has not a doubt of it now, knew. All these years presiding serenely over his growing up and knowing the truth and shielding him from it.

Dan takes the brass button from his pocket and turns it over in the sunlight. He squeezes its surface tightly between his palms. He will have to make sure, of course, back in England, but Dan is in no doubt about this either. He is looking at a relic of that absurdly outdated uniform in which his father gathered his troop of irregulars to fight against the German paratroopers, in which he withdrew to the mountains when the fighting was over at Ano Meri, to organize his guerrilla force on the Nida Plateau.

As the lines of the button's embossed insignia fade from his hand, Dan stares wide-eyed beyond the casement window of the Cabin, oblivious to the sunlight. What was it he once said to Lucy: the solution to one mystery is only another mystery?

'You see, Milica, this turns everything on its head. To hell with the enquiry, to hell with the bones we know were deposited in Bothros 2. They must be still there, of course. Lower down. *He* guarantees that, you might say. No, Milica, we'll have to leave the archaeology to Horst now. But what *I* want to know is, how in the name of God did he get there? With his faithful gundog Tzak at his feet? It beggars belief, Milica, I don't know what to think.'

But in the course of the day, amid the solemnly prescribed farewells to their hosts, Dan's thoughts have hardened. Every sinew in his body on fire from the night's exertions, Dan has kept his hands self-consciously in his pockets as much as possible throughout the formalities of his leave-taking, lest some eagle-eye should spot the recent contusions, the lingering traces of the dust of Ano Meri so recently ingrained there. And among the smiles and the goodwill – even the Mayor's gold tooth flashes with a grin that could be of pure friendliness – Dan cannot help scanning the faces that have become almost familiar in the past week: the suited figures running to fat, the thick moustaches drooping defiantly; there is a toughness in the swarthy features, a wiry pride inherited from generations of hill-fighters. As he shakes hands with the men (they nearly all are men) of the village, of the prefecture, of his own profession, Dan has felt his own venial guilt crying out in the spring sunshine. And even while he clasps their hands in his, Dan is now convinced that any one of them may be the son or grandson, the cousin or the friend, may be the heir to the confidences, of his father's murderer.

It is a relief at last to rejoin Milica on the quayside. She had taken herself off, somewhat mysteriously, earlier in the day.

Now, as the already darkening Venetian fortress of Kastro fades away astern into the flat grey sea and the cool mist of evening, she explains. 'I went to the village.'

Dan looks at her questioningly.

'The women will tell us more than the men,' she explains. And as he still stares blankly she prompts him. 'You know, the next stage of the enquiry. *Your* enquiry, but I'm your assistant, remember? There will be people still living, Dan, who can tell us how he died. Isn't that what you want to find out?'

Milica had been, Dan has admiringly to admit, rather astute. 'Women always want to talk about their families, don't they? Well,' she goes on, 'I've been tracking down the younger generation. Nobody very young lives in the village now, you'll have noticed that? But I've got names and addresses written down – daughters, cousins, nieces, studying or married and settled down in Athens, Ljubljana, Leeds, Manchester, Düsseldorf, Melbourne, Baltimore. Take a look, Dan.'

Darkness has fallen, the moon is not yet up. Above their heads the stars are swimming in the slight haze. Here on the lee side of the ship, away from the rail, under the ship's lights, the air is almost balmy. Milica takes a notebook from her bag and flips through its pages. Dan looks at the names and addresses scrawled in ungainly block capitals. The village of the Laskaris has indeed reached out to conquer the world.

She turns to him, her eyes shining with something that it shocks him to realize must be excitement.

'You see,' Milica edges confidentially closer to him, 'these are people who will *want* to talk about their home and their families back in Crete, and the history of their village. The women will, you'll see. If we have the time, Dan, and the patience, we can find out what happened.'

None of this is quite real for Dan. A terrible lassitude has come over him. His body aches from top to toe, his senses are dulled. Only his mind has been working ceaselessly throughout the night and day, lucidly detached from the rest of him. He cannot take it in yet, obscurely he senses that there will be pain to come. The hateful certainty that has been forming all day finally breaks through into words, he finds himself speaking calmly, almost easily. Milica's solid presence beside him by the ship's rail may have something to do with that. But his thoughts today have been moving in a tight circle, and they have not been of Milica.

Dan's eyes as he speaks are fixed on the distant lights of the shore. 'For him to come down from the mountains, and wearing his uniform, which everybody must have known in the district, it would have had to be at night. Maybe on his way to the Cabin, maybe after he'd left it to go back to the mountains. Either way, somebody was waiting for him. Someone who knew the place well. Someone, what's more, who needed to conceal what he had done. So not the Germans. And not a collaborator. A collaborator would simply have denounced him to the Germans, which would have come to the same thing. To bury him like that could only have been the work of someone from his own side, a comrade, someone who was equally at risk from the Germans himself. I don't think there can be much doubt, Milica. My father was murdered by a Cretan patriot.' In all probability one of those commemorated in the brazen assurance of Manolis Laskaris' memorial outside the town hall.

'I understand, Dan. But *why*, can you tell me that? They were on the same side, he was fighting with the partisans after all. Why should they kill him?'

'They're a proud lot, the Cretans, and they're supposed to have long memories. My father never got on with the villagers, and Manolis (the original Manolis) in particular. He took up their cause in his last years, certainly, but that doesn't make him one of them. The Mayor is proof of that, if proof were needed. I'm sure those people never forgot that Ano Meri belonged to them, that the Laskaris' land had been taken from them by guile and force. Think what a fortune old Manolis could have made for himself and his brother – and they *knew*, don't forget, there were antiquities buried there before ever Lionel came along. Nobody seems to have dared raise a finger against the old rogue. But my father was a different matter. Imagine him, in the conditions of occupation and resistance, coming down from the mountains to visit his wife at Ano Meri, fearlessly – we know about the risks he took, but *trusting*, do you see? thinking himself safe among the people he thought were his own. And it's too easy, isn't it, on a dark night . . .'

Dan's voice tails off. They are standing close together now by the rail, in the moist gale of the ship's motion. Her face is very close to his; it isn't easy to be heard over the ship's engines and the blowing of the gale. A long way below them the rush of foaming water is a brilliant white as far as the ship's lights reach. Further out is blackness.

'I think I know now why he died,' Dan says, but his words are not really intended for Milica and the wind has whipped them away almost before they are uttered. Dan continues to stare beyond the round rim of Milica's face, beyond the white water, into the empty darkness. He knows now what it is to come out of nothing. To stare into an open grave, to return the empty gaze of his grandfather's bronze bust that guards the gate to Ano Meri, and see in that emptiness his own beginning. And out of that emptiness reaches, with all the terrible power of a vacuum, the desire whose shadow has been teasing him for so long. The desire that in his time led Daniel Robertson, a wanted man, a guerrilla leader in an occupied land, to the door of the Cabin, right next to the German command post at the Villa, the very heart of enemy territory. And why? So that he, Dan, might have life.

No wonder the name of his father could not be spoken ever after.

And now Dan can focus on the strong brown gaze of Milica's eyes upon him; his life is suddenly full, something within himself that he didn't know was there is brimming over. Dan is tongue-tied, tremulous with a desire that is at last inexplicably purged of shame. She has undone her headband and her hair is blowing thickly backward, the last strands straggling loosely over her face. The wind of the ship's motion fills out the white shirt she wears tightly tucked into her jeans, emphasizing the small curve of her breasts. Her face is tilted slightly upward, he has always admired Milica's disdain of makeup. She wrinkles her nose at him now, it may have been involuntary; a ghost of a grin, a wistful flicker, seems to pass across her broad features. Dan opens his arms to her and she comes into his embrace, nestling her head against his shoulder, bracing her thighs against his. For a long moment he strokes her hair that seems alive in the gale. With all the time in the world he gently raises her chin until her face is an inch from his own.

'Yes?' he whispers.

'Yes,' she breathes back and he kisses her long and deeply.

Later, before settling himself for sleep, Dan stands for a moment at the porthole of the little cabin. The moon has risen and its path reaches across the ruffled sea straight towards him, like a scroll unfurled. Only, he cannot read the shifting hieroglyphs of silver on black; he remembers the gramophone records he used to watch on the turntable, with his mother at Upland Grange, and his fascination then with the mysterious grooves that the needle could read and turn into music. But where *is* the music? he had demanded to know. He had been fascinated by the process that could stamp such wonderful sounds into plastic. It is with such a script that the moonlight teases him tonight. Could he but read it (his mind is already dissolving towards sleep) perhaps the whole mystery of what happened at Ano Meri during those blank years of occupation, years of legend, of heroism, of betrayal, would unravel before his eyes. The impartial moon that watched him and Milica last night, has no doubt seen all, and all it once saw it holds out to him now, faithfully engraved on the moving surface of the sea, in the beam of light that is destined for this porthole alone.

The sleep that has eluded him for so long now gently takes Dan and lays him sprawling in the lower bunk. Above him in the darkness Milica is breathing softly. He has been surprised by the simplicity of their lovemaking, her legs planted squarely, wide apart, her body barely moving under his, the only light the moonlight from the porthole.

When it was over and he still held her close in the enclosed space of the lower bunk, she grinned happily and said, 'Didn't Lucy ever tell you I like older men?'

He winced at that. Lucy has no business here, she should have known. But he has also seen beneath the remark, to the game attempt at sophistication. It touched him, that, as a reminder of how unsophisticated Milica really is, and what a wonderful thing is her trust.

Dan has no qualms any more about Lady Ottoline and the Institute's code of practice for sexual harassment. He has gone beyond the pale, now. It seems, as he sinks deeply into sleep, rather a nice place to be.

Dan can sense the change in the air the moment he steps inside the hall where Foucault's pendulum still mutely testifies to the planet's trajectory through space and time. Going to collect his mail and fumbling in his pocket for the correct change to put in the machine for his first plastic-tasting coffee of the day, he can't quite define it. He has only been away three weeks. But it's as though the secretaries he passes in the corridor, the colleagues he nods to as they hurry past with bent heads and sheaves of papers in their hands, have all somehow aged in his absence. Their backs are stooping, their hair grey. Has so much time gone by in only three weeks?

By lunchtime he has had to correct the impression. He collides with Jennifer in the canteen. 'Oh, I didn't see you.' She lets out a little shriek and the tray in her hand wobbles precariously, precipitating a bread roll in a long arc that takes it under the feet of the Nanosecond Technology men who are in a huddle at the far side of the room, recognizable at a distance by their close-cropped heads and day-glo tee-shirts. 'My goodness, Dan, I think we'd all about given you up as lost in the wilds of Crete or some such place.' There is no alternative now but to sit down with Jennifer. He makes a detour first by the counter to purchase her a new bread roll. As he does so, he feels like a ghost. That's it: he's become invisible.

Jennifer has recovered herself sufficiently to interrogate him brightly. He gives her the edited version of his trip he has also prepared for Dingo Cathcart, and will shortly be typing out to accompany his expenses form to send to Luxembourg. Jennifer chews lustily, and fires sharp questions at him with her mouth full. A projectile of white bread lands on the side of his plate and he covertly conceals it under a blighted chip. 'And that student of yours – your assistant, isn't she? Did you find her much help?'

He has probably only imagined the gleam in the anthropophagous spinster's eye, but he feels something unaccustomed and discomfiting happening to his face, a hot, crawling sensation in his cheeks.

Trying as best he can to look as though his mind was on something else, Dan nods. 'She's had to go back to Yugoslavia for a bit. Some trouble at home, I gather.'

Milica in fact has parted from him in Athens, changing her flight at the last minute for one to Ljubljana. Dan has been on hot coals ever since. She has assured him it is not because of him. Apparently she has a brother in Ljubljana, she is vague about what the trouble is. Dan, to his shame, came close to pleading with her. 'It's not that, it's not that,' she kept saying, shaking her head very far from side to side, and he has almost believed her. He has believed her because they made love again in the Athens hotel before she left to catch her plane. Twice, in fact. The second time just after the first. She will be back in London in two, three weeks at most. She has promised. And walked out of his life with, he is ready to swear, a tear of genuine affection for him in her eye.

That, to be fair, was less than a week ago, but this is how it already seems to Dan. And as he cannot dislodge that early morning in the Athens hotel from his memory, he again feels that unfamiliar, uncontrollable thing happening to his face.

It is because of Paola, he supposes. What Paola has left behind, in fading out

320

of his life, and what has triggered his panic now at Milica's desertion, is her *absence*. For a dizzying moment the idea comes to him of making a clean breast to Jennifer. Instead he talks to her, with an urgency that is new to him, about Ano Meri. About how changed it all was after thirty years. He wants at all costs to deflect her from the subject that will expose him in the blushing of his cheeks. He tells her about the socialist Mayor with the gold eye-tooth, who had the same name as the old *phýlax* at the site. Was Jennifer ever at Ano Meri? Yes, she gives him a crooked smile, concealing what strangely wistful memories, Dan finds time to wonder? She remembers Manolis well, the old *phýlax* with the cough. 'His bark was certainly worse than his bite,' says Jennifer now, and her words send Dan back through thirty years to his very first morning in Crete, and Garel Thomas' cheerful encouragement: 'Don't mind old Manolis. His bark's worse than his bite.' Manolis' bark, it was true, could be heard on a still day, from the *phýlax*'s hut, all over the excavation.

A knife-wound, Dan recalls for Jennifer now, from a skirmish during the war, had left Lionel's former foreman with a collapsed lung and the irritable, wheezing cough that invariably announced his presence. Doggedly he clung to the meagre privilege of his post guarding Ano Meri, though his age and the state of his health suggested he should long since have retired. 'Got two children to bring up, haven't I,' he would growl when anyone ever raised the subject. Manolis' nephew was rarely to be seen in the village – he had gone to Athens to study, and to his uncle's disgust seemed to prefer the delights of the metropolis even in summer. The girl, who must have been about fifteen, seemed to be always indoors: sick, or sewing, or for some reason indisposed. Dan had never seen her. Their mother was *kyrá* Maria who kept the café in the village, and day in day out wore black with a black scarf over her head for Yannis Laskaris, descendant, so he had dreamed, of emperors and murdered in a back street of Kastro by fascist thugs in 1946.

It was to this tiny, fly-blown café that some of the archaeologists would come to fraternize after supper at the Villa, in a distant, easy way, with the villagers who worked on the site. Dan rarely went along. The thick, guttural Greek that the others seemed able to follow, and some of them even to make jokes in, from the response they seemed to arouse, went over his head. When he did go it was more often than not as a chaperone for one of the girls, to whom he would talk quietly as the alien speech, with its strange rhythms of rapid-fire explosion alternating with deep, ruminative silence, rumbled on around them. The chairs were ranged in the dust outside the little café, *kyrá* Maria went round with a watering can at sunset, laying the dust around the tables and, if any was left over, giving a drop to the withered geraniums in tin cans that lined the steps to the upper storey where the family lived. Electricity had not yet come to the village, and when the sun set and the lamps were lit Dan was conscious of the deep darkness, only just held at bay. Sometimes, on those evenings in the village, Dan was certain he could feel the *phýlax*'s eyes upon him, boring into him from the spartan interior of the café.

'He always used to give me the creeps,' Dan confides now to Jennifer, as he gets up to go back to his office.

'Funny you should say that,' says Jennifer. 'He did have a way of peering at the young men, on the dig. Shouldn't say such a thing of course, but I always thought he was queer. Never caused any trouble, though. Harmless old ruffian really. Almost as though he was looking out for someone to turn up. The blond youth of his dreams. Never did so far as I know, poor old Manolis.'

In the event Milica's absence lasts two months. During that time Dan has received a number of postcards from her which he takes to be encouraging, though they give little away. A date has been fixed for Slovenia's independence; she will return by then, she has promised. She has also written to him more formally at the Institute, to ask for leave of absence from the investigation. She has, she indicates, found a lead in Ljubljana she will follow up, but she is very doubtful whether it will yield results relevant to the main report. Decoded, this suggests to Dan that when at last she does get back, she may not come empty-handed. But it is herself he misses, and he cannot, either on a postcard or, once, when he was overjoyed to hear her voice on a crackling phone line, find a way of saying so. No, she explained then through the long-distance distortions, she is not staying away at the other end of Europe to wave a little flag. But there may be trouble. Dan is still not clear whether the trouble is the family trouble she mentioned before, or something else. Yugoslavia has been on the television news lately. Outbreaks of violence in faraway places are nothing new these days. But Slavonia is not at all the same thing as Slovenia, it seems, and Milica should be well away from it all, in the Slovenian capital, Ljubljana.

The Adria Airways flight from Ljubljana has been delayed for the fourth time. Gatwick Airport is full of holidaymakers this Wednesday afternoon. Milica has telephoned again at last, to say she will be on today's flight. The line is more crackly than ever, he can't make out half of what she says. She sounds anxious, 'How was Independence Day?' he remembered to ask.

'Independence was today, it is over. Tomorrow I leave for England.'

Only nobody, it seems, will fly out of Ljubljana this Wednesday afternoon in June 1991. Tanks have taken over the runway at Brnik airport. The first Dan knows of this is an overheard conversation between two men half his age, whom he knows instinctively must be journalists. To their evident embarrassment he accosts them. 'Aye, it's trew,' says one, with a strong Glasgow accent, 'but for Goad's sake dinna go tellin' folks, will ye? It's no' official yet.'

322

Dan finds himself in the grip of an anxiety he knows is unreasonable. Blindly he stumbles through the crowds of holidaymakers streaming up the escalators towards the consumer delights of Gatwick Village, and makes his way down into the gloom from which a fast train will take him to Victoria or a slow one to London Bridge. Back in town it is the rush hour; squeezed and sweating on a succession of trains, Dan arrives at last in the sepulchral quiet of his own front room, with the familiar sound of his mother's grandfather clock ticking in the hall. He is in time for the six o'clock news. There are no pictures from Ljubljana as yet, but what the Glaswegian has told him is true enough: the Yugoslav Federal Army has moved into the city and taken over the airport. There *are* pictures from Austria, though – of a blocked customs post and on the other side an unfamiliar flag waving gently in the breeze. Dan in his present state doesn't recognize this world. He recognizes fear flaring in his nostrils – fear of losing himself in the loneliness watched over by the ticking of the grandfather clock, fear of what might happen to Milica. He is appalled at how much he needs Milica, misses her, but she is right in there, in the thick of this new world with its unfamiliar flags where tanks can take over the runways of an international airport. He daren't switch off the television for fear of missing some new development, some news flash interrupting programmes, though the style of the coverage from Yugoslavia so far scarcely warrants such a degree of urgency. He finds himself nostalgic for the wall-to-wall relays from CNN during the Gulf War. He should have sodded his vague principles and bought a satellite dish after all. Lucy has one, he seems to remember.

It is half past two in the morning when a sleepless Dan picks up the phone and dials Lucy's number. Before she rings off he fancies he has heard a cross male voice in the background. Lucy's life is her own affair, he's pleased for her if she's got someone just now; she hasn't said anything but there's no reason why she should. As Dan rolls over in the empty bed that was once his mother's and tries to curl himself into a tight ball beneath the duvet, the way he used to as a child when he was afraid of the huge darkness of Upland Grange, he feels his nakedness shredded almost to the bone. It is not fair of him to cast Lucy in this light, he knows that perfectly well. But tonight he feels himself deserted even by his daughter.

Milica, when she finally does arrive, is subtly changed. It is as though she has been through some sort of crucible and come out of it with a new hardness, a new brittle surface. She talks with a kind of defeated cynicism he has never heard from her before. Her nails are bitten to the quick, and in slack moments her fingers will worry at her mouth even in front of him. She must have taken up smoking again while she has been away, he notices the new nicotine stains on her fingers. There is a darkness, almost a furtiveness, in the patient depths of her eyes, and with a degree of panic he recognizes in them the reflection of his own fear, although from what she has to tell him it is a fear far better grounded.

He has set himself, this first evening, to reassure her. The European Community has mediated to bring an end to the flare-up in Slovenia. And she herself is safe in London.

Her eyes where she sits half curled up on the sofa next to him, are enormous. 'Oh Dan, you don't understand anything, do you? In my country it is only just beginning. And "safe"! What is it you say: safe as houses? What use is it if *I* am safe? Yes, for a time, in London I am safe. My father and brothers are not safe. My grandfather's grave, with the red star of the army he gave his life to, is not safe. I will try to explain it for you, Dan, if you will be patient. I am a Yugoslav, and already I am a foreigner in half my country. Soon, there may be nowhere in the world where I can be what I am: a Yugoslav. My father, my brothers, my aunt in Sarajevo, they will all have to choose. To be Slovenes, Croatians, Serbs, to be Muslims or Orthodox or Catholic, although they may not have been inside a church or a mosque for twenty years. Dan, if this goes on I will be cut in little pieces. And it is only beginning, I tell you.'

She is wearing the same faded jeans she wore in Crete. Dan longs to reach across the sofa and enfold her, to hold out the reassurance of his South London home where time moves stolidly in the measure of the grandfather clock and his mother's ghost watches over him benignly, her love, he has so often felt, too strong to be extinguished by mere death. If only he could resume with Milica from where they left off that morning in the Athens hotel. But he doesn't yet know how she has changed. She seems to him wary, like a frightened horse. Normally taciturn, now she is close to him, biting her nails, sitting on the sofa with one leg curled under her, and she needs to talk. So let her talk. And Dan listens.

She tells a tale of petty spite and conflicting loyalties – a family affair until in the last weeks of June it spilled over to become the story of a people and a new country was born, Slovenia. Janko, Milica's youngest brother, is a conscript in the federal army serving outside Ljubljana. He's got involved with a local girl, but the local people hate the federal army. The girl is thrown out by her father. Janko is confined to barracks for breaking discipline. Milica has tried to mediate, to use her influence. Her family is well known in military circles, Janko's sentence can be bought off. But the girl turns out to be pregnant. He's crazy about her. He wants to marry her. Her people give him an ultimatum: he *can* marry her, but only if he deserts and joins the new Slovene Defence Force.

'What do you do, Dan, when your life is suddenly cut in two like that?'

Dan, despite everything, is intrigued by the story. 'What *did* he do?'

'I don't know, Dan, that's the worst thing. The last week when I was there, the barracks was like a fortress. Nobody could get in. There were people gathered outside, the phone lines were cut. Now the federal regiments are withdrawing from Slovenia. I cannot find out if Janko has deserted. If he has, my father will never speak to him again.'

It turns out it is this stern and, Dan is beginning to divine, also military figure, who has in effect ordered Milica back to London on the day that Slovenian independence finally became a reality. She is supposed to resume her studies. There is nothing more she can do in Ljubljana. And Dan begins to guess also at the bitterness behind Milica's bland words, the shadow of this peremptory father at whose bidding, it now appears, she parted from him so suddenly in Athens, and by whose will she is now restored to him.

She has brought him a bottle of *slivovic*, and he has kept refilling their glasses while she has been talking. The sharp, rancid taste is not much to his liking, but Dan has had enough to make him feel quite drunk. He will answer for this in the morning. But with the sensation and the unfamiliar taste comes a sense of exotic comradeship that warms him. Milica must have got through half the bottle. He hadn't noticed, but all at once her face has a fiercely dishevelled look, her eyes are slightly bloodshot, her hair has begun to escape from her headband.

'Dan,' she kneels up suddenly on the sofa facing him. 'Dan, will you make love to me?'

Despite everything he is taken aback by the abruptness of it. He reaches out an arm. 'Shall we go to bed?'

But she is kneeling up rigid on the sofa. 'No, Dan. Have to go home . . .'

Dan can see another abyss opening before him. 'Not tonight, Milica, you can't go anywhere in this state.'

But already Milica has torn the headband from her hair and thrown it on the floor. 'Here, Dan. Now. Please.' Her look is suddenly so appealing, so vulnerable and at the same time so full of hard, passionate desire, it seems all at once absurd to try to argue with her. Already she is leaning forward and unsteadily undoing the buttons of his shirt.

Dan wakes with the first dawn chorus. Something is pounding behind his forehead, his mouth is dry with a strange, sour taste. He looks around the bedroom in the growing light that filters through the curtains. Something is missing; and then memory comes back and he leaps up in a panic. Where is Milica? But the pounding in his head is much worse, the room is reeling, he can feel the nausea start to rise. Steadying himself by the doorjamb, Dan pads across the landing to the bathroom and struggles briefly, inconclusively with the child-proof top of the paracetamol bottle. Desperate now, he cracks the bottle against the side of the bath and is childishly delighted at the cascade of round white tablets and chunks of brown glass. Have to clear this up by morning. He dusts off two of the tablets and washes them down with a gulp of water straight from the tap.

And now Dan is entirely purposive. Pulling on his dressing gown over his nakedness, he makes his way quietly downstairs. Milica's clothes are all over the sitting room. It comes to him with something approaching terror that Mrs McKenzie, the elderly cleaning lady bequeathed him by his mother, will be here at eight thirty. Mrs McKenzie has a key and is used to letting herself in. Wide awake now, Dan tiptoes among the wreckage of last night's lovemaking. He feels oddly squeamish, gathering up Milica's empty clothes. In their scattered dismemberment he reads again the traces of violence, of desperation even, in their repeated lovemaking. As she looked up at him from the sofa her eyes had seemed to penetrate behind his, but it was as though his skull had become transparent. In her search for him she was seeing right through him. He wanted more than anything to be there for her, to give of himself, but her body was heaving beneath his too fast for him, her breathing had turned too soon into a whistling gasp, he felt the seed flowing out of him and wanted to cry from frustration. This was not what his anxiety for Milica and his own newfound vulnerability had nurtured through the months of her absence. It was a crude, desperate coupling and yes, he needed that too, and responded to it, but it wasn't enough; the cry that broke from her at the moment of climax was the cry of someone who had lost more than he could ever make up to her, it went past him, it wasn't for him, he couldn't answer it. It is Milica herself, no more and no less, that he loves. And there, almost aloud against the chorus of fledgelings under the eaves waiting to be brought this dawn's early half-digested worms, the word is spoken. Milica, where are you?

He runs her to earth eventually in the spare bedroom. She is lying sprawled on her front, she has kicked off the covers. Her long dark auburn hair straggles down her back and overflows on to the pillow. Her buttocks and thighs look strong and relaxed. Her breathing is slow and gentle. Quietly Dan deposits her clothes at the end of the bed. Then he leans over the pillow, kisses her on the forehead, barely brushing her skin with his lips. She stirs, mutters something in a language he doesn't understand.

In the gathering light Dan tiptoes back to his room.

It is a sunny Monday morning in July, in Dingo Cathcart's office. Facing his Head of Level, as the measured words fall one by one into his consciousness and the abyss that has haunted him for years at last opens up at his feet, Dan is mildly surprised to find it happening in a way so different from his anxious imaginings. All those years, walking up through Covent Garden from Charing Cross with the knotted feeling in his stomach. All those nightmares of collecting his mail from his pigeonhole, opening the sealed buff transit envelope, *Dear Dr Robertson, I regret to have to inform you* . . . But it hasn't been like that at all, he could have spared himself the anguish. Also, all these mornings with the twisted feeling in his gut, he needn't have worried. He was, had he but known it, perfectly safe on every one of them. It is only *this* morning, which has begun with a quite jovial phone call from Cathcart; is he very busy right now, can he spare a minute? It seems Dan can spare a minute and more. The rest of his working life in fact.

'The nub of the matter is this,' says Dingo, his elbows planted squarely on the desk and his fingertips together: 'we can go through the whole dismissal routine. As I've indicated to you, there are grounds. None of this need be necessary, though. You sign a voluntary severance agreement, your pension is secure, you get a lump sum under redundancy provisions, which is quite generous when you think of investing it at current interest rates. Date of leaving, well there could be some flexibility there. In effect we'd be looking at the end of the year. Of course, you'd be free to make your own arrangements as soon as you like.'

Dan is looking very intently at the speaker of these words. Cathcart with his palely glinting spectacles seems a thousand miles away on the other side of the desk. This is what it really feels like to be beyond the pale. On the wrong side of a light-coloured, softwood-veneer desk like Cathcart's.

'I don't like innuendo,' says Dan, doggedly sticking up for himself, as much for something to say as with any expectation that anything he does say will alter the outcome. 'Before I sign that document I think the least I can expect is to know precisely what it is that will, as you put it, not be held against me.'

Cathcart sighs, as though he had expected this. 'I have had a series of telephone conversations with Horst Wesenthal of the University of Düsseldorf. You will be hearing independently from the EC Bureau in charge of the investigation you have been seconded to. You will, I under-stand – I'm sorry about this, Dan, I really am, but you have to see it from their point of view, and of course it reflects very much on the Institute too – you'll have to resign from the investigation. Oh – and repay all expenses received.'

'But Dingo – I just don't believe I'm hearing this. *Why*, for God's sake?'

Cathcart looks up sharply, as if briefly wondering whether to attach any weight to this apparent protestation of innocence, then goes on. 'It seems that only you can fully answer that question, Dan. I'm not asking you to, I hope that's quite clear. Lady Ottoline doesn't want some kind of witch hunt, and I'm sure you'll respect that. Obviously, what's said now is between these four walls. All we are asking – all I'm asking of you, Dan, is to sign that severance agreement. Your conscience is your own affair. I've no business interfering.'

'So Horst has something against me, has he?'

'I should say he has, Dan. His people were tipped off by the local Mayor at Ano Meri, apparently. Someone had tampered with the site. They've just completed an emergency excavation. Something or somewhere called Bothros 2. Mean anything to you, Dan?'

'Of course it does, it's central to the enquiry. It was excavated in 1939 and filled in again some time afterwards. I don't know if Horst knew that, but it's ridiculous to accuse—'

'Steady on, Dan. This isn't a court of law and nobody's accusing you of anything. Bothros 2 or whatever it's called had been interfered with very recently. The surface soil was found to be disturbed within days of your being there. It wasn't done by vandals or treasure hunters, the Greeks recognized the work of a trained archaeologist who'd taken some trouble to cover his tracks. Does the cap fit, Dan – you or your nice young assistant?'

'Let's leave my assistant out of this, shall we?'

'We'll come to that in a moment, I'm afraid. Now, Wesenthal didn't tell me what he found down there, but he gave me to understand it was something pretty surprising. He doesn't think anything was stolen, and he's asking the Greeks not to press charges. I think that's pretty reasonable, don't you?'

'I don't know about Greece, but in this country a man's supposed to be innocent until he's proved guilty, isn't he?'

Cathcart smiles, and his mouth is full of teeth. 'Obviously if you were – innocent, it could be a complicated business. The Greek courts, the EC Bureau, industrial tribunal. Let's get things straight can we, Dan? If Lady Ottoline were to be persuaded this is a put-up job, you've been framed or something, there's more to it than meets the eye, you haven't broken the law of an EC member state and double-crossed an EC committee of enquiry, to say nothing of the reputation of the institution that employs you, well, I can't speak for the Director, of course, but I know where *I* would stand, I'd back you to the hilt. Now what about it, Dan? Don't let's use emotive terms like innocence and guilt. Do you have a case?'

For a long moment Dan stares stupidly at his Head of Level. Does he have a case that might prompt Lady Ottoline to throw the weight of the Institute behind him? He thinks back to that dinner in the Bayswater square, to the stiletto gaze with which his Director followed Milica's retreating back at the Europa Exhibition in Cambridge.

And before he can reply, into the silence drops the final, poisoned barb. 'And of course, there is the matter of your relations with your assistant, a student of the Institute. The Director would have to take a serious view of that, a very serious view indeed.'

Dan takes up the pen and signs away the job for life that is his no longer.

18 ARIADNE'S THREAD

IT is Lucy who has galvanized him into holding this little dinner party, to welcome Milica back, but also, Dan divines, to draw him back himself from the no-man's-land of invisibility that yawns before him, this summer of 1991. It has been difficult for him to see Milica, since his interview with Cathcart. Not that he blames her. Quite the contrary, he has insisted that her own position at the Institute should not be jeopardized by what has happened, and this, he supposes, must inevitably put some distance between them. Lucy's tact, he concludes, is beyond praise.

Dan sees no point these days in keeping his customary hours at the Institute, nor, it seems, does anyone expect him to. Sooner or later he will have some 'tidying up' to do, as Cathcart has drily put it, but to all intents and purposes Dan is already a free man. With so much time stretching before him, it scarcely seems worthwhile to make decisions. Lucy has already tried unsuccessfully to brace him up: how old are you, Dan, you'll be forty-nine in a week, life begins at forty-nine; you've got six months' notice for heaven's sake, *use* them, you'll find another job, but you've got to get out and *look* for one.

But Dan doesn't see it that way at all. He has been touched with the stigma of Unemployment. He has become a ghost. There are, Dan is reliably informed by the daily newspapers, some three million such ghosts in Great Britain today. He has stepped over some of them in doorways in the Strand, he knows what these ghosts look like. What he didn't know was how it would feel to be one.

Present in Dan's South London home tonight are Milica, Lucy, and Mark. This is the first Dan has heard of Mark, unless a suspected male grunt behind Lucy's voice on the end of the phone at half past two in the morning can be counted, and Dan has reacted to the prospect of meeting him with mixed feelings. Included in these feelings is an acute sense of his own hypocrisy in having such feelings at all. But Lucy's supreme tact, he has already had to acknowledge to himself, has another side to it.

In the event, the evening passes off pleasantly enough. Dan has taken the precaution of locking away what remains of the *slivovic*. He has provided Bulgarian Cabernet with a supermarket label on it, and laid a freshly-ironed cloth on the table. Lucy and Mark have brought a bottle each, Mark rather a nice one, and Dan has been quite successful in following the cooking and serving instructions on a complicted array of tin-foil trays and cling-wrapped containers he has bought from the same supermarket. Mark is, inevitably Dan supposes, a psychologist ('not at all the same as a psychiatrist, please!'). He sports a shock of pepper-and-salt hair and a wispy, tapering beard of the same hue. Dan has to concede that he is actually rather striking, and throughout the meal Mark is unfailingly affable, and pleasingly solicitous towards Lucy. Dan scrutinizes him covertly for signs of his age. The hair is misleading, he quickly realizes. Mark has some self-deprecating anecdote about his mother being surprised by a badger while he was *in utero*; his hair has always been like this, and certainly it gives him a look both startled and startling. Dan relaxes.

After dinner the conversation turns, as sooner or later it must, to Ano Meri. Dan has not told Lucy everything about his visit to Crete with Milica, but the discovery of his father's body has been much too important to keep back. Mark too, it seems, is familiar with the story. Or perhaps he's a well-trained listener. Milica reminds Dan of her promise, overshadowed by the pace of events but by no means forgotten, to follow up a lead in Ljubljana. There is, it turns out, quite a large Greek population among the students at the University there.

'They fail in their examinations at home, and to study in Yugoslavia is very cheap. They bring foreign currency to my country, they stay three or more years. I didn't find out what they do. They don't learn the language. Anyway,' Milica likes this locution. It sounds idiomatic, and it launches her on her tale. While in Ljubljana with time on her hands she has befriended Sonia, who was christened Athanasia but that is too much for Slovenian tongues to get round. Sonia's grandmother has for longer than anyone can remember been the chief mourner in the village back in Crete. When the village people die, Milica explains, the women of the village gather round the deathbed and tear their hair and keen terribly ('It is the same in my country,' she adds). One of the women takes the lead, while the body is being laid out and washed and dressed for burial, in the screeching songs for the dead. It is, Milica assures them, a frightening experience to be present at such a wake. Anyway, chief among the mourners in Sonia's village is her grandmother, whom Milica has also met while they were at Ano Meri: a little woman like a crow, she describes her.

Sonia's grandmother has laid to rest in her time almost two generations of villagers – those who came to the end of their allotted span, and those others, so many, who were cut down in the prime of life. Sonia's grandmother has seen the chariot-wheels of war galloping through the villages, has buried two sons of her own. She has keened the most shrilly of all the mourners, for her own kin and strangers alike. Sonia, from what Milica can make out, is glad to be away from her village, though naturally she misses it and is easily encouraged to talk. She herself likes discos, dresses well, is studying to become an engineer. Anyway. The turn of Manolis Laskaris, the *phýlax* with the cough, Lionel Robertson's sometime foreman, came in 1967. Sonia seemed a bit vague about this, she herself wasn't born then, but it had been something to do with tanks in the streets down in Kastro, a military takeover throughout the country. It was all a long time ago, according to Sonia. But the new people in power, according to her parents anyway, still nursed grievances that went back to the War. (This war, for Sonia, was clearly the equivalent of prehistory.) Manolis was rounded up in the first days after the coup. With a handful of others from the villages he was taken to jail in the military barracks outside Kastro. His health had been terrible for years. Probably he was roughly treated. In any case, he died.

Lucy and Dan have exchanged glances while Milica has been talking. Lucy was born that year, on 21 April. On trips to Greece with Margaret while Lucy was a toddler, they had been amused as well as saddened to see the brashly militarist slogans everywhere proclaiming the date of Lucy's birth as the day of national salvation.

So Manolis Laskaris returned to Ano Meri for the last time. Sonia's grandmother led the mourning while Maria and the other women relatives stripped and washed the corpse. And when they had stripped him, the women of the village who had seen death close to in all its hideous forms, stopped in their wailing, and an unaccustomed silence fell upon the house. A miracle, someone said. Fetch the priest. No wait, said another. A third grossly ran a hand through the thick hair of the dead man's chest. The wound. The wartime wound that had destroyed a whole lung, and left Manolis Laskaris a semi-invalid for more than twenty years, where was it? Surely a miracle?

This version of the story was still told in the village, Sonia had assured Milica. But she herself had heard the truth from her grandmother, and this was only darkly spoken of, if at all. In due course, having washed the front of the body, the women had turned it over. The scar of a terrible knife-gash was clearly visible, below the left shoulder. Manolis Laskaris had been stabbed in the back.

'Yes, this is Dan Robertson speaking.'
  'Oh hullo there. Lambert here. Sidney Lambert. We met, you remember?'
Dan remembers.
  'I've a piece of sad news for you. Well, maybe it is, maybe it isn't, if you

know what I mean.'

Dan doesn't. Patiently, he waits.

'It's about the old girl. My mother, you remember? – who took such a shine to you?'

Dan doesn't think Sidney Lambert likes him very much.

'Well, the old girl's taken a turn for the worse. Doctors don't reckon she's going to hang on much longer, poor thing.'

Dan is sorry to hear it. Actually, behind his guarded words, he finds this news more disturbing than he could easily explain. Sarah Jane is the only living link to 'them Robertsons', her half-crazed clinging to her birthright the last visible, painful witness to the futile passions of a generation.

'Wants to see you, she does.' The voice at the other end sounds positively nasty now. 'Don't ask me why, I've no idea. The old girl won't say, not to anybody. I don't see it'll do her any good seeing you, do you? But there you are, she will insist and it's about all we *can* do for her, see? I'm sorry it's short notice like this but it isn't me, you understand. The grim reaper waits for no man,' and Sidney laughs shortly. 'If you're coming, it'll have to be in the next few days.'

'I'll come,' says Dan, his mind racing. It's not as though he is exactly burdened with commitments. But even if he had still been at the Institute and subject to the daily humdrum pressures of full-time employment, he would as surely have dropped everything to obey such a summons.

'Where is she?' he thinks to ask.

Again that dry, mirthless laugh at the end of the line. 'There's only one way the old girl's going to leave Upland Grange, she's said it often enough herself. And that's feet first. You'll find us just like last time.'

Milica will be at the Institute at this hour. With a clumsy attempt to disguise his voice (he doesn't want the people on the switchboard tittering and reviving the no doubt rumoured causes of his dismissal), he dials the number.

'Will you hold, please?'

The decorous strains of Haydn's 'Clock' symphony come to him, grotesquely distorted, down the line.

Eventually he recognizes the voice of Rex Prebble.

'Damn,' says Dan.

'I beg your pardon?'

'Sorry, I mean Dan. Dan here. I was trying to find Milica.'

But Milica has already left for the afternoon, or is in the library. Dan is not jealous of the independence that Milica has insisted on, indeed he is rather proud of it. She continues to live in her student bedsit in town; when she spends the night with him, which is quite often, she sleeps in the spare room. He has once heard her call it 'her room' before she realized and in embarrassment tried to cover up her gaffe, and was secretly pleased. No, he is

332

not trying to check up on Milica. He just needs to find her.

'So how's the life of Riley?' Rex seems disposed to chat.

'It has its moments, I suppose. Reports of ease and luxury are grossly exaggerated though.'

'Oh, I don't know. If I could afford it, I'd take early retirement like a shot.'

Who says I can afford it? Dan is about to protest, but stops himself. Can it be that Cathcart and Lady Ottoline have kept their word?

'Is there news from Horst, Rex? He should be back from Crete by now.'

'Haven't a clue, sorry. Oh yes, I did see something, what was it? That's right, Horst's sent samples of everything they found in the disturbed layers of Bothros 2 for radio-carbon dating. That should resolve the most important doubts, don't you think?'

As easily as that, modern archaeological science will be able to determine the truth about Laura's grisly find. Horst will have identified the relics by now, in the resting place they have shared for half a century with Daniel Robertson. Radio-carbon dating will pinpoint exactly when life stopped in them – correct to within a hundred and fifty years. If the bones are a hoax, as Lionel died believing, Horst will be able to prove it. But Dan's interest isn't in these relics any longer. He needs, more urgently than ever now, to know about his father. Horst will be thorough, the mortal remains of Daniel Robertson will assuredly pass through the same process. *And when precisely, doctor, would you say was the time of death? Well, Mr Poirot, plus or minus one hundred and fifty years of course, I'd say death occurred . . .*

'What did you say?'

'Sorry Rex, I wasn't concentrating. When d'you think Horst will have the results?'

'Usual thing. About a year, I suppose?'

The poplars lining the drive at Upland Grange are almost bare of leaves. As Dan gets out of his 2CV, he recognizes Pat's voice marshalling a hubbub of dogs, but otherwise the house has a subdued, doleful air. If there are guests staying at the hotel they must be having a thin time of it, Dan remarks under his breath to Milica as they stand in the gloom of the reception hall.

The upstairs room is almost dark, the smell that he remembers from before catches Dan by the throat. The shape in the bed seems to have shrunk, to take up less space. Sarah Jane has been propped up on high pillows. Somebody has done her hair and made up her face. The result is a cruel caricature of the life that is visibly ebbing. Across the bed sits Sidney Lambert, frowning. His eyes move rapidly from his mother to Dan and back again, like the parts of a mechanical toy. Dan holds forward the bunch of freesias and unseasonable gladioli he has brought. The face so cruelly disfigured with lipstick shows no sign of registering his presence, or the flowers. Excepting his mother's last illness, which was mercifully short, Dan has not been this close to death before. It is as though the features staring at a point on the far wall, midway between himself and Sidney, are only a crude representation of life, a deathmask stuck inexpertly over the empty skull beneath. But a twisted blue vein beats in the temple; the temple is deeply sunken, it is as though the skin has been stretched taut for too long and will give way at any moment. Dan is afraid. Surreptitiously he reaches out a hand and finds Milica's, where she is standing silently just behind him. She gives it a little squeeze. The air escaping from Sarah Jane's lips is forming words. He bends to hear.

'. . . knew you was an impostor. But you've got nice daughters. Will say that for you.' Guiltily, Dan lets go of Milica's hand. A shiver runs over him. It is hard to tell which side of death this unearthly monologue is coming from.

'. . . was Sidney found the proof, though, wasn't it, Sid? Grubbing about in the attic, things hadn't been disturbed for donkey's years. Came down all over in cobwebs, didn't you, thought I was seeing a ghost. Such a shriek.'

Despite his reluctance. Dan finds himself inching closer towards the death's head that is uttering these words. The head it seems cannot move, the eyes are all but fixed. He bends forward to stare into them; there is a thin film over the blue, he wonders if she's blind. And as he looks into them he sees something else that is quite incongruous, he sees into the life that is still there in their depths, he sees the living Sarah Jane who was once a child on the steps of this same house holding a discarded letter in her hand; he sees the cheeky, snub-nosed little girl catching crabs from the rickety wooden pier where he used to play so often himself. In the very presence of death he sees a spark, a gleam of mischief. All at once he is touched with something that might be admiration, might almost be complicity. He can see into the old girl's still living skull: in there Sarah Jane is playing the big scene of her life, and enjoying every minute of it. And Dan is seized with dread.

'You see,' – staring as though mesmerized into those eyes Dan finds the inflection, the hint even of a chuckle behind the flat, barely audible words – 'I know and Sidney here knows. Daniel Robertson didn't have no son. The last of the Robertsons, young man, you see before you. Last of the Robertsons, that's me, Sarah Jane. Thought they could turn me out of my birthright, they did. Had to buy with Bud's ill-gotten gains what was mine by right. Never mind. Much good it's done me, as you can see for yourself. But listen here, when all's said and done, Sarah Jane has lived a slut for an awful lot of years, but she's going to die a lady. Ain't she, Sid?' Dan can imagine the self-approving nods of the immobile head. 'The last of the Robertsons. Yes, young man, a lady. That's me.' And there is at this even some tiny muscular contraction that chips the powder covering the indrawn cheeks.

Dan feels himself turned to stone; where his insides used to be is a weight of solid ice.

'. . . had to be an impostor, you see. 'Cos of this. This is what Sid found.

Smart boy, aren't you, Sid? Like I said, Daniel Robertson didn't have no son.'

On cue Sidney proffers across the bed a small notebook. With a start, Dan recognizes it as just like the ones his mother used for her diaries throughout fifteen years of married life. The hand that reaches out to take it is not steady. Sidney's eyes are on him, willing him to open it.

With nervous impatience, Dan flips through the pages. Like the ones he has read so carefully already and all but memorized, they are brittle, yellow-brown. He leafs through the little book again, puzzled, ready to be angry. There is nothing written in the notebook.

Sidney, without a flicker of expression on his face, reaches over to point towards the back cover. As he does so, a piece of torn paper slips to the floor. Stop the scene here, everything in Dan is screaming inside him, let me walk away from this now, with Milica, and never see this triumphant death's head or Upland Grange or ghastly smug Sidney Lambert again. Anything, not to pick up that paper off the floor.

Dan bends down and picks up the scrap of paper.

Smudgily printed at the top where the paper has been torn is part of an insignia, the German eagle perhaps, and below it the words *Fallschirmjäger Rgt. III.* Dan can hardly make out the faded scrawl that has been traced in large, cursive letters across the bottom half of the page. He holds it up to the light. Carefully, he mouths the German words. Dan's is a reading German, he is used to picking his way through technical papers in the archaeological journals, though he would be embarrassed to try to communicate with Horst Wesenthal in his own language. It doesn't take him long to decipher what is written there.

Permission is hereby given for the burial of an English officer in irregular uniform. Villa Europa, Crete.

And the date, that at a stroke writes Dan out of history: *30. Mai 1941.*

Very carefully, as though in slow motion, Dan replaces the scrap of paper in the notebook. He turns over each of its pages. The dry sound of the aged paper seems deafening in the silence of the room. It is all, in this awful moment following revelation, frighteningly simple. He is turning over the record of those blank months, of those unfathomable, unbridgeable fourteen months that separate his father's death from his own beginning. Every nerve in his body is strained to draw out of the empty pages any clue, anything at all to make sense of his presence here on the planet. *Who am I?* The agonized question sounds deafeningly inside his head, over and over again, louder and louder; soon it must break out and be heard in this room which is still here in the same place and time, with the same people motionlessly watching him, only *he* is not here any more, the centre of their silent attention is no longer Dan Robertson; they are still staring at him and God alone knows who or what they see, sitting bent over the bed in exactly the attitude of Dan Robertson only a moment before. *Who am I?*

His face is very close to Sarah Jane's, her eyes fill up his entire vision. He can feel the sweat breaking out on his forehead. 'For God's sake, tell me,' he pleads. '*Who am I?*'

But the voice is silent, the eyes empty. Sarah Jane has played her big scene to the end.

Sidney's chair scrapes on the floor. 'My mother's exhausted herself, I'm afraid. We'll have to . . .'

But it is not quite over. Dan, still frozen close to the bed, with his face a few inches from Sarah Jane's, can feel something moving drily, sideways, close to him. He is ready to cry out with terror, but he stays quite still. It is the claws of a river crab that inch their way across his hair, to touch his face, it is all he can do not to raise his hand to protect his eyes. But he submits to the touch of Sarah Jane's desiccated fingers and he alone hears the words from those barely moving lips: 'The last of the Robertsons.'

'I don't want to appear crude over this, you understand.' Sidney is walking them out to the car. 'But whatever cracked ideas the old girl may have got into that head of hers, there is no possibility of a claim on Upland Grange.'

'Did you think I was contemplating one?'

Sidney is huffy now. 'It seemed a bit odd, your suddenly wanting to rake up that stuff after all these years. So I had a mosey round before you came up for the season of goodwill. I took legal advice of course, they charge a fortune for research, these people. "Research" they call it. Only needed to find someone can crack the damn' lingo. Still, there you are. No claim. And now you know.'

The thought of Sidney pawing his way through the volumes of his mother's diaries makes Dan's skin crawl. He feels his knuckles tightening. All of a sudden it would give him an unexpected pleasure to smash his fist into those slick, hard features. It is neither the knowledge that Sidney is younger and fitter, nor any lingering sense of good manners, that restrains him: Dan has not engaged in fisticuffs since his schooldays, he is unsure how to go about it. It would actually be rather horrible to touch that flesh at all. So the moment passes, in social awkwardness, and Milica tucks her long legs into the front seat of the 2CV.

'I assure you it never crossed my mind,' says Dan curtly as he rejects the proffered hand and slams the driver's door. As he starts the engine, and the car starts to buck down the drive, he drags open the window and shouts out, 'And I hope it falls down on you, you bastard!'

The childish insult rebounds to hit Dan full in the solar plexus. It is not Sidney who is a bastard.

Out of sight beyond the top of the drive, Dan pulls in and sits shaking, hunched over the wheel. *Who am I? I am no one. Milica, I don't exist, they've taken even that from me. And why? Just so they can feel secure in their bloody, rat-infested . . .*

From a long way off he hears Milica's voice: 'I think I'd better drive, Dan.'

There are dark days of winter ahead for Dan. Milica is going to Yugoslavia to spend Christmas and New Year. With her he has followed on the television news the nightly devastation of the war in Croatia. The long litany of exotic names, of towns destroyed, of sieges and heroic, futile defences (it's like the Middle Ages, but with modern weapons and colour photography), is almost as deeply engraved in his own mind as he knows it is in Milica's: Osijek, Vukovar, Vinkovci already destroyed, the medieval citadel of Dubrovnik (Lionel's Ragusa) pounded from the land while impotent EC monitors watched from the sea and journalists sent back pictures. Now over Christmas it has been the turn of Karlovac. Most of them places Dan had never heard of. But for Milica, he would still have only the haziest idea of where they are. For her these are towns as familiar as Basingstoke or Chelmsford, they are places where friends, acquaintances, relatives have lived, where she has gone to visit them, everyday memories, parts of her life. And nobody, it seems, lives any more in the ruins of Osijek and Vukovar.

Zaga, Milica's cousin, has fled with her two young children to her mother in Sarajevo. Zaga's husband, a Croatian journalist, sent them away before the siege started: Zaga is a Serb. Her husband stayed behind, you see, Milica has explained to Dan, he wasn't a fighting man but he stayed anyway. After the fall of the town, when the remnant of the defenders had given themselves up and were being taken away on lorries, Zaga's husband was seized, put up against a wall and shot. He was quite well known, you see, he'd done a lot of broadcasts on the local Croatian radio. Taken off a lorry in the mist of a December morning, the roads full of shell-holes, the ruins still smouldering. And shot in cold blood. At least, was Milica's only comment, he died at once. I am afraid for Zaga, Milica has told Dan simply, and though he will miss her very much he has put a brave face on her going. Just over Christmas, and into the New Year.

Sarajevo, she has assured him, is a civilized city, where they had the Winter Olympics not so long ago, remember? He is not to worry about her. Sarajevo is a long way from the action and not in the news.

It is Milica's last night in London.

'Don't go,' he murmurs to her gently, as he cradles her head against his shoulder. The night is cold, but both of them are perspiring under the duvet. The erogenous smell of her young body still feels strong and close. Usually, she says little after lovemaking, just smokes a cigarette with her head leaning back against him, blowing smoke-rings towards the ceiling. Dan at these moments is content to drift. The cigarette finished, she will lean over him, her hair deliciously covering his face and smelling of smoke and shampoo, like the morning after a party in his student days, and kiss him on the mouth. Then, without covering her nakedness, she will leave him, to sleep chastely in the spare bedroom for the remainder of the night. But tonight she stiffens at his words, his eyes are closed, but he can feel her scrabbling anxiously for cigarette and lighter.

'I *have* to go, Dan.'

He relaxes. 'I didn't mean that. I know you do. I meant, don't go now. Stay with me tonight.'

Her cigarette lit, she settles back against him. She says nothing, and he opens his eyes to search her face. She looks content, dreamy. Dan lies back, wondering.

'Dan?'

'Mm?'

Out of the emptiness of his present life has come the overwhelming urge to protect Milica. His arm is firmly round the bare soft skin of her shoulder and upper arm. He loves this girl who is warm and there, with her long legs and ox-like eyes, who has quietly, methodically, kept him company on his journey into the past, who has shared his quest, his terrors and his hopes, and has unhesitatingly held out her hand to guide him through the private darkness of the last few months.

'Dan, if someone in my country was to marry an English person, would they be free to come and live in England?'

Dan's heart is suddenly full. He sits up, facing her. 'Oh Milica, *would you?*'

But Milica's hand has gone to her mouth in the slightly comical, crestfallen gesture with which she acknowledges one of her gaffes. 'Oh God, Dan, I didn't mean – I'm sorry, I didn't think. Oh Dan,' and she throws her arms round his neck, 'oh Dan, I'm so worried, it's awful, you'll never forgive me—' For the first time since he has known her he feels Milica's tears flowing against his breast. He tries mechanically to comfort her, but something that had barely taken root has already withered inside him.

'It's Zaga, you see. Her husband is dead, her children are still little. The Serbs in Bosnia have declared their own republic, I am terrified for what will happen. Zaga was married to a Croatian, do you understand? Her children have Croatian names, they will not be safe. Even in Sarajevo they will not be safe.'

Milica stays with Dan that night in his bed, tightly held in his arms. Early in the morning, before he is properly awake, she will creep out quietly to catch her flight to Belgrade and Sarajevo.

Dan's will be a lonely Christmas.

And now in the dark, silent hours after New Year's Eve has turned into New Year's Day and the *ceilidh* and the chat shows have faded from the television screens, Dan cannot find the strength to take himself up to bed. He lies back in the leather armchair that was, like most things in this house, his mother's. The *slivovic* bottle is at his elbow; he has seen the New Year in with a toast – it isn't meant to be valedictory, but it feels that way – to the absent Milica. And another to Lucy and Mark, who are in Barbados. At the last moment Lucy tried to get him to come with them, she had tactfully assumed (he supposes) that he would be spending the festive season with Milica and when she found he wasn't, surprised him with her invitation. Dan's refusal was firm. Assuredly he is sorry for himself these days; if he allows others to be sorry for him too, to take pity on him· and drag him along to Barbados, an inconvenient third, that will be the beginning of the end. He doesn't know how much of this Lucy will have understood – how do you second-guess a trainee psychoanalyst? – but at least she didn't seem offended. It's better this way.

The *slivovic* is little more than a ritual gesture. Forewarned of its power, he has sipped it in a most un-Balkan way. Its warmth has coursed through him, but he has no intention of celebrating tomorrow with a hangover. As the television screen has gone dark at the touch of the remote control in his hand, Dan feels an unconquerable lethargy steal over him, but mentally he is wide awake. There is nothing to do now except go to bed. But there is no hurry, and the actual physical motion required eludes him. Dan experiences again a sensation that came to him in Crete, with Milica in the moonlight on their clandestine excavation. He can look down from somewhere near the ceiling and see his own body sprawled in the armchair. The sensation lasts only a moment, but it prompts in Dan a sense almost of well-being, of equilibrium, of forces temporarily in perfect balance. This moment before getting up out of the chair may only last thirty seconds in reality, but sitting there in no hurry to move, Dan can imagine time endlessly dilating around this here and now, the single moment could last for ever (for as long as it lasts, it *does* last forever), there is no need of a yesterday or tomorrow. Movement, in such a state, is unthinkable. And unnecessary.

Dan's mind, alert from the *slivovic*, flits across the weeks and years, gathers together the shreds of information that he owes in such large measure to Milica's indefatigable persistence. He feels Milica's absence almost more strongly, now, than her presence throughout these past months: Milica, with tender firmness and implacable logic, tracing connections, confronting him with deductions. It hadn't seemed so at the time, but now, out of her words and the tingling memory of her body close to him in this same room, in front of the empty television screen he finds himself tracing glowing lines of meaning, the way he once could on the Institute computer, with a purely private pride he now misses, at times, more than he can say. Dan watches fascinated as the lines in his imagination break up and diverge, come back together again, in kaleidoscopic chaos. From Milica's words, from the rustle of Sarah Jane's dry lips at the threshold of death, from the suave, incomprehending professionalism of Horst Wesenthal in Düsseldorf – inexorably the evidence has gathered and comes together now in the lines of light taking shape before Dan's eyes on the empty screen. And this time he can read those lines, they take the form of images almost familiar, like the images earlier in the evening of the smashed heart of Karlovac in central Croatia. Now that even Milica has gone, Dan is as hard and empty as the gramophone head with its miraculous needle remembered from childhood, he is an instrument finely honed and whetted, to ride the path of the moon across the Cretan sea that night when he and Milica made love, to hear and lucidly to dissect Milica's words reverberating inside his skull. Time, dilated, is now dissolving. In the emptiness before him, *it is all there*. It is all still there as it will, in some way, Dan knows, be there for all eternity.

There is no mystery any more. Dan knows.

19 THE NAME OF THE FATHER

LAURA Robertson lay wide awake in the darkness. The moon, small and distant, shone through the uncurtained window of the Cabin, striking a shimmer of palest gossamer from the end of the mosquito net that still hung tentlike over the bed. This was the legacy Daniel had left her: to lie awake like this and hear the mysterious life of the night. And in a perverse way she found these sleepless nights brought him close again. She wouldn't, for as long as she could, let go of him, though as night succeeded night and now, with summer over, there was longer each time to wait for dawn, she had begun to sense his presence dissolving, even as the body that had been hard and firm and part of her life and her dreams for so long must be dissolving in its makeshift grave close by, up at the site. No, she would not let go of him, but all that remained of him now was the dry taste of sleepless nights – and his nightmares. Laura too, by this time, had been marked by battle and the presence of violent death. By day, a black headscarf wound round her head, she would perform the tasks allotted her with an unsmiling, unbending precision, worthy of the conquerors her masters. When it had all been over, and Lieutenant Colonel Meyerhof had moved into the Villa with his staff, it had been something between an order and a tacit expectation that she should continue to supervise Aspasia and her young niece Maria at the Villa, with the general, if ill-defined, duties of housekeeper. 'Of course,' the Commandant had mused in her presence, in an elegant if clipped French, his eyes fixed on the craggy peak of Iouktas beyond the window, 'I could send you to the Italian zone.' Afterwards Laura was never quite sure if she had been asked to state a preference, or if indeed her silence had been taken for one. Meyerhof had scrutinized the Italian passport that had already been taken from her at the time of the Villa's capture. No doubt, along with the passport had come some intelligence from the paratroop Major whose name she never knew, that there was more to her case than met the eye. But so what, the lady's English husband was dead and buried, she herself had nowhere else to go; an Italian housekeeper in an occupied zone where the population had turned out to be so unexpectedly hostile was surely to be preferred to a Greek one. Or so Laura supposed the Commandmant's thoughts must have run. Nothing more was said. She avoided the Commandant's eyes as he appeared to do hers, and never spoke in the presence of the German officers who now moved into the Villa, unless they addressed her directly. Before long, she began to realize that for them, most of the time, she simply didn't exist.

And it suited her well enough not to exist. In her operatic imagination she was a mortal woman, a captive in war no doubt, waiting upon the table of the undying heroes in Valhalla. The soldiers, she noticed, often lounged about in various stages of undress; but the officers who were her charge were always meticulously turned out, their uniforms tightly buttoned even when the summer heat soared into the hundreds. They strode about the Villa and the courtyard, leaping into the back of jeeps that took off with roaring engines in a cloud of dust; they expected their table linen to be washed and ironed daily, the silver polished. Mealtimes were strictly observed, leave to go down to the cinemas and, no doubt, the army brothels, in Kastro was rationed. The Wehrmacht ruled the Villa Europa with a discipline even tighter than Lionel's, but not, it both alarmed and comforted Laura to realize, so utterly different in kind. Aspasia and Maria, and the other village women she only now got to know, from shopping with them on the black market (at the Commandant's behest: in little things the Commandant was infinitely corruptible, but if his men caught a local farmer selling his produce at an illegal profit, as likely as not the farmer would be shot). Laura would share her own meagre rations with them when she could, including the leftovers from the officers' table. Laura found herself experiencing life at the Villa much as it had always been, but from the other side.

Except that it wasn't quite the other side. As summer wore on, Laura had noticed the increasing reserve of the village women towards her. *They don't know where I belong*, she thought to herself with something approaching terror. She herself scarcely knew either. Only Aspasia shared her secret: when the occasional taciturn shepherd would pass through the village and in conversation with Yannis Laskaris introduce the word *eleftheria* – freedom, hidden in the cigarette packet which Yannis would slip into the shepherd's pocket would be Laura's notes written out in a tiny hand on cigarette paper, everything she had been able to glean that she could understand from the conversation and the activities of the officers at the Villa; once, on an occasion that still made her tremble to remember it, an inventory of the contents of Meyerhof's safe. And only Aspasia, among the women, could guess that these notes were destined for the guerrillas in the mountains and even, who knew, if they were important enough, for the British High Command in Cairo. Laura had no illusions about what would happen to her if she were caught. But however much the women, apart from Aspasia, might distrust her, she would be putting more than her own life at risk if she were to seek their trust by so much as a single confidence.

The nights were never silent. Even when the noise of jeeps and the clipped shouts, the tread of military boots, had subsided and the mechanized presence of the invader had succumbed to the deep darkness of the Cretan night, the Cabin and the hilltop of Ano Meri had their own sounds. It may have been the faintest footfall of a gecko, darting across the roof, the whir of a bat by the open window, the screech owls in the dry riverbed below the site, even the ripening of the grapes on the vines, the nighttime breathing of the earth that was parched by day, now opening its pores to the infinitesimal summer dew descending with infinite gentleness out of a clear sky full of stars, and always, everywhere, at any hour of the night, the braying of a donkey stirring in its sleep, the precocious cry of a cockerel impatient for the dawn, the howl of a dog chained up on guard – but to guard what, when the land was plundered and the invader held the low-lying farmlands in an iron grip?

Only once had Meyerhof behaved towards her with less than the icy correctness she had come to associate with her masters at the Villa. She had been doing the accounts, and as Aspasia was banging about in the kitchen, Meyerhof had told her she could bring her notebooks and work on them at the end of the long polished table. Lionel had furnished the Villa in style. Meyerhof, with his own papers strewn in front of him and his flat monocle (did he wear it only for effect?) screwed into his eye, sat a good fifteen feet from her at the table's other end. After a time she became conscious that he was staring at her. This in itself was unusual, and surprised her. It also made her feel uncomfortable, vulnerable in a way she had not consciously thought about before. She tried to keep her head bent; irritably she licked the end of her pencil as though to concentrate on the figures before her. But she could feel the force of his gaze on her. In the end, flushing, she looked up.

He had moved from the end of the table and was standing above her, about half way down its length. '*Madame.*' Laura's German belonged to the whimsical wonderland of Wagnerian opera; its use in the real world in which she found herself was severely limited. There was also perhaps an obscure principle at work: it was better to converse with the enemy in a neutral language. Her dealings with her masters had always been conducted in stiffly formal French. He had removed the monocle, it hung round his neck. His eyes looked tired. He must be suffering from the unaccustomed heat, though he gave no outward sign of it. Even as she thought this, Laura refused him the least shred of sympathy in her heart. She stared back at him, something she had never done before either. Perhaps encouraged, perhaps indifferent to her lack of encouragement, Meyerhof pulled a wallet from his tunic. 'Forgive me, *madame*, it is that you resemble my dear wife in Aachen very much. May I?' And already he was pulling out a tiny photograph, and other photographs: his children. 'That is my Margarethe, my Gretchen. And my two little ones.

Hans was born just when war was declared. He will be two years old this month, and he has never known peace. My God, *madame*, when will it end?'

With disgust, Laura thought she detected a tear of sentimentality in the Lieutenant Colonel's eye. He reached forward as though to take her hand where it rested on the table; she withdrew it, not sharply, but firmly, and lowered her eyes to her papers. '*Mon colonel*, I have lost a husband in this war and will never know what it is to have children like your charming sons.' Suddenly, Laura could no longer control the shaking of her shoulders, for shame she put her hands up over her face to hide from him the hot tears that nothing could staunch. She had been like this since Daniel was killed; it came over her at moments when she least expected it, sometimes with Aspasia who understood and clucked soothingly over her, usually on her own in the privacy of the Cabin. Grief surged triumphant through her body, forcing her vision to cloud and her eyes to overflow; it was nothing to do with remembering Daniel or even with sorrow as she had ever known it, it was a physical pain, it was something terrifying in its power to take hold of her body, to shake it and wring it out. There was nothing to do at such moments but surrender to it, and only when the surge had receded and she was left with the bitter flatness of finding the world stolidly unchanged around her, then would come the time for memories, for self-accusation, for a deep bitter rage that sometimes attached itself to Daniel for being dead, for having stupidly, needlessly sacrificed himself when all that mattered – good God had he *ever* really understood that? – was to be alive, to be there under the sun. But more often her anger was at herself for somehow having failed him, for failing to penetrate the darkness of his dreams; how different it might have been if they had had a child. And crimson from the shame of breaking down like this in front of the enemy with his easy sentimentality, Laura could do no more than bury her face in her arms and let the storm of grief blow through her.

It was almost over, her eyes were hot but there were no more tears to flow. The aching desolation that she knew would inevitably follow was already beginning to reach out ahead of her to the empty horizon. She tasted blood on her lip. And then she felt him coming closer, standing behind her, the touch of the hated uniform clumsily, not unkindly, brushing her shoulder. In an instant she had sprung to her feet. 'No,' she cried, 'I beg of you.' And she stared at him wild-eyed, holding the back of a chair as a flimsy protection against his presence.

Lieutenant Colonel Meyerhof appeared surprised, but not put out. '*Madame*, I did not wish to offend you. If ever you need me, I beg that you will come to me. You are a very beautiful woman, and the very likeness of my dear wife in Aachen. Come to me when you are ready. Then, if you wish, I can send you to the Italian zone.'

There may even have been genuine kindness in the cold blue eyes that gazed for a moment longer into hers, but Laura still retained enough of her pride not to put it to the test. Then the Commandant turned briskly on his heel and returned to his papers at the head of the table.

The moonlight was advancing slowly up the bed. In its light the mosquito net had become a silver shroud. Outside there were frogs croaking somewhere nearby. An eddy of night air entered the room, bringing with it the distant sound of singing. Surely the officers weren't having another schnapps night? When that happened the sounds came very clearly over the open ground to the Cabin where Laura lay hoping in vain for sleep to take her: the stamping feet, the swaying, solid rhythm, the brash masculinity of the voices raised with drink and the solidarity of the Corps, the military fists beating her once cherished piano in the songs of the invaders' homeland. Laura clenched her teeth on such nights and held the pillow over her ears, and still the slobbering nostalgia, the triumphal stamping of military boots on Lionel's costly parquet floor, came through the soft down and penetrated her consciousness. But no, this was singing much further off, the night had fallen still again and the sound was gone. Then Laura remembered. All last month the men of the village, and many of the women too, had been harvesting and treading the grapes. By now the must had been poured into vats and the mystery of fermentation would be under way, to produce in a few months' time the new, light-red, slightly effervescent, vintage – the first fruits, Laura thought to herself in the darkness, of slavery. Aspasia had told her there would be celebrations in the village, muted, of course, but the curfew wasn't strictly enforced this far from town, and even under enemy occupation life had to go on, didn't it. Tonight was the night the lees of the must would be boiled up in great cauldrons, and the first *tsikoudia* distilled. Everybody got a little drunk then, Aspasia had told her, and grinned hugely.

The grapes had been hardly formed on the vine, then. Tiny clusters, no bigger than peppercorns. Parachutists had landed among those vines, trampling them. Daniel's Cretan irregulars had stalked the parachutists under cover of the broad green leaves. As Laura's convoy of wounded bumped its way up the rutted track to Ano Meri that Sunday morning, bursts of firing had broken out from the vineyards to right and left. The hunted were becoming the hunters. The Cretans, with their silent, deadly knives, no longer pounced with impunity on lone paratroopers hampered by their harness, dazed and bewildered by the behaviour of a population they had been told would be friendly. By now the survivors among the paratroopers, reinforced, were forming up into units; the isolated, sporadic fire of ancient rifles had given way to the raking of machine-guns from dug-in positions, from abandoned farm buildings. By the time she arrived at Ano Meri, to Daniel's displeasure, Laura already knew the battle was lost.

But as the sounds of firing came closer, and the Villa Europa began to shake from the impact of mortar shells, Laura was fully occupied with a battle of her own. Several of the wounded in her charge had travelled badly. They had all spent a night in the open on the way here, some of the bandages were beginning to stink. Water had to be fetched from the well, but at least at Ano Meri there was water in abundance. One of the two drivers, who had been co-opted as orderlies, was hit while zigzagging across the open ground from the well; the precious liquid he was carrying poured all over the ground and was soaked up in seconds. That made one more of the wounded, and Laura gave the order that no one was to venture out of doors now. It couldn't last much longer. She understood that Daniel and his irregulars would inflict as much damage on the enemy as they could, before melting away through the olive groves, retreating one by one round the perimeter of the site, to make their way down into the ravine, then, under cover of darkness, to regroup on higher ground. Where, no doubt, the whole desperate, pointless business would begin again. She understood, she saw it could not be otherwise. But what had occupied Laura every day and every minute since the bombing began in Kastro was not the necessity of it nor any thought of what victory or defeat might mean when it was over, but only the evidence that affronted her senses, of what bullets and shrapnel, fire and falling buildings do to the human beings they so casually, so randomly strike in their path. Laura had learnt to stare into the eyes of pain, not to flinch before the terror of a living body knowing itself broken beyond repair, and to know that nothing she could say could lessen the anguish, could right the wrong. When the pastors came in and for a few moments held the hands of the dying, she would look away. Even if there were an afterlife, what would it be to live forever with a smashed spine, with a face wiped almost smooth by fire? If there was a soul to be released from these poor, mangled bodies, as her Catholic upbringing had taught her, its invisible deformities were surely the most terrible and irrevocable of all. With a clear head and steady gaze, Laura learnt to watch the disintegration of the human form, of human reason, the abolition of every feeling or sentiment other than pain and fear, and sometimes, in the less serious cases, the seeds beginning to grow of a corrosive, burning anger that she could see already, if her patients lived, would never die.

Everyone was now confined to Lionel's earthquake-proof basement. Even down here Laura could feel the house trembling from the hail of machine-gun bullets, the dull thud of a grenade bursting on the ground not far from her head. The long narrow room was crowded, the only light came from candles that Aspasia had enterprisingly 'borrowed' from the church down in the village. Alongside her feelings of claustrophobia, Laura was obsessed throughout that day – the longest day of her life – by the fear of fire. The wounded in her charge complained. From the slender, flickering candles came a soft fragrance of incense; Laura was grateful for it, it helped mask the raw stench of injured bodies packed together, but for the Greeks among them the odour of church candles was the odour of death, and they accused her, some deliriously, almost violently, of consigning them to life in the tomb. Laura bit her lip and went about her tasks. It couldn't last much longer. But all the time half of her mind was with Daniel, up on the roof terrace, willing him to escape under cover of the continuing fire. So long as the battle raged above her head, Laura prayed that Daniel would still have time to make good his escape. And perversely she became convinced that if the shooting was still going on up there, that meant he must be alive, it was not too late for him to escape and regroup with his comrades in the mountains, he could still fulfil that breezy promise flung over his shoulder as he bounded up the steps out of her sight, Tzak at his heels: he'd be back.

It had scarcely occurred to Laura to fear for her own safety. But suddenly that was all there was to think about. The firing outside rose in a crescendo, there was a crash and the sounds of boots running just over their heads. And still the shooting went on. The door at the top of the stairs was pulled open, letting a sudden shaft of light and the hot afternoon air into the basement. Behind the sunlight came a powerful torchbeam, harsh voices Laura couldn't understand. The thud of boots was on the stairway now, torchbeams crisscrossed the enclosed space. And somehow all around her in the cramped space were running feet; they were still firing, even down here among the wounded; who were they shooting at? Why? The questions ran through her bruised brain like jagged splinters; it didn't matter in the slightest, it was the merest, absurdest habit of the brain to keep functioning even when there was nothing for it to do any more, it didn't matter *why*, instinct had taken over – Laura, like the rest of them who could move at all, had flung herself behind the corner of a table and cowered there, her hands over her ears and head. The stampede seemed to go on for ever, then the thunder of boots returned to the wooden stairs and the firing stopped. Laura's ears were ringing, red sparks exploded in front of her eyes, for a moment she wondered if she had been hit. As she slumped forward her forehead hit the concrete floor and as though from a great distance she heard the crack. A chill began to spread through her limbs, it would be blissful to surrender to it, out of the heat and the stifling air and the pain; if she woke up there would be pain and more pain to come, her own and others', better surely to let the chill rise through her bones from the concrete floor, let the blood that she could feel begin to flow warm and wet from her forehead soak down into the foundations. Yes, thought Laura, you *can* die willingly, the music that she had heard all these years ago was swelling to a roar, soon it would overwhelm everything, it didn't matter, this was surrender, this was the end, it was better so.

But it wasn't over, not yet. Her senses were still alert, the raucous voice and the waving torchbeam from the head of the stairs meant nothing to her but she couldn't shut them out. *'Raus, 'raus.* One of the orderlies had her by the shoulders. She felt her head lolling loose, then with a tremendous effort she shook herself and jerked upright, suddenly panicstricken. Nausea spread through her, forcing its way with a bitter taste into the back of her mouth. Desperately she fought it down. The horror of that moment when she had all but surrendered would never leave her. It had been so easeful a betrayal. And she had so nearly succumbed.

Slowly, painfully, the basement was evacuated under the eyes of the German soldiers who had ransacked it only a few moments before. Laura stood with the rest of them, those who could still walk or crawl, blinking in the late afternoon sunlight that was still fierce. Blood kept trickling into the corner of her eye; someone, it must have been Dimitris the orderly who had got her off the floor, had tied a makeshift bandage round her head. Her head still throbbed terribly, the ground was unsteady beneath her feet. There were soldiers everywhere, she had never seen German soldiers so close. There was no more shooting. Even the running boots were beginning to run out of steam. A terrific pall of weariness seemed to settle over the Villa Europa.

Wildly, in the unaccustomed sunlight, Laura looked about her. *Daniel, Daniel,* a forlorn voice inside her was calling out, but of course she could make no sound. It was all over now. Either he had made good his escape while the battle was at its height, or— she could not allow herself to think of that. There were bodies laid out in the Villa already, she noticed. All of them in uniform. And all of them German.

There were more orders roughly shouted, that Laura couldn't understand. People were moving all around her, some bumped into her, nobody apologized. There was a coming and going, stretchers were being carried this way and that. Laura couldn't make it out. Then suddenly she could. She would have to stop it. Summoning the most basic German she could muster, Laura launched herself towards the officer she had already singled out as the one in command. '*Herr Major!*' In an indignant flow of Italian, Laura began to expostulate. She invoked the Geneva Convention, the rights of wounded civilians and military personnel in wartime (a subject of which she knew much at first hand but next to nothing of the legalities she invoked). As she heard the torrent of her own words, and experienced a kind of necessary release in giving tongue like this, Laura was appalled to think how she must appear in the eyes of the victors. Her uniform was a mess, covered in the dust of the basement floor, her forehead tied up in a bloody bandage, a trickle of dried blood seeping down her face. Evidently the Major had not expected this at the end of a hard-fought battle.

But he did, fortunately, understand Italian, at least enough to question her about herself. A soldier was despatched to the Cabin to check her identity, and came back a few moments later with the Italian passport she had last renewed that winter when – how farcical it seemed now – she had thought she might be leaving Daniel for ever. The Major could make no sense of it. An Italian in the service of the Greek Red Cross, standing up to him in no uncertain terms to block his eviction of a ragbag of civilian and enemy casualties from a field hospital that had suddenly offered itself as a godsend to his men. 'I have lost ten men killed and twenty-five wounded here today,' the Major shouted furiously in a mixture of Italian and his own language. 'So – *you* must care for them. *Si?*'

It was a strange confrontation, fought out under the stares of the silent German soldiers and those of Laura's charges who had not already been booted down the steps and, if they were able to walk at all, melted into the shadows of the olive trees. The Major was visibly in a state of exhaustion, he wanted nothing more than to jump into his sidecar and be driven back to his command post wherever it was, to report that a nest of *francs-tireurs* had been smoked out, but at a cost. He wanted to be rid of Laura. In the end a bargain was struck, one of those strange, uneasy truces that can come about in wartime between people who recognize that each, even so, has something which the other needs. Pending the arrival of a German medical unit, Laura and her team could continue to look after their own wounded, on condition that they devoted themselves, as a first priority, to the German casualties who were even now being carried into the Villa. A paratroop guard would remain, to make sure these orders were carried out, and to secure the Villa against further incursions by *francs-tireurs*. Laura in the meantime would be answerable to the paratroopers, and through them, to the Major.

When this had been concluded, a proclamation was made, to be translated into Greek and pinned on the plane trees and cried aloud in village squares: the burial of *francs-tireurs* killed in the recent skirmish was forbidden on pain of death. Laura had heard of these edicts, many had been issued in the past week. She thought of the men she had known for years, wielding picks and shovels at the excavation, now in days to come lying out bloated under the olive trees. And the pitiful attempts that would be made by the survivors, some of whom might well be shot for their efforts, to dig makeshift graves where their kinsmen had fallen, to cover them from the elements and the wild dogs and carrion crows. One of the soldiers who had been on the roof clattered down the steps and whispered something in the Major's ear. The Major's eyebrows shot up. '*Was?*' The man nodded vigorously.

The Major turned a glance of intense suspicion at Laura. 'Wait,' he said curtly, and followed the soldier back up the steps.

Laura's heart was pounding, the blood was throbbing in her head, she could feel it once again bursting through the bandage that bound her forehead. But already she could feel that icy sensation returning to her legs and stomach, and found herself furiously hating her own weakness. It was all unfolding very slowly in front of her, this wasn't happening to her at all, she could see herself very clearly standing stupidly, dazed in the midst of the soldiers, all eyes turned towards the steps leading up to the roof, where the Major must shortly reappear. A part of her already knew what must happen next. Whatever was up there, on the roof, she would have to face it.

What, not who.

The Major, a strange expression on his face, was beckoning from the top of the steps.

If it hadn't been for those years of rigorous training for the diva parts on the operatic stage that would never be hers in real life, Laura was sure she couldn't have mustered the iron control it took to climb those steps. There was no room in her consciousness for anything but the next whitewashed tread, and at the end of the line of treads the dusty boots of the Major. She looked no higher than his boots. Each step was a procrastination, each step might, with luck, last for ever, she need never reach the black dusty leather, those boots whose weight was even now bearing down, in careless triumph, on the ruins of her life.

When she reached the Major, it seemed for a cruel, dizzying moment as though the flat expanse of the roof was empty. Spent cartridges littered the surface, here and there the sandbags had been blown backwards by a mortar blast or a grenade, the white pebbly earth of Ano Meri had spilled everywhere. Then she saw him. He was so small lying there, her first glance hadn't taken in the human form prostrate behind the highest part of the sandbags. With the same interminably slow step, as though wading through warm water, Laura crossed the roof and looked down into Daniel's face. His open eyes were full of the blue of the sky – even the tiny flecks of cirrus high above, that she hadn't noticed in the sky itself, were there in the blue of his eyes. The lines of strain that she knew so well from so many conflicting, passing moods had disappeared from his face. His features were boyish; what hurt her suddenly with the pain of a knife-blow was to recognize before her a Daniel younger than she had ever known in life, to glimpse only now an innocence and an ease inside his own body that the Daniel she had known had never possessed. Before her she saw the lineaments of a life that might have been, the gaze of the wide-eyed youth who had volunteered for training on Salisbury Plain, who had exulted in being himself and alive, proud to be wearing his uniform. Yes, ridiculously under the Cretan sun and the dispassionate puzzlement of the modern German war machine, it was the same uniform he had shown her, that had lain concealed at the bottom of his trunk for all the long years of their married life. He had been proud to be in uniform, marching to the Rhine and to victory, a march that would turn out to have no end, a march that she knew to her cost had gone on and on in the dreams of every night, in the strange states – neither sleeping nor waking – that had so terrified her in their first years together, when he was out of her reach entirely – a march that only now had ended in the only way it could ever end. And Daniel dead was Daniel released, restored to the boyhood she would have given everything that had ever been hers to have known. This was the Daniel who had always been beyond the reach of her love, and she loved him all at once, now, a whole lifetime of love pouring out in this

350

moment as the white plumes of cirrus drifted across the infinite depths of the dead man's eyes. A life that might have been. And caring nothing now for the Major and the two helmeted soldiers who stood at ease, leaning on their rifles, Laura turned her eyes upwards and followed the gaze of those dead eyes, up beyond the wisps of white cloud, on and up into the pale blue, and as she continued to gaze with eyes that were also, in that moment, Daniel's, her vision was crisscrossed with lines and a misty film swam in front of her aching retinas; she couldn't go on looking, she had lost him, he was far beyond her, but *yes*, she whispered, *yes, it goes on. For ever and ever, it goes on.*

She heard someone say, simply, without inflection, in answer to the Major's interrogative glance, 'He is my husband.' The voice was her own, but it seemed to be coming from a long way off. 'He was a soldier in the last war.' In such blank, bland ways can a lifetime be put into words.

The Major continued to study the uniform. He was young, perhaps he'd never seen one like it before. 'This is not the regular uniform of the English army.' He seemed unsure whether to make it a question.

Laura shook her head. 'Not nowadays, no.' She was entirely clear-headed, calm had descended on her. There were some things to do, she would have to exert herself, busy herself: they were important, it wouldn't do to fail. But they were all quite trivial, nothing really mattered alongside the salient, simple fact: Daniel was all right. The rest she could handle.

'Major,' she said, almost briskly, 'I have to ask you a favour. By the laws of war I do not know if this man is an enemy officer or what you call a *franc-tireur*. I request permission for him to be buried.'

The Major seemed almost relieved. He was once again impatient to be off, he was losing interest already.

'Permission granted,' he said curtly.

'One thing more.' The tone of Laura's voice held him back. 'You are leaving. There will be other soldiers here, you have given an order forbidding the burial of *francs-tireurs*. How may I rely on your permission being respected?'

Not bothering to conceal his impatience any longer, the Major pulled a notepad and pencil from the pocket of his tunic. He scribbled something quickly in a long, scrawling hand. Then with a quick movement he tore out the page and handed it to Laura. Laura noticed that the German eagle in the top right-hand corner was torn in half.

'Safe conduct for your husband,' he muttered sardonically. 'And remember, you are answerable to my men until the relief comes. The relieving force will decide what to do with you.'

And with a sign to the two soldiers, the Major went clattering down the steps, leaving Laura alone with the inert bundle that was Daniel, and the wide-open sky.

★

351

It was Spinalonga helped her bury him, Spinalonga who chose the spot. He must have been hiding in the olive trees. Perhaps when the Major in his sidecar and the half dozen jeeps and an armoured car drove off in a swirl of dust, he thought the Germans had gone. Anyway, there he was, silent and gangling in the doorway, the soldiers prodding him with their rifle butts and threatening to burn his tongue with their cigarettes unless he answered their questions. Laura intervened to vouch for him. Listlessly they abandoned their half-hearted sport.

Propped against Spinalonga's long back, Daniel made his last journey down the steps from the roof of the Villa Europa. Outside, his heels dragged in the dust, leaving tracks like some vehicle with wobbly wheels. There were sentries posted up at the site, keeping a watchful eye on the countryside below. Three times Laura had wordlessly to produce the scrap of paper given her by the Major. Three times she found herself staring into a pair of unblinking eyes over the naked steel of a bayonet. They must have cut a strange figure, the three of them, she and Spinalonga with Daniel lolling on his back. With nods and a little sarcastic laughter they were allowed to pass. Laura had realized where Spinalonga was heading. There was a kind of ironic justice in it. It was hardly a soldier's grave, but even as a temporary resting place, it was fitting. The relics that had caused the final, fatal rift between father and son were still down there, still open to the elements. The body of Daniel Robertson, that she and Spinalonga now laid out with care, would cover the secret of the excavation. Daniel's dead body would keep prying eyes and inquisitive spirits from the terrible evidence that had shaken Ariadne's Summer Palace to its foundations. None of them would ever know the truth; for as long as Daniel rested there in peace no one ever would know. And that, as Laura prepared to bid a dry-eyed farewell, was fitting too.

There was no time to lose. The sun was going down, and the petrified stillness of afternoon, that had come down like a pall once the guns had fallen silent, was giving way to the stirrings and sounds of the coming night. The birds had come back, she couldn't identify notes but there was birdsong from the branches of the olive trees, the deep note of a hoopoe from the ravine. Swallows were darting about above the open grave. The ground-smell of wild mint and thyme was rising into the air. Spinalonga had loaded a rusty wheelbarrow with earth from the spoilheap nearby. Time to fill in Bothros 2 that was now, though the word meant nothing to her yet, a war grave. Suddenly a movement caught the corner of her eye. She gripped Spinalonga's shoulder and pointed. Round the corner of the trees where they concealed the Villa Europa, some three hundred yards or so down the slope, came a hurtling shape. The furious barking, that could be heard quite clearly where she stood, arrested Laura at once. This was no part of the background noises of evening. It was a sound directed straight at her and she stiffened instinctively in response: Tzak, that had been given to her as a puppy to help her get well; Tzak, Daniel's faithful sheepdog turned gundog who had become his closest companion these last few months. Where had he been? What had happened to him? How had he escaped unscathed from the maelstrom on the roof of the Villa? But here he was, scrambling over branches and boulders, his pale golden hair sleeked back with the speed of his flight, following in the tracks left by Daniel's heels in the dust. As he vanished for a moment behind the reconstructed north portico of the palace, to reappear a second later at the far end of the Great Court, stopping for a moment to sniff the ground and the air, then starting forward again with a huge bound and a volley of barking, Laura opened her arms to him and cried out joyfully, 'Tzak!'

Too late she saw the sentry turn and take aim. Tzak was a fast-moving target but an easy one at that range, and he had not the human guile or sense of danger to swerve out of his course. Too late Laura screamed, began to run towards the sentry – it was probably the closest to death she came that day. Tzak's sleek body was at full stretch, all four paws off the ground, his ears laid back, his muzzle high. Tzak was returning to his master, his flying momentum to be forever etched, frozen, in Laura's memory. Two shots rang out, and a second later Tzak lay curled in the dust, his blood only the latest to soak into the parched ground of Ano Meri, his eyes already glazed but his legs still futilely, impotently pawing the air, still carrying him towards his master.

Laura, whose deep calm in the face of Daniel's death had not yet broken, was beside herself. She hurled herself at the sentry and would have scratched his eyes out, or been bayoneted on the spot, had Spinalonga not come limping behind to grasp her with an unexpectedly strong arm and drag her away, still helplessly shouting all the imprecations, English, Italian, French and German, that she knew.

She couldn't bring herself to touch the corpse. But she showed Spinalonga how to lay it, the way she had seen carved on the tombs of knights in English cathedrals, at Daniel's feet.

Then at last the grave was filled in.

Spinalonga, she knew, could tell no one what had happened. Already Daniel had begun to live again in the heroic legends of wartime Crete. And Laura, with nowhere to go in a world at war, had no wish to leave him while his body dissolved among the bones of Bothros 2. She would play her part to the end. Gradually she found herself fostering the tales that were told: that he had a guerrilla base on the Nida Plateau, that he had entered Kastro in disguise and escaped detection, even, delicately, that he had visited her at dead of night here at Ano Meri, in the Cabin. In Laura's mind these were not untruths, though she never used them to deceive herself. They were true to the spirit of the time, the spirit of resistance. Daniel, even dead, continued to give her strength and a sense of purpose (it was for Daniel, purely and simply, to keep faith with all that he had planned and confided in her when he was alive, that she took the risks she did). And she believed that in the world of rumours, legends and tall tales that now took the place of hard facts and real news, even as a legend he could still inspire the guerrilla forces he had hoped to lead in life. So Laura, throughout that summer, silently kept watch, protectively nurturing this other, this legendary Daniel who might possibly give comfort to others but never to herself. It was a way of keeping faith. And in return, he had bequeathed her his nightmares, the terror of sleep that would keep her awake, the images of those past months flickering incessantly behind her eyelids in the darkness.

The nights were getting longer. Soon the autumn rains and the gales from the mountains would lash the exposed parts of the site and buffet the wooden walls of the Cabin. Time to let Daniel go in peace, she told herself, not for the first time, as the moonlight, filtered through the fine strands of mosquito net, reached her face and she stared back at the cold silver disk, small in the sky and not quite full. She closed her eyes without turning her head away, so that a pale radiance suffused her lids. But peace was not to be found so easily. In a moment she had jerked upright, staring at the dark square of the window. This often happened now, she would be near to sleep and suddenly imagine the sound of voices whispering in the darkness outside. She had dreamt – had she dreamt it? – of hideous faces craning round the uncurtained, open casement, mouthing at her horribly. She had dreamt, certainly, of swimming round and round in a deep tank, with seaweed and bubbles and tropical fish and she was a fish or a mermaid or some kind of monstrosity; she was warm and safe in the tank, but outside, distorted by water and glass, were ranged the faces of the idlers, onlookers, rough unshaven men, old women like the stallkeepers she remembered from street markets in her childhood, with sprouting hairs on chins that wobbled and rheumy eyes; they meant her no harm but they ogled and pointed, she was different, they'd paid a penny to crowd round the tank and see her. Laura would wake up breathless and draw in frantic, long gulps of air into her lungs. It had been only a dream, but she never felt she had slept, there was no rest in dreams such as these.

She forced herself to lie back and close her eyes. The moon was full on the pillow, but this time she turned away. A second later she was sitting up again, staring into the open square of the window. She was sure there was a scuffling in the darkness. Geckoes? A stray dog? The nights were full of such sounds. Her senses, her imagination, were at full stretch. There was a face, there were faces, at the window. She couldn't see their features against the moonlight, but this was no dream, they were there, peering in. 'Who's there?' Laura called out sharply, in Greek.

The faces disappeared, but she could hear movement, a scurry of footsteps, a snatch of tuneless song, abruptly hushed as though someone had put a hand over the singer's mouth. Then out of the darkness came a fierce whisper, the voice sounded the worse for drink, but there was no mistaking the venom in it. 'Collaborator!' She had seen the Greek word daubed on walls – usually (and this told its own story and froze her blood now) of houses that were empty and blackened. There came a sound of male giggling, of tipsy altercation, followed by a sharp crack from the outer room and the whole Cabin shook. 'Traitor! Collaborator! We want the macaroni-eater!'

Again there were shushing sounds, they seemed to be arguing amongst themselves. Terrified, Laura leapt out of bed, upsetting the mosquito net, threw a dressing gown over her shoulders and went out into the corridor. She huddled for a moment against the wall. Here there was no window, they couldn't see her. Outside, the sounds continued, listless, desultory, swaying now this way now that. Fresh from celebrating the first of the year's *tsikoudiá*, they couldn't know what they were doing. Every nerve in her body strained to hear the confused sounds from beyond the fragile shelter of the Cabin. Her fate hung in the balance.

Then the sharp sound of a blow on wood was repeated. As the outer door splintered, spilling the pitiless moonlight and an indeterminate crew of dark shapes into the room, Laura strode forward to meet them, a lighted oil lamp in her hand.

But they were too many for her, and too far gone with drink or changed by war to fall back into the sullen deference of those vanished years. The lamp was prised loose from her fingers, held close to her face – they seemed to be inspecting her as they might a prize ewe or kid, joking, egging each other on as they did so. Their faces were still indistinct, although some she thought she knew. The stench of stale alcohol and aniseed invaded her senses. In the first moment Laura knew, with terror, that she had lost control, that nothing she could say now would have its customary effect, that the sound of her voice merely drove them on to frenzy. The room dipped and swayed out of sight, they had her down on the floor, in the mocking band of moonlight. There was no escape. Rough, strong male hands held her now, she was their victim and they plunged into her one after the other. She was lucid enough to think: she must not struggle, it only seemed to excite them more and no, even while their overpowering bodies tore the very self from her, and she was half fainting from pain and humiliation, she would not scream or cry out, not even in this the worst moment of her life would she call for help from Meyerhof and his men a stone's throw away at the Villa.

It seemed it was over, the panting stench had withdrawn from her nostrils, the shapes in the moonlight were fading away. Did she imagine it, or was that gleam the bald pate of Hadzi-Aga, the old barrow boy from Smyrna? If it was, she couldn't tell if he was wringing his hands or buttoning his trousers. At the thought she began to retch. Again and again in the middle of the floor in the track of the moon, doubled up with pain and disgust, Laura vomited back what she could of the outrage that had been done to her.

She must have fainted. There was someone here, standing over her. Powerful hands grasped her by the shoulders; this time she couldn't help a stifled cry as she tore herself away. But the hands were firm, and not ungentle. They took her below the shoulders and raised her from the floor. Still shuddering uncontrollably, Laura allowed herself to be half carried, half dragged down the corridor and laid on her bed among the ruins of the mosquito net. Anything to be left alone, just let him leave her alone. He had the same smell as the others. His touch was rough but somehow also tender, wondering. She stared at his dark, broad face bending over her in the moonlight. She knew who it was, though nobody was who they had been any more, everything was different, everybody was someone else in wartime. And she herself was nothing at all, they had taken what was hers and made it vile and hateful. For the first and only time in her life Laura wanted to die. She wanted it passionately. Her eye flew to the short-handled Cretan knife in his belt. Anything was possible. His gentleness, so unexpected after what had happened, made her flesh creep, she could not yield to it. Did he mean to kill her? And all at once life, even the bereft, shredded husk of a life that remained to her, was better, was infinitely better than to have her throat cut like a lamb.

'Thank you,' she stammered through chattering teeth. If only he would go now. But he didn't, he was lying down in the narrow bed alongside her, taking up hardly any space, just being there, watching over her in the darkness. She was powerless, her world had turned a somersault, she dared not ask him to leave, the smell of raw alcohol and aniseed was close to her, she felt nausea rising again but choked it down. He was quiet at her side. It was a moment of oasis. Into her mind came the notion of climbers who can sleep on a narrow ledge halfway up a rock face, where just to roll over in their sleep would send them hurtling into the abyss. It was like that with Laura. Sleep, or oblivion, overcame her.

She awoke with a cry of fear, and found herself staring into the bloodshot eyes of Lionel's former foreman. He too, it seemed, had been roused by her cry and sudden movement. Not much time could have passed. The moon was still high in the sky, perhaps there was a pre-dawn scent in the air from the open window. Everything came back to her, the stale smell was still there on his breath. In panic she jerked away from him. She saw her own horror mirrored in his face. She saw there the Manolis who had been moved almost to tears by her tale of the Old Man of Crete, who had stolidly led the mules to the Nida Plateau. And she saw too the thickset bull-head go down, she saw the fierce pride of the Laskarids, cheated and bullied by Lionel, of the lonely male who had offered her his protection and provoked only her violent, instinctive revulsion. Terror overcame her once again as she saw all this, she could see the blood rising in his face, the veins swelling in his neck. 'No,' she had barely strength to move, let alone to struggle. 'Manolis, by all that's sacred to you.'

With a bellow that might have been of pain he bestrode her, pinioning her legs. 'Don't blaspheme,' he grunted. She tossed this way and that, she had no thought now of holding back her screams, she was in agony but his hand was firmly clasped over her mouth, his trousers were about his knees, his thighs were as thick as treetrunks and covered with thick black hair; she squirmed away from him but knew that she was helpless. He was pounding into her now, her scream went on and on, soundlessly, gagged by that huge hand. And at last it came to her: flooding, invading every crevice of her violated body and soul, came hatred, perfect and absolute. And with hatred came, in the midst of her powerlessness, power. Laura opened her eyes. The belt with the handle of the Cretan knife was at his knees. He was breathing loudly, furiously; at any moment his seed would be exploding within her, and her hatred would be consummated. Laura drew the knife from its sheath, held it in both hands behind his back. And as his humped flank arched in the moment of triumph, she drove its blade with all that remained of her strength into his body, below the left shoulder.

The breath burst out of him, hitting her in the face like a wave. A moment later, as the weight of his body collapsed on top of her, came an outpouring of hot blood and mucus, the stale stench overcoming her in a torrent. The nightmare that she would be pinioned there for ever, beneath the weight of his corpse, never afterwards left her. She freed herself only by the strength of despair. There was no pride left now. Inside Laura was a great emptiness. She must have blundered across the open ground to the Villa, past the water-trough where once she and Daniel had tried to catch a star.

As the sun came up she was found there, huddled on the steps, by Meyerhof's men.

Laura gave birth on that same bed, helped only by Aspasia and a tight-lipped Maria, on the fourth of July, 1942. This is the birthday that Dan Robertson, now in his fiftieth year, has celebrated ever since. She had accepted the fact of her pregnancy, when at last it could no longer be denied, with quiet disgust. At first, she had not been able to believe it. Then as month followed month, a strange slippage occurred, she found she was nursing with more care and attention than ever, not the thing inside her but the legend that was Daniel, her only link to the self she had once been. In a way that she scarcely understood yet, this monstrous growth within her kept her husband – her shadowy, legendary husband – alive. She had longed so much for Daniel's child, it was of Daniel she thought constantly as her body swelled.

Meyerhof had accepted her arrival at the Villa with a raising of his thin, sandy eyebrows. No questions had been asked of her, and she had volunteered nothing. Tacitly, permission was given for her to lay her mattress in a corner of the kitchen. The officers clattered by at all hours of the day and night; she had to serve them on their drunken schnapps nights. Something had gone wrong with her reflexes: each one of them was not just the enemy but male, the most savage enemy of all. As she went about her tasks she shied away from them, she couldn't help herself, as though she were a zookeeper in a cage of wild beasts.

But, whatever they understood or even noticed, they left her alone. Meyerhof she caught looking at her appraisingly more than once, but she avoided him as much as possible, and his offer to send her to the Italian zone was not repeated.

So Laura stayed. A collaborator in the eyes of the village, she never went there now if she could help it. She had never been so lonely in her life. She could only guess how much the women knew. Maria wouldn't speak to her at all, even Aspasia seemed to have lost her tongue. Slowly it dawned on her that, whatever they knew or suspected, in the eyes of the village women it was she who was to blame for their menfolk's fall from grace. When her condition could no longer be concealed, and Aspasia had eyed her middle with a calculating stare for the fifth time in a morning, Laura pre-empted her with a wan smile of triumph. 'I told you Daniel came down to the Cabin in the autumn. Well, you see what happened!'

She felt Aspasia's gaze probing behind her eyes, she could sense the ray of hope in the old woman's shrewd mind. 'And *kyr* Daniel? Is he alive? In hiding? Where?'

Laura nodded slowly. 'I don't know,' she said with a lessening of conviction. The women continued to stare at one another for some time, it was a silent communion.

'So,' said Aspasia at last, sucking a long breath through her teeth, 'the young *milord* lives. Yes?'

What Spinalonga had done and seen he had not the words to tell. The secret of Daniel's burial was surely safe. But what might not a mother, who lived for her last-born, idiot son be able to understand by instinct, by osmosis, from the gestures and the inarticulate sounds she doted on? All this passed through Laura's mind as she returned Aspasia's penetrating, less than trusting gaze.

Then the older woman crossed herself several times, muttering silently. Aspasia was suddenly effusive, tears sprang into her eyes. She embraced Laura, she summoned Maria, confronted her with the news. Maria had to be nudged, Laura noticed, before a slow smile spread across her face too; she went so far as to peck Laura drily on the cheek before backing off to a safe distance.

None of them was deceived. But a pact had been sealed. The child Laura was carrying was the son (what else?) of the *milord*. All was well. And Daniel would live a few months longer.

It lasted until the birth. The child was not yet born when Aspasia came to her, breathless, risking the curfew at dead of night. She bent over Laura in the darkness of the kitchen, kneading her swollen eyes with her hands. There was evil talk down in the village. Manolis was near to death from a terrible stab wound. The men held Laura responsible. If he died, they would 'take back the blood'. Her child would not be safe at Ano Meri. She must beg Meyerhof to send her to the Italian zone as soon as it was born. They will kill the child.

Laura's blood froze. The child, that had been conceived in pure hate, was growing big inside her. The terror that struck at her heart now was the terror of love. Love had not, after all, been extinguished in her. This child, if only it could be spared, would restore to her the love that had been so savagely taken from her. Suddenly she knew she would devote the rest of her life to this child. She would wrap him in this new love that grew strongly within her even as the child grew; there was nothing else left, she had nothing else left to give but this, her love. Only let her child be spared.

Lieutenant Colonel Meyerhof was shot by firing squad in an Athens prison yard in January 1947, without ever seeing his wife in Aachen and his children again. At his trial there had been no one to come forward and testify to his one undoubted act of mercy. With great secrecy, on the ninth of July, 1942, the housekeeper of the Villa Europa, with her five-day-old son, had been whisked to the safety of the Italian zone in the east of the island. She had begged to go, for the sake of the child, whom the local villagers had threatened to kill in a blood feud. These things happen in Crete; and the sentimental Meyerhof, who a year later would play his part in the deportation of the Jews from Kastro, appears to have been motivated by nothing other than compassion.

As the military jeep drove east into the eye of the sun, Laura kept her grip as tight as ever upon the tiny living bundle in her arms. It was the last checkpoint. Levelly she stared at the flaring disk, staring it out until her vision went black. The child in her arms was Daniel's child, born of a legend. The child of this alien, terrifying land, conceived in murderous hate. She loved this tiny creature, the issue of all those years just ended, she loved him so much that it hurt: nothing, surely, not even her own death, could take away that tenderness, that terror of any harm coming to him, that longing to give him the world into his hands. It couldn't, could it?

The child was sleeping, its gums lazily drew comfort from Laura's little finger. An innocent snatched from violent death. He was safe now, this little Dan, as safe as anyone could hope to be while this war still went on. But even as she dedicated what remained to her of life – her vision seared by the sun that had now risen clear of the rim of the sea – to the helpless creature in her arms,

Laura could not deceive herself. Can there be innocence in a world where nothing, not even love, is truly lost?

In her arms she cradled Daniel's child. Daniel's monster child. The child that would never know its father's name.

20 RETURN TO SARAJEVO

THE young year is wet and foggy. Lucy is back from Barbados. Mark, it seems, is moving in with her, has already moved in perhaps. Dan is glad for them, he likes Mark. Everybody is back, Milica too. The New Year hangovers are over, the world is turning once again.

Life, Dan has discovered, goes on. Life, looking back over nearly fifty years, is very long. All that time being somebody else and not knowing it. Dan is free now. Free of the past that has sucked him down and chewed him and mangled him and now spat out the hard empty shell that is Dan in the first months of 1992. He is free of the past now, free even of the self that was his for half a century. Loyal at last to the name of no father. The shadow, the provocation and prohibition of desire, has evaporated into air. Dan is as free as air. He is drunk on air. Life goes on.

'So you see,' he has explained it all to Lucy, 'if there's a Minotaur at the heart of this labyrinth: you're looking at him!'

She got up then impulsively and kissed him on the forehead. 'I think you make a lovely Minotaur, Dan. Did you ever know how fierce you are?' But she has studied him carefully, peering, with an anxiety he has found rather touching in her green eyes, round the corner of his wry jocularity. He is if anything reassured by her scrutiny. Dan for the first time in his life feels instinctively he has nothing to hide.

Her inspection over, Lucy merely nods. 'They're all dead now, those people, Dan. Leave them in peace,' she says earnestly.

'Even Sarah Jane,' he breaks in. 'The last of the Robertsons.'

For on Christmas Day, having held on to life for longer than anyone thought possible, Sarah Jane has gone at last to meet the Robertsons who haunted the last years of her life. Dan has wondered if they will treat her any better there, and is inclined to doubt it. He himself bears no grudge. Not against Sarah Jane, whose eyes he likes to think must have held that hidden gleam to the end, whose claw-like hand touched his hair in mischievous

361

benediction. Sidney is a different matter, but he is confident he will never cross paths with Sidney Lambert again.

'And what's left?' he muses, half to himself.

'Why, you and me, of course.'

'And an awful lot of ghosts.'

'Don't, Dan. I believe in ghosts too. There are enough ghosts and monsters in anyone's unconscious, believe me. You've seen. Now let them go.'

Dan nods. 'Doesn't it worry you to have a monster for a father?'

'I worry about *you*, Dan. It's as simple as that.'

And oddly enough, it is. Dan rests a hand, not paternally, more in complicity of understanding, on his daughter's shoulder. 'I'm all right, Lucy. But thank you.'

This is, as Milica would be sure to say, an understatement of the English. But it is true. At nearly fifty-something, Dan is a worrier no longer. Now that he no longer has an income, he has taken to giving the change in his pocket to the homeless who accost him. He has taken up amateur boxing, and gets a buzz out of the blows to the head and chest that send him spinning. He doesn't resent them, and gives as good as he gets. There is an entirely new satisfaction in showering down at the end of a session, grinning ruefully at the occasional black eye or blue-black bruise on his forehead in the mirror, and feeling the tingling relaxation of sinews he never knew he had. Dan has never in his life been so unselfconsciously aware of his own body. It won't go on like this, of course: soon he'll have to start taking decisions again, exercise this extraordinary freedom that has come to him from nowhere, and then (he can see this quite clearly) he won't be free any more, he'll have a new self to build up and protect, a new pride to hem him in, new fears to allay, expectations to live up to. But for the moment, while it lasts, Dan is free to make of himself what he will, and it has given him some satisfaction to start with the body he inhabits but has scarcely noticed for so long. It is an intoxicating sensation, not at all unpleasant.

It is not long before Lucy comments on it, with evident pleasure. 'I can't remember you being in such good form, Dan. When are you going to start finding something to do?'

He is glad she hasn't said 'find a job'. Dan isn't sure whether he dare admit it, but after little more than six months out of work, he can barely remember what all the fuss was about. He no longer describes himself as 'unemployed'. Consultancy work is what Dan does now. And it's true that on occasion he has been rung up by museums and archaeological services in different countries: would he oversee a project, give advice on setting up a database? It seems his professional reputation has not been irrevocably tarnished after all. He rather enjoys these small commissions. They give him a sense of being wanted, which he never had at the Institute. Of course, he can't see that they will ever generate enough income to pay his bills. He has no illusions about

362

what it means to do 'consultancy work' in the 1990s. But Dan, on the brink of serious poverty, has never worried less about money.

Milica sits facing him on the sofa, one long leg tucked under her. She smokes heavily now; he misses the strong smell of Balkan Sobranie when she isn't there. Often she will leave him, almost abruptly, to catch the last train after the ten o'clock news. It has occurred to him to wonder if she has someone else, but he hasn't the courage to ask. He is not absolutely certain that he would mind if she did, and wonders what this might mean. If he loves her enough to contemplate her being happy with someone nearer her own age, does that mean that he loves her more or loves her less? Dan was never one for self-delusion. Any more than his mother.

Milica's face, as she talks, is set. Her cheeks are drawn, her lips pinched. She has lost weight too. This is not the Milica who gave herself to him with such tender simplicity on the ship from Crete.

'But surely,' Dan tries to be bracing, 'there's a ceasefire agreed in Croatia. Nothing's happening in Bosnia. You said yourself, Sarajevo is civilization.'

Milica bites the nail of her index finger irritably.

Then it all comes out in a rush: the JNA (sorry Dan, the Yugoslav Federal Army) has been pulling back its forces into Bosnia, Croats and Muslims are being intimidated in Banja Luka, and now the EC deadline for recognition. 'Everybody knows Bosnia is going to go up in flames. Except in Europe. They think because they got it wrong over Croatia they can make things better by recognizing Bosnia. It will be Europe's fault. Not only, of course. Everyone is at fault really. But anyone who can is getting out. You cannot be a Yugoslav in Bosnia any more. And my cousin Zaga's children are Yugoslavs, Dan. We haven't much time,' she prompts him. 'They've fixed a date for the referendum. The first of March.'

'Well, better than the first of April, I suppose.'

But Milica is not in a mood for joking. 'I have been asking my friends. I have Zaga's photograph. I have been reading there are agencies, brides from eastern Europe are in demand in Britain – can that be true? But oh Dan, I'm so worried.'

If Bosnia goes up in flames, there are how many – four million? five million? – human beings trapped together in that small, landlocked country. And Milica will worry herself to death for the whole lot of them. Dan cannot cope with large numbers, at least where people are concerned. He knows his own strength, which is the strength of a fifty-year-old man in good health but with a poor history of exercise. This body is not going to take on an army, save a country from destruction. He would do a lot for Milica, but if she is right about the disaster that is coming, he is as powerless as the big battalions around the world who couldn't do a thing to stop the massacres in Croatia. It is Milica Dan loves. Not her interminable family, which to makes matters worse seems to be spread pretty thinly through half the republics of the defunct Yugoslav federation. And, though he remembers distant trips with Margaret and an infant Lucy to Greece, when they used to drive from end to end of that federation without the least idea of how many republics there were or where one finished and another began, with no more anxiety in their heads than whether their allowance of petrol coupons would last them to the frontier, and how long it would be before they could next find disposable nappies in the shops, Dan cannot find an answering echo in himself to the misty-eyed gloom that will overcome Milica when she contemplates the demise of Yugoslavia.

And so, although it touches a raw nerve, he has seized upon the idea of Zaga. He knows no more of her than Milica has told him. The smudgy passport-type photograph shows a woman probably getting on for forty, with a heavy face and a high perm that reminds Dan of movies from the Elvis Presley age. There is, perhaps, a family resemblance to Milica, but he may be imagining that: the broad cheeks, a quizzical lifting of the left eyebrow? Perhaps.

'Does she *want* to come and live in England? What about finding her a rich American?'

'*Are* Americans rich nowadays? I don't know any, do you Dan?' Milica can sound so comical, without the hint of a smile on her face, he has still not learnt for certain when she is joking.

'Well *I'm* certainly not rich,' he quips back.

Milica is sitting very still, staring at him. He hadn't thought anything about it; it was what Lucy would no doubt call a Freudian slip, a mere accident of the conversation.

Is she conscious of echoing his own words? 'Dan,' her eyes are glowing with admiration, '*would you?*'

And all at once Dan is seized with the most terrific sense of *déjà vu*. He has been here before. With Paola. Loving Paola and being married to Margaret. Loving Margaret but unable to let go the quicksilver evanescent figure of Paola and the strange dream of a Cretan night under the orange trees. What was it Lucy told him once: men always make the same mistake twice? And women too, she had been generous enough to concede. But Dan is concerned about men. Dan is concerned about himself. He can see the pattern in the kaleidoscope scattering only to repeat itself in different colours. He has the choice, of course, that's the whole nature of this freedom he temporarily enjoys. But the tidal wave of his new-found freedom is gathering ready to break. It may break anywhere, that is his choice. But break it must. And why not here? More than most, he knows the likely consequences; after all, he has been here before. Nature abhors the vacuum that is in him, that he knows too. Hard and empty, like a shell singing on the beach. But no longer quite empty: the true nadir, the moment when time opened out without duration, is already past. He loves this girl who is hardly more than half his age. And he is old enough, and wise enough, to know it can't go on. For her sake it can't go on. But this love for her buoys him up, crowding, pouring through the emptiness that is in him.

And so Dan's unconscious (how unconscious was it really?) has seized upon Zaga.

'A marriage in form only? Is that what you mean? Just to bring your cousin out of Sarajevo?'

'More than that, Dan. Her children need a home, so does she. The Home Office people would check I think, they're terribly nosey.'

But Dan has caught sight of a future. Children romping through the garden, muddy wellies in the kitchen. The ticking of the grandfather clock pushed back into the silence by the sound of cries and running feet. The companionship of a maturer, a more world-weary version of Milica, a recent widow who would surely, despite Milica's evasion, be well content with the outward forms of marriage.

Milica is miserably chewing a finger-end. In a moment she has gone from glowing enthusiasm to the verge of tears.

'You don't like the idea?' he challenges her.

She takes his hand on the sofa now. 'Oh Dan,' she gulps. 'I think it's a wonderful idea.' And she cries as he has never known her cry, bent double with her hands clamped over her face. When they come away her features are streaked like shapeless, wet clay. There is a bitter little twist to her mouth. 'It's my fault, Dan, isn't it? There was a moment, remember? Oh if only we could undo that moment!'

He takes her gently in his arms. 'Milica, listen,' he whispers in her ear. But no more words come. She is right. He owes so much to Milica. It was Milica who led him unerringly into the heart of the labyrinth. But it was her *absence* that brought him face to face with the empty television screen and the truth of his own beginning. There was no malice, no calculation in that, of course. She couldn't have known. If Milica had stayed over Christmas, if he had been ready, *then*, to put into words his love for her, all of it, what it might mean, the future it might have contained, it could all have been so different. And he might still have been spared the knowledge that has set him free. But she had asked a different question. It was only her anxiety about her cousin that put that future into words for Dan at all. And then, already, it had been too late. He cannot tell her these thoughts, he cannot tell her to her face the sacrifice he means to make. This way, *she* will be free, and his love for her will not be exhausted when their lovemaking comes, as in the nature of things it surely will, to an end.

The envelope lies on the mat. Everything about it is official and officious. The paper is of high quality, starched, the typing on the outside straitlaced and upright. As he gingerly turns it over, Dan is impressed by the ostentatious modesty of the letterhead. With more curiosity than anything else he slits it open, standing there in the hallway.

Sarah Jane Lambert deceased. Pursuant to the last Will and Testament of the aforementioned . . .

Oh God. Dan's eyes begin to swim, he blunders into the sunlight of the sitting room and falls backwards on to the sofa, still holding the letter rigidly out in front of him. His first reaction is actually annoyance. *Them Robertsons,* he can hear Sarah Jane's East Anglian vowels quite clearly. Why won't they leave him alone?

Translated out of legalese, the letter seems to be telling him that his exile is over. Under the terms of the will, and subject to probate, the buildings and adjacent parkland of Upland Grange are his to inherit.

Sitting on the sofa Dan laughs aloud. Of course he has no intention of snatching the inheritance of those two boorish Lamberts from under their noses. Whatever daft ideas the old girl, the last of the Robertsons, may have got into her head, Upland Grange belongs by right to them. What would he want with a pile like that?

But Dan spends a good part of the day on the phone. Lucy is wildly excited by his news. 'Well that certainly solves your career problem for you, doesn't it?' she tells him admiringly. 'You can live out your days in splendid isolation in Suffolk or you can sell it or rent it out and do very nicely on the income. Lucky old you!'

Milica's silences on the phone can be trying. Dan can't quite be sure she hasn't hung up. At length she says slowly, 'A house that size, Dan: just think. We could set up a centre for refugees from eastern Europe.'

'*We* could, could *we*?' he responds with an irony he knows is unfair.

'Dan,' she reproves him quite sharply, 'that is nasty of you. Would you do this really?'

No sooner has he put the phone down than it rings again. Picking it up, he holds the instrument away from his ear. He knows this voice, has promised himself that he will never have to hear it again. He tries not to listen, but the words come tumbling out of the receiver, like a noxious spray. '. . . be contested you know . . . every step of the way . . . injunction . . . High Court . . . cannot at this stage exclude the possibility of criminal charges . . . malign influence . . . essential you notify soonest . . .'

At the end of more than five minutes, Dan's generous resolve of the morning is seriously weakened.

'I have written to Zaga.' Milica looks up at him from the sofa with a shy grin. 'I have not explained everything – how could I? But I think she will accept.'

'And your father?' Dan is more conscious than ever of this upstanding marionette-master in the wings. From his new vantage point he can recognize all too clearly the contours of the shadow that still holds Milica in thrall.

'He has already given his blessing. Only Dan . . .' she touches his arm.

He finishes for her, 'He mustn't ever know – about us. Is that right?'

Milica nods.

He draws her over to him so that she is lying on his chest, looking up into his face. 'I love you, Milica. You and no one else. I just wanted you to know that.'

'So do I, Dan.'

And a long while later: 'Now for your first lesson in Serbo-Croat.'

Dan feels only relief as the plane soars out of Heathrow and up into the sunlight. For what may be the first time in his life, Dan is doing something for no better reason than that he has decided to do it. Nobody's productivity curve, no country's GDP, will be in the least enhanced by any of this activity. Once, he would have been appalled to be pleasing himself in this way. Now he basks in a secret glow of pride. Dan has escaped from the imperatives that have governed his first half century. Dan is flexing those muscles he never knew he had, it may be no more than shadow-boxing but Dan doesn't mind that: he knows he is tilting at windmills but they are *his* windmills, he is flying towards them at five hundred and thirty-five miles per hour (there is a lighted indicator above his seat to give him this information with categorical precision) and as he settles back to watch the changing shapes of the clouds below, it gives Dan considerable pleasure to reflect that whatever else it may be, his mission is not a selfish one.

Only Lucy, before his departure, has seriously tried to talk him out of his harebrained scheme. But once she saw how firmly he was resolved, she has been as supportive as ever. 'A brand plucked from the burning, is that it, Dan?' she has taken to teasing him since. 'If just one soul can be saved . . . ? You'll be taking up religion next.'

But Dan has been content to smile benignly. He knows it is a quixotic mission. But not – with the referendum in Bosnia still a week away – a dangerous one. And it has occurred to him to wonder if those Robertsons who are really no business of his, have after all quite let go of him. If Milica's cousin had taken refuge in Banja Luka instead of Sarajevo, would he have set out for the travel agent's with such a determined spring in his step? The first wind-battered crocuses were out in the front gardens of South London that day. It had been the deadest time, the turning point of the year.

'Are you a journalist?' the girl in the travel agent's had asked.

Dan shook his head.

'Sarajevo? You're sure?'

Dan has got used to that look by the time his plane touches down, several hours late, in Belgrade.

'*Zhurnalist?*' the young woman at the transit desk asks him now.

And it is true that his few fellow passengers all have that hunted look, have fussed about taking their overweight cameras and equipment on board with them, and spent the whole of the short flight drinking and conferring worriedly in low tones.

As a result of the delays, Dan's first sight of Sarajevo is in darkness. Milica has commandeered a taxi to meet him at the airport, and silently holds his hand for most of the journey. It seems an interminable distance. At last the lights of the city are around them, traffic is hooting everywhere. Dan cannot conceal his anxiety as Milica helps him carry his things into the draughty stairwell of a high-rise concrete building. Impatiently she jabs her finger again and again at the button which calls the lift, but which remains obstinately unlighted. The building seems unnaturally silent after the bustle of traffic outside. A strong smell of frying onions mingled with something indefinably sweet wafts past his nostrils and reminds him that he has eaten only airline food, at the whimsical times of day dictated by delayed flights and a longer-than-expected stop-over at Belgrade airport. Even Milica, in this strange environment, seems different. In the pale light of the stairwell he realizes why: she is wearing earrings and lipstick, a skirt instead of the jeans he is used to, which makes her middle look much thicker. Milica on her home ground is smarter than at home. And, to his critical eye, less herself.

He is about to suggest walking up, the lift obviously isn't working, but she squeezes his hand again. 'It's the twelfth floor, Dan. Relax, it'll come.'

But Dan has rarely felt so unrelaxed in all his life. In a few moments he will come face to face with the family he has pledged, from the other end of Europe, to make his own. In the desolation of the stairwell the full folly and absurdity of what he is doing descends on Dan with clammy panic. He shouldn't be here, in this strange city, waiting amid the unfamiliar smells of cooking and . . . can it perhaps be drains? He doesn't belong, he oughtn't to be here. He should be disentangling the mess left behind by Sarah Jane's will. He should, in Lucy's carefully chosen words, be finding 'something to do'. Dan has used up his freedom to the length of his chain. Here it stops. The lives he is about to walk into, a stranger free as air, he cannot afterwards turn and walk away from. Dan grits his teeth, and steps into the lift.

On the twelfth floor a door stands wide open, pouring a wedge of light into the darkness. There are figures here, and voices, all talking at once. Some words seem to be in English, but most of it goes past him. An excited crush hastens him over the threshold into the brightly lighted room. Limply he feels himself passed from one strong handclasp to another. To his embarrassment a huge man with a beard that tickles his ear grasps him by both shoulders and kisses him full on each cheek. He is not at first sure which of the women is Zaga, which of the several children who are all talking at once and jumping up and down are about to become his stepsons. The bearded man pushes forward two boys of perhaps seven and four (Dan isn't very good at telling children's ages) wearing matching American-style jeans and check shirts with black armbands. Suddenly shy, the boys are introduced as Andrej and Franjo. There is a moment of embarrassed stiffness, until the younger stands back a pace, pointing his little fist at Dan's face, and pipes up something shrilly in Serbo-Croat. The adults roar with mirth and the ice is broken, everybody is again talking at once, Dan is at the centre of things but nobody seems to be quite noticing him either; he takes advantage of the oasis to try to get his bearings.

'What did he say?' he whispers to Milica.

'He wanted to know where you've left your top hat. All the English people in the storybooks we have wear top hats and frock coats. The English are still imperialists here, you know. Now, come and meet Zaga.'

Zaga looks younger than he had expected, a more compact, a rounder, rosy-cheeked version of Milica. She wears restrained mourning: a grey dress with black scarf. She is perhaps in her mid thirties. 'You are welcome, Dan. I may call you Dan?' She extends her hand the full length of her arm, as though half wishing to ward him off, then, as he takes it gingerly in his, draws him towards her, her eyes intently appraising his face. As he approaches, she twinkles at him and presents her cheek to be kissed. Applause and a cheer go up as Dan obliges. 'We will be quite terrific friends. I can feel it already.' It is so simple and so gauche, his heart turns over. Then she lets go of him and suddenly there are glasses chinking everywhere, the rancid, pungent smell of *slivovic* invades the room, a tiny glass is pressed into Dan's hand, and he finds himself invited to help it down with little cubes of goat cheese and tiny aromatic meatballs.

In a strange, light-headed way, Dan begins to feel at home.

Pavel, the man in the beard, and Milica take it on themselves to be his guides around the city. There is still a powdering of snow on the hills and the Miljacka River bounds between its concrete banks and beneath the bridges in the city centre, its waters dark yellow and foaming, carrying in its course branches and trunks of trees and here and there a dead sheep. In daylight the block of flats where Zaga and her family live is an easy landmark, painted on the outside an only slightly brighter shade of yellow than the river water, and rising high above the cosmopolitan skyline of the city centre, with its Austrian pitched roofs, tapering minarets and socialist squared-off concrete. 'No risk of getting lost,' Pavel has assured him.

On Saturday the bustle and the noise of the city have suddenly become subdued. The referendum, which will take two whole days, has begun. The normally extrovert Bosnians seem to take their electoral responsibilities with a solemnity Dan can hardly credit – and this even though a third of the population, the Serbs, won't be voting. Pavel has been helpful in explaining the politics, but Dan has to admit he is often left behind. Pavel's gratitude to Dan, his painful pleasure that, thanks to him, Zaga and her boys will be safe in England, is openly expressed and embarrassing. Dan has preferred to talk about the city, to be shown the sights. With a more than dutiful interest he has followed his guides round the Princip Museum, built on the spot where on a June morning all those years ago an Englishman six foot three in his socks stood eyeing the cakes in an old-fashioned Viennese pastry shop. More arresting than the partly faded photographs of the archduke's assassins, Dan has found a commemorative set of footprints pressed into new concrete at the corner where the riverside Quay meets Yugoslav Federal Army Street, better known to the world by its long defunct name of Franz Josef Strasse. Here, Pavel has explained without disguising a perfunctory pride, Gavrilo Princip stood and pulled the trigger on that morning in 1914. Dan has taken in the scene, it is an ordinary, busy street corner now.

And he will never know what it was that brought the future excavator of Ano Meri to this spot on that fateful June morning.

The wedding is to take place tomorrow, the second day of the referendum. Apparently the churches will be doing a brisk trade. In the anxieties surrounding the outcome, lots of weddings have been brought forward, Pavel has told Dan. Theirs is to be a subdued affair, but he has been taken to the little dark Orthodox church behind the broken-down wall that once protected it from the Turkish masters of the city; he has met the priest with his tall square-domed hat, and drawn into his lungs the close, powerful scent of incense. Round the walls the frescoes of the saints have been darkened by the smoke of centuries of candles. While they were rehearsing and he was being shown the motions he will need to make, the cantor was practising in the apse, and the sonorous unaccompanied voice set the whole enclosed space vibrating like an echo chamber. It transports Dan straight back to the Russian basses he used to admire, with Paola, at Covent Garden. He can imagine himself on the set of *Boris Godunov*: at the centre of the sound, in the heart of the action. Dan finds himself strangely drawn to the unfamiliar ritual that will be enacted here tomorrow.

Dan has been left rather on his own, this final evening, as the family makes its preparations around him. After a Lenten evening meal he went out with Milica for a drink in a half-deserted bar. He has found it difficult to talk to Milica here, though he is deeply grateful for her presence. But for her, he couldn't possibly go through with it. In the glum surroundings of the bar he has sat on a stool in the flashing lights of a video-game arcade, and placed her hand on his knee. They have sat like that, saying little, for some time, mixing *slivovic* with the local Pilsner beer. It would not do to be incapacitated tomorrow. But Dan is fast developing a Balkan constitution, and needs the warming reassurance of alcohol and the closeness of Milica's body. It will not be like this again.

As they leave the bar a sharp report rings out from the streets higher up the hill, followed in quick succession by several more. Dan stops abruptly. '*What was that?*' He is quite shaken.

Milica takes his arm. 'People are very nervous these days. Let us hope it is nothing. But we should be indoors now.'

As he settles himself on the trestle bed in the tiny room that has been given up for him, Dan fancies he hears more gunshots, further away this time. His brain is active, *slivovic* has that effect on him, but he is dog-tired.

And now in the troubled twilight that is not quite waking, not quite sleeping, Dan finds himself driving once more, as he did with Pavel and Milica earlier today, along the riverside Quay. The river has subsided while he has been here, the sky has turned cold and grey. The car moves in slow motion over the cobbled street, Pavel at the wheel, Milica beside him in the back. Dan is leaning anxiously forward, looking for something, there is something he is trying to recognize. It is the street corner by the bridge, where they got out to look round the museum yesterday and Pavel pointed to the imprint of the assassin's feet. Only it seems different now. The open car as it approaches the turning is reflected in the plate glass window of a shop with golden curlicues scrolled on the glass. Dan has no difficulty in recognizing – he has seen the photographs in the museum just yesterday – the slight Charlie Chaplin figure who now stands forward. And just behind him, occupying all of Dan's attention, a tall man in Edwardian whites and straw hat, six foot three and more, who suddenly turns from inspecting the wares in the shop to face him. The eyes that stare into his in the instant of recognition are an icy, brilliant blue. Too late Dan catches sight of the assassin's arm, the revolver raised, the barrel pointed straight towards him.

Dan turns restlessly on the lumpy mattress. More gunfire, closer this time: the rattling of metal leaves down the empty streets and the echoing passages of Dan's head.

CPSIA information can be obtained at www.ICGtesting.com
Printed in the USA
LVOW11s2259050816

499278LV00001B/40/P